D0985438

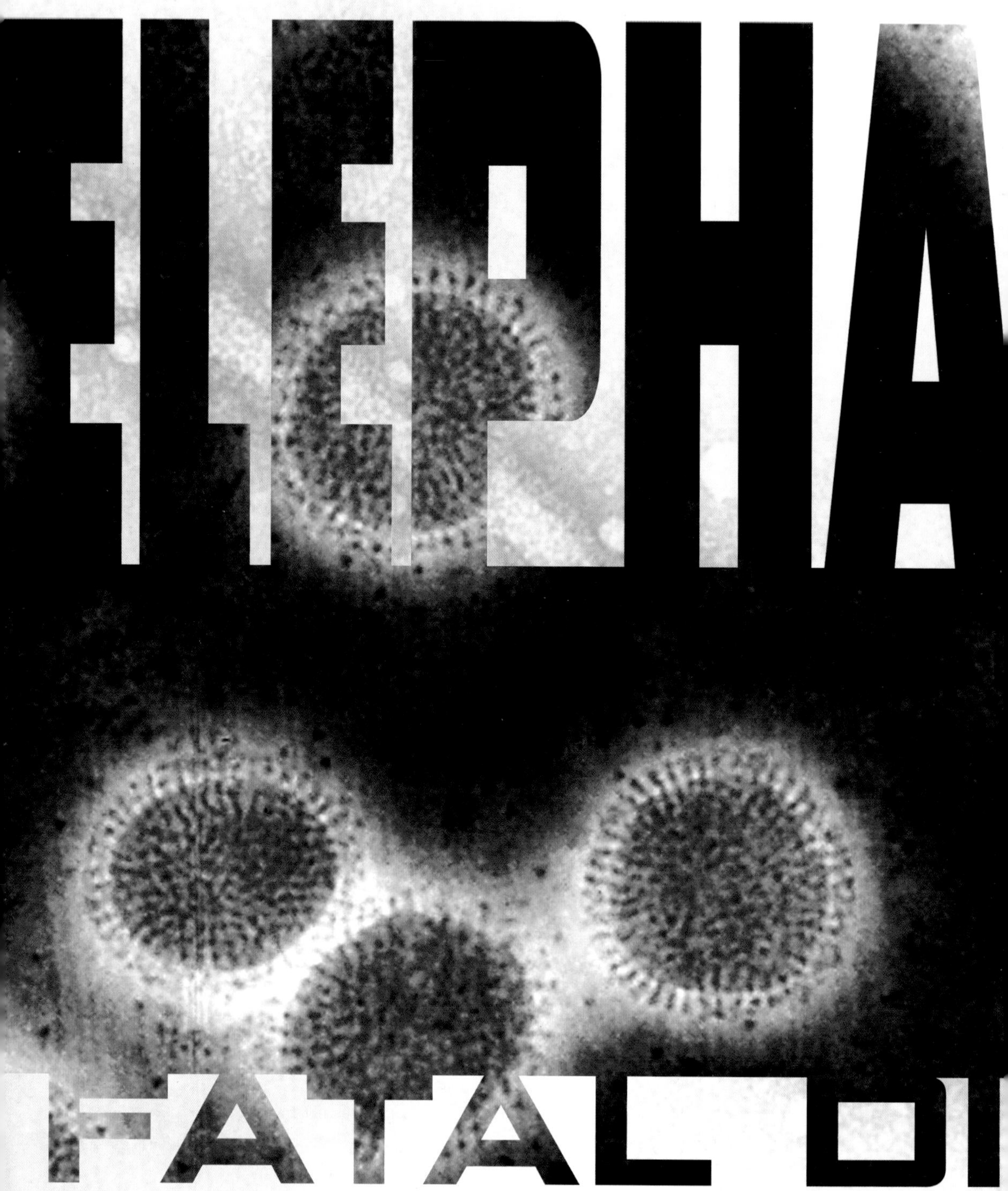
ELEPHA
FATAL DI

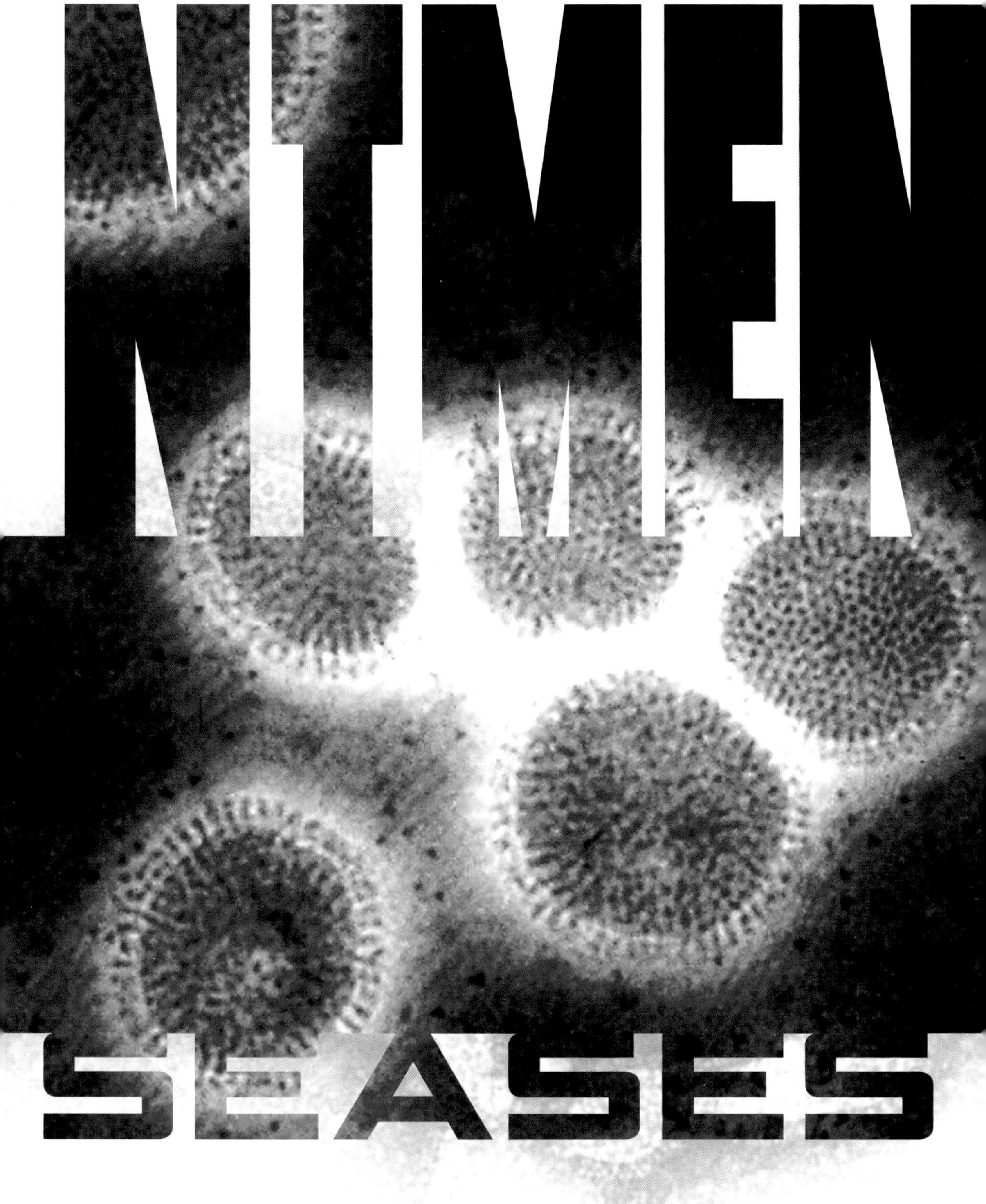
NTMEN
SEASES

STORY & LETTERING
RICHARD STARKINGS

WITH THANKS TO
KURT BUSIEK
JOE KELLY
JEPH LOEB

ARTWORK
MORITAT
IAN CHURCHILL
AXEL MEDELLIN
ROB STEEN
BOO COOK
LADRÖNN

STEVE BUCCELLATO
CHRIS BURNHAM
PETER GROSS
STUART IMMONEN
RYAN KELLY

DESIGN
J.G. ROSHELL
of COMICRAFT

WITH HELP FROM THE
CENTER FOR DISEASE CONTROL
WWW.CDC.GOV

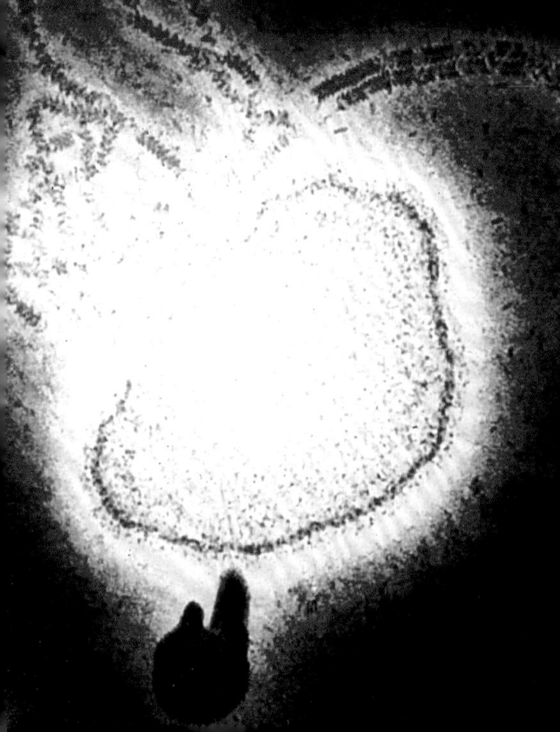

image

COO
ROBERT KIRKMAN

CFO
ERIK LARSEN

President
TODD McFARLANE

CEO
MARC SILVESTRI

Vice-President
JIM VALENTINO

Publisher
ERIC STEPHENSON

Sales & Licensing Coordinator
TODD MARTINEZ

PR & Marketing Coordinator
SARAH DELAINE

Accounts Manager
BRANWYN BIGGLESTONE

Administrative Assistant
EMILY MILLER

Marketing Assistant
JAMIE PARRENO

Digital Rights Coordinator
KEVIN YUEN

Production Manager
TYLER SHAINLINE

Art Director
DREW GILL

Senior Production Artist
JONATHAN CHAN

Production Artists
MONICA GARCIA
VINCENT KUKUA
JANA COOK

ELEPHANTMEN VOL. 2: FATAL DISEASES. Second printing. Published by
Image Comics, Inc., Office of publication: 2134 Allston Way, Second
Floor, Berkeley, California 94704. Copyright © 2011 Active Images.
Originally published in single magazine form as ELEPHANTMEN #8-15
and ELEPHANTMEN: PILOT. All rights reserved. HIP FLASK®, MYSTERY
CITY™ and ELEPHANTMEN™ (including all prominent characters featured
in this issue), its logo and all character likenesses are trademarks of
Active Images, unless otherwise noted. Image Comics® is a trademark
of Image Comics, Inc. All rights reserved. No part of this publication
may be reproduced or transmitted, in any form or by any means
(except for short excerpts for review purposes) without the express
written permission of Image Comics, Inc. All names, characters, events
and locales in this publication are entirely fictional. Any resemblance
to actual persons (living or dead), events or places, without satiric
intent, is coincidental. PRINTED IN KOREA • ISBN 978-160706-394-0

ACTIVE IMAGE

APPROVED BY THE COMICRAFT AUTHORITY

SCIENCE, ENTERTAINMENT and PINK ELEPHANTS

AN INTRODUCTION BY JANET ZUCKER

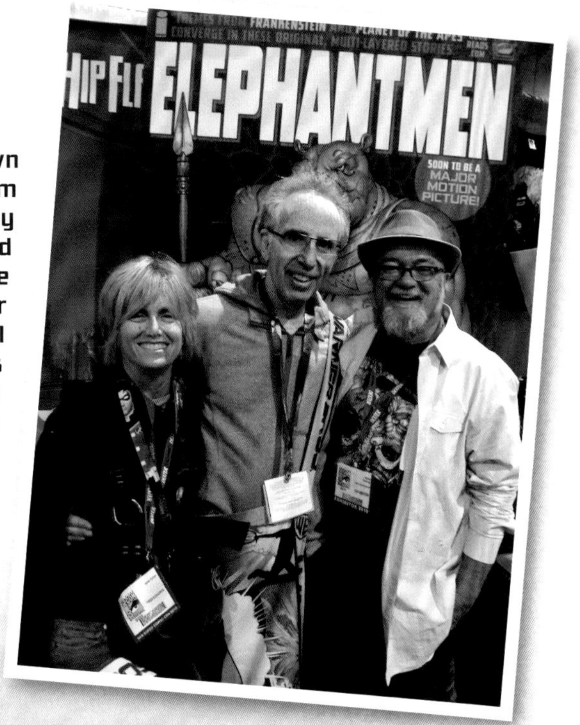
ELEPHANTMEN
SOON TO BE A MAJOR MOTION PICTURE!

As Richard Starkings and I sat down for our weekly **ELEPHANTMEN** film development session, he casually informed me that he wanted me to write the intro for the reissue of Volume 2. How could I ever say anything but yes to the thoughtful Buddhist Englishman whose eyes always have a twinkle and who has a mind like a steel trap? Our collaboration has been like the odd couple; I have been in the film business for thirty years, working on my own and with my husband Jerry Zucker [*Airplane!, Ghost, Rat Race*], while Richard has spent the same time span immersed in the world of comic books, as an editor, cartoonist, letterer, writer and creator.

I first picked up *Hip Flask: Unnatural Selection* and Hip's soulful face stared back at me. The world of a film noir human/animal hybrid is one we've never seen before in cinema. I remembered the wonderment we all felt the first time we saw the Brachiosaurus lumber across the savannah in *Jurassic Park*. **ELEPHANTMEN** takes this exploration one step further; the Elephantmen are essentially beings that have had human and animal DNA melded together. And it raises the questions: do they have the same rights, impulses and attitudes as humans? Which side is dominant? What is the interplay between animal instinct and human reason?

All dramatic themes and questions, but who was the audience? I showed my eighteen year-old son the series, and his comment was "well, it's obvious...it's really cool watching giant animals battle man and machine." Hip and Horn, Ebony and Sahara, Silencer and Yvette -- these are more than just cool characters, they are the multi-layered protagonists and antagonists that anchor movies and draw us into their world. The ability to tell a story that addresses moral issues and the horrors of war, yet still allow moments where Hip can battle crocs in the sewers, really excited me, both as a film lover and producer. My passion for the project was instant.

Unlike some producers, I am not steeped in graphic novel lore, but what I do have is a love of science and entertainment, with a deep commitment to storytelling and compelling characters. I saw that one could care about these lonely animals caught between two worlds, struggling to find love, dealing with their rage and anger. Hip has decided to toe the line, not rock the boat.

Horn is filled with rage and a desire to dominate and engulf, tempered by his humanizing love for Sahara. Yet they are not allowed to marry and have children, which is a natural instinct for humans and animals alike. I find it interesting to consider what would happen when the inextinguishable drive to preserve our species is frustrated. Whether we are human or Elephantman, would we toe the line?

These characters are set up to travel down paths resulting in colliding consequences -- death, destruction, broken dreams and love unrequited and then consummated. I have encouraged Richard not to ignore the "pink elephant" in the room, the sexuality and desire between the two species because after all, they are human and animals, species that both feel desire, love and parental drive.

Richard Starkings has created a world that is dark and vibrant, violent yet compassionate, and forces us to confront our own narrow world views. How could anyone not want to read this comic book...or see this movie!

Janet Zucker
Los Angeles, CA
May 2011

JANET ZUCKER HAS BEEN PRODUCING AND MANAGING IN THE ENTERTAINMENT BUSINESS FOR OVER TWO DECADES. SHE CO-HEADS ZUCKER PRODUCTIONS WITH HER HUSBAND, WRITER/DIRECTOR JERRY ZUCKER, AND MOST RECENTLY PRODUCED FAIR GAME STARRING SEAN PENN AND NAOMI WATTS AND DIRECTED BY DOUG LIMAN.

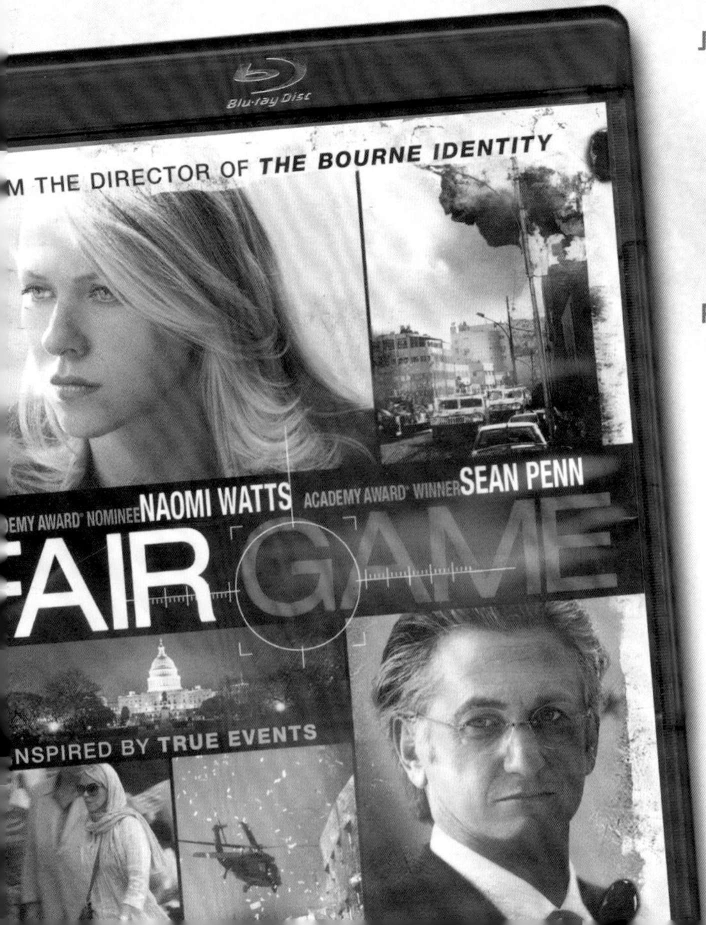
Blu-ray Disc
M THE DIRECTOR OF THE BOURNE IDENTITY
EMY AWARD NOMINEE NAOMI WATTS
ACADEMY AWARD WINNER SEAN PENN
AIR GAME
NSPIRED BY TRUE EVENTS

JANET IS ALSO A PASSIONATE ADVOCATE FOR STEM CELL RESEARCH, AND IN 2004, SHE AND JERRY, ALONG WITH TWO OTHER FAMILIES, STARTED PROPOSITION 71, THE CALIFORNIA STEM CELL RESEARCH AND CURES INITIATIVE. JANET IS THE PRESIDENT OF CURESNOW, A NON-PROFIT ORGANIZATION, AS WELL AS A CO-CREATOR OF THE SCIENCE & ENTERTAINMENT EXCHANGE, A COMMUNICATIONS INITIATIVE DESIGNED TO OPEN UP LINES OF DIALOGUE BETWEEN ENTERTAINMENT INDUSTRY PROFESSIONALS AND THE SCIENCE COMMUNITY. FOR HER CONTRIBUTIONS TO THE SCIENTIFIC COMMUNITY, JANET HAS BEEN INDUCTED INTO THE NATIONAL ACADEMY OF SCIENCES' EINSTEIN SOCIETY.

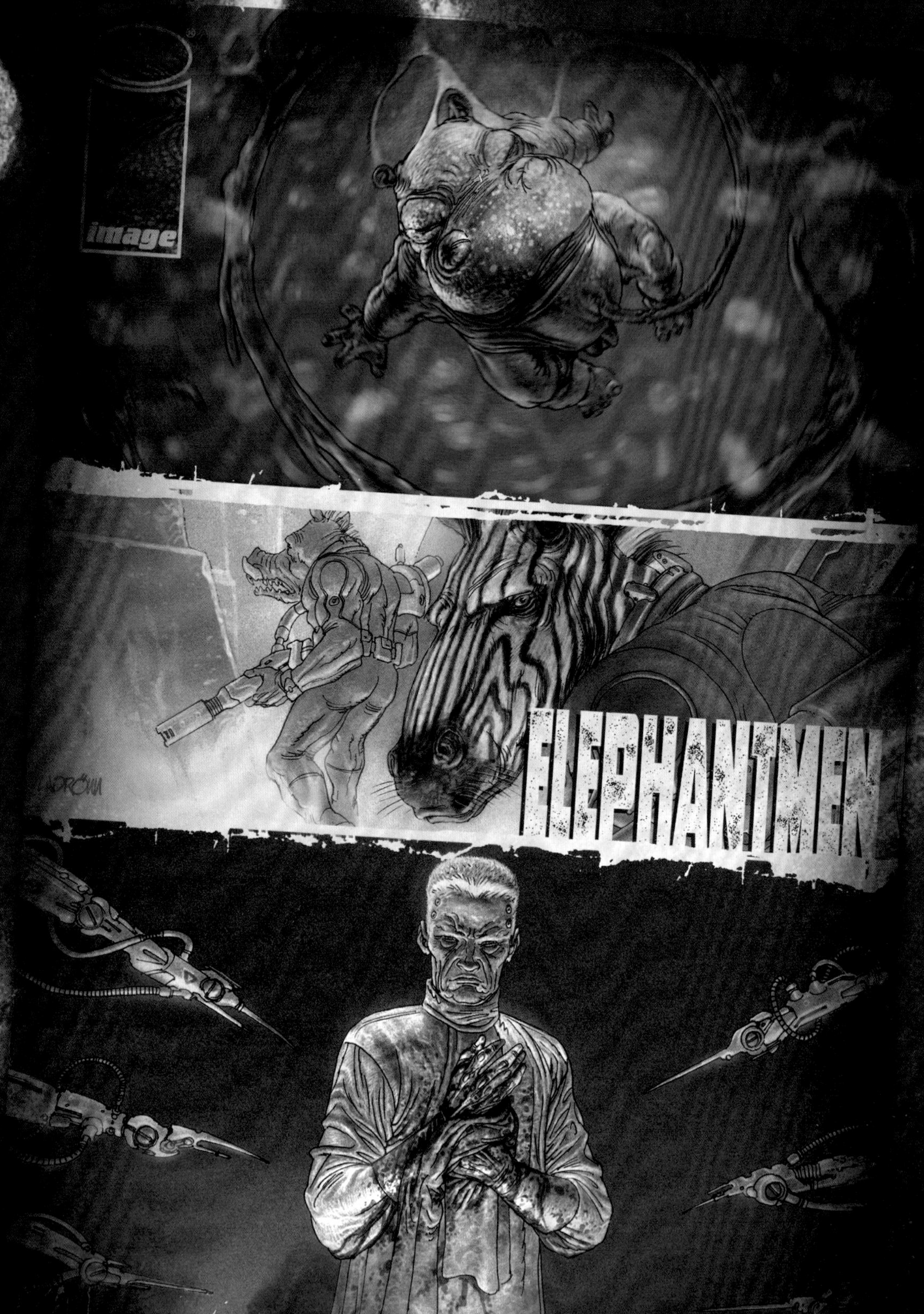
image
ELEPHANTMEN

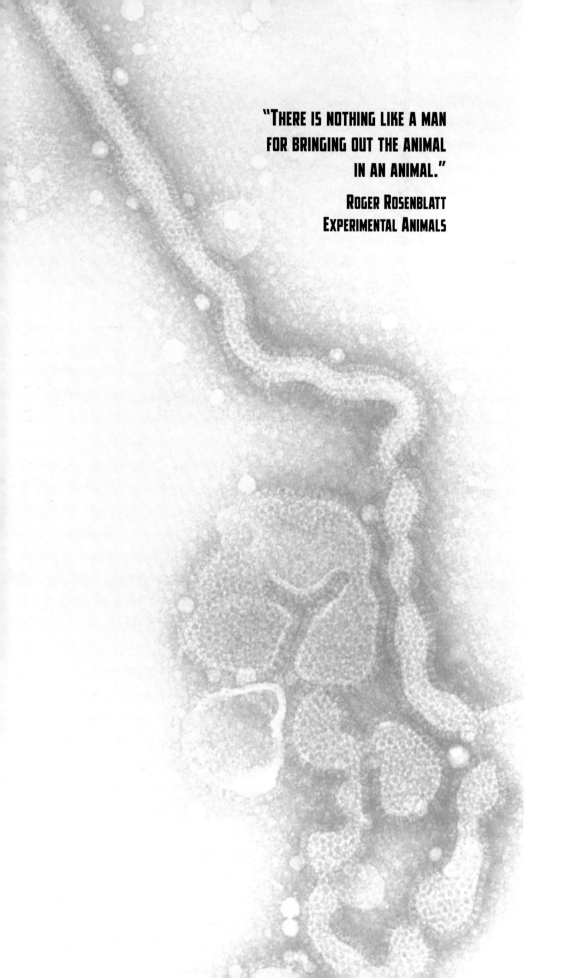

"THERE IS NOTHING LIKE A MAN
FOR BRINGING OUT THE ANIMAL
IN AN ANIMAL."

ROGER ROSENBLATT
EXPERIMENTAL ANIMALS

QUI TACET CONSENTIRE VIDETUR

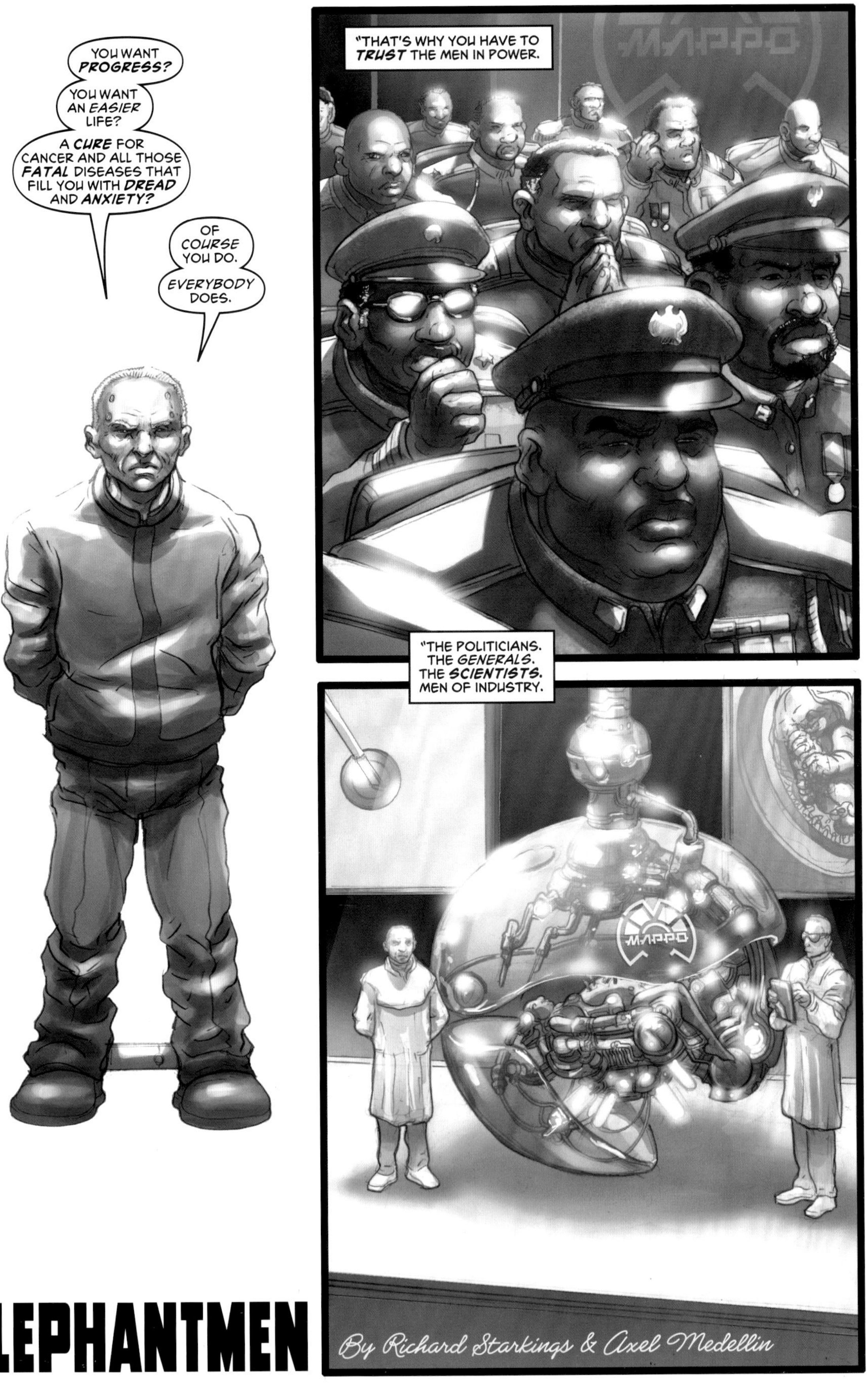

YOU WANT PROGRESS?
YOU WANT AN EASIER LIFE?
A CURE FOR CANCER AND ALL THOSE FATAL DISEASES THAT FILL YOU WITH DREAD AND ANXIETY?
OF COURSE YOU DO.
EVERYBODY DOES.
"THAT'S WHY YOU HAVE TO TRUST THE MEN IN POWER.
MAPPO
"THE POLITICIANS. THE GENERALS. THE SCIENTISTS. MEN OF INDUSTRY.
MAPPO
By Richard Starkings & Axel Medellin

ELEPHANTMEN

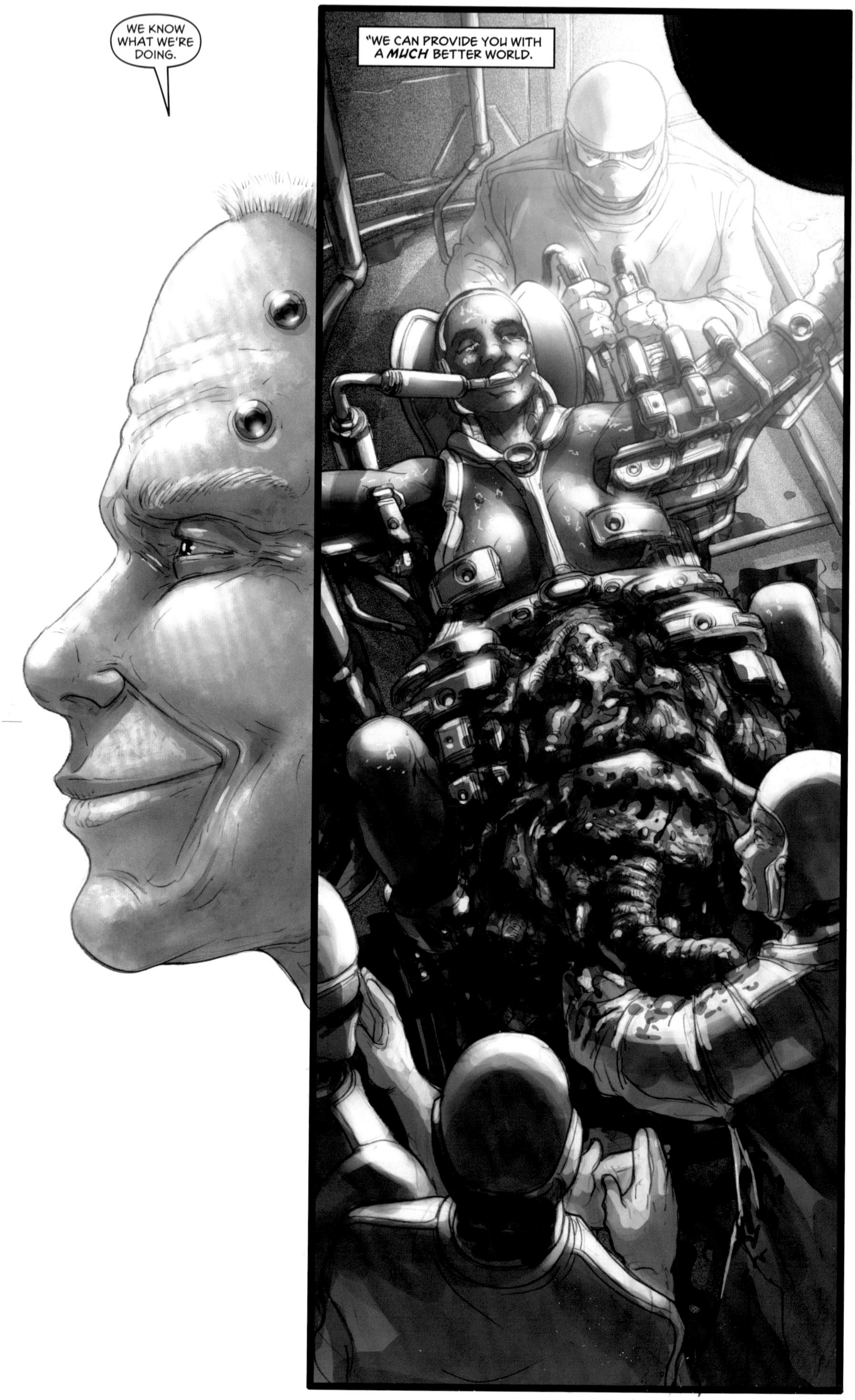
WE KNOW WHAT WE'RE DOING.
"WE CAN PROVIDE YOU WITH A *MUCH* BETTER WORLD.

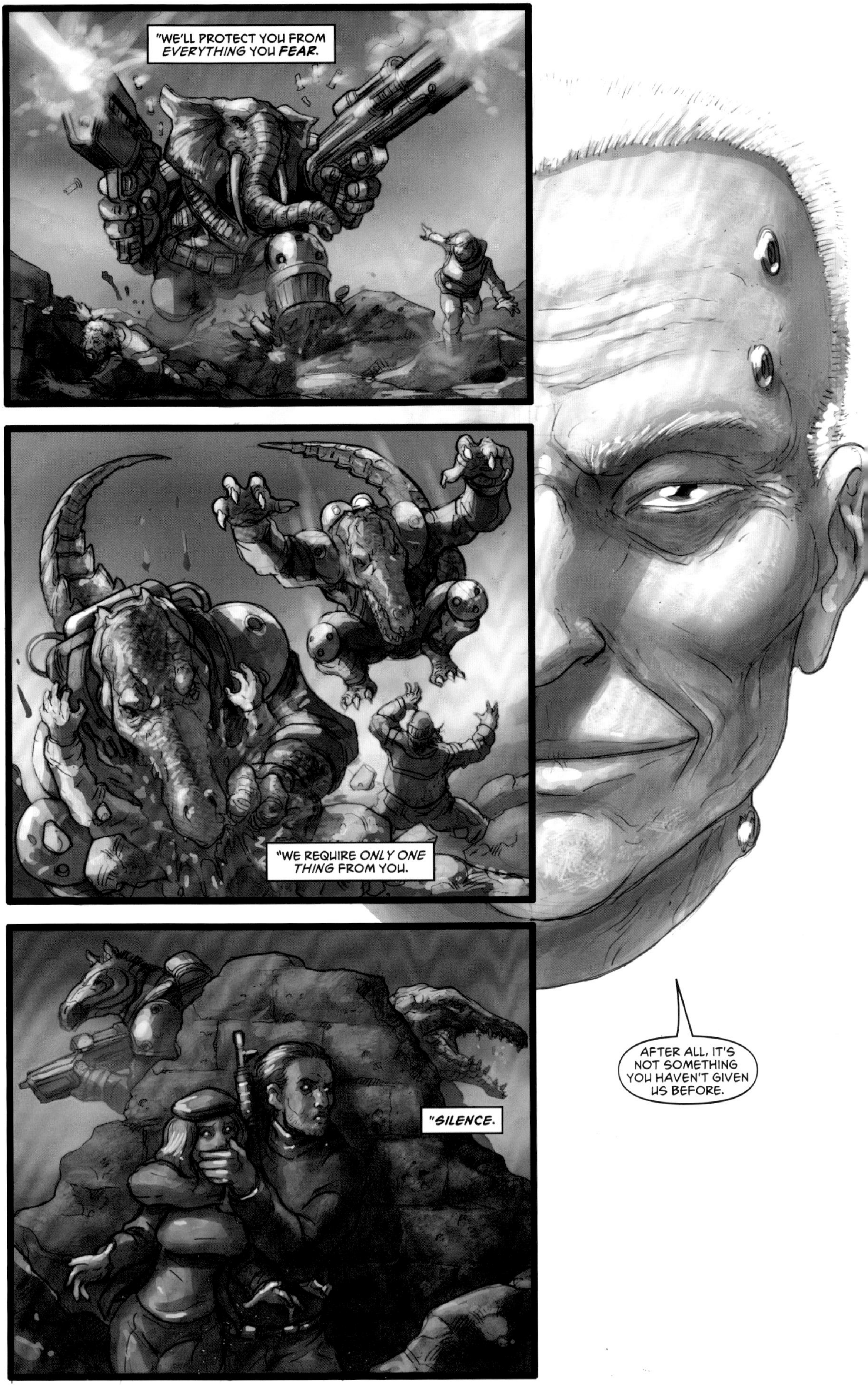
"WE'LL PROTECT YOU FROM *EVERYTHING* YOU ***FEAR***.
"WE REQUIRE *ONLY ONE THING* FROM YOU.
"***SILENCE***.
AFTER ALL, IT'S NOT SOMETHING YOU HAVEN'T GIVEN US BEFORE.

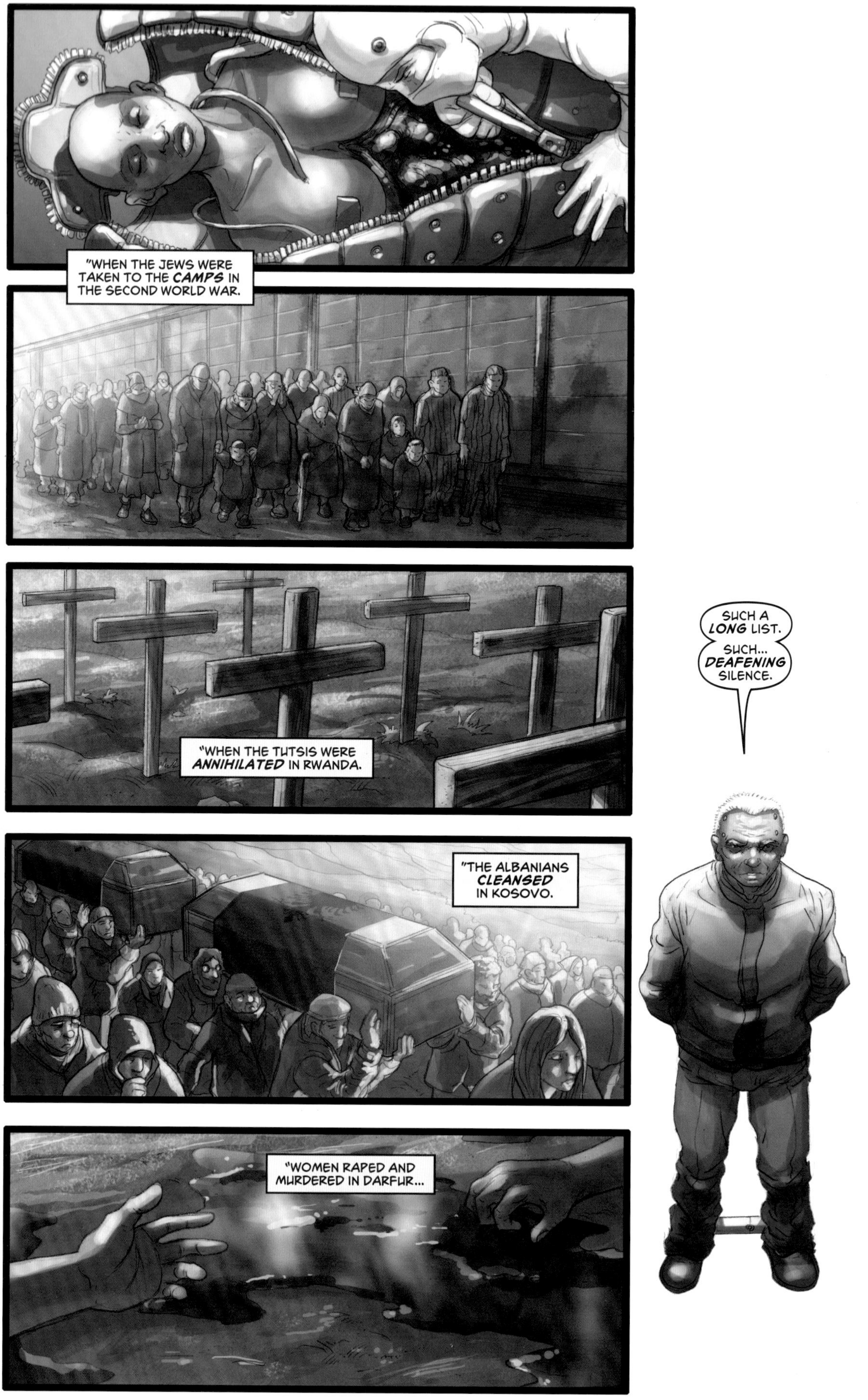
"WHEN THE JEWS WERE TAKEN TO THE CAMPS IN THE SECOND WORLD WAR.
"WHEN THE TUTSIS WERE ANNIHILATED IN RWANDA.
"THE ALBANIANS CLEANSED IN KOSOVO.
"WOMEN RAPED AND MURDERED IN DARFUR...
SUCH A LONG LIST. SUCH... DEAFENING SILENCE.

SO, REST ASSURED, THE MEN IN POWER ARE *ALWAYS* WORKING FOR THE GREATER *GOOD.*

AND IF DEVELOPMENTS IN THE WORLD ARE NOT TO YOUR *LIKING...*

"IF THE PATH OF PROGRESS MAKES YOU... *UNCOMFORTABLE.*

"JUST... LOOK THE OTHER WAY. EVERYTHING IS UNDER CONTROL.

"PUT ANOTHER GALLON OF GAS IN YOUR CAR.

"HAVE ANOTHER BEER.

"ENJOY A BALLGAME.

"KEEP QUIET."

H+ WHu ΓΕΕΓ⊓ ΓΙLΕΓT ΑΓΓΕΑΓΓ Tu 'uⁿΓΓT

HORN · SAHARA · SERENGHETI · EBONY · GRUENWALD · MIKI · DELANEY · FLASK

THE STORY
SO FAR...

2259: HIP FLASK, EBONY HIDE and OBADIAH HORN are Elephantmen, survivors of a war fought between Africa and China over the European countries ravaged by the deadly MCN virus. That war is long since over and over 15,000 Elephantmen have been rehabilitated by the United Nations and scattered throughout the globe to live peacefully among humans.

Flask and Hide work for THE INFORMATION AGENCY as Crime Scene Investigators. Flask has been recovering from injuries sustained in an altercation with croc ELIJAH DELANEY, an employee of Obadiah Horn. Ebony Hide has been recovering from injuries sustained during a run in with JOSHUA SERENGHETI, a Los Angeles-based crimelord dealing in the illegal buying and selling of Elephantmen body parts. GRUENWALD, director of the L.A. arm of the Information Agency, is now keeping a closer eye on Flask and Hide, who have also attracted the attention of SKYCAB driver HIROMI "MIKI" KIYOKO.

Obadiah Horn, perhaps the most celebrated Elephantmen of all, has become a popular socialite, screen personality and business magnate; he is the Chairman and CEO of HORN INDUSTRIES, a global business dealing in imports, exports and real estate development. Horn is also the founder of IVORY TOWERS, which operates numerous casinos and hotels across the world. Horn's extravagant lifestyle, outspoken manner and his engagement to U.N. Refugee Spokesperson SAHARA, have made him the subject of intense scrutiny by the media. Some suspect that his business dealings are not entirely legal and it is true that those who speak out against him have been known to disappear without trace, or die in mysterious circumstances.

ELEPHANTMEN
Tales from Mystery City & the World of
IN THE
THE ONE-EYED

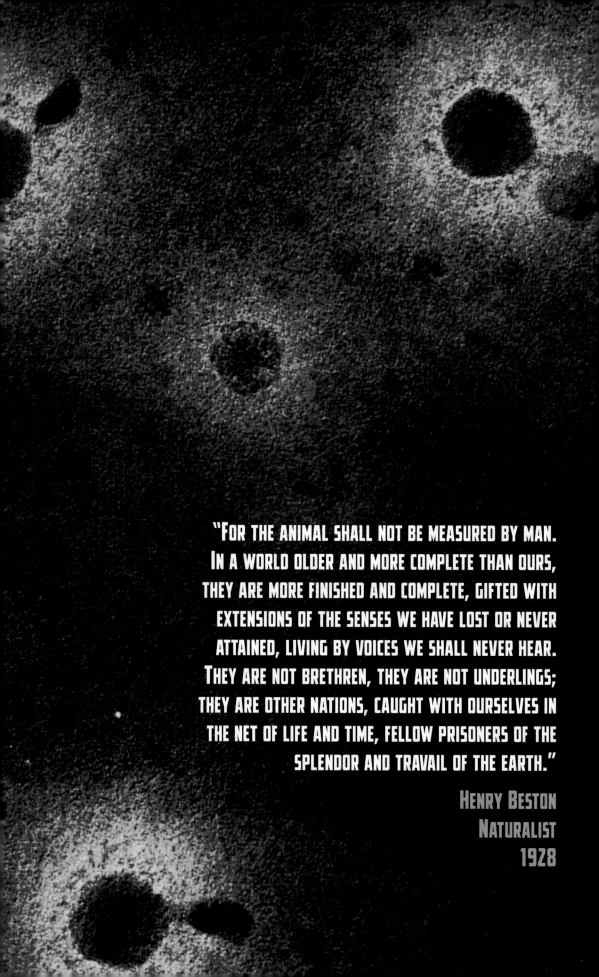

"FOR THE ANIMAL SHALL NOT BE MEASURED BY MAN.
IN A WORLD OLDER AND MORE COMPLETE THAN OURS,
THEY ARE MORE FINISHED AND COMPLETE, GIFTED WITH
EXTENSIONS OF THE SENSES WE HAVE LOST OR NEVER
ATTAINED, LIVING BY VOICES WE SHALL NEVER HEAR.
THEY ARE NOT BRETHREN, THEY ARE NOT UNDERLINGS;
THEY ARE OTHER NATIONS, CAUGHT WITH OURSELVES IN
THE NET OF LIFE AND TIME, FELLOW PRISONERS OF THE
SPLENDOR AND TRAVAIL OF THE EARTH."

HENRY BESTON
NATURALIST
1928

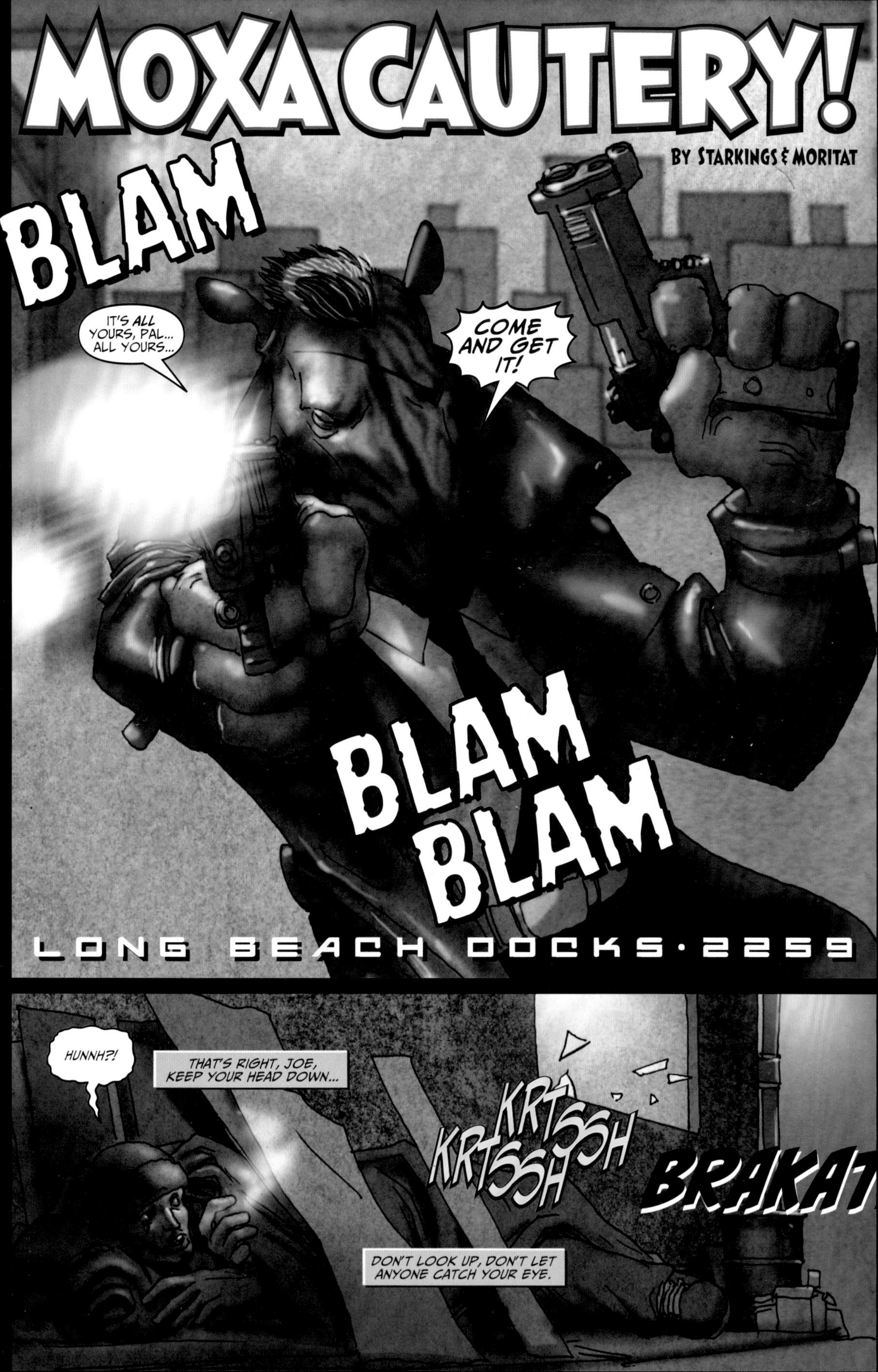
MOXA CAUTERY!
BY STARKINGS & MORITAT
BLAM
IT'S ALL YOURS, PAL... ALL YOURS...
COME AND GET IT!
BLAM
BLAM
LONG BEACH DOCKS · 2259
HUNNH?!
THAT'S RIGHT, JOE, KEEP YOUR HEAD DOWN...
KRTSSH
KRTSSH
BRAKAT
DON'T LOOK UP, DON'T LET ANYONE CATCH YOUR EYE.

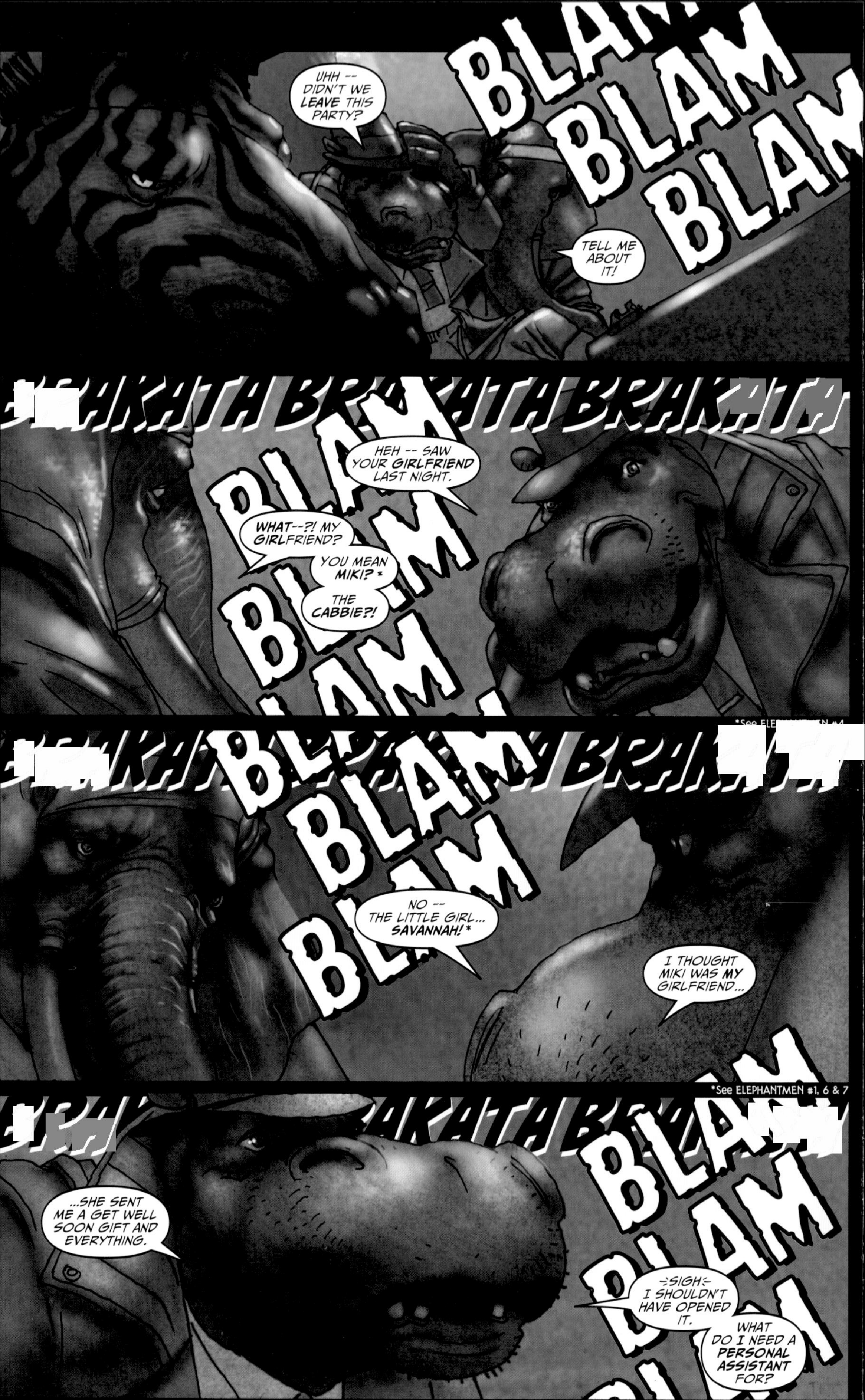

BLAM BLAM BLAM
UHH -- DIDN'T WE LEAVE THIS PARTY?
TELL ME ABOUT IT!
BLAM BLAM BLAM
HEH -- SAW YOUR GIRLFRIEND LAST NIGHT.
WHAT--?! MY GIRLFRIEND?
YOU MEAN MIKI? *
THE CABBIE?!
BLAM BLAM
NO -- THE LITTLE GIRL... SAVANNAH! *
I THOUGHT MIKI WAS MY GIRLFRIEND...
*See ELEPHANTMEN #1, 6 & 7
BLAM BLAM
...SHE SENT ME A GET WELL SOON GIFT AND EVERYTHING.
-SIGH- I SHOULDN'T HAVE OPENED IT.
WHAT DO I NEED A PERSONAL ASSISTANT FOR?

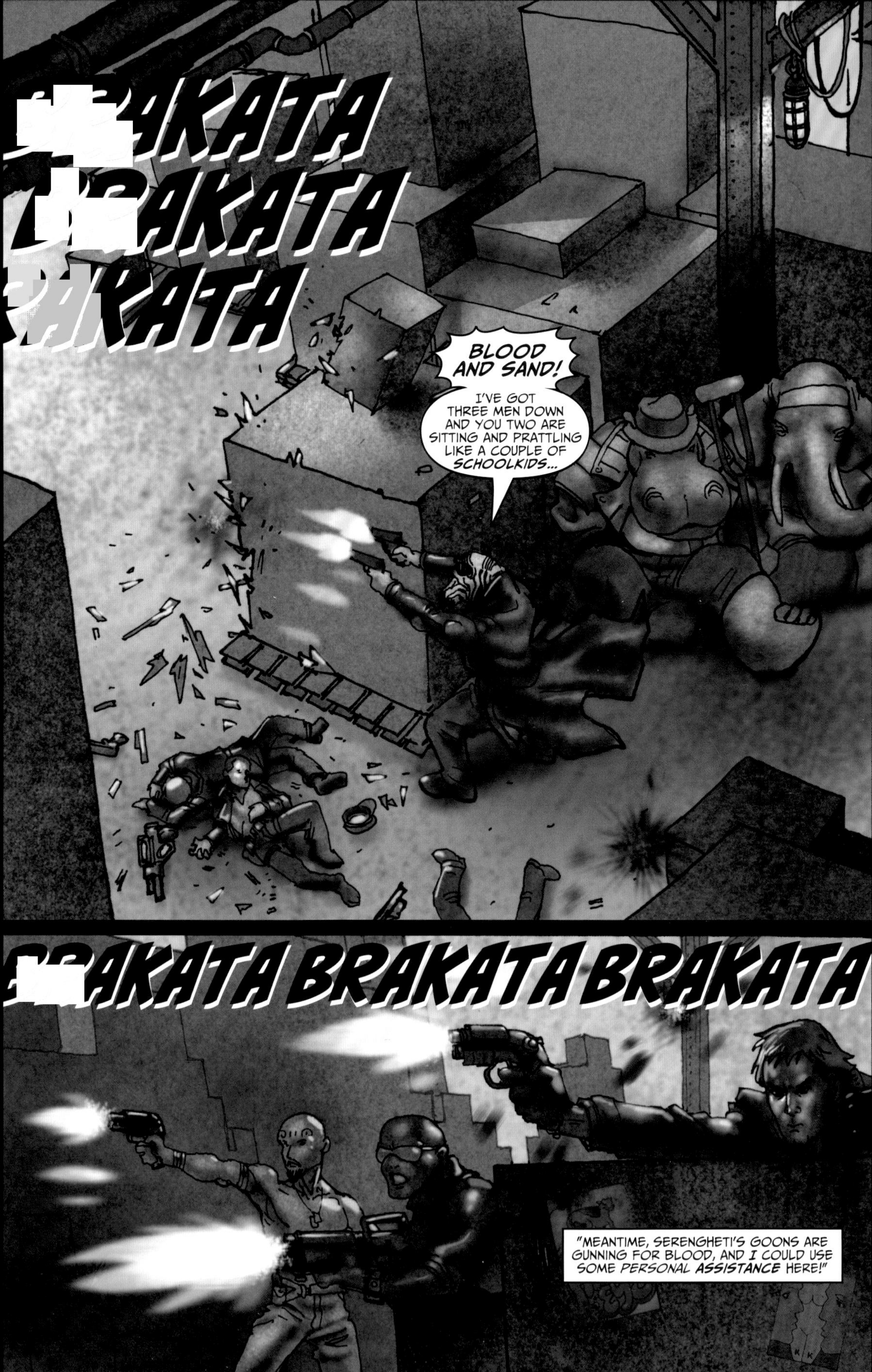
AKATA
AKATA
AKATA
BLOOD AND SAND!
I'VE GOT THREE MEN DOWN AND YOU TWO ARE SITTING AND PRATTLING LIKE A COUPLE OF SCHOOLKIDS...
AKATA BRAKATA BRAKATA
"MEANTIME, SERENGHETI'S GOONS ARE GUNNING FOR BLOOD, AND I COULD USE SOME PERSONAL ASSISTANCE HERE!"

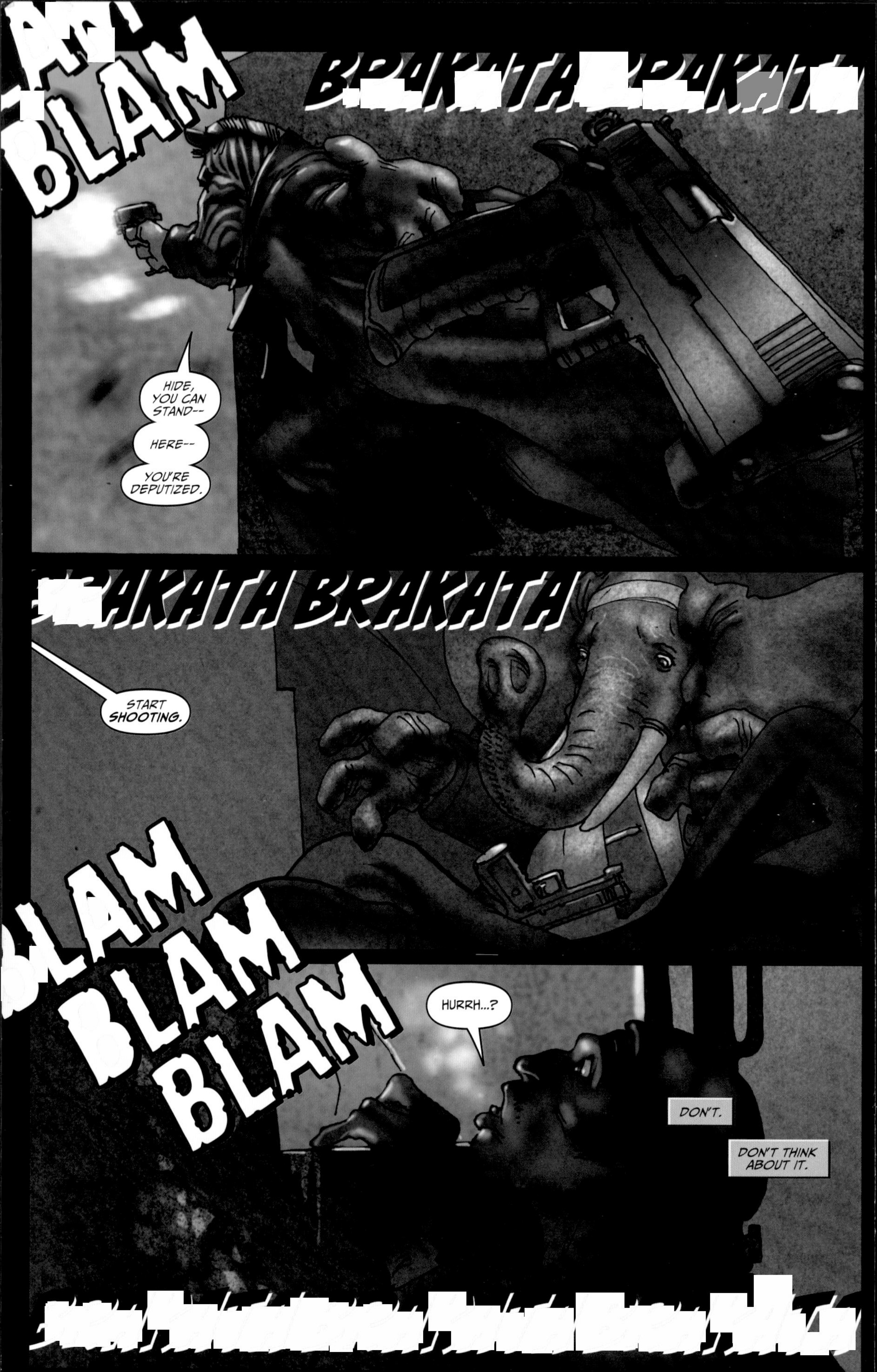
BLAM
HIDE, YOU CAN STAND--
HERE--
YOU'RE DEPUTIZED.
BRAKATA
START SHOOTING.
BLAM
BLAM
BLAM
HURRH...?
DON'T.
DON'T THINK ABOUT IT.

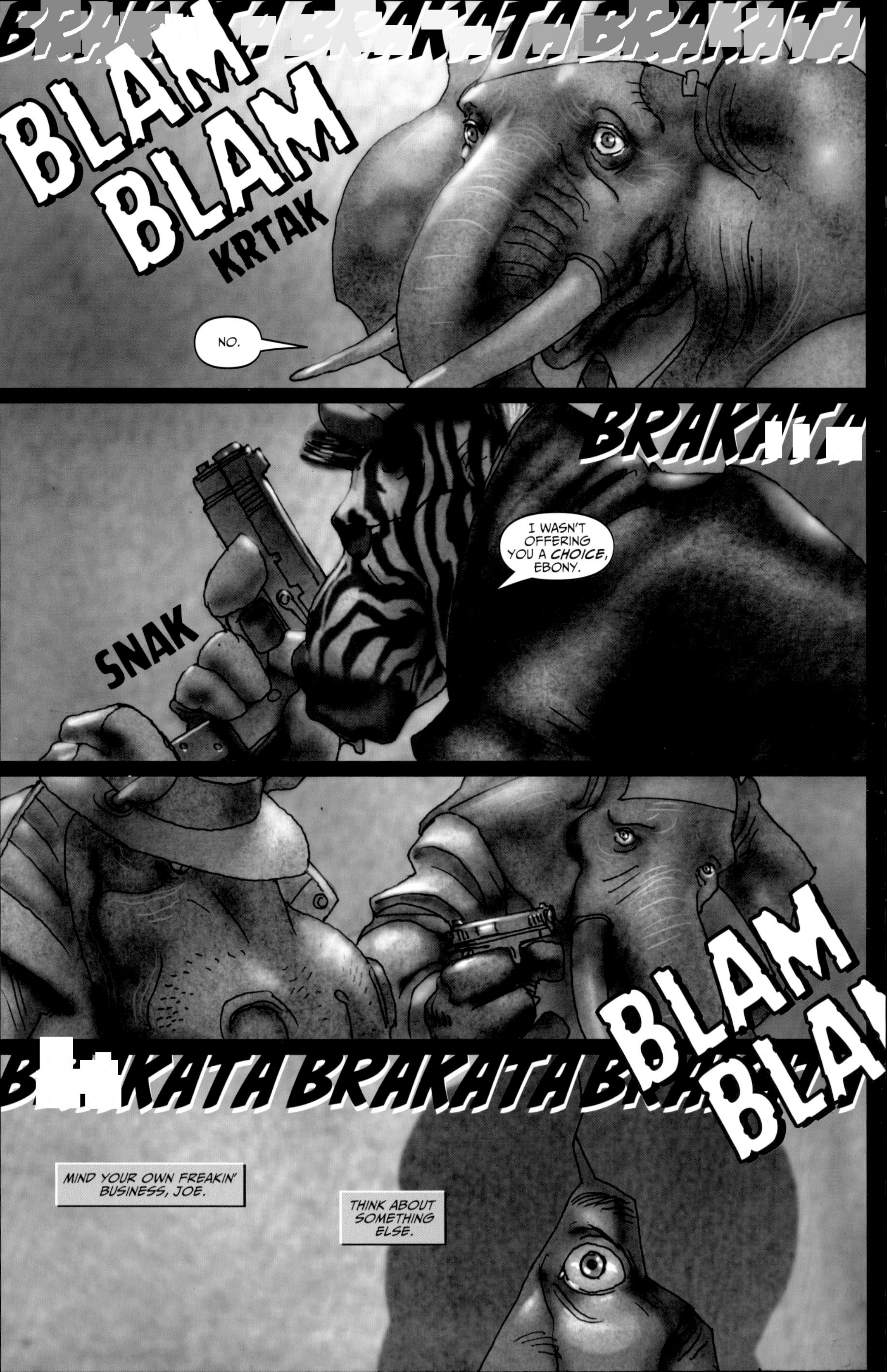
BLAM
BLAM
KRTAK
NO.
I WASN'T OFFERING YOU A CHOICE, EBONY.
SNAK
BLAM
BRAKATA
MIND YOUR OWN FREAKIN' BUSINESS, JOE.
THINK ABOUT SOMETHING ELSE.

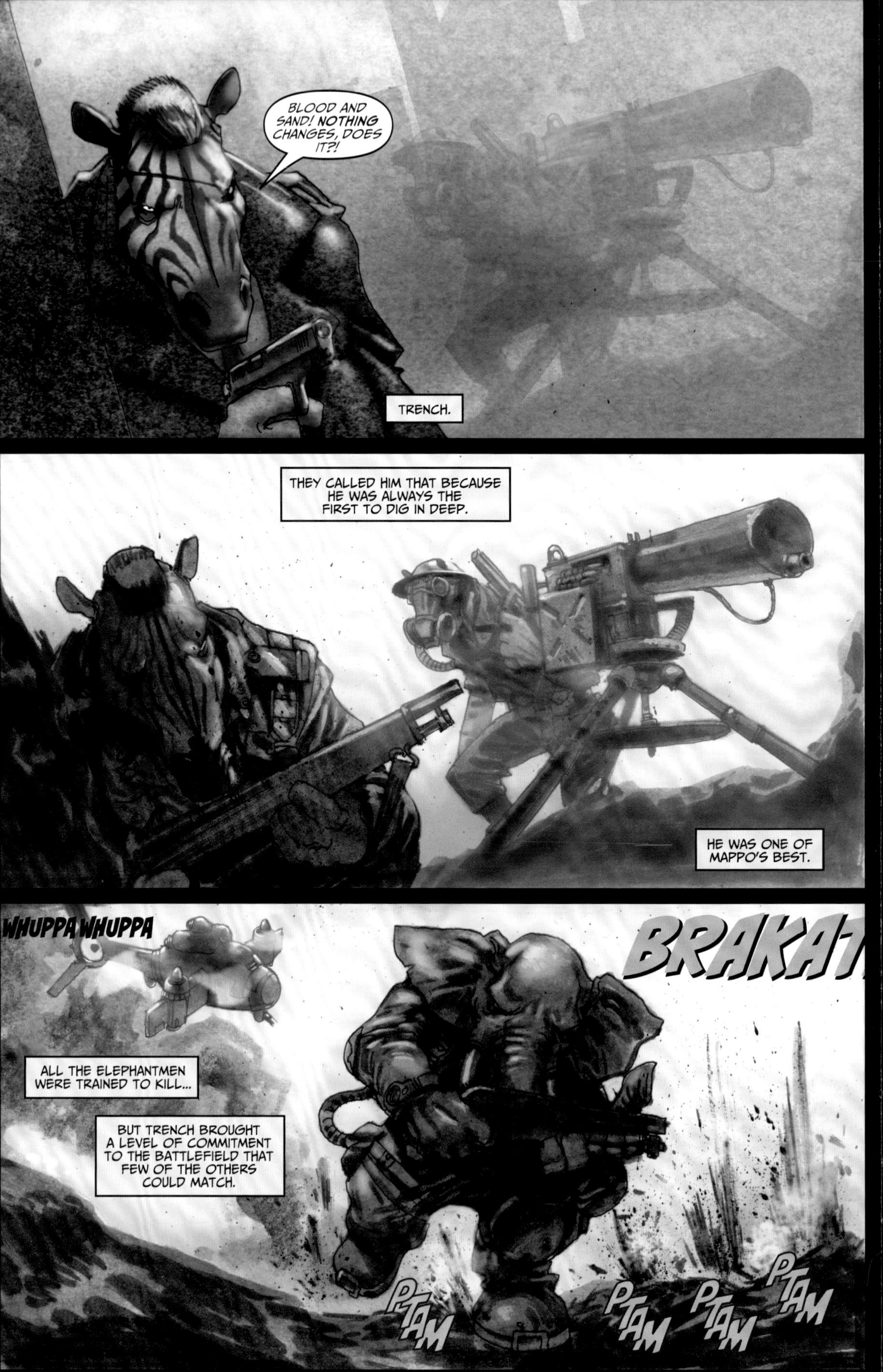
BLOOD AND SAND! NOTHING CHANGES, DOES IT?!
TRENCH.
THEY CALLED HIM THAT BECAUSE HE WAS ALWAYS THE FIRST TO DIG IN DEEP.
HE WAS ONE OF MAPPO'S BEST.
WHUPPA WHUPPA
BRAKAT
ALL THE ELEPHANTMEN WERE TRAINED TO KILL...
BUT TRENCH BROUGHT A LEVEL OF COMMITMENT TO THE BATTLEFIELD THAT FEW OF THE OTHERS COULD MATCH.
PTAM
PTAM
PTAM
PTAM

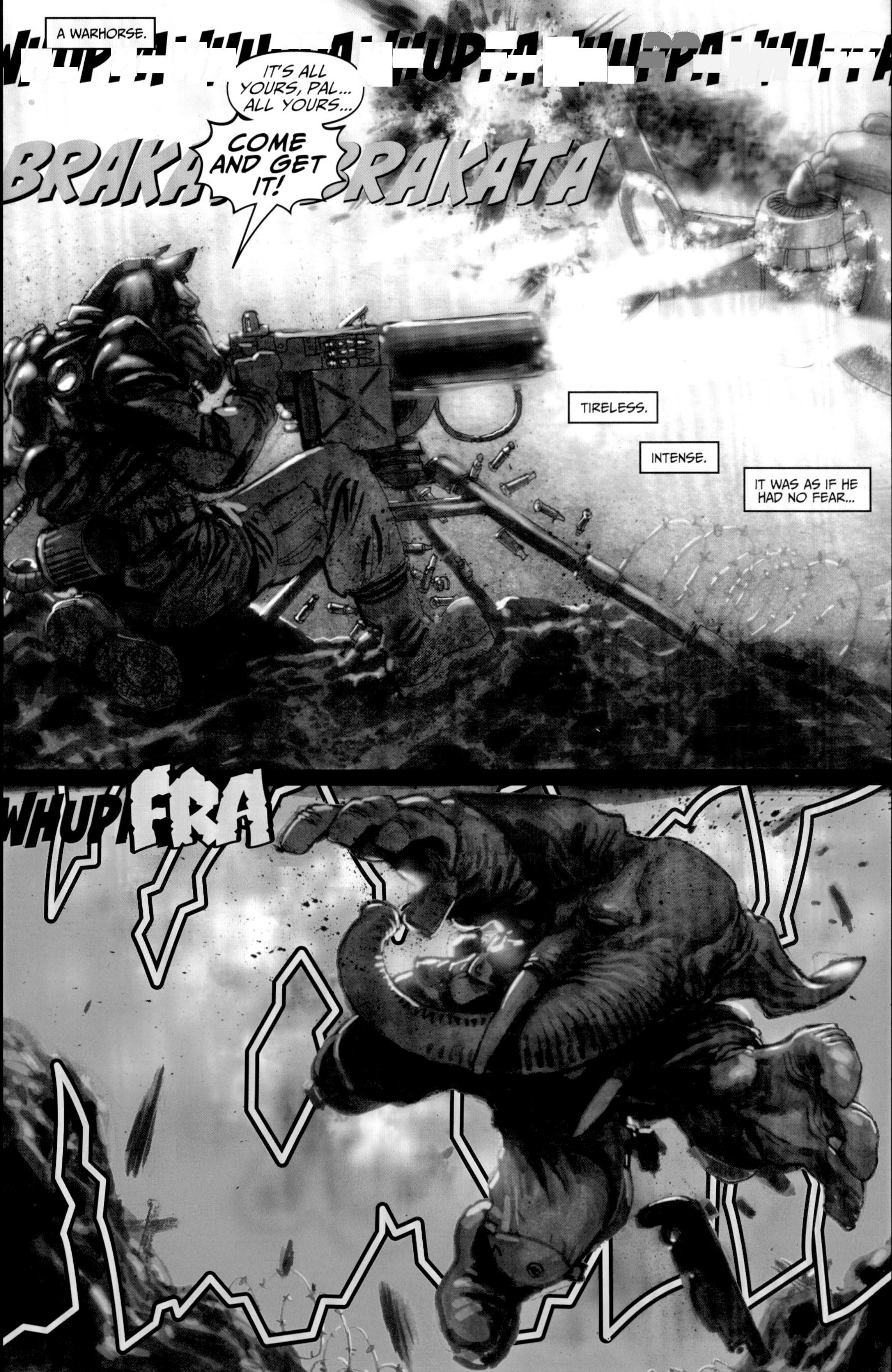
A WARHORSE.
IT'S ALL YOURS, PAL... ALL YOURS...
COME AND GET IT!
BRAKA
RAKATA
TIRELESS.
INTENSE.
IT WAS AS IF HE HAD NO FEAR...
WHUPFRA

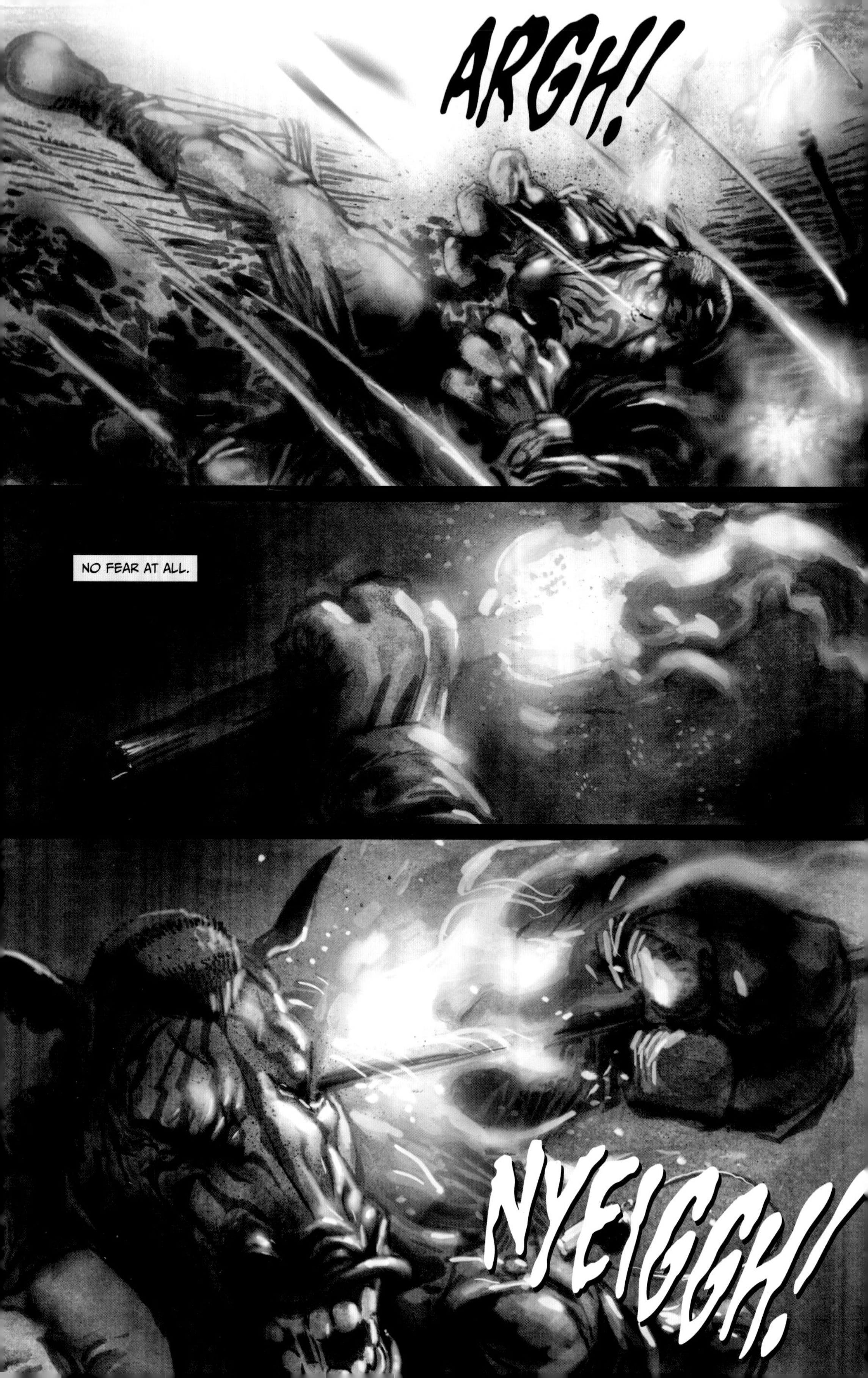
ARGH!
NO FEAR AT ALL.
NYEIGGH!

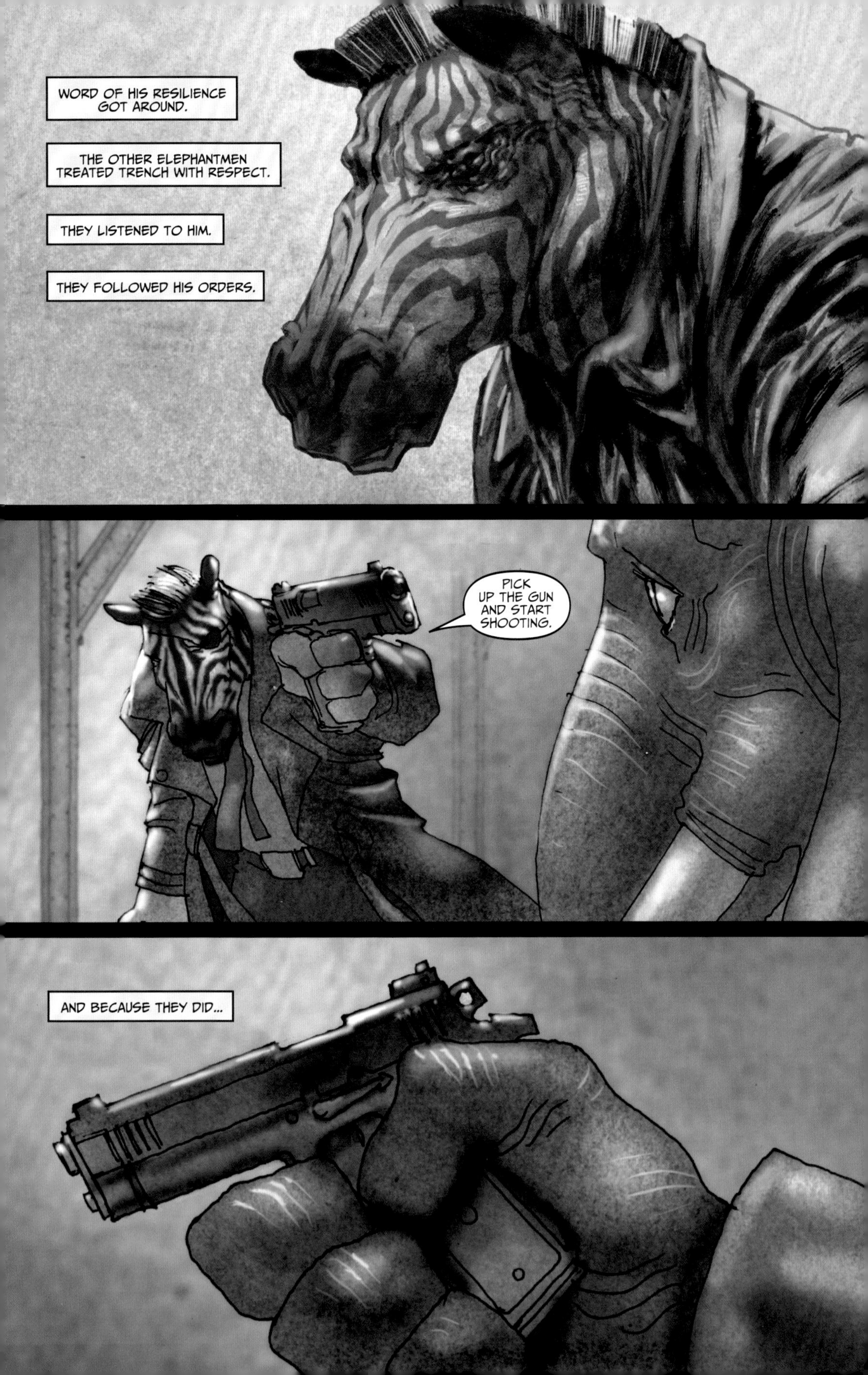
WORD OF HIS RESILIENCE GOT AROUND.
THE OTHER ELEPHANTMEN TREATED TRENCH WITH RESPECT.
THEY LISTENED TO HIM.
THEY FOLLOWED HIS ORDERS.
PICK UP THE GUN AND START SHOOTING.
AND BECAUSE THEY DID...

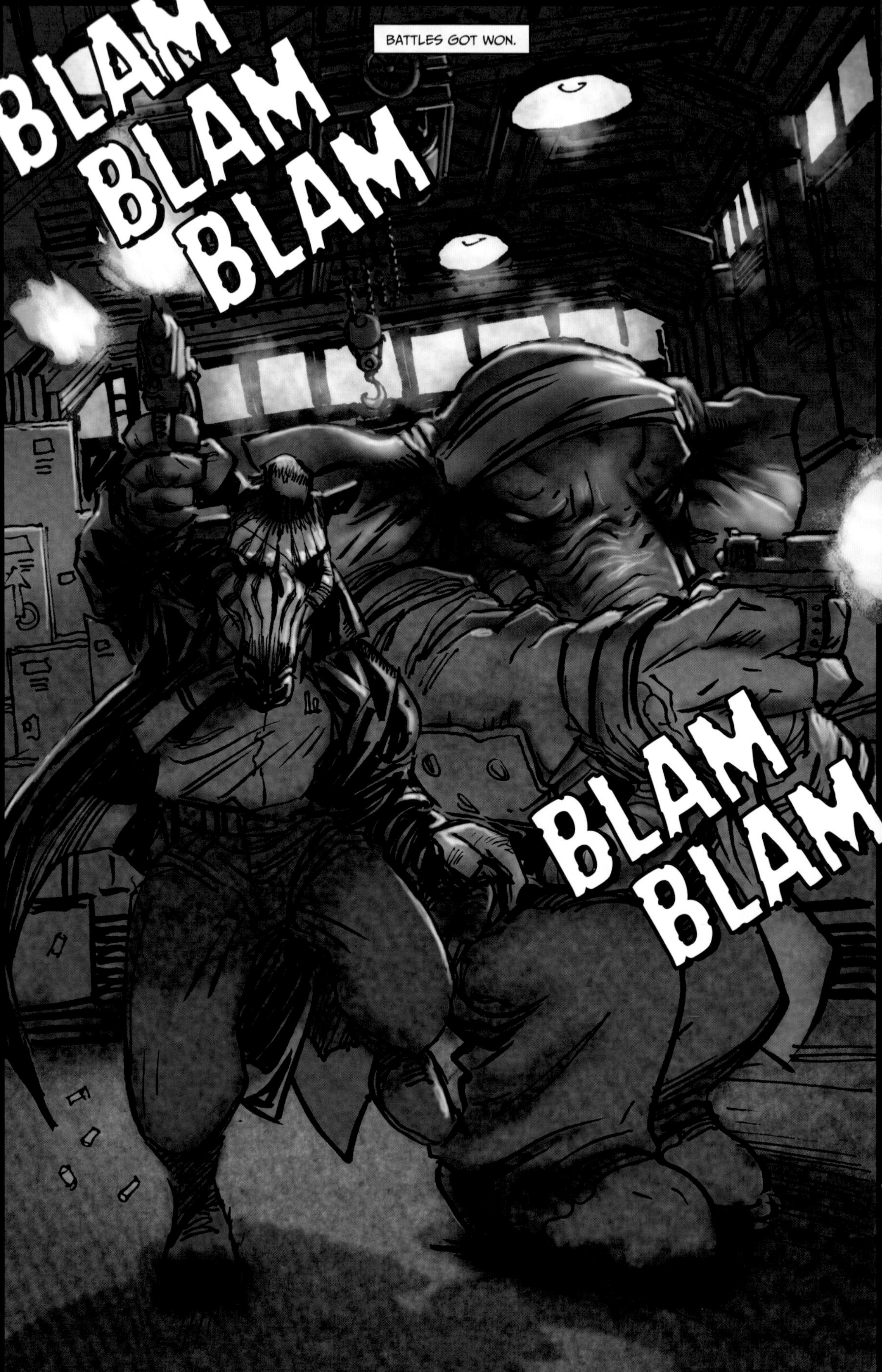
BATTLES GOT WON.
BLAM
BLAM
BLAM
BLAM
BLAM

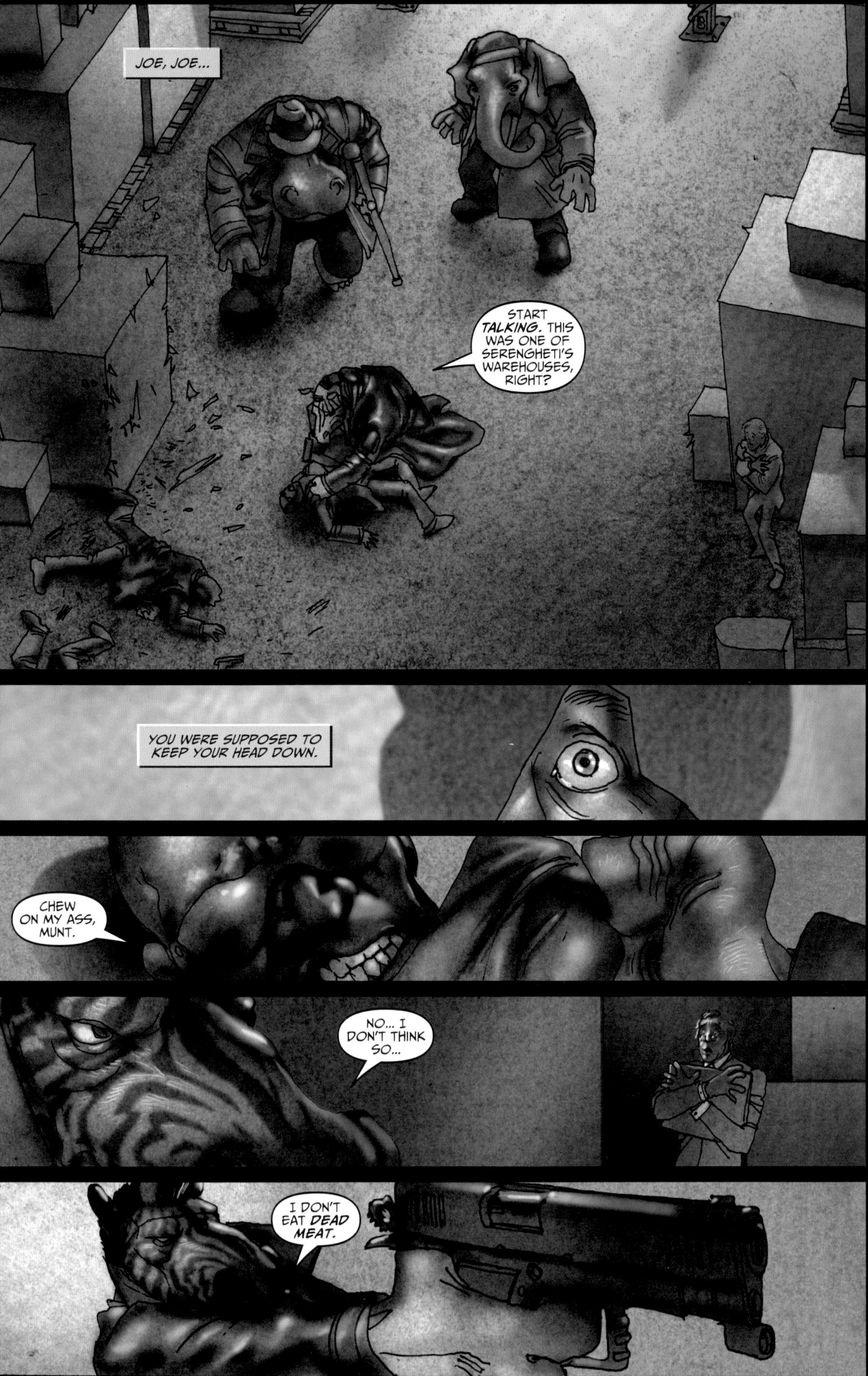
JOE, JOE...
START TALKING. THIS WAS ONE OF SERENGHETI'S WAREHOUSES, RIGHT?
YOU WERE SUPPOSED TO KEEP YOUR HEAD DOWN.
CHEW ON MY ASS, MUNT.
NO... I DON'T THINK SO...
I DON'T EAT DEAD MEAT.

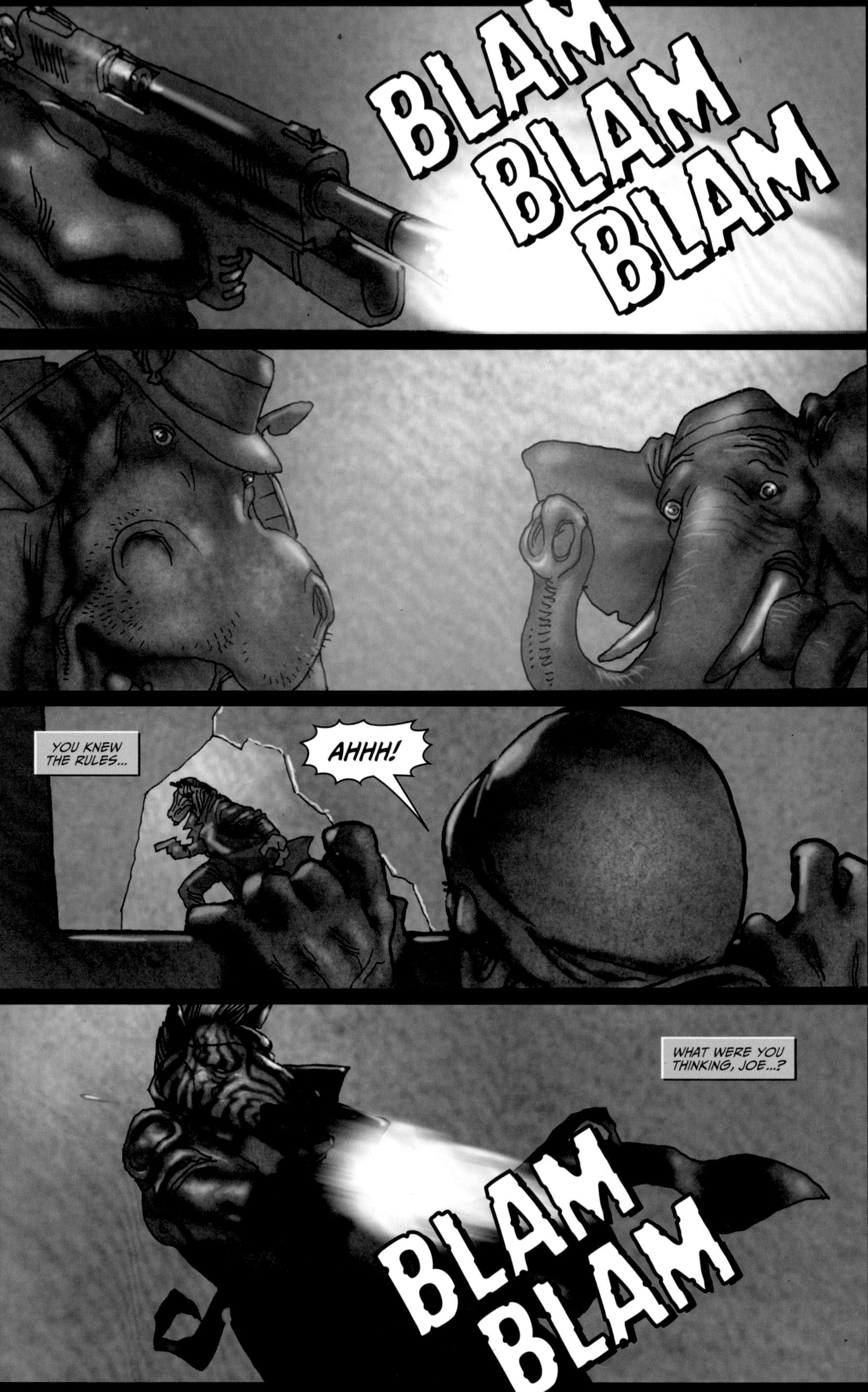
BLAM
BLAM
BLAM
YOU KNEW THE RULES...
AHHH!
WHAT WERE YOU THINKING, JOE...?
BLAM
BLAM

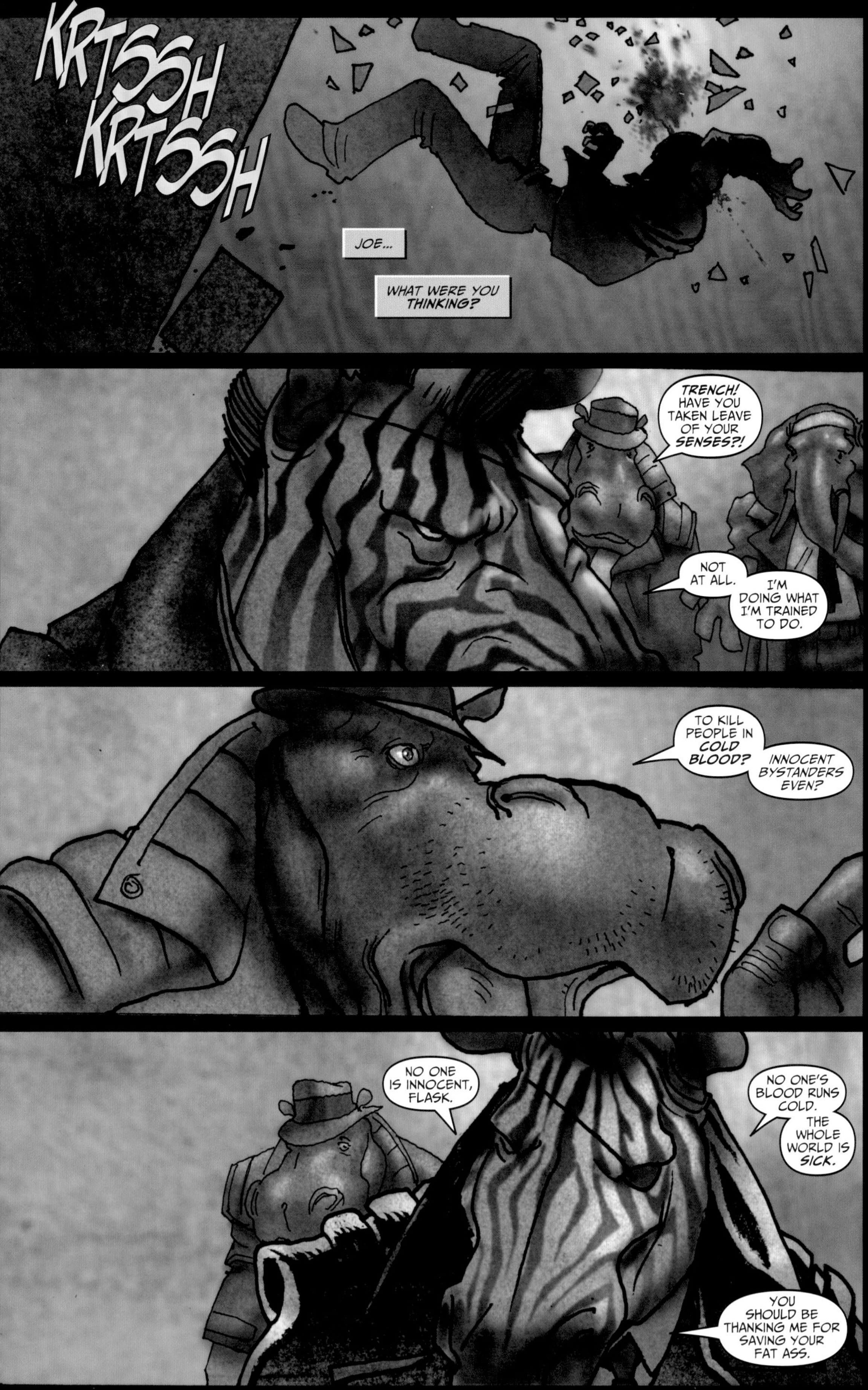
KRTSSH KRTSSH
JOE...
WHAT WERE YOU THINKING?
TRENCH! HAVE YOU TAKEN LEAVE OF YOUR SENSES?!
NOT AT ALL.
I'M DOING WHAT I'M TRAINED TO DO.
TO KILL PEOPLE IN COLD BLOOD?
INNOCENT BYSTANDERS EVEN?
NO ONE IS INNOCENT, FLASK.
NO ONE'S BLOOD RUNS COLD.
THE WHOLE WORLD IS SICK.
YOU SHOULD BE THANKING ME FOR SAVING YOUR FAT ASS.

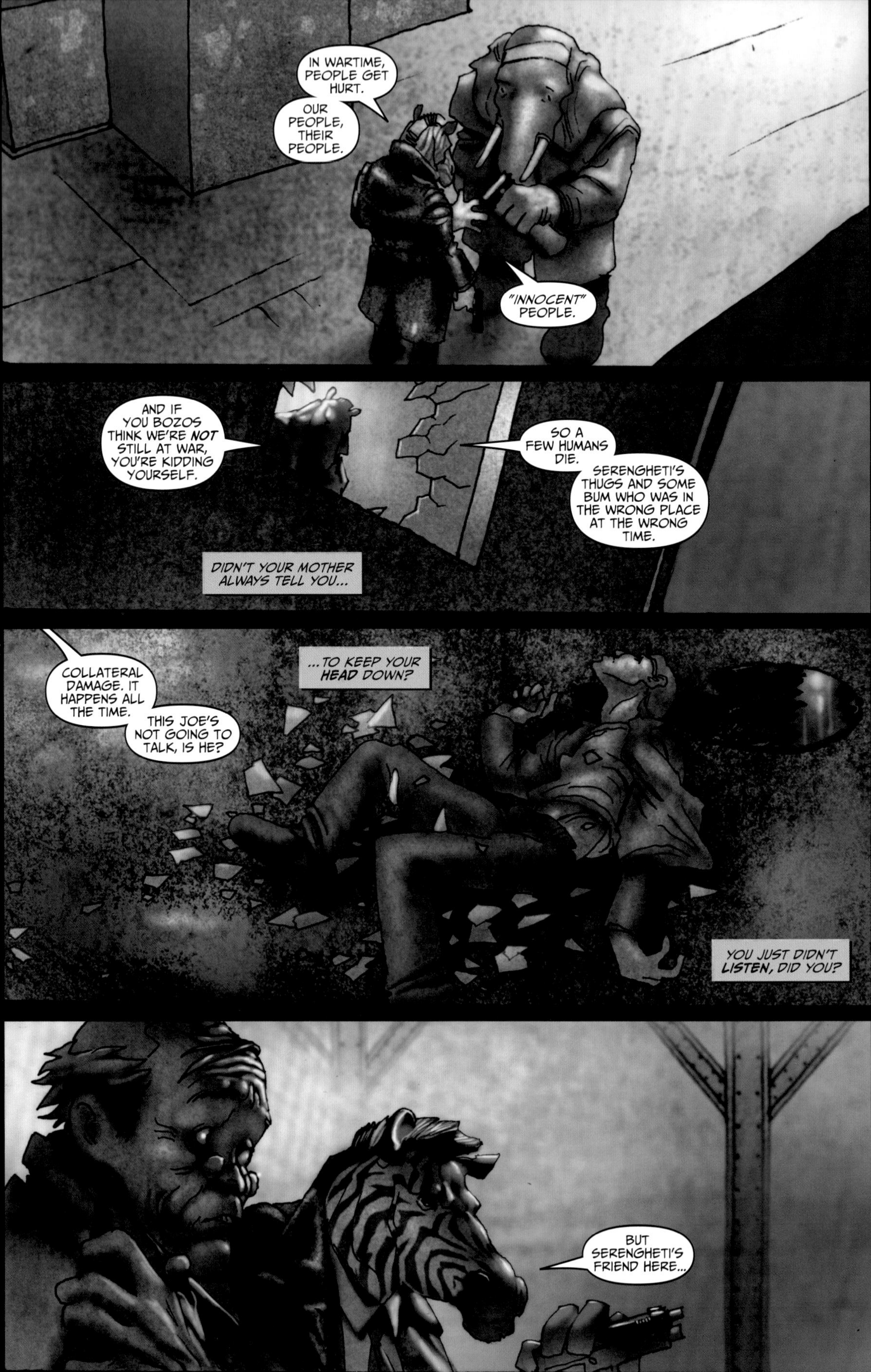
IN WARTIME, PEOPLE GET HURT.
OUR PEOPLE, THEIR PEOPLE.
"INNOCENT" PEOPLE.
AND IF YOU BOZOS THINK WE'RE **NOT** STILL AT WAR, YOU'RE KIDDING YOURSELF.
SO A FEW HUMANS DIE.
SERENGHETI'S THUGS AND SOME BUM WHO WAS IN THE WRONG PLACE AT THE WRONG TIME.
DIDN'T YOUR MOTHER ALWAYS TELL YOU...
COLLATERAL DAMAGE. IT HAPPENS ALL THE TIME.
THIS JOE'S NOT GOING TO TALK, IS HE?
*...TO KEEP YOUR **HEAD** DOWN?*
*YOU JUST DIDN'T **LISTEN,** DID YOU?*
BUT SERENGHETI'S FRIEND HERE...

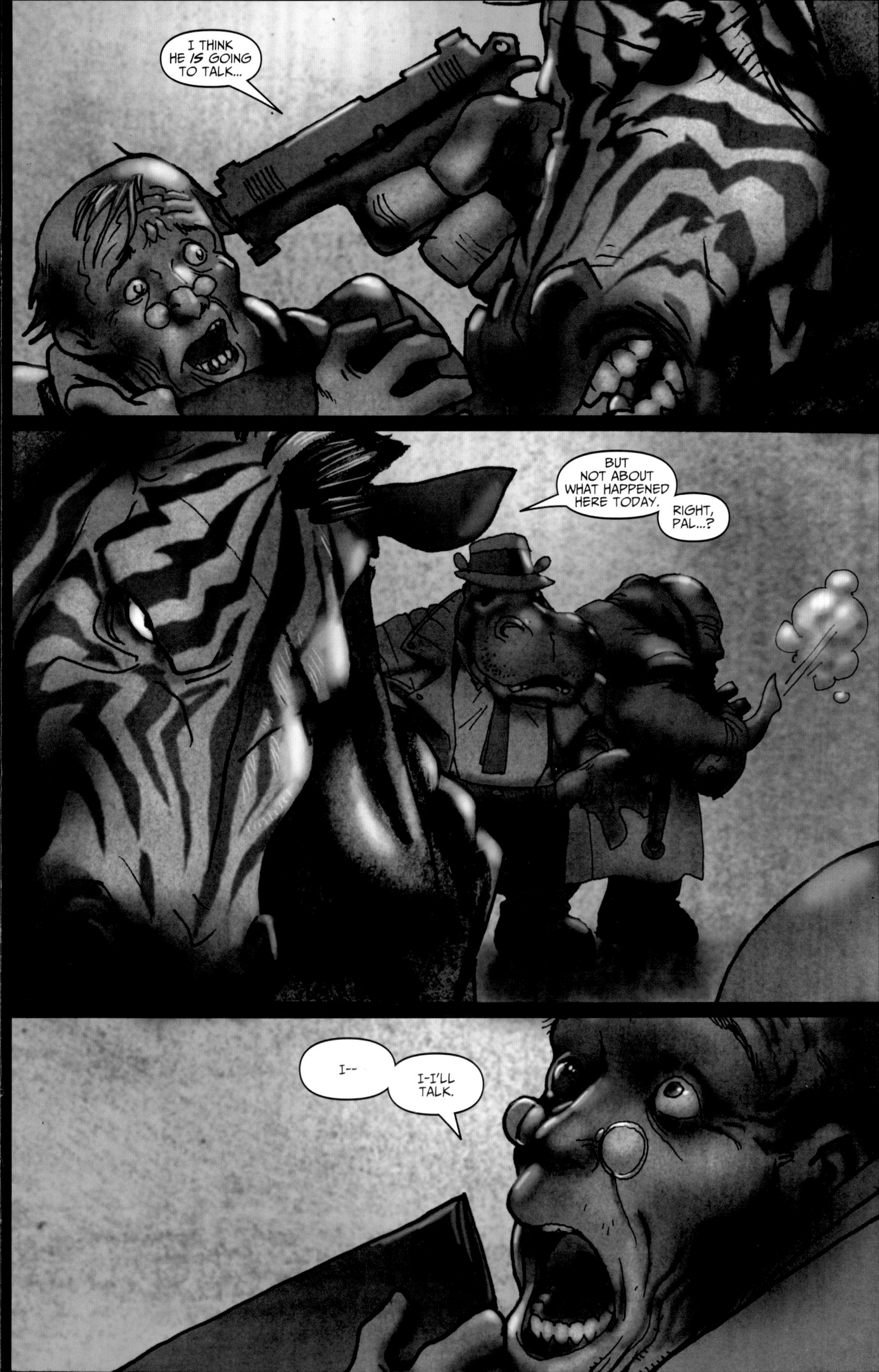
I THINK HE IS GOING TO TALK...
BUT NOT ABOUT WHAT HAPPENED HERE TODAY.
RIGHT, PAL...?
I--
I-I'LL TALK.

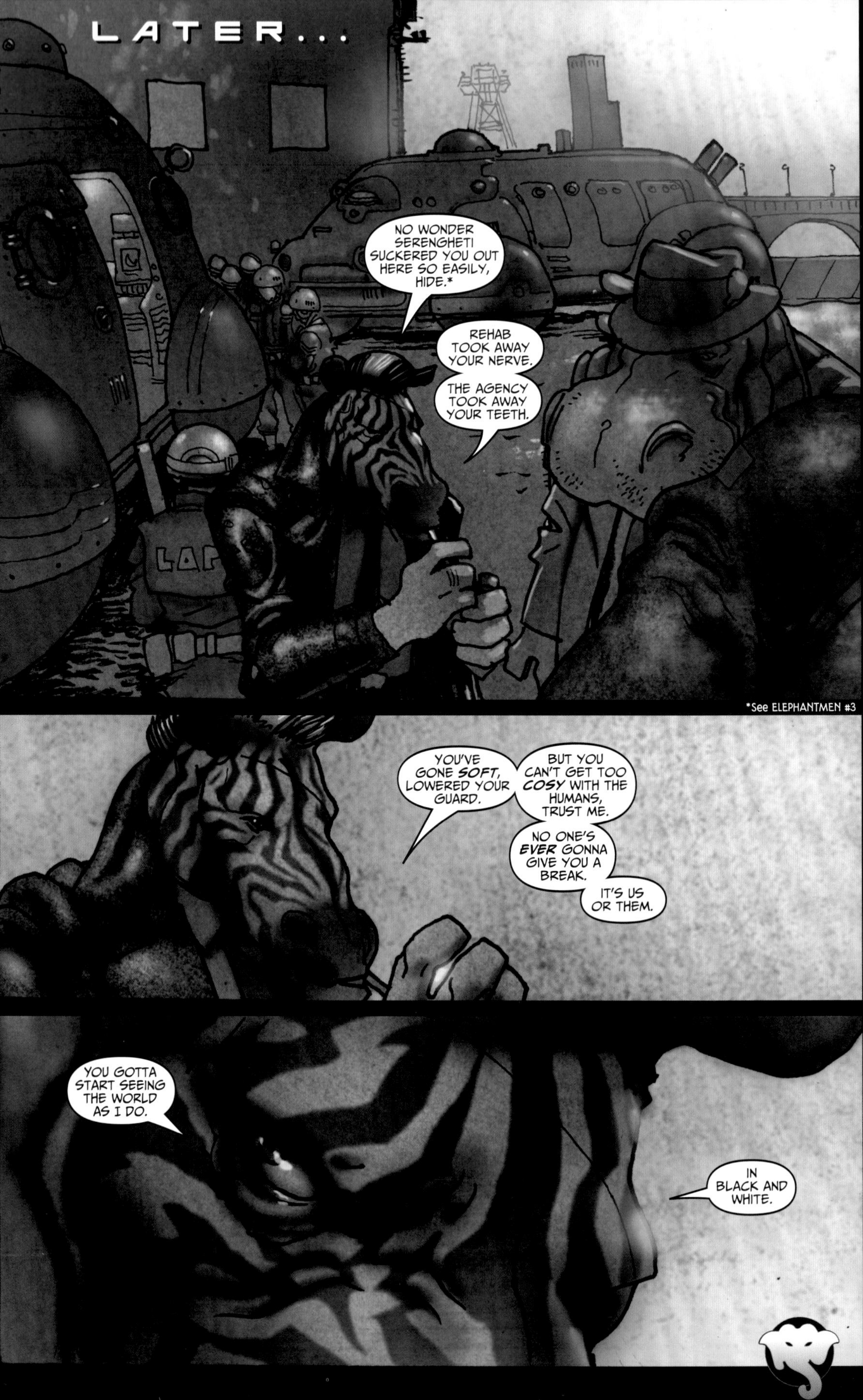
LATER...
NO WONDER SERENGHETI SUCKERED YOU OUT HERE SO EASILY, HIDE.*
REHAB TOOK AWAY YOUR NERVE.
THE AGENCY TOOK AWAY YOUR TEETH.
*See ELEPHANTMEN #3
YOU'VE GONE SOFT, LOWERED YOUR GUARD.
BUT YOU CAN'T GET TOO COSY WITH THE HUMANS, TRUST ME.
NO ONE'S EVER GONNA GIVE YOU A BREAK.
IT'S US OR THEM.
YOU GOTTA START SEEING THE WORLD AS I DO.
IN BLACK AND WHITE.

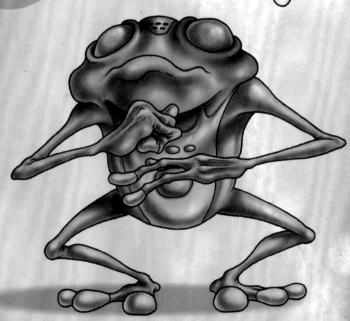

Elephantmen

WAGNER the iFROG | Father

IN HIS OWN ADVENTURE AT LAST!
WAGNER
THE iFROG IN
MONKEY BUSINESS

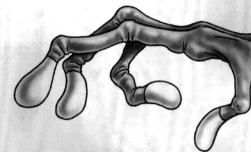

JILL FRESHNEY & ROB STEEN

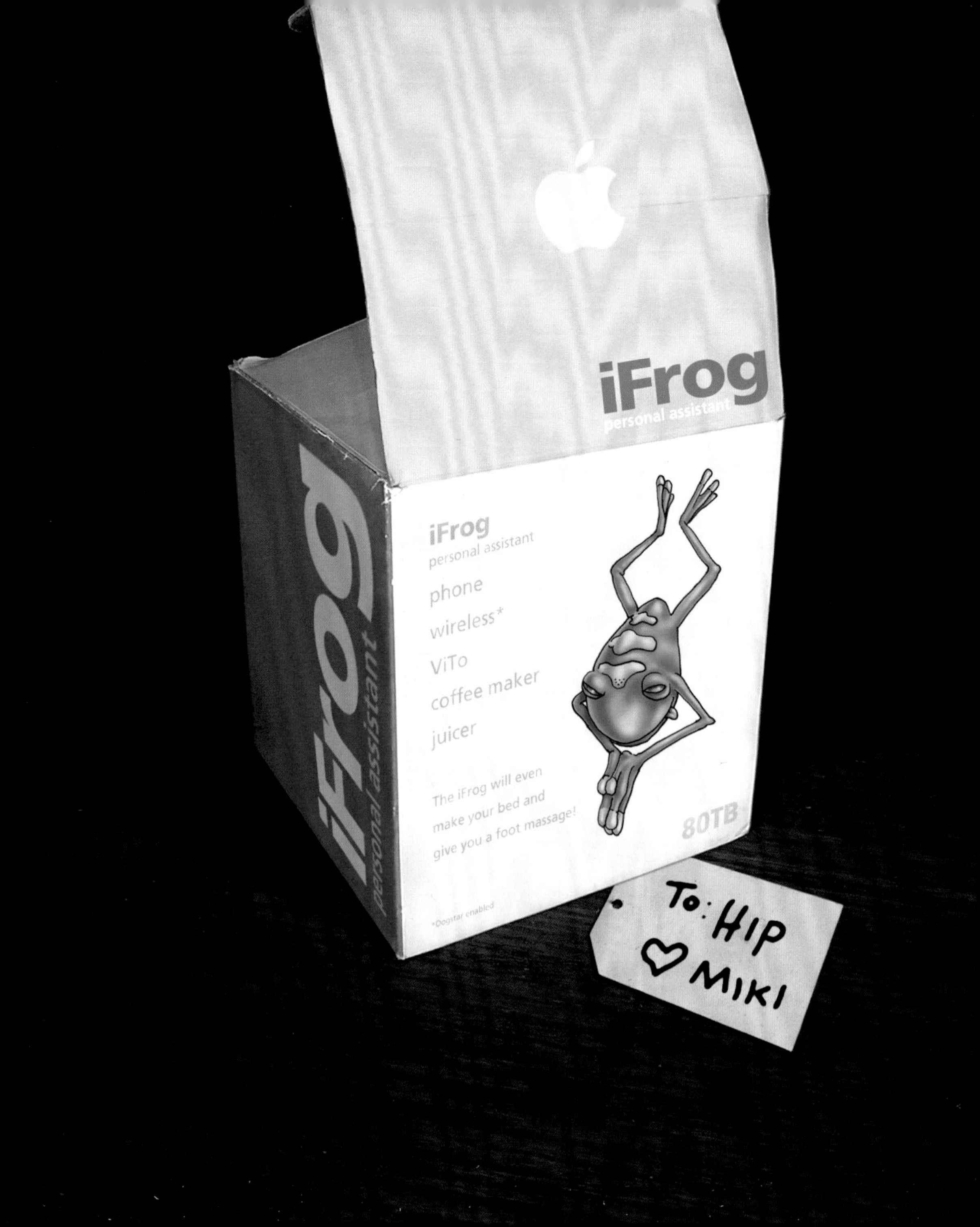
iFrog
personal assistant
iFrog
personal assistant
iFrog
personal assistant
phone
wireless*
ViTo
coffee maker
juicer
The iFrog will even
make your bed and
give you a foot massage!
80TB
*Dogstar enabled
To: Hip
♡ Miki

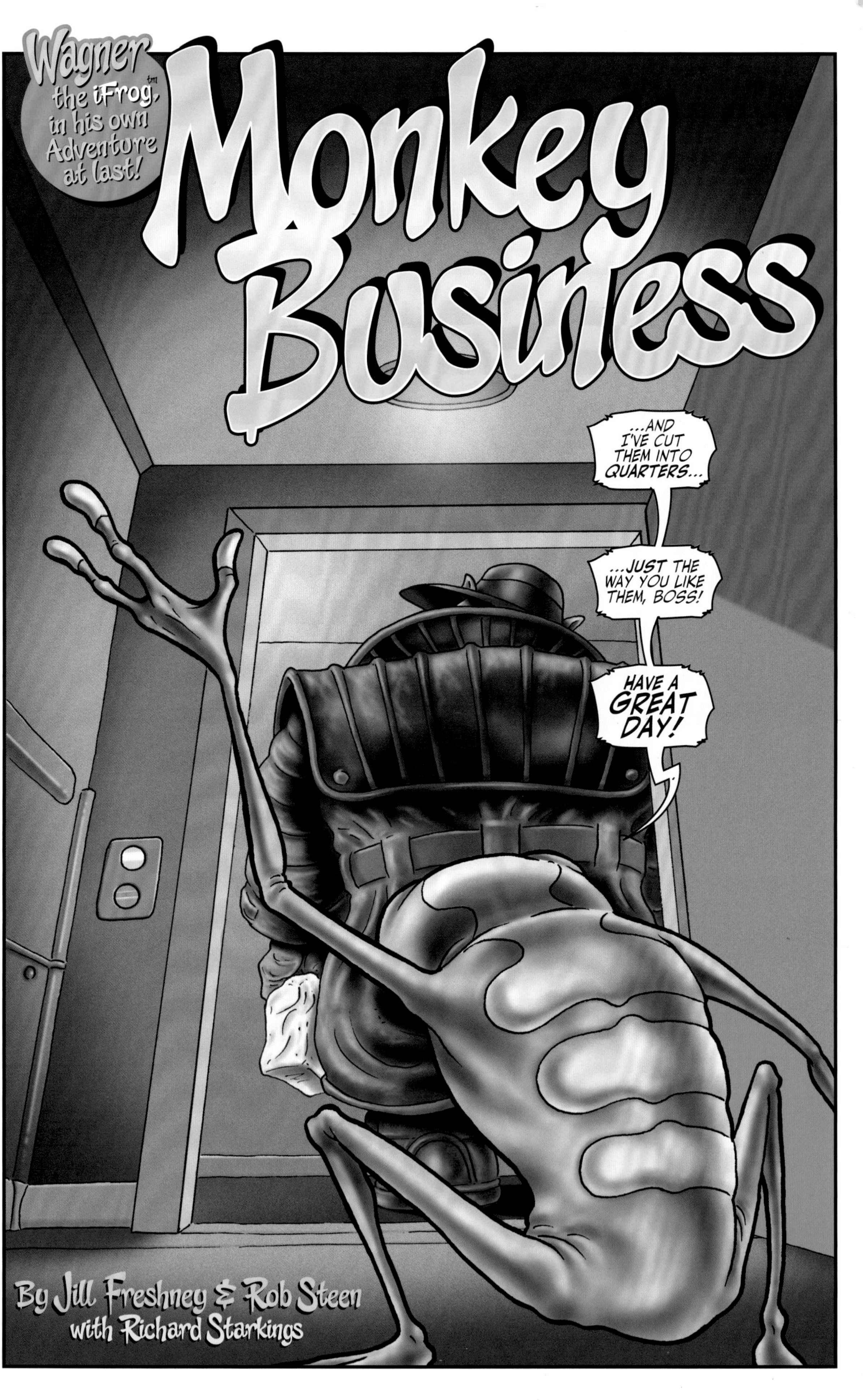
Wagner the iFrog, in his own Adventure at last!
tm
Monkey Business
...AND I'VE CUT THEM INTO QUARTERS...
...JUST THE WAY YOU LIKE THEM, BOSS!
HAVE A GREAT DAY!
By Jill Freshney & Rob Steen
with Richard Starkings

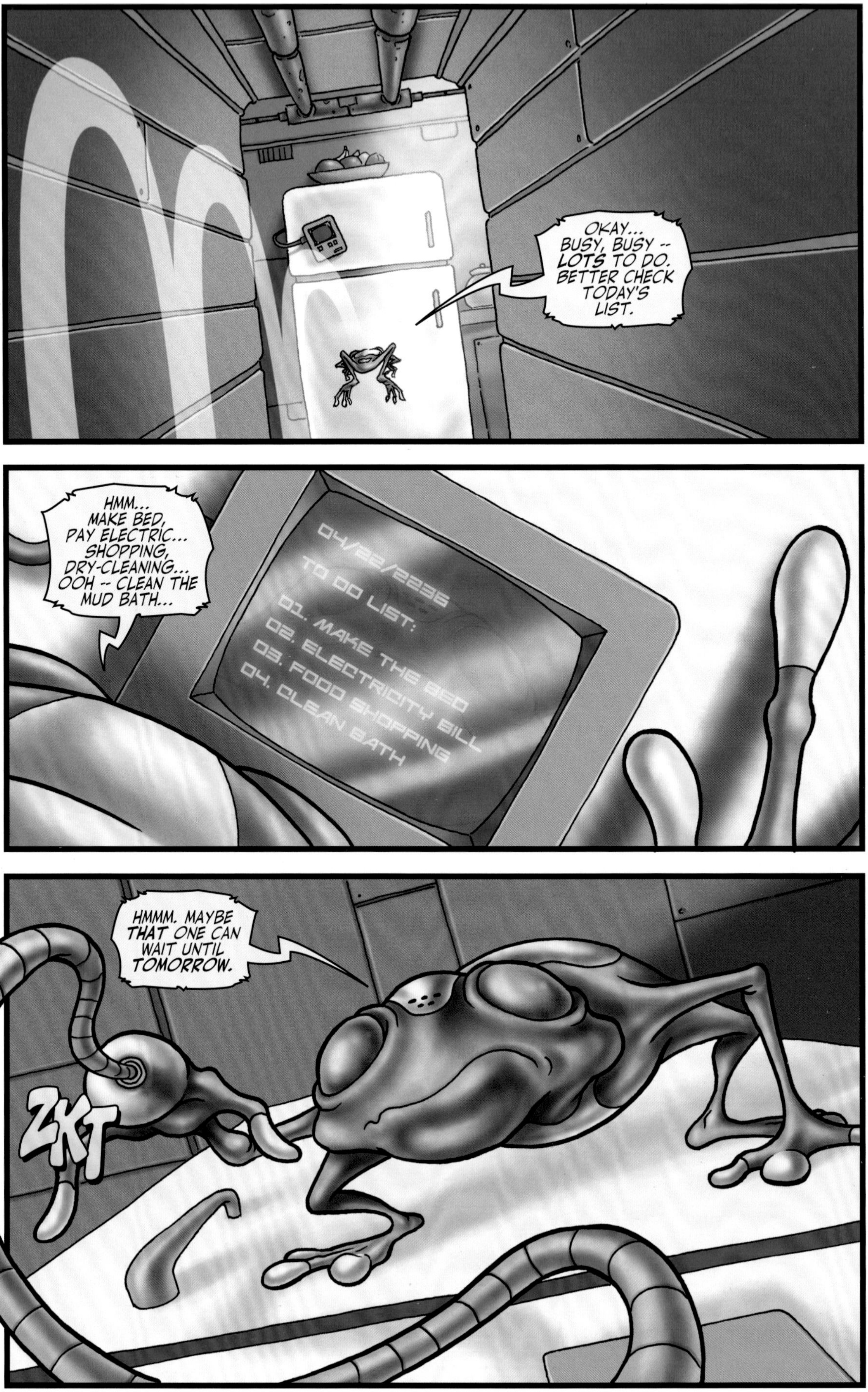
OKAY... BUSY, BUSY -- LOTS TO DO. BETTER CHECK TODAY'S LIST.
HMM... MAKE BED, PAY ELECTRIC... SHOPPING, DRY-CLEANING... OOH -- CLEAN THE MUD BATH...
04/22/2236
TO DO LIST:
01. MAKE THE BED
02. ELECTRICITY BILL
03. FOOD SHOPPING
04. CLEAN BATH
HMMM. MAYBE THAT ONE CAN WAIT UNTIL TOMORROW.
ZKT

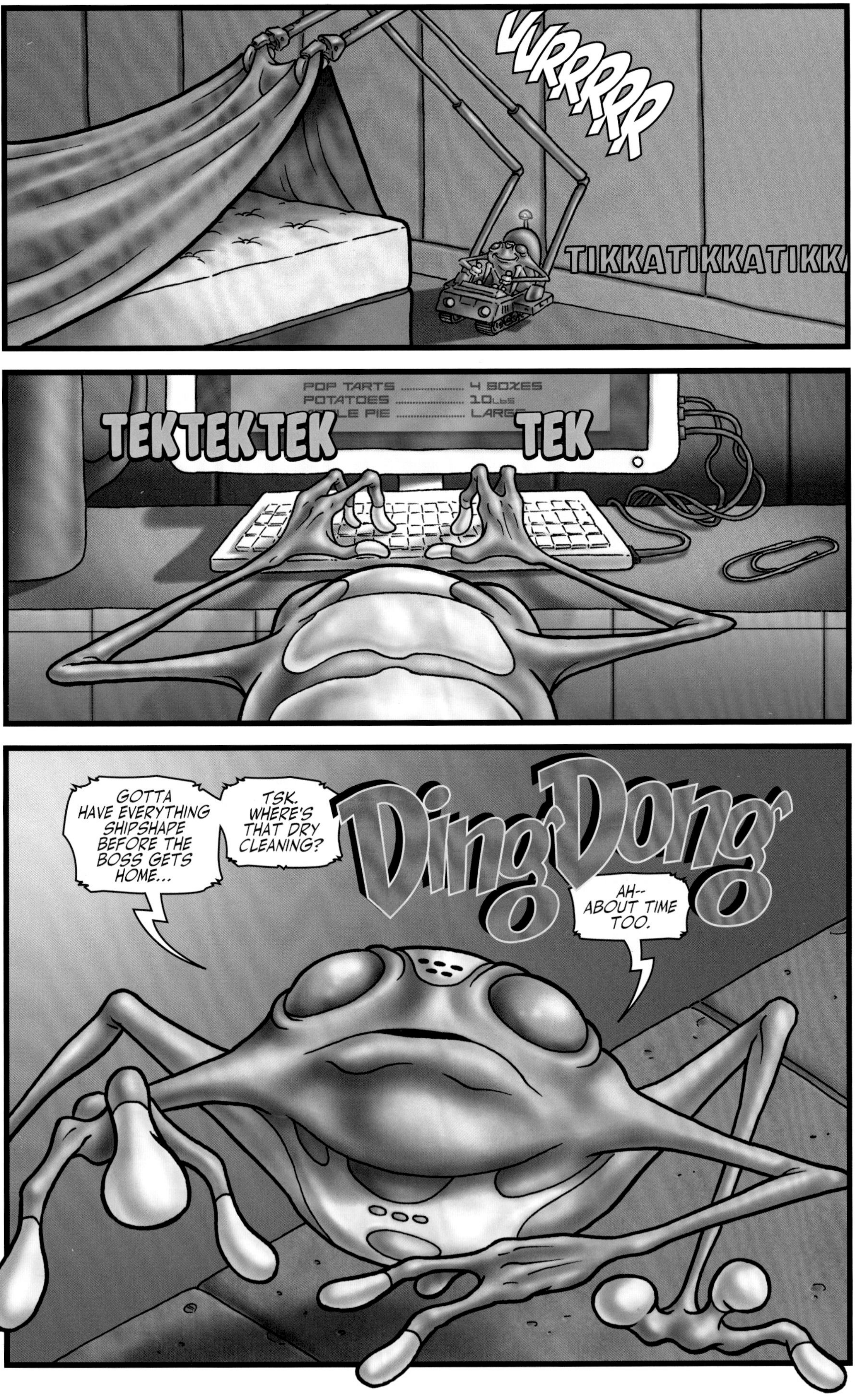
VVRRRRRR
TIKKATIKKATIKKA
POP TARTS .... 4 BOXES
POTATOES 10Lbs
TEKTEKTEK
TEK
GOTTA HAVE EVERYTHING SHIPSHAPE BEFORE THE BOSS GETS HOME...
TSK. WHERE'S THAT DRY CLEANING?
Ding Dong
AH-- ABOUT TIME TOO.

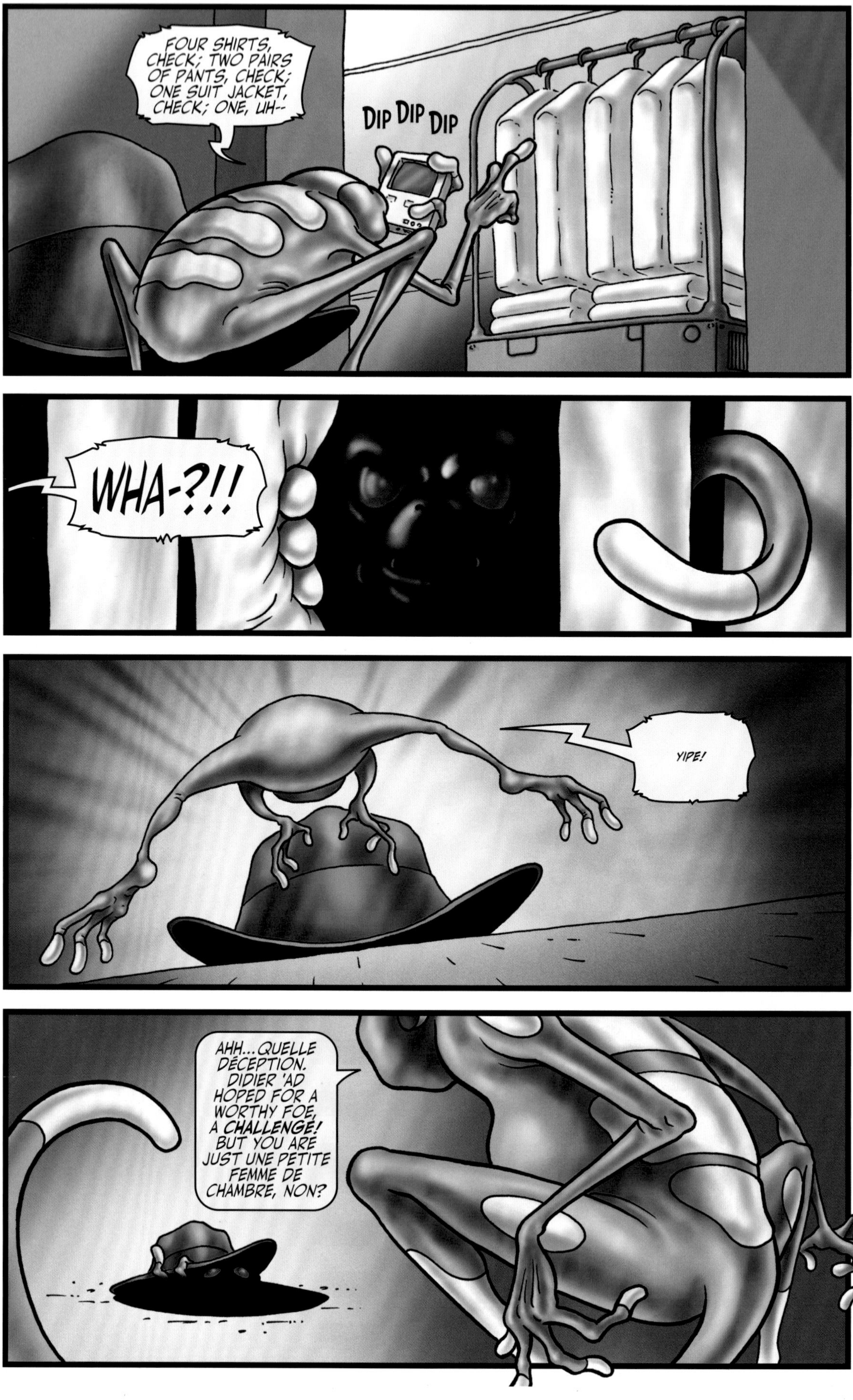
FOUR SHIRTS, CHECK; TWO PAIRS OF PANTS, CHECK; ONE SUIT JACKET, CHECK; ONE, UH--
DIP DIP DIP
WHA-?!!
YIPE!
AHH... QUELLE DÉCEPTION. DIDIER 'AD HOPED FOR A WORTHY FOE, A **CHALLENGE!** BUT YOU ARE JUST UNE PETITE FEMME DE CHAMBRE, NON?

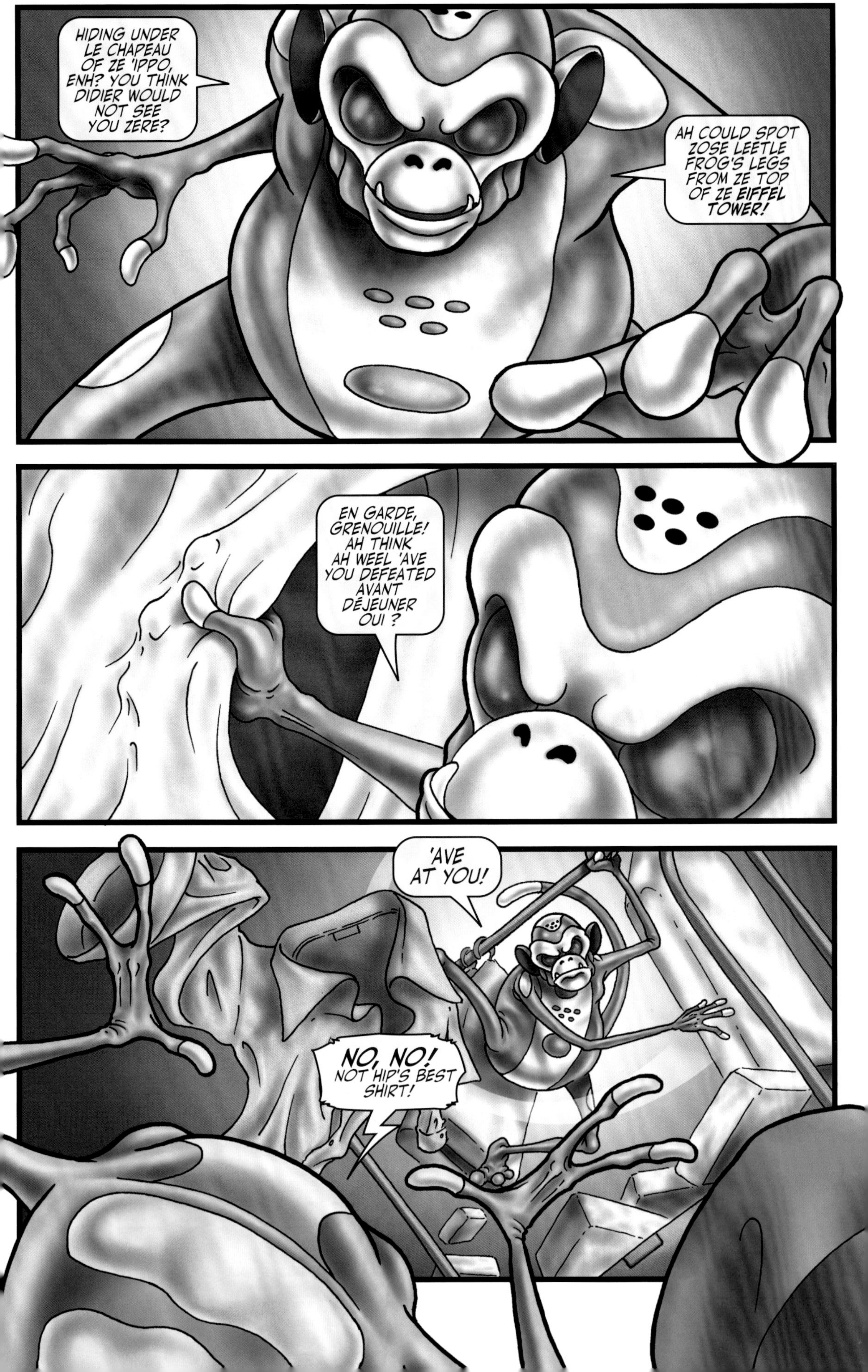
HIDING UNDER LE CHAPEAU OF ZE 'IPPO, ENH? YOU THINK DIDIER WOULD NOT SEE YOU ZERE?
AH COULD SPOT ZOSE LEETLE FROG'S LEGS FROM ZE TOP OF ZE EIFFEL TOWER!
EN GARDE, GRENOUILLE! AH THINK AH WEEL 'AVE YOU DEFEATED AVANT DÉJEUNER OUI ?
'AVE AT YOU!
NO, NO! NOT HIP'S BEST SHIRT!

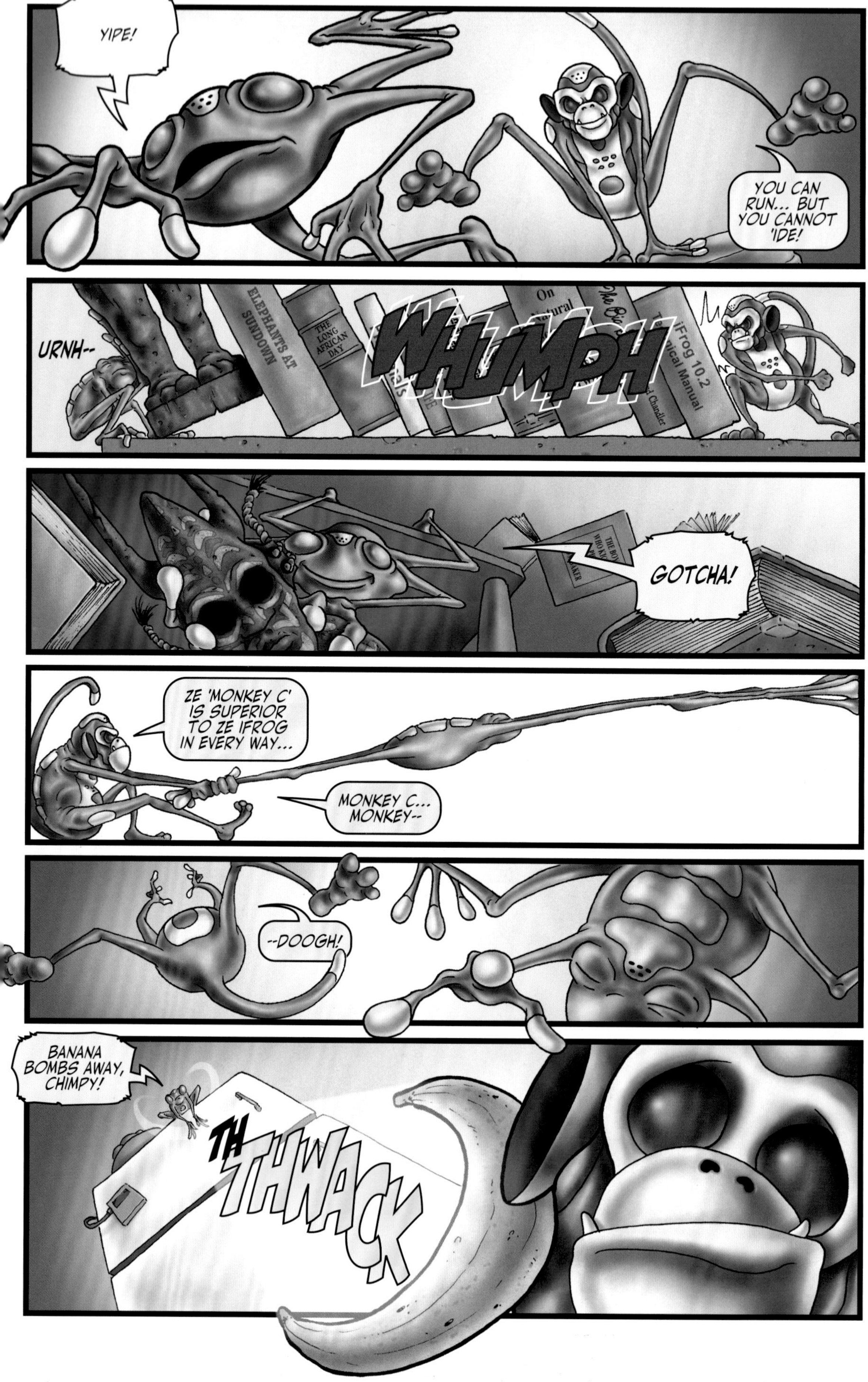
YIPE!
YOU CAN RUN... BUT YOU CANNOT 'IDE!
URNH--
WHUMPH
ELEPHANTS AT SUNDOWN
THE LONG AFRICAN DAY
iFrog 10.2 Technical Manual
GOTCHA!
ZE 'MONKEY C' IS SUPERIOR TO ZE IFROG IN EVERY WAY...
MONKEY C... MONKEY--
--DOOGH!
BANANA BOMBS AWAY, CHIMPY!
THTHWACK

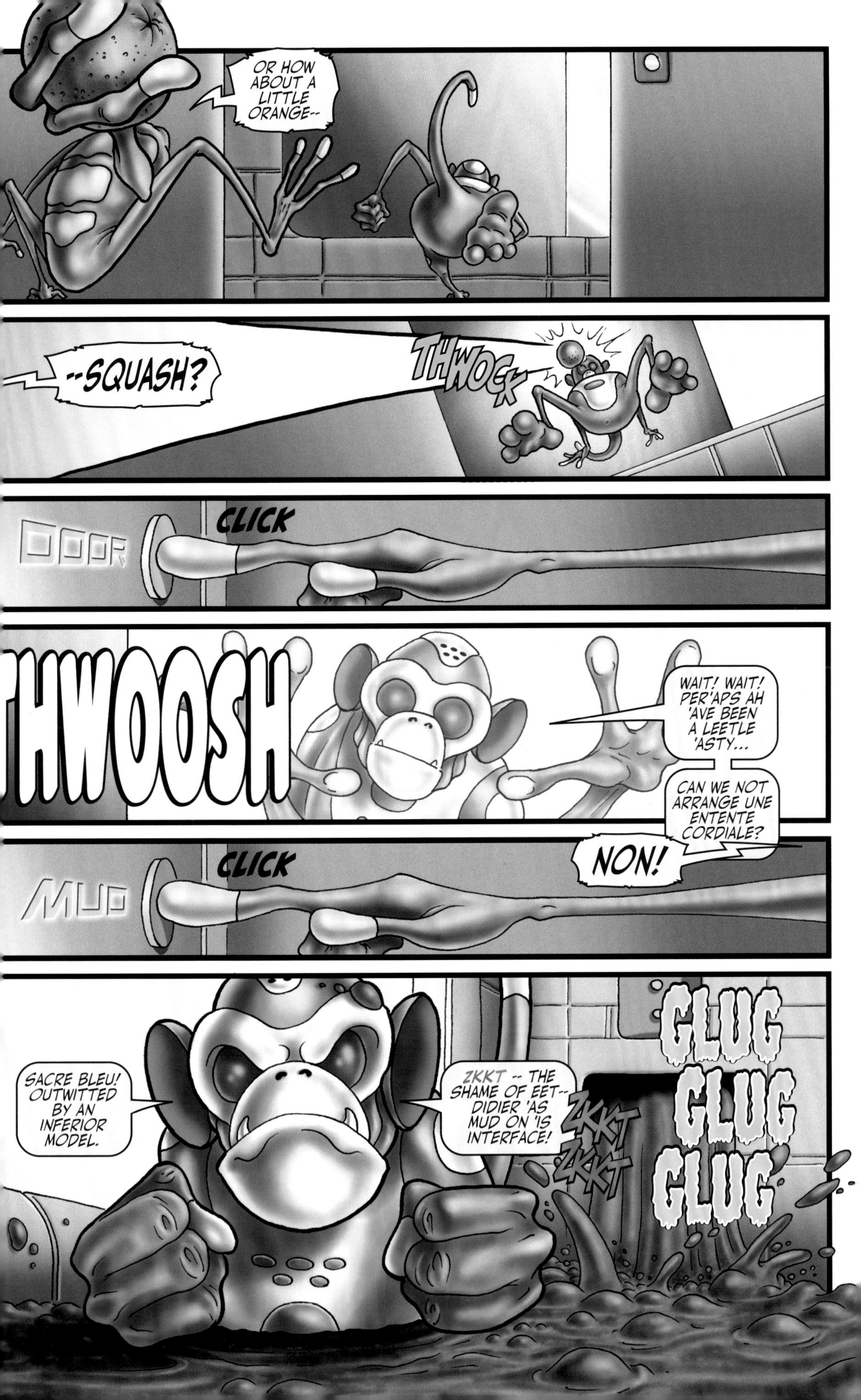
OR HOW ABOUT A LITTLE ORANGE--
--SQUASH?
THWOCK
DOOR
CLICK
THWOOSH
WAIT! WAIT! PER'APS AH 'AVE BEEN A LEETLE 'ASTY...
CAN WE NOT ARRANGE UNE ENTENTE CORDIALE?
NON!
MUD
CLICK
GLUG
GLUG
GLUG
SACRE BLEU! OUTWITTED BY AN INFERIOR MODEL.
ZKKT -- THE SHAME OF EET-- DIDIER 'AS MUD ON 'IS INTERFACE!
ZKKT
ZKKT

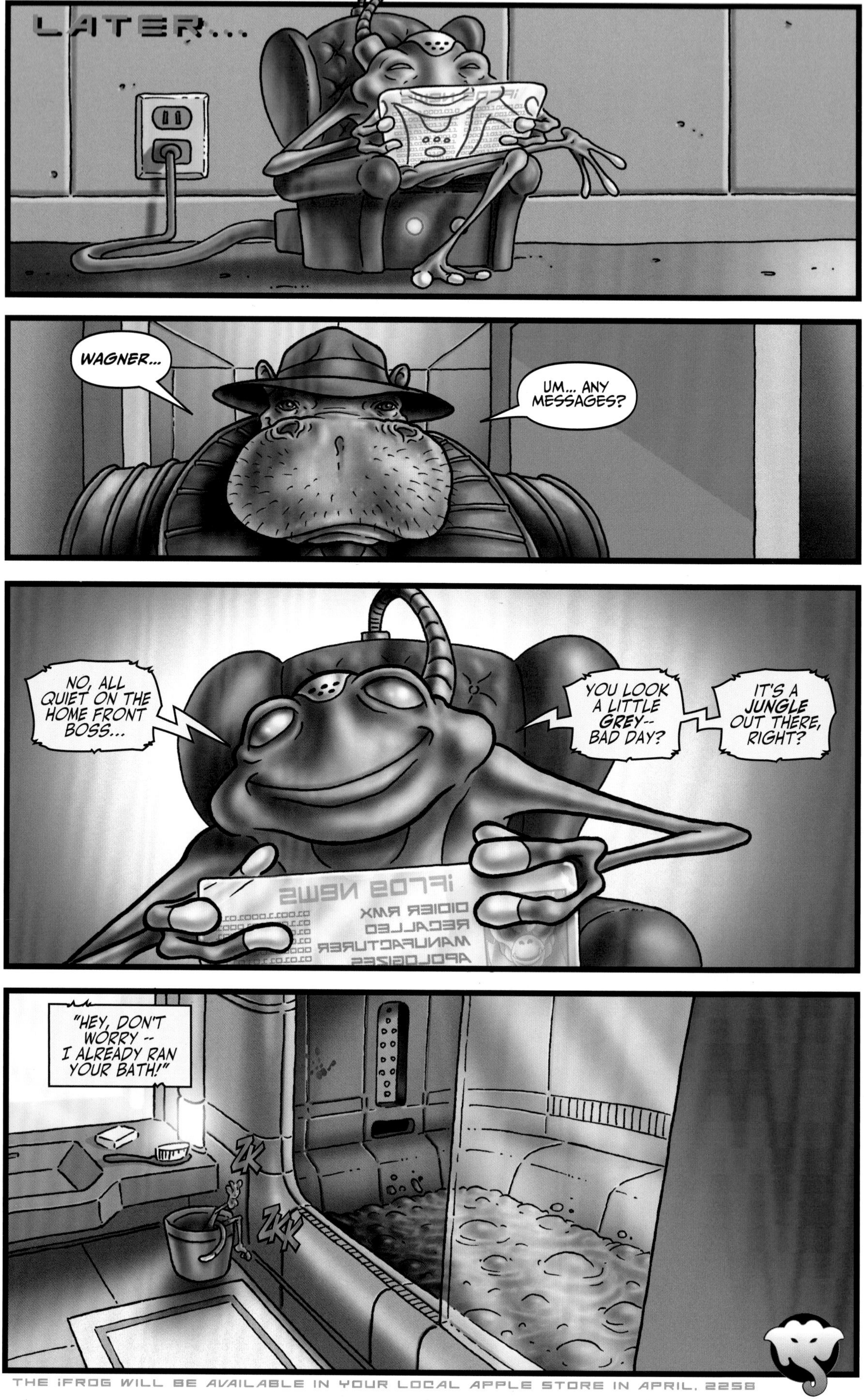
LATER...
WAGNER...
UM... ANY MESSAGES?
NO, ALL QUIET ON THE HOME FRONT BOSS...
YOU LOOK A LITTLE GREY-- BAD DAY?
IT'S A JUNGLE OUT THERE, RIGHT?
"HEY, DON'T WORRY -- I ALREADY RAN YOUR BATH!"
ZK
ZKK

THE iFROG WILL BE AVAILABLE IN YOUR LOCAL APPLE STORE IN APRIL, 2258

ELEPHANTMEN

Tales from Mystery City & the World of HIP FLASK™

$2.99
$3.50 CAN
APR
2007
#009

KABA

Your Local Hippo

MARKINGS · HABITAT · COMICRAFT · LADRÖNN

LADRÖNN 2007

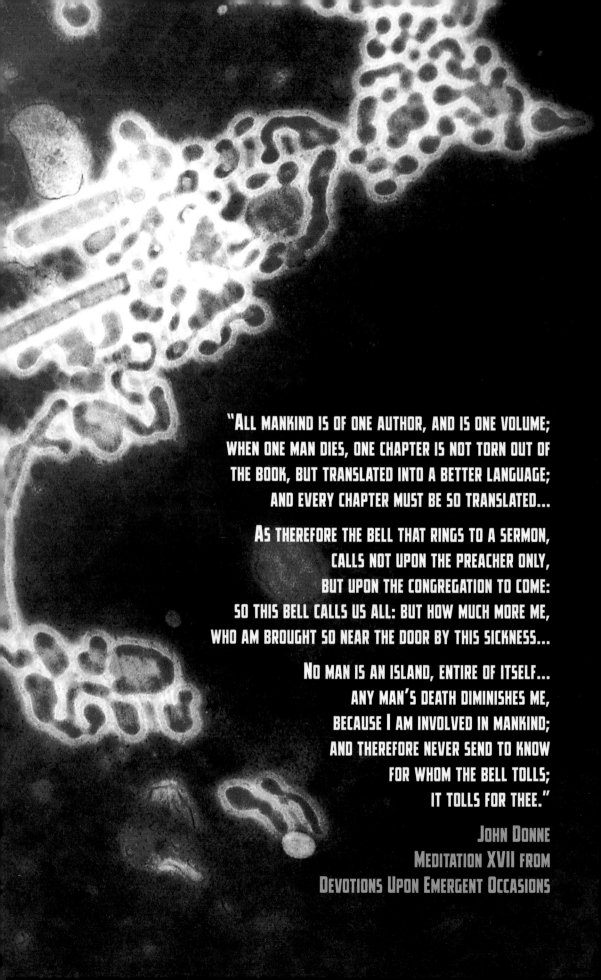

"ALL MANKIND IS OF ONE AUTHOR, AND IS ONE VOLUME;
WHEN ONE MAN DIES, ONE CHAPTER IS NOT TORN OUT OF
THE BOOK, BUT TRANSLATED INTO A BETTER LANGUAGE;
AND EVERY CHAPTER MUST BE SO TRANSLATED...

AS THEREFORE THE BELL THAT RINGS TO A SERMON,
CALLS NOT UPON THE PREACHER ONLY,
BUT UPON THE CONGREGATION TO COME:
SO THIS BELL CALLS US ALL: BUT HOW MUCH MORE ME,
WHO AM BROUGHT SO NEAR THE DOOR BY THIS SICKNESS...

NO MAN IS AN ISLAND, ENTIRE OF ITSELF...
ANY MAN'S DEATH DIMINISHES ME,
BECAUSE I AM INVOLVED IN MANKIND;
AND THEREFORE NEVER SEND TO KNOW
FOR WHOM THE BELL TOLLS;
IT TOLLS FOR THEE."

JOHN DONNE
MEDITATION XVII FROM
DEVOTIONS UPON EMERGENT OCCASIONS

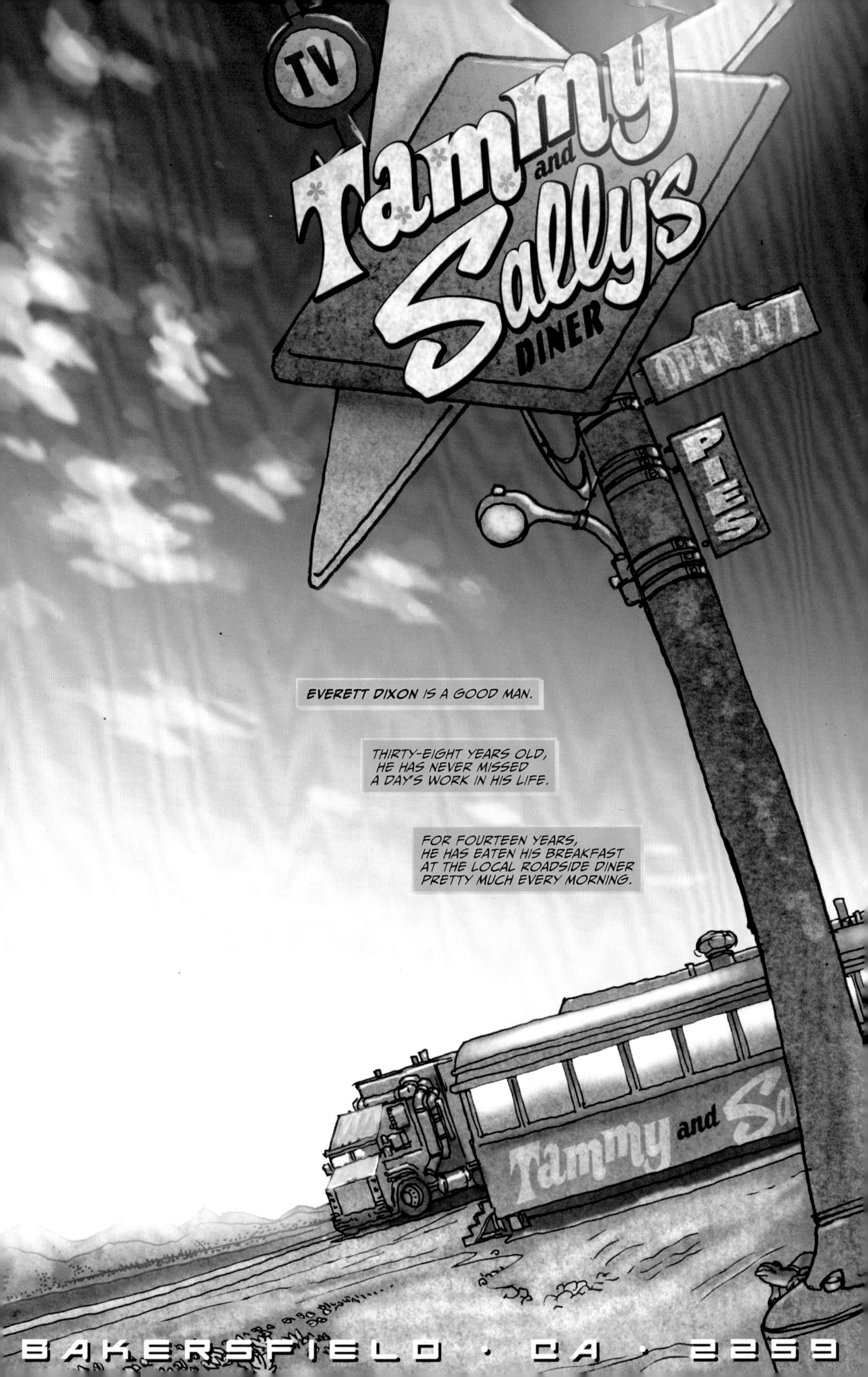
TV
Tammy and Sally's DINER
OPEN 24/7
PIES
EVERETT DIXON IS A GOOD MAN.
THIRTY-EIGHT YEARS OLD, HE HAS NEVER MISSED A DAY'S WORK IN HIS LIFE.
FOR FOURTEEN YEARS, HE HAS EATEN HIS BREAKFAST AT THE LOCAL ROADSIDE DINER PRETTY MUCH EVERY MORNING.
Tammy and Sa
BAKERSFIELD · CA · 2259

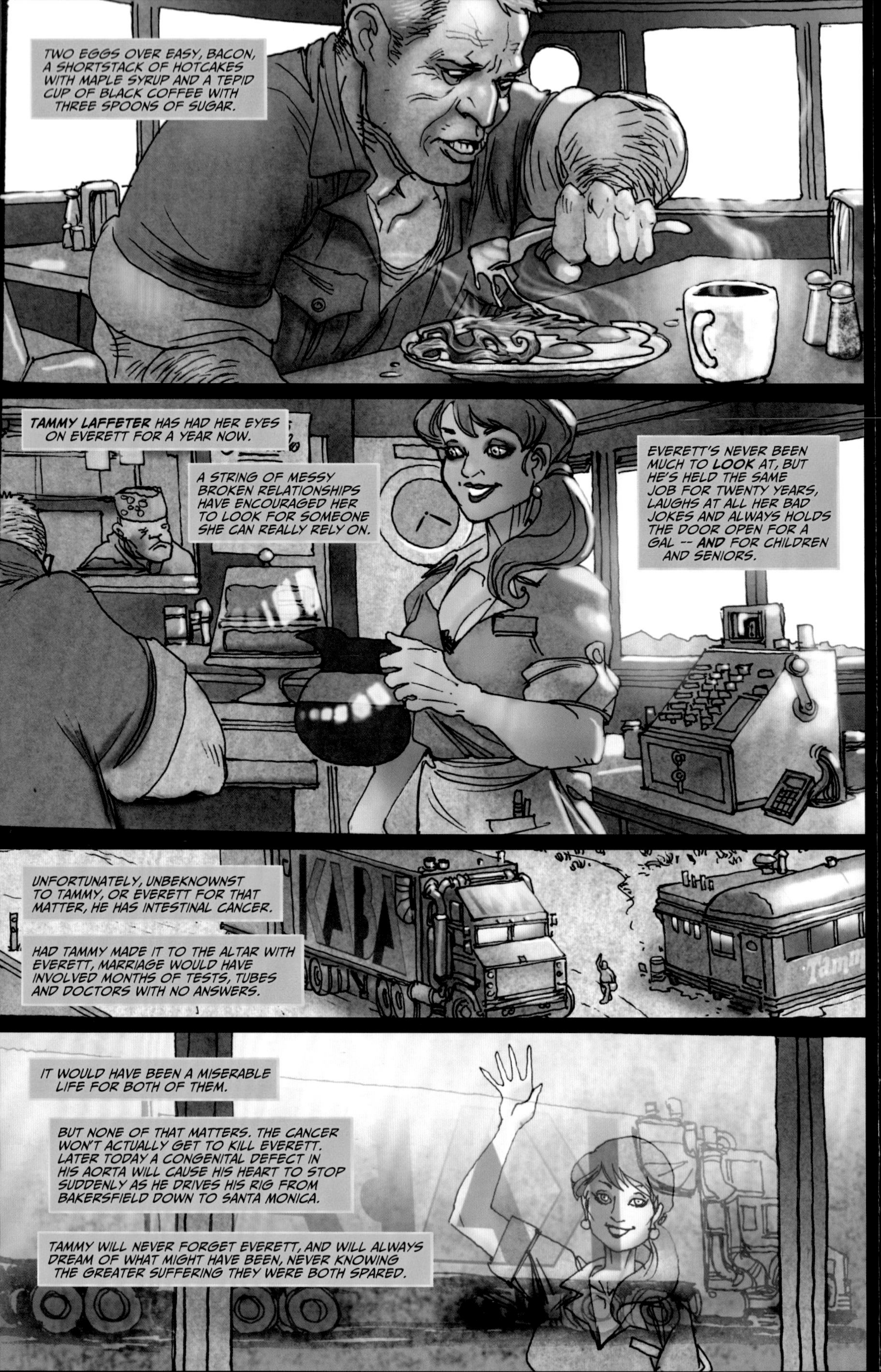
TWO EGGS OVER EASY, BACON, A SHORTSTACK OF HOTCAKES WITH MAPLE SYRUP AND A TEPID CUP OF BLACK COFFEE WITH THREE SPOONS OF SUGAR.
TAMMY LAFFETER HAS HAD HER EYES ON EVERETT FOR A YEAR NOW.
A STRING OF MESSY BROKEN RELATIONSHIPS HAVE ENCOURAGED HER TO LOOK FOR SOMEONE SHE CAN REALLY RELY ON.
EVERETT'S NEVER BEEN MUCH TO LOOK AT, BUT HE'S HELD THE SAME JOB FOR TWENTY YEARS, LAUGHS AT ALL HER BAD JOKES AND ALWAYS HOLDS THE DOOR OPEN FOR A GAL -- AND FOR CHILDREN AND SENIORS.
UNFORTUNATELY, UNBEKNOWNST TO TAMMY, OR EVERETT FOR THAT MATTER, HE HAS INTESTINAL CANCER.
HAD TAMMY MADE IT TO THE ALTAR WITH EVERETT, MARRIAGE WOULD HAVE INVOLVED MONTHS OF TESTS, TUBES AND DOCTORS WITH NO ANSWERS.
IT WOULD HAVE BEEN A MISERABLE LIFE FOR BOTH OF THEM.
BUT NONE OF THAT MATTERS. THE CANCER WON'T ACTUALLY GET TO KILL EVERETT. LATER TODAY A CONGENITAL DEFECT IN HIS AORTA WILL CAUSE HIS HEART TO STOP SUDDENLY AS HE DRIVES HIS RIG FROM BAKERSFIELD DOWN TO SANTA MONICA.
TAMMY WILL NEVER FORGET EVERETT, AND WILL ALWAYS DREAM OF WHAT MIGHT HAVE BEEN, NEVER KNOWING THE GREATER SUFFERING THEY WERE BOTH SPARED.

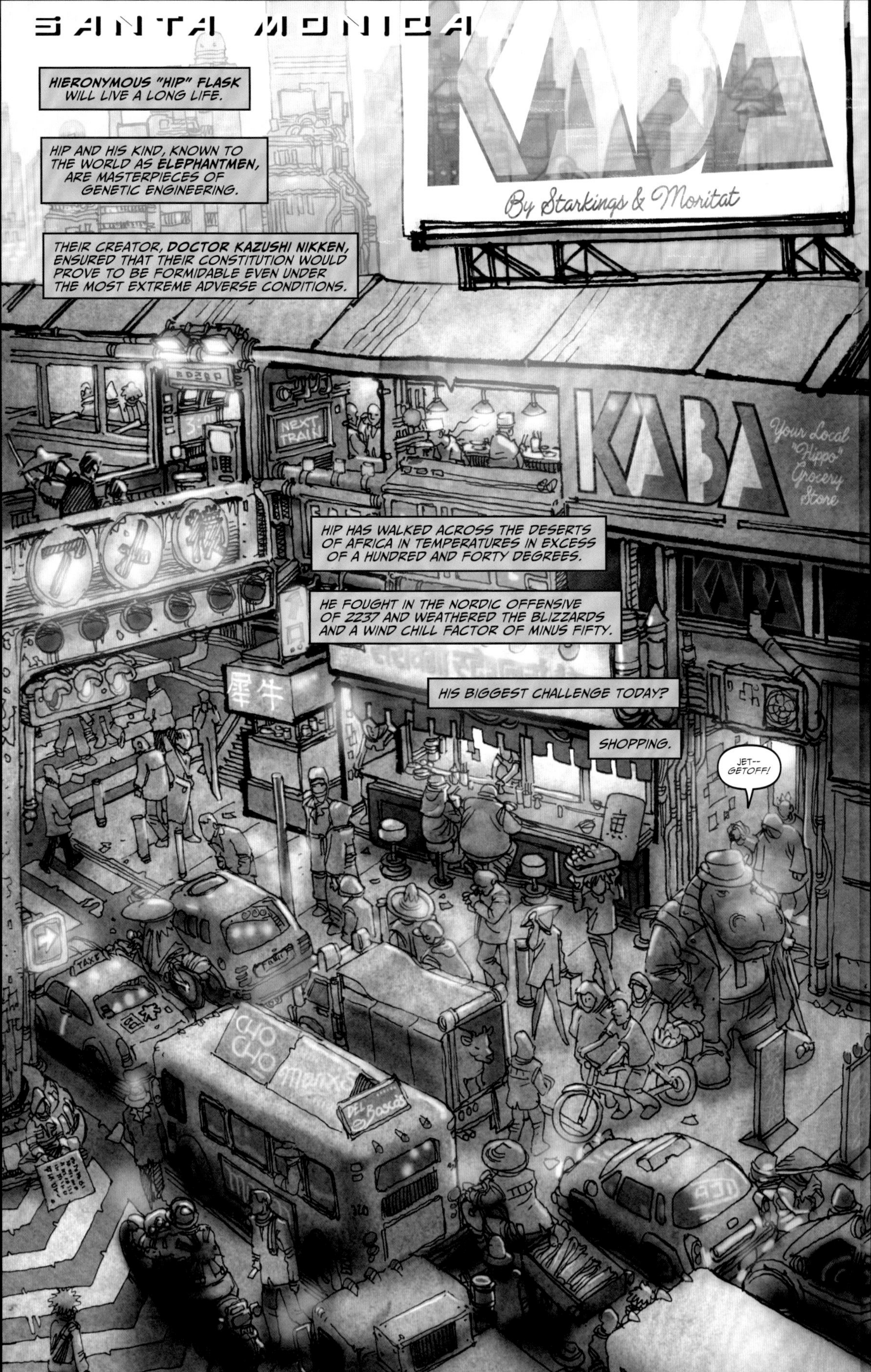
SANTA MONICA
HIERONYMOUS "HIP" FLASK WILL LIVE A LONG LIFE.
HIP AND HIS KIND, KNOWN TO THE WORLD AS ELEPHANTMEN, ARE MASTERPIECES OF GENETIC ENGINEERING.
THEIR CREATOR, DOCTOR KAZUSHI NIKKEN, ENSURED THAT THEIR CONSTITUTION WOULD PROVE TO BE FORMIDABLE EVEN UNDER THE MOST EXTREME ADVERSE CONDITIONS.
KABA
By Starkings & Moritat
NEXT TRAIN
KABA
Your Local "Hippo" Grocery Store
HIP HAS WALKED ACROSS THE DESERTS OF AFRICA IN TEMPERATURES IN EXCESS OF A HUNDRED AND FORTY DEGREES.
KABA
HE FOUGHT IN THE NORDIC OFFENSIVE OF 2237 AND WEATHERED THE BLIZZARDS AND A WIND CHILL FACTOR OF MINUS FIFTY.
HIS BIGGEST CHALLENGE TODAY?
SHOPPING.
JET-- GETOFF!
TAXI
CHO CHO
DEL Bosco's

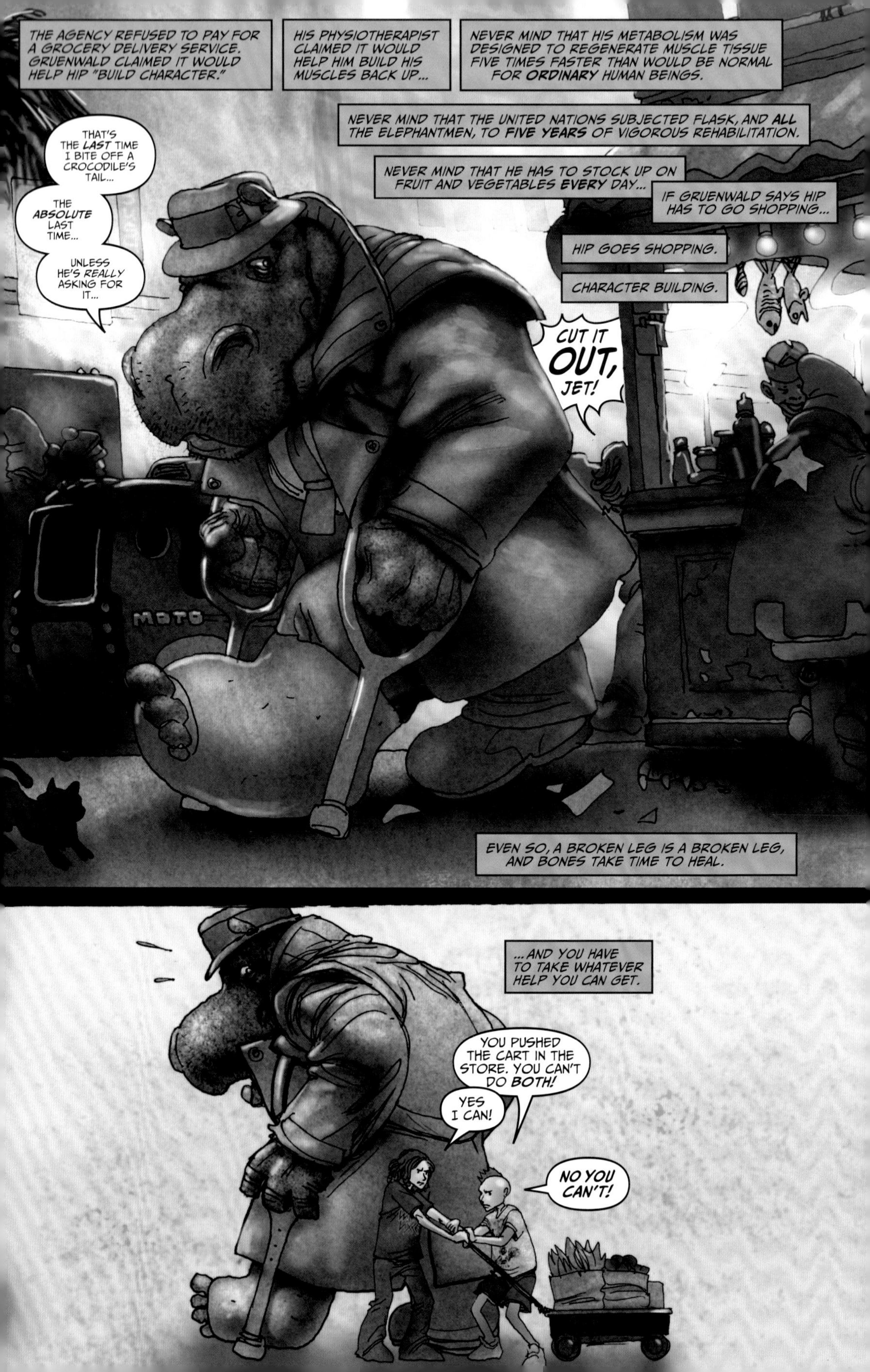
THE AGENCY REFUSED TO PAY FOR A GROCERY DELIVERY SERVICE. GRUENWALD CLAIMED IT WOULD HELP HIP "BUILD CHARACTER."
HIS PHYSIOTHERAPIST CLAIMED IT WOULD HELP HIM BUILD HIS MUSCLES BACK UP...
NEVER MIND THAT HIS METABOLISM WAS DESIGNED TO REGENERATE MUSCLE TISSUE FIVE TIMES FASTER THAN WOULD BE NORMAL FOR ORDINARY HUMAN BEINGS.
NEVER MIND THAT THE UNITED NATIONS SUBJECTED FLASK, AND ALL THE ELEPHANTMEN, TO FIVE YEARS OF VIGOROUS REHABILITATION.
NEVER MIND THAT HE HAS TO STOCK UP ON FRUIT AND VEGETABLES EVERY DAY...
IF GRUENWALD SAYS HIP HAS TO GO SHOPPING...
HIP GOES SHOPPING.
CHARACTER BUILDING.
THAT'S THE LAST TIME I BITE OFF A CROCODILE'S TAIL...
THE ABSOLUTE LAST TIME...
UNLESS HE'S REALLY ASKING FOR IT...
CUT IT OUT, JET!
MOTO
EVEN SO, A BROKEN LEG IS A BROKEN LEG, AND BONES TAKE TIME TO HEAL.
...AND YOU HAVE TO TAKE WHATEVER HELP YOU CAN GET.
YOU PUSHED THE CART IN THE STORE. YOU CAN'T DO BOTH!
YES I CAN!
NO YOU CAN'T!

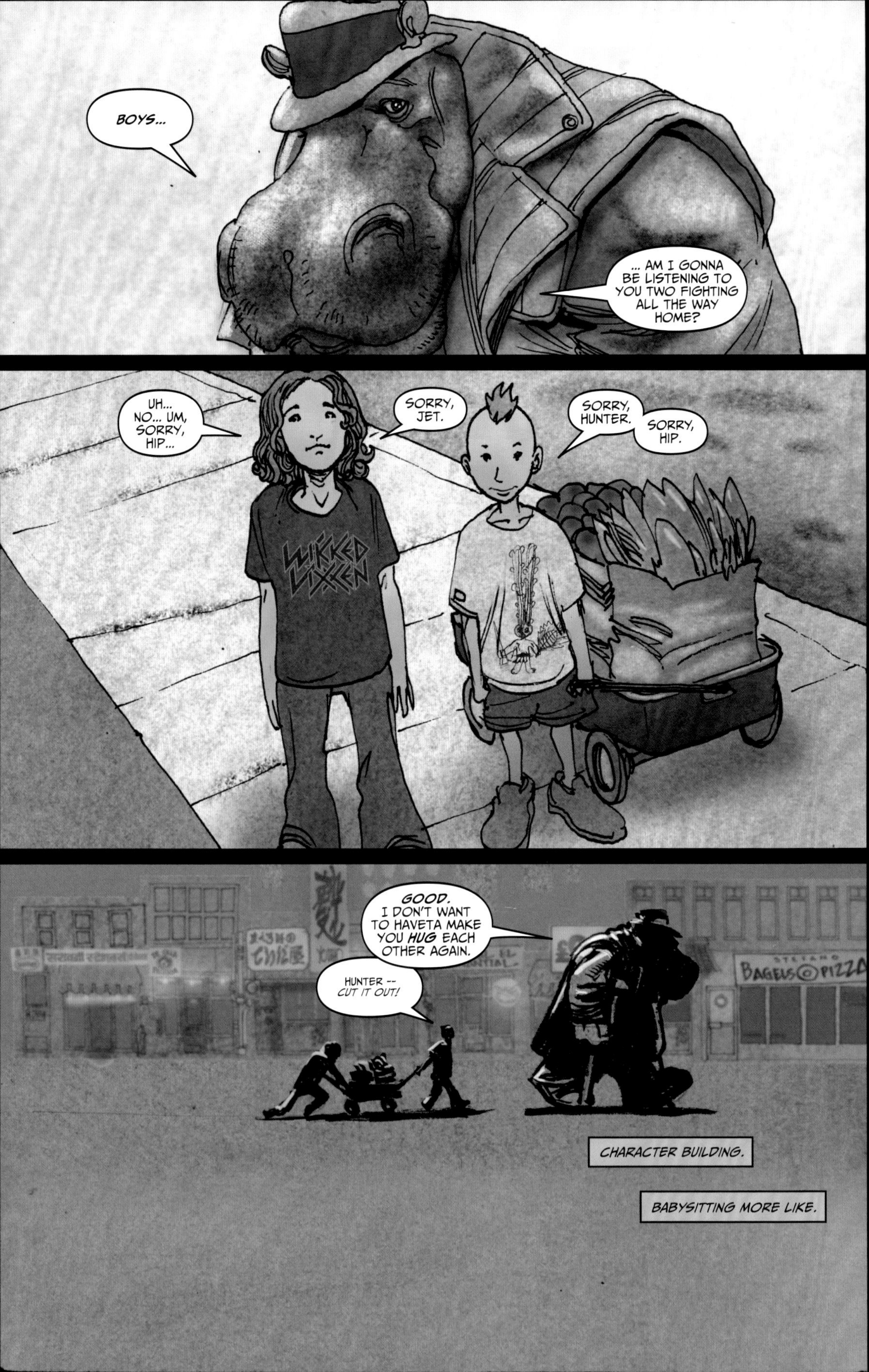
BOYS...
... AM I GONNA BE LISTENING TO YOU TWO FIGHTING ALL THE WAY HOME?
UH... NO... UM, SORRY, HIP...
SORRY, JET.
SORRY, HUNTER.
SORRY, HIP.
GOOD. I DON'T WANT TO HAVETA MAKE YOU HUG EACH OTHER AGAIN.
HUNTER -- CUT IT OUT!
BAGELS @ PIZZA
CHARACTER BUILDING.
BABYSITTING MORE LIKE.

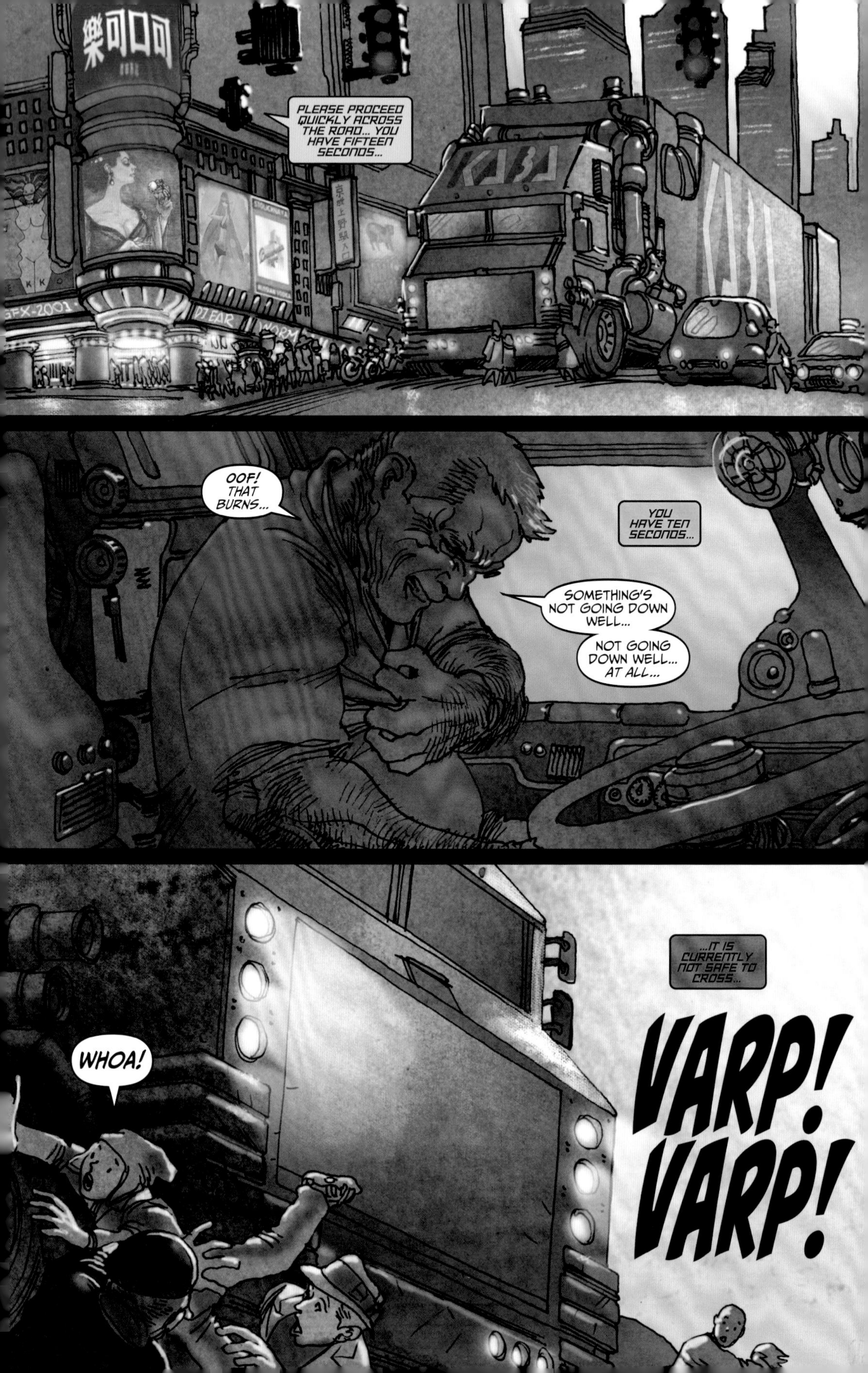
PLEASE PROCEED QUICKLY ACROSS THE ROAD... YOU HAVE FIFTEEN SECONDS...
OOF! THAT BURNS...
YOU HAVE TEN SECONDS...
SOMETHING'S NOT GOING DOWN WELL...
NOT GOING DOWN WELL... AT ALL...
...IT IS CURRENTLY NOT SAFE TO CROSS...
WHOA!
VARP! VARP!

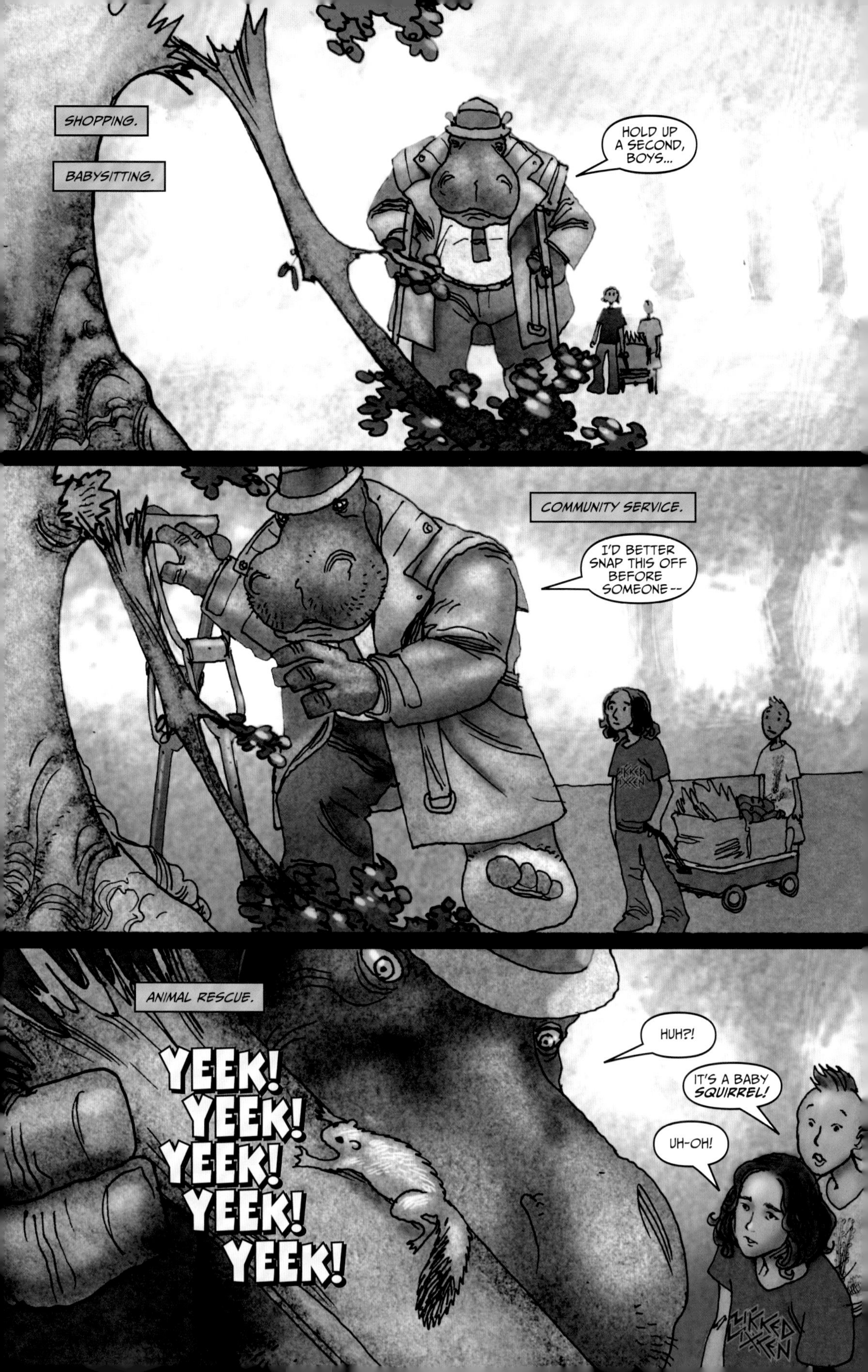
SHOPPING.
BABYSITTING.
HOLD UP A SECOND, BOYS...
COMMUNITY SERVICE.
I'D BETTER SNAP THIS OFF BEFORE SOMEONE--
ANIMAL RESCUE.
YEEK! YEEK! YEEK! YEEK! YEEK!
HUH?!
IT'S A BABY SQUIRREL!
UH-OH!

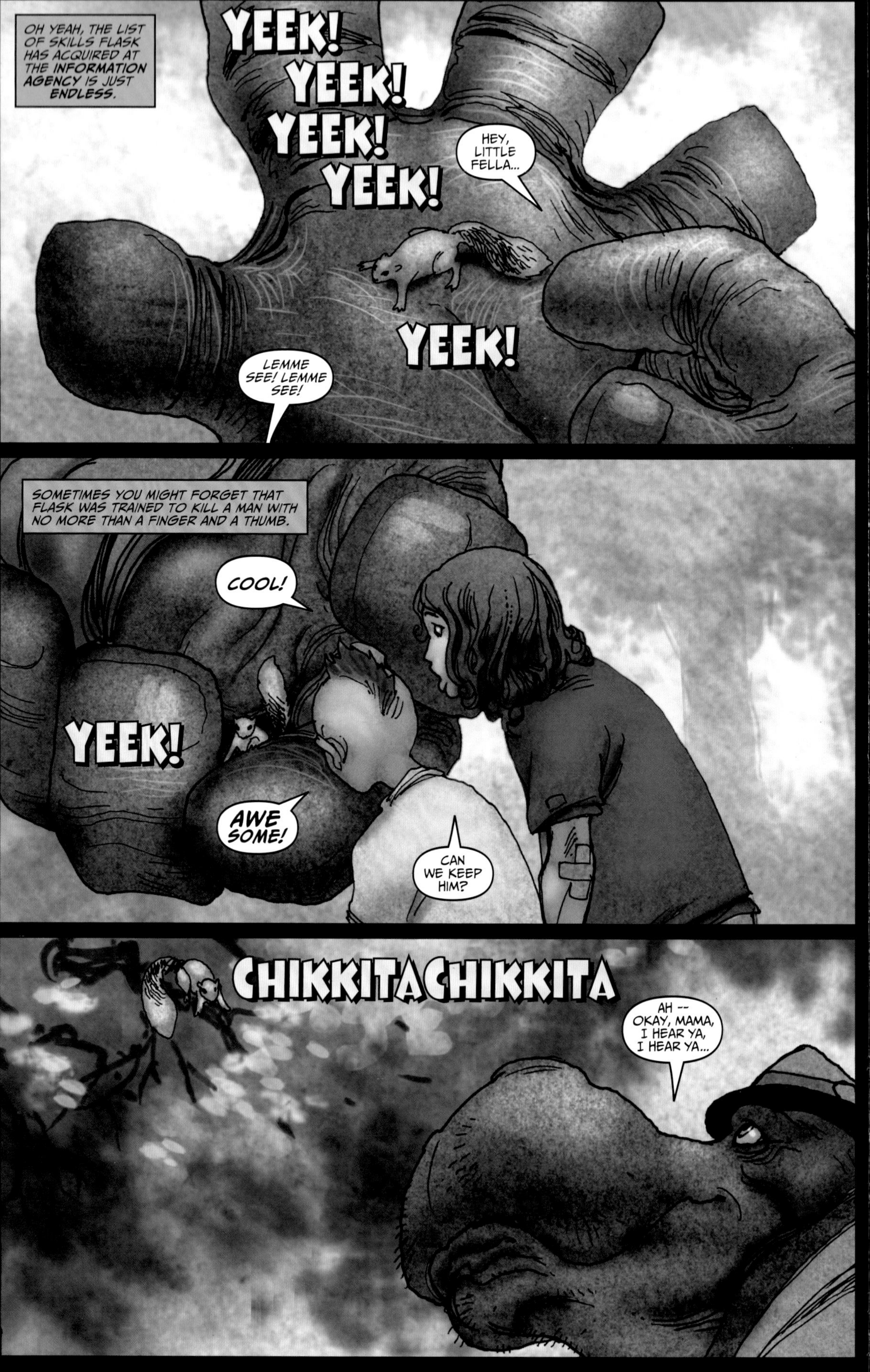

OH YEAH, THE LIST OF SKILLS FLASK HAS ACQUIRED AT THE INFORMATION AGENCY IS JUST ENDLESS.
YEEK!
YEEK!
YEEK!
YEEK!
HEY, LITTLE FELLA...
YEEK!
LEMME SEE! LEMME SEE!
SOMETIMES YOU MIGHT FORGET THAT FLASK WAS TRAINED TO KILL A MAN WITH NO MORE THAN A FINGER AND A THUMB.
COOL!
YEEK!
AWE SOME!
CAN WE KEEP HIM?
CHIKKITACHIKKITA
AH -- OKAY, MAMA, I HEAR YA, I HEAR YA...

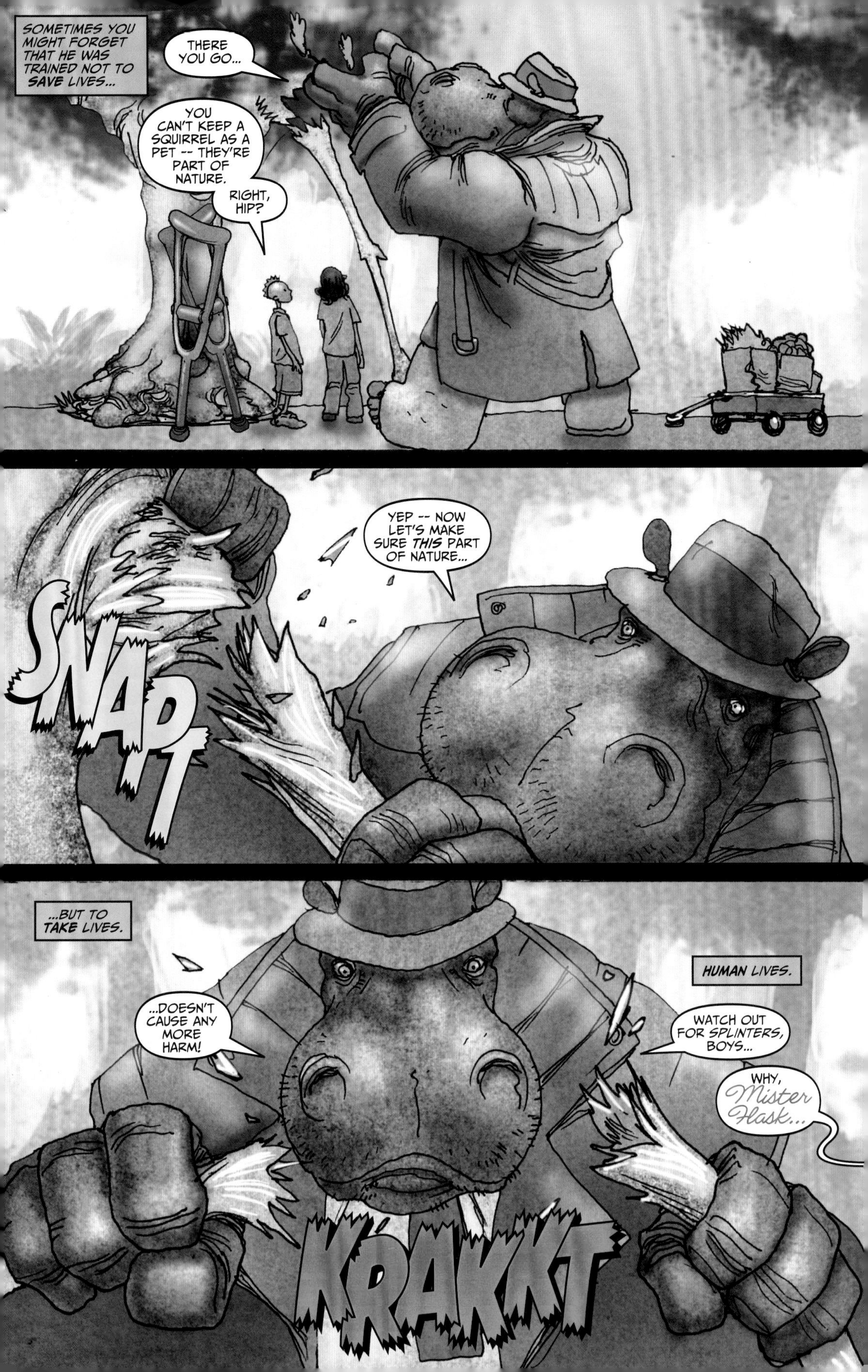
SOMETIMES YOU MIGHT FORGET THAT HE WAS TRAINED NOT TO SAVE LIVES...
THERE YOU GO...
YOU CAN'T KEEP A SQUIRREL AS A PET -- THEY'RE PART OF NATURE.
RIGHT, HIP?
YEP -- NOW LET'S MAKE SURE THIS PART OF NATURE...
SNAP
...BUT TO TAKE LIVES.
HUMAN LIVES.
...DOESN'T CAUSE ANY MORE HARM!
WATCH OUT FOR SPLINTERS, BOYS...
WHY, Mister Hask...
KRAKKT

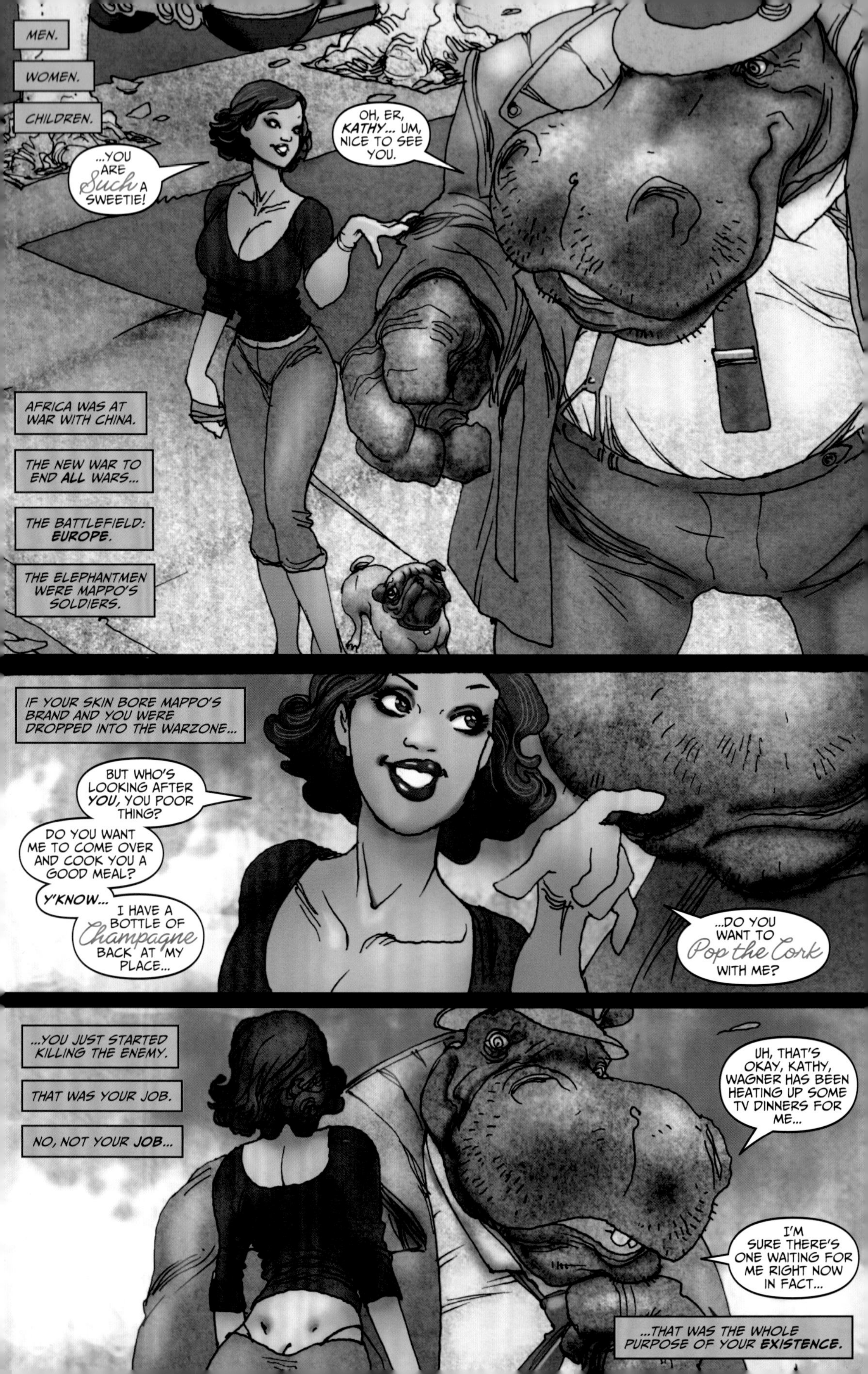
MEN.
WOMEN.
CHILDREN.
...YOU ARE Such A SWEETIE!
OH, ER, KATHY... UM, NICE TO SEE YOU.
AFRICA WAS AT WAR WITH CHINA.
THE NEW WAR TO END ALL WARS...
THE BATTLEFIELD: EUROPE.
THE ELEPHANTMEN WERE MAPPO'S SOLDIERS.
IF YOUR SKIN BORE MAPPO'S BRAND AND YOU WERE DROPPED INTO THE WARZONE...
BUT WHO'S LOOKING AFTER YOU, YOU POOR THING?
DO YOU WANT ME TO COME OVER AND COOK YOU A GOOD MEAL?
Y'KNOW... I HAVE A BOTTLE OF Champagne BACK AT MY PLACE...
...DO YOU WANT TO Pop the Cork WITH ME?
...YOU JUST STARTED KILLING THE ENEMY.
THAT WAS YOUR JOB.
NO, NOT YOUR JOB...
UH, THAT'S OKAY, KATHY, WAGNER HAS BEEN HEATING UP SOME TV DINNERS FOR ME...
I'M SURE THERE'S ONE WAITING FOR ME RIGHT NOW IN FACT...
...THAT WAS THE WHOLE PURPOSE OF YOUR EXISTENCE.

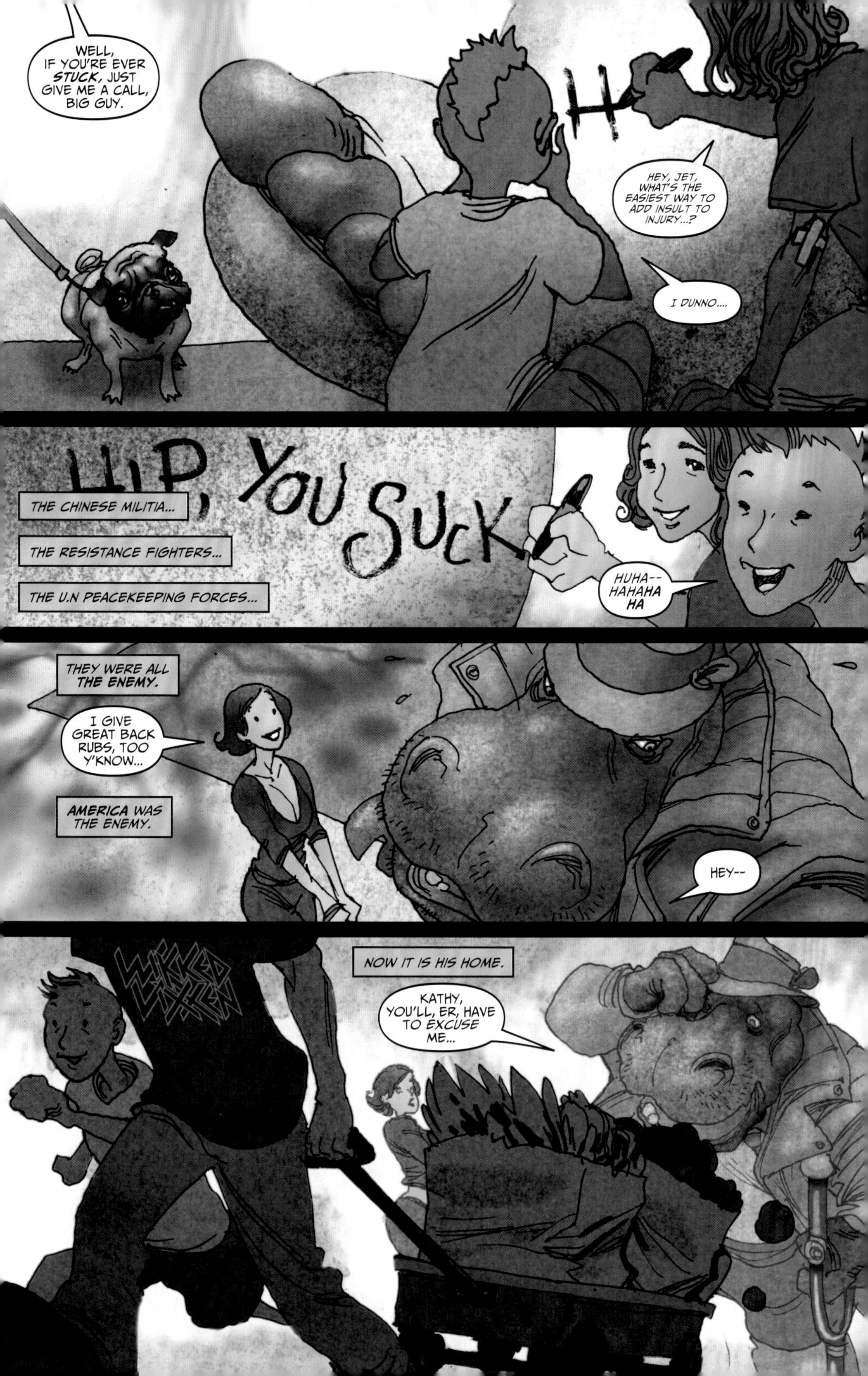
WELL, IF YOU'RE EVER STUCK, JUST GIVE ME A CALL, BIG GUY.
HEY, JET, WHAT'S THE EASIEST WAY TO ADD INSULT TO INJURY...?
I DUNNO....
HIP, YOU SUCK
THE CHINESE MILITIA...
THE RESISTANCE FIGHTERS...
THE U.N PEACEKEEPING FORCES...
HUHA--HAHAHAHA HA
THEY WERE ALL THE ENEMY.
I GIVE GREAT BACK RUBS, TOO Y'KNOW...
AMERICA WAS THE ENEMY.
HEY--
NOW IT IS HIS HOME.
KATHY, YOU'LL, ER, HAVE TO EXCUSE ME...

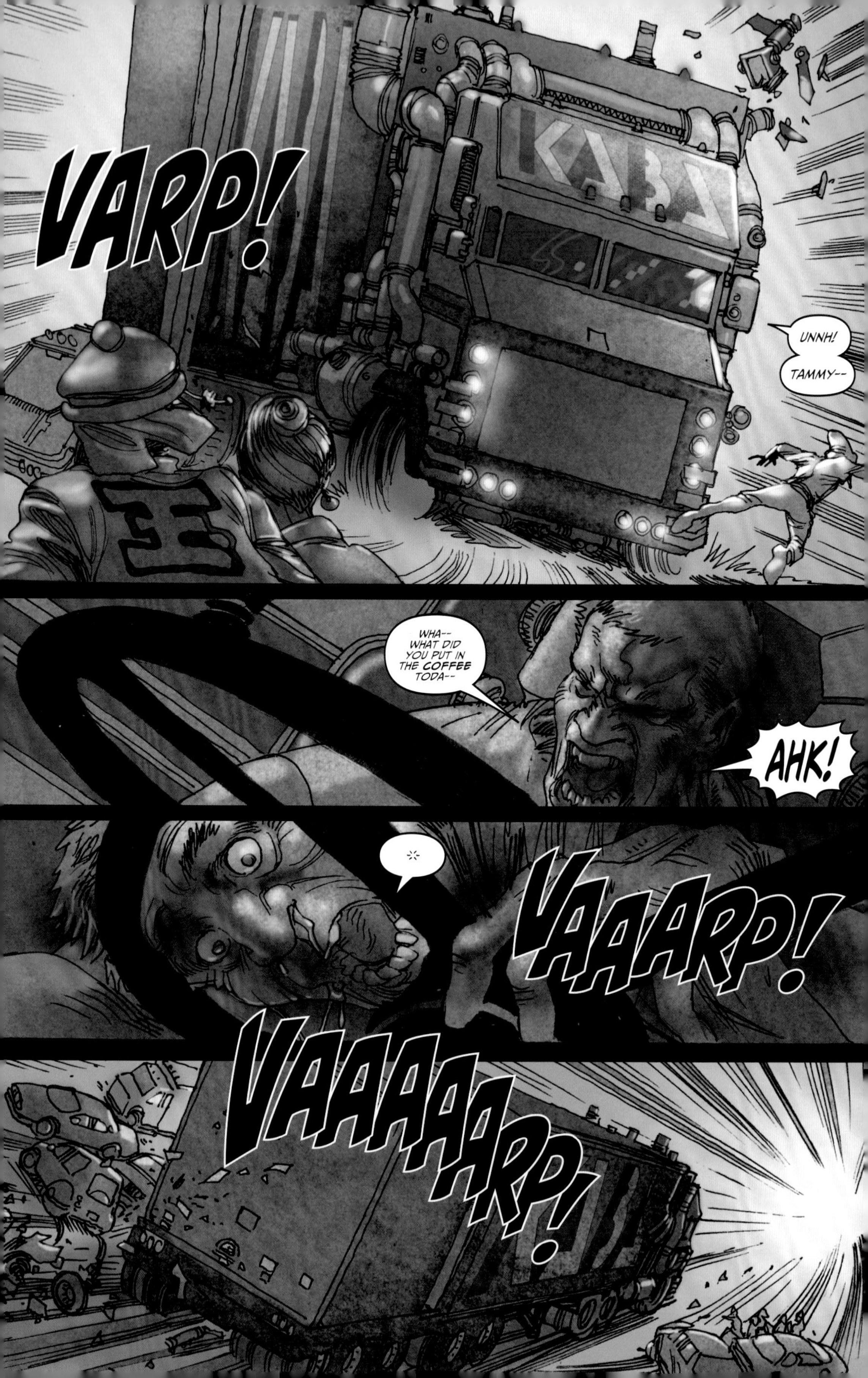
VARP!
UNNH!
TAMMY--
WHA-- WHAT DID YOU PUT IN THE COFFEE TODA--
AHK!
VAAARP!
VAAAAAARP!

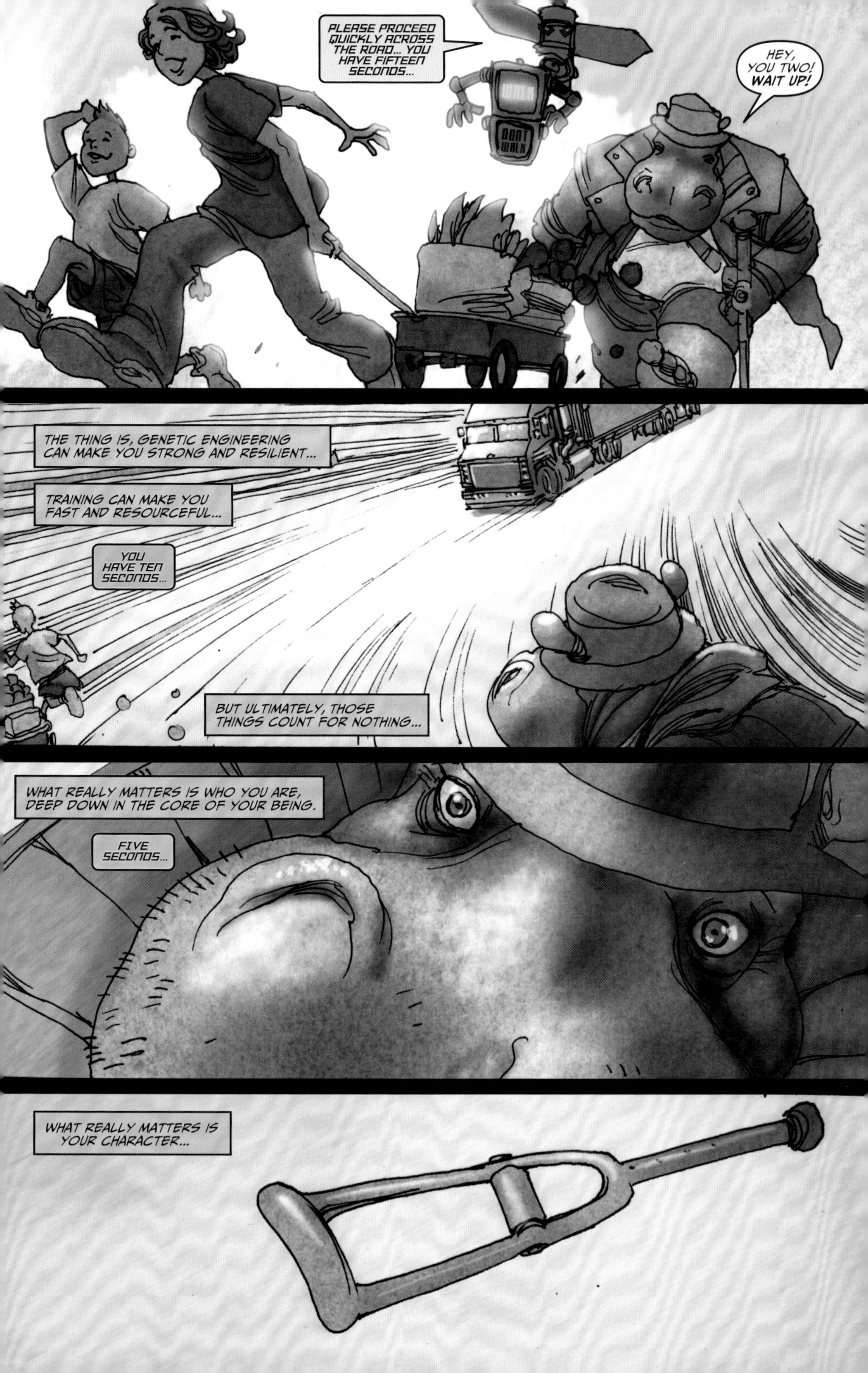
PLEASE PROCEED QUICKLY ACROSS THE ROAD... YOU HAVE FIFTEEN SECONDS...
WALK
DONT WALK
HEY, YOU TWO! **WAIT UP!**
THE THING IS, GENETIC ENGINEERING CAN MAKE YOU STRONG AND RESILIENT...
TRAINING CAN MAKE YOU FAST AND RESOURCEFUL...
YOU HAVE TEN SECONDS...
BUT ULTIMATELY, THOSE THINGS COUNT FOR NOTHING...
WHAT REALLY MATTERS IS WHO YOU ARE, DEEP DOWN IN THE CORE OF YOUR BEING.
FIVE SECONDS...
WHAT REALLY MATTERS IS YOUR CHARACTER...

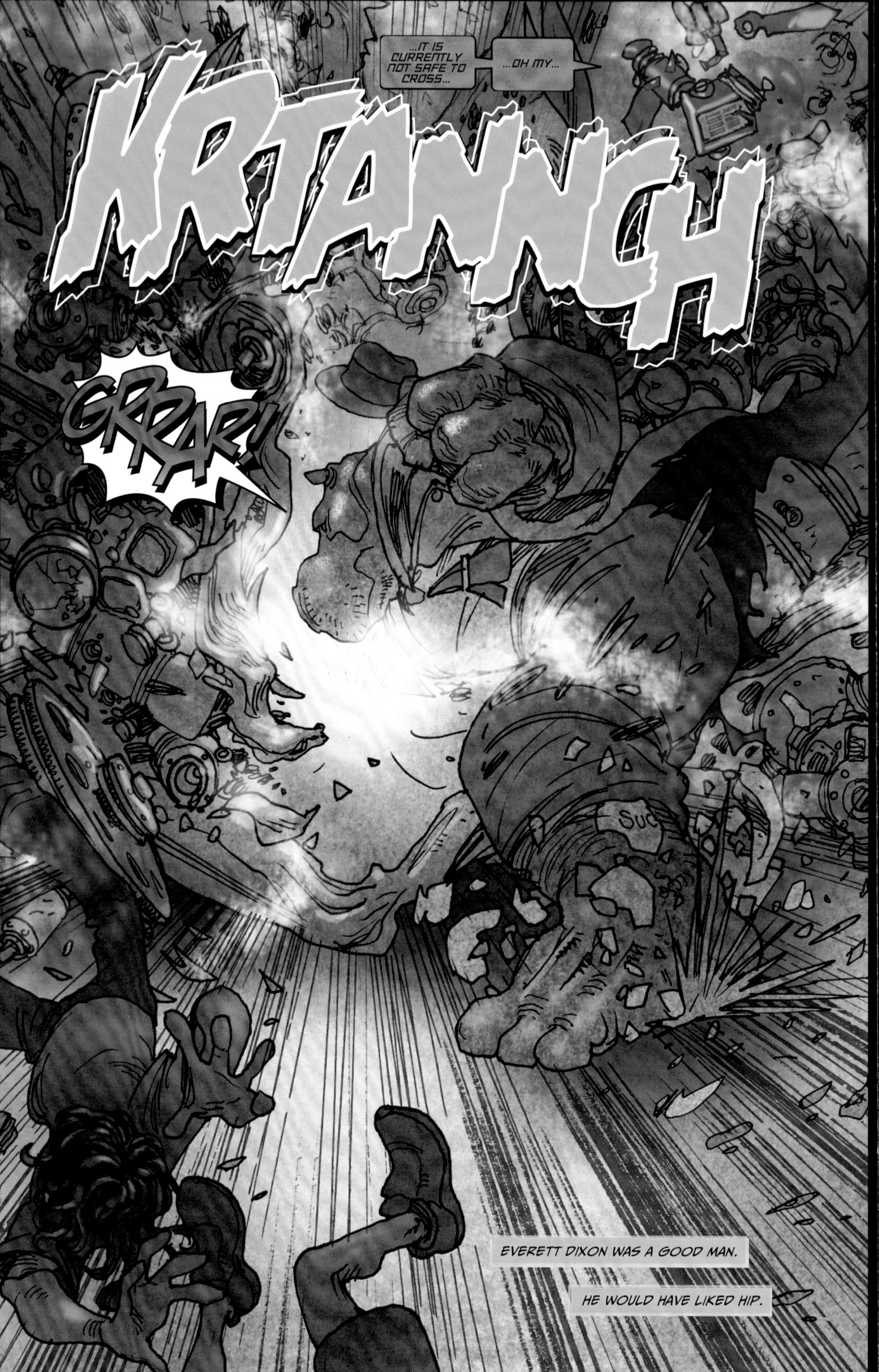
...IT IS CURRENTLY NOT SAFE TO CROSS...
...OH MY...
KRTANNCH
GRRAR!
EVERETT DIXON WAS A GOOD MAN.
HE WOULD HAVE LIKED HIP.

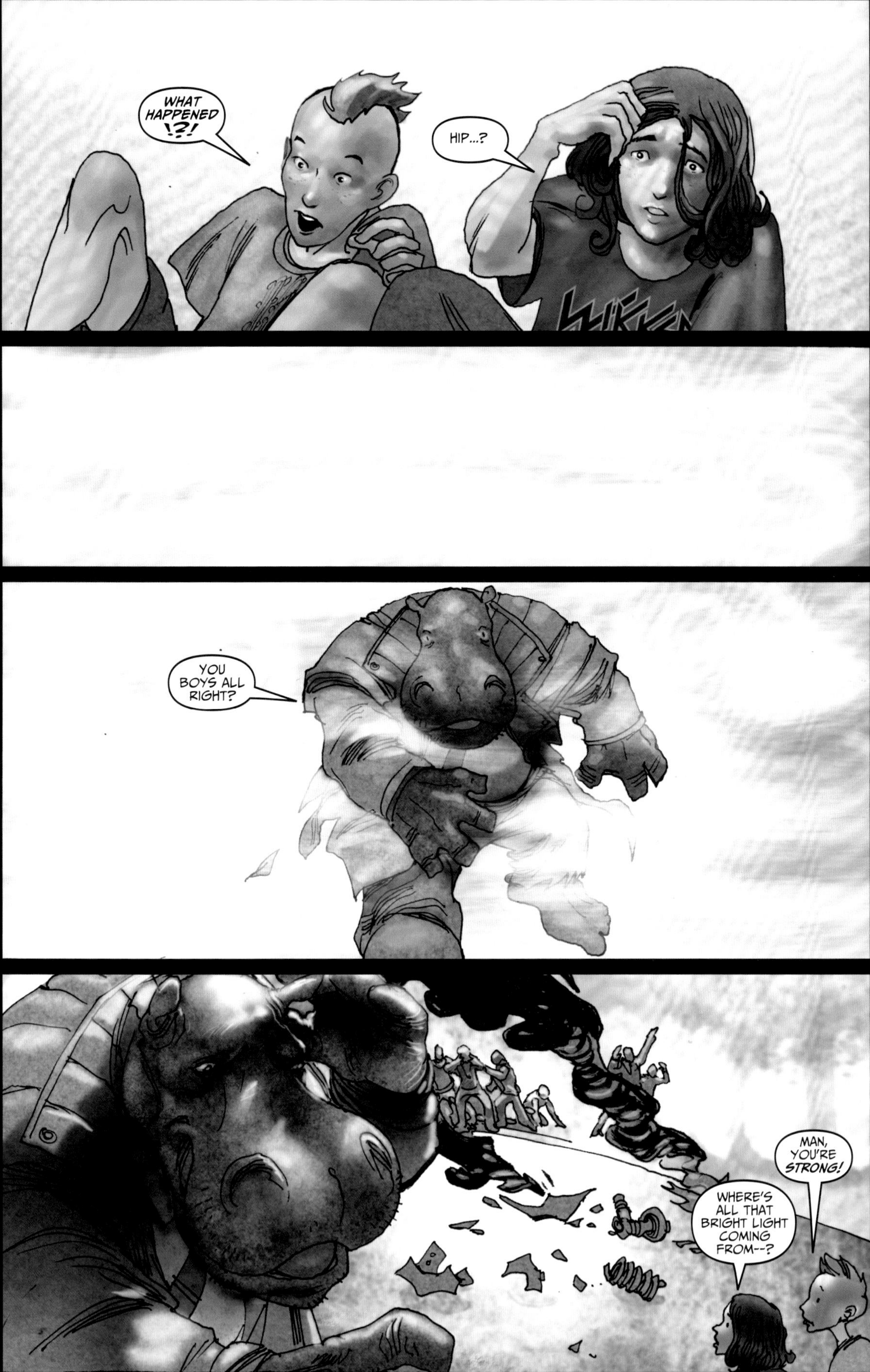
WHAT HAPPENED !?!
HIP...?
YOU BOYS ALL RIGHT?
MAN, YOU'RE STRONG!
WHERE'S ALL THAT BRIGHT LIGHT COMING FROM--?

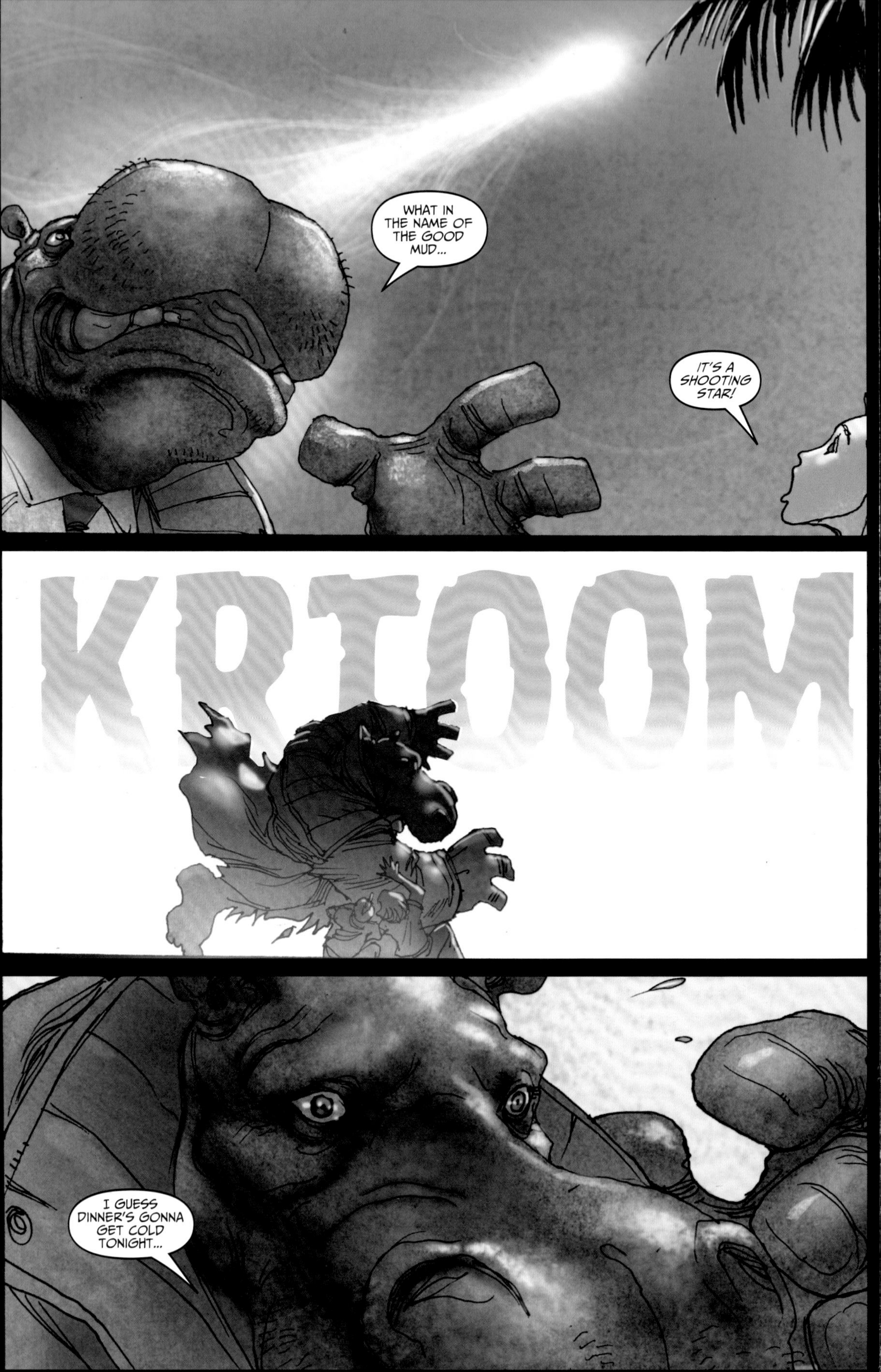
WHAT IN THE NAME OF THE GOOD MUD...
IT'S A SHOOTING STAR!
KRTOOM
I GUESS DINNER'S GONNA GET COLD TONIGHT...

To Be Continued!

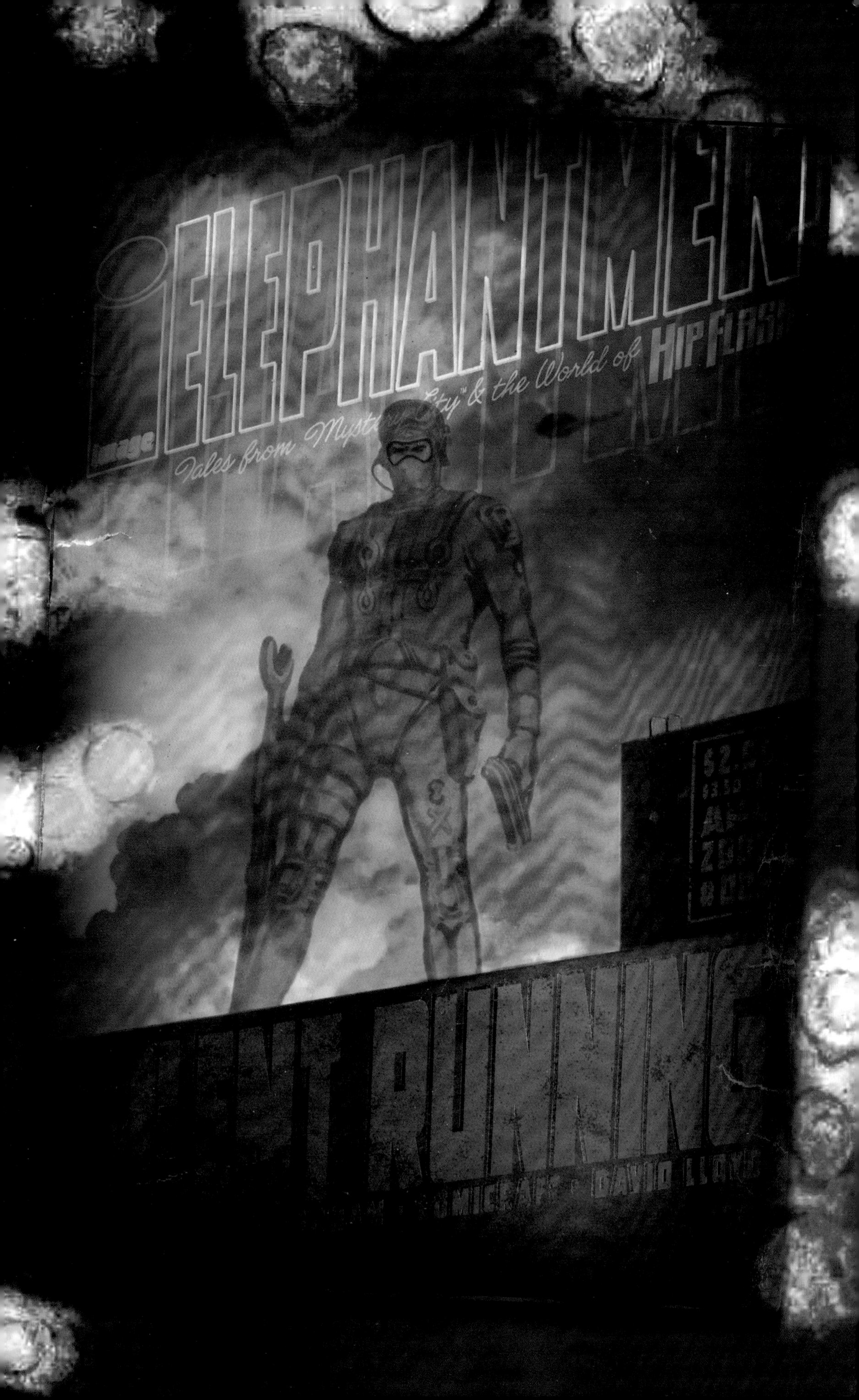
Tales from
& the World of

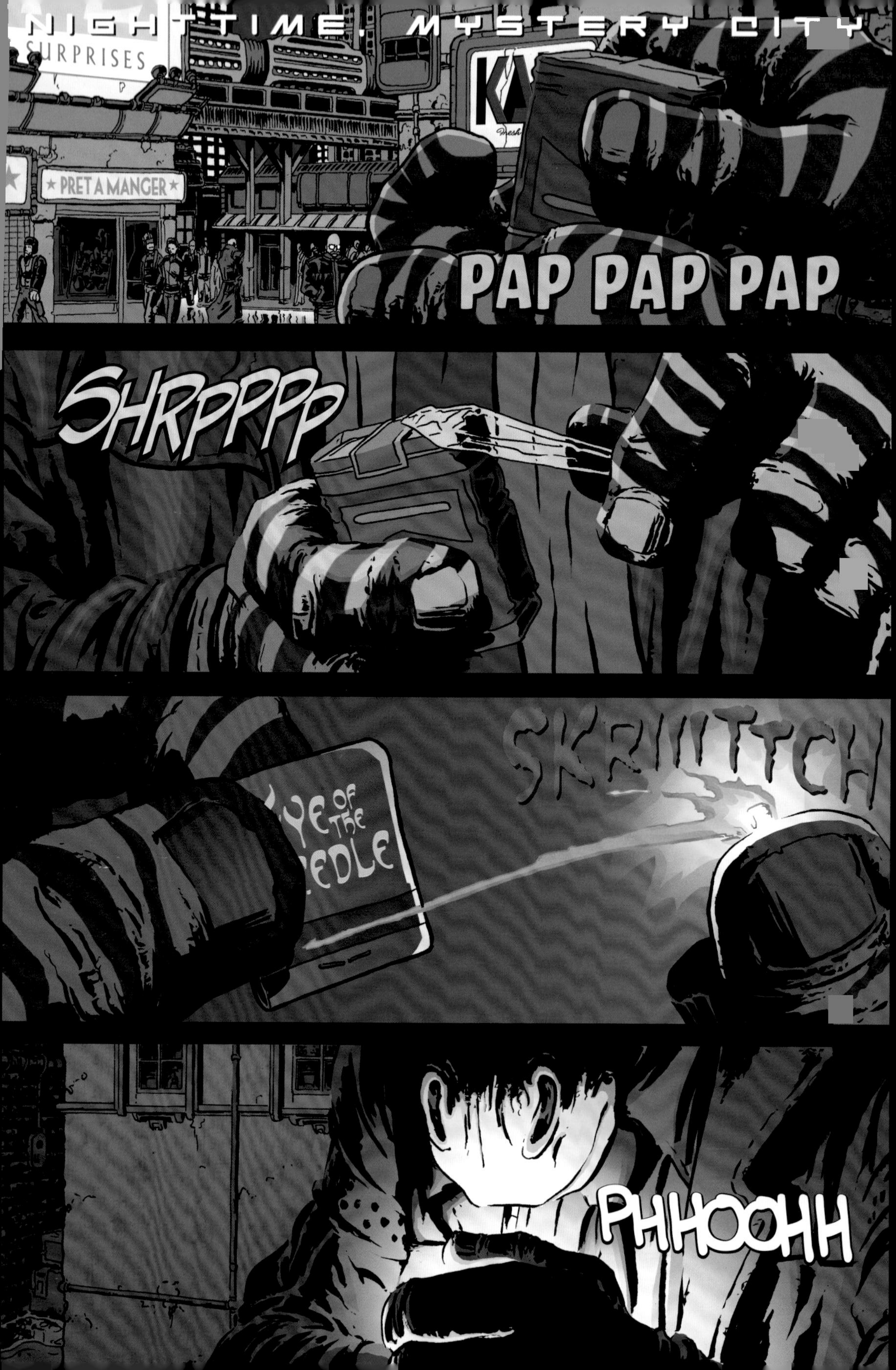
NIGHTTIME, MYSTERY CITY
SURPRISES
PRET A MANGER
PAP PAP PAP
SHRPPPP
OF THE
SKRIITTCH
PHHOOHH

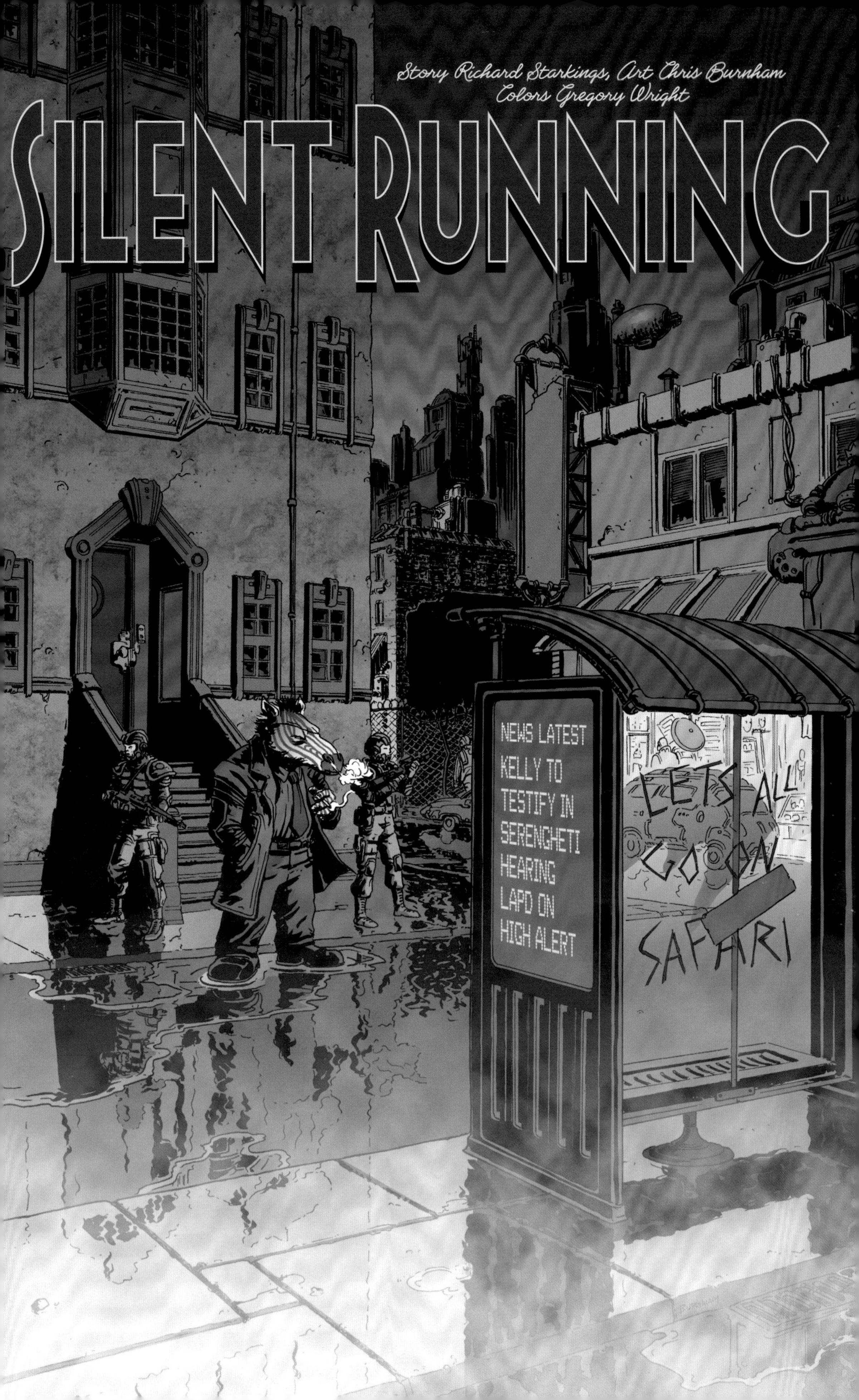

Story Richard Starkings, Art Chris Burnham
Colors Gregory Wright
SILENT RUNNING
NEWS LATEST
KELLY TO
TESTIFY IN
SERENGHETI
HEARING
LAPD ON
HIGH ALERT
LETS ALL GO ON SAFARI

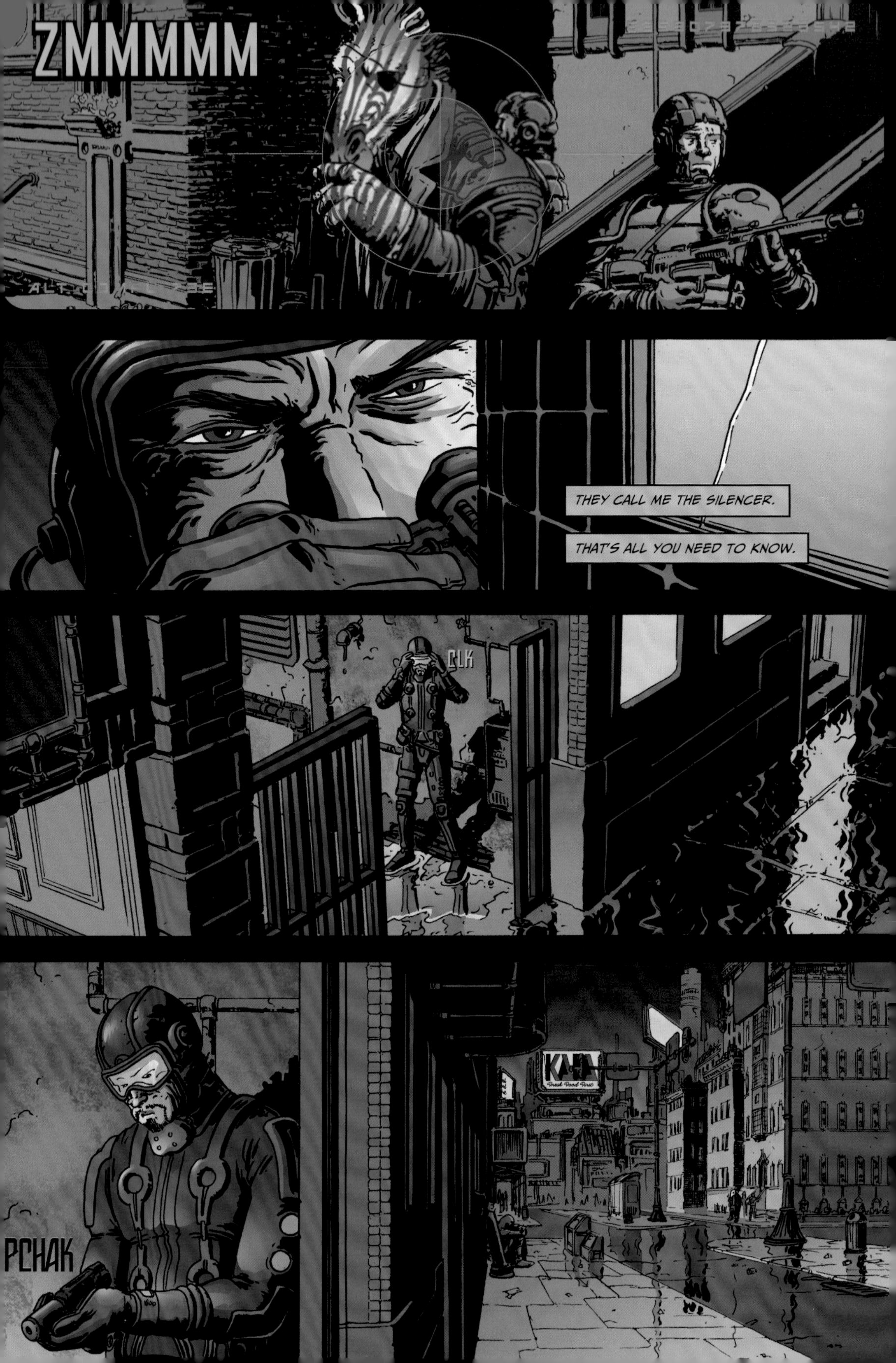
ZMMMMM
THEY CALL ME THE SILENCER.
THAT'S ALL YOU NEED TO KNOW.
CLK
PCHAK

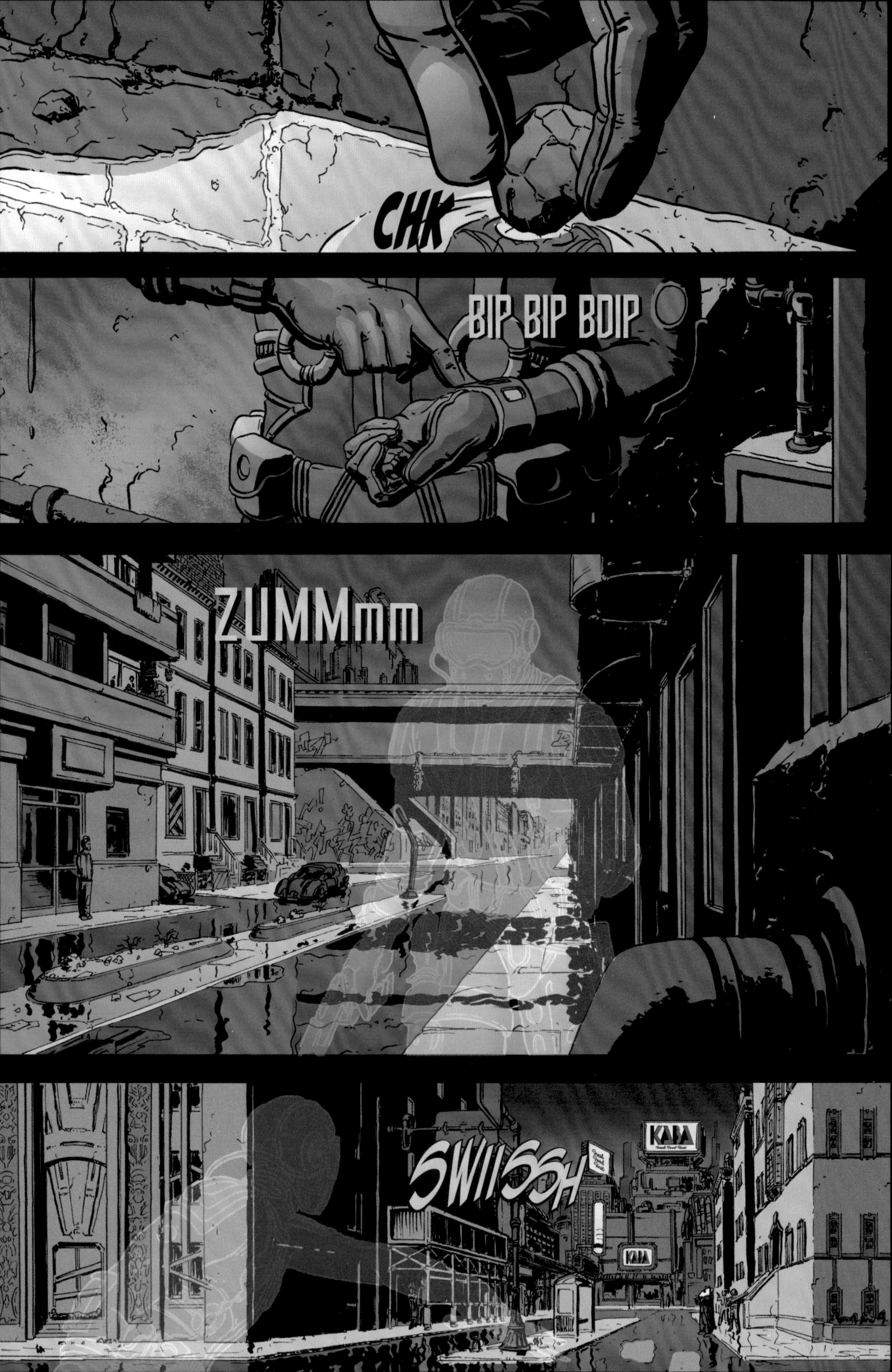
CHK
BIP BIP BDIP
ZUMMmm
SWIISSH
KABA
KABA

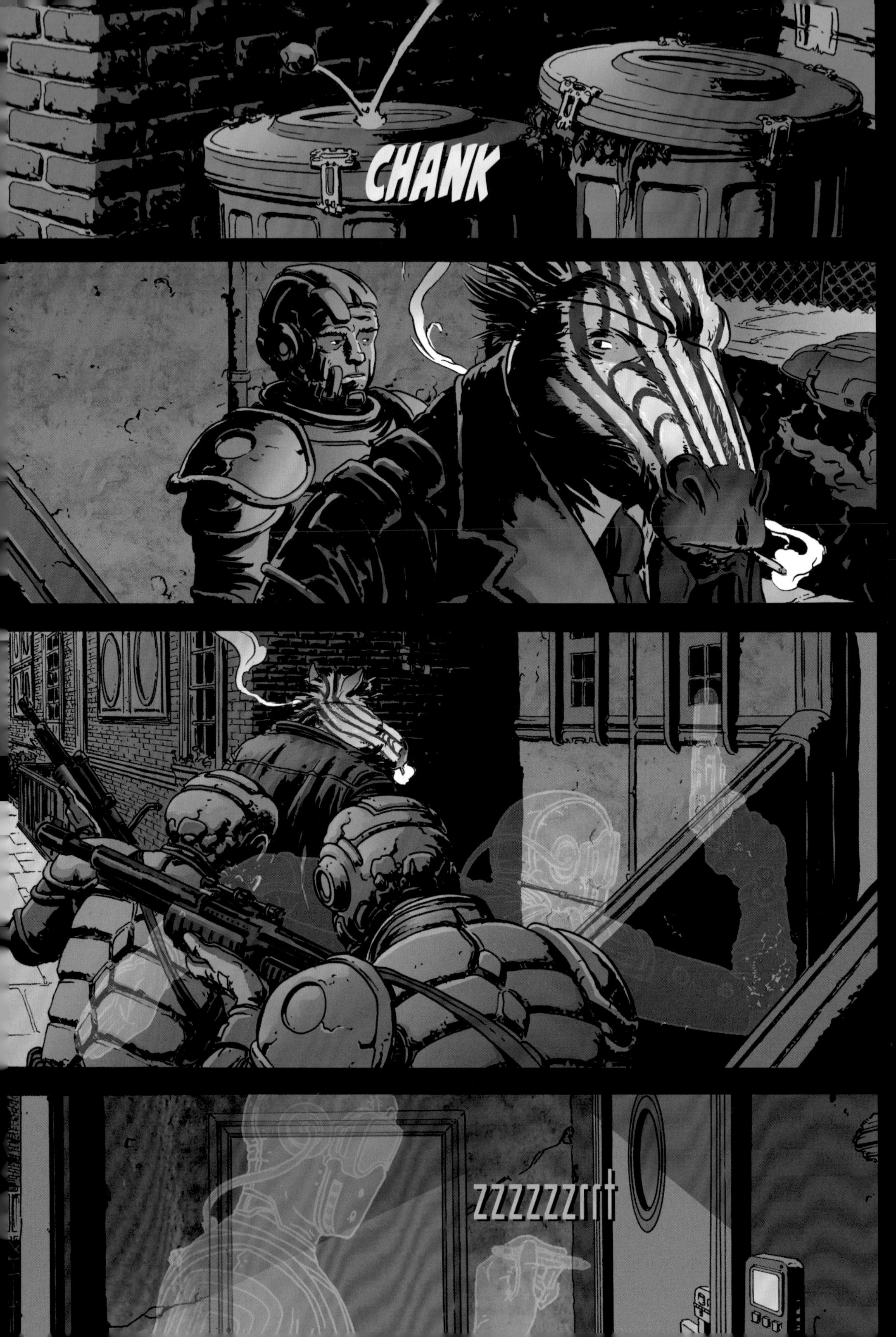
CHANK
zzzzzzrrt

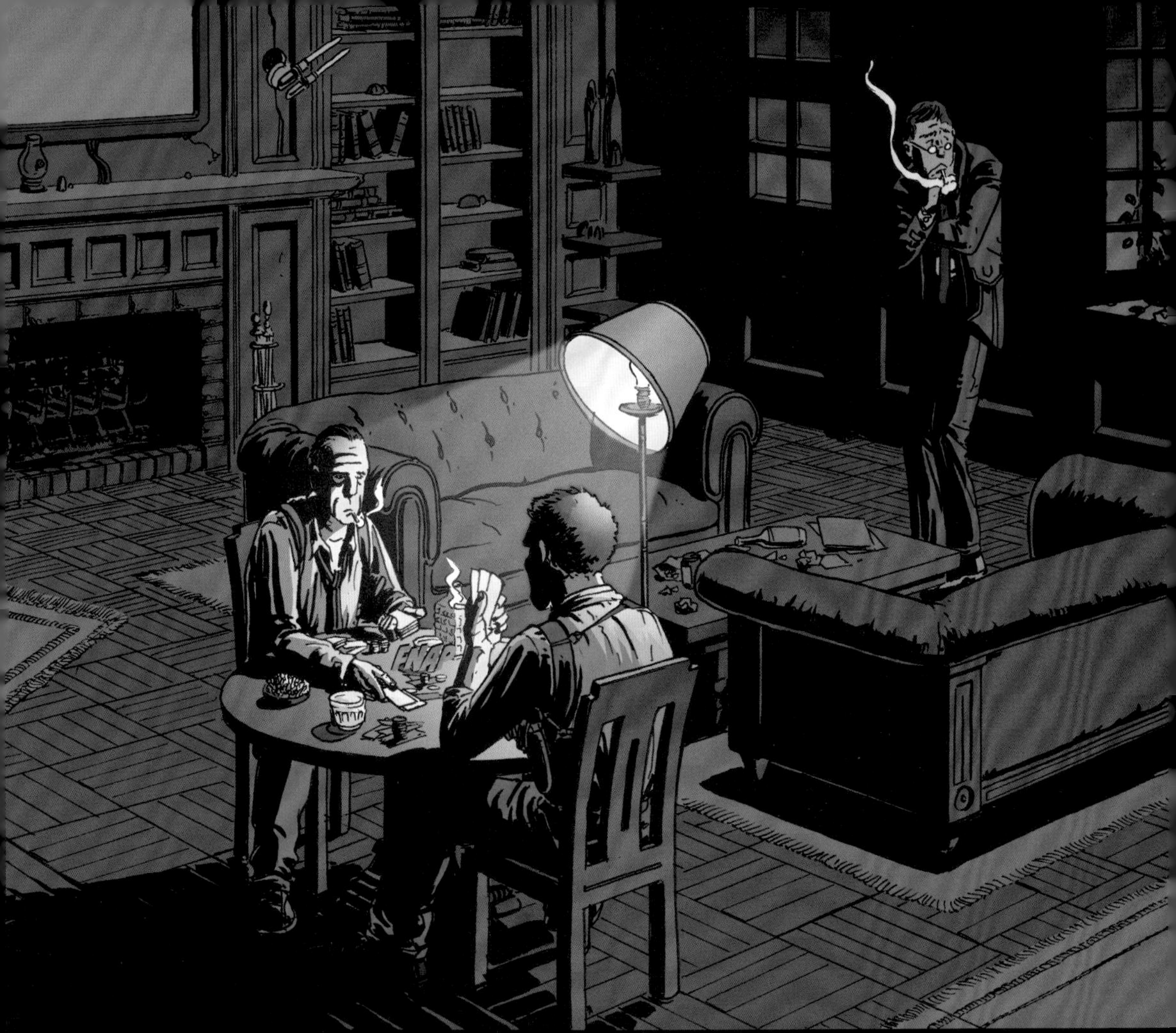
ENAP
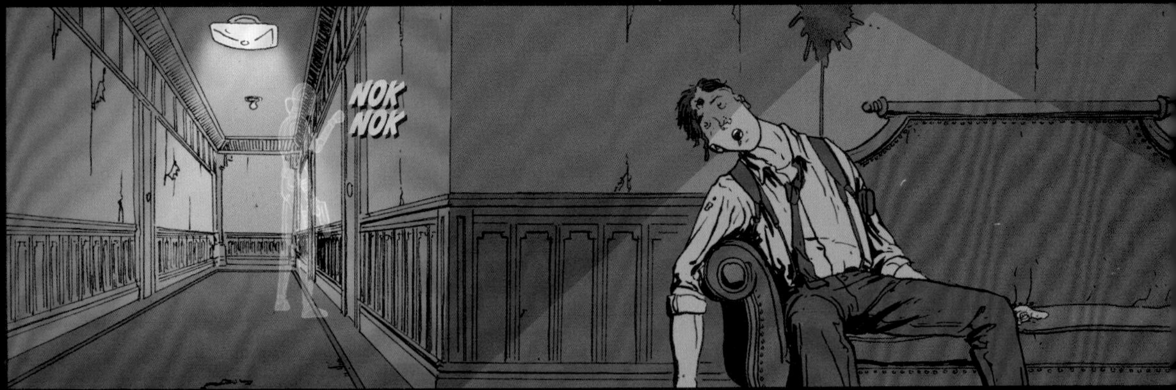
NOK
NOK
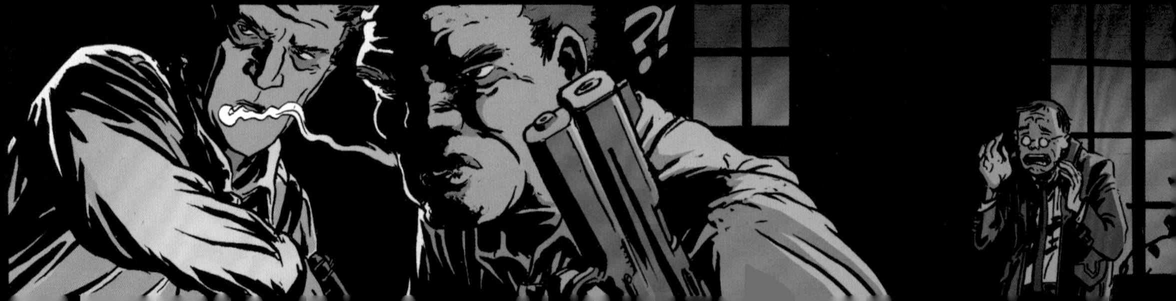
?!

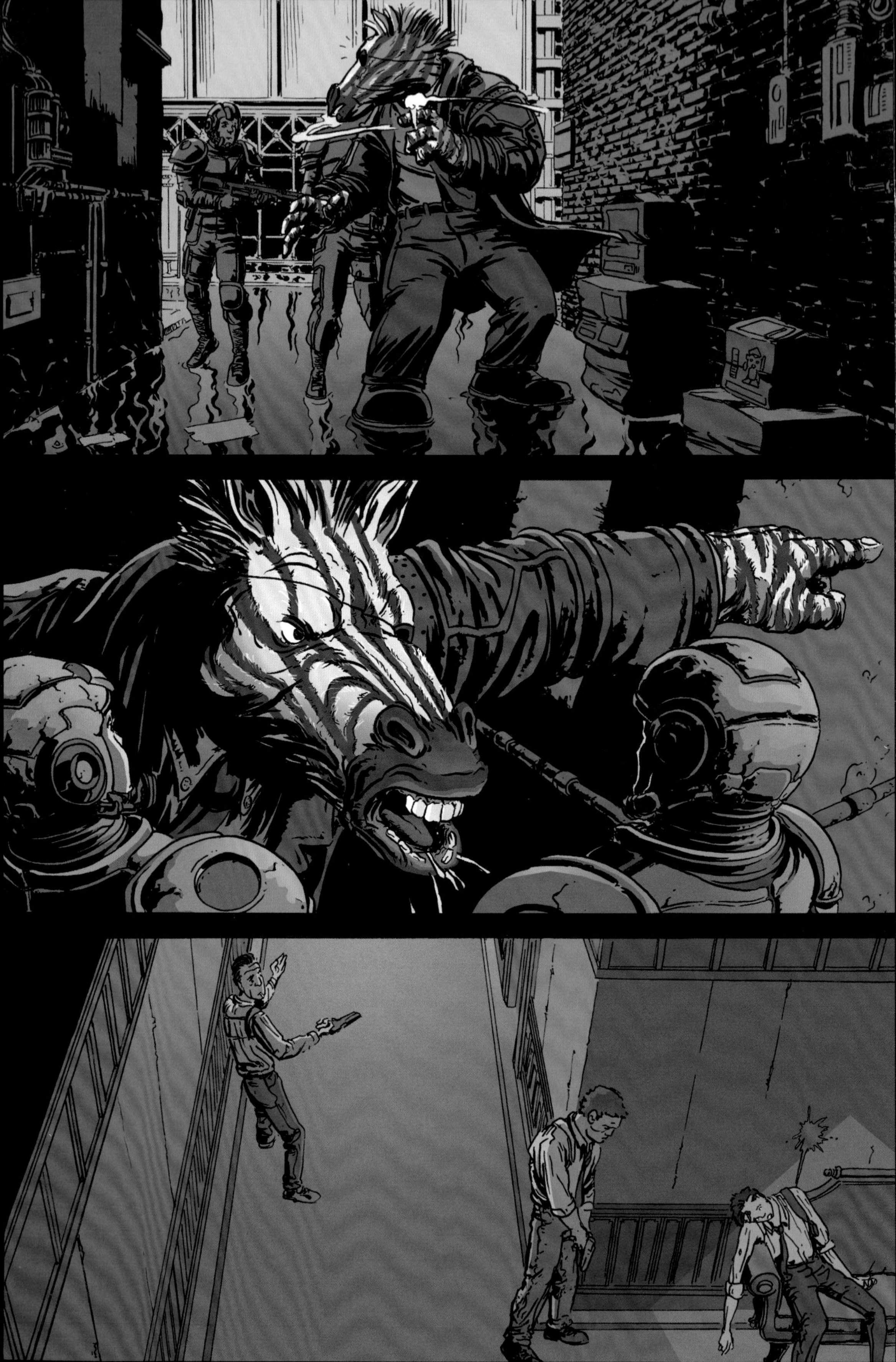

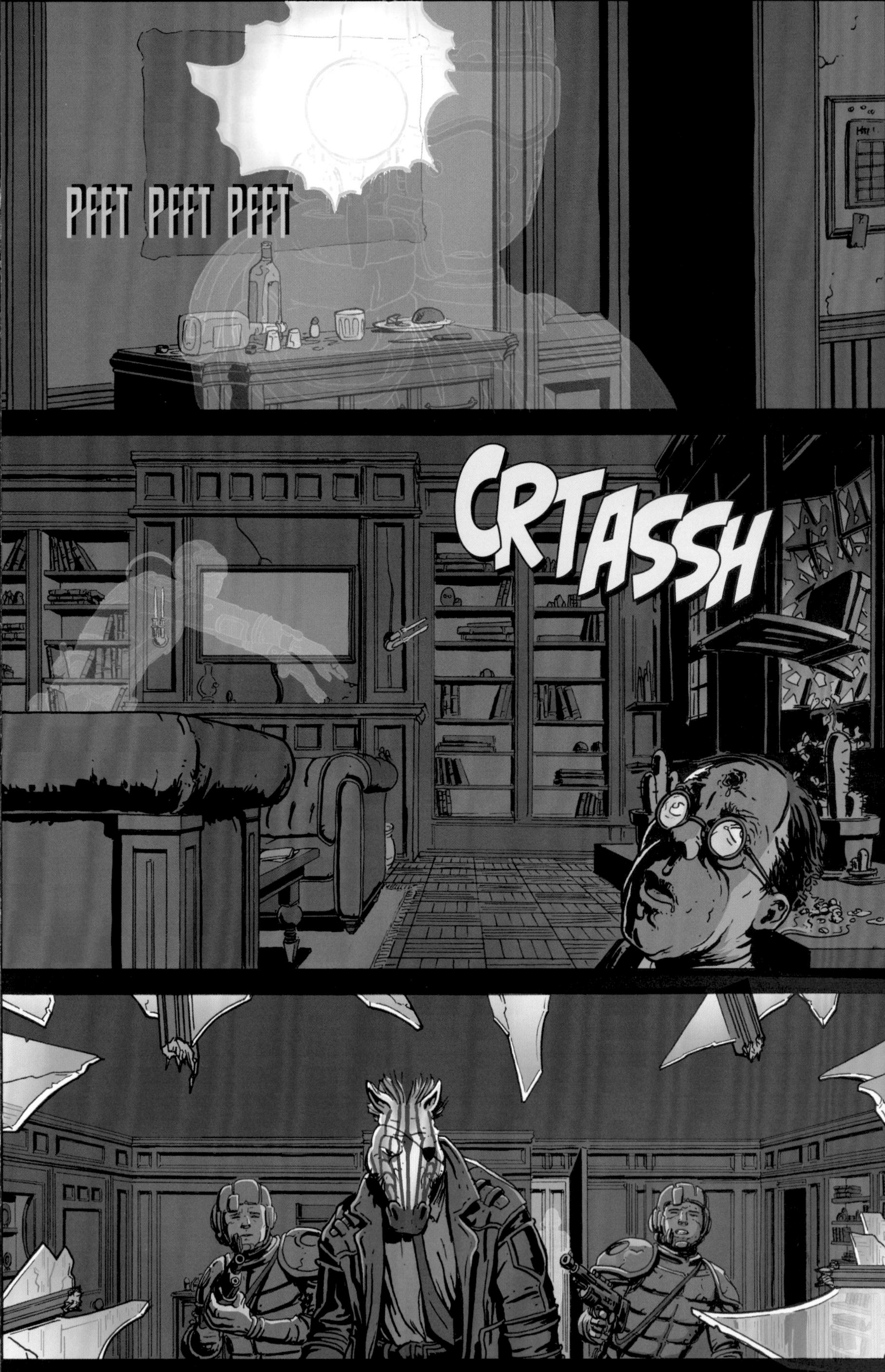
PFFT PFFT PFFT
CRTASSH

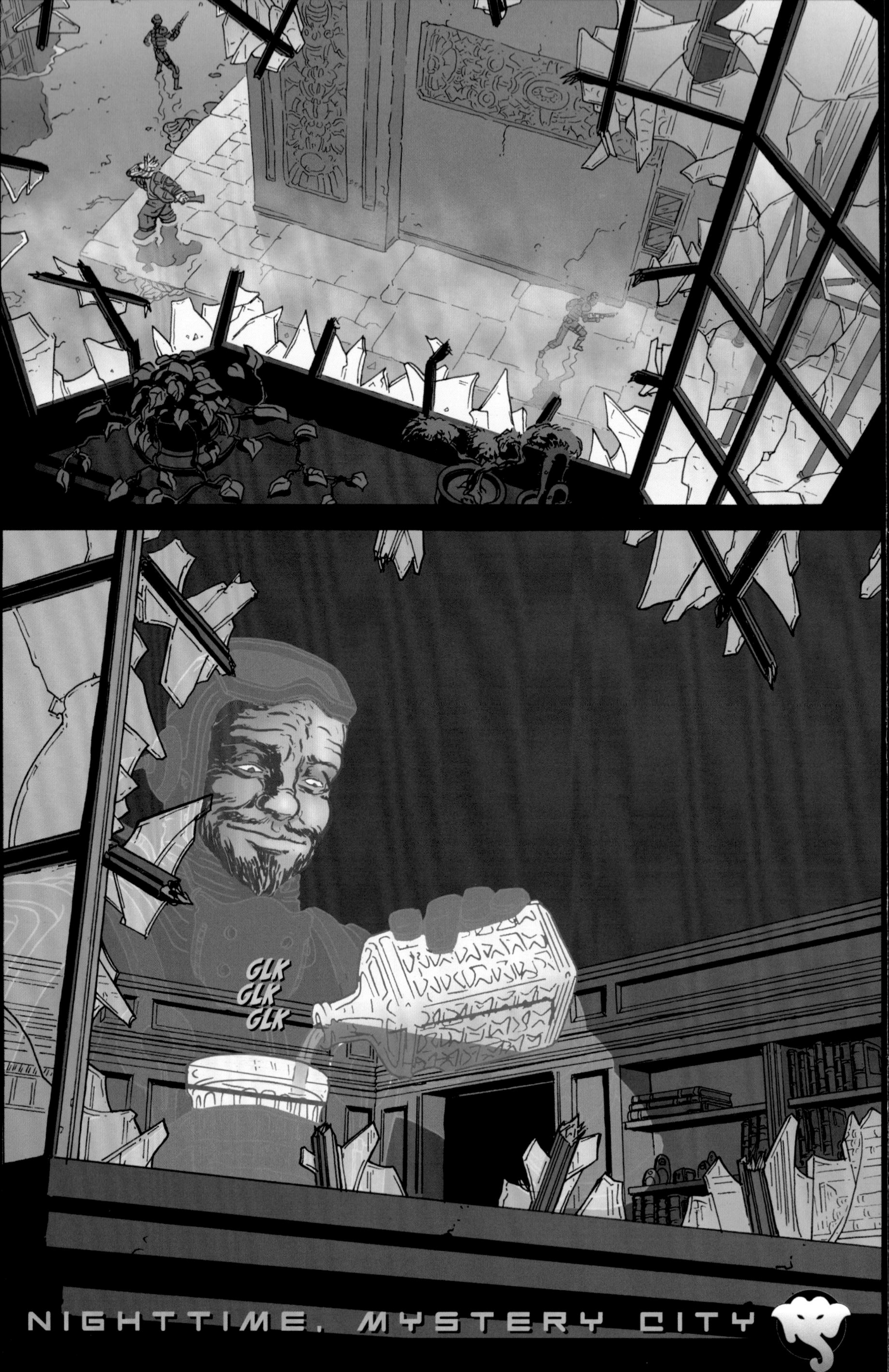
GLK
GLK
GLK
NIGHTTIME, MYSTERY CITY

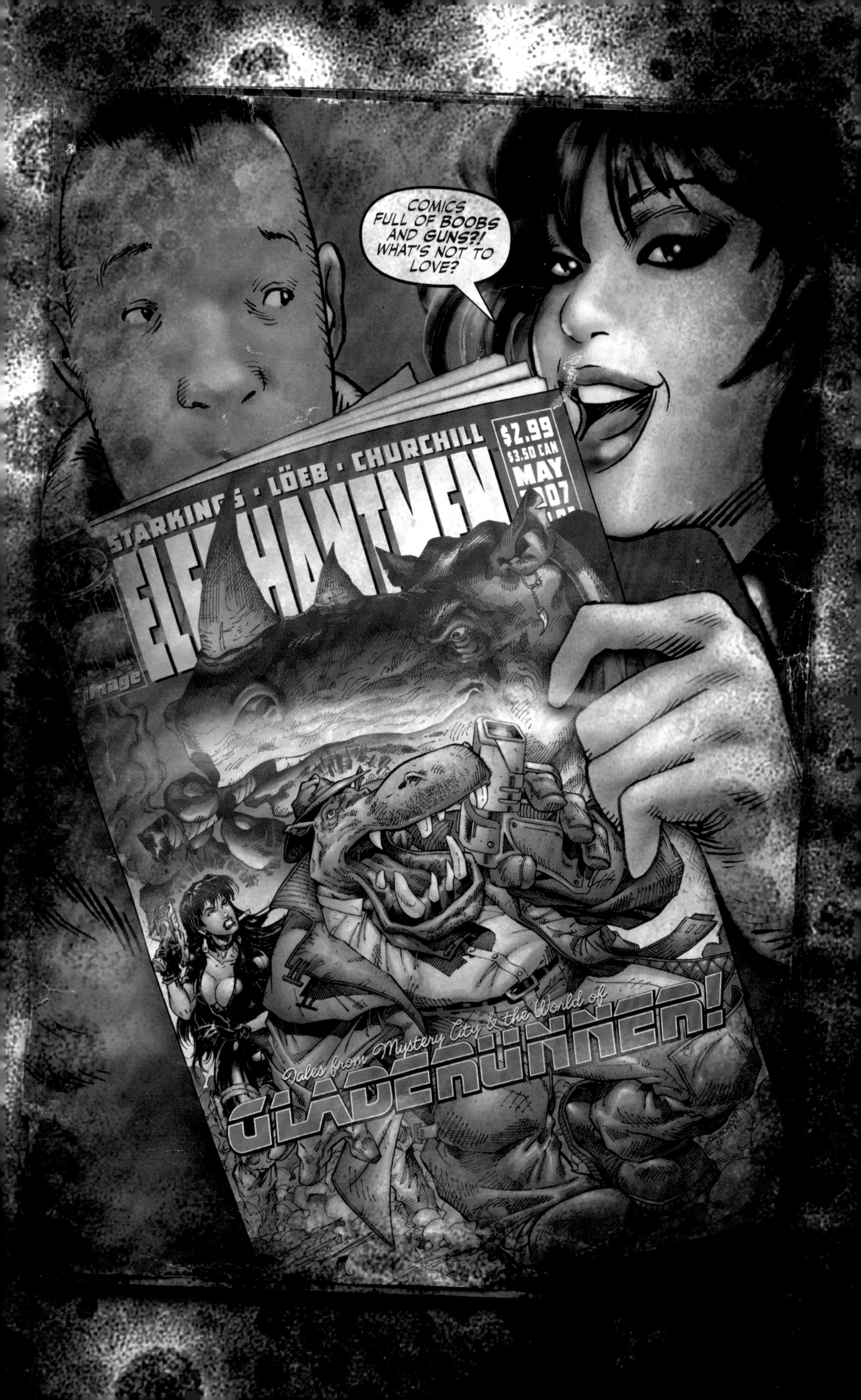
COMICS FULL OF BOOBS AND GUNS?! WHAT'S NOT TO LOVE?
STARKINGS · LÖEB · CHURCHILL
$2.99
$3.50 CAN
MAY
Tales from Mystery City & the World of
GLADERÜNNER!

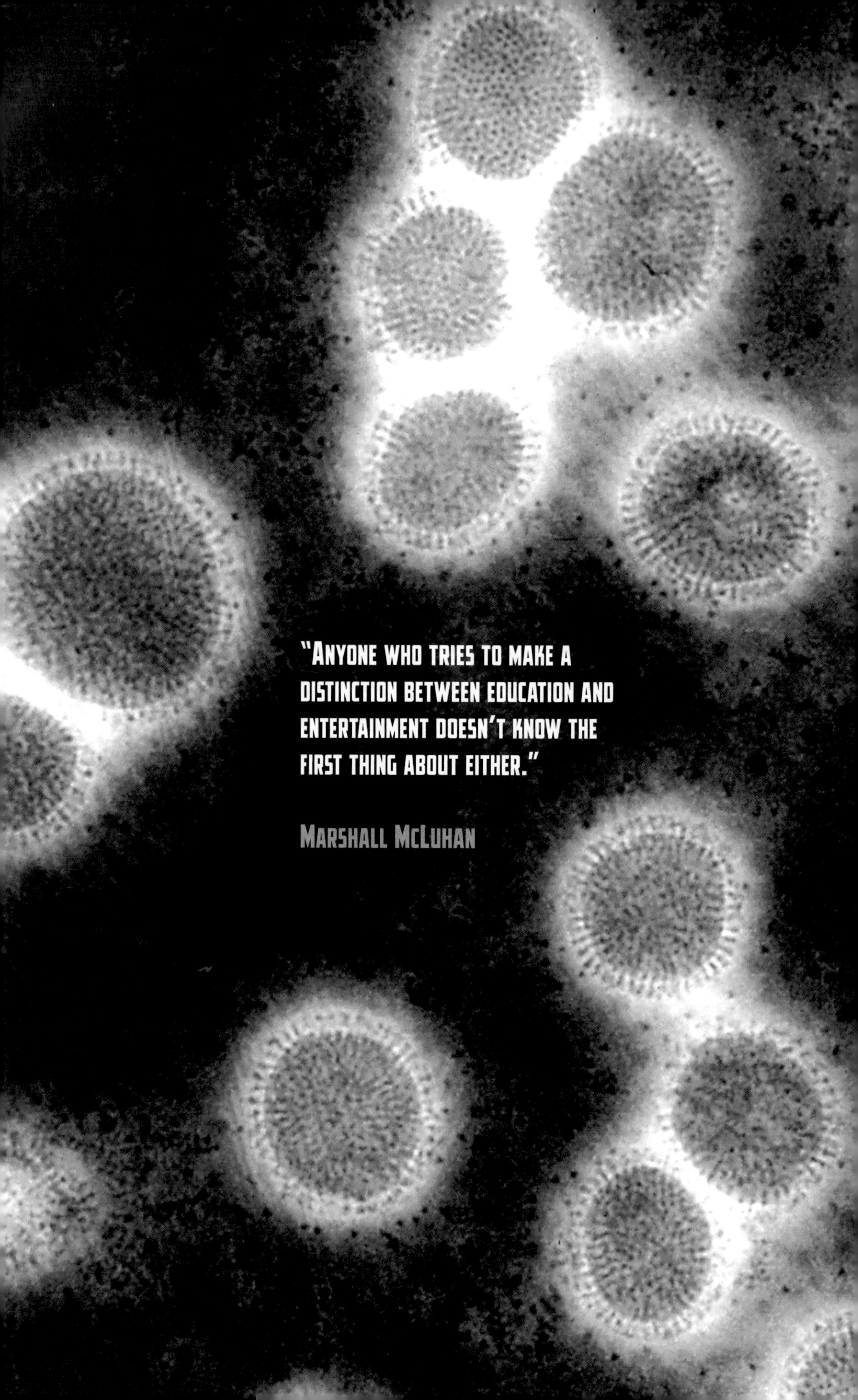

"Anyone who tries to make a distinction between education and entertainment doesn't know the first thing about either."

Marshall McLuhan

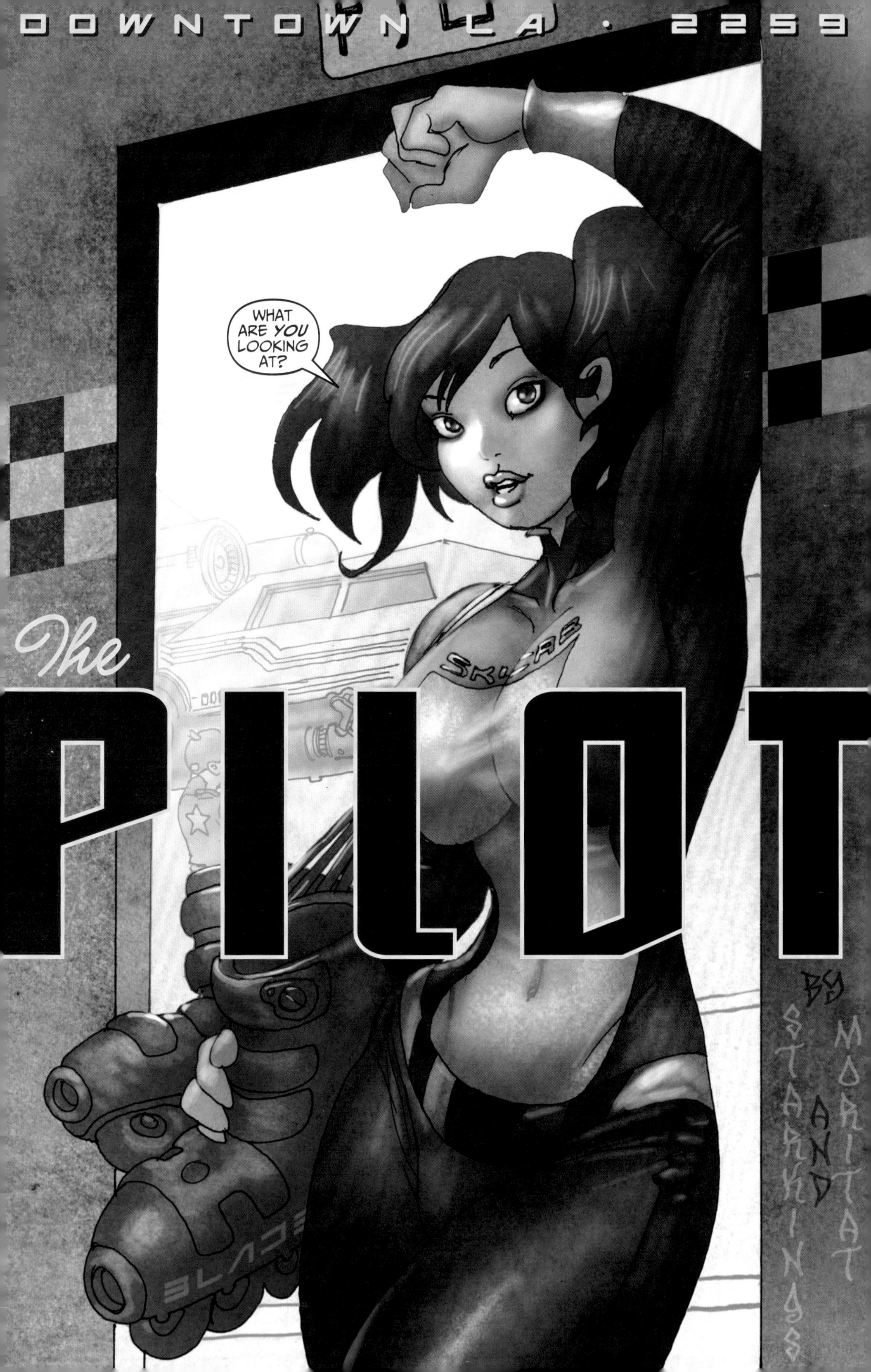
DOWNTOWN LA · 2259
WHAT ARE YOU LOOKING AT?
The PILOT
BY STARKINGS AND MORITAT

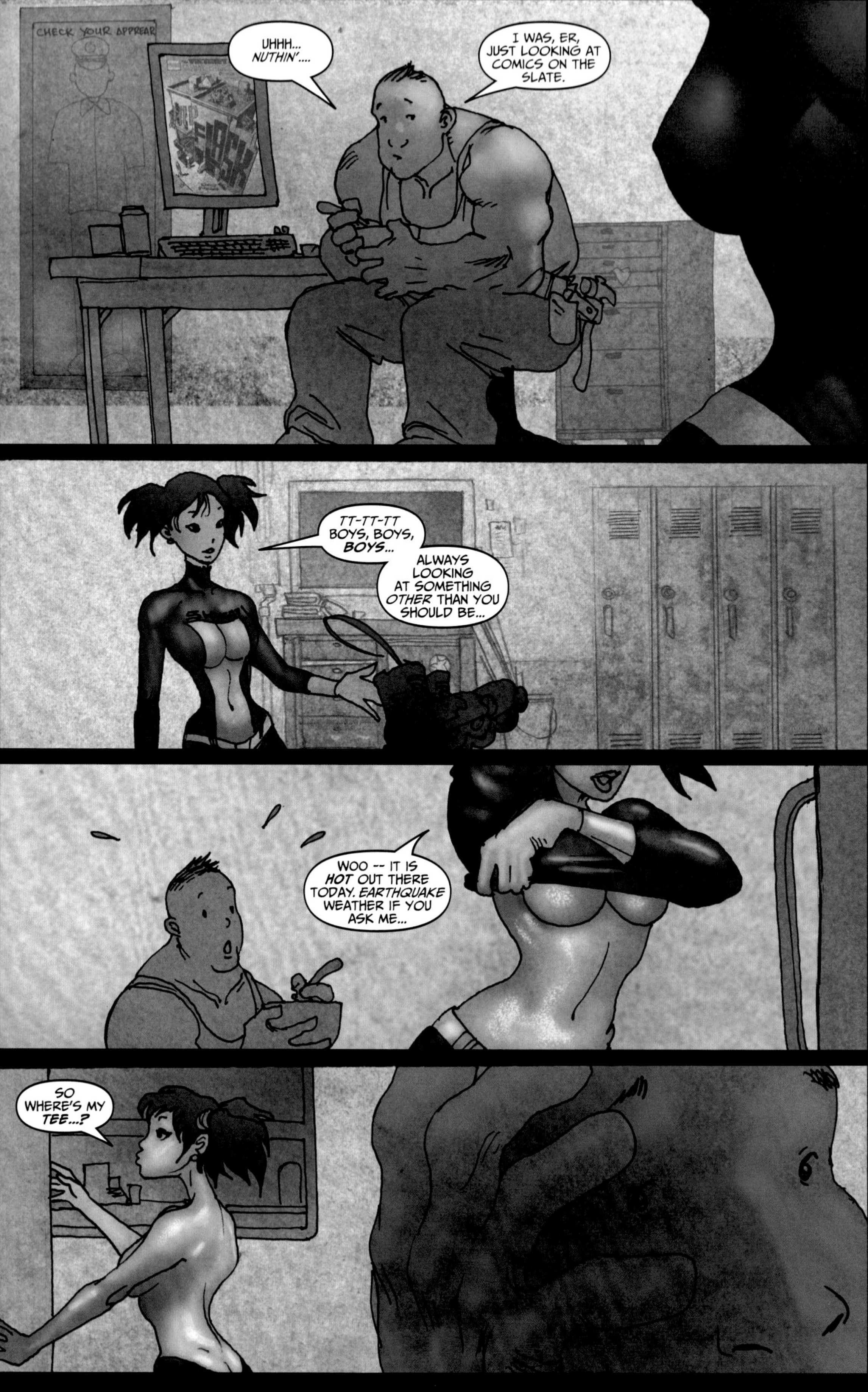
CHECK YOUR APPREAR
UHHH... NUTHIN'....
I WAS, ER, JUST LOOKING AT COMICS ON THE SLATE.
TT-TT-TT BOYS, BOYS, BOYS...
ALWAYS LOOKING AT SOMETHING OTHER THAN YOU SHOULD BE...
WOO -- IT IS HOT OUT THERE TODAY. EARTHQUAKE WEATHER IF YOU ASK ME...
SO WHERE'S MY TEE...?

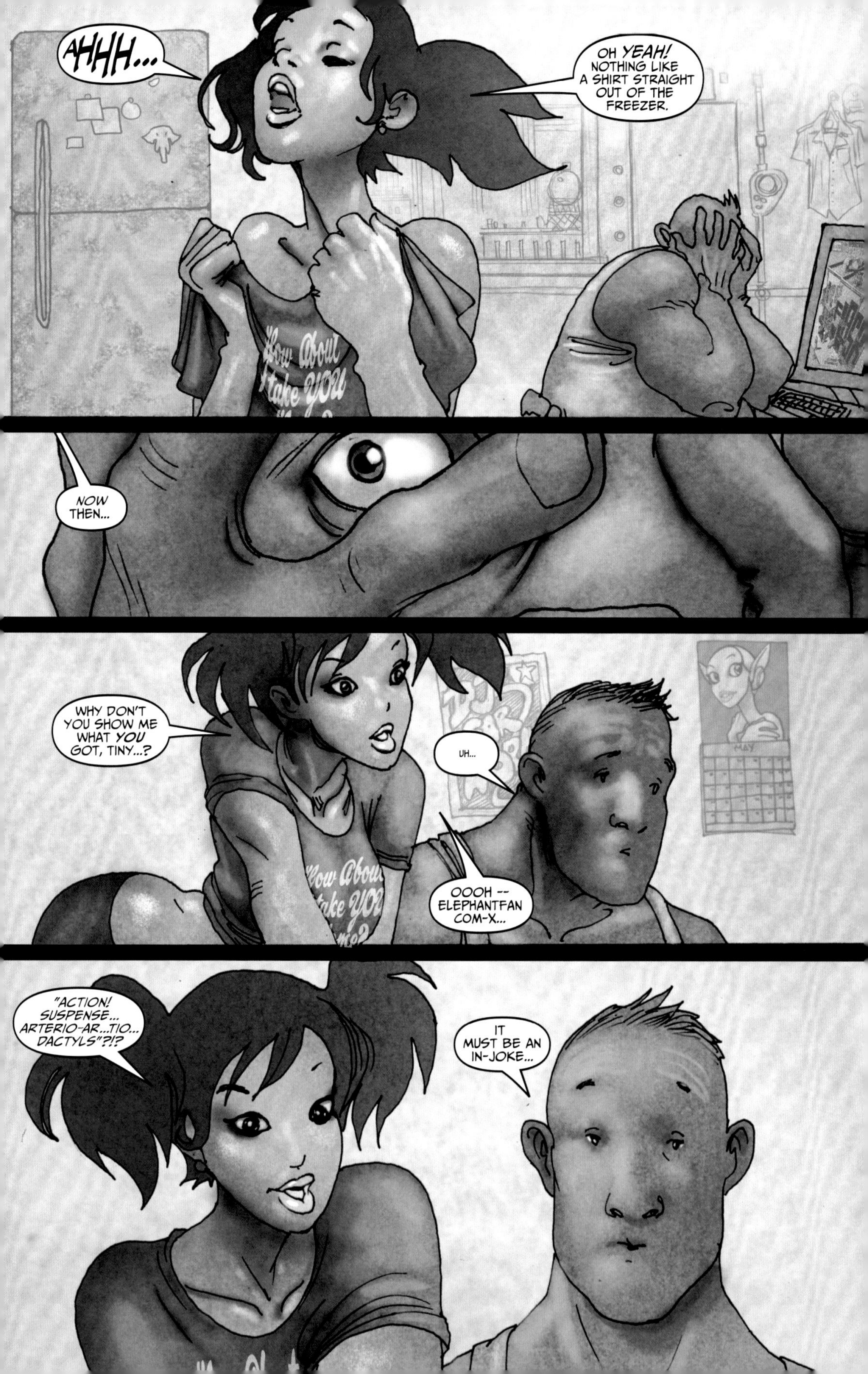
AHHH...
OH YEAH! NOTHING LIKE A SHIRT STRAIGHT OUT OF THE FREEZER.
NOW THEN...
WHY DON'T YOU SHOW ME WHAT YOU GOT, TINY...?
UH...
OOOH -- ELEPHANTFAN COM-X...
"ACTION! SUSPENSE... ARTERIO-AR...TIO... DACTYLS"?!?
IT MUST BE AN IN-JOKE...

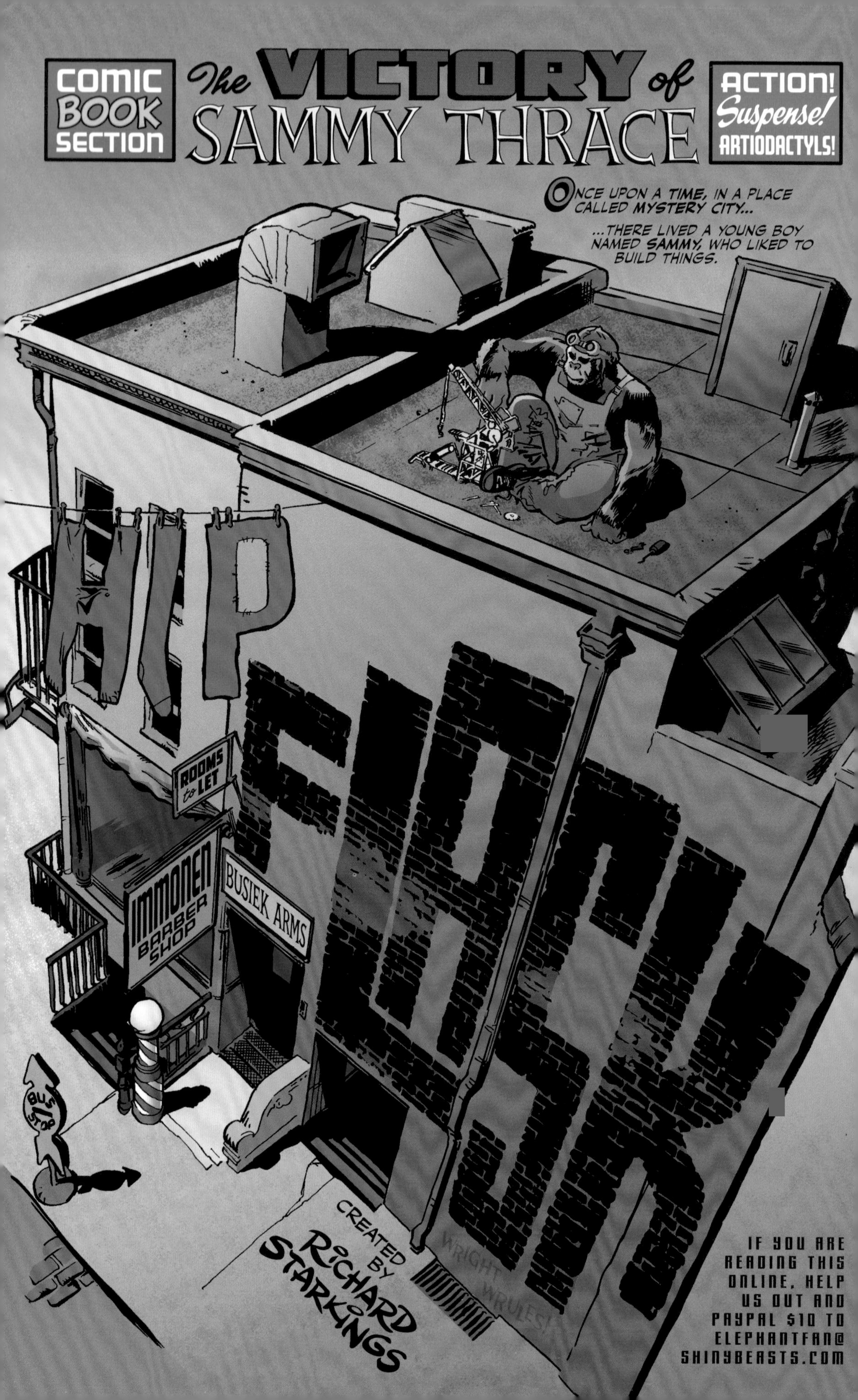
COMIC BOOK SECTION
The VICTORY of SAMMY THRACE
ACTION! Suspense! ARTIODACTYLS!
ONCE UPON A TIME, IN A PLACE CALLED MYSTERY CITY...
...THERE LIVED A YOUNG BOY NAMED SAMMY, WHO LIKED TO BUILD THINGS.
HIP
FLASK
ROOMS to LET
IMMONEN BARBER SHOP
BUSIEK ARMS
BUS STOP
CREATED BY RICHARD STARKINGS
WRIGHT RULES!
IF YOU ARE READING THIS ONLINE, HELP US OUT AND PAYPAL $10 TO ELEPHANTFAN@SHINYBEASTS.COM

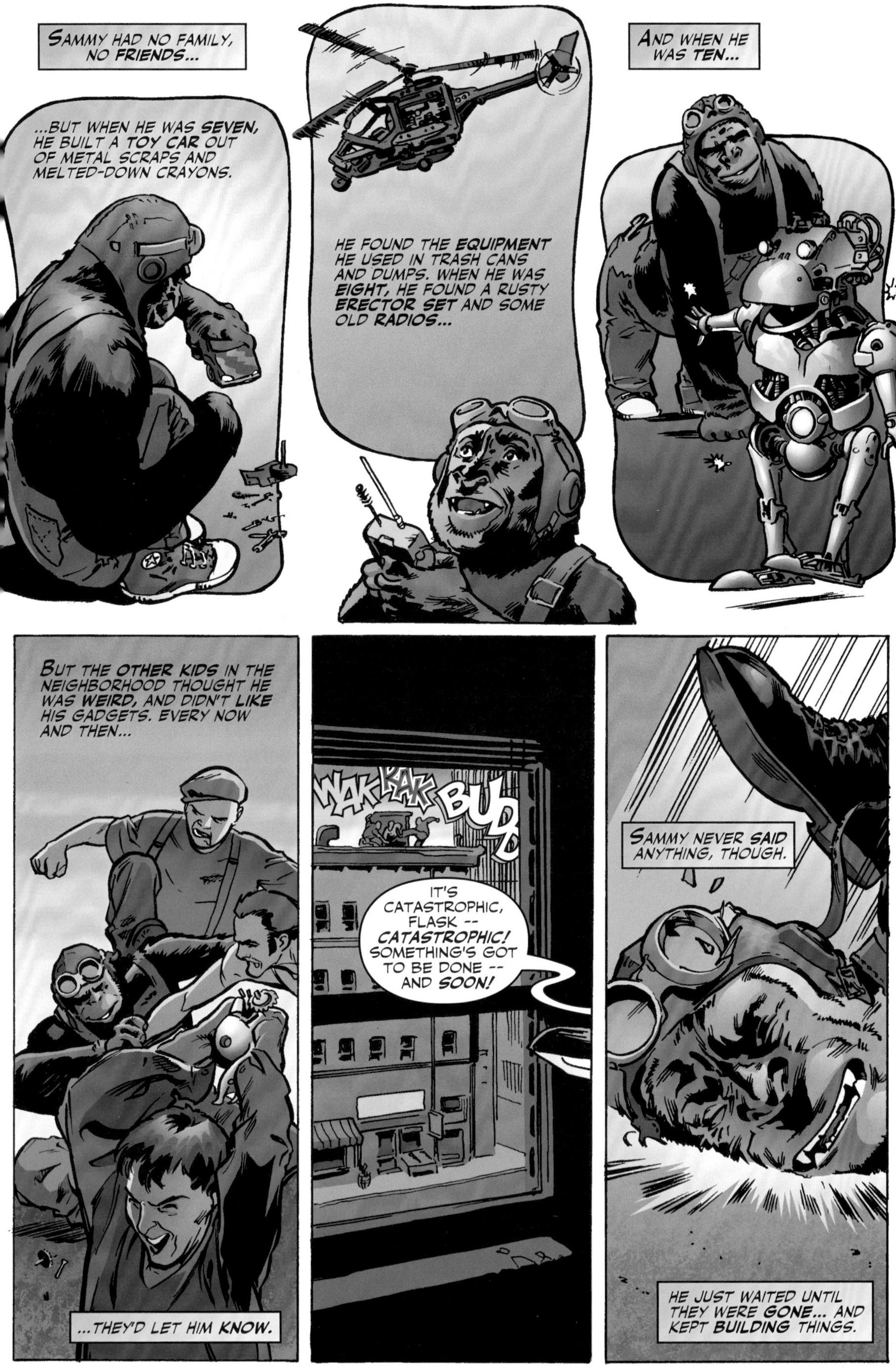
SAMMY HAD NO FAMILY, NO FRIENDS...
...BUT WHEN HE WAS SEVEN, HE BUILT A TOY CAR OUT OF METAL SCRAPS AND MELTED-DOWN CRAYONS.
HE FOUND THE EQUIPMENT HE USED IN TRASH CANS AND DUMPS. WHEN HE WAS EIGHT, HE FOUND A RUSTY ERECTOR SET AND SOME OLD RADIOS...
AND WHEN HE WAS TEN...
BUT THE OTHER KIDS IN THE NEIGHBORHOOD THOUGHT HE WAS WEIRD, AND DIDN'T LIKE HIS GADGETS. EVERY NOW AND THEN...
...THEY'D LET HIM KNOW.
WAK KAK BUD
IT'S CATASTROPHIC, FLASK -- CATASTROPHIC! SOMETHING'S GOT TO BE DONE -- AND SOON!
SAMMY NEVER SAID ANYTHING, THOUGH.
HE JUST WAITED UNTIL THEY WERE GONE... AND KEPT BUILDING THINGS.

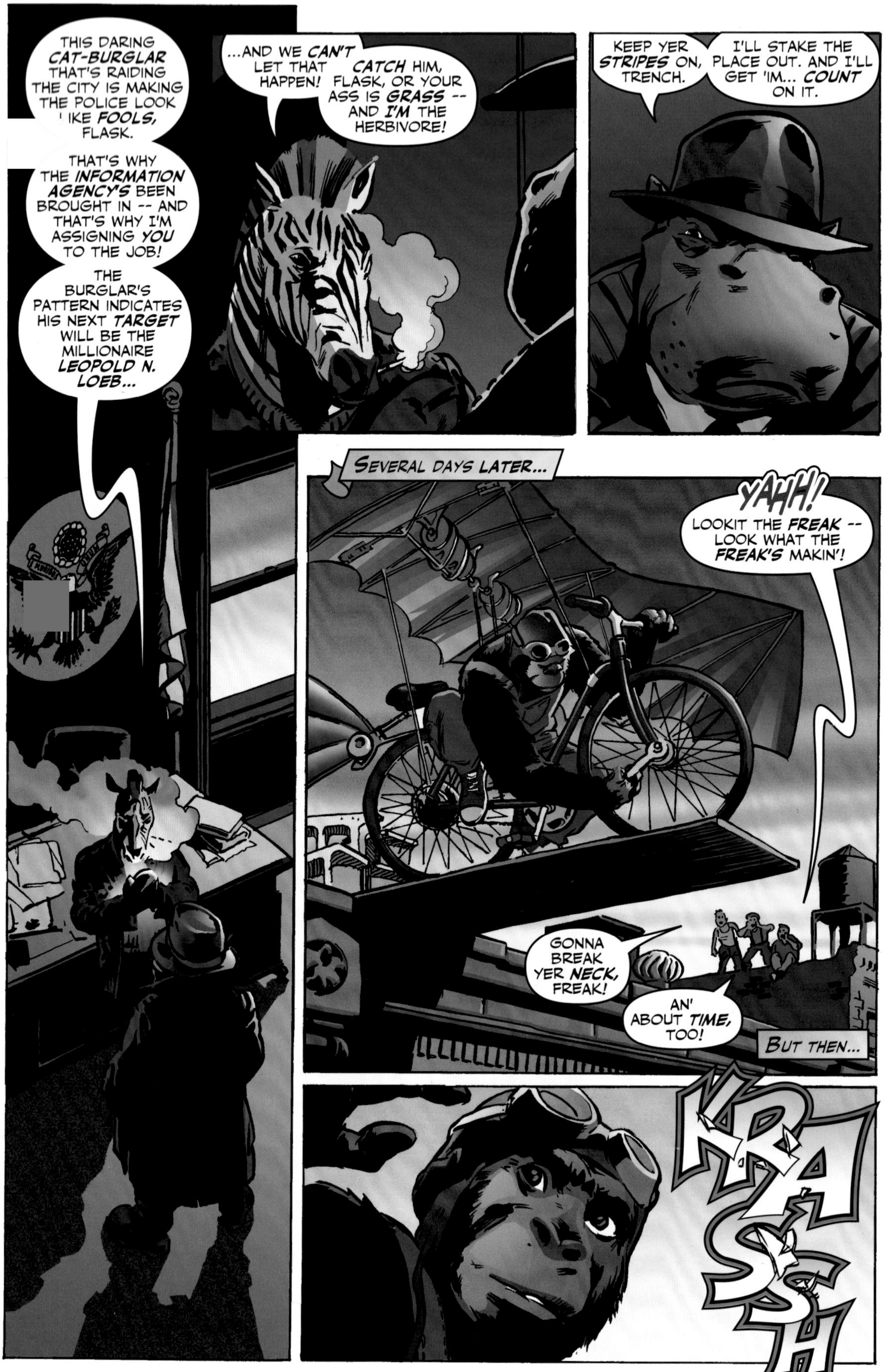
THIS DARING CAT-BURGLAR THAT'S RAIDING THE CITY IS MAKING THE POLICE LOOK LIKE FOOLS, FLASK.
THAT'S WHY THE INFORMATION AGENCY'S BEEN BROUGHT IN -- AND THAT'S WHY I'M ASSIGNING YOU TO THE JOB!
THE BURGLAR'S PATTERN INDICATES HIS NEXT TARGET WILL BE THE MILLIONAIRE LEOPOLD N. LOEB...
...AND WE CAN'T LET THAT HAPPEN!
CATCH HIM, FLASK, OR YOUR ASS IS GRASS -- AND I'M THE HERBIVORE!
KEEP YER STRIPES ON, TRENCH.
I'LL STAKE THE PLACE OUT. AND I'LL GET 'IM... COUNT ON IT.
SEVERAL DAYS LATER...
YAHH!
LOOKIT THE FREAK -- LOOK WHAT THE FREAK'S MAKIN'!
GONNA BREAK YER NECK, FREAK!
AN' ABOUT TIME, TOO!
BUT THEN...
KRASSH

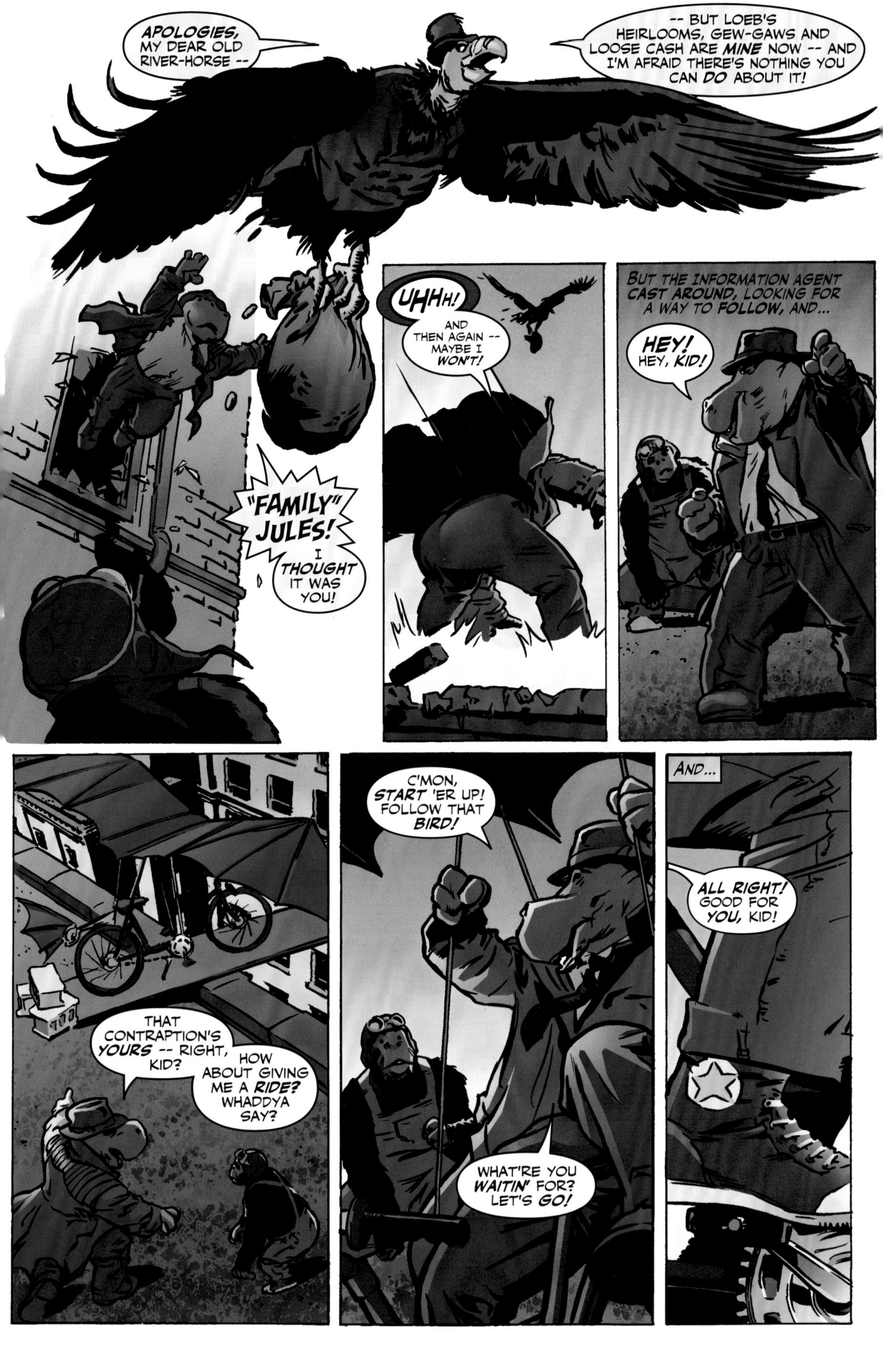
APOLOGIES, MY DEAR OLD RIVER-HORSE --
-- BUT LOEB'S HEIRLOOMS, GEW-GAWS AND LOOSE CASH ARE MINE NOW -- AND I'M AFRAID THERE'S NOTHING YOU CAN DO ABOUT IT!
"FAMILY" JULES!
I THOUGHT IT WAS YOU!
UHHH!
AND THEN AGAIN -- MAYBE I WON'T!
BUT THE INFORMATION AGENT CAST AROUND, LOOKING FOR A WAY TO FOLLOW, AND...
HEY! HEY, KID!
THAT CONTRAPTION'S YOURS -- RIGHT, KID?
HOW ABOUT GIVING ME A RIDE? WHADDYA SAY?
C'MON, START 'ER UP! FOLLOW THAT BIRD!
WHAT'RE YOU WAITIN' FOR? LET'S GO!
AND...
ALL RIGHT! GOOD FOR YOU, KID!

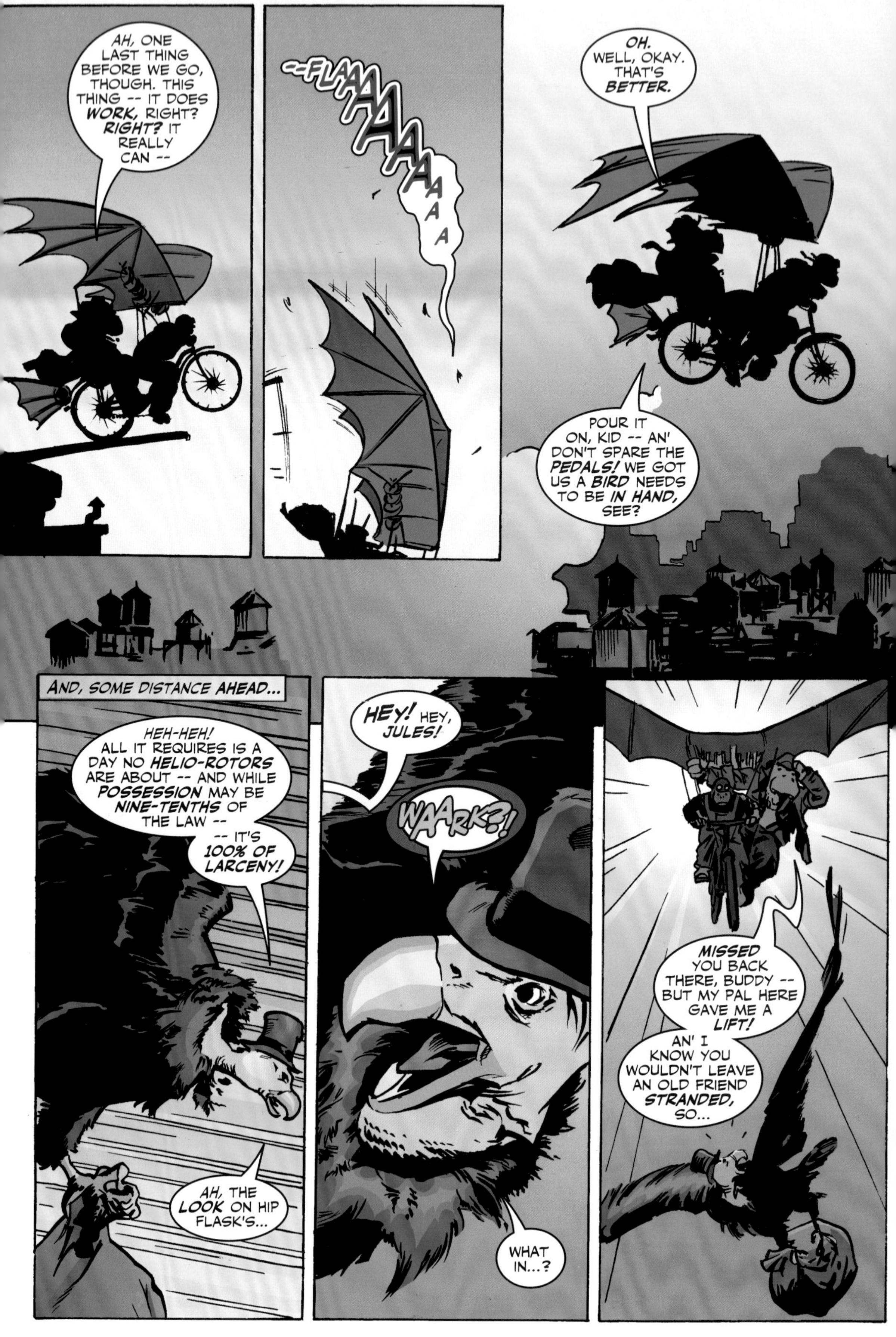
AH, ONE LAST THING BEFORE WE GO, THOUGH. THIS THING -- IT DOES WORK, RIGHT? RIGHT? IT REALLY CAN --
--FLAAAAAAAAA
OH. WELL, OKAY. THAT'S BETTER.
POUR IT ON, KID -- AN' DON'T SPARE THE PEDALS! WE GOT US A BIRD NEEDS TO BE IN HAND, SEE?
AND, SOME DISTANCE AHEAD...
HEH-HEH! ALL IT REQUIRES IS A DAY NO HELIO-ROTORS ARE ABOUT -- AND WHILE POSSESSION MAY BE NINE-TENTHS OF THE LAW --
-- IT'S 100% OF LARCENY!
AH, THE LOOK ON HIP FLASK'S...
HEY! HEY, JULES!
WAARK?!
WHAT IN...?
MISSED YOU BACK THERE, BUDDY -- BUT MY PAL HERE GAVE ME A LIFT!
AN' I KNOW YOU WOULDN'T LEAVE AN OLD FRIEND STRANDED, SO...

...GOING MY WAY?!

AWRK! NO... NO!

WHUMP

IN YOU GO, JULIUS. AND THANKS, FLASK.

NO SWEAT, BRUNO. BUT I'LL TELL YOU...

...I COULDN'T'A DONE IT WITHOUT THE KID HERE! HIM AN' HIS CONTRAPTION -- THEY'RE THE REAL HEROES HERE!

GOWAN, NEWSHAWKS -- GET A PIC!

SAMMY GOT HIS PICTURE IN THE PAPER, AND A REWARD FROM MR. LOEB.

formation Agent

CITY - Samuel Thrace, ensie Avenue in the section of Mystery City, aided Information Agent mous P. Flask in the ension of Julius n-Byrd, a.k.a. "Family" the notorious burglar that had plaguing Mystery City's thiest, of late.

Carrion-Byrd had just burglarized e home of local financier, philanthropist and political aspirant Leopold N. Loeb, and was escaping by air, pursued over the rooftops by Agent Flask. Further pursuit would have bee ssible, however, due to Carr ian nature, if not for ornithopter young Thrace had buildin on recovery of th

Samuel K. Thrace, youthful inventor

AND IF YOU THINK THAT WOULD IMPRESS THE OTHER KIDS, MAKE THEM REASSESS SAMMY...

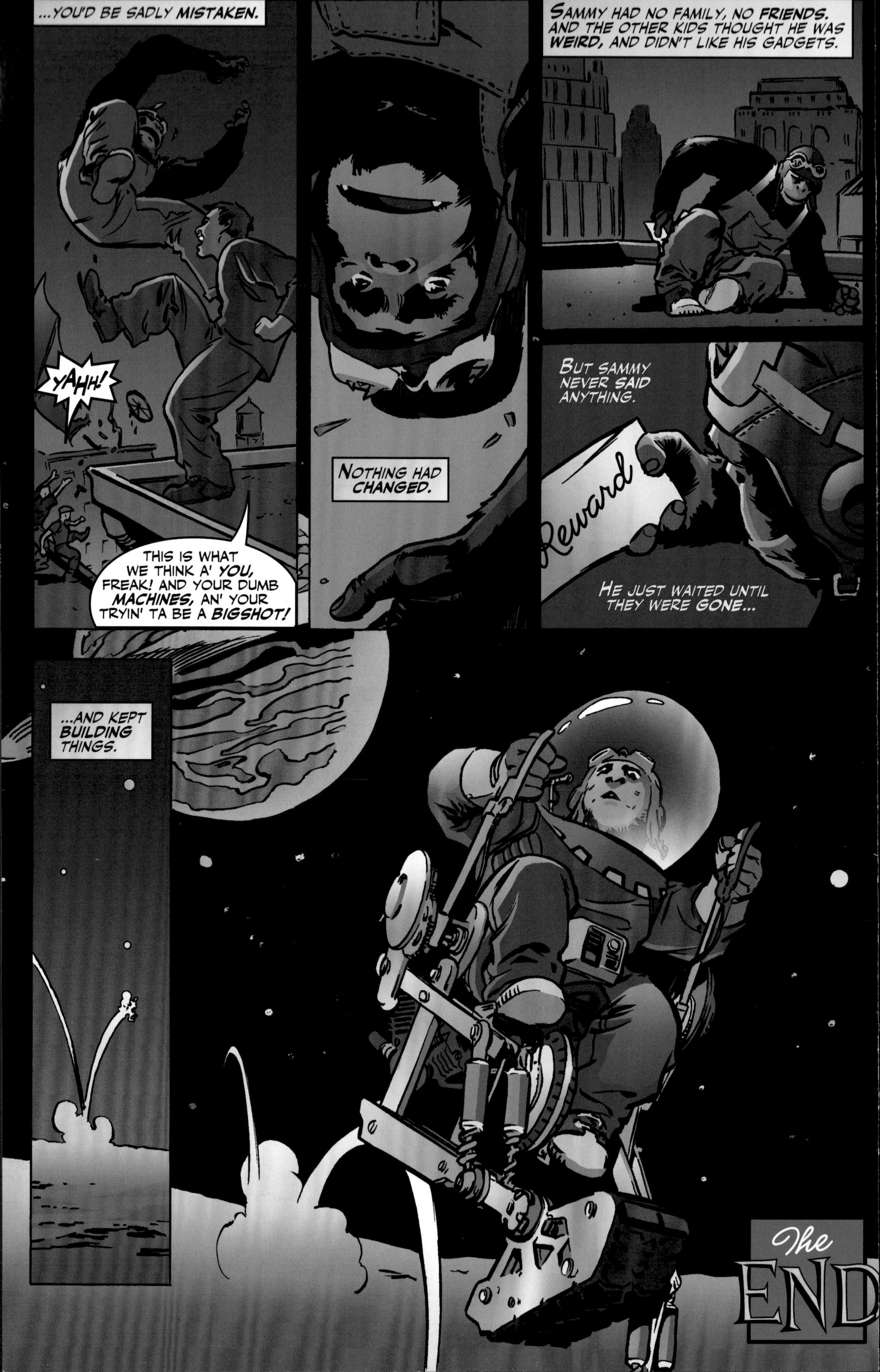
...YOU'D BE SADLY MISTAKEN.
YAHH!
THIS IS WHAT WE THINK A' YOU, FREAK! AND YOUR DUMB MACHINES, AN' YOUR TRYIN' TA BE A BIGSHOT!
NOTHING HAD CHANGED.
SAMMY HAD NO FAMILY, NO FRIENDS. AND THE OTHER KIDS THOUGHT HE WAS WEIRD, AND DIDN'T LIKE HIS GADGETS.
BUT SAMMY NEVER SAID ANYTHING.
Reward
HE JUST WAITED UNTIL THEY WERE GONE...
...AND KEPT BUILDING THINGS.
The END

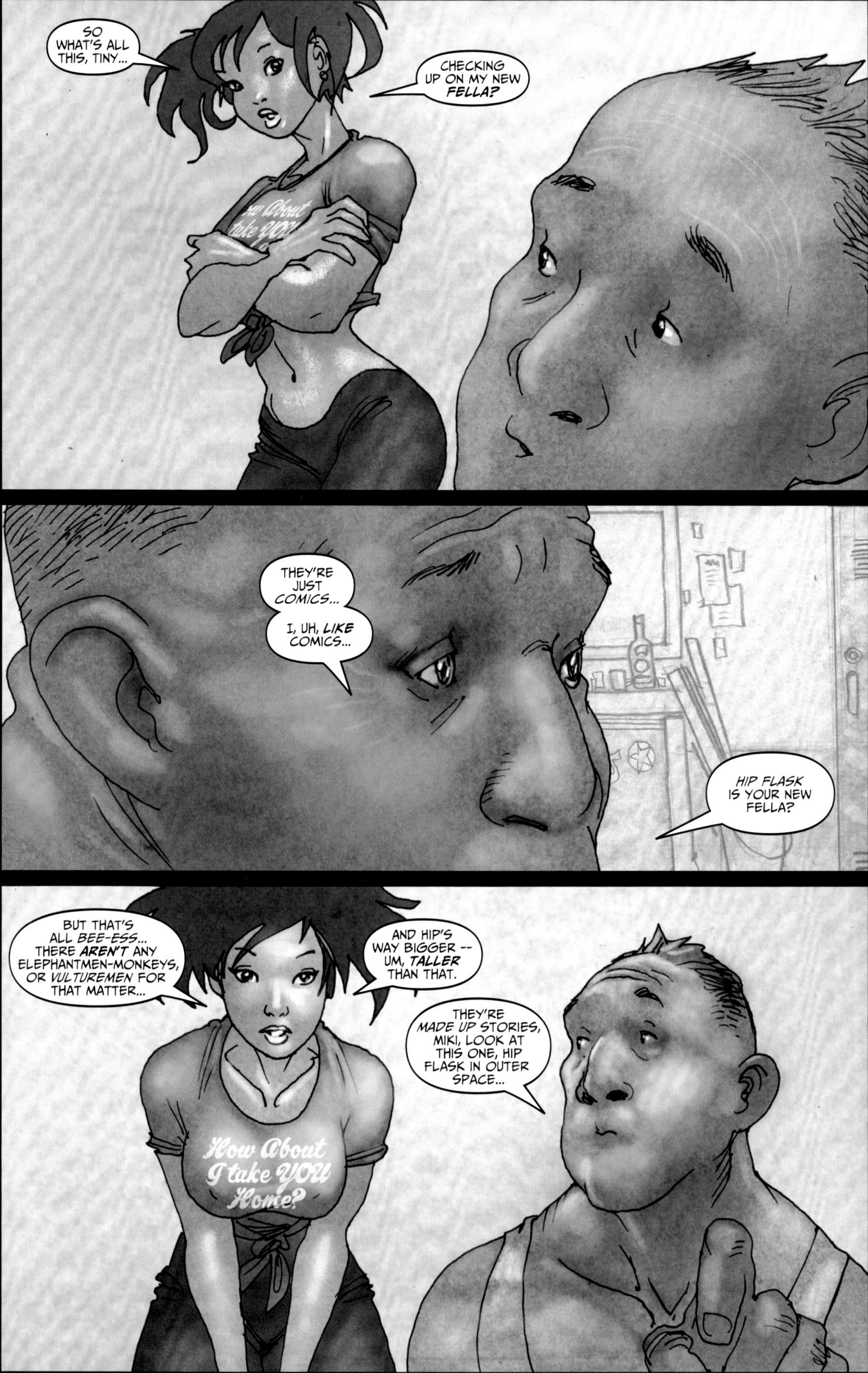
SO WHAT'S ALL THIS, TINY...
CHECKING UP ON MY NEW *FELLA?*
THEY'RE JUST *COMICS...*
I, UH, *LIKE* COMICS...
HIP FLASK IS YOUR NEW FELLA?
BUT THAT'S ALL *BEE-ESS...* THERE ***AREN'T*** ANY ELEPHANTMEN-MONKEYS, OR *VULTUREMEN* FOR THAT MATTER...
AND HIP'S WAY BIGGER -- UM, *TALLER* THAN THAT.
THEY'RE *MADE UP* STORIES, MIKI, LOOK AT THIS ONE, HIP FLASK IN OUTER SPACE...
How About I take YOU Home?

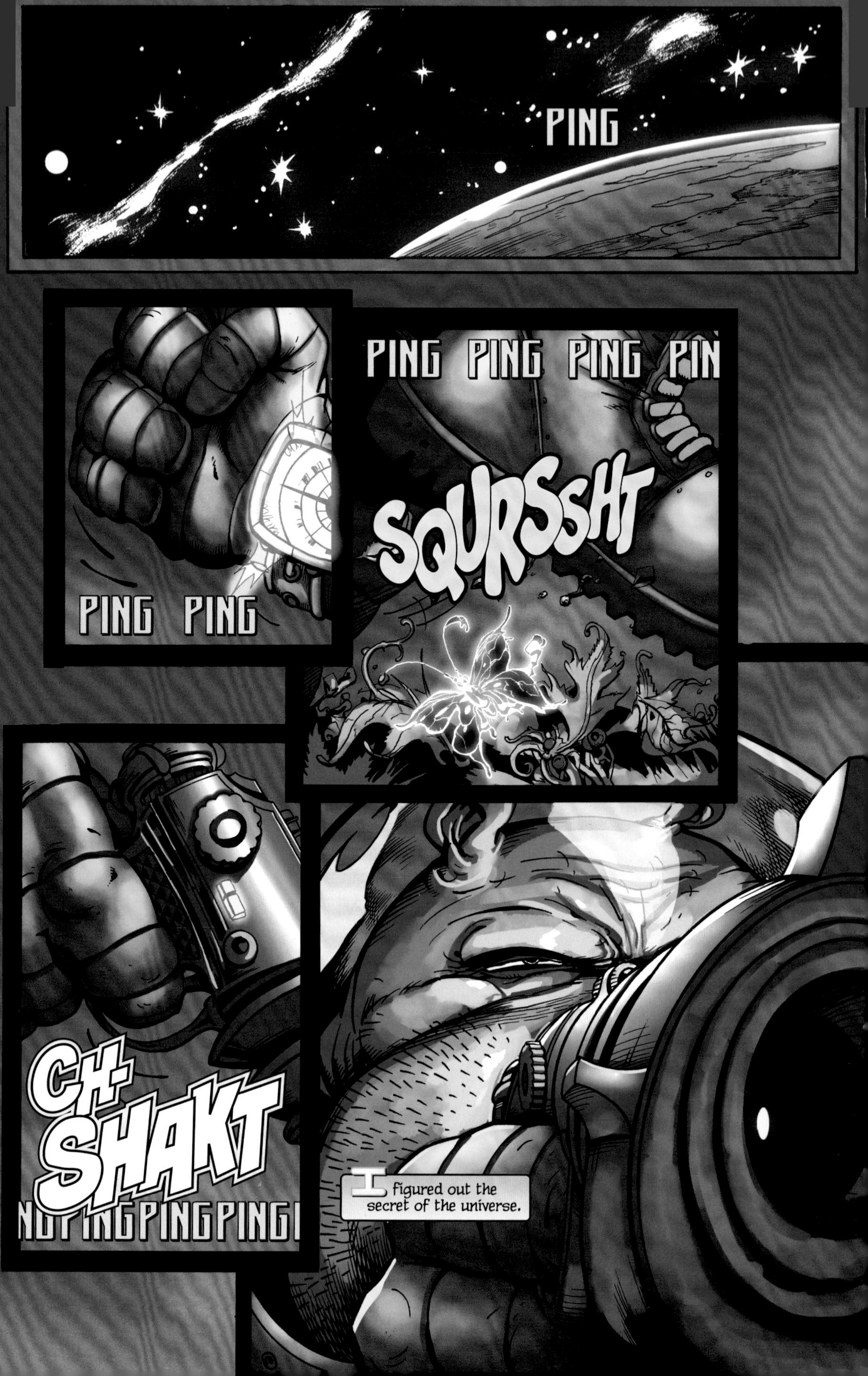
PING
PING PING
PING PING PING PIN
SQURSSHT
CH-SHAKT
NGPINGPINGPINGP
I figured out the secret of the universe.

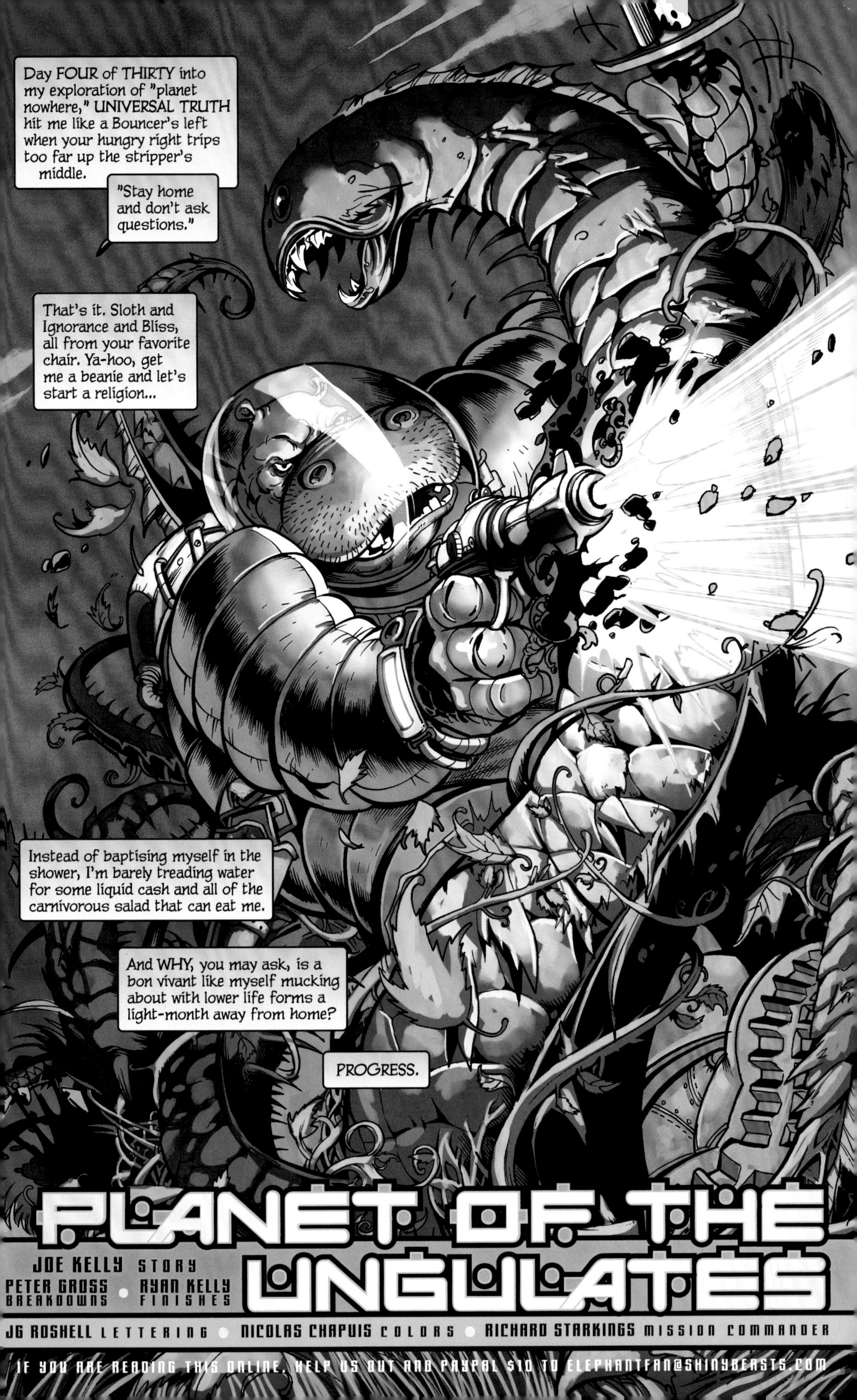
Day FOUR of THIRTY into my exploration of "planet nowhere," UNIVERSAL TRUTH hit me like a Bouncer's left when your hungry right trips too far up the stripper's middle.
"Stay home and don't ask questions."
That's it. Sloth and Ignorance and Bliss, all from your favorite chair. Ya-hoo, get me a beanie and let's start a religion...
Instead of baptising myself in the shower, I'm barely treading water for some liquid cash and all of the carnivorous salad that can eat me.
And WHY, you may ask, is a bon vivant like myself mucking about with lower life forms a light-month away from home?
PROGRESS.
PLANET OF THE UNGULATES
JOE KELLY STORY
PETER GROSS BREAKDOWNS
RYAN KELLY FINISHES
JG ROSHELL LETTERING
NICOLAS CHAPUIS COLORS
RICHARD STARKINGS MISSION COMMANDER
IF YOU ARE READING THIS ONLINE, HELP US OUT AND PAYPAL $10 TO ELEPHANTFAN@SHINYBEASTS.COM

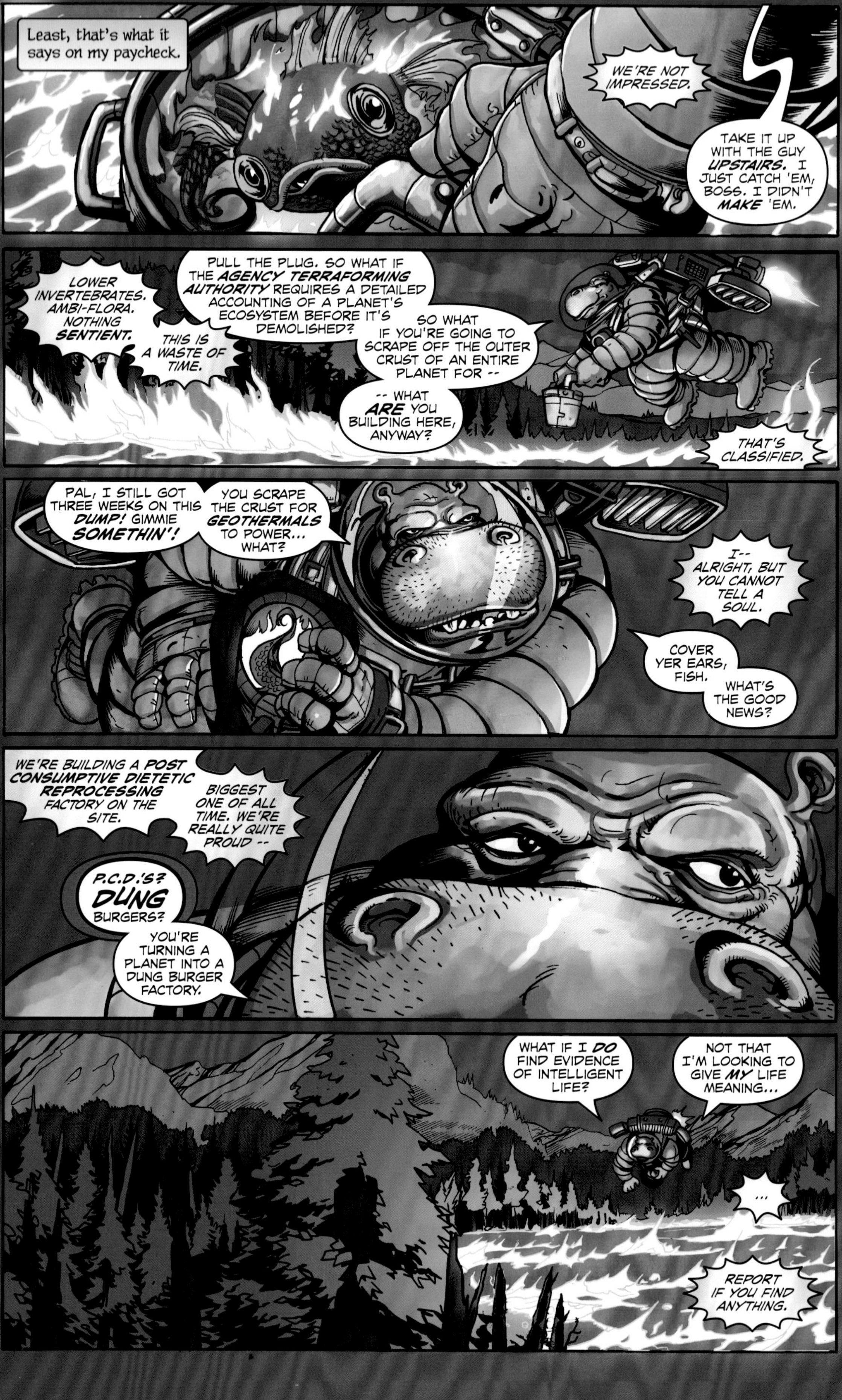
Least, that's what it says on my paycheck.
WE'RE NOT IMPRESSED.
TAKE IT UP WITH THE GUY UPSTAIRS. I JUST CATCH 'EM, BOSS. I DIDN'T MAKE 'EM.
LOWER INVERTEBRATES. AMBI-FLORA. NOTHING SENTIENT.
THIS IS A WASTE OF TIME.
PULL THE PLUG. SO WHAT IF THE AGENCY TERRAFORMING AUTHORITY REQUIRES A DETAILED ACCOUNTING OF A PLANET'S ECOSYSTEM BEFORE IT'S DEMOLISHED?
SO WHAT IF YOU'RE GOING TO SCRAPE OFF THE OUTER CRUST OF AN ENTIRE PLANET FOR --
-- WHAT ARE YOU BUILDING HERE, ANYWAY?
THAT'S CLASSIFIED.
PAL, I STILL GOT THREE WEEKS ON THIS DUMP! GIMMIE SOMETHIN'!
YOU SCRAPE THE CRUST FOR GEOTHERMALS TO POWER... WHAT?
I-- ALRIGHT, BUT YOU CANNOT TELL A SOUL.
COVER YER EARS, FISH.
WHAT'S THE GOOD NEWS?
WE'RE BUILDING A POST CONSUMPTIVE DIETETIC REPROCESSING FACTORY ON THE SITE.
BIGGEST ONE OF ALL TIME. WE'RE REALLY QUITE PROUD --
P.C.D.'S? DUNG BURGERS?
YOU'RE TURNING A PLANET INTO A DUNG BURGER FACTORY.
WHAT IF I DO FIND EVIDENCE OF INTELLIGENT LIFE?
NOT THAT I'M LOOKING TO GIVE MY LIFE MEANING...
...
REPORT IF YOU FIND ANYTHING.

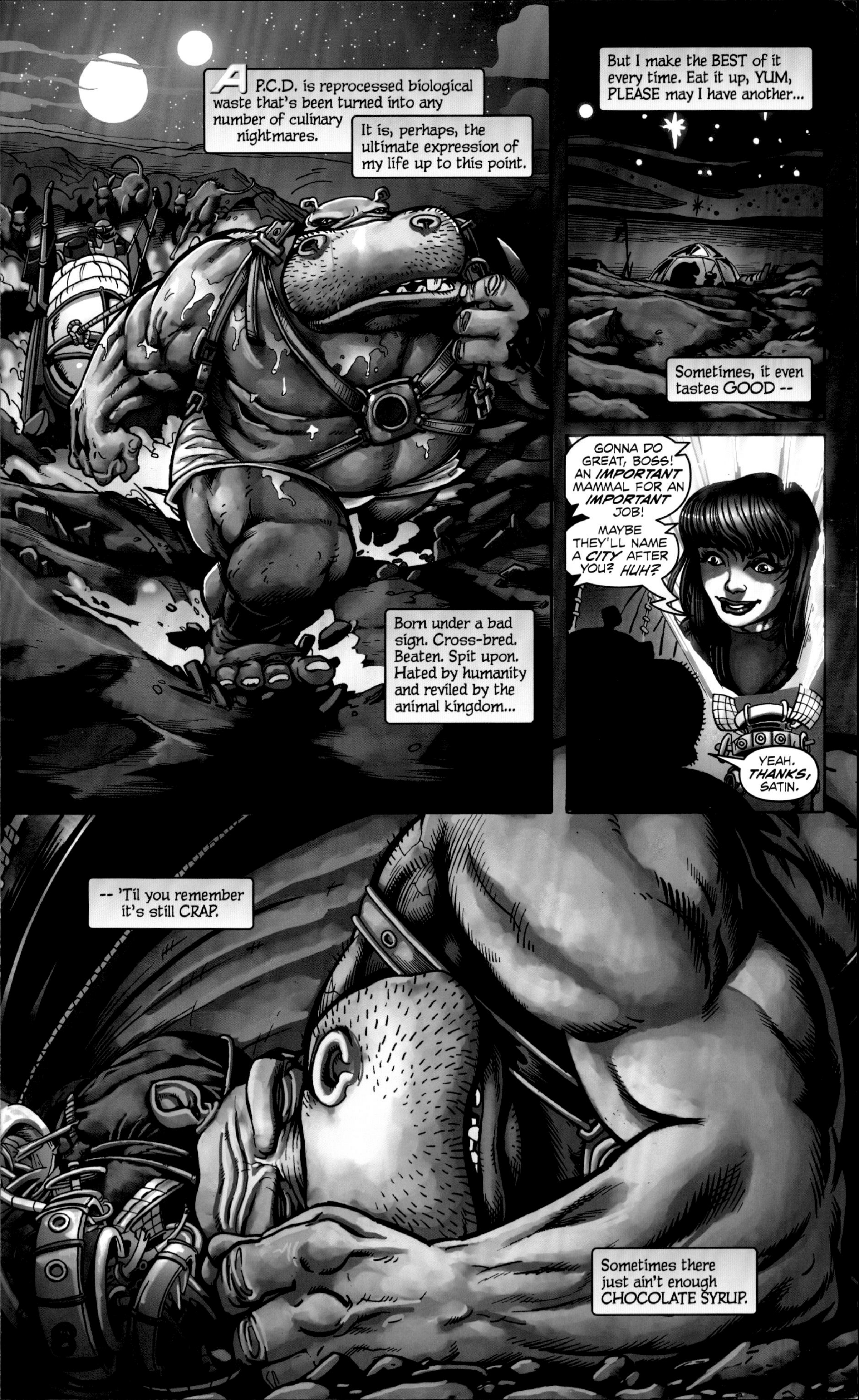
A P.C.D. is reprocessed biological waste that's been turned into any number of culinary nightmares.
It is, perhaps, the ultimate expression of my life up to this point.
Born under a bad sign. Cross-bred. Beaten. Spit upon. Hated by humanity and reviled by the animal kingdom...
But I make the BEST of it every time. Eat it up, YUM, PLEASE may I have another...
Sometimes, it even tastes GOOD --
GONNA DO GREAT, BOSS! AN IMPORTANT MAMMAL FOR AN IMPORTANT JOB!
MAYBE THEY'LL NAME A CITY AFTER YOU? HUH?
YEAH. THANKS, SATIN.
-- 'Til you remember it's still CRAP.
Sometimes there just ain't enough CHOCOLATE SYRUP.

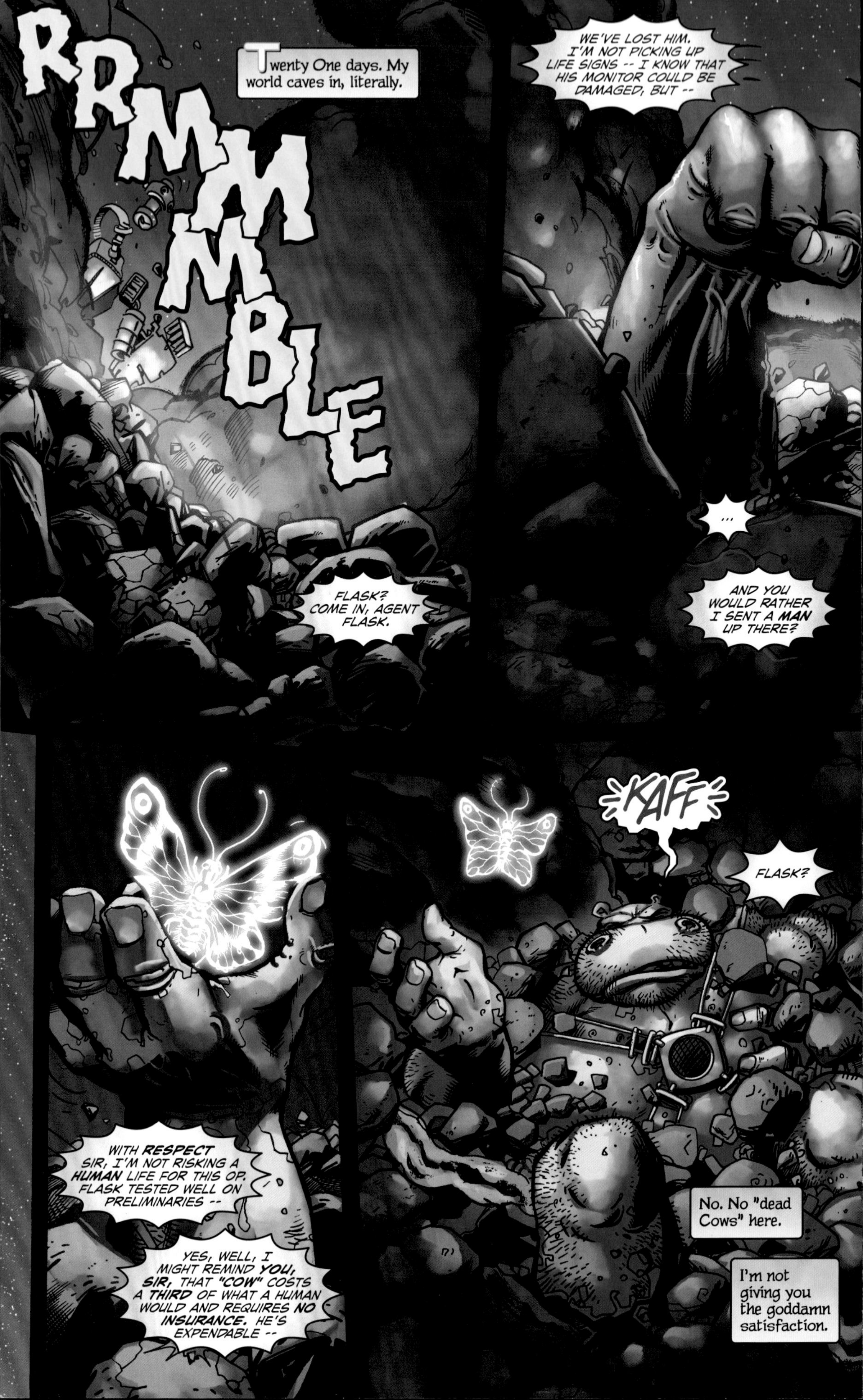
RRMMMBLE
Twenty One days. My world caves in, literally.
FLASK? COME IN, AGENT FLASK.
WE'VE LOST HIM. I'M NOT PICKING UP LIFE SIGNS -- I KNOW THAT HIS MONITOR COULD BE DAMAGED, BUT --
...
AND YOU WOULD RATHER I SENT A MAN UP THERE?
WITH RESPECT SIR, I'M NOT RISKING A HUMAN LIFE FOR THIS OP. FLASK TESTED WELL ON PRELIMINARIES --
YES, WELL, I MIGHT REMIND YOU, SIR, THAT "COW" COSTS A THIRD OF WHAT A HUMAN WOULD AND REQUIRES NO INSURANCE. HE'S EXPENDABLE --
KAFF
FLASK?
No. No "dead Cows" here.
I'm not giving you the goddamn satisfaction.

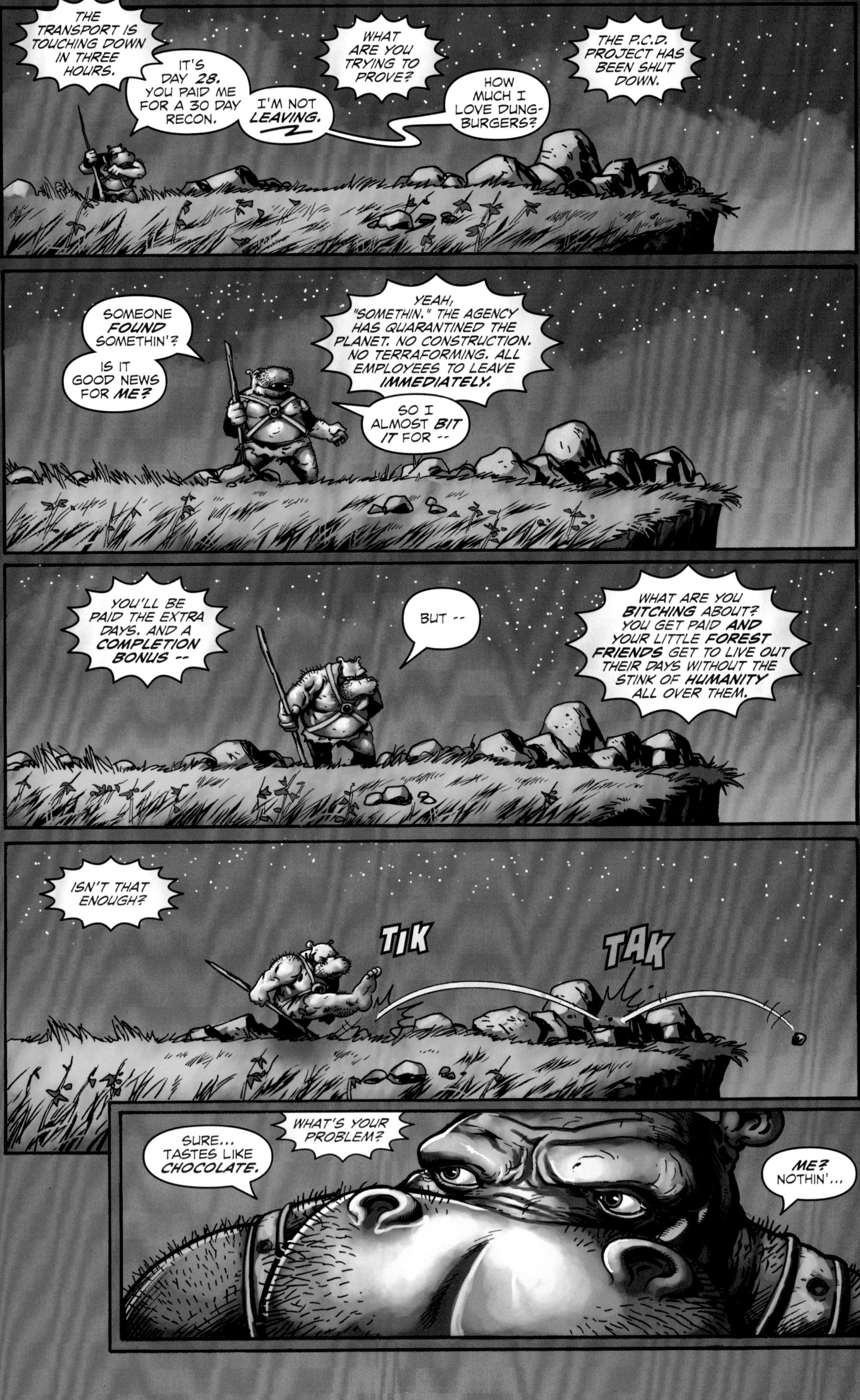
THE TRANSPORT IS TOUCHING DOWN IN THREE HOURS.
IT'S DAY 28. YOU PAID ME FOR A 30 DAY RECON.
I'M NOT LEAVING.
WHAT ARE YOU TRYING TO PROVE?
HOW MUCH I LOVE DUNG-BURGERS?
THE P.C.D. PROJECT HAS BEEN SHUT DOWN.
SOMEONE FOUND SOMETHIN'?
IS IT GOOD NEWS FOR ME?
YEAH, "SOMETHIN." THE AGENCY HAS QUARANTINED THE PLANET. NO CONSTRUCTION. NO TERRAFORMING. ALL EMPLOYEES TO LEAVE IMMEDIATELY.
SO I ALMOST BIT IT FOR --
YOU'LL BE PAID THE EXTRA DAYS. AND A COMPLETION BONUS --
BUT --
WHAT ARE YOU BITCHING ABOUT? YOU GET PAID AND YOUR LITTLE FOREST FRIENDS GET TO LIVE OUT THEIR DAYS WITHOUT THE STINK OF HUMANITY ALL OVER THEM.
ISN'T THAT ENOUGH?
TIK
TAK
SURE... TASTES LIKE CHOCOLATE.
WHAT'S YOUR PROBLEM?
ME? NOTHIN'...

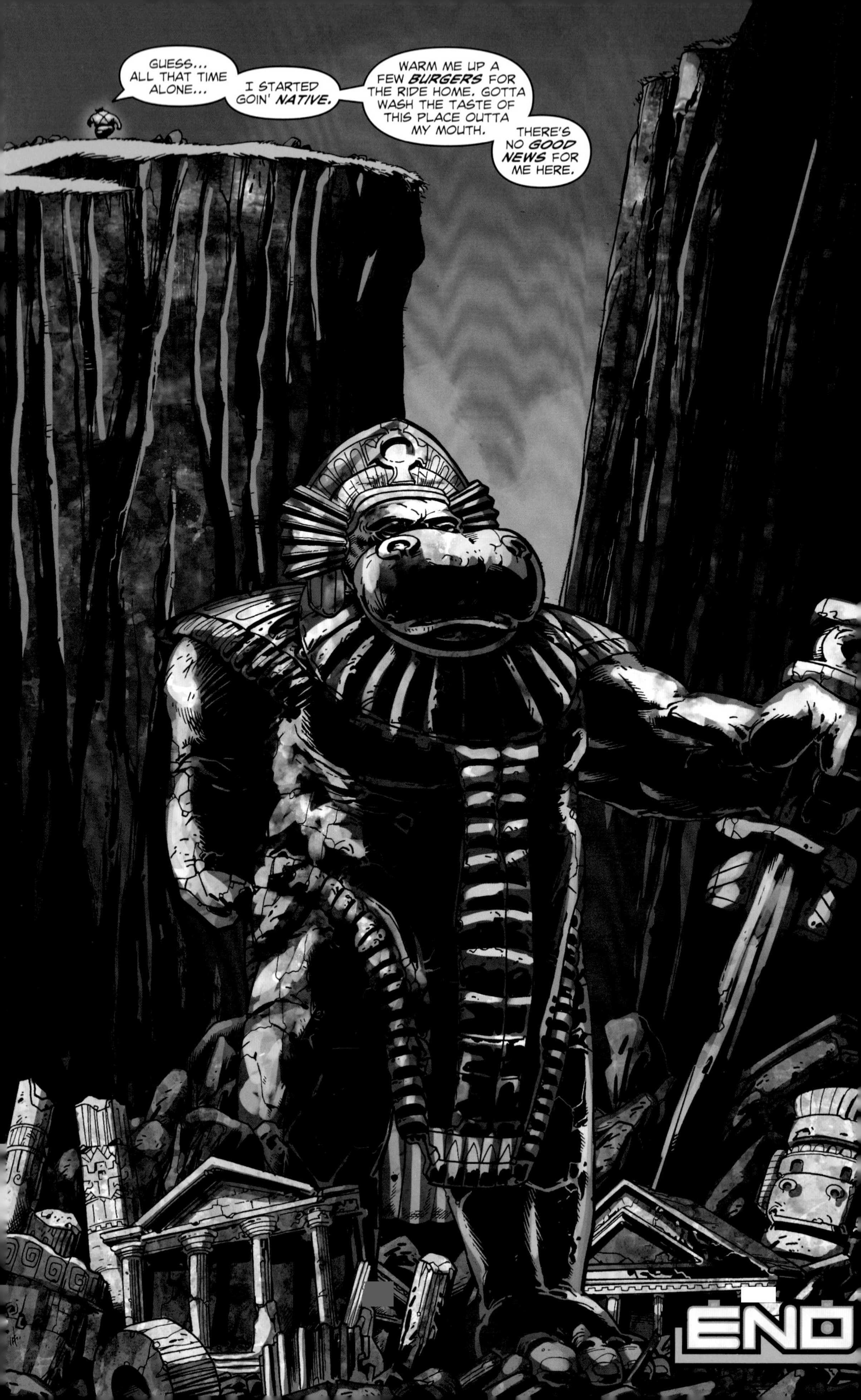
GUESS... ALL THAT TIME ALONE...
I STARTED GOIN' NATIVE.
WARM ME UP A FEW BURGERS FOR THE RIDE HOME. GOTTA WASH THE TASTE OF THIS PLACE OUTTA MY MOUTH.
THERE'S NO GOOD NEWS FOR ME HERE.
END

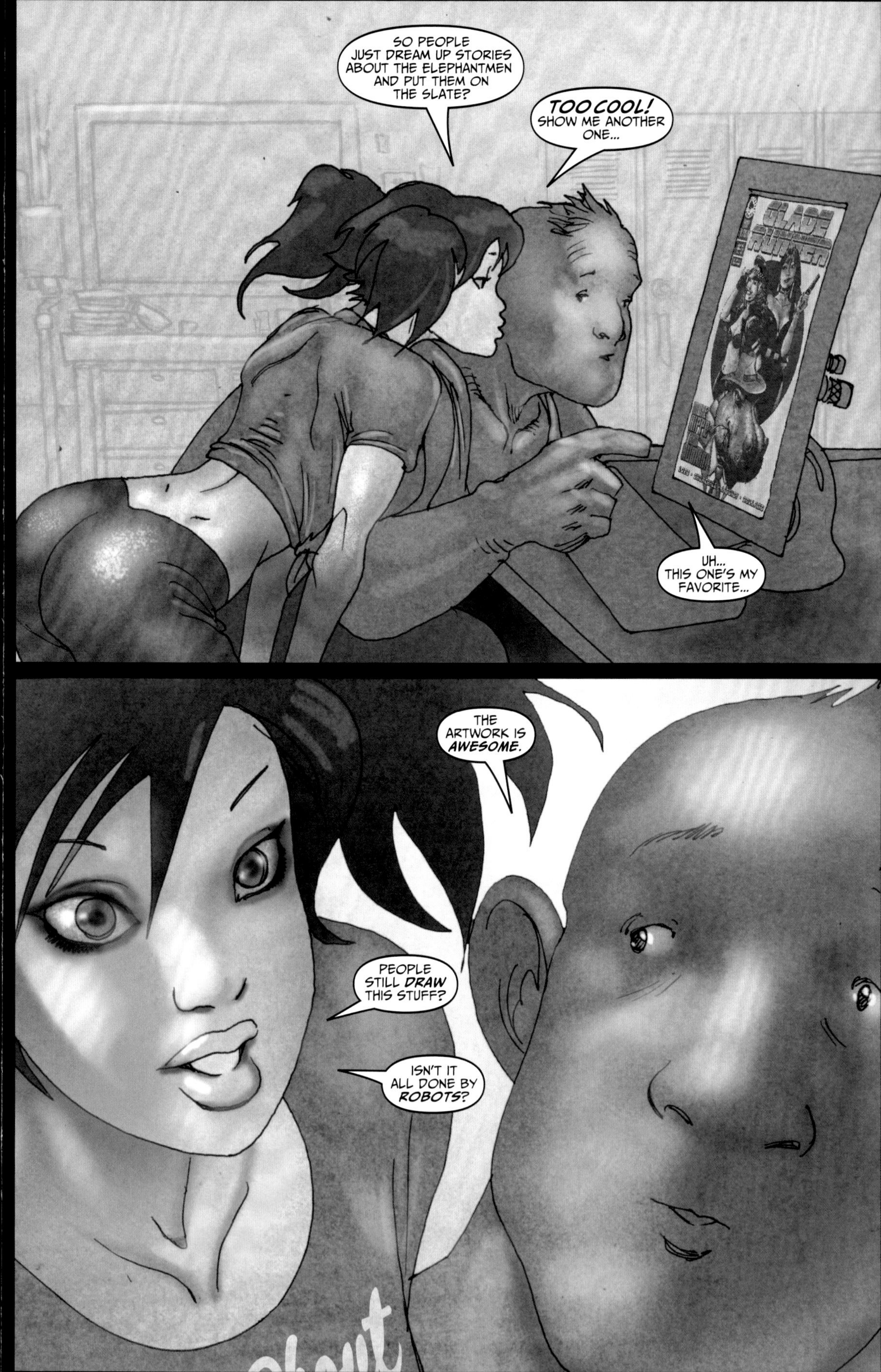

SO PEOPLE JUST DREAM UP STORIES ABOUT THE ELEPHANTMEN AND PUT THEM ON THE SLATE?
TOO COOL! SHOW ME ANOTHER ONE...
UH... THIS ONE'S MY FAVORITE...
THE ARTWORK IS AWESOME.
PEOPLE STILL DRAW THIS STUFF?
ISN'T IT ALL DONE BY ROBOTS?

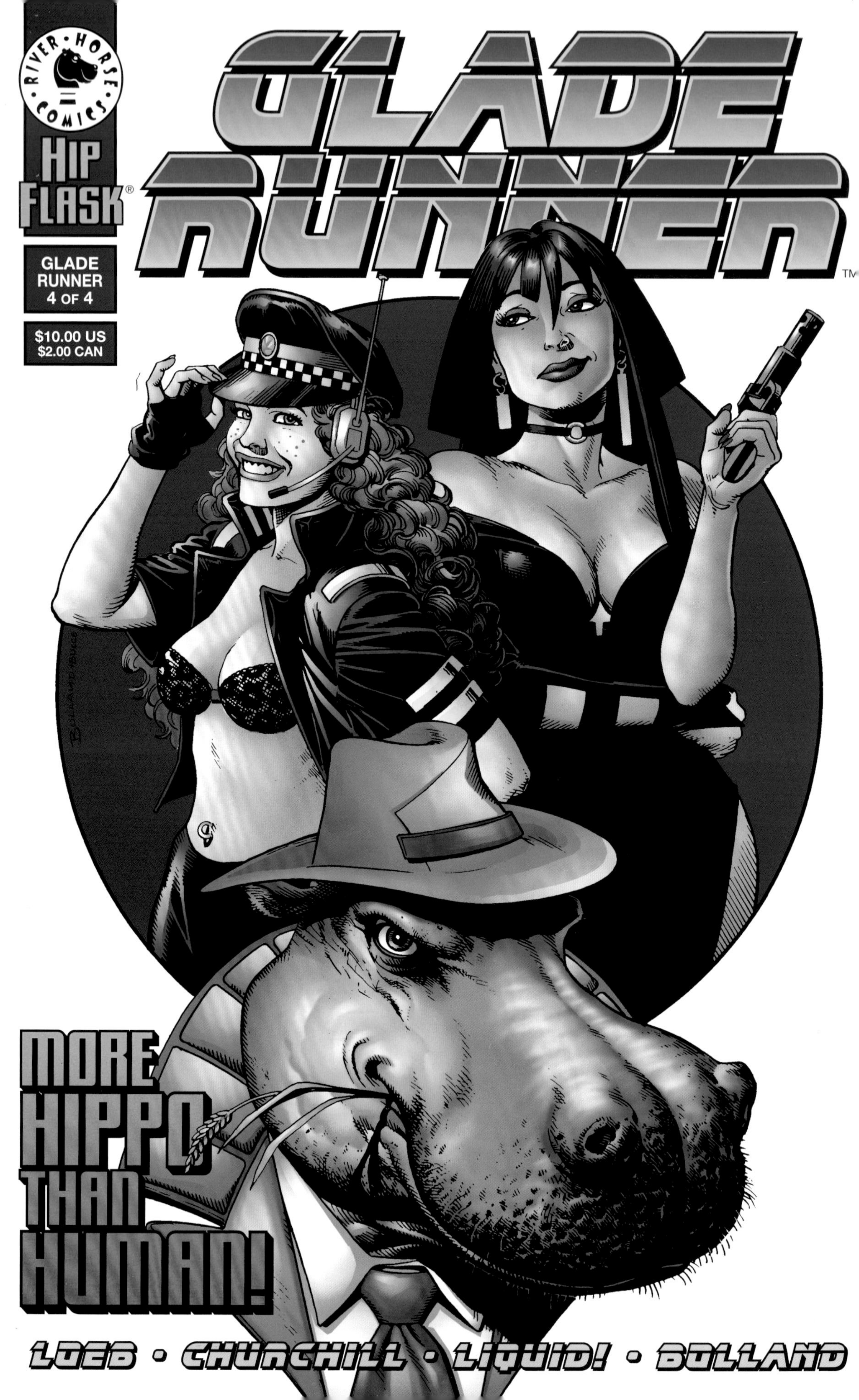
RIVER · HORSE · COMICS
HIP FLASK®
GLADE RUNNER 4 OF 4
$10.00 US
$2.00 CAN
GLADE RUNNER™
MORE HIPPO THAN HUMAN!
LOEB · CHURCHILL · LIQUID! · BOLLAND

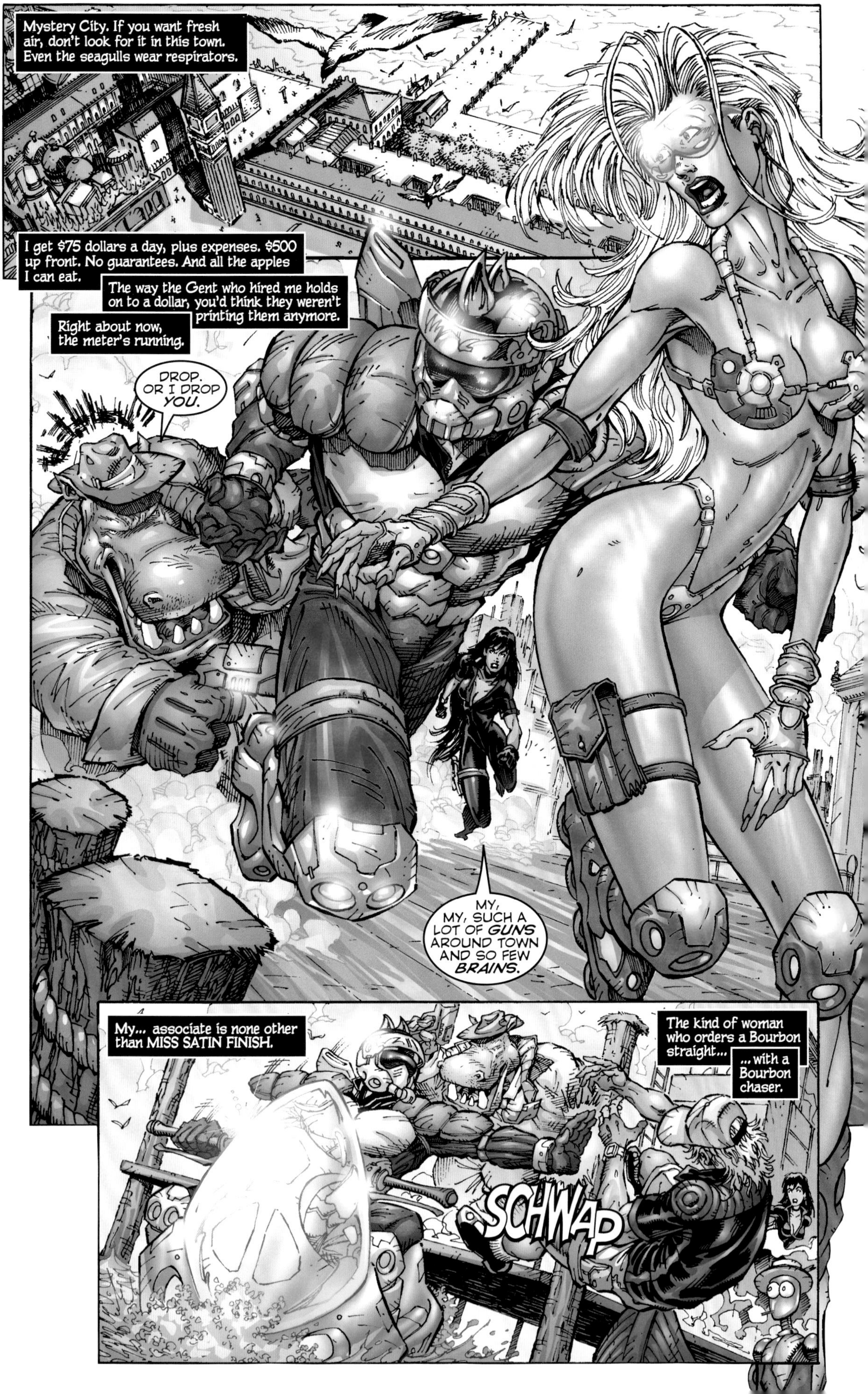
Mystery City. If you want fresh air, don't look for it in this town. Even the seagulls wear respirators.
I get $75 dollars a day, plus expenses. $500 up front. No guarantees. And all the apples I can eat.
The way the Gent who hired me holds on to a dollar, you'd think they weren't printing them anymore.
Right about now, the meter's running.
DROP. OR I DROP YOU.
MY, MY, SUCH A LOT OF GUNS AROUND TOWN AND SO FEW BRAINS.
My... associate is none other than MISS SATIN FINISH.
The kind of woman who orders a Bourbon straight...
...with a Bourbon chaser.
SCHWAP

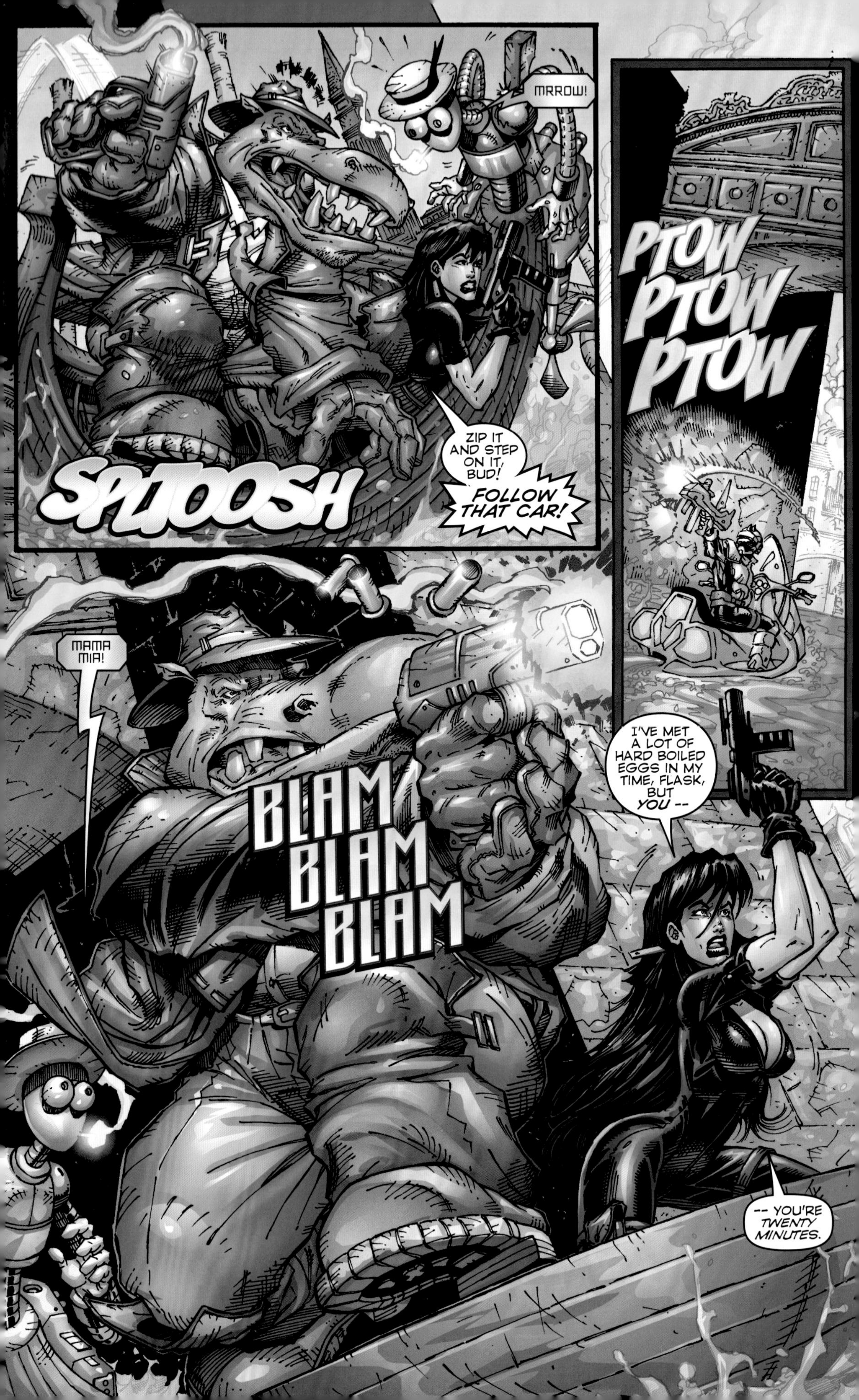
MRROW!
ZIP IT AND STEP ON IT, BUD!
FOLLOW THAT CAR!
SPLOOSH
PTOW PTOW PTOW
MAMA MIA!
BLAM BLAM BLAM
I'VE MET A LOT OF HARD BOILED EGGS IN MY TIME, FLASK, BUT YOU --
-- YOU'RE TWENTY MINUTES.

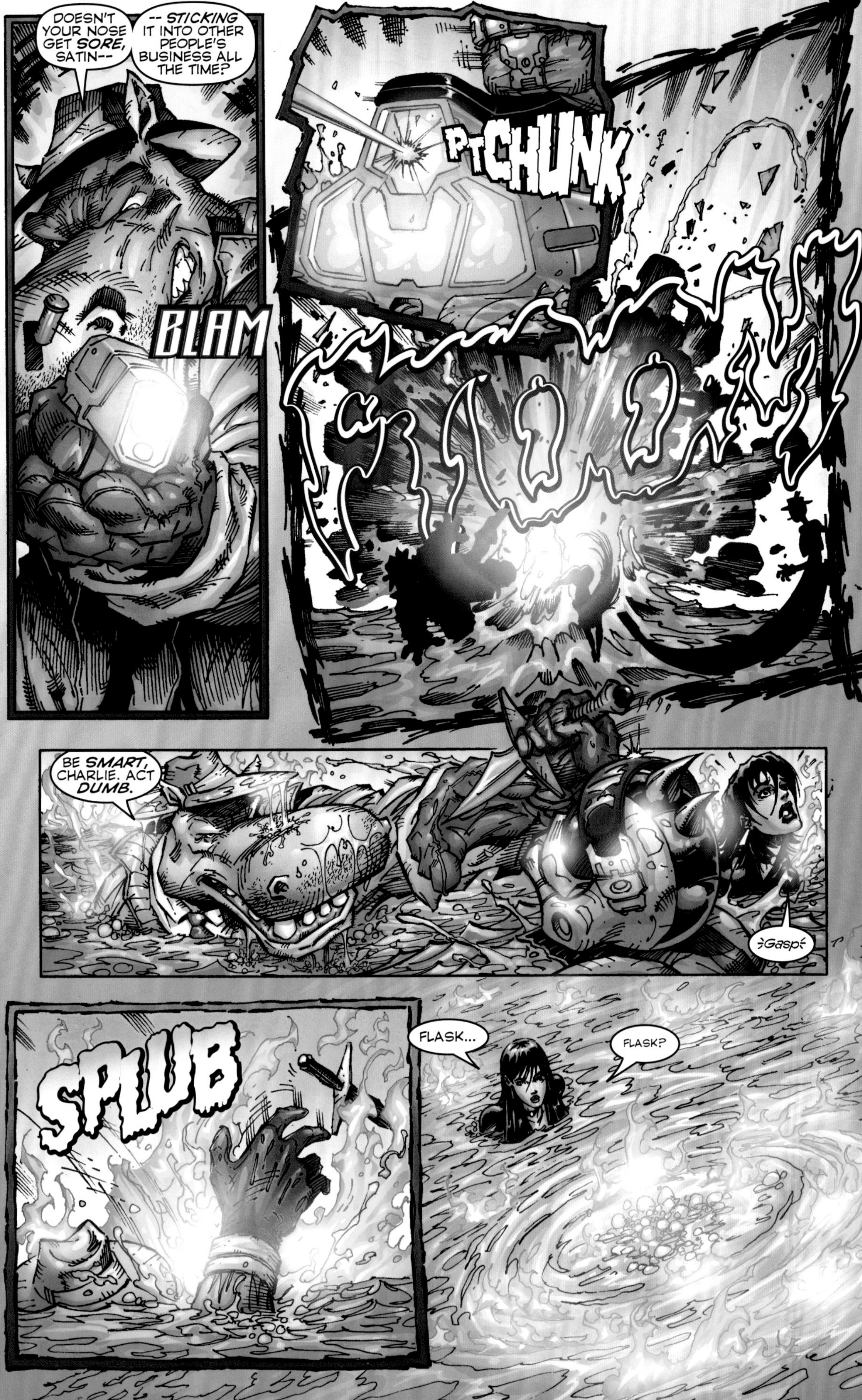
DOESN'T YOUR NOSE GET SORE, SATIN--
-- STICKING IT INTO OTHER PEOPLE'S BUSINESS ALL THE TIME?
BLAM
PTCHUNK
BE SMART, CHARLIE. ACT DUMB.
Gasp
SPLUB
FLASK...
FLASK?

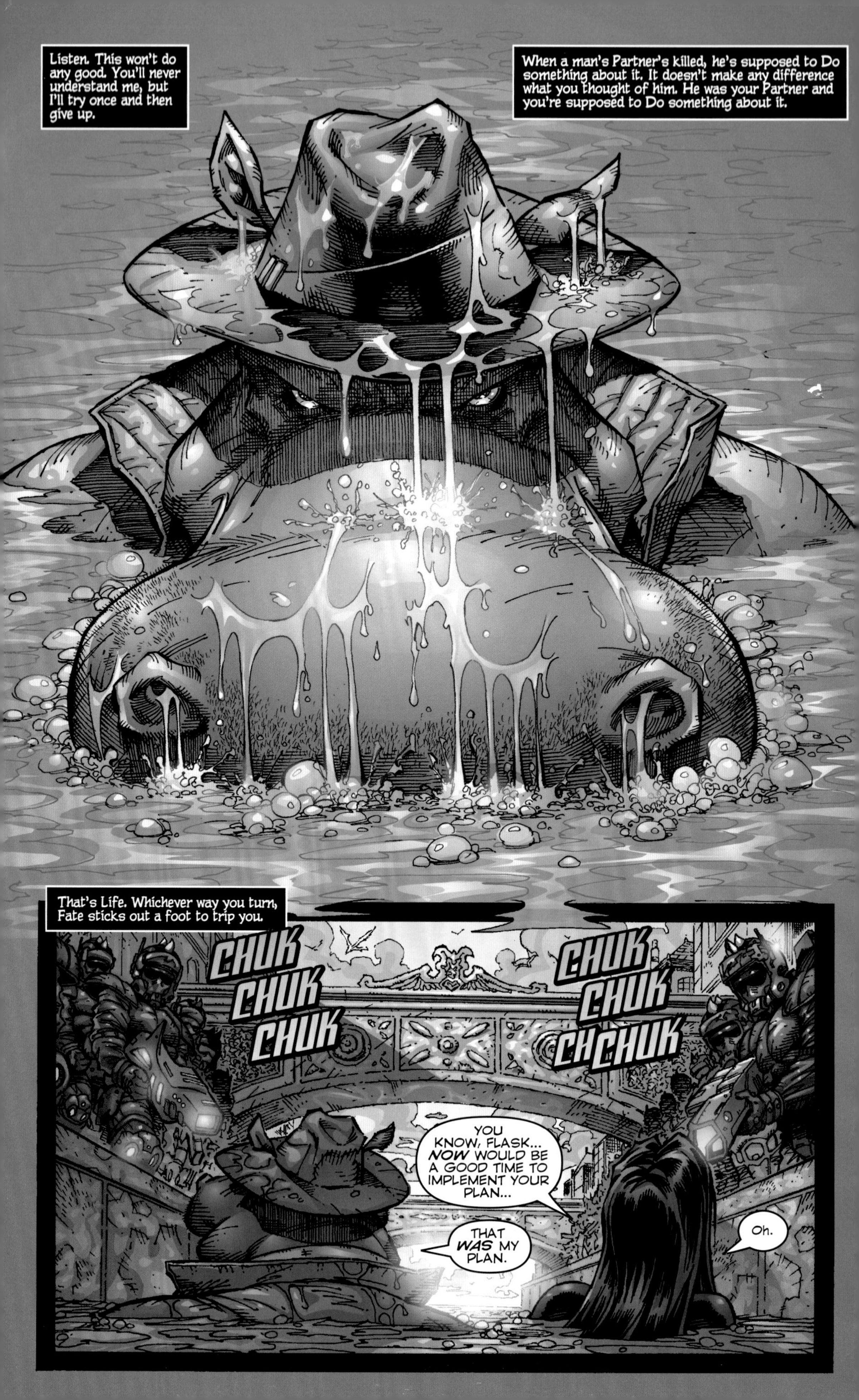
Listen. This won't do any good. You'll never understand me, but I'll try once and then give up.
When a man's Partner's killed, he's supposed to Do something about it. It doesn't make any difference what you thought of him. He was your Partner and you're supposed to Do something about it.
That's Life. Whichever way you turn, Fate sticks out a foot to trip you.
CHUK CHUK CHUK
CHUK CHUK CHCHUK
YOU KNOW, FLASK... NOW WOULD BE A GOOD TIME TO IMPLEMENT YOUR PLAN...
THAT WAS MY PLAN.
Oh.

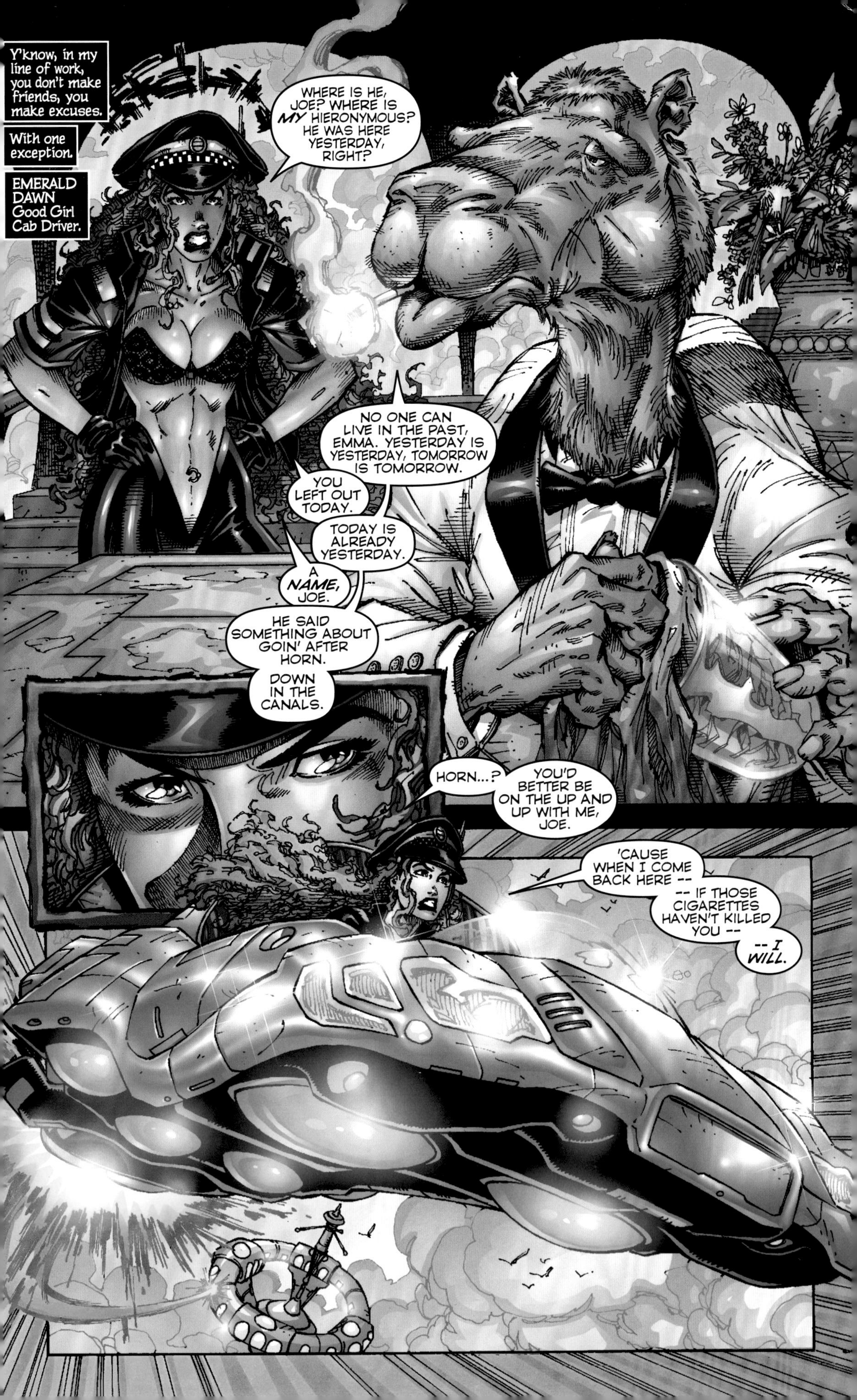
Y'know, in my line of work, you don't make friends, you make excuses.
With one exception.
EMERALD DAWN Good Girl Cab Driver.
WHERE IS HE, JOE? WHERE IS MY HIERONYMOUS? HE WAS HERE YESTERDAY, RIGHT?
NO ONE CAN LIVE IN THE PAST, EMMA. YESTERDAY IS YESTERDAY, TOMORROW IS TOMORROW.
YOU LEFT OUT TODAY.
TODAY IS ALREADY YESTERDAY.
A NAME, JOE.
HE SAID SOMETHING ABOUT GOIN' AFTER HORN.
DOWN IN THE CANALS.
HORN...?
YOU'D BETTER BE ON THE UP AND UP WITH ME, JOE.
'CAUSE WHEN I COME BACK HERE --
-- IF THOSE CIGARETTES HAVEN'T KILLED YOU --
-- I WILL.

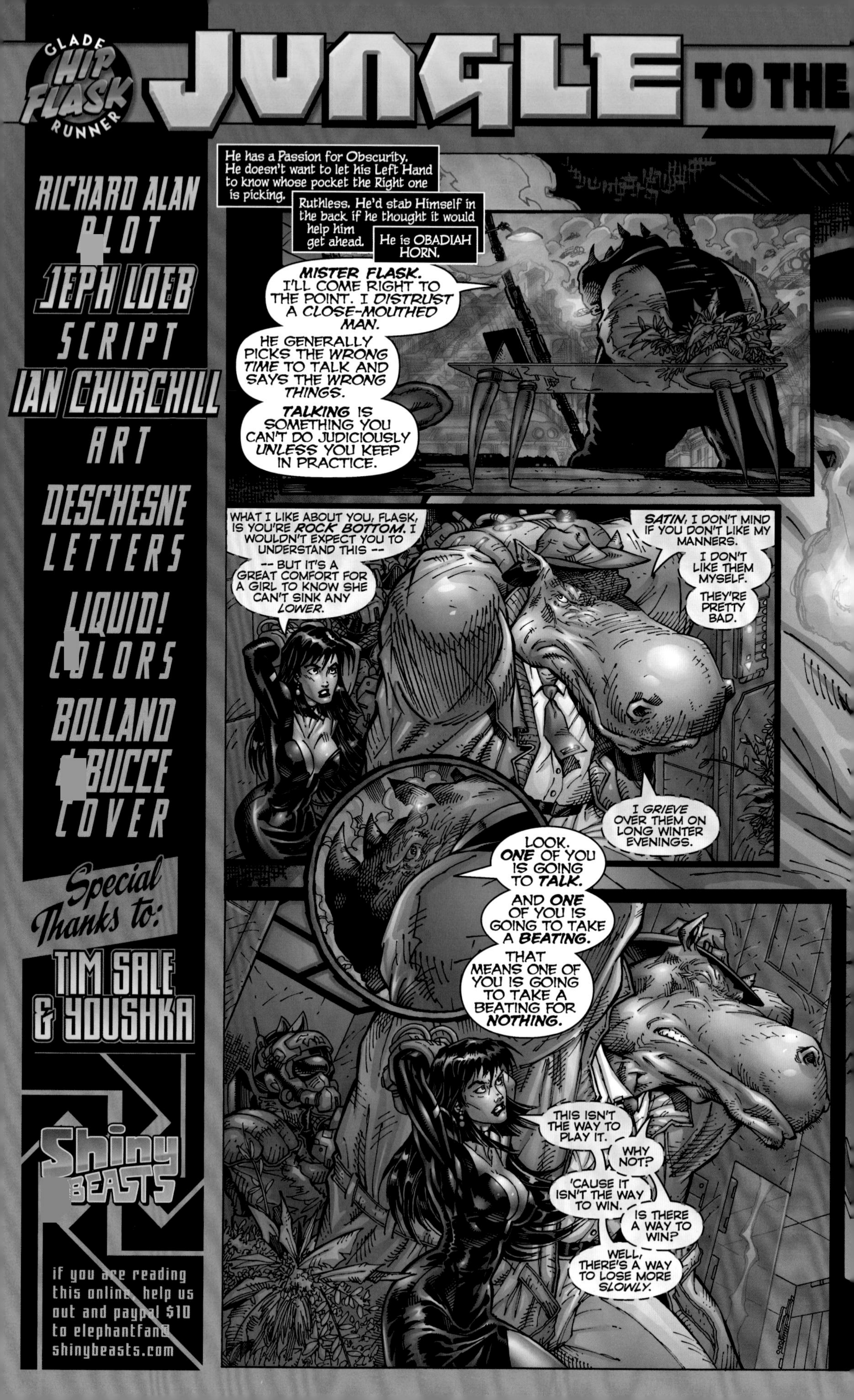

GLADE HIP FLASK RUNNER
JUNGLE TO THE
RICHARD ALAN PLOT
JEPH LOEB SCRIPT
IAN CHURCHILL ART
DESCHESNE LETTERS
LIQUID! COLORS
BOLLAND & BUCCE COVER
Special Thanks to:
TIM SALE & YOUSHKA
He has a Passion for Obscurity. He doesn't want to let his Left Hand to know whose pocket the Right one is picking.
Ruthless. He'd stab Himself in the back if he thought it would help him get ahead.
He is OBADIAH HORN.
MISTER FLASK. I'LL COME RIGHT TO THE POINT. I DISTRUST A CLOSE-MOUTHED MAN.
HE GENERALLY PICKS THE WRONG TIME TO TALK AND SAYS THE WRONG THINGS.
TALKING IS SOMETHING YOU CAN'T DO JUDICIOUSLY UNLESS YOU KEEP IN PRACTICE.
WHAT I LIKE ABOUT YOU, FLASK, IS YOU'RE ROCK BOTTOM. I WOULDN'T EXPECT YOU TO UNDERSTAND THIS --
-- BUT IT'S A GREAT COMFORT FOR A GIRL TO KNOW SHE CAN'T SINK ANY LOWER.
SATIN, I DON'T MIND IF YOU DON'T LIKE MY MANNERS.
I DON'T LIKE THEM MYSELF.
THEY'RE PRETTY BAD.
I GRIEVE OVER THEM ON LONG WINTER EVENINGS.
LOOK. ONE OF YOU IS GOING TO TALK.
AND ONE OF YOU IS GOING TO TAKE A BEATING.
THAT MEANS ONE OF YOU IS GOING TO TAKE A BEATING FOR NOTHING.
THIS ISN'T THE WAY TO PLAY IT.
WHY NOT?
'CAUSE IT ISN'T THE WAY TO WIN.
IS THERE A WAY TO WIN?
WELL, THERE'S A WAY TO LOSE MORE SLOWLY.
Shiny BEASTS
if you are reading this online, help us out and paypal $10 to elephantfan@shinybeasts.com

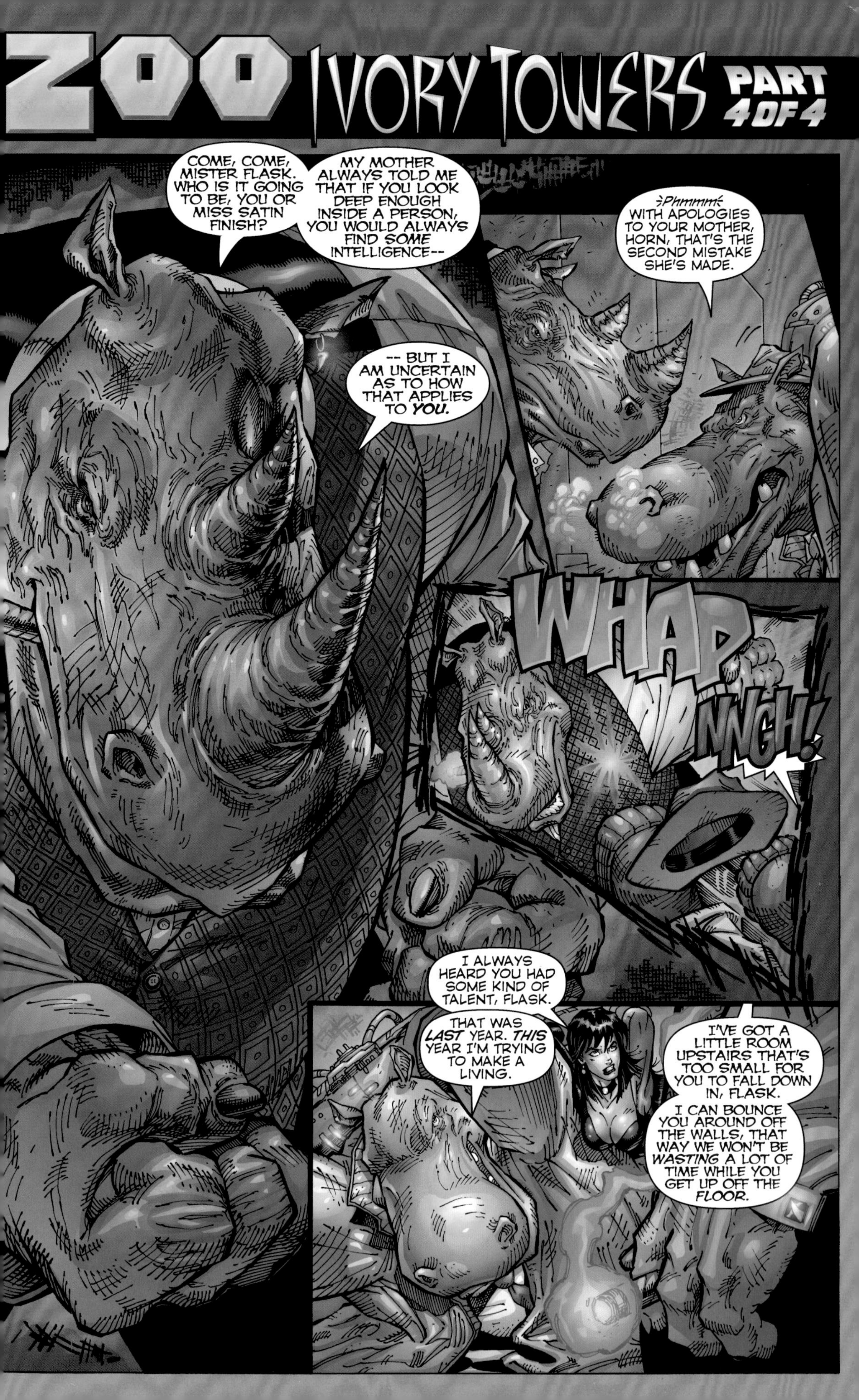
ZOO IVORY TOWERS PART 4 OF 4
COME, COME, MISTER FLASK. WHO IS IT GOING TO BE, YOU OR MISS SATIN FINISH?
MY MOTHER ALWAYS TOLD ME THAT IF YOU LOOK DEEP ENOUGH INSIDE A PERSON, YOU WOULD ALWAYS FIND SOME INTELLIGENCE--
-- BUT I AM UNCERTAIN AS TO HOW THAT APPLIES TO YOU.
Phmmm
WITH APOLOGIES TO YOUR MOTHER, HORN, THAT'S THE SECOND MISTAKE SHE'S MADE.
WHAP
NNGH!
I ALWAYS HEARD YOU HAD SOME KIND OF TALENT, FLASK.
THAT WAS LAST YEAR. THIS YEAR I'M TRYING TO MAKE A LIVING.
I'VE GOT A LITTLE ROOM UPSTAIRS THAT'S TOO SMALL FOR YOU TO FALL DOWN IN, FLASK.
I CAN BOUNCE YOU AROUND OFF THE WALLS, THAT WAY WE WON'T BE WASTING A LOT OF TIME WHILE YOU GET UP OFF THE FLOOR.

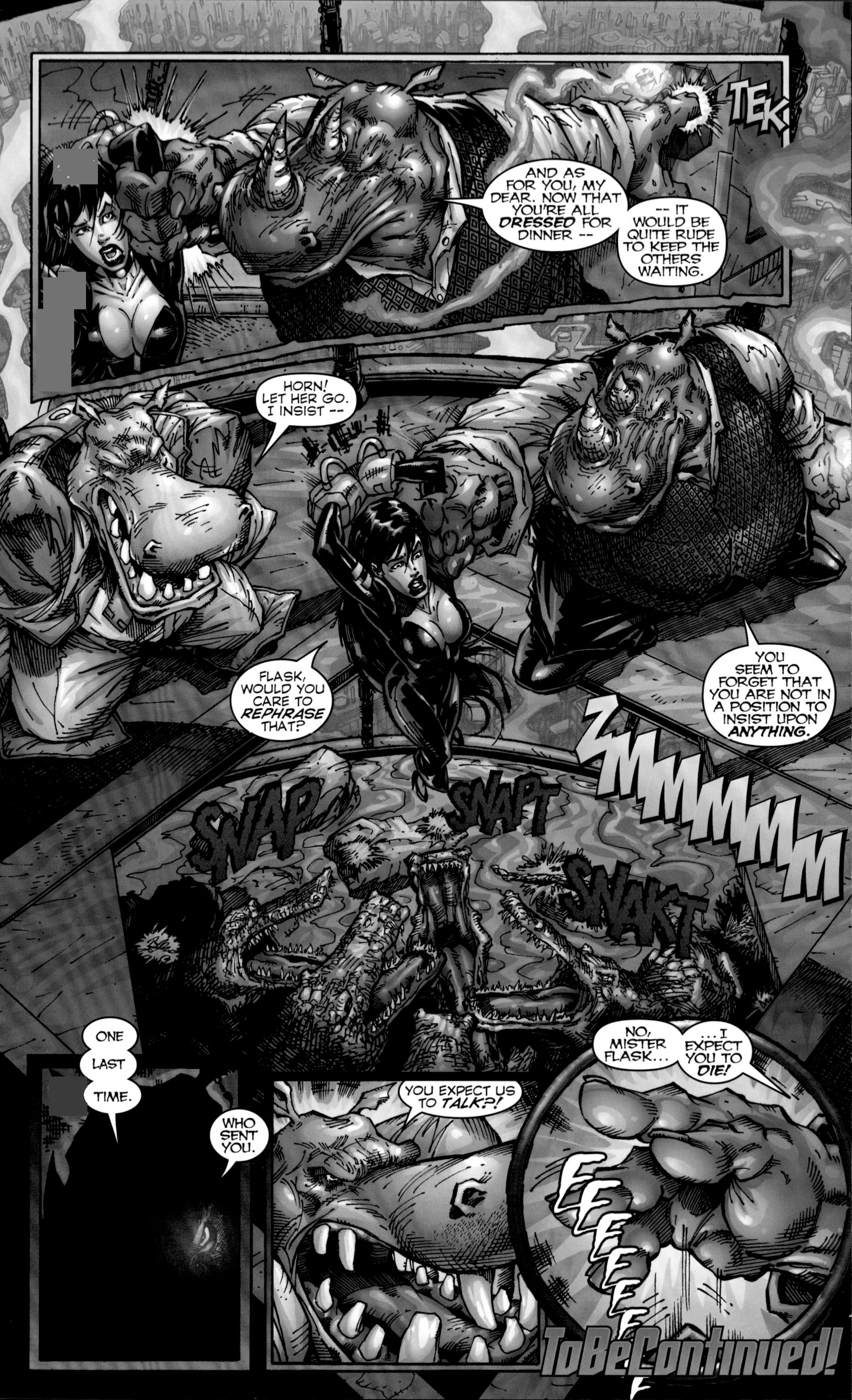
TEK
AND AS FOR YOU, MY DEAR. NOW THAT YOU'RE ALL DRESSED FOR DINNER --
-- IT WOULD BE QUITE RUDE TO KEEP THE OTHERS WAITING.
HORN! LET HER GO. I INSIST --
FLASK, WOULD YOU CARE TO REPHRASE THAT?
YOU SEEM TO FORGET THAT YOU ARE NOT IN A POSITION TO INSIST UPON ANYTHING.
ZMMMMMMMM
SNAP
SNAPT
SNAKT
ONE LAST TIME.
WHO SENT YOU.
YOU EXPECT US TO TALK?!
NO, MISTER FLASK...
...I EXPECT YOU TO DIE!
EEEEEE
To Be Continued!

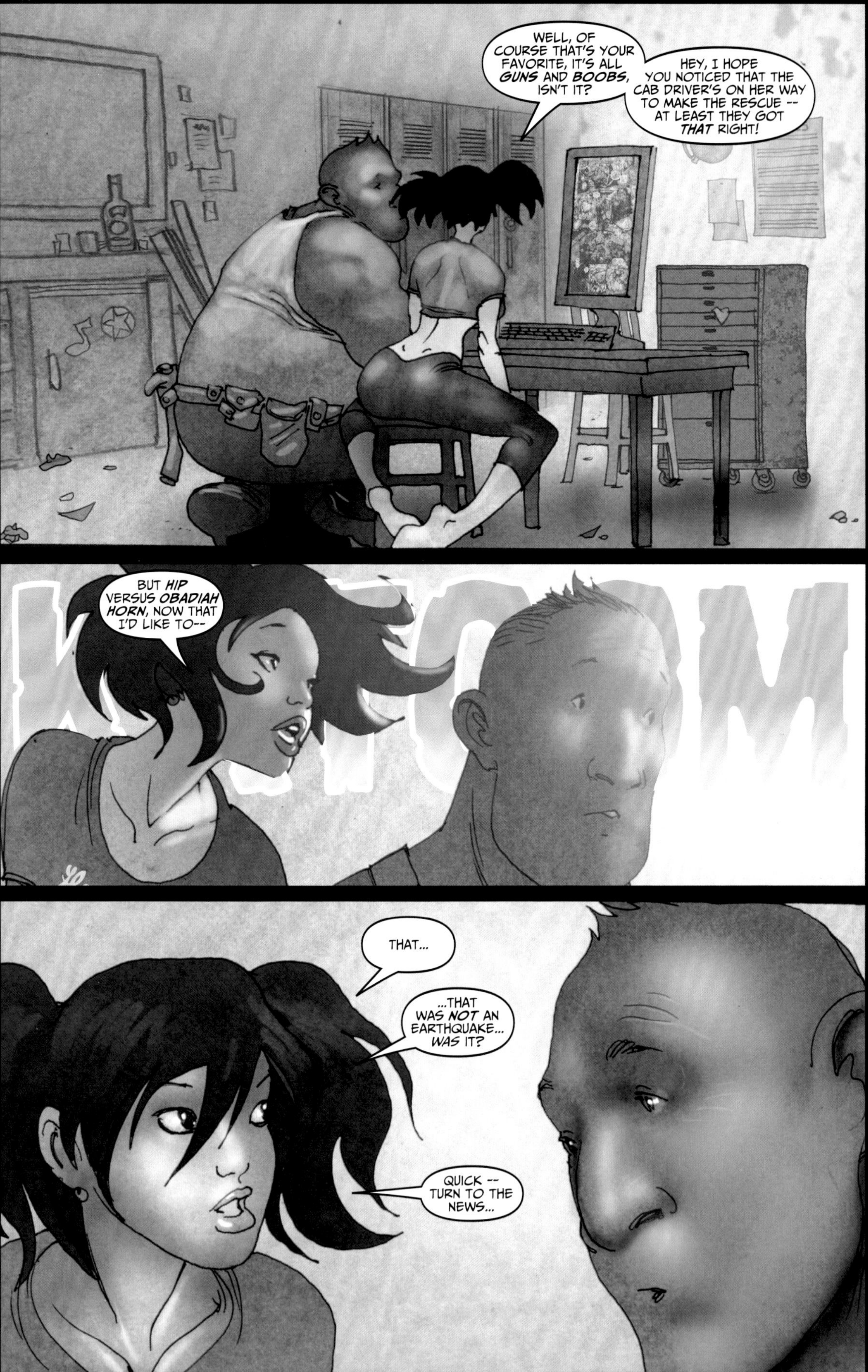

WELL, OF COURSE THAT'S YOUR FAVORITE, IT'S ALL GUNS AND BOOBS, ISN'T IT?
HEY, I HOPE YOU NOTICED THAT THE CAB DRIVER'S ON HER WAY TO MAKE THE RESCUE -- AT LEAST THEY GOT THAT RIGHT!
BUT HIP VERSUS OBADIAH HORN, NOW THAT I'D LIKE TO--
THAT...
...THAT WAS NOT AN EARTHQUAKE... WAS IT?
QUICK -- TURN TO THE NEWS...

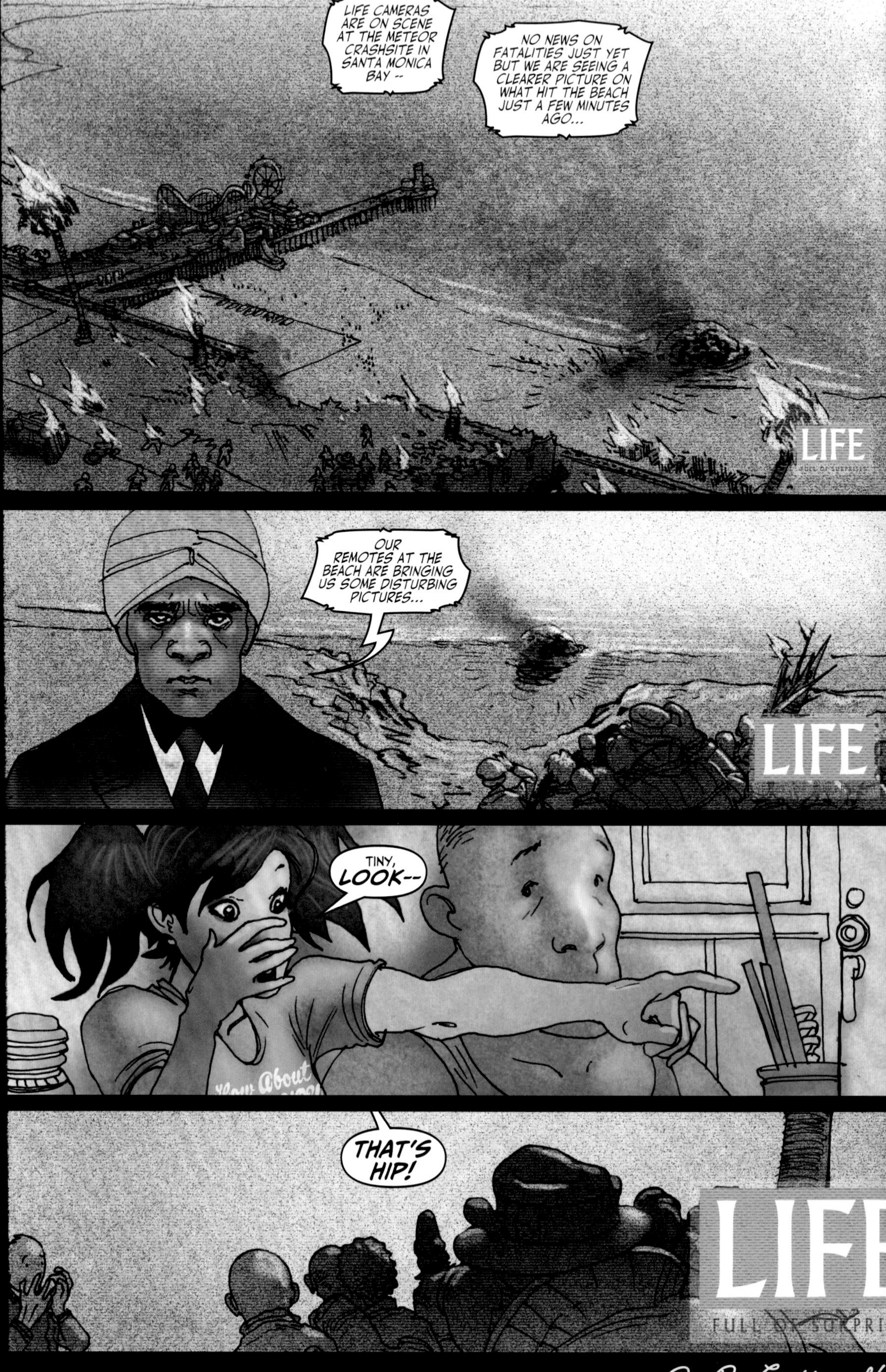
LIFE CAMERAS ARE ON SCENE AT THE METEOR CRASHSITE IN SANTA MONICA BAY --
NO NEWS ON FATALITIES JUST YET BUT WE ARE SEEING A CLEARER PICTURE ON WHAT HIT THE BEACH JUST A FEW MINUTES AGO...
LIFE
OUR REMOTES AT THE BEACH ARE BRINGING US SOME DISTURBING PICTURES...
LIFE
TINY, LOOK--
THAT'S HIP!
LIFE

To Be Continued!

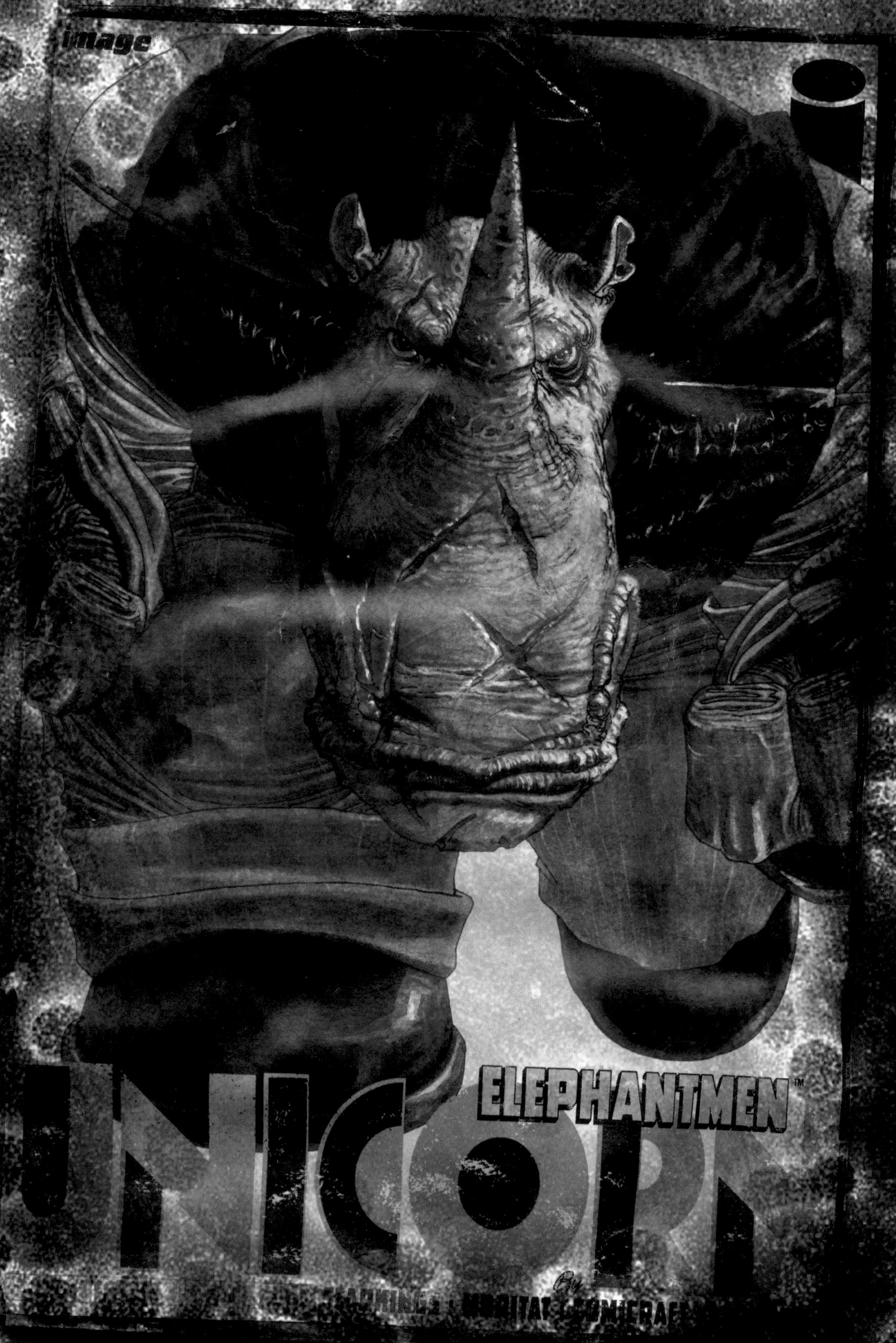
image
ELEPHANTMEN™
UNICORN

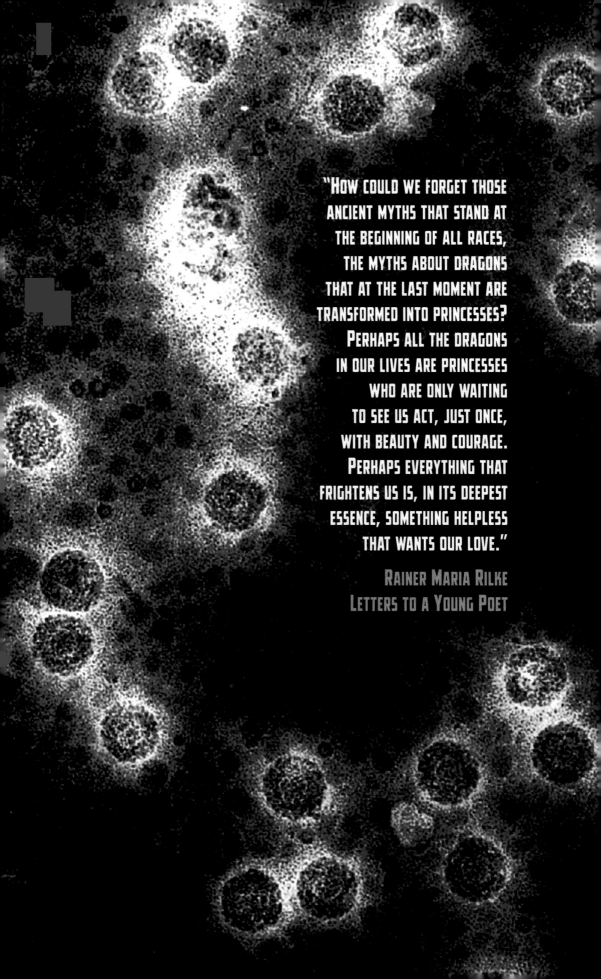

"How could we forget those ancient myths that stand at the beginning of all races, the myths about dragons that at the last moment are transformed into princesses? Perhaps all the dragons in our lives are princesses who are only waiting to see us act, just once, with beauty and courage. Perhaps everything that frightens us is, in its deepest essence, something helpless that wants our love."

Rainer Maria Rilke
Letters to a Young Poet

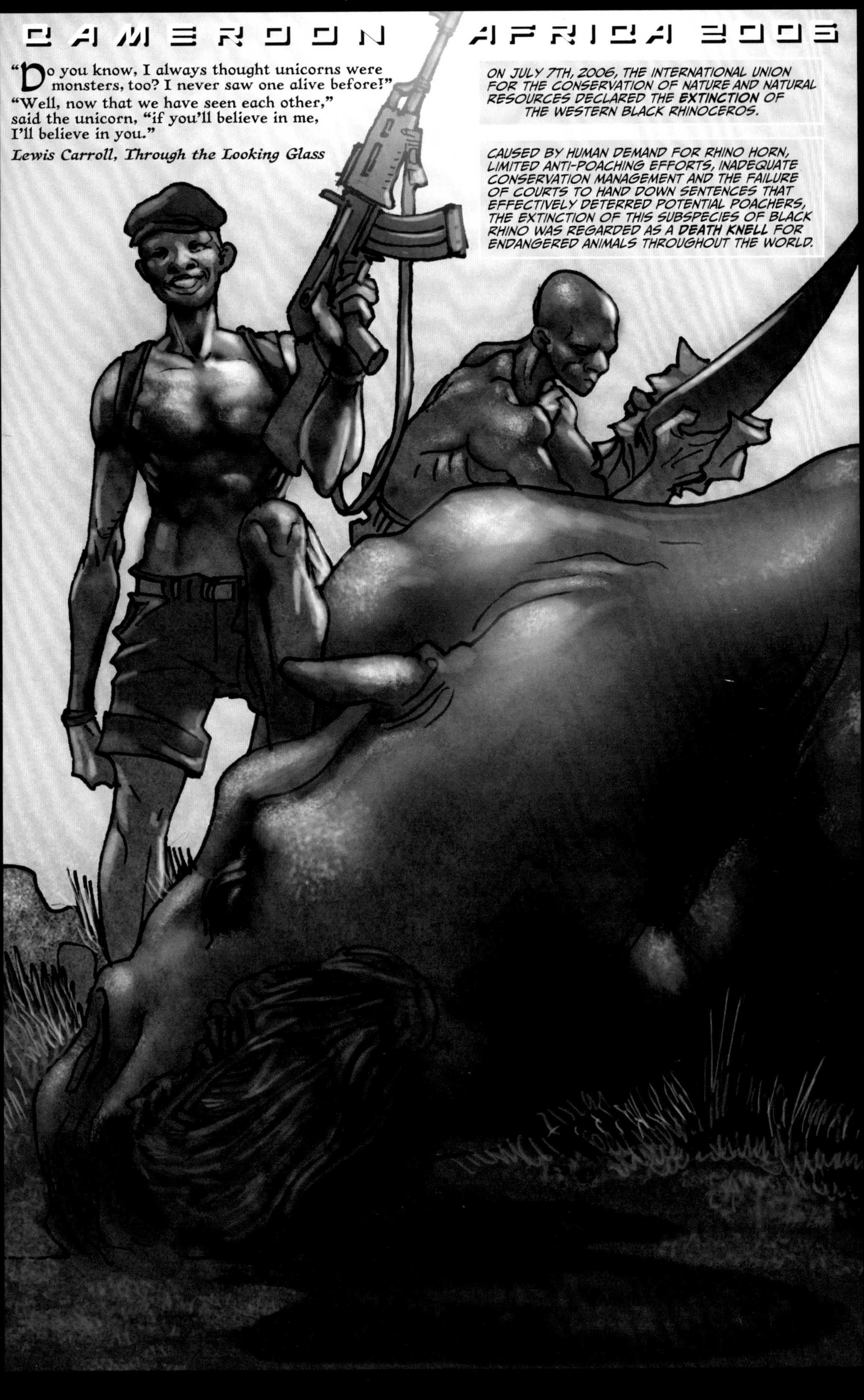
CAMEROON AFRICA 2006
"Do you know, I always thought unicorns were monsters, too? I never saw one alive before!"
"Well, now that we have seen each other," said the unicorn, "if you'll believe in me, I'll believe in you."
Lewis Carroll, Through the Looking Glass
ON JULY 7TH, 2006, THE INTERNATIONAL UNION FOR THE CONSERVATION OF NATURE AND NATURAL RESOURCES DECLARED THE EXTINCTION OF THE WESTERN BLACK RHINOCEROS.
CAUSED BY HUMAN DEMAND FOR RHINO HORN, LIMITED ANTI-POACHING EFFORTS, INADEQUATE CONSERVATION MANAGEMENT AND THE FAILURE OF COURTS TO HAND DOWN SENTENCES THAT EFFECTIVELY DETERRED POTENTIAL POACHERS, THE EXTINCTION OF THIS SUBSPECIES OF BLACK RHINO WAS REGARDED AS A DEATH KNELL FOR ENDANGERED ANIMALS THROUGHOUT THE WORLD.

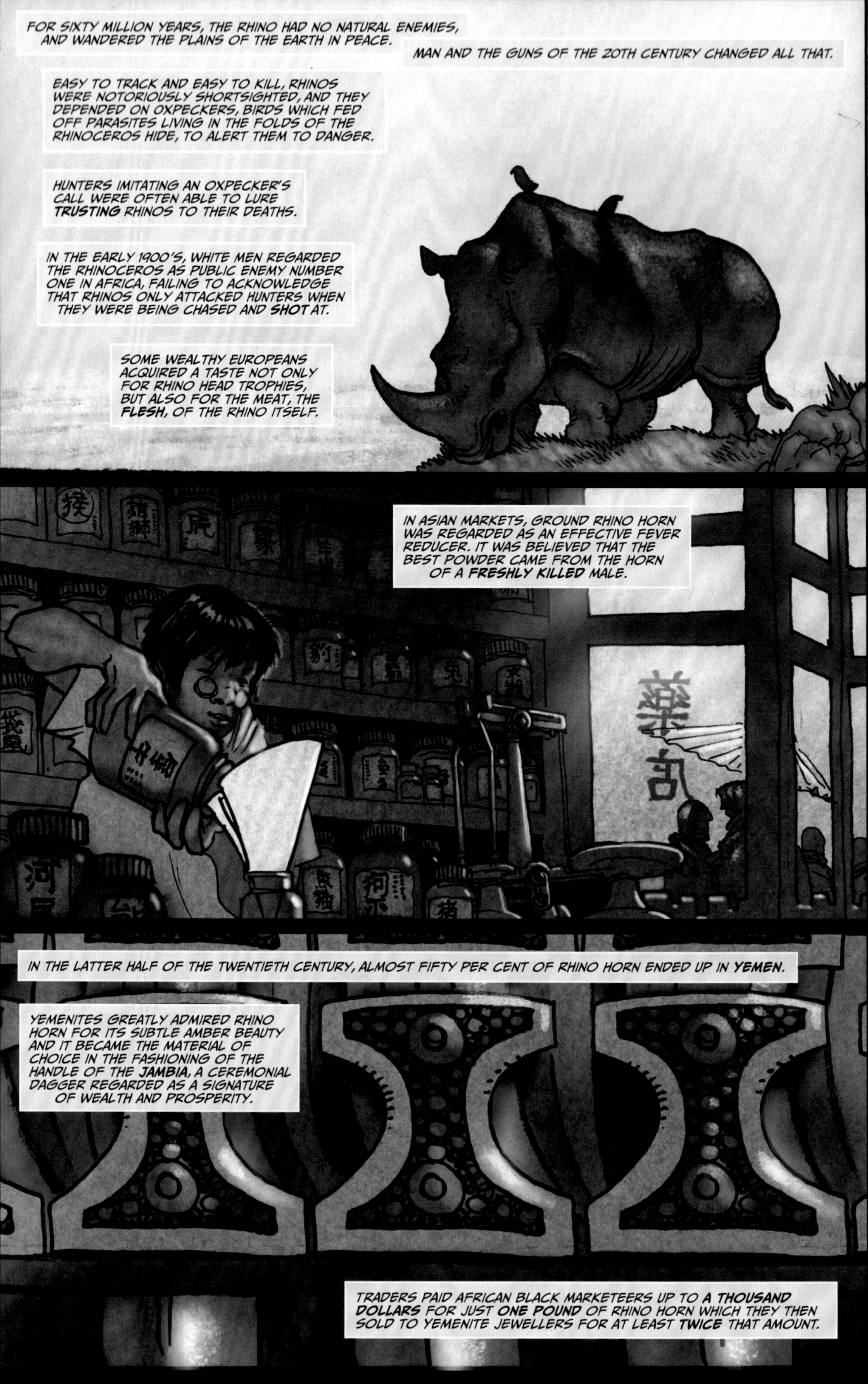
FOR SIXTY MILLION YEARS, THE RHINO HAD NO NATURAL ENEMIES, AND WANDERED THE PLAINS OF THE EARTH IN PEACE.
MAN AND THE GUNS OF THE 20TH CENTURY CHANGED ALL THAT.
EASY TO TRACK AND EASY TO KILL, RHINOS WERE NOTORIOUSLY SHORTSIGHTED, AND THEY DEPENDED ON OXPECKERS, BIRDS WHICH FED OFF PARASITES LIVING IN THE FOLDS OF THE RHINOCEROS HIDE, TO ALERT THEM TO DANGER.
HUNTERS IMITATING AN OXPECKER'S CALL WERE OFTEN ABLE TO LURE **TRUSTING** RHINOS TO THEIR DEATHS.
IN THE EARLY 1900'S, WHITE MEN REGARDED THE RHINOCEROS AS PUBLIC ENEMY NUMBER ONE IN AFRICA, FAILING TO ACKNOWLEDGE THAT RHINOS ONLY ATTACKED HUNTERS WHEN THEY WERE BEING CHASED AND **SHOT** AT.
SOME WEALTHY EUROPEANS ACQUIRED A TASTE NOT ONLY FOR RHINO HEAD TROPHIES, BUT ALSO FOR THE MEAT, THE **FLESH**, OF THE RHINO ITSELF.
IN ASIAN MARKETS, GROUND RHINO HORN WAS REGARDED AS AN EFFECTIVE FEVER REDUCER. IT WAS BELIEVED THAT THE BEST POWDER CAME FROM THE HORN OF A **FRESHLY KILLED** MALE.
IN THE LATTER HALF OF THE TWENTIETH CENTURY, ALMOST FIFTY PER CENT OF RHINO HORN ENDED UP IN **YEMEN**.
YEMENITES GREATLY ADMIRED RHINO HORN FOR ITS SUBTLE AMBER BEAUTY AND IT BECAME THE MATERIAL OF CHOICE IN THE FASHIONING OF THE HANDLE OF THE **JAMBIA**, A CEREMONIAL DAGGER REGARDED AS A SIGNATURE OF WEALTH AND PROSPERITY.
TRADERS PAID AFRICAN BLACK MARKETEERS UP TO **A THOUSAND DOLLARS** FOR JUST **ONE POUND** OF RHINO HORN WHICH THEY THEN SOLD TO YEMENITE JEWELLERS FOR AT LEAST **TWICE** THAT AMOUNT.

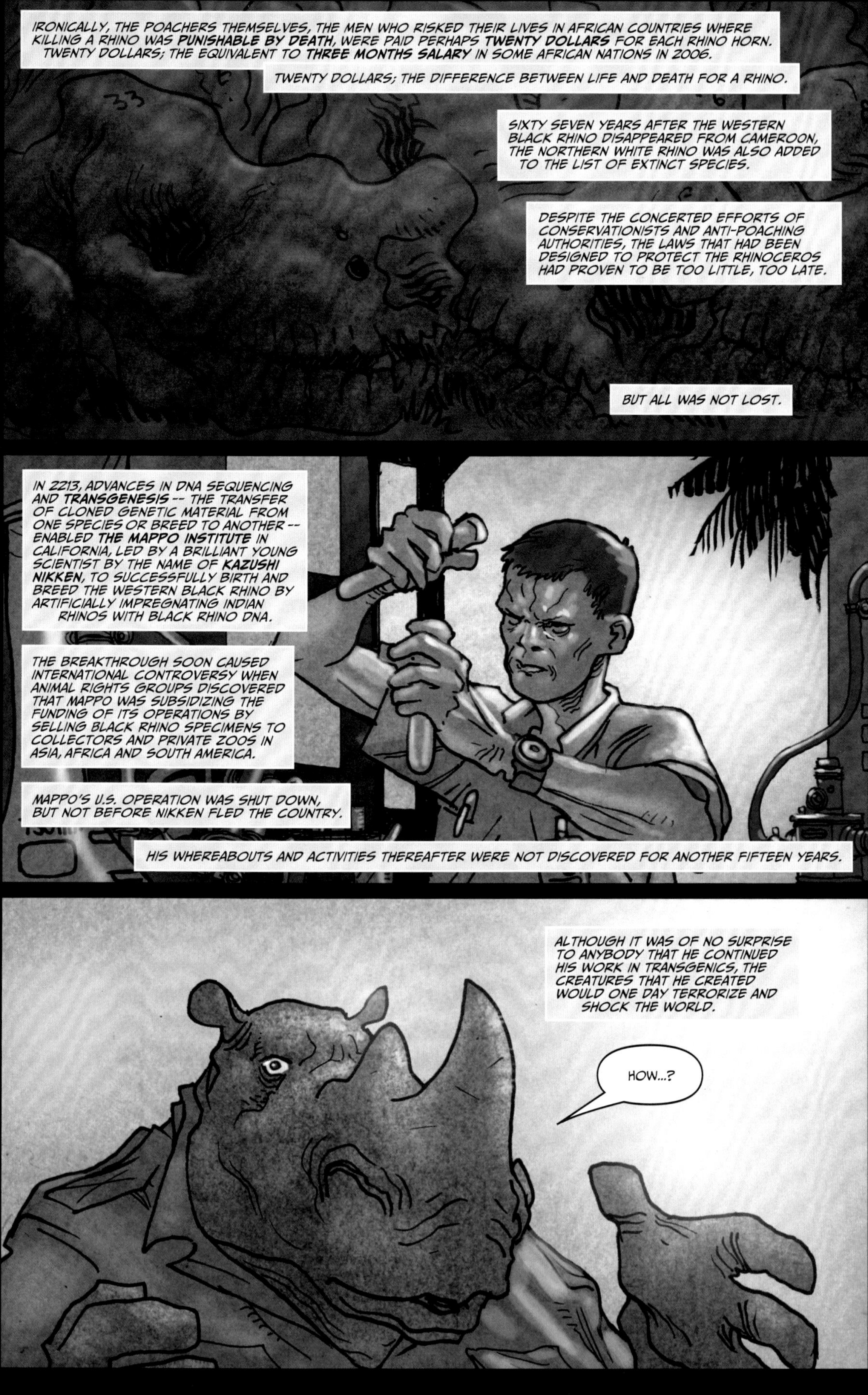

IRONICALLY, THE POACHERS THEMSELVES, THE MEN WHO RISKED THEIR LIVES IN AFRICAN COUNTRIES WHERE KILLING A RHINO WAS **PUNISHABLE BY DEATH**, WERE PAID PERHAPS **TWENTY DOLLARS** FOR EACH RHINO HORN. TWENTY DOLLARS; THE EQUIVALENT TO **THREE MONTHS SALARY** IN SOME AFRICAN NATIONS IN 2006.
TWENTY DOLLARS; THE DIFFERENCE BETWEEN LIFE AND DEATH FOR A RHINO.
SIXTY SEVEN YEARS AFTER THE WESTERN BLACK RHINO DISAPPEARED FROM CAMEROON, THE NORTHERN WHITE RHINO WAS ALSO ADDED TO THE LIST OF EXTINCT SPECIES.
DESPITE THE CONCERTED EFFORTS OF CONSERVATIONISTS AND ANTI-POACHING AUTHORITIES, THE LAWS THAT HAD BEEN DESIGNED TO PROTECT THE RHINOCEROS HAD PROVEN TO BE TOO LITTLE, TOO LATE.
BUT ALL WAS NOT LOST.
IN 2213, ADVANCES IN DNA SEQUENCING AND **TRANSGENESIS** -- THE TRANSFER OF CLONED GENETIC MATERIAL FROM ONE SPECIES OR BREED TO ANOTHER -- ENABLED **THE MAPPO INSTITUTE** IN CALIFORNIA, LED BY A BRILLIANT YOUNG SCIENTIST BY THE NAME OF **KAZUSHI NIKKEN**, TO SUCCESSFULLY BIRTH AND BREED THE WESTERN BLACK RHINO BY ARTIFICIALLY IMPREGNATING INDIAN RHINOS WITH BLACK RHINO DNA.
THE BREAKTHROUGH SOON CAUSED INTERNATIONAL CONTROVERSY WHEN ANIMAL RIGHTS GROUPS DISCOVERED THAT MAPPO WAS SUBSIDIZING THE FUNDING OF ITS OPERATIONS BY SELLING BLACK RHINO SPECIMENS TO COLLECTORS AND PRIVATE ZOOS IN ASIA, AFRICA AND SOUTH AMERICA.
MAPPO'S U.S. OPERATION WAS SHUT DOWN, BUT NOT BEFORE NIKKEN FLED THE COUNTRY.
HIS WHEREABOUTS AND ACTIVITIES THEREAFTER WERE NOT DISCOVERED FOR ANOTHER FIFTEEN YEARS.
ALTHOUGH IT WAS OF NO SURPRISE TO ANYBODY THAT HE CONTINUED HIS WORK IN TRANSGENICS, THE CREATURES THAT HE CREATED WOULD ONE DAY TERRORIZE AND SHOCK THE WORLD.
HOW...?

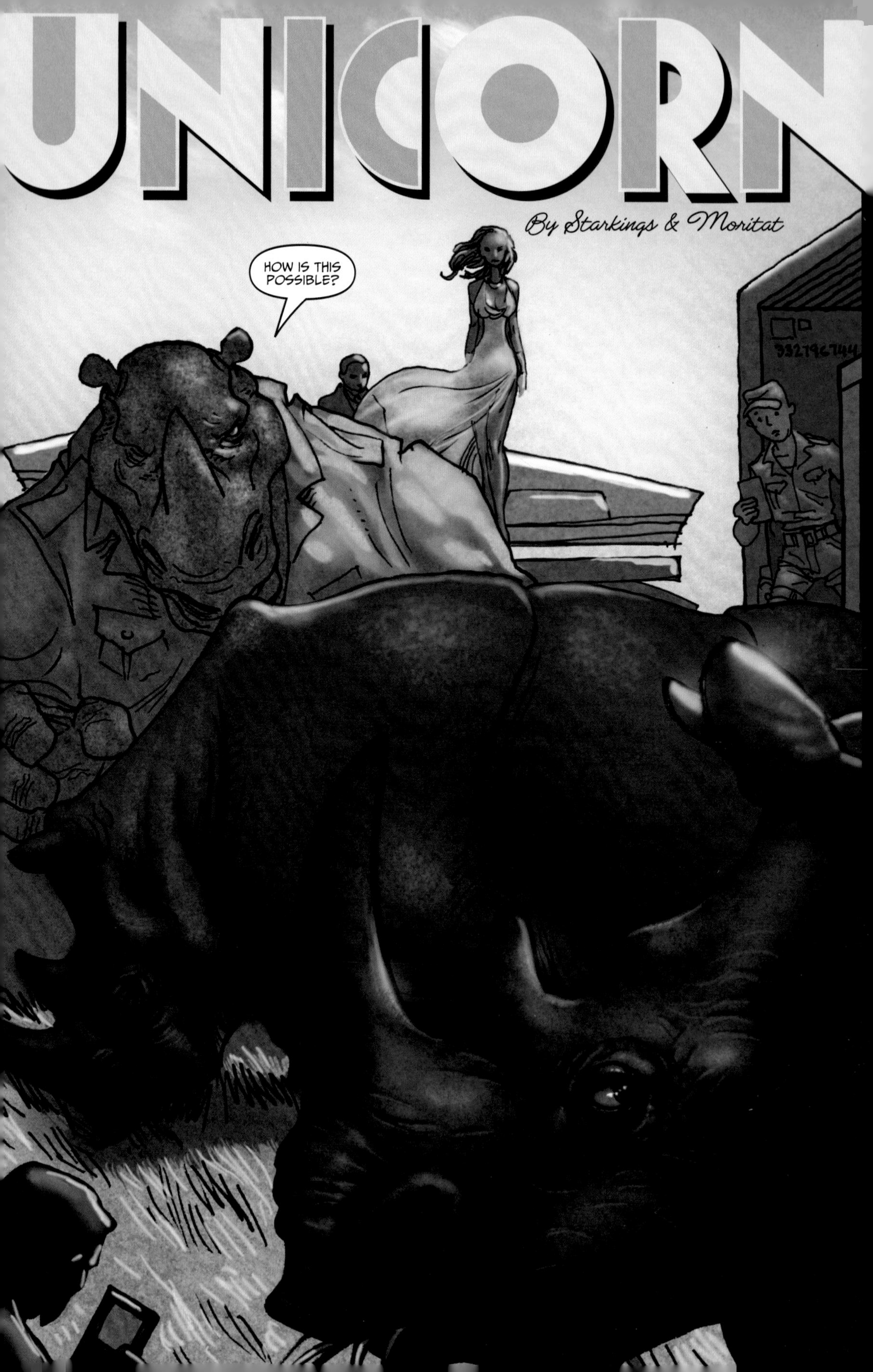
UNICORN
By Starkings & Moritat
HOW IS THIS POSSIBLE?

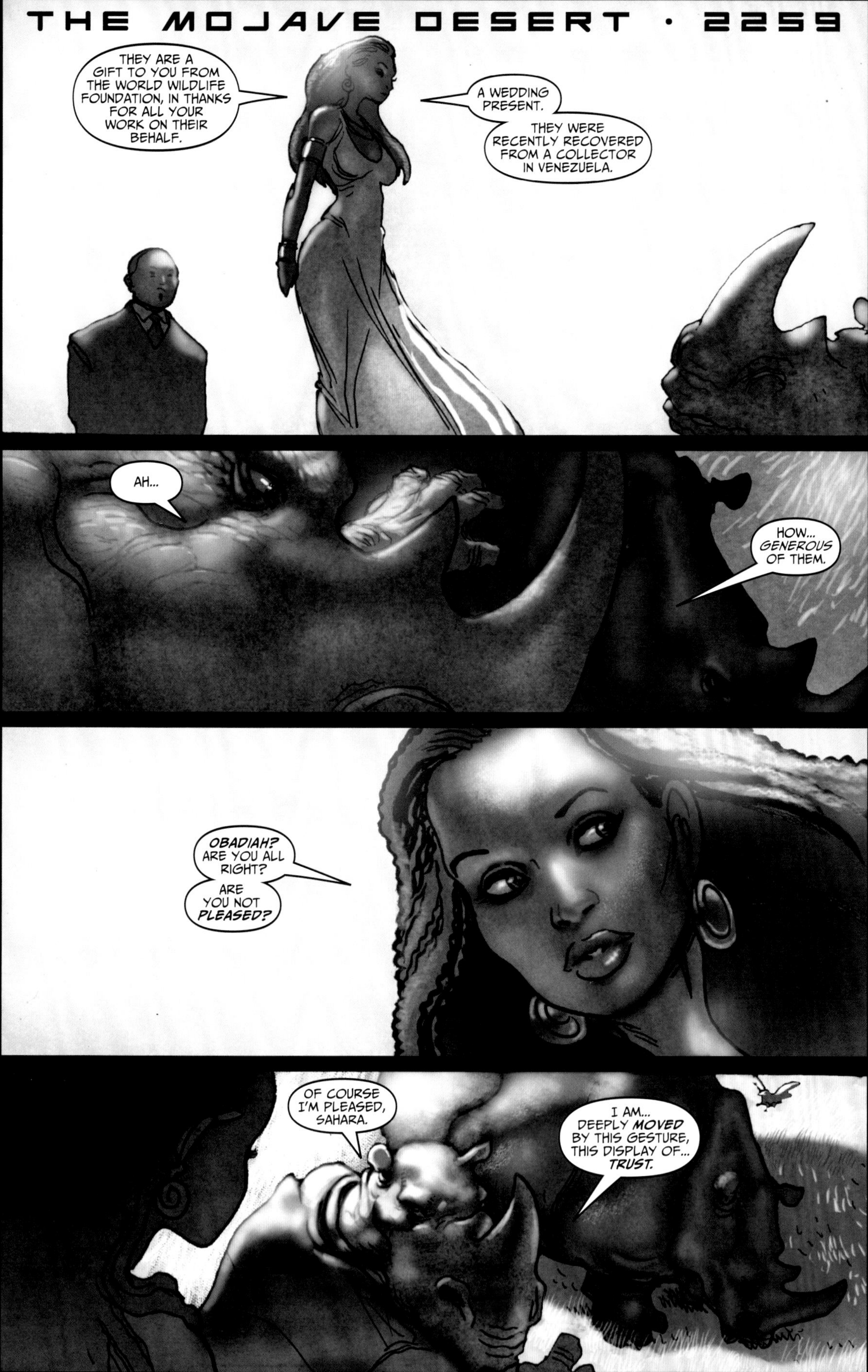
THE MOJAVE DESERT · 2259
THEY ARE A GIFT TO YOU FROM THE WORLD WILDLIFE FOUNDATION, IN THANKS FOR ALL YOUR WORK ON THEIR BEHALF.
A WEDDING PRESENT.
THEY WERE RECENTLY RECOVERED FROM A COLLECTOR IN VENEZUELA.
AH...
HOW... GENEROUS OF THEM.
OBADIAH? ARE YOU ALL RIGHT?
ARE YOU NOT PLEASED?
OF COURSE I'M PLEASED, SAHARA.
I AM... DEEPLY MOVED BY THIS GESTURE, THIS DISPLAY OF... TRUST.

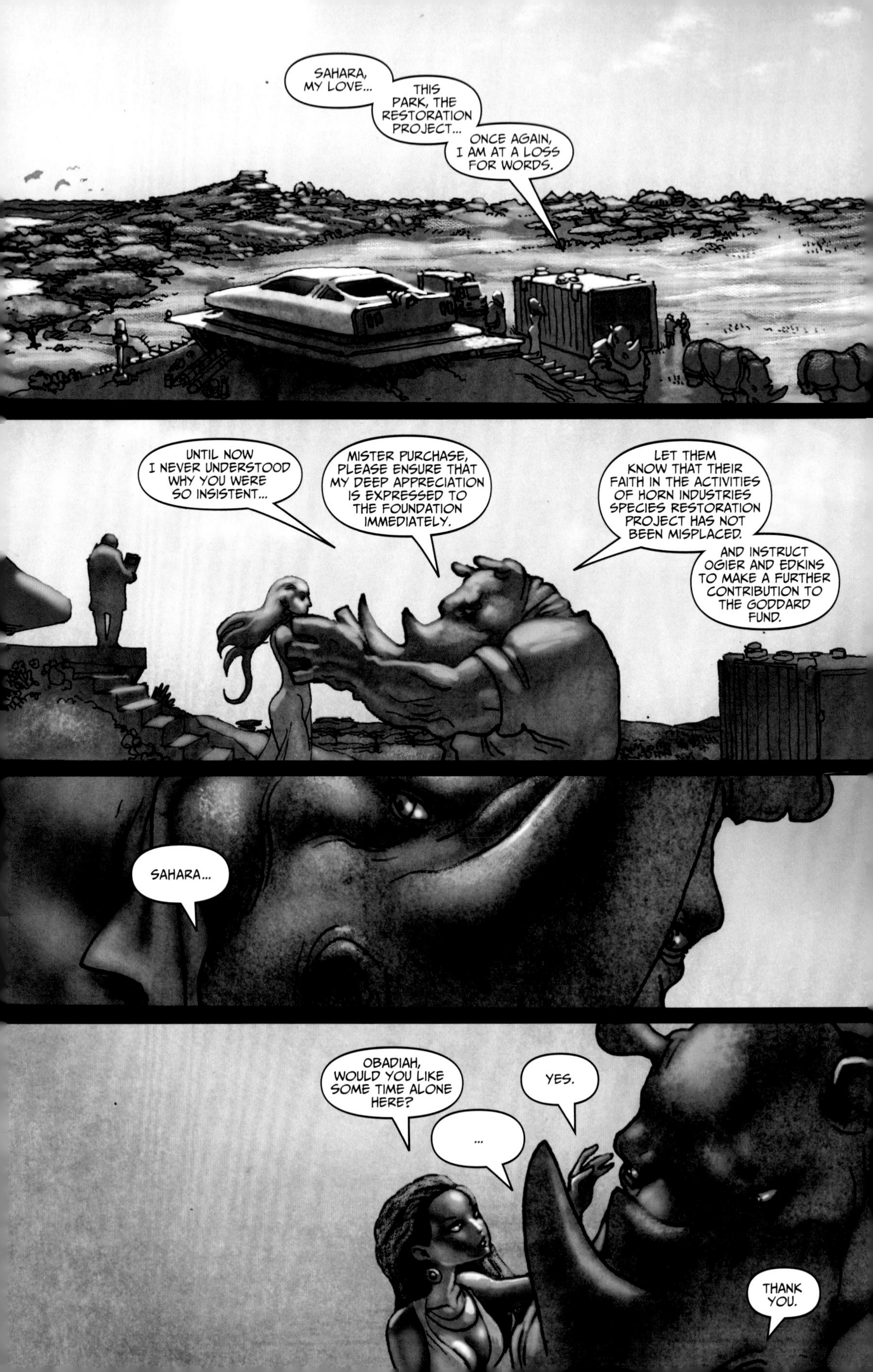
SAHARA, MY LOVE...
THIS PARK, THE RESTORATION PROJECT...
ONCE AGAIN, I AM AT A LOSS FOR WORDS.
UNTIL NOW I NEVER UNDERSTOOD WHY YOU WERE SO INSISTENT...
MISTER PURCHASE, PLEASE ENSURE THAT MY DEEP APPRECIATION IS EXPRESSED TO THE FOUNDATION IMMEDIATELY.
LET THEM KNOW THAT THEIR FAITH IN THE ACTIVITIES OF HORN INDUSTRIES SPECIES RESTORATION PROJECT HAS NOT BEEN MISPLACED.
AND INSTRUCT OGIER AND EDKINS TO MAKE A FURTHER CONTRIBUTION TO THE GODDARD FUND.
SAHARA...
OBADIAH, WOULD YOU LIKE SOME TIME ALONE HERE?
...
YES.
THANK YOU.

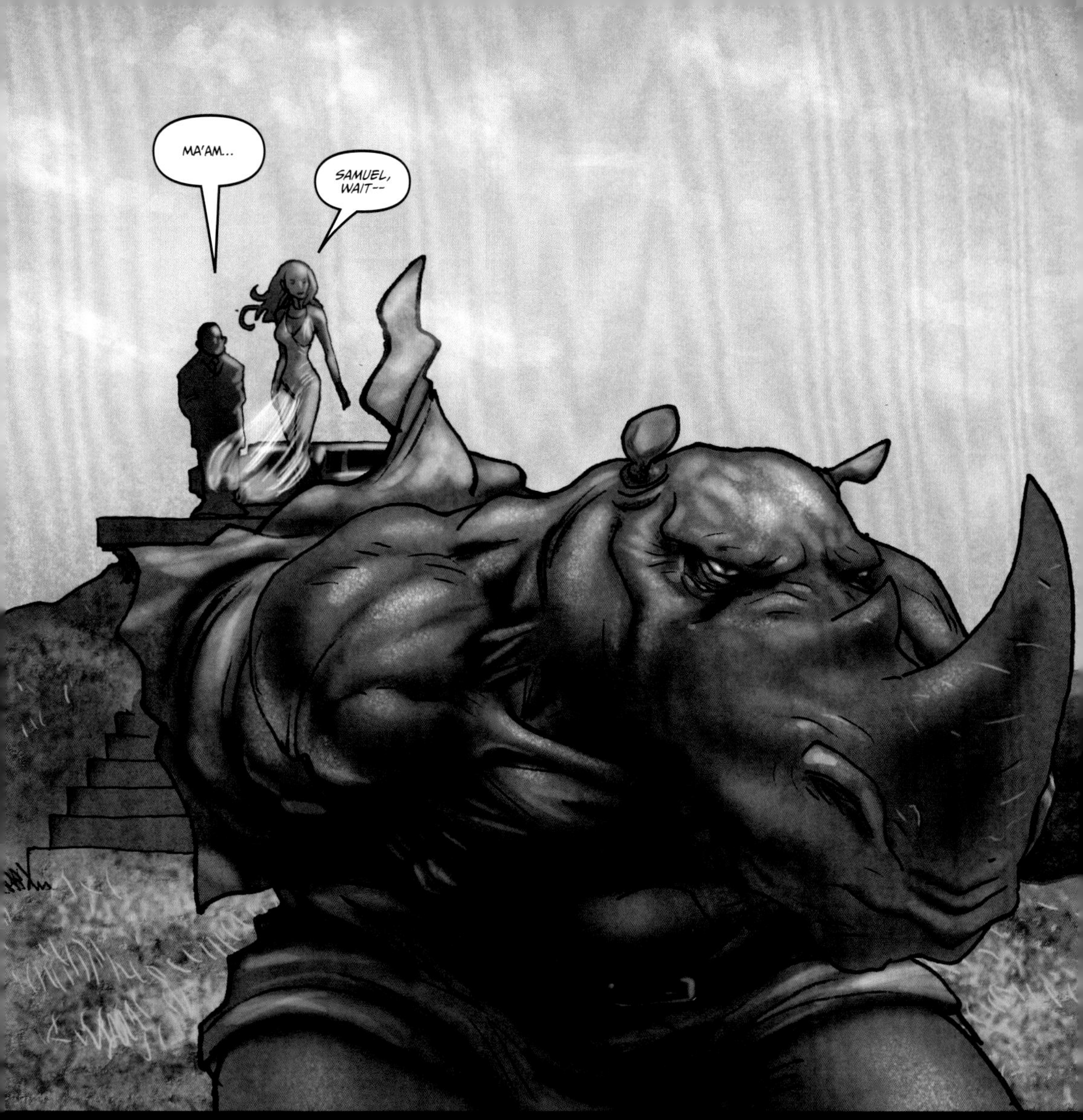
MA'AM..
SAMUEL, WAIT--
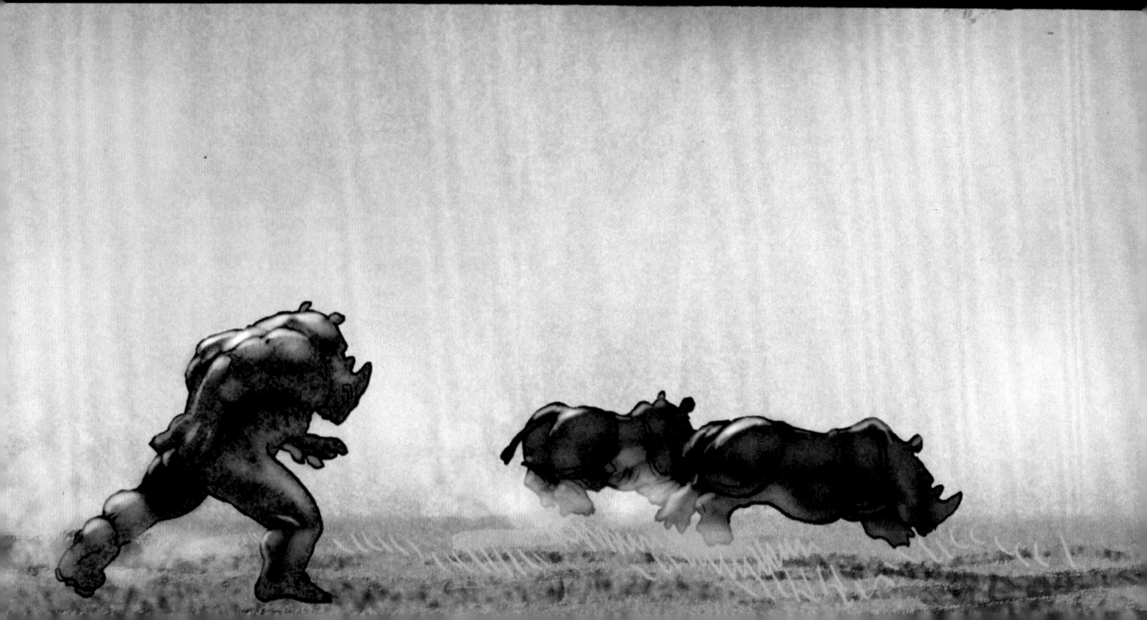

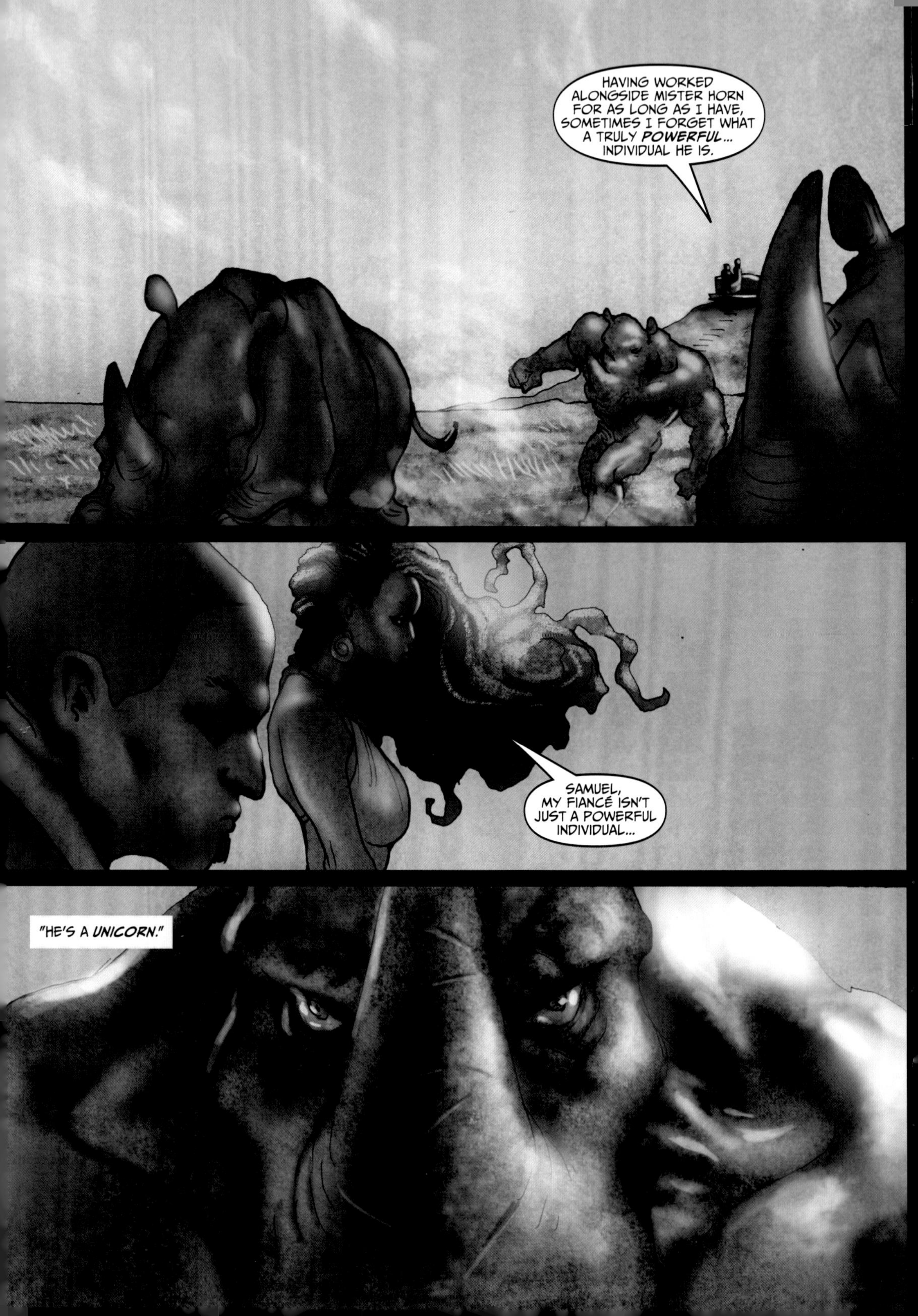
HAVING WORKED ALONGSIDE MISTER HORN FOR AS LONG AS I HAVE, SOMETIMES I FORGET WHAT A TRULY *POWERFUL*... INDIVIDUAL HE IS.
SAMUEL, MY FIANCÉ ISN'T JUST A POWERFUL INDIVIDUAL...
"HE'S A *UNICORN*."

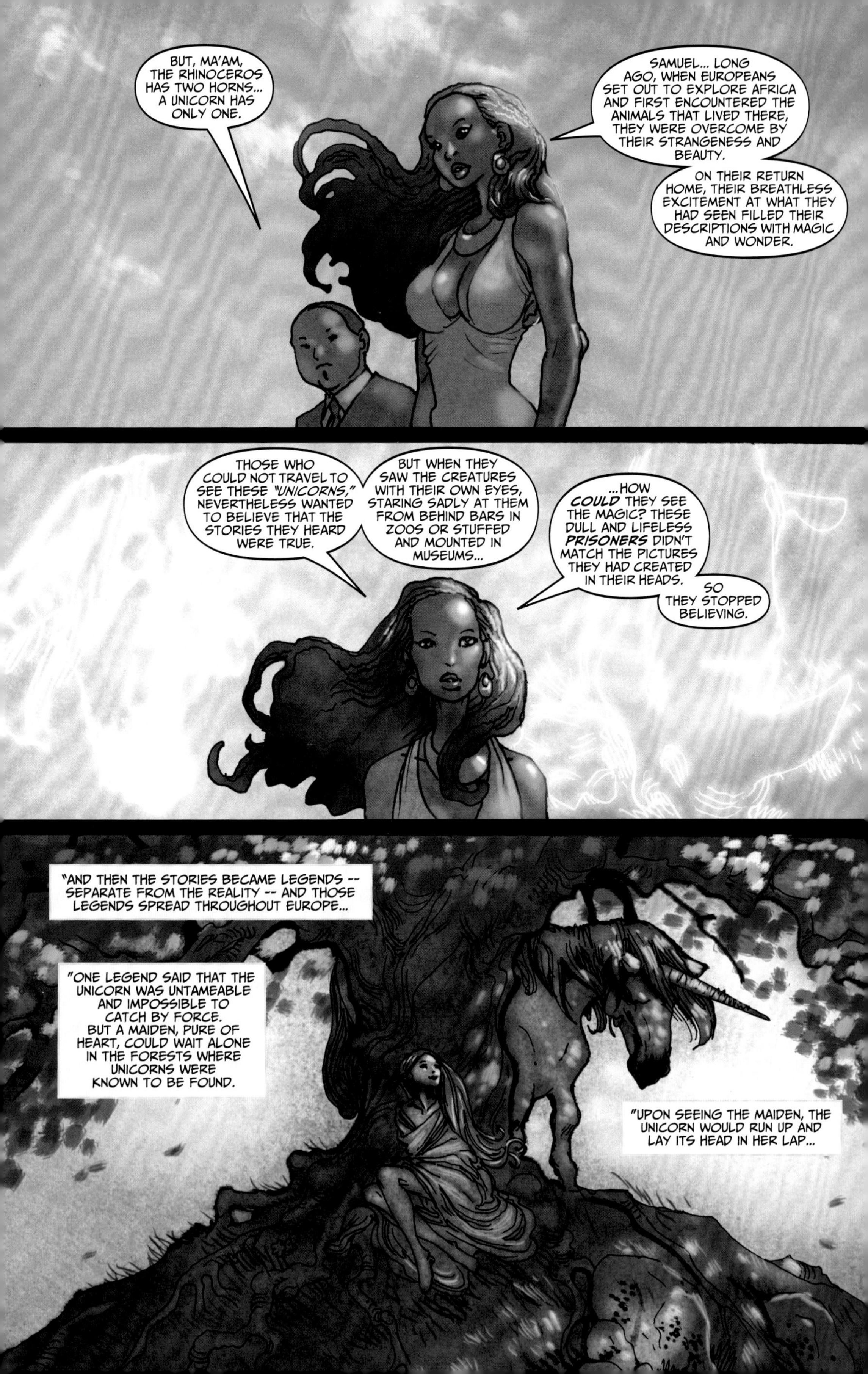
BUT, MA'AM, THE RHINOCEROS HAS TWO HORNS... A UNICORN HAS ONLY ONE.
SAMUEL... LONG AGO, WHEN EUROPEANS SET OUT TO EXPLORE AFRICA AND FIRST ENCOUNTERED THE ANIMALS THAT LIVED THERE, THEY WERE OVERCOME BY THEIR STRANGENESS AND BEAUTY.
ON THEIR RETURN HOME, THEIR BREATHLESS EXCITEMENT AT WHAT THEY HAD SEEN FILLED THEIR DESCRIPTIONS WITH MAGIC AND WONDER.
THOSE WHO COULD NOT TRAVEL TO SEE THESE *"UNICORNS,"* NEVERTHELESS WANTED TO BELIEVE THAT THE STORIES THEY HEARD WERE TRUE.
BUT WHEN THEY SAW THE CREATURES WITH THEIR OWN EYES, STARING SADLY AT THEM FROM BEHIND BARS IN ZOOS OR STUFFED AND MOUNTED IN MUSEUMS...
...HOW ***COULD*** THEY SEE THE MAGIC? THESE DULL AND LIFELESS ***PRISONERS*** DIDN'T MATCH THE PICTURES THEY HAD CREATED IN THEIR HEADS.
SO THEY STOPPED BELIEVING.
"AND THEN THE STORIES BECAME LEGENDS -- SEPARATE FROM THE REALITY -- AND THOSE LEGENDS SPREAD THROUGHOUT EUROPE...
"ONE LEGEND SAID THAT THE UNICORN WAS UNTAMEABLE AND IMPOSSIBLE TO CATCH BY FORCE. BUT A MAIDEN, PURE OF HEART, COULD WAIT ALONE IN THE FORESTS WHERE UNICORNS WERE KNOWN TO BE FOUND.
"UPON SEEING THE MAIDEN, THE UNICORN WOULD RUN UP AND LAY ITS HEAD IN HER LAP...

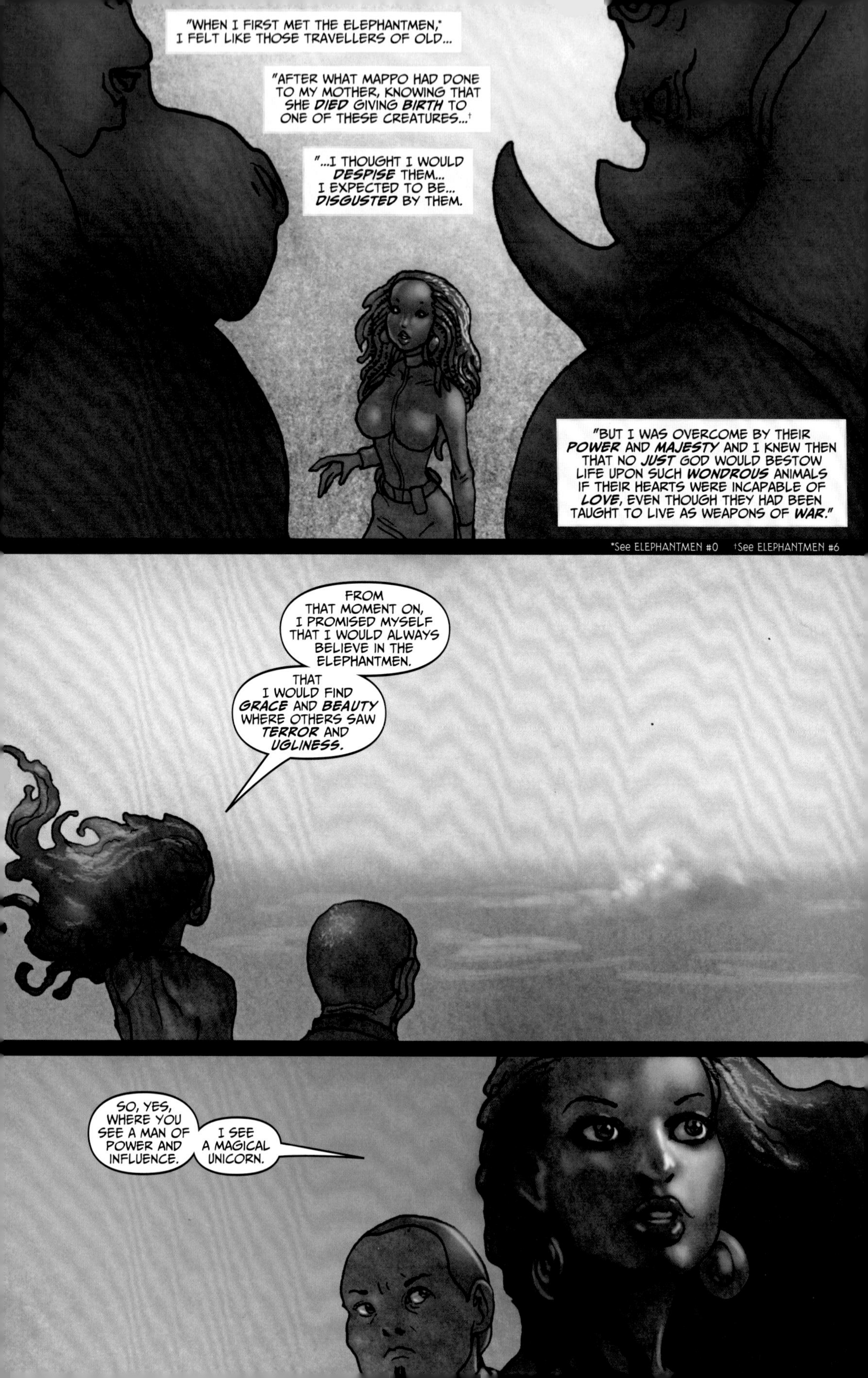
"WHEN I FIRST MET THE ELEPHANTMEN,* I FELT LIKE THOSE TRAVELLERS OF OLD...
"AFTER WHAT MAPPO HAD DONE TO MY MOTHER, KNOWING THAT SHE DIED GIVING BIRTH TO ONE OF THESE CREATURES...†
"...I THOUGHT I WOULD DESPISE THEM... I EXPECTED TO BE... DISGUSTED BY THEM.
"BUT I WAS OVERCOME BY THEIR POWER AND MAJESTY AND I KNEW THEN THAT NO JUST GOD WOULD BESTOW LIFE UPON SUCH WONDROUS ANIMALS IF THEIR HEARTS WERE INCAPABLE OF LOVE, EVEN THOUGH THEY HAD BEEN TAUGHT TO LIVE AS WEAPONS OF WAR."
*See ELEPHANTMEN #0 †See ELEPHANTMEN #6
FROM THAT MOMENT ON, I PROMISED MYSELF THAT I WOULD ALWAYS BELIEVE IN THE ELEPHANTMEN.
THAT I WOULD FIND GRACE AND BEAUTY WHERE OTHERS SAW TERROR AND UGLINESS.
SO, YES, WHERE YOU SEE A MAN OF POWER AND INFLUENCE.
I SEE A MAGICAL UNICORN.

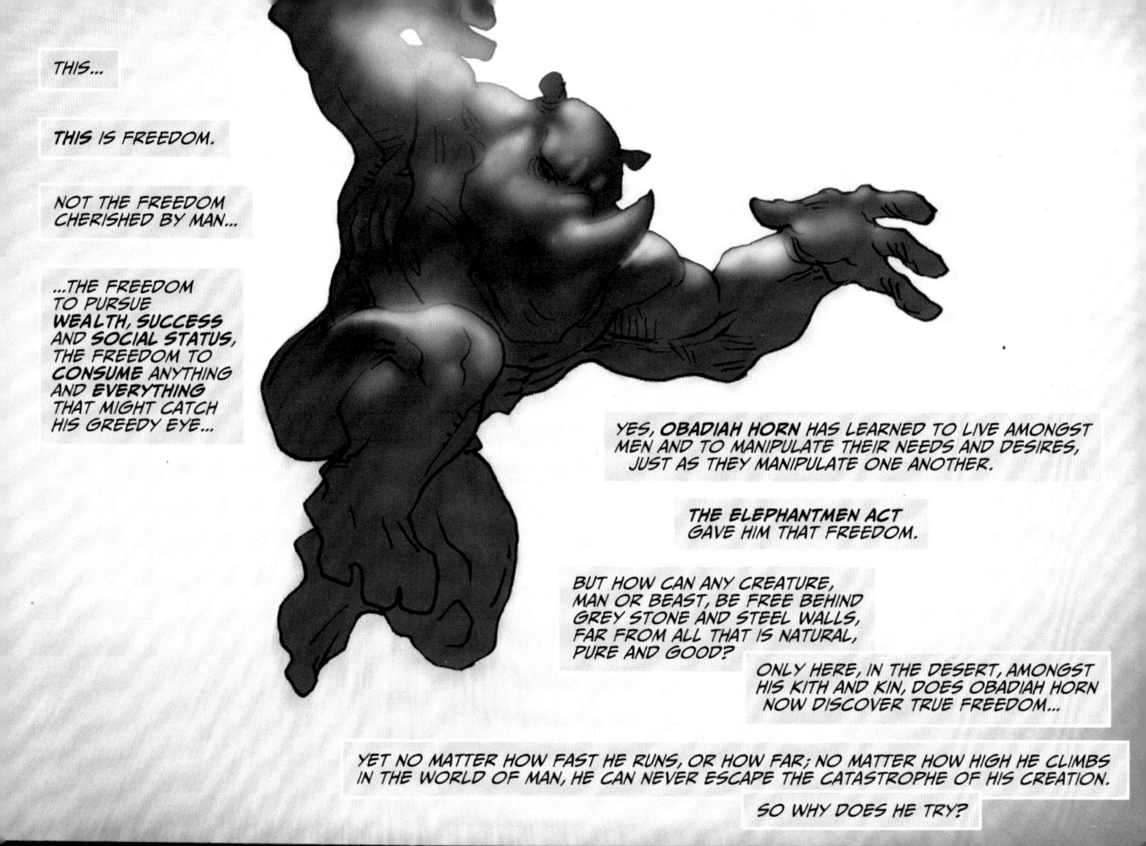
THIS...
THIS IS FREEDOM.
NOT THE FREEDOM CHERISHED BY MAN...
...THE FREEDOM TO PURSUE WEALTH, SUCCESS AND SOCIAL STATUS, THE FREEDOM TO CONSUME ANYTHING AND EVERYTHING THAT MIGHT CATCH HIS GREEDY EYE...
YES, OBADIAH HORN HAS LEARNED TO LIVE AMONGST MEN AND TO MANIPULATE THEIR NEEDS AND DESIRES, JUST AS THEY MANIPULATE ONE ANOTHER.
THE ELEPHANTMEN ACT GAVE HIM THAT FREEDOM.
BUT HOW CAN ANY CREATURE, MAN OR BEAST, BE FREE BEHIND GREY STONE AND STEEL WALLS, FAR FROM ALL THAT IS NATURAL, PURE AND GOOD?
ONLY HERE, IN THE DESERT, AMONGST HIS KITH AND KIN, DOES OBADIAH HORN NOW DISCOVER TRUE FREEDOM...
YET NO MATTER HOW FAST HE RUNS, OR HOW FAR; NO MATTER HOW HIGH HE CLIMBS IN THE WORLD OF MAN, HE CAN NEVER ESCAPE THE CATASTROPHE OF HIS CREATION.
SO WHY DOES HE TRY?

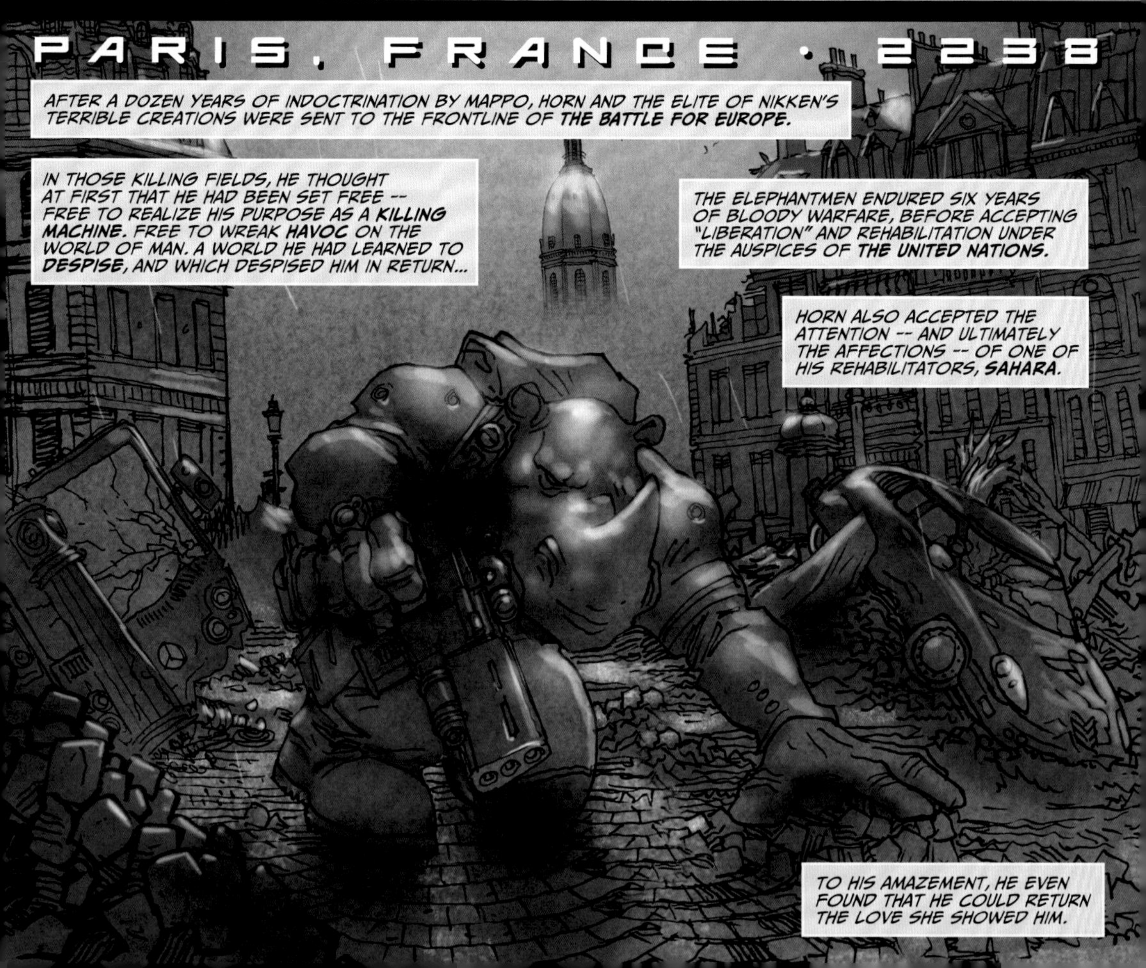
PARIS, FRANCE · 2238
AFTER A DOZEN YEARS OF INDOCTRINATION BY MAPPO, HORN AND THE ELITE OF NIKKEN'S TERRIBLE CREATIONS WERE SENT TO THE FRONTLINE OF THE BATTLE FOR EUROPE.
IN THOSE KILLING FIELDS, HE THOUGHT AT FIRST THAT HE HAD BEEN SET FREE -- FREE TO REALIZE HIS PURPOSE AS A KILLING MACHINE. FREE TO WREAK HAVOC ON THE WORLD OF MAN. A WORLD HE HAD LEARNED TO DESPISE, AND WHICH DESPISED HIM IN RETURN...
THE ELEPHANTMEN ENDURED SIX YEARS OF BLOODY WARFARE, BEFORE ACCEPTING "LIBERATION" AND REHABILITATION UNDER THE AUSPICES OF THE UNITED NATIONS.
HORN ALSO ACCEPTED THE ATTENTION -- AND ULTIMATELY THE AFFECTIONS -- OF ONE OF HIS REHABILITATORS, SAHARA.
TO HIS AMAZEMENT, HE EVEN FOUND THAT HE COULD RETURN THE LOVE SHE SHOWED HIM.

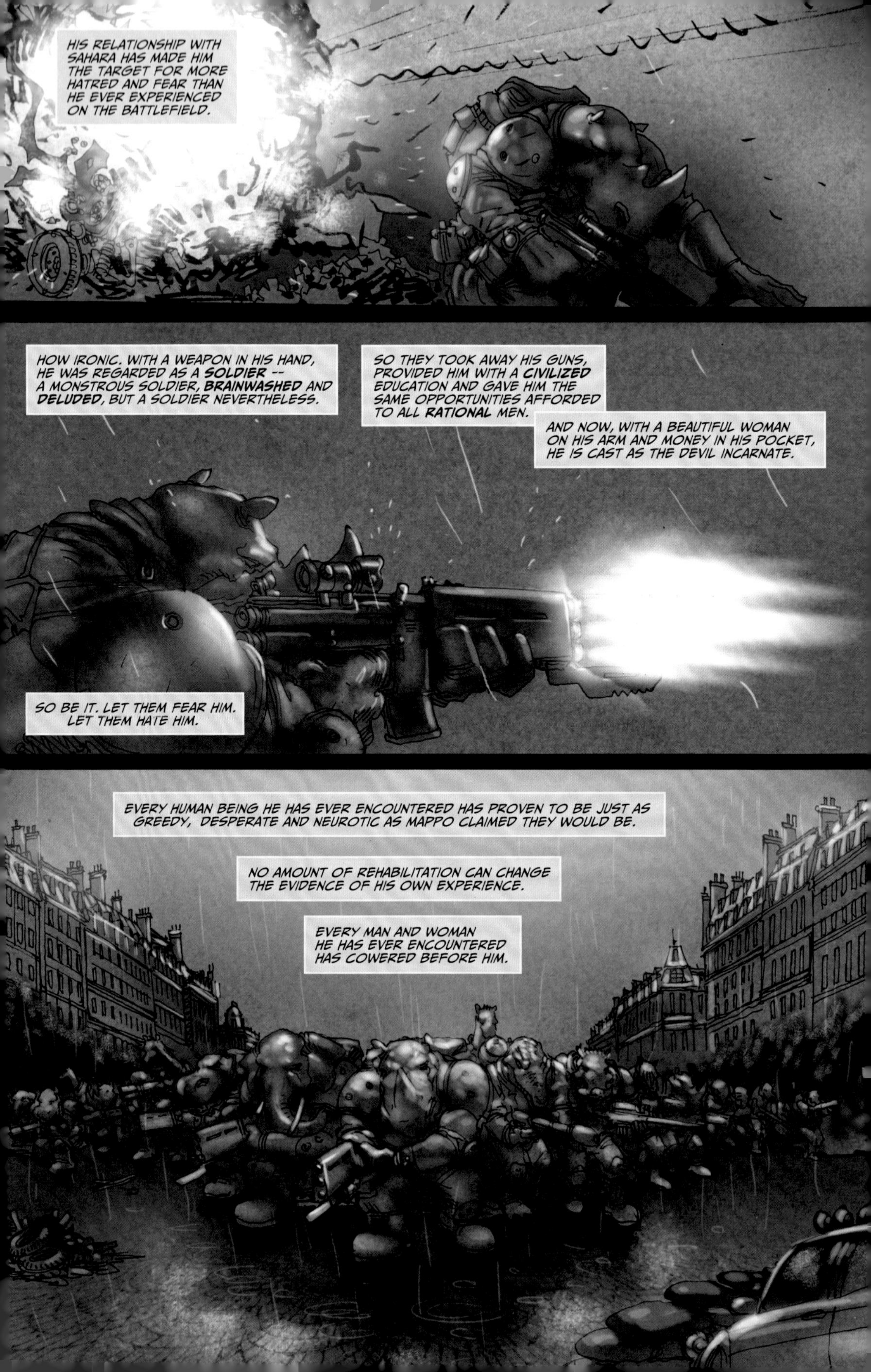
HIS RELATIONSHIP WITH SAHARA HAS MADE HIM THE TARGET FOR MORE HATRED AND FEAR THAN HE EVER EXPERIENCED ON THE BATTLEFIELD.
HOW IRONIC. WITH A WEAPON IN HIS HAND, HE WAS REGARDED AS A SOLDIER -- A MONSTROUS SOLDIER, BRAINWASHED AND DELUDED, BUT A SOLDIER NEVERTHELESS.
SO THEY TOOK AWAY HIS GUNS, PROVIDED HIM WITH A CIVILIZED EDUCATION AND GAVE HIM THE SAME OPPORTUNITIES AFFORDED TO ALL RATIONAL MEN.
AND NOW, WITH A BEAUTIFUL WOMAN ON HIS ARM AND MONEY IN HIS POCKET, HE IS CAST AS THE DEVIL INCARNATE.
SO BE IT. LET THEM FEAR HIM. LET THEM HATE HIM.
EVERY HUMAN BEING HE HAS EVER ENCOUNTERED HAS PROVEN TO BE JUST AS GREEDY, DESPERATE AND NEUROTIC AS MAPPO CLAIMED THEY WOULD BE.
NO AMOUNT OF REHABILITATION CAN CHANGE THE EVIDENCE OF HIS OWN EXPERIENCE.
EVERY MAN AND WOMAN HE HAS EVER ENCOUNTERED HAS COWERED BEFORE HIM.

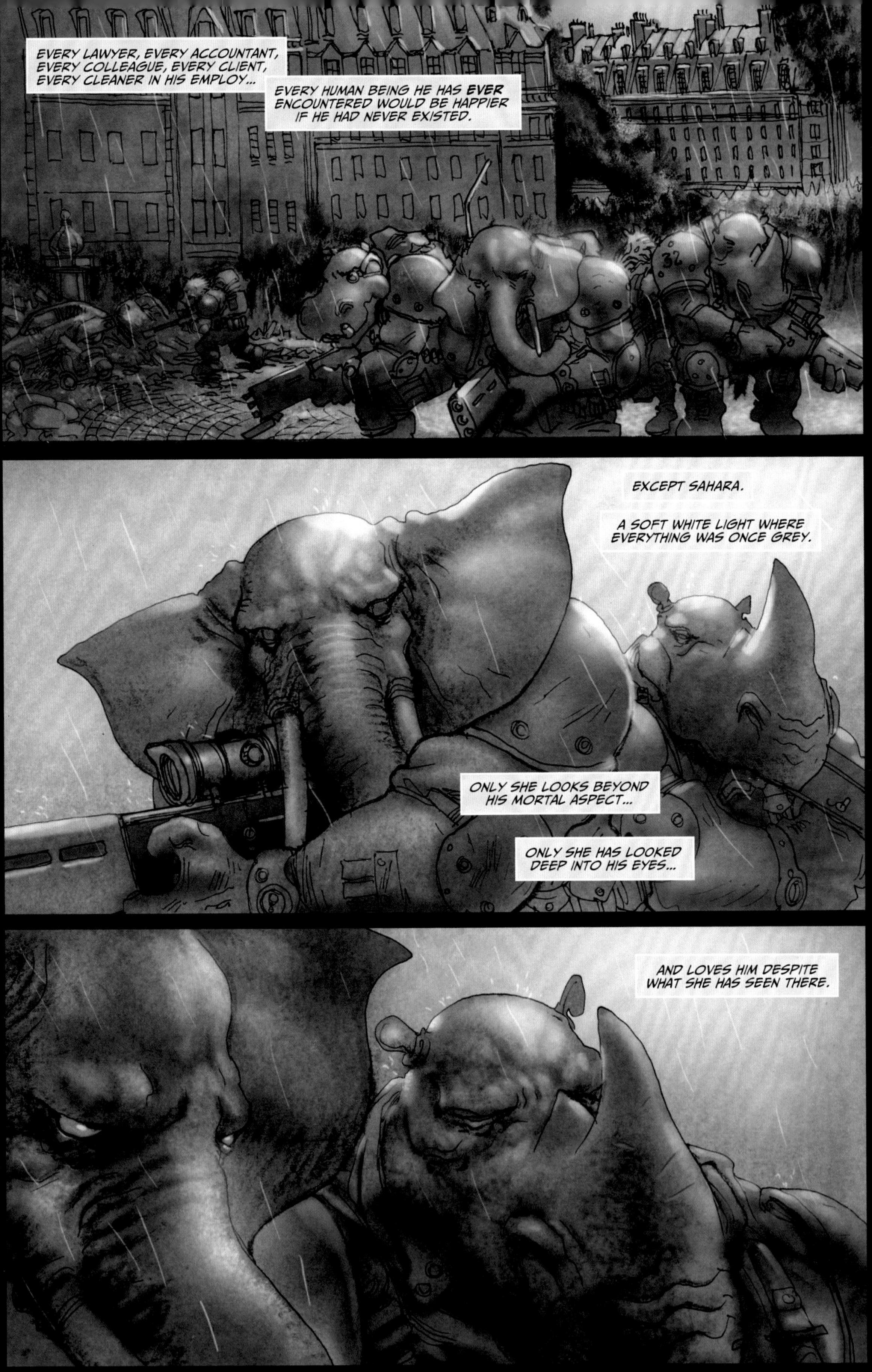
EVERY LAWYER, EVERY ACCOUNTANT, EVERY COLLEAGUE, EVERY CLIENT, EVERY CLEANER IN HIS EMPLOY...
EVERY HUMAN BEING HE HAS EVER ENCOUNTERED WOULD BE HAPPIER IF HE HAD NEVER EXISTED.
EXCEPT SAHARA.
A SOFT WHITE LIGHT WHERE EVERYTHING WAS ONCE GREY.
ONLY SHE LOOKS BEYOND HIS MORTAL ASPECT...
ONLY SHE HAS LOOKED DEEP INTO HIS EYES...
AND LOVES HIM DESPITE WHAT SHE HAS SEEN THERE.

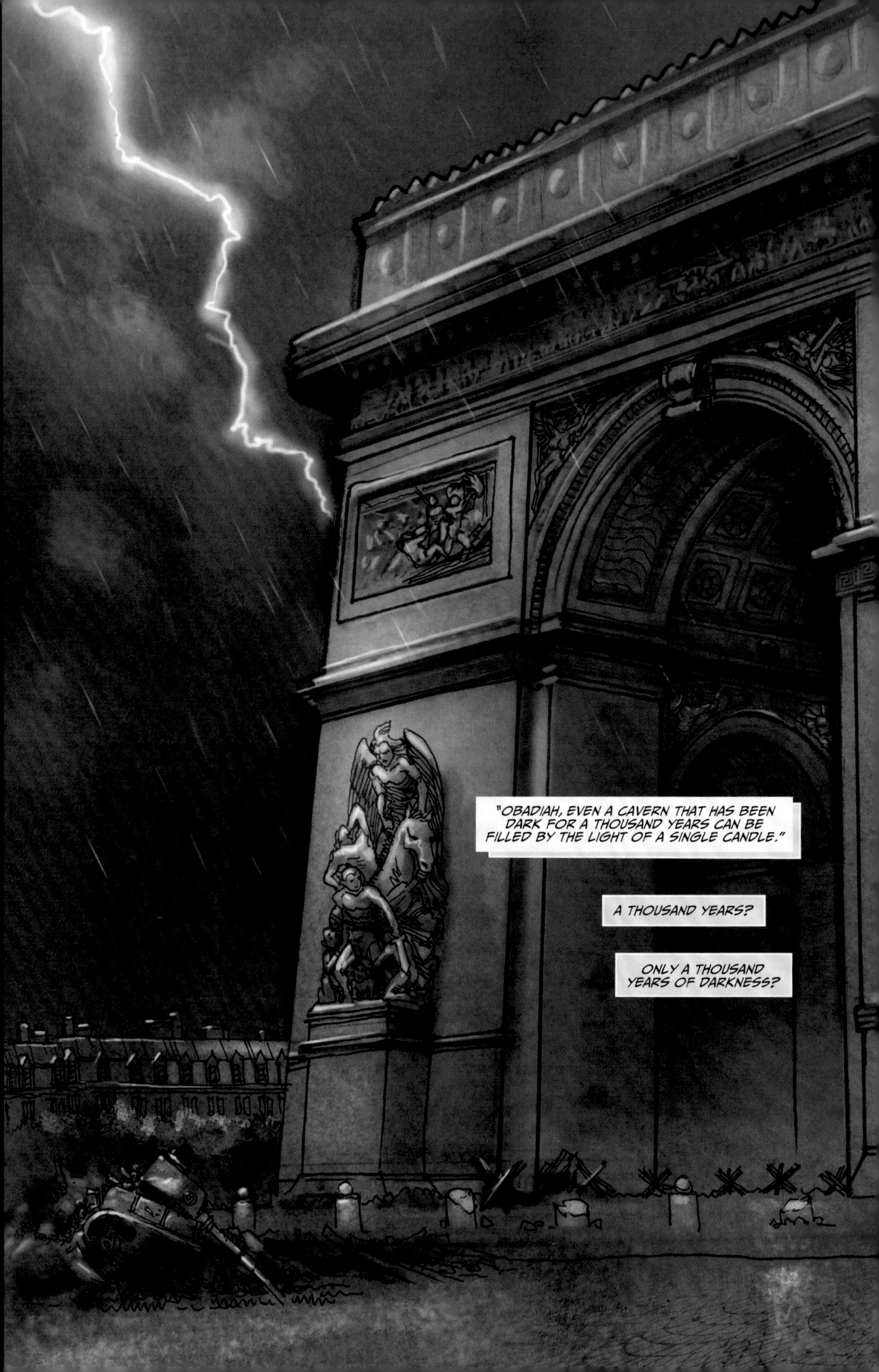
"OBADIAH, EVEN A CAVERN THAT HAS BEEN DARK FOR A THOUSAND YEARS CAN BE FILLED BY THE LIGHT OF A SINGLE CANDLE."
A THOUSAND YEARS?
ONLY A THOUSAND YEARS OF DARKNESS?

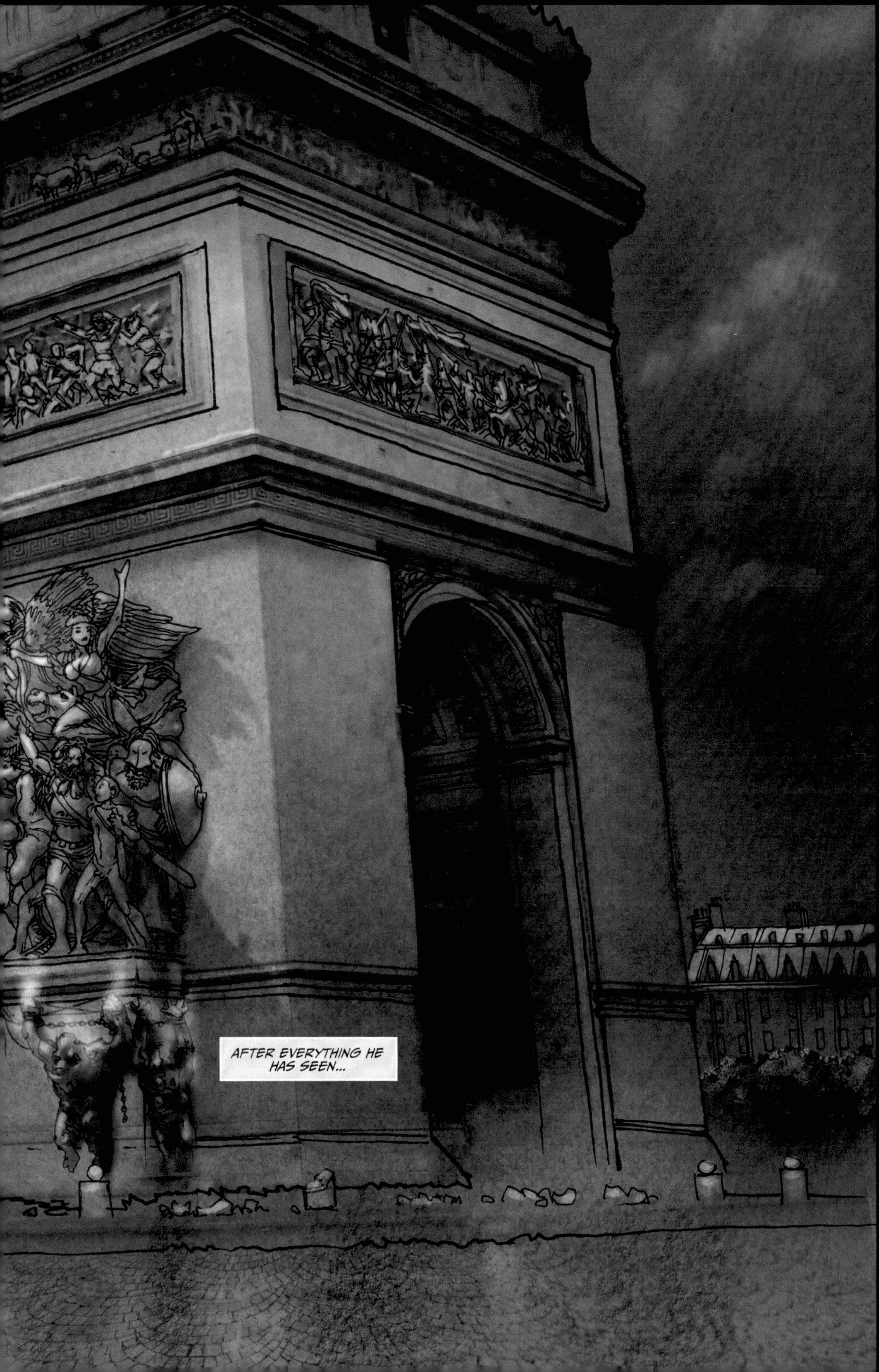
AFTER EVERYTHING HE HAS SEEN...

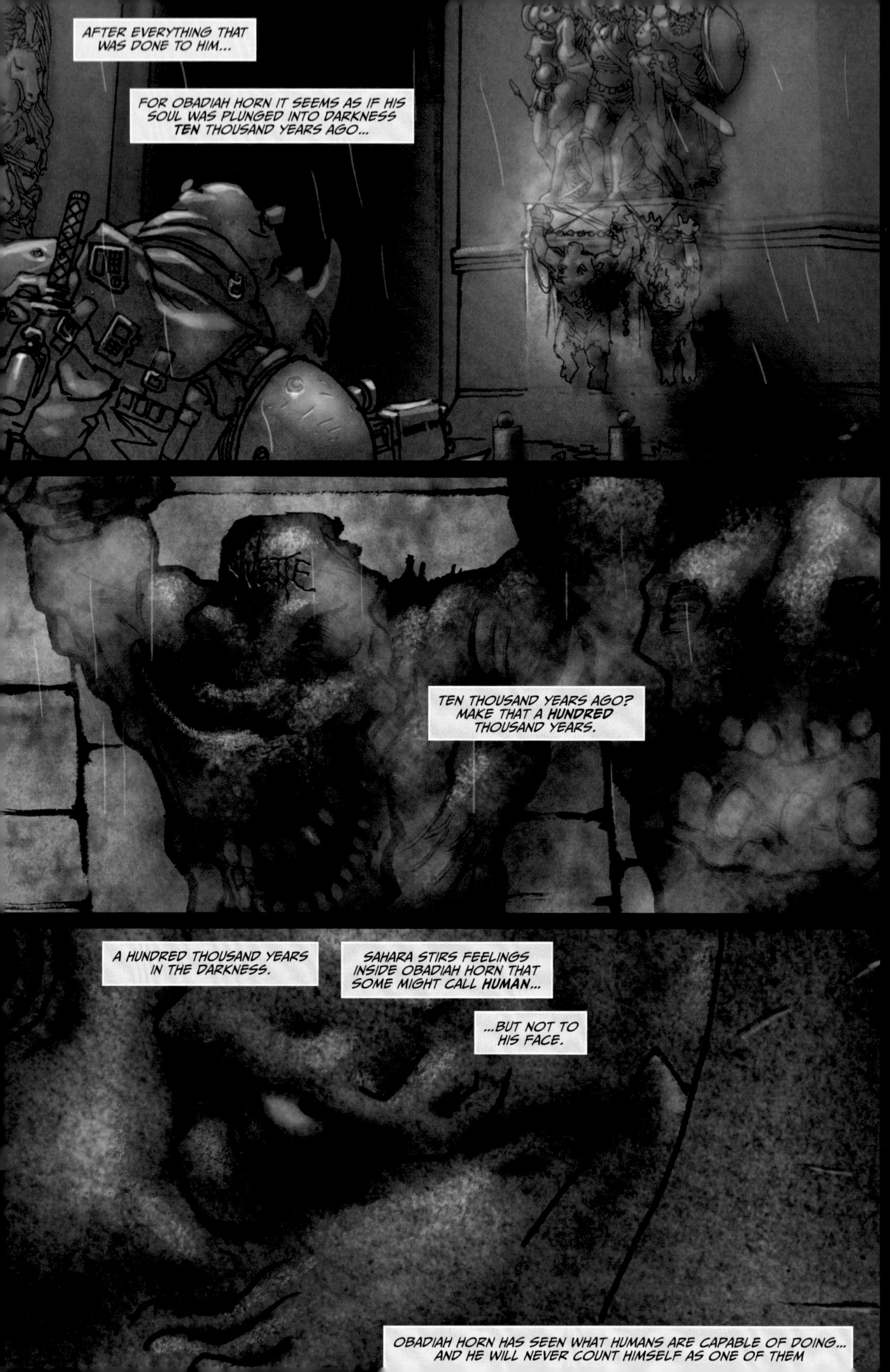
AFTER EVERYTHING THAT WAS DONE TO HIM...
FOR OBADIAH HORN IT SEEMS AS IF HIS SOUL WAS PLUNGED INTO DARKNESS TEN THOUSAND YEARS AGO...
TEN THOUSAND YEARS AGO? MAKE THAT A HUNDRED THOUSAND YEARS.
A HUNDRED THOUSAND YEARS IN THE DARKNESS.
SAHARA STIRS FEELINGS INSIDE OBADIAH HORN THAT SOME MIGHT CALL HUMAN...
...BUT NOT TO HIS FACE.
OBADIAH HORN HAS SEEN WHAT HUMANS ARE CAPABLE OF DOING... AND HE WILL NEVER COUNT HIMSELF AS ONE OF THEM

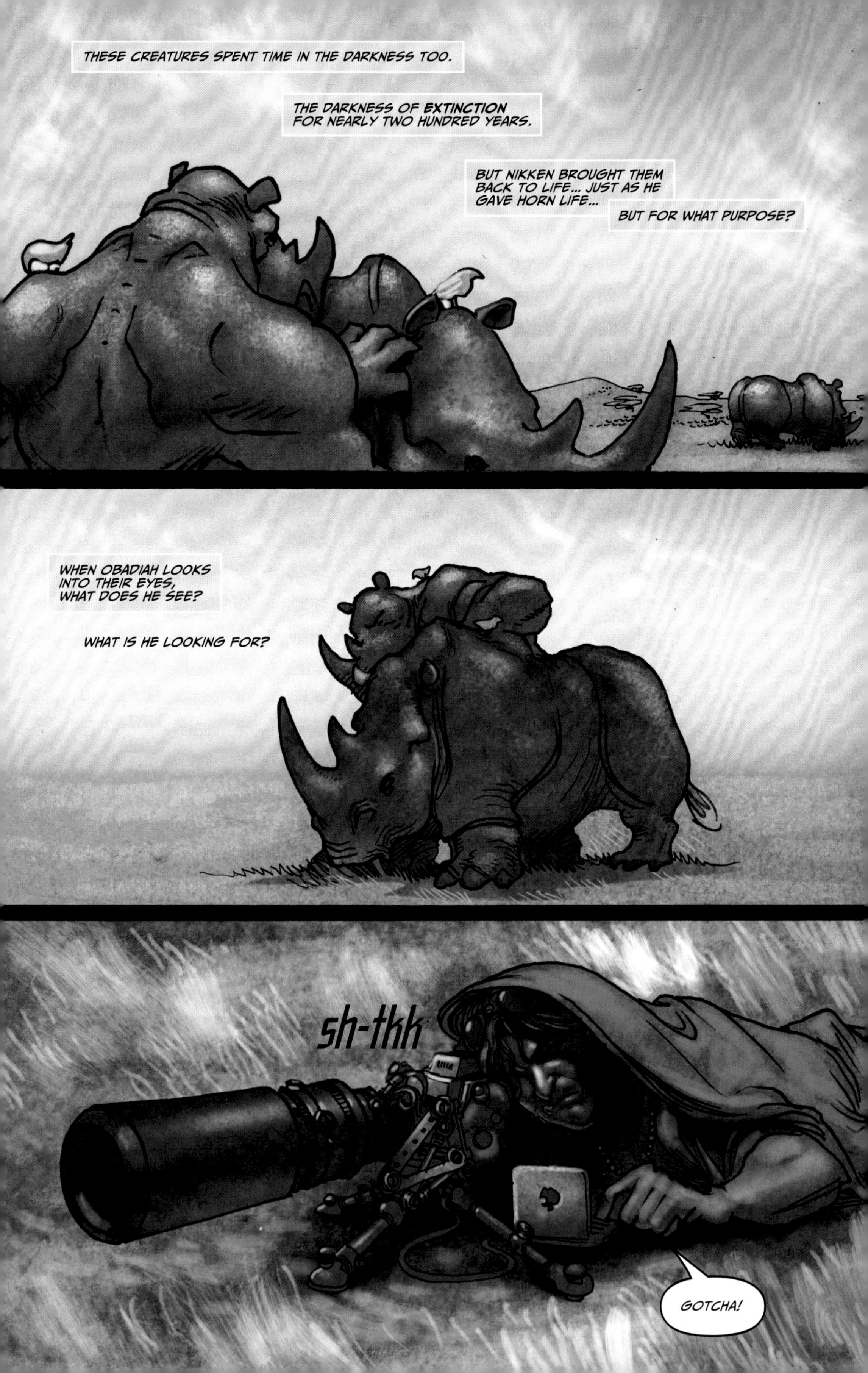
THESE CREATURES SPENT TIME IN THE DARKNESS TOO.
THE DARKNESS OF EXTINCTION FOR NEARLY TWO HUNDRED YEARS.
BUT NIKKEN BROUGHT THEM BACK TO LIFE... JUST AS HE GAVE HORN LIFE...
BUT FOR WHAT PURPOSE?
WHEN OBADIAH LOOKS INTO THEIR EYES, WHAT DOES HE SEE?
WHAT IS HE LOOKING FOR?
sh-tkk
GOTCHA!

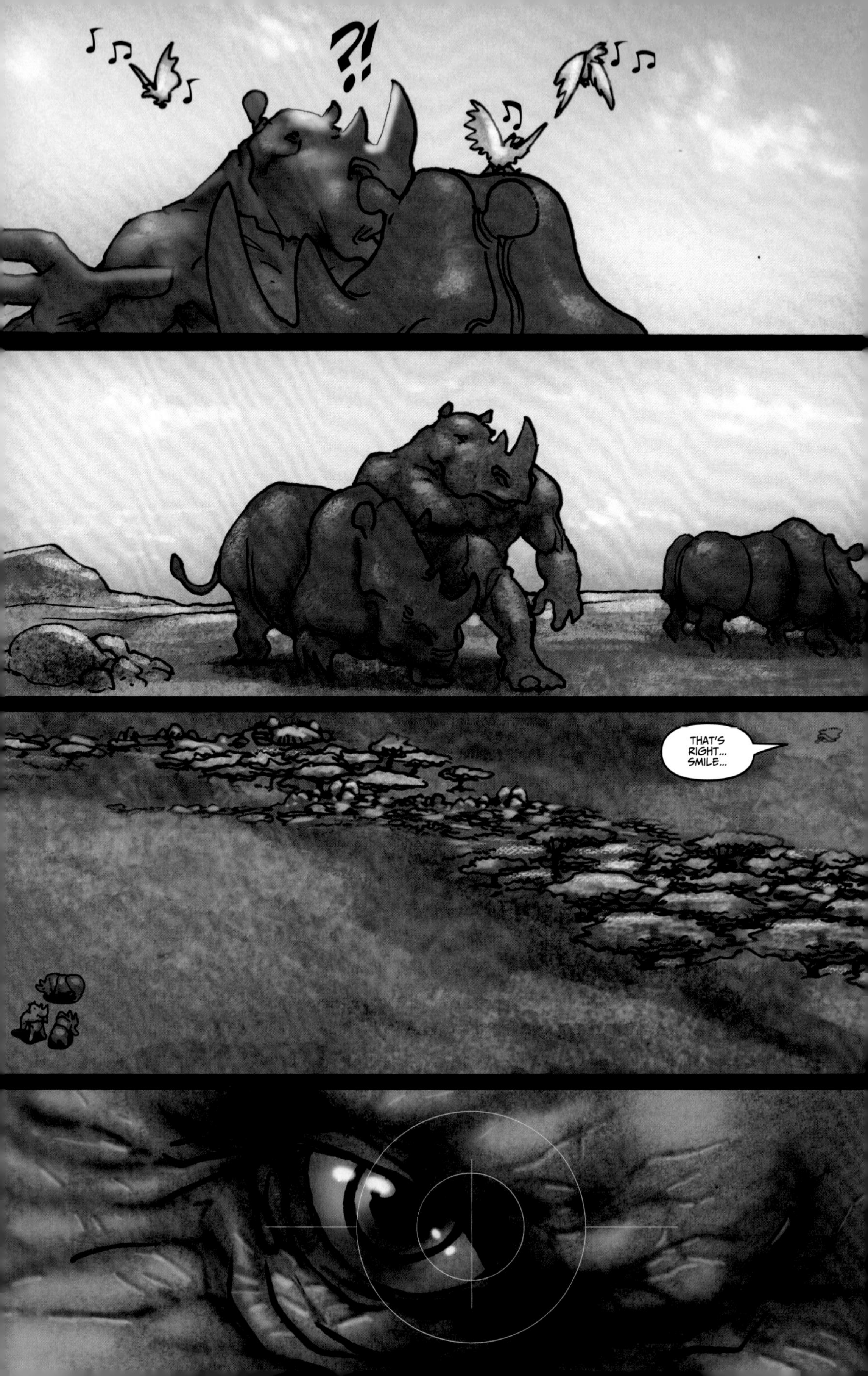
?!
THAT'S RIGHT... SMILE...

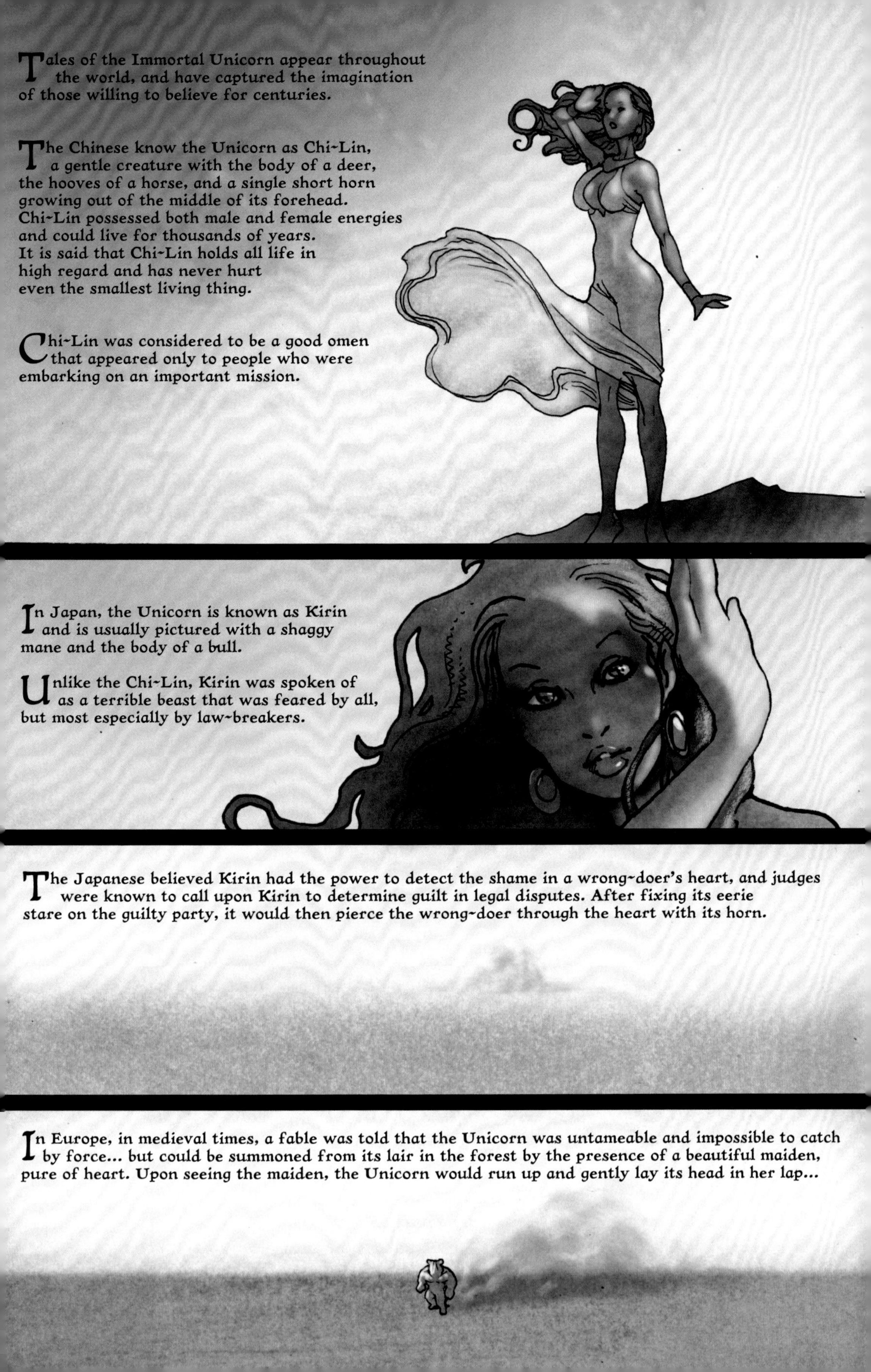
Tales of the Immortal Unicorn appear throughout the world, and have captured the imagination of those willing to believe for centuries.
The Chinese know the Unicorn as Chi-Lin, a gentle creature with the body of a deer, the hooves of a horse, and a single short horn growing out of the middle of its forehead. Chi-Lin possessed both male and female energies and could live for thousands of years. It is said that Chi-Lin holds all life in high regard and has never hurt even the smallest living thing.
Chi-Lin was considered to be a good omen that appeared only to people who were embarking on an important mission.
In Japan, the Unicorn is known as Kirin and is usually pictured with a shaggy mane and the body of a bull.
Unlike the Chi-Lin, Kirin was spoken of as a terrible beast that was feared by all, but most especially by law-breakers.
The Japanese believed Kirin had the power to detect the shame in a wrong-doer's heart, and judges were known to call upon Kirin to determine guilt in legal disputes. After fixing its eerie stare on the guilty party, it would then pierce the wrong-doer through the heart with its horn.
In Europe, in medieval times, a fable was told that the Unicorn was untameable and impossible to catch by force... but could be summoned from its lair in the forest by the presence of a beautiful maiden, pure of heart. Upon seeing the maiden, the Unicorn would run up and gently lay its head in her lap...

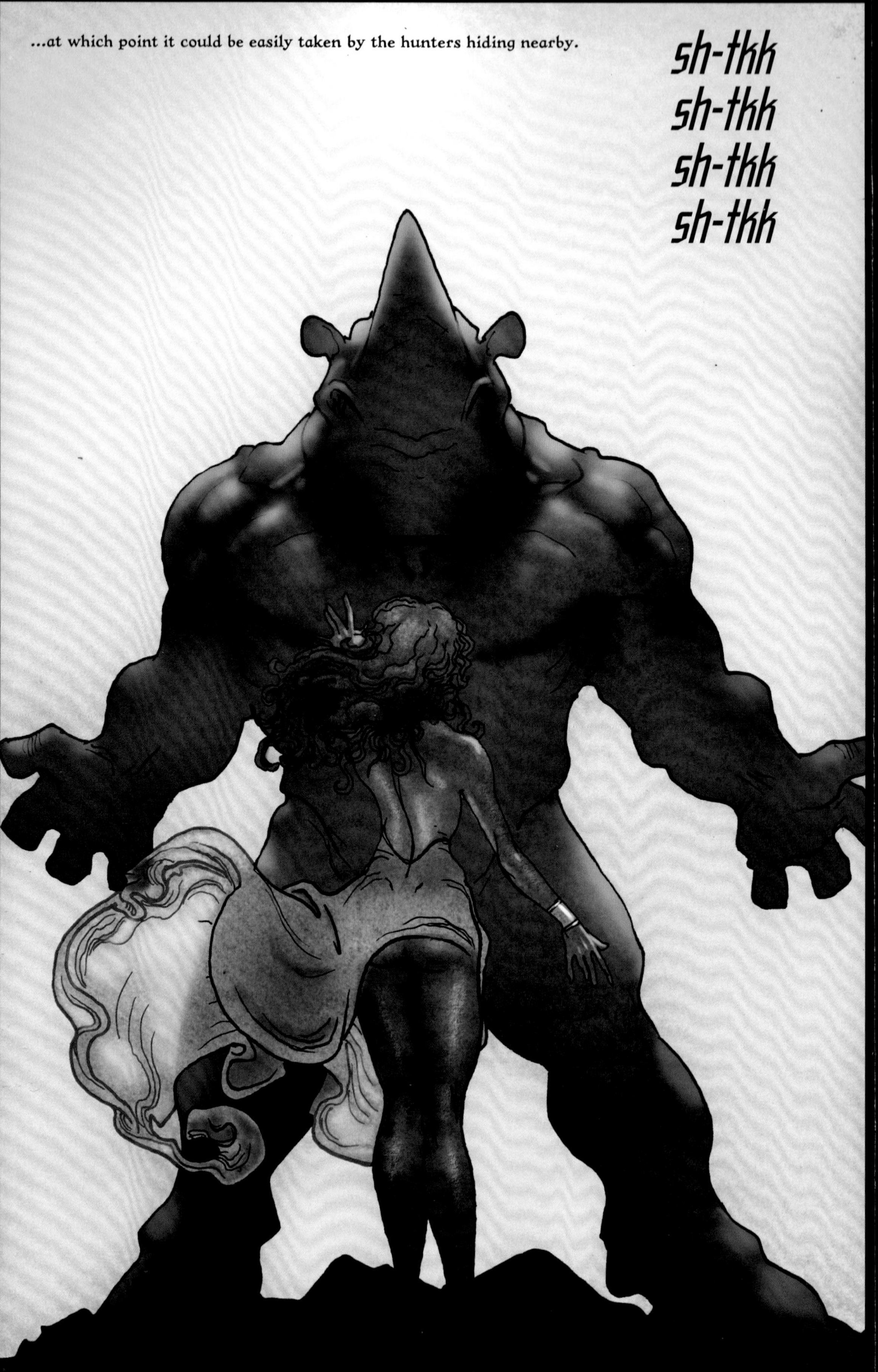
...at which point it could be easily taken by the hunters hiding nearby.
sh-tkk
sh-tkk
sh-tkk
sh-tkk

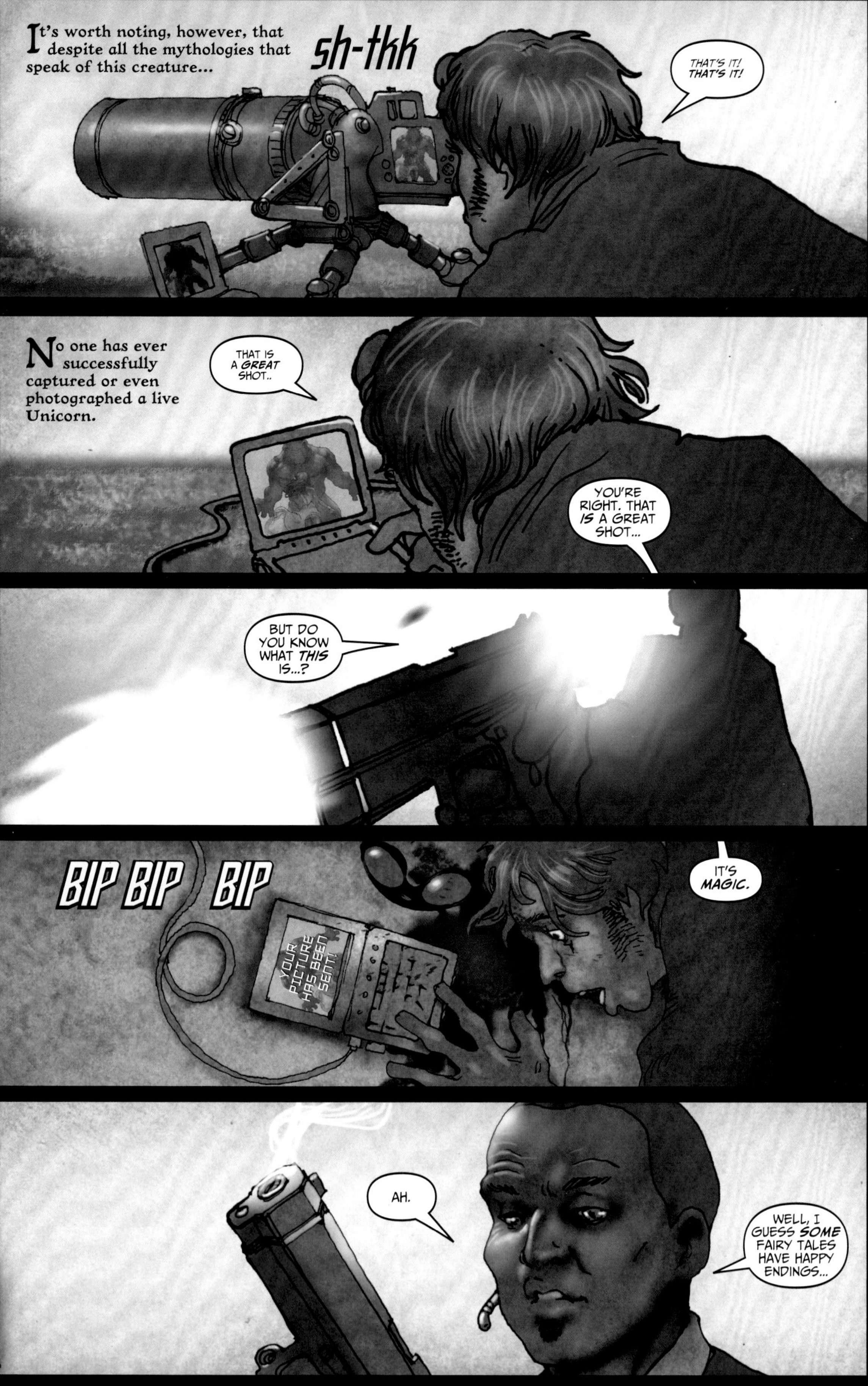
It's worth noting, however, that despite all the mythologies that speak of this creature...
sh-tkk
THAT'S IT! THAT'S IT!
No one has ever successfully captured or even photographed a live Unicorn.
THAT IS A GREAT SHOT..
YOU'RE RIGHT. THAT IS A GREAT SHOT...
BUT DO YOU KNOW WHAT THIS IS...?
BIP BIP BIP
YOUR PICTURE HAS BEEN SENT!
IT'S MAGIC.
AH.
WELL, I GUESS SOME FAIRY TALES HAVE HAPPY ENDINGS...

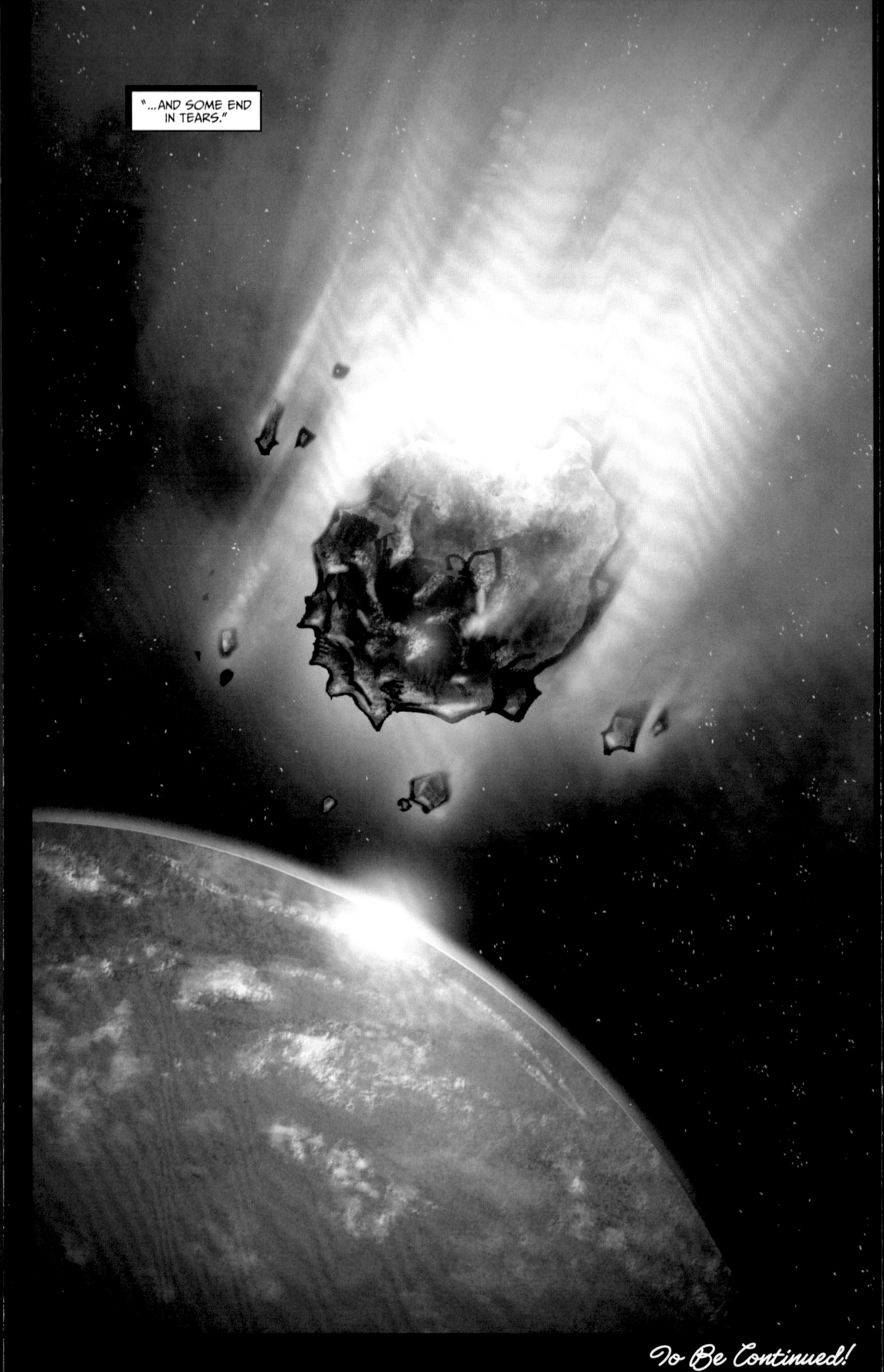
"...AND SOME END IN TEARS."
To Be Continued!

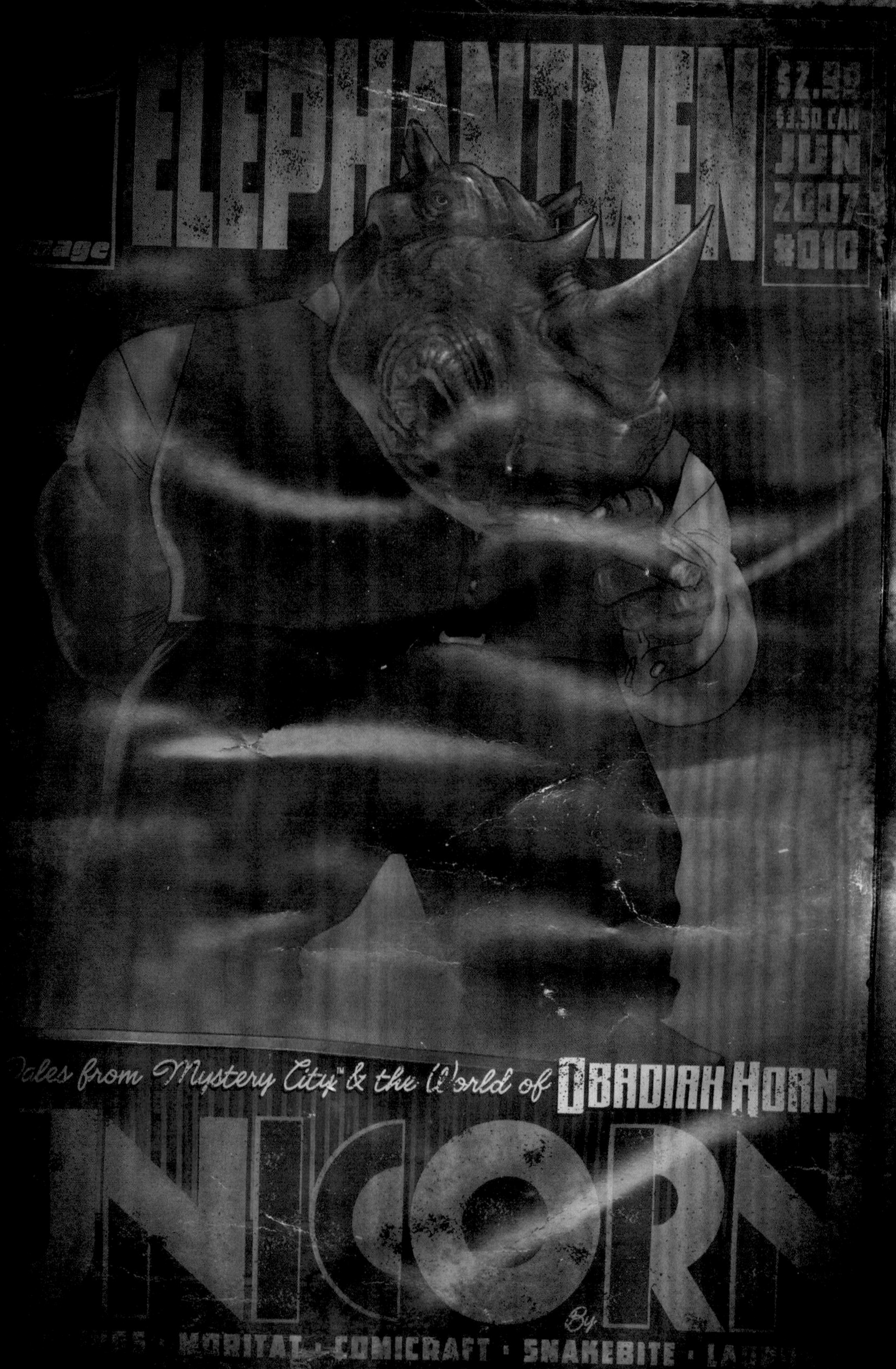
ELEPHANTMEN
$2.99
$3.50 CAN
JUN
2007
#010
Tales from Mystery City™ & the World of OBADIAH HORN
By
MORITAT · COMICRAFT · SNAKEBITE

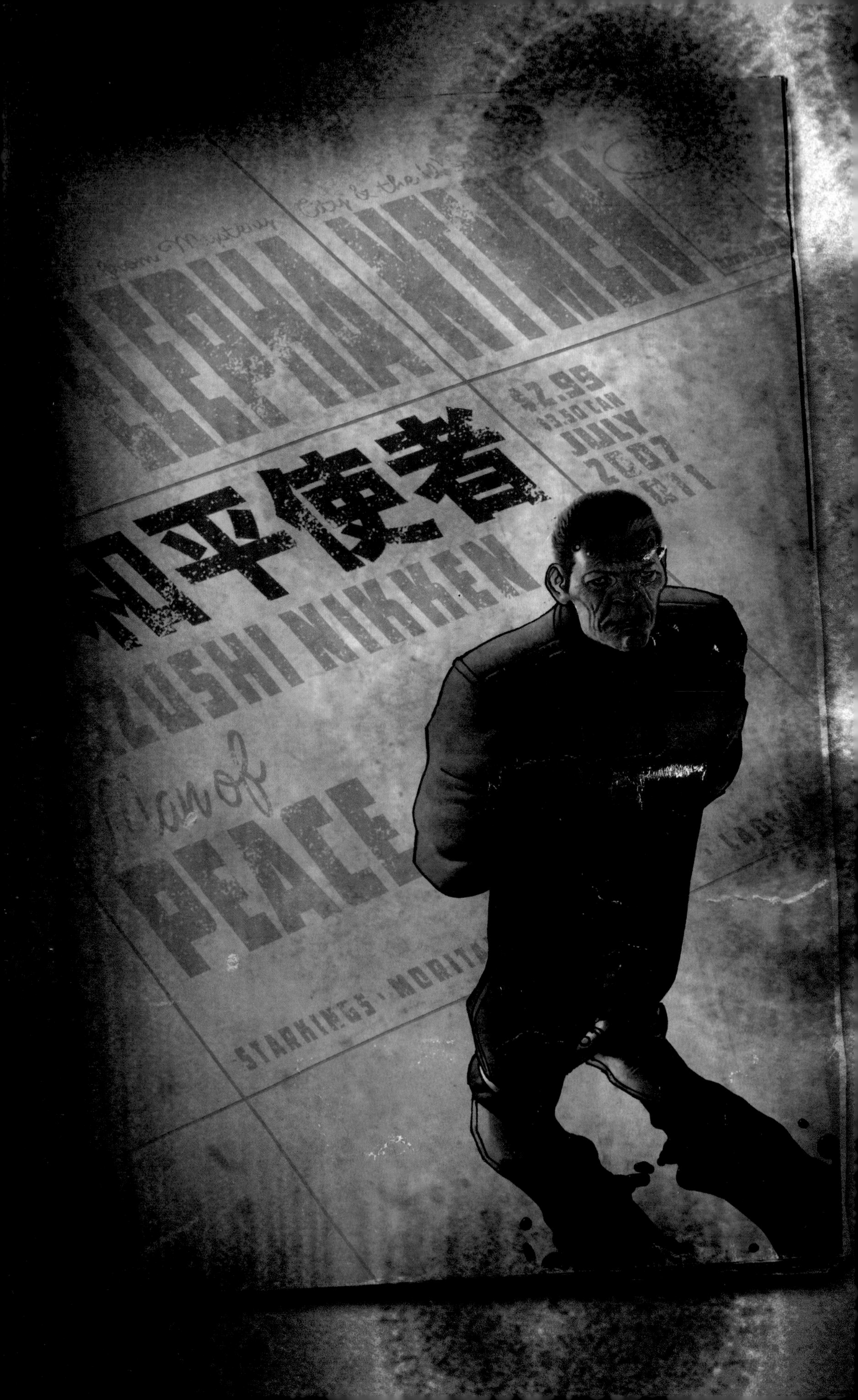

$2.95
$3.50 CAN
JULY
2007
和平使者
NIKKEN
PEACE

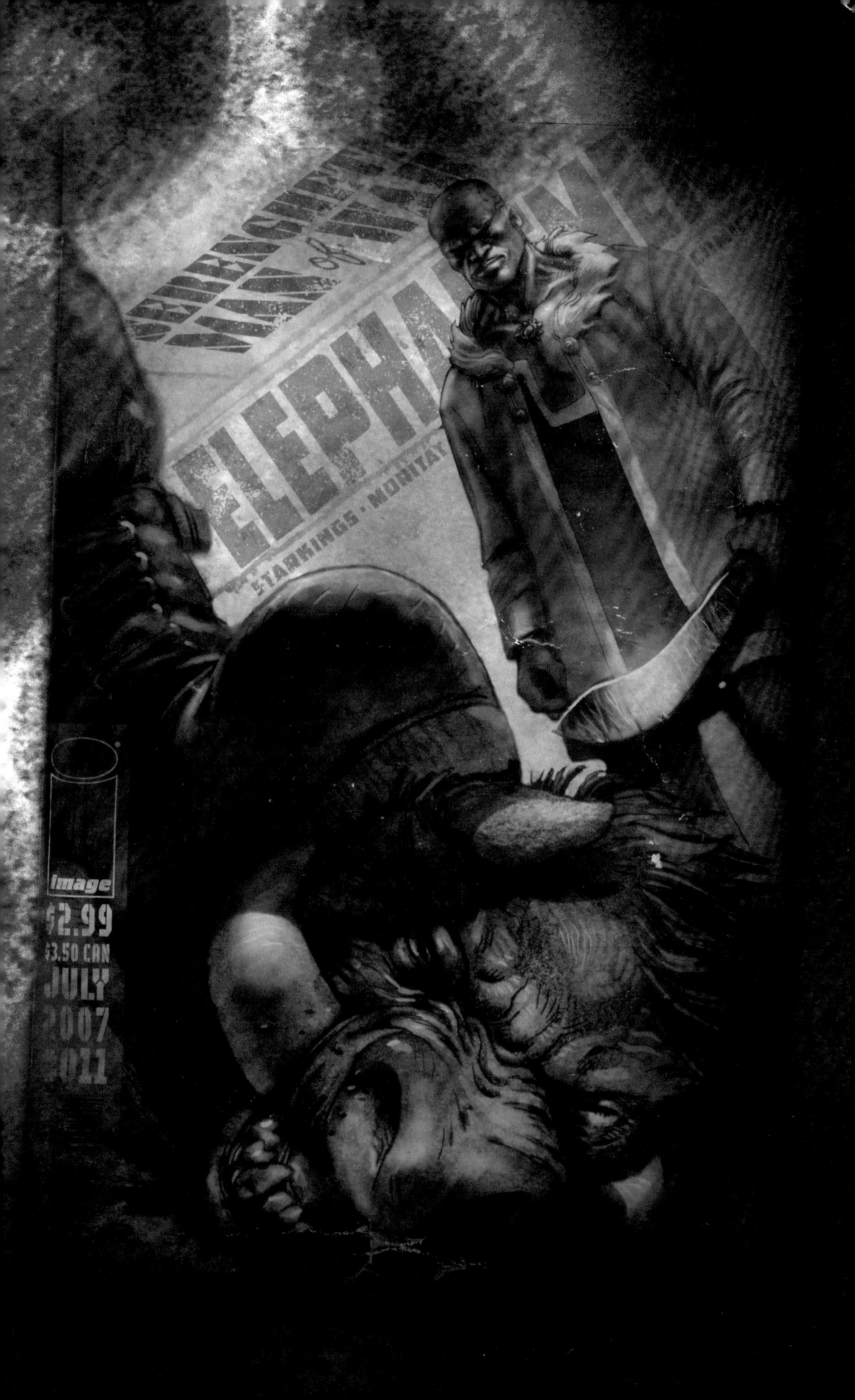
ELEPH
STARKINGS · MORITAT
image
$2.99
$3.50 CAN
JULY
2007
#011

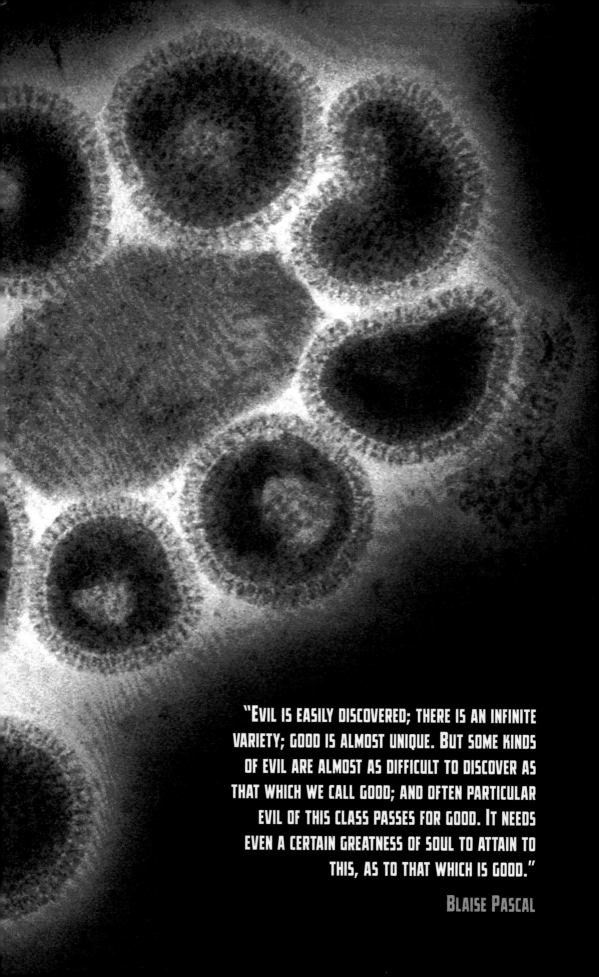

"EVIL IS EASILY DISCOVERED; THERE IS AN INFINITE VARIETY; GOOD IS ALMOST UNIQUE. BUT SOME KINDS OF EVIL ARE ALMOST AS DIFFICULT TO DISCOVER AS THAT WHICH WE CALL GOOD; AND OFTEN PARTICULAR EVIL OF THIS CLASS PASSES FOR GOOD. IT NEEDS EVEN A CERTAIN GREATNESS OF SOUL TO ATTAIN TO THIS, AS TO THAT WHICH IS GOOD."

BLAISE PASCAL

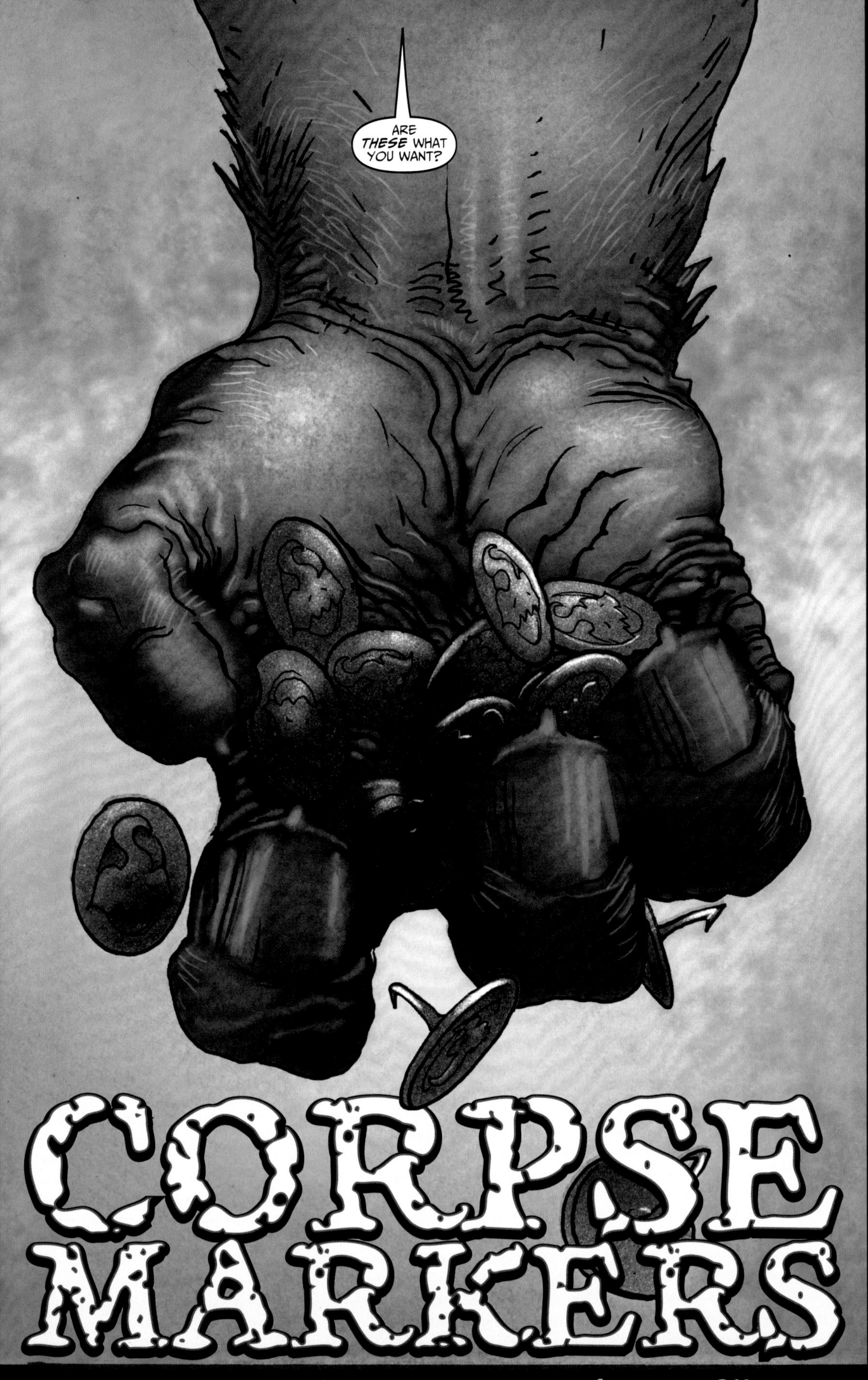
ARE THESE WHAT YOU WANT?
CORPSE MARKERS

By Starkings & Moritat

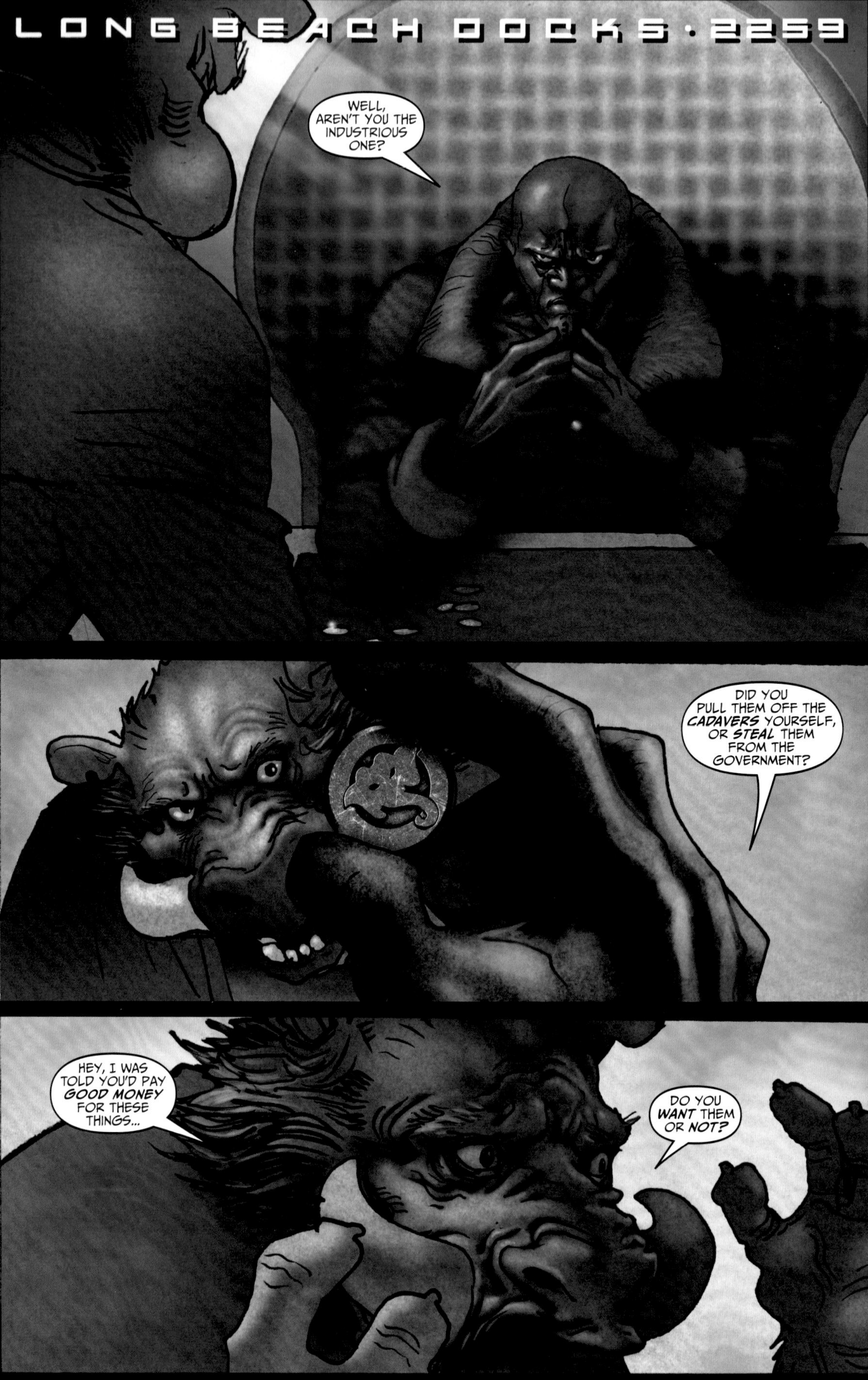
LONG BEACH DOCKS · 2259
WELL, AREN'T YOU THE INDUSTRIOUS ONE?
DID YOU PULL THEM OFF THE CADAVERS YOURSELF, OR STEAL THEM FROM THE GOVERNMENT?
HEY, I WAS TOLD YOU'D PAY GOOD MONEY FOR THESE THINGS...
DO YOU WANT THEM OR NOT?

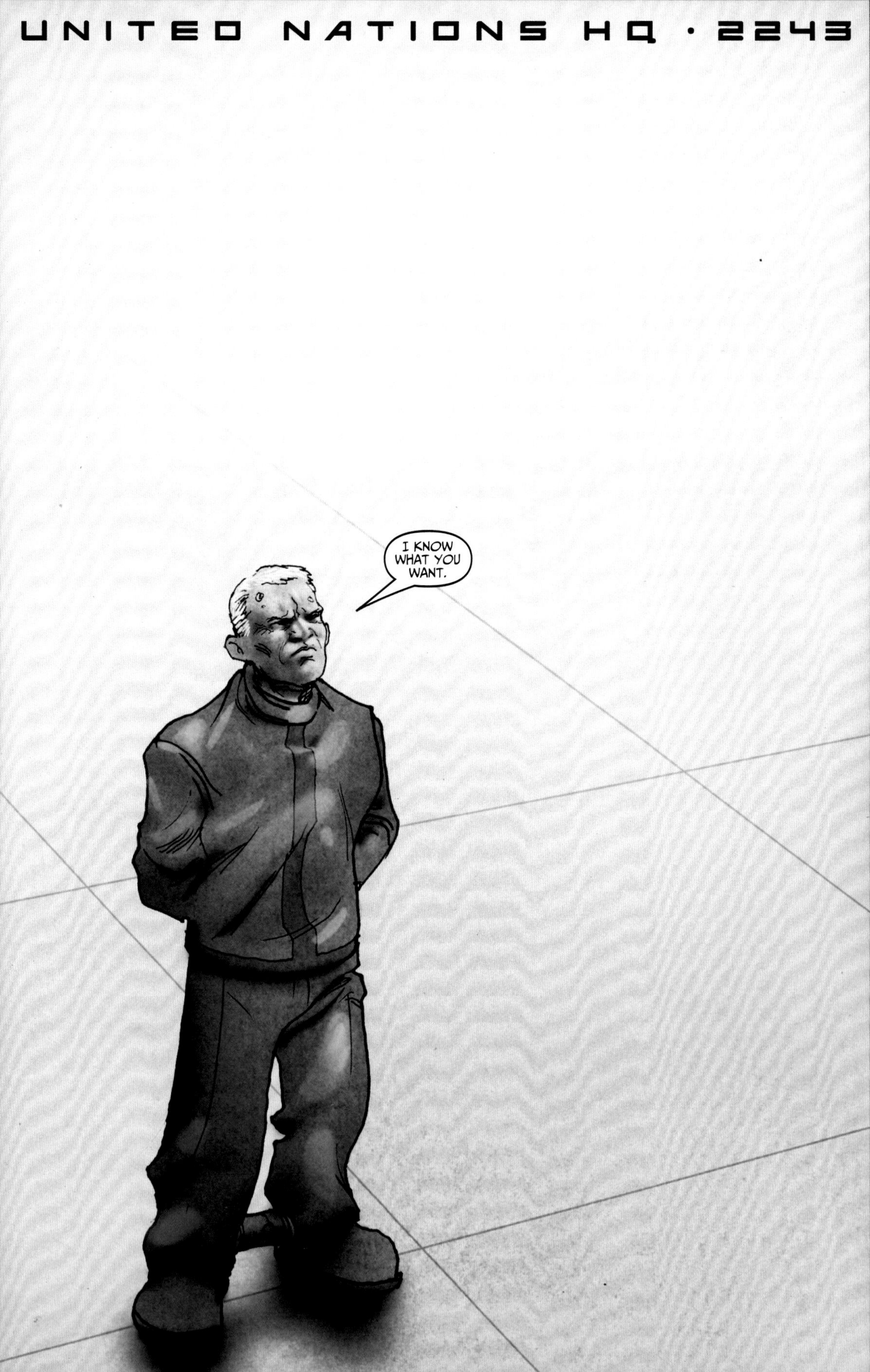
UNITED NATIONS HQ · 2243
I KNOW WHAT YOU WANT.

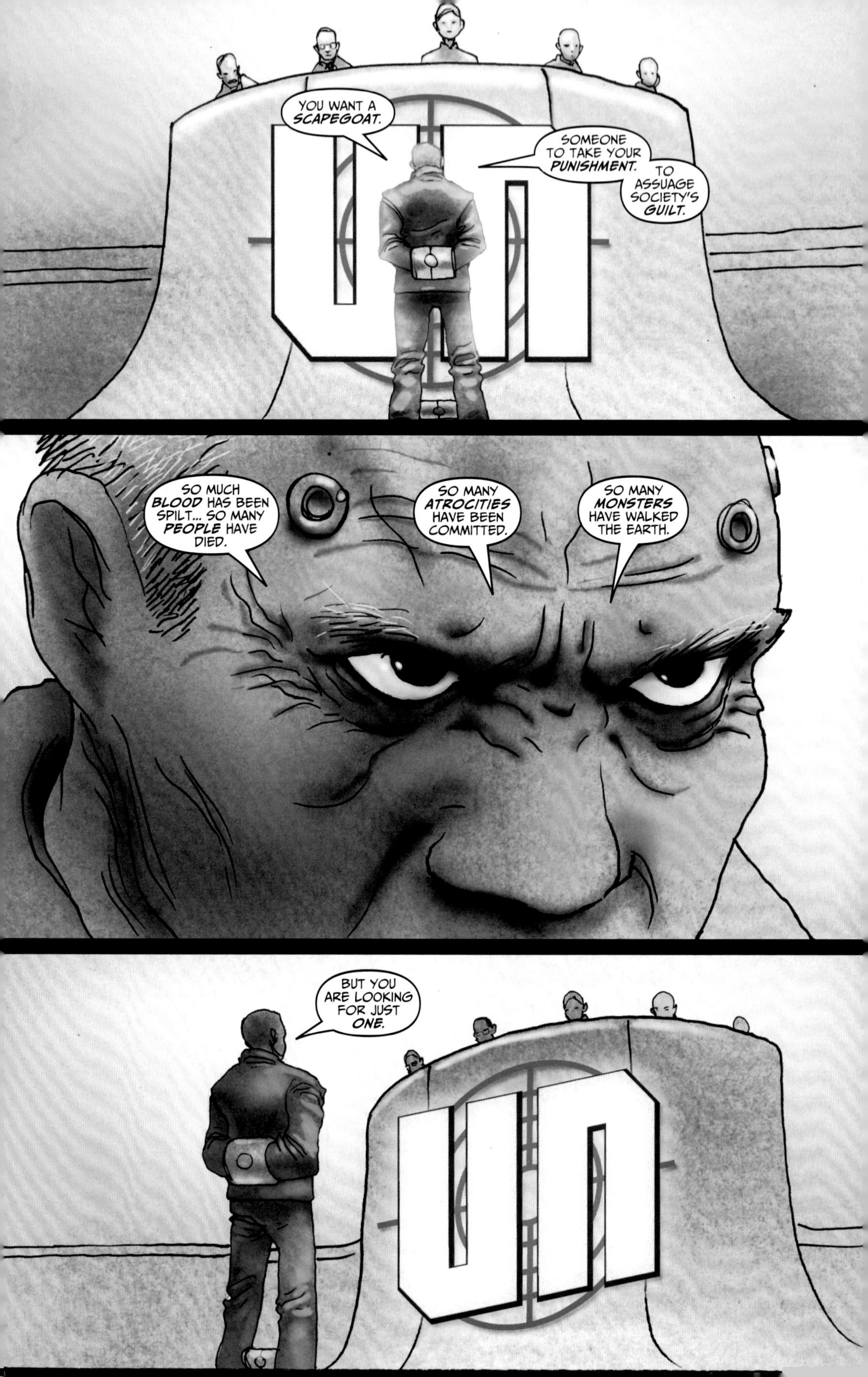
YOU WANT A SCAPEGOAT.
SOMEONE TO TAKE YOUR PUNISHMENT.
TO ASSUAGE SOCIETY'S GUILT.
SO MUCH BLOOD HAS BEEN SPILT... SO MANY PEOPLE HAVE DIED.
SO MANY ATROCITIES HAVE BEEN COMMITTED.
SO MANY MONSTERS HAVE WALKED THE EARTH.
BUT YOU ARE LOOKING FOR JUST ONE.

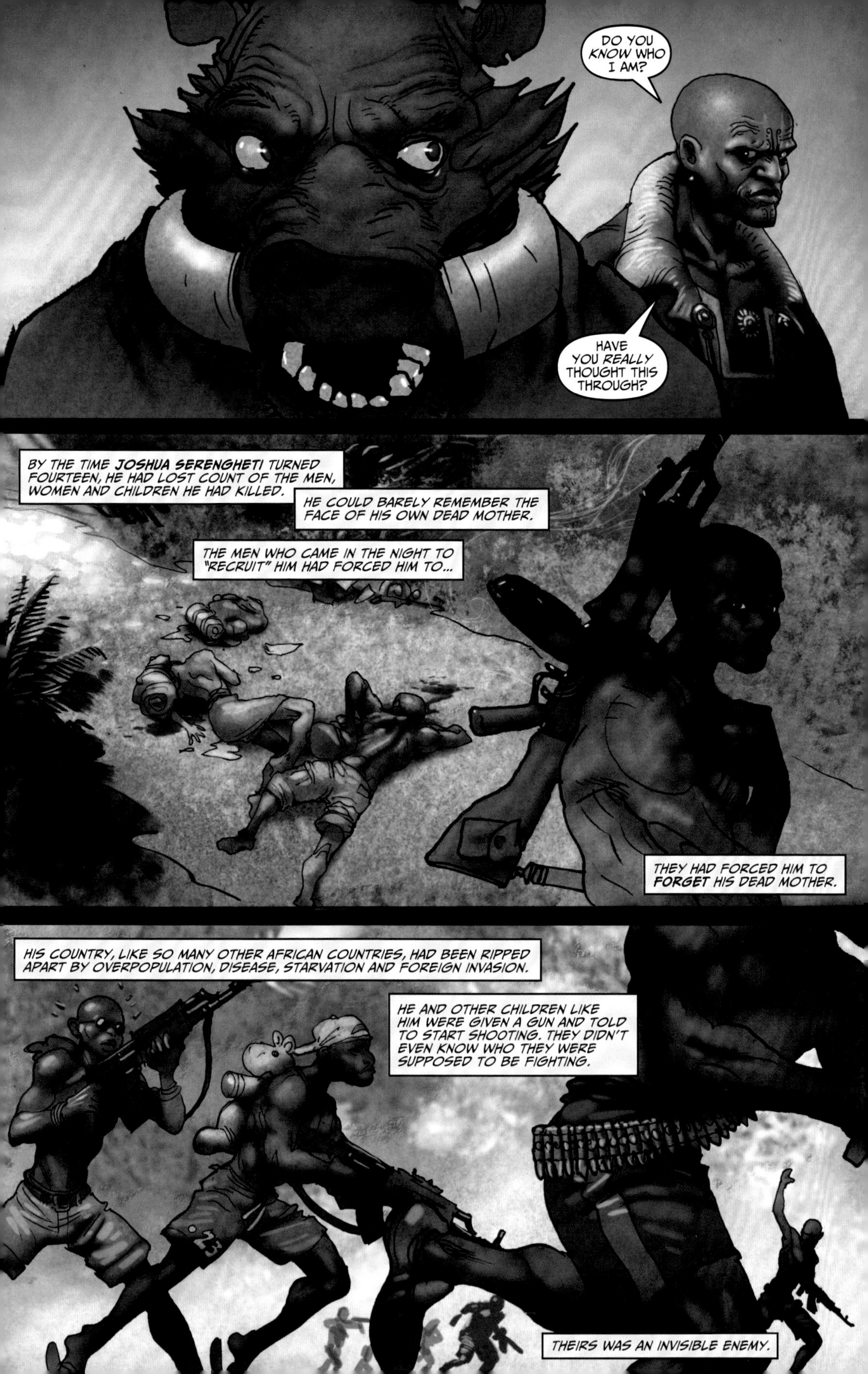
DO YOU KNOW WHO I AM?
HAVE YOU *REALLY* THOUGHT THIS THROUGH?
BY THE TIME **JOSHUA SERENGHETI** TURNED FOURTEEN, HE HAD LOST COUNT OF THE MEN, WOMEN AND CHILDREN HE HAD KILLED.
HE COULD BARELY REMEMBER THE FACE OF HIS OWN DEAD MOTHER.
THE MEN WHO CAME IN THE NIGHT TO "RECRUIT" HIM HAD FORCED HIM TO...
THEY HAD FORCED HIM TO **FORGET** HIS DEAD MOTHER.
HIS COUNTRY, LIKE SO MANY OTHER AFRICAN COUNTRIES, HAD BEEN RIPPED APART BY OVERPOPULATION, DISEASE, STARVATION AND FOREIGN INVASION.
HE AND OTHER CHILDREN LIKE HIM WERE GIVEN A GUN AND TOLD TO START SHOOTING. THEY DIDN'T EVEN KNOW WHO THEY WERE SUPPOSED TO BE FIGHTING.
THEIRS WAS AN INVISIBLE ENEMY.

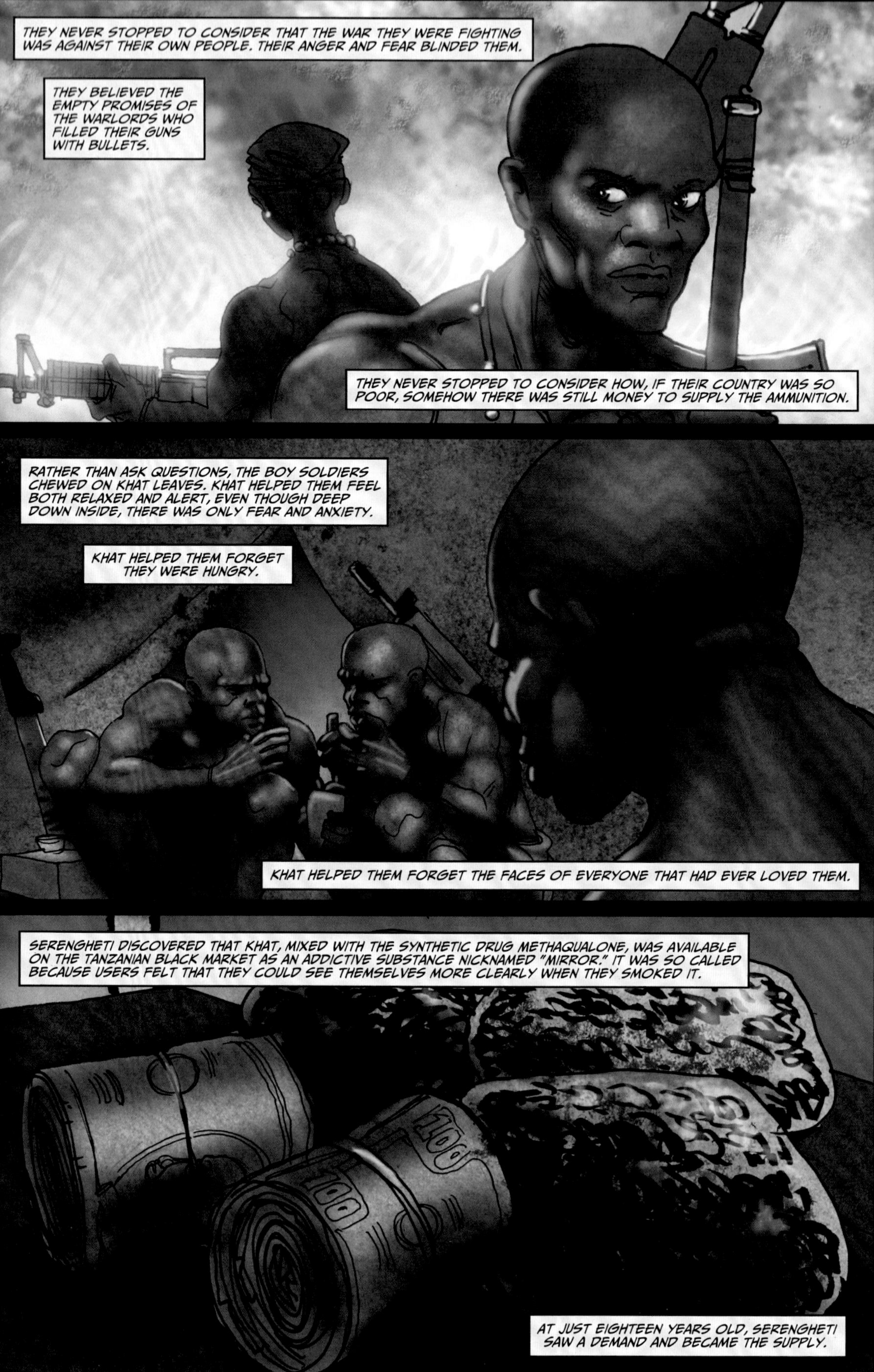
THEY NEVER STOPPED TO CONSIDER THAT THE WAR THEY WERE FIGHTING WAS AGAINST THEIR OWN PEOPLE. THEIR ANGER AND FEAR BLINDED THEM.
THEY BELIEVED THE EMPTY PROMISES OF THE WARLORDS WHO FILLED THEIR GUNS WITH BULLETS.
THEY NEVER STOPPED TO CONSIDER HOW, IF THEIR COUNTRY WAS SO POOR, SOMEHOW THERE WAS STILL MONEY TO SUPPLY THE AMMUNITION.
RATHER THAN ASK QUESTIONS, THE BOY SOLDIERS CHEWED ON KHAT LEAVES. KHAT HELPED THEM FEEL BOTH RELAXED AND ALERT, EVEN THOUGH DEEP DOWN INSIDE, THERE WAS ONLY FEAR AND ANXIETY.
KHAT HELPED THEM FORGET THEY WERE HUNGRY.
KHAT HELPED THEM FORGET THE FACES OF EVERYONE THAT HAD EVER LOVED THEM.
SERENGHETI DISCOVERED THAT KHAT, MIXED WITH THE SYNTHETIC DRUG METHAQUALONE, WAS AVAILABLE ON THE TANZANIAN BLACK MARKET AS AN ADDICTIVE SUBSTANCE NICKNAMED "MIRROR." IT WAS SO CALLED BECAUSE USERS FELT THAT THEY COULD SEE THEMSELVES MORE CLEARLY WHEN THEY SMOKED IT.
AT JUST EIGHTEEN YEARS OLD, SERENGHETI SAW A DEMAND AND BECAME THE SUPPLY.

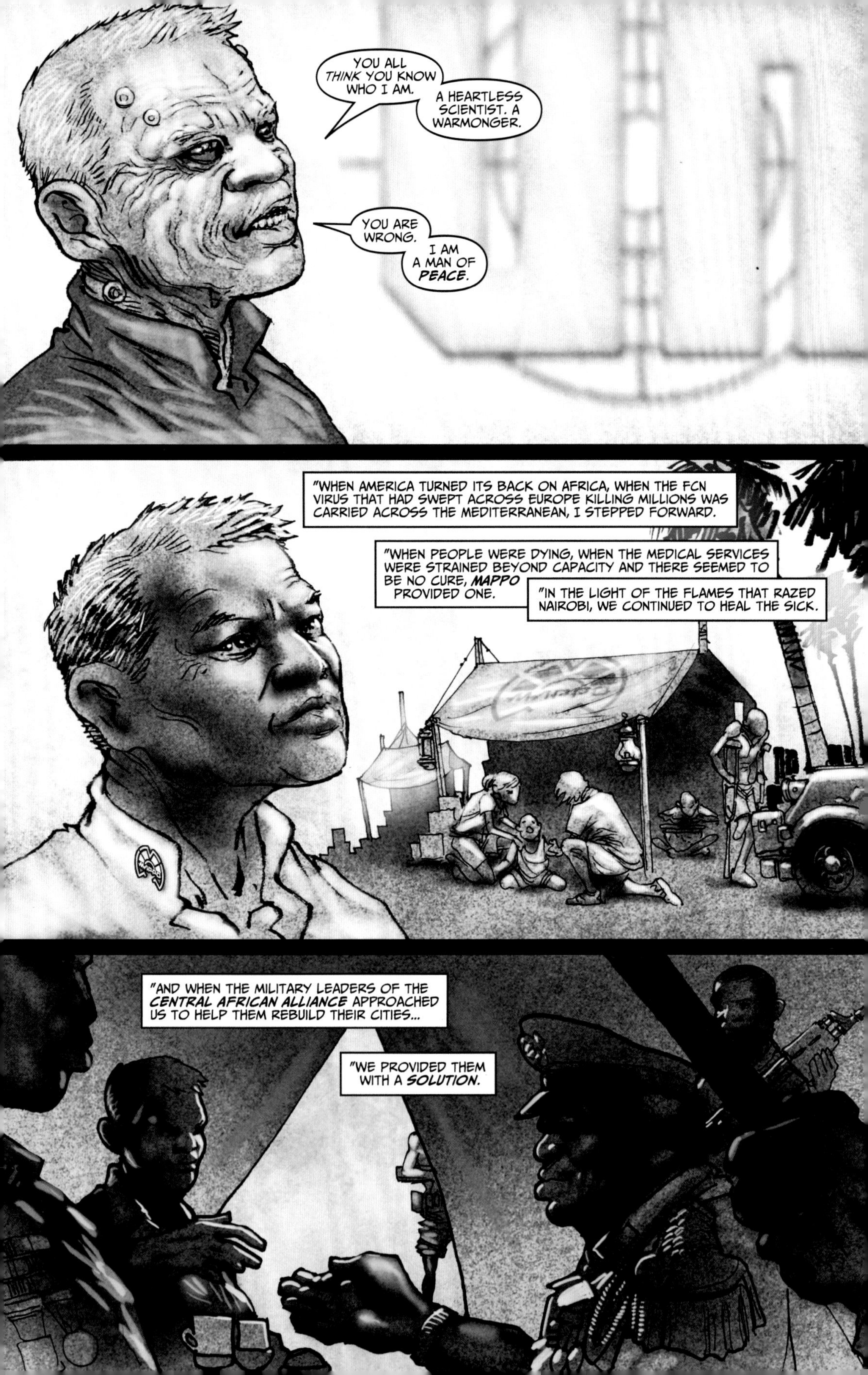
YOU ALL THINK YOU KNOW WHO I AM.
A HEARTLESS SCIENTIST. A WARMONGER.
YOU ARE WRONG.
I AM A MAN OF PEACE.
"WHEN AMERICA TURNED ITS BACK ON AFRICA, WHEN THE FCN VIRUS THAT HAD SWEPT ACROSS EUROPE KILLING MILLIONS WAS CARRIED ACROSS THE MEDITERRANEAN, I STEPPED FORWARD.
"WHEN PEOPLE WERE DYING, WHEN THE MEDICAL SERVICES WERE STRAINED BEYOND CAPACITY AND THERE SEEMED TO BE NO CURE, MAPPO PROVIDED ONE.
"IN THE LIGHT OF THE FLAMES THAT RAZED NAIROBI, WE CONTINUED TO HEAL THE SICK.
"AND WHEN THE MILITARY LEADERS OF THE CENTRAL AFRICAN ALLIANCE APPROACHED US TO HELP THEM REBUILD THEIR CITIES...
"WE PROVIDED THEM WITH A SOLUTION.

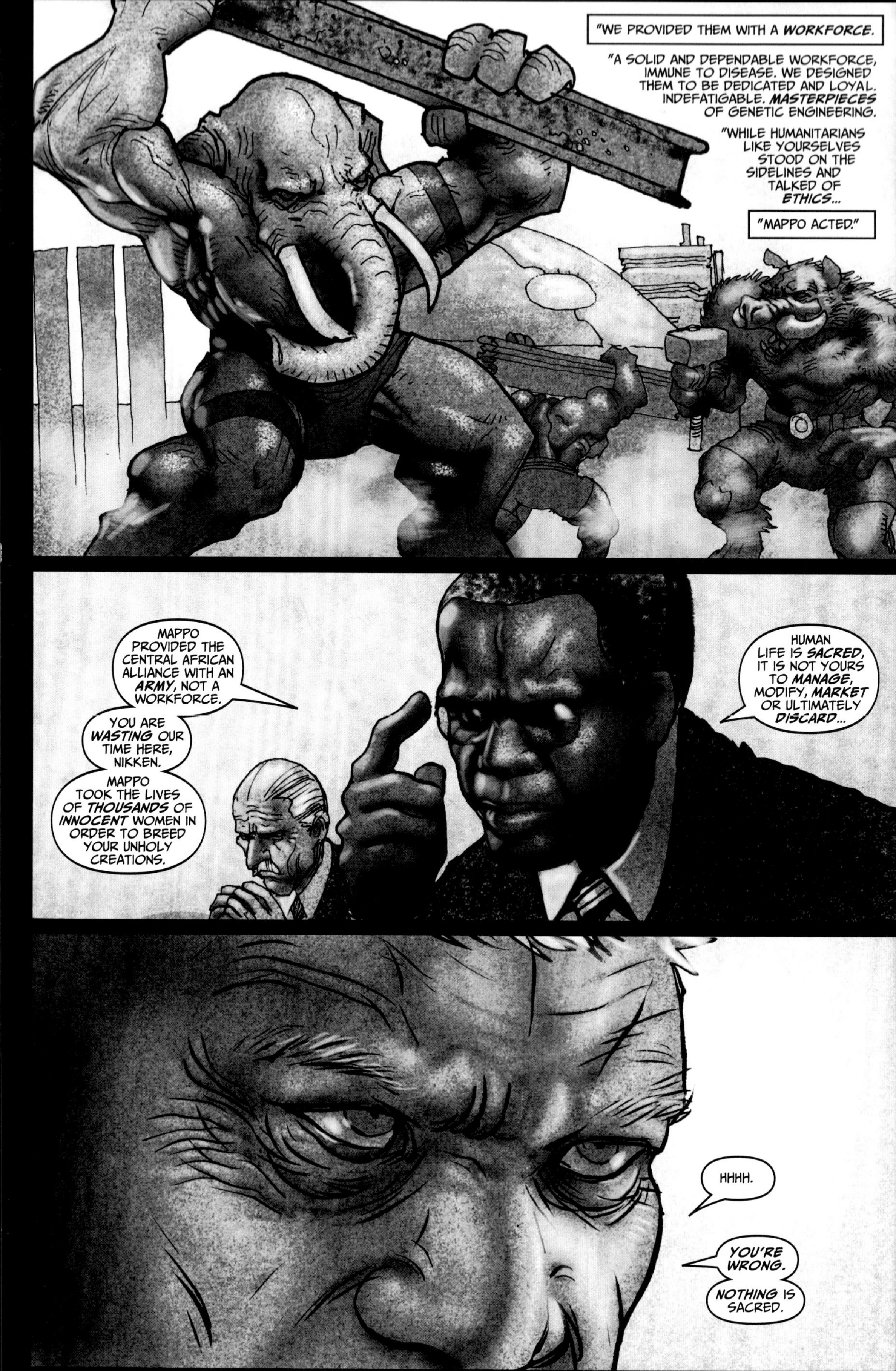
"WE PROVIDED THEM WITH A WORKFORCE.
"A SOLID AND DEPENDABLE WORKFORCE, IMMUNE TO DISEASE. WE DESIGNED THEM TO BE DEDICATED AND LOYAL. INDEFATIGABLE. MASTERPIECES OF GENETIC ENGINEERING.
"WHILE HUMANITARIANS LIKE YOURSELVES STOOD ON THE SIDELINES AND TALKED OF ETHICS...
"MAPPO ACTED."
HUMAN LIFE IS SACRED, IT IS NOT YOURS TO MANAGE, MODIFY, MARKET OR ULTIMATELY DISCARD...
MAPPO PROVIDED THE CENTRAL AFRICAN ALLIANCE WITH AN ARMY, NOT A WORKFORCE.
YOU ARE WASTING OUR TIME HERE, NIKKEN.
MAPPO TOOK THE LIVES OF THOUSANDS OF INNOCENT WOMEN IN ORDER TO BREED YOUR UNHOLY CREATIONS.
HHHH.
YOU'RE WRONG.
NOTHING IS SACRED.

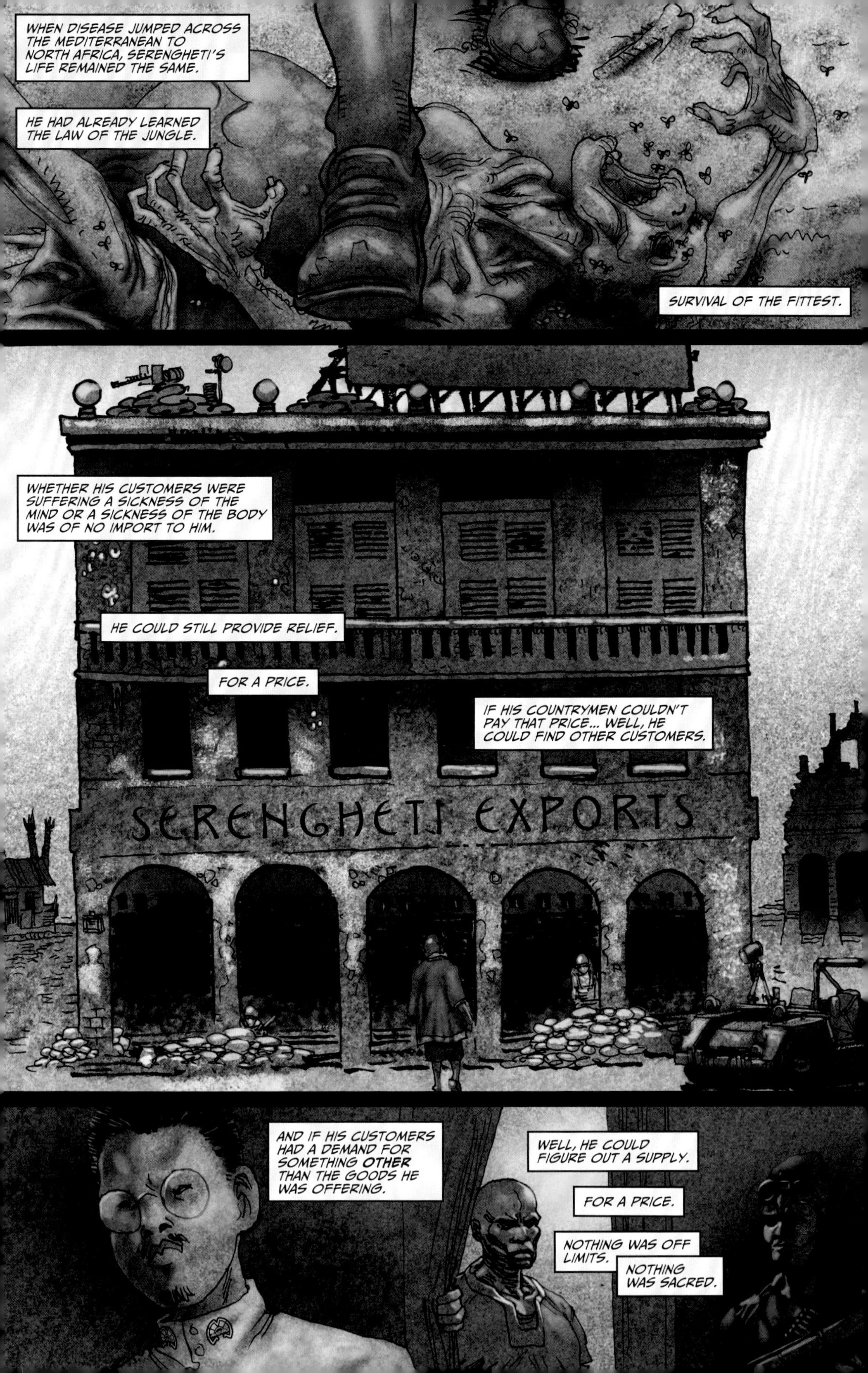

WHEN DISEASE JUMPED ACROSS THE MEDITERRANEAN TO NORTH AFRICA, SERENGHETI'S LIFE REMAINED THE SAME.
HE HAD ALREADY LEARNED THE LAW OF THE JUNGLE.
SURVIVAL OF THE FITTEST.
WHETHER HIS CUSTOMERS WERE SUFFERING A SICKNESS OF THE MIND OR A SICKNESS OF THE BODY WAS OF NO IMPORT TO HIM.
HE COULD STILL PROVIDE RELIEF.
FOR A PRICE.
IF HIS COUNTRYMEN COULDN'T PAY THAT PRICE... WELL, HE COULD FIND OTHER CUSTOMERS.
SERENGHETI EXPORTS
AND IF HIS CUSTOMERS HAD A DEMAND FOR SOMETHING **OTHER** THAN THE GOODS HE WAS OFFERING.
WELL, HE COULD FIGURE OUT A SUPPLY.
FOR A PRICE.
NOTHING WAS OFF LIMITS.
NOTHING WAS SACRED.

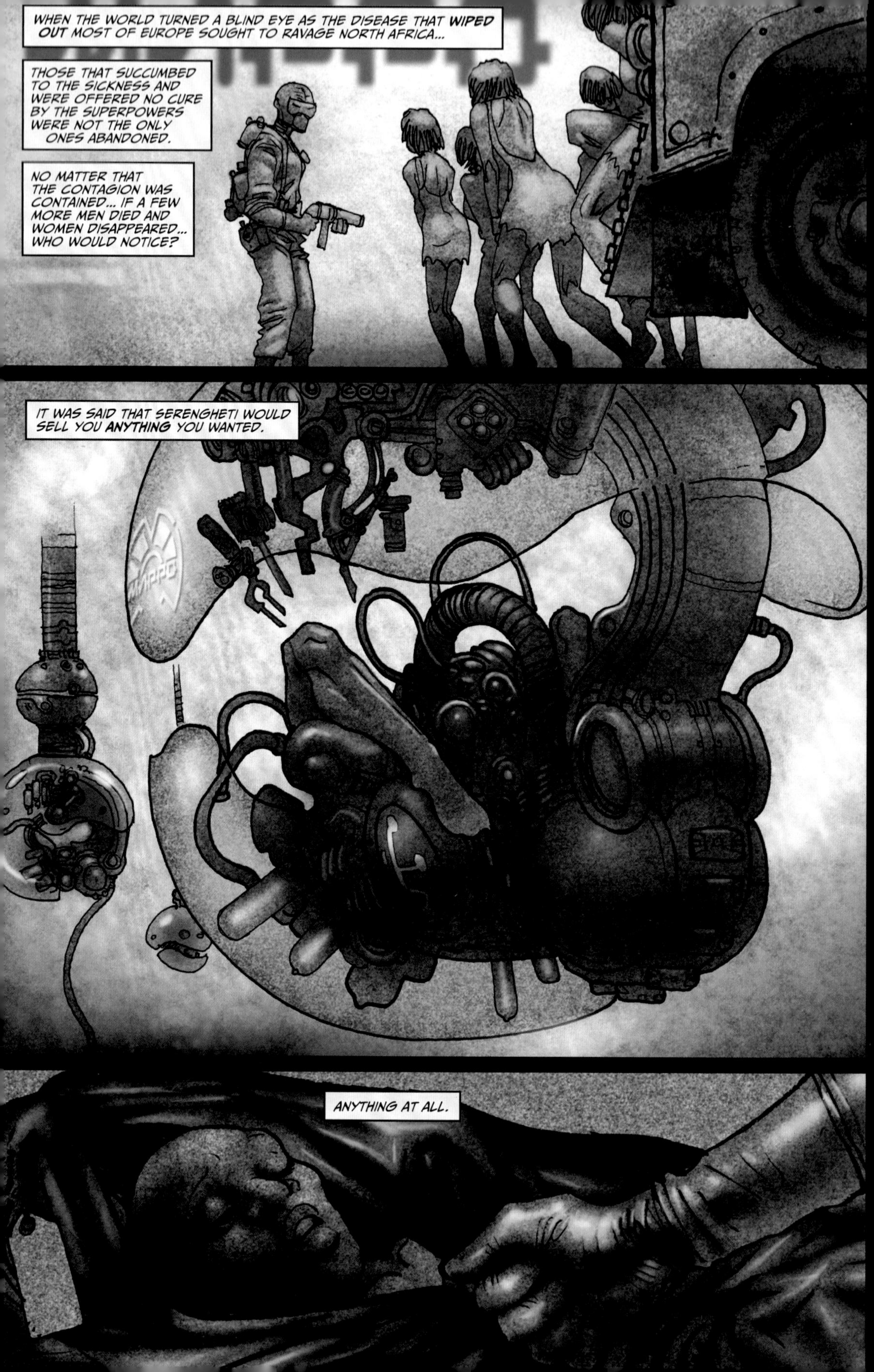
WHEN THE WORLD TURNED A BLIND EYE AS THE DISEASE THAT WIPED OUT MOST OF EUROPE SOUGHT TO RAVAGE NORTH AFRICA...
THOSE THAT SUCCUMBED TO THE SICKNESS AND WERE OFFERED NO CURE BY THE SUPERPOWERS WERE NOT THE ONLY ONES ABANDONED.
NO MATTER THAT THE CONTAGION WAS CONTAINED... IF A FEW MORE MEN DIED AND WOMEN DISAPPEARED... WHO WOULD NOTICE?
IT WAS SAID THAT SERENGHETI WOULD SELL YOU ANYTHING YOU WANTED.
ANYTHING AT ALL.

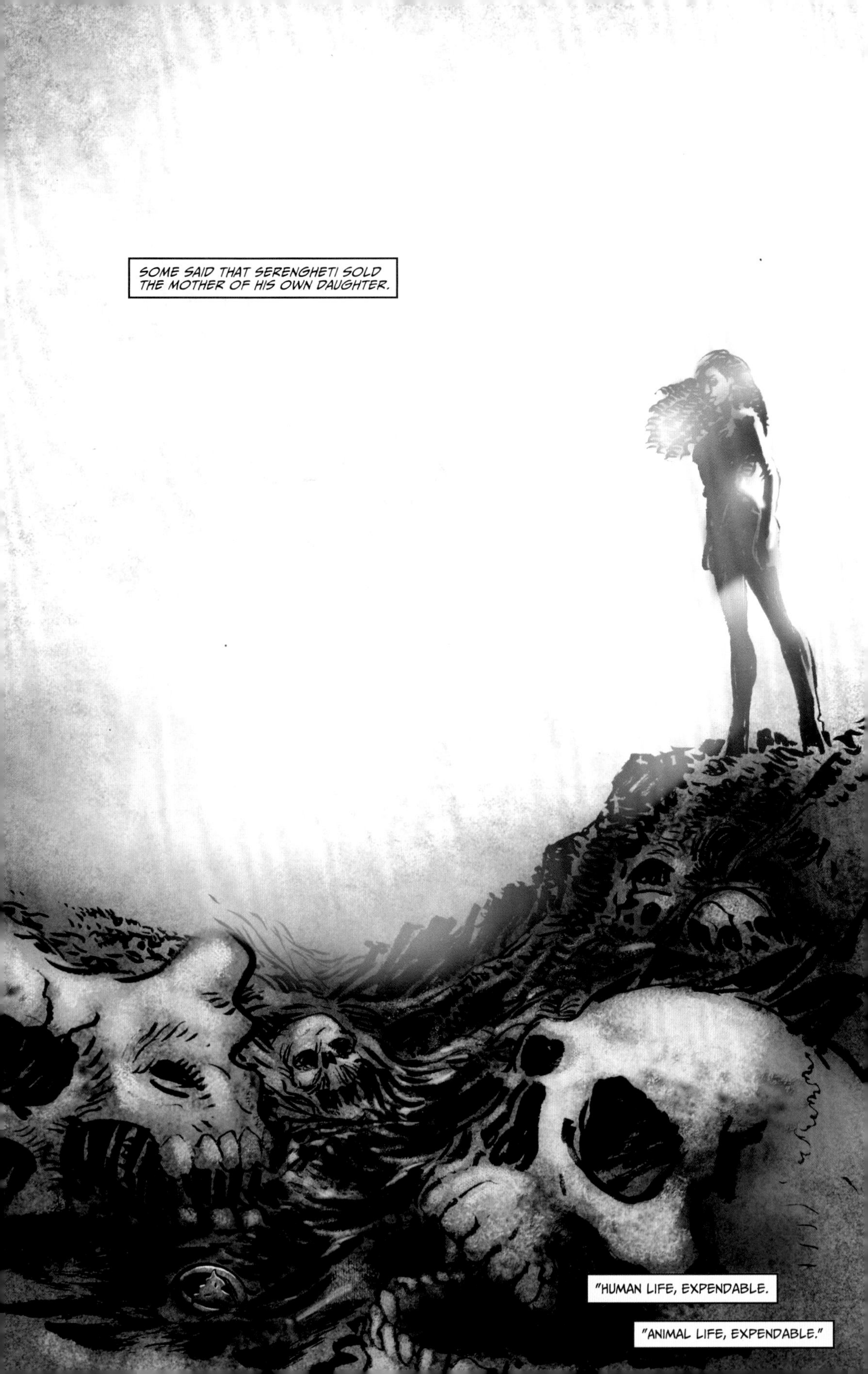
SOME SAID THAT SERENGHETI SOLD THE MOTHER OF HIS OWN DAUGHTER.
"HUMAN LIFE, EXPENDABLE.
"ANIMAL LIFE, EXPENDABLE."

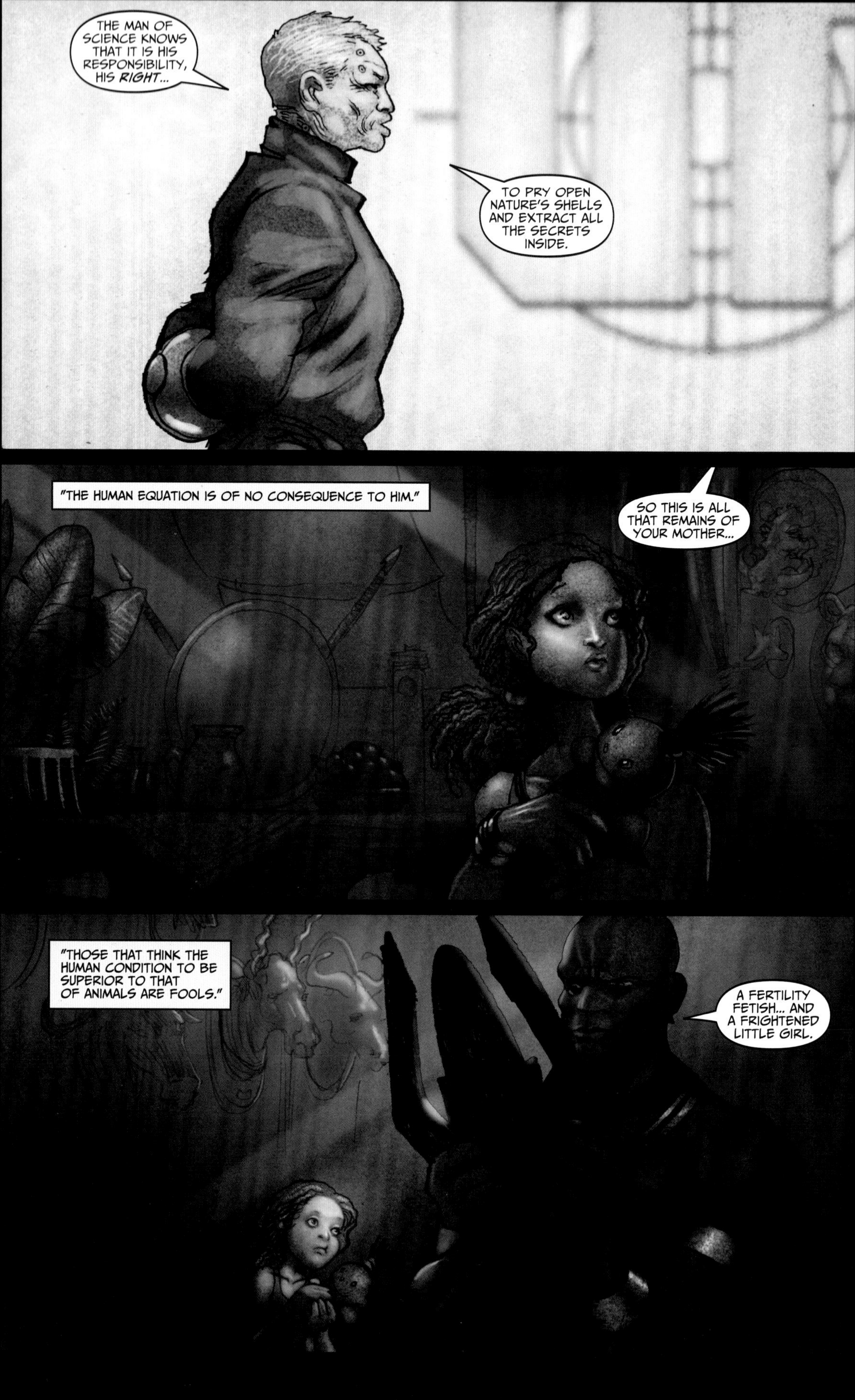
THE MAN OF SCIENCE KNOWS THAT IT IS HIS RESPONSIBILITY, HIS *RIGHT*...
TO PRY OPEN NATURE'S SHELLS AND EXTRACT ALL THE SECRETS INSIDE.
"THE HUMAN EQUATION IS OF NO CONSEQUENCE TO HIM."
SO THIS IS ALL THAT REMAINS OF YOUR MOTHER...
"THOSE THAT THINK THE HUMAN CONDITION TO BE SUPERIOR TO THAT OF ANIMALS ARE FOOLS."
A FERTILITY FETISH... AND A FRIGHTENED LITTLE GIRL.

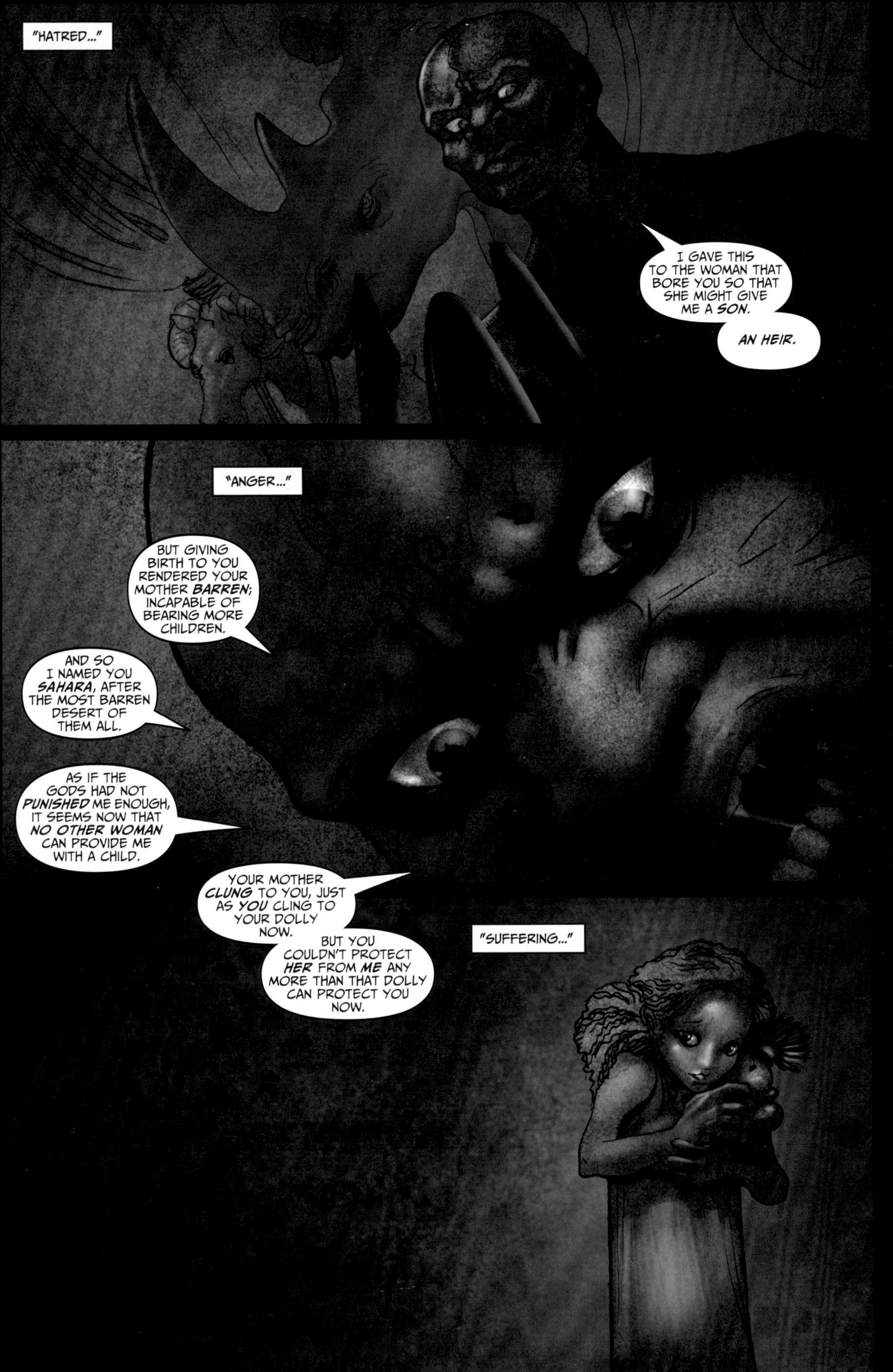
"HATRED..."
I GAVE THIS TO THE WOMAN THAT BORE YOU SO THAT SHE MIGHT GIVE ME A SON.
AN HEIR.
"ANGER..."
BUT GIVING BIRTH TO YOU RENDERED YOUR MOTHER BARREN; INCAPABLE OF BEARING MORE CHILDREN.
AND SO I NAMED YOU SAHARA, AFTER THE MOST BARREN DESERT OF THEM ALL.
AS IF THE GODS HAD NOT PUNISHED ME ENOUGH, IT SEEMS NOW THAT NO OTHER WOMAN CAN PROVIDE ME WITH A CHILD.
YOUR MOTHER CLUNG TO YOU, JUST AS YOU CLING TO YOUR DOLLY NOW.
BUT YOU COULDN'T PROTECT HER FROM ME ANY MORE THAN THAT DOLLY CAN PROTECT YOU NOW.
"SUFFERING..."

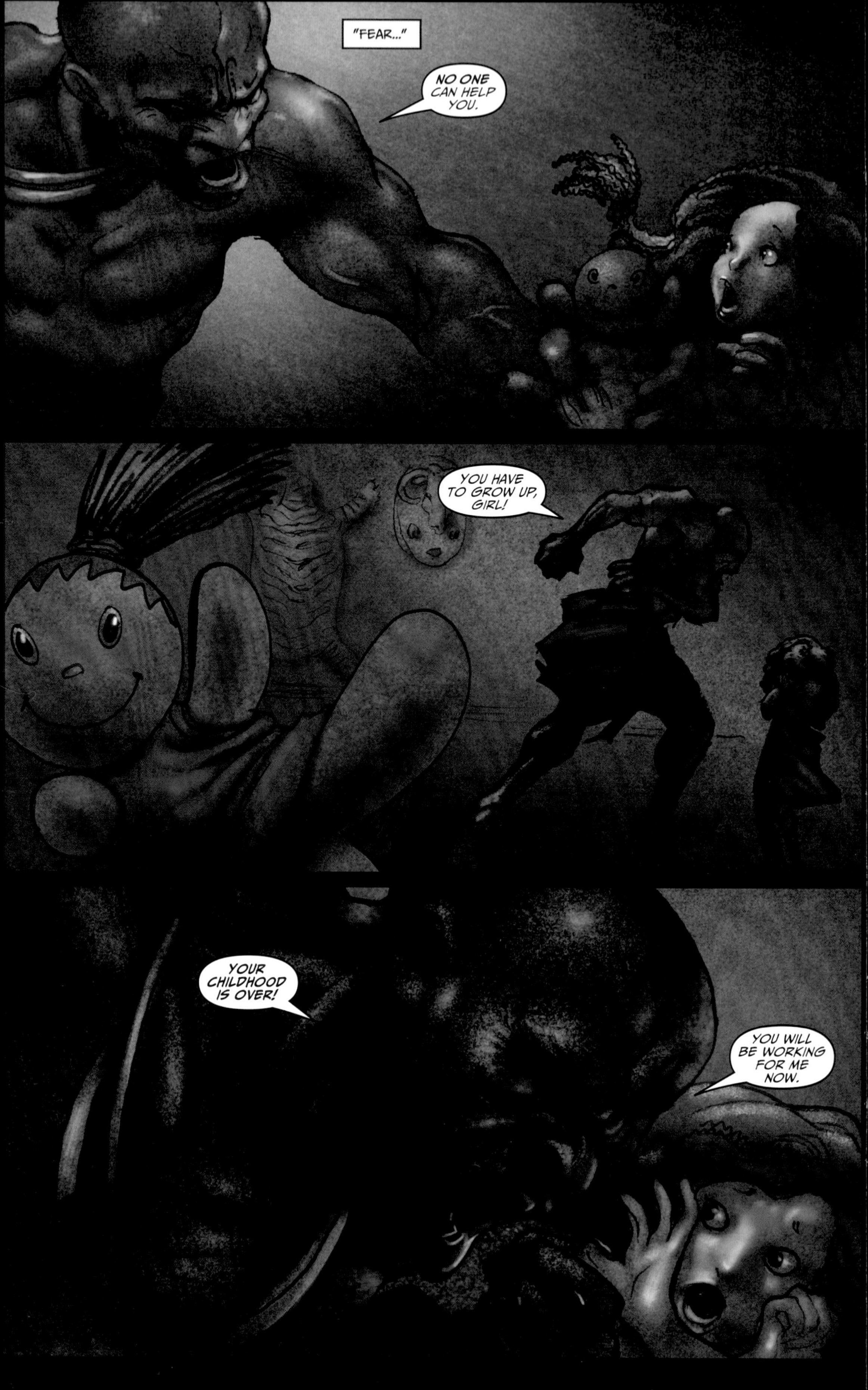
"FEAR..."
NO ONE CAN HELP YOU.
YOU HAVE TO GROW UP, GIRL!
YOUR CHILDHOOD IS OVER!
YOU WILL BE WORKING FOR ME NOW.

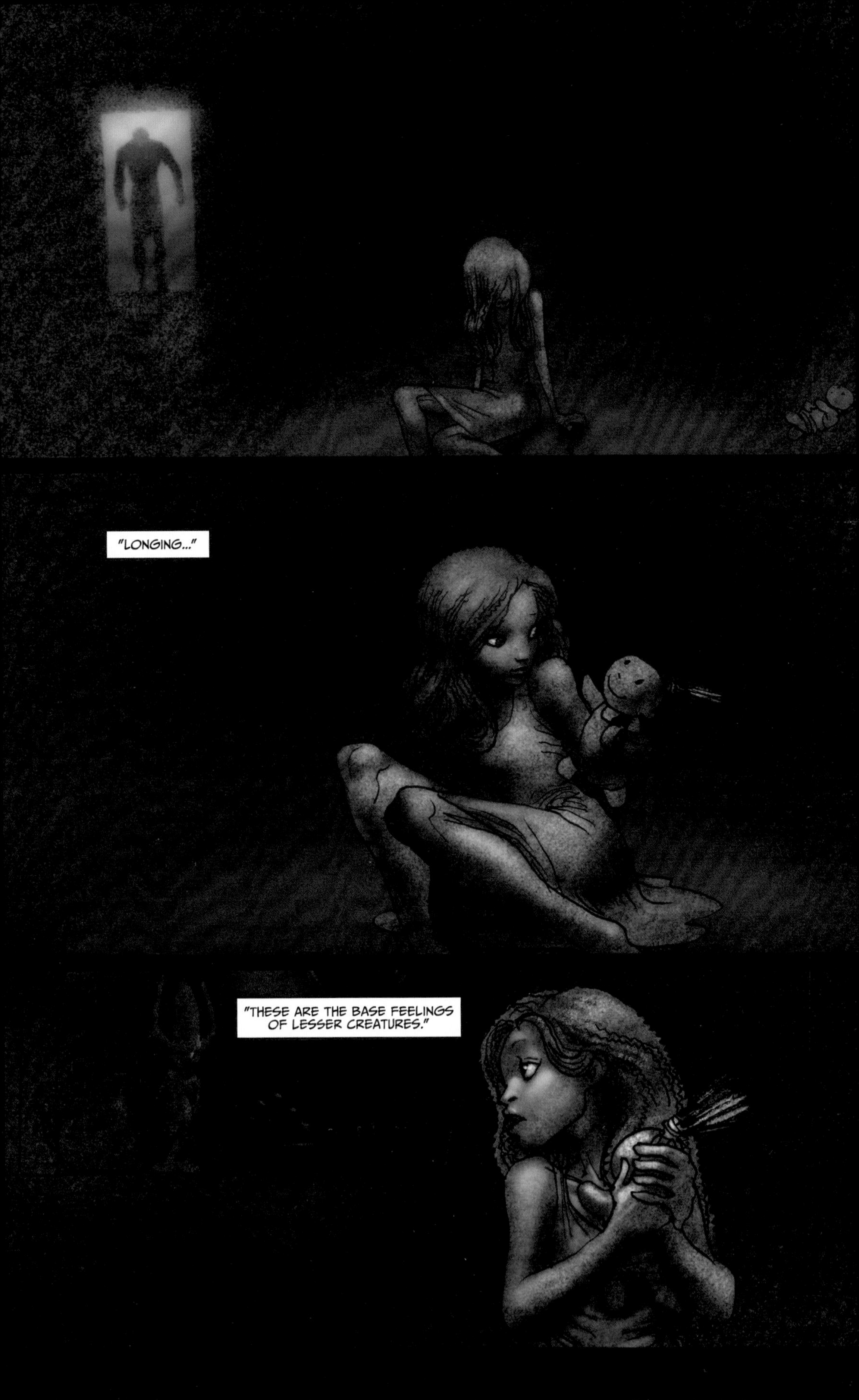
"LONGING..."
"THESE ARE THE BASE FEELINGS OF LESSER CREATURES."

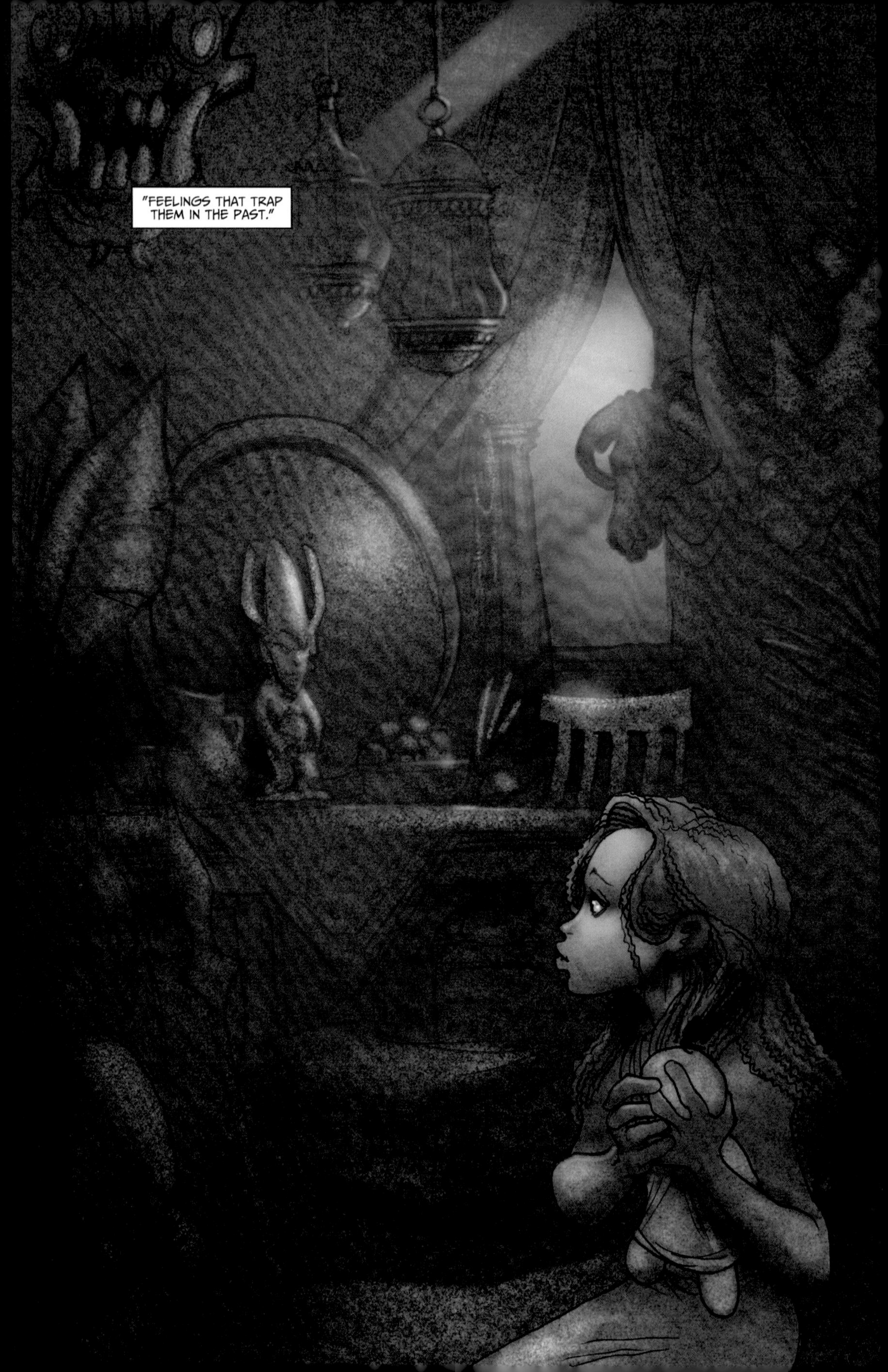
"FEELINGS THAT TRAP THEM IN THE PAST."

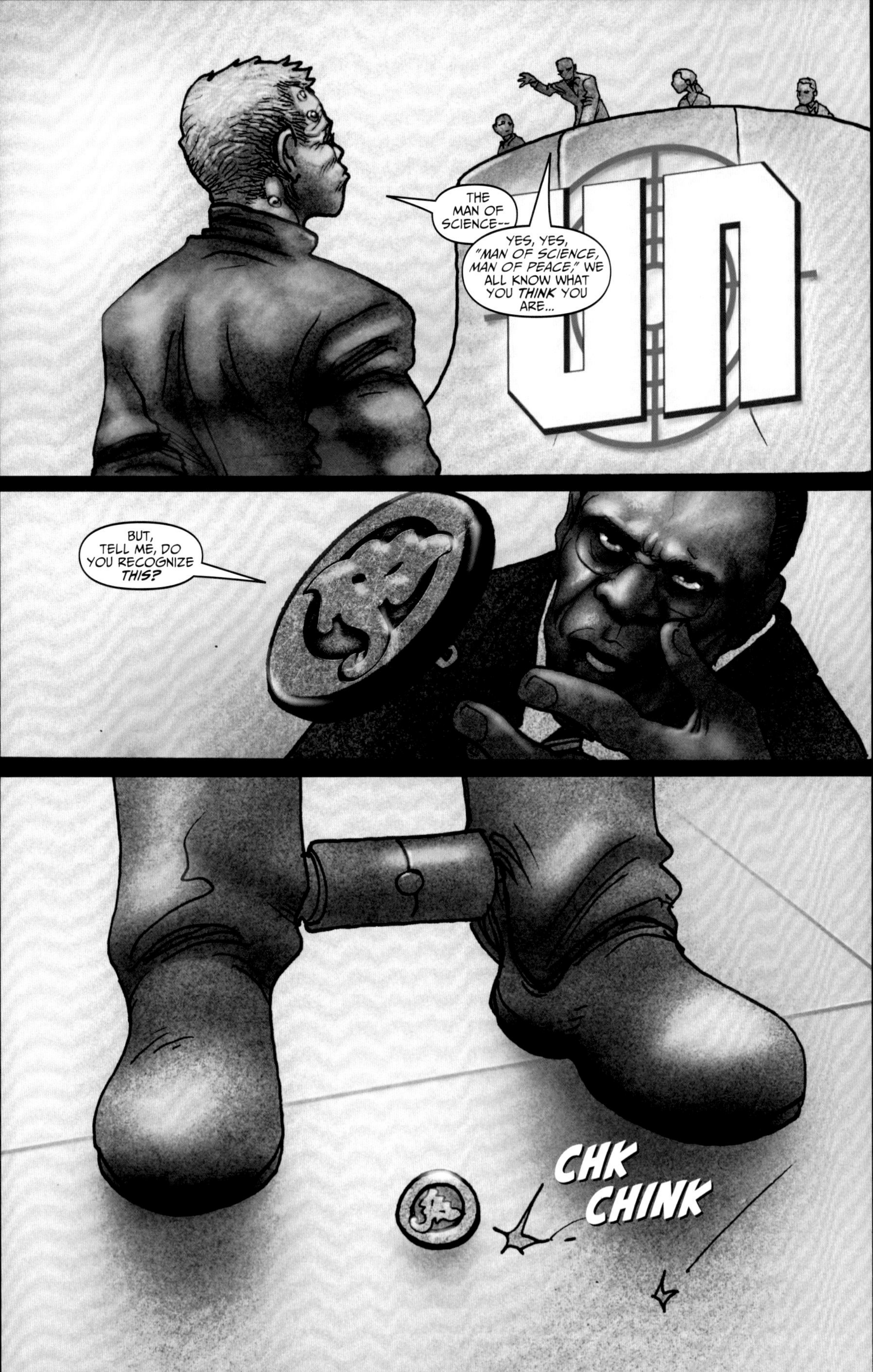
THE MAN OF SCIENCE--
YES, YES, "MAN OF SCIENCE, MAN OF PEACE," WE ALL KNOW WHAT YOU *THINK* YOU ARE...
UN
BUT, TELL ME, DO YOU RECOGNIZE *THIS?*
CHK CHINK

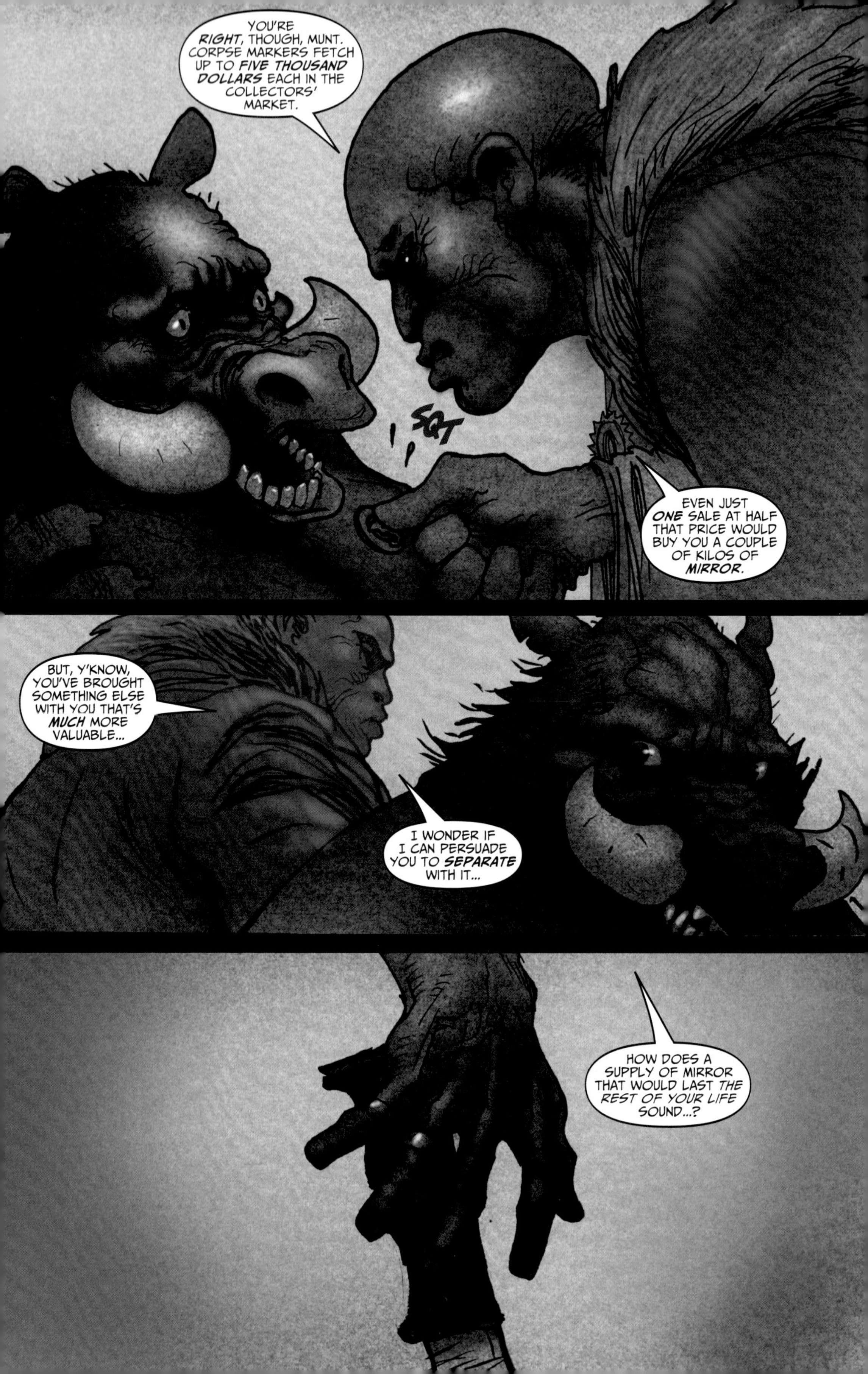
YOU'RE **RIGHT**, THOUGH, MUNT. CORPSE MARKERS FETCH UP TO ***FIVE THOUSAND DOLLARS*** EACH IN THE COLLECTORS' MARKET.
SQT
EVEN JUST ***ONE*** SALE AT HALF THAT PRICE WOULD BUY YOU A COUPLE OF KILOS OF ***MIRROR***.
BUT, Y'KNOW, YOU'VE BROUGHT SOMETHING ELSE WITH YOU THAT'S ***MUCH*** MORE VALUABLE...
I WONDER IF I CAN PERSUADE YOU TO ***SEPARATE*** WITH IT...
HOW DOES A SUPPLY OF MIRROR THAT WOULD LAST *THE REST OF YOUR LIFE* SOUND...?

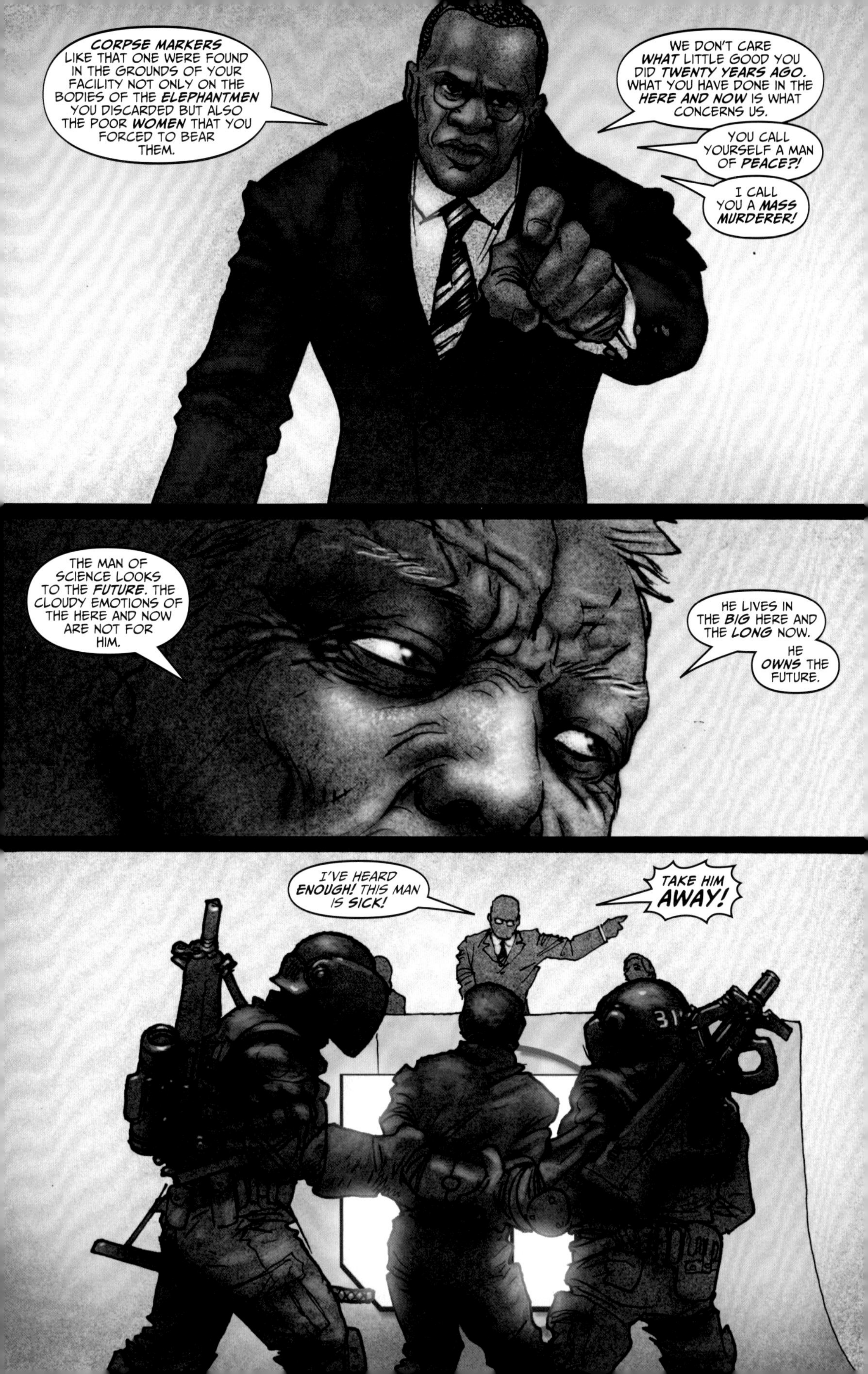
CORPSE MARKERS LIKE THAT ONE WERE FOUND IN THE GROUNDS OF YOUR FACILITY NOT ONLY ON THE BODIES OF THE ELEPHANTMEN YOU DISCARDED BUT ALSO THE POOR WOMEN THAT YOU FORCED TO BEAR THEM.
WE DON'T CARE WHAT LITTLE GOOD YOU DID TWENTY YEARS AGO. WHAT YOU HAVE DONE IN THE HERE AND NOW IS WHAT CONCERNS US.
YOU CALL YOURSELF A MAN OF PEACE?!
I CALL YOU A MASS MURDERER!
THE MAN OF SCIENCE LOOKS TO THE FUTURE. THE CLOUDY EMOTIONS OF THE HERE AND NOW ARE NOT FOR HIM.
HE LIVES IN THE BIG HERE AND THE LONG NOW.
HE OWNS THE FUTURE.
I'VE HEARD ENOUGH! THIS MAN IS SICK!
TAKE HIM AWAY!
31

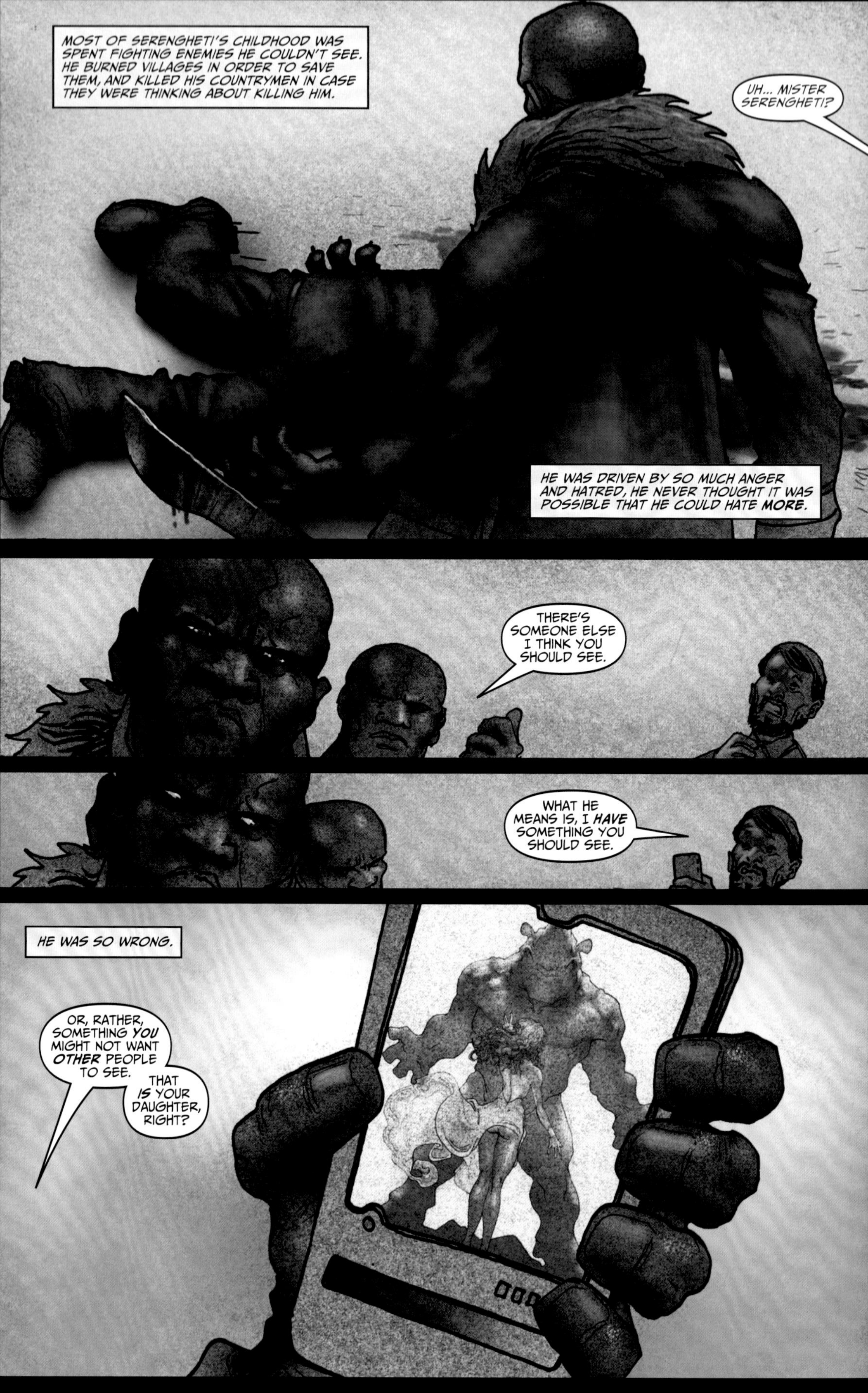

MOST OF SERENGHETI'S CHILDHOOD WAS SPENT FIGHTING ENEMIES HE COULDN'T SEE. HE BURNED VILLAGES IN ORDER TO SAVE THEM, AND KILLED HIS COUNTRYMEN IN CASE THEY WERE THINKING ABOUT KILLING HIM.
UH... MISTER SERENGHETI?
HE WAS DRIVEN BY SO MUCH ANGER AND HATRED, HE NEVER THOUGHT IT WAS POSSIBLE THAT HE COULD HATE MORE.
THERE'S SOMEONE ELSE I THINK YOU SHOULD SEE.
WHAT HE MEANS IS, I HAVE SOMETHING YOU SHOULD SEE.
HE WAS SO WRONG.
OR, RATHER, SOMETHING YOU MIGHT NOT WANT OTHER PEOPLE TO SEE.
THAT IS YOUR DAUGHTER, RIGHT?

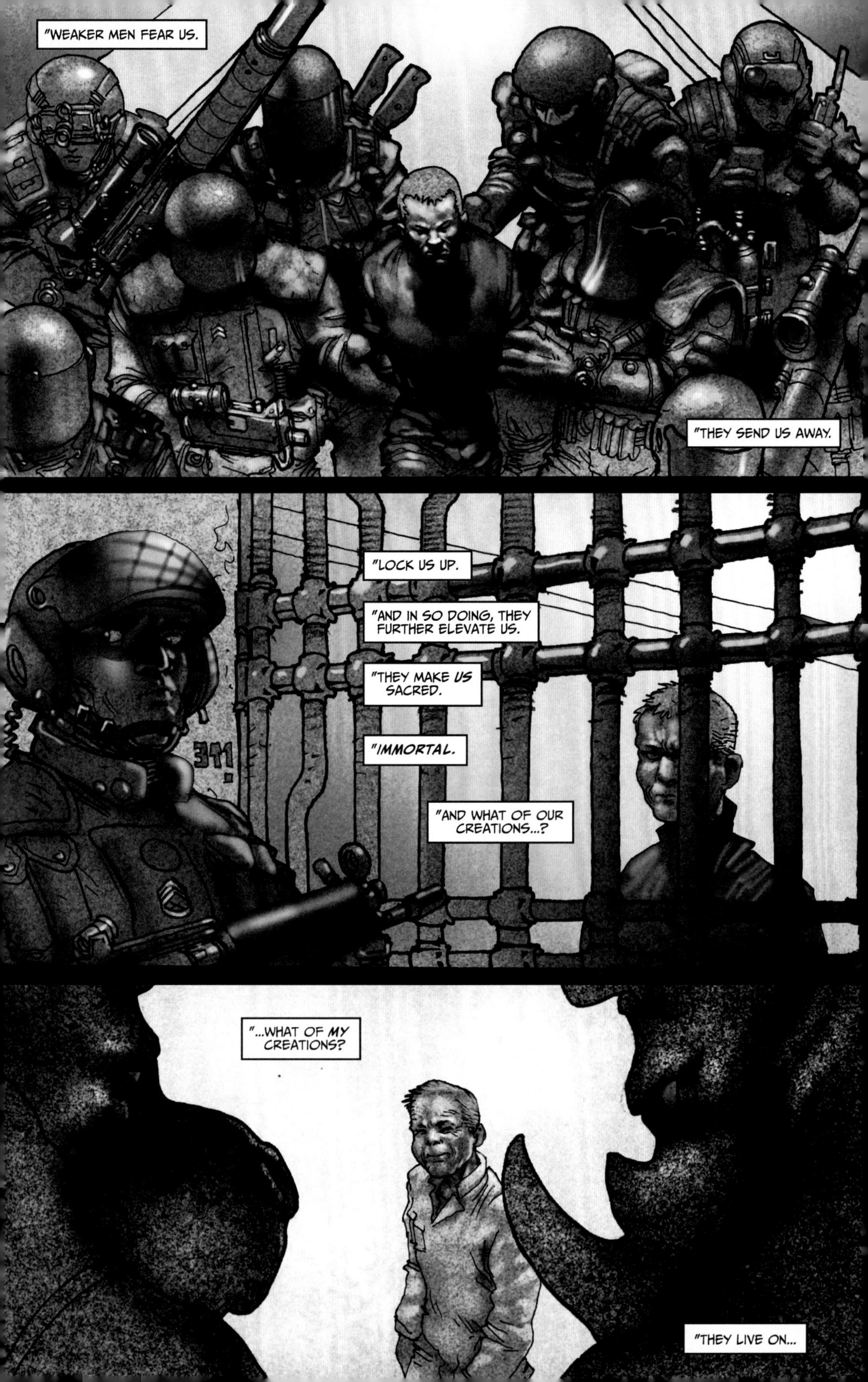
"WEAKER MEN FEAR US.
"THEY SEND US AWAY.
"LOCK US UP.
"AND IN SO DOING, THEY FURTHER ELEVATE US.
"THEY MAKE *US* SACRED.
"*IMMORTAL.*
"AND WHAT OF OUR CREATIONS...?
"...WHAT OF *MY* CREATIONS?
"THEY LIVE ON...

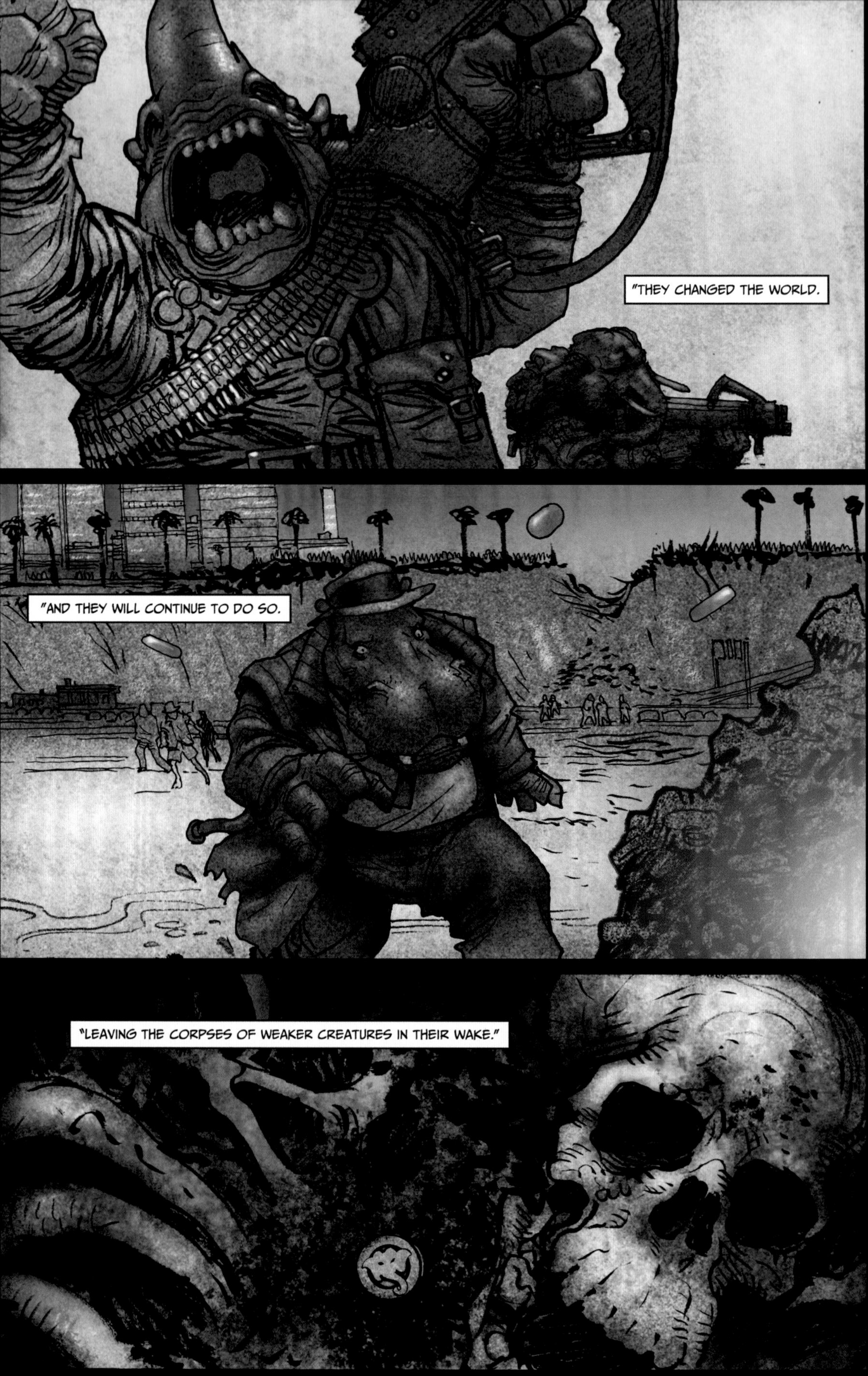
"THEY CHANGED THE WORLD.
"AND THEY WILL CONTINUE TO DO SO.
"LEAVING THE CORPSES OF WEAKER CREATURES IN THEIR WAKE."

To Be Continued!

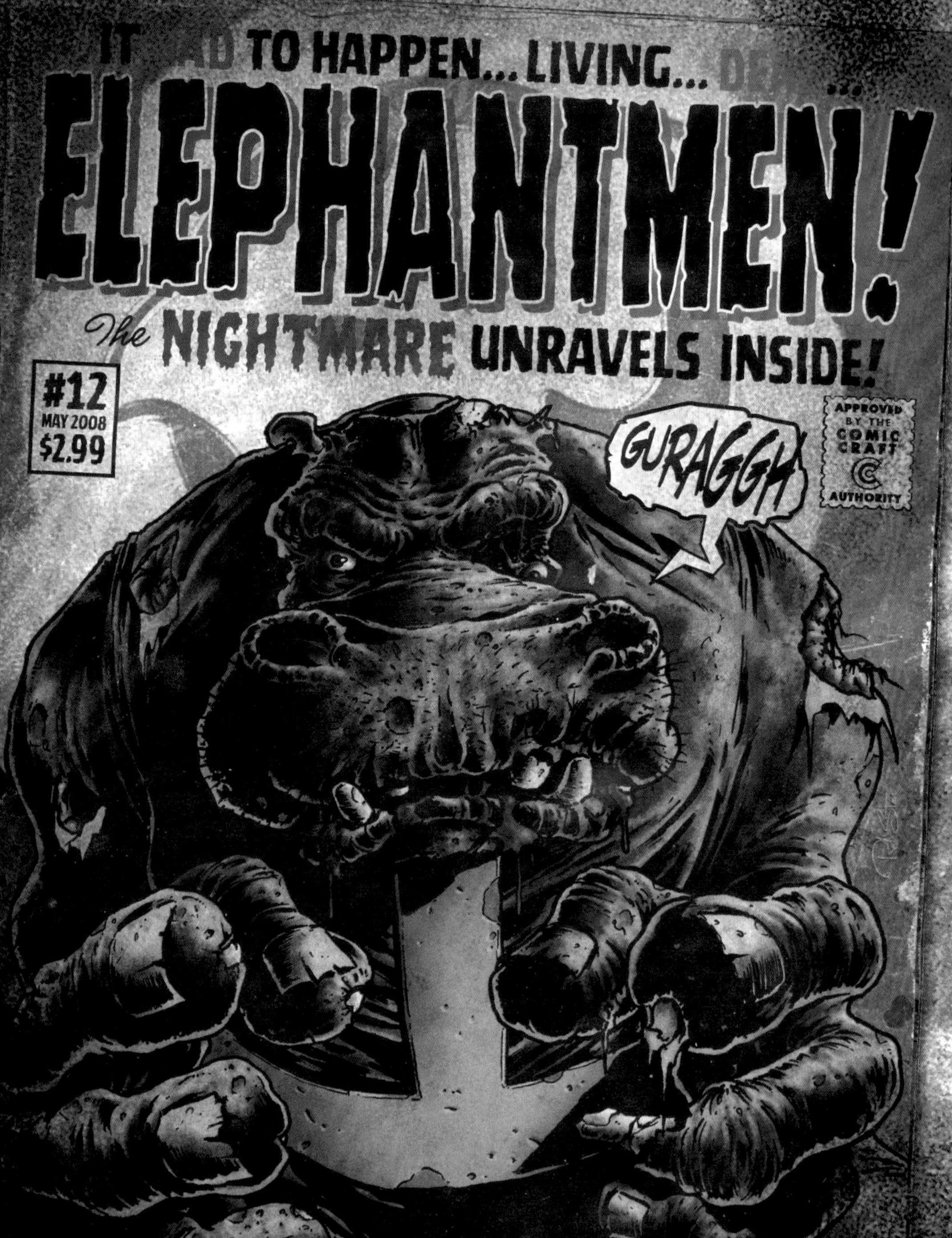

TO HAPPEN... LIVING...
ELEPHANTMEN!
The NIGHTMARE UNRAVELS INSIDE!
#12
MAY 2008
$2.99
GURAGGH
APPROVED BY THE COMIC CRAFT AUTHORITY
STARKINGS! Rob STEEN! John ROSHELL!
image

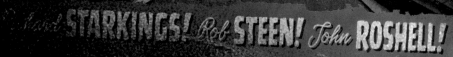

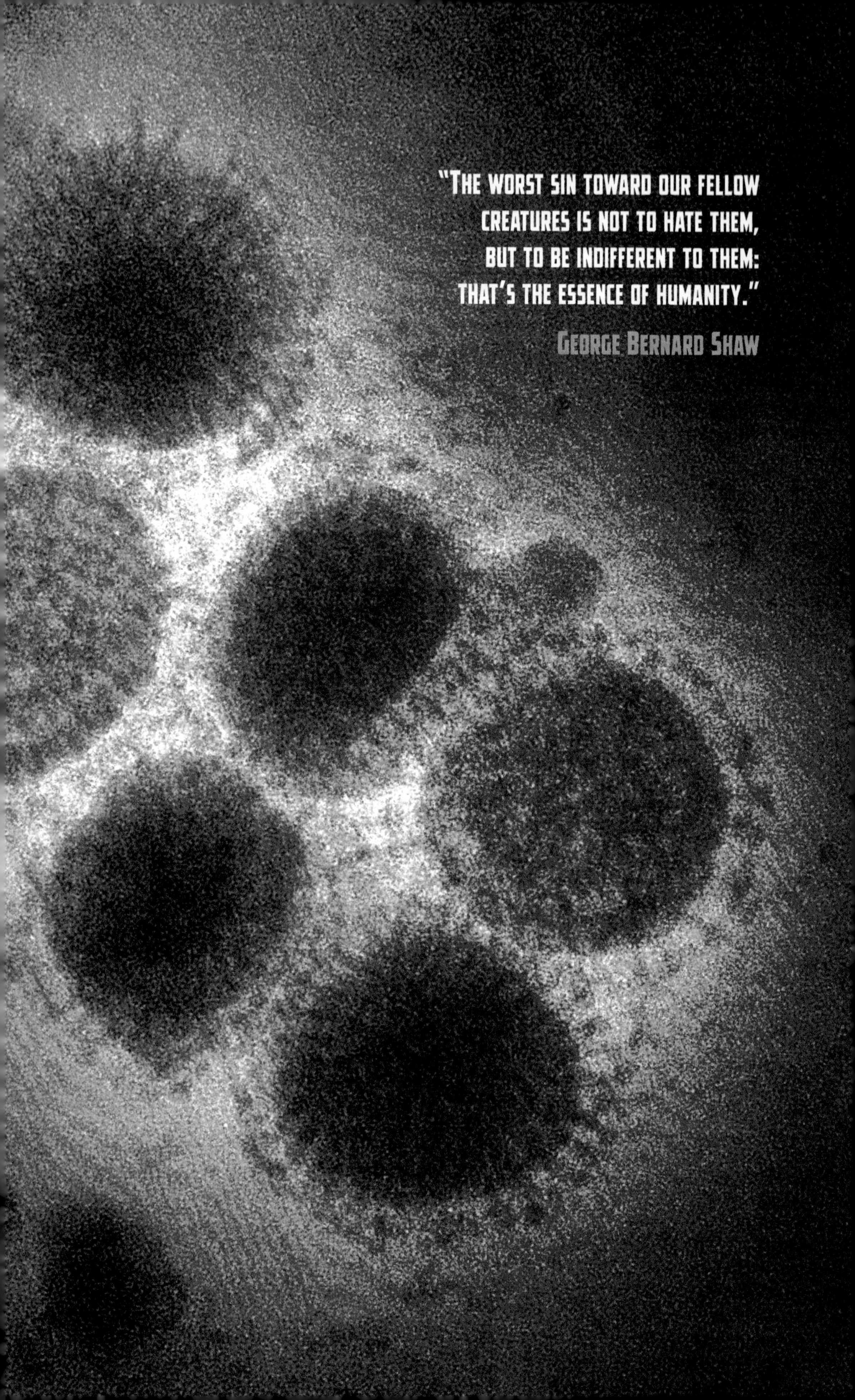

"The worst sin toward our fellow creatures is not to hate them, but to be indifferent to them: that's the essence of humanity."

George Bernard Shaw

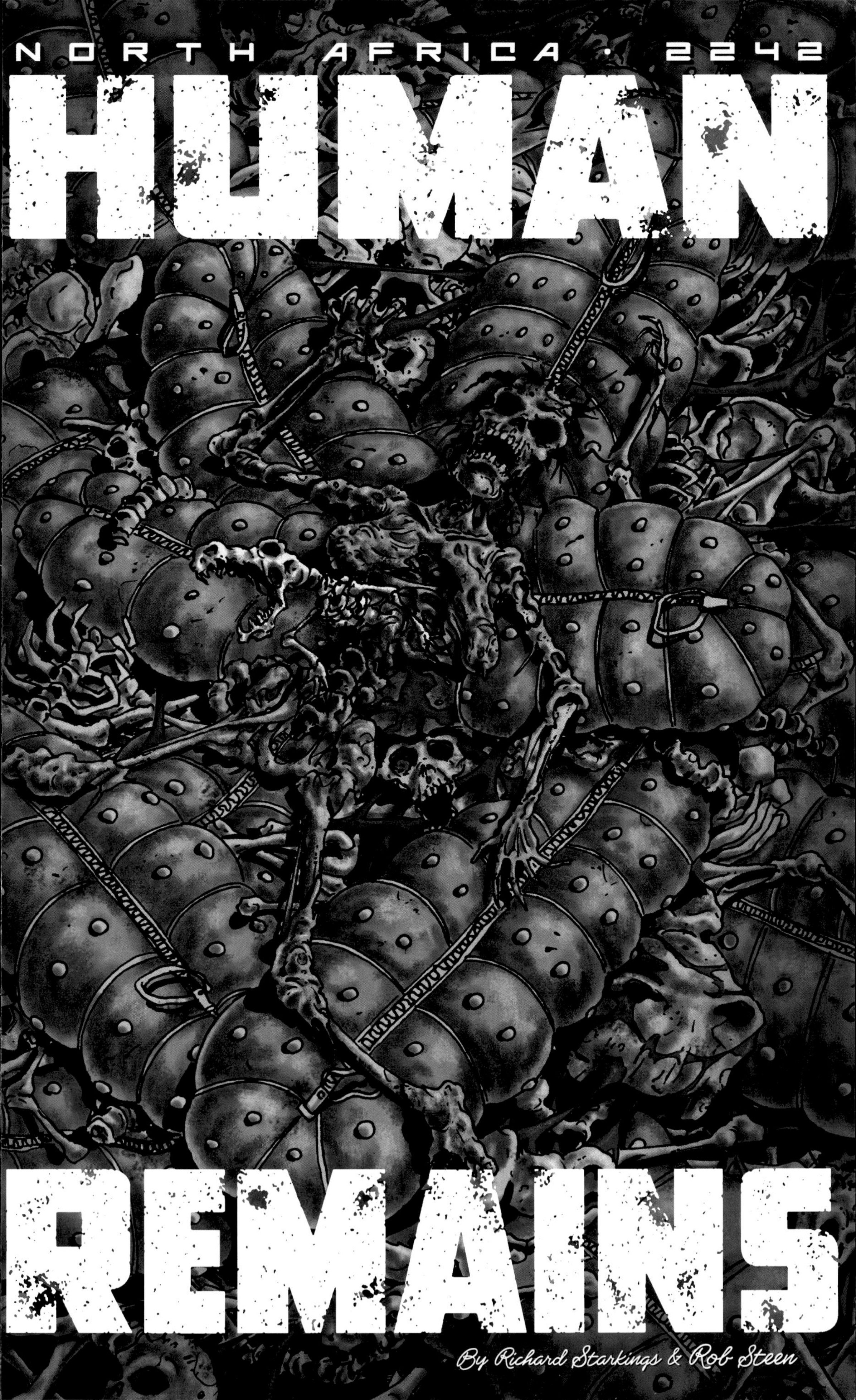
NORTH AFRICA · 2242
HUMAN
REMAINS
By Richard Starkings & Rob Steen

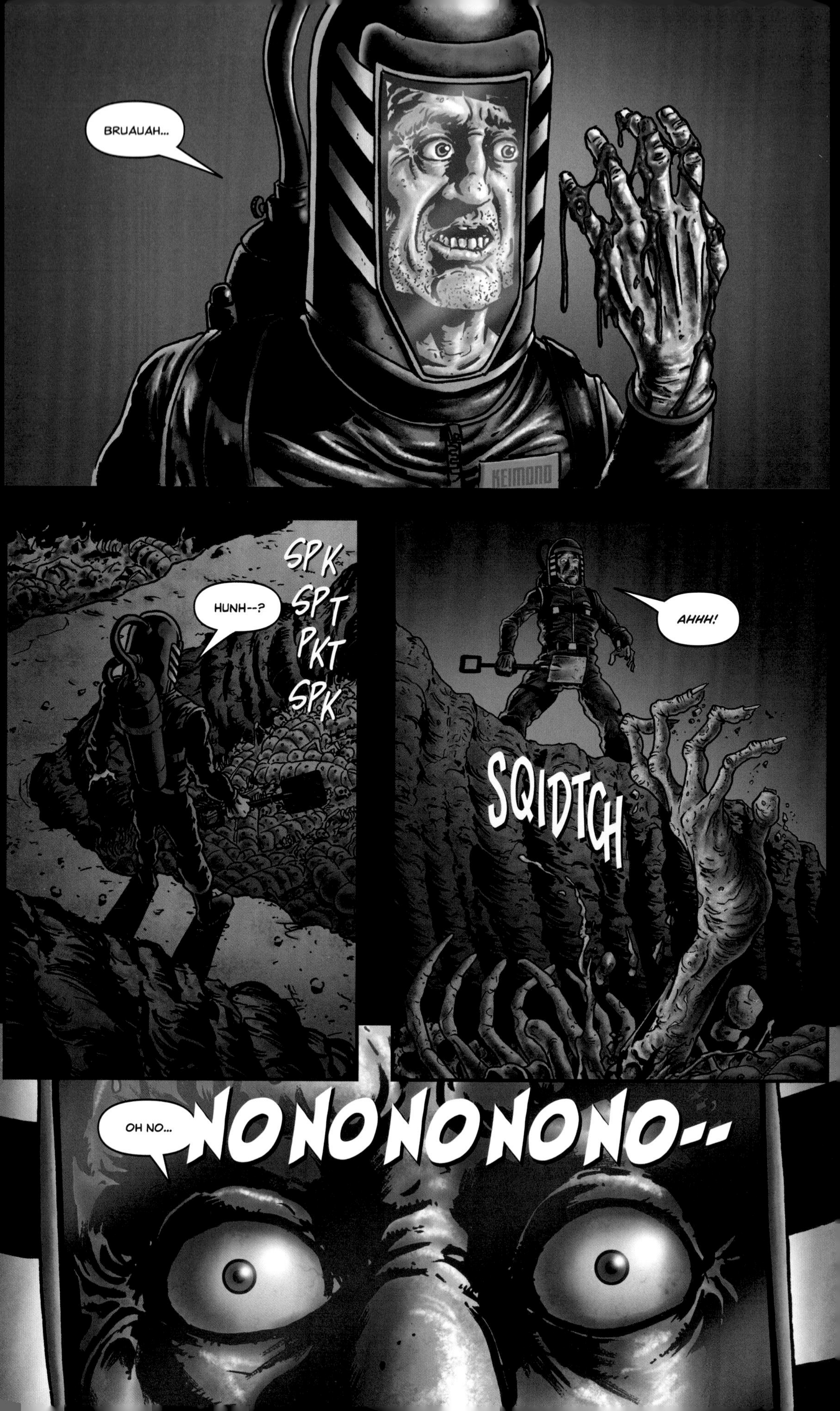

BRUAUAH...
KEIMOND
HUNH--?
SPK
SPT
PKT
SPK
AHHH!
SQIDTCH
OH NO...
NO NO NO NO NO NO NO--

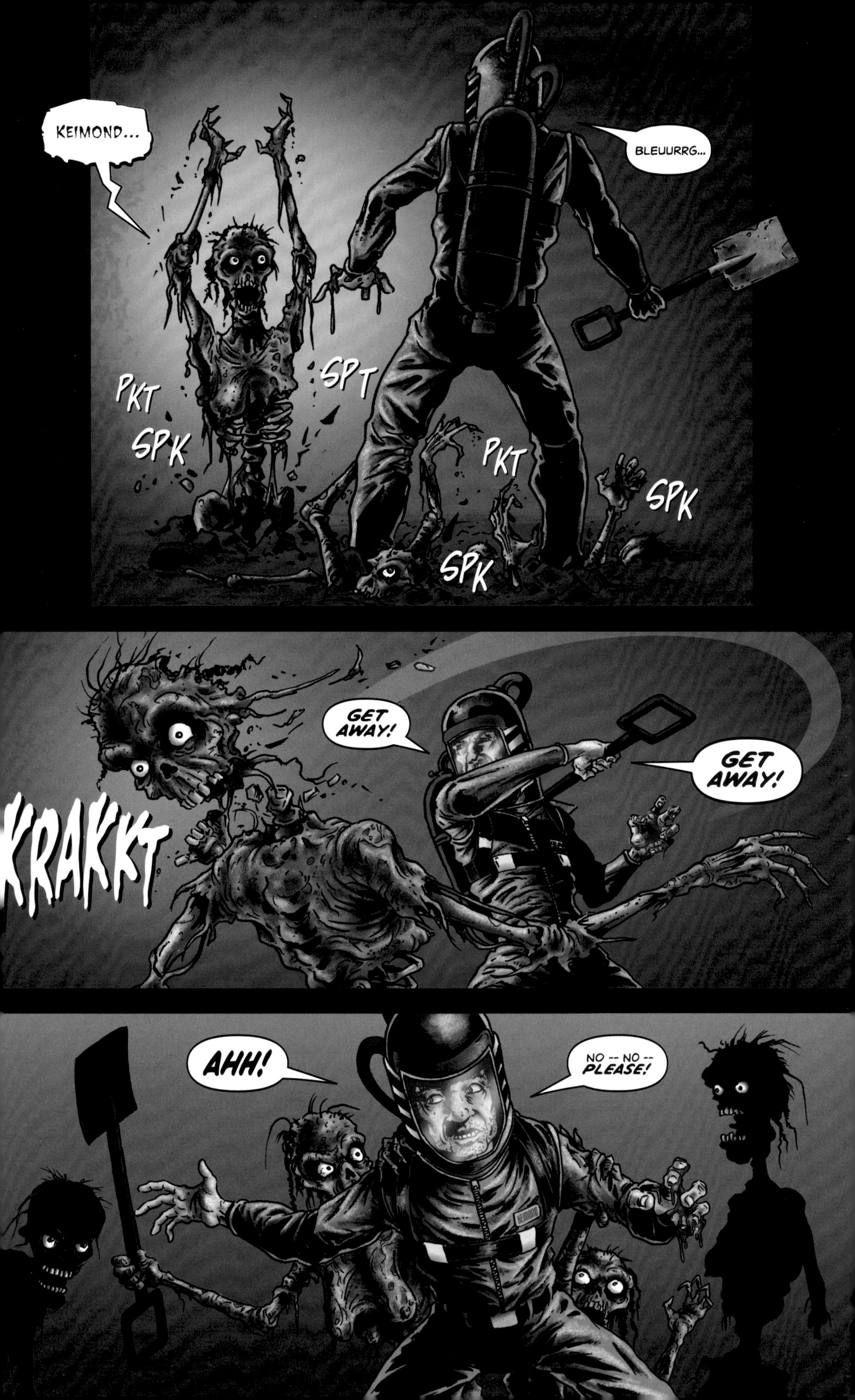
KEIMOND...
BLEUURRG...
PKT
SPT
SPK
PKT
SPK
SPK
KRAKKT
GET AWAY!
GET AWAY!
AHH!
NO -- NO -- PLEASE!

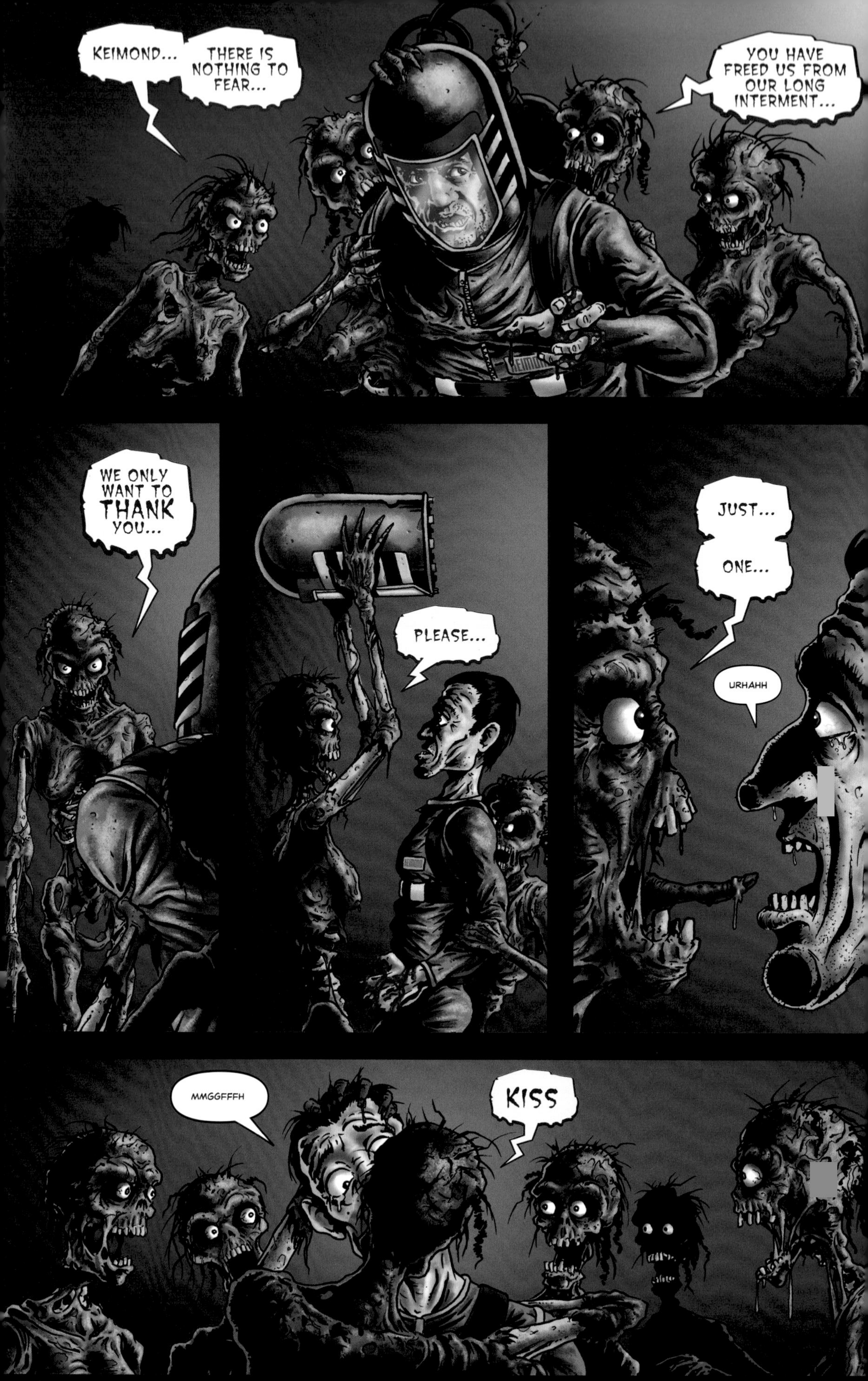
KEIMOND...
THERE IS NOTHING TO FEAR...
YOU HAVE FREED US FROM OUR LONG INTERMENT...
WE ONLY WANT TO THANK YOU...
PLEASE...
JUST...
ONE...
URHAHH
MMGGFFFH
KISS

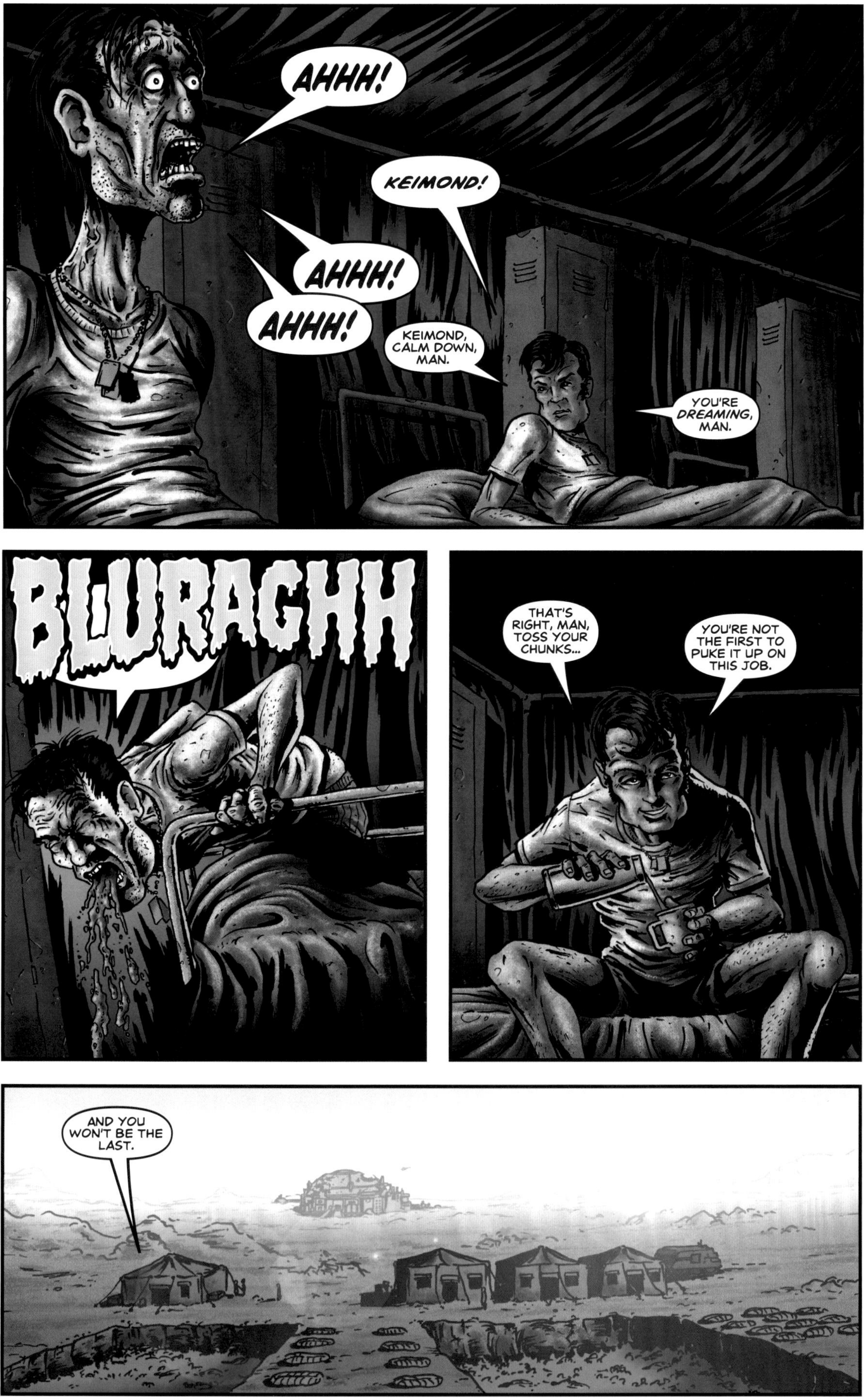
AHHH!
KEIMOND!
AHHH!
AHHH!
KEIMOND, CALM DOWN, MAN.
YOU'RE DREAMING, MAN.
BLURAGHH
THAT'S RIGHT, MAN, TOSS YOUR CHUNKS...
YOU'RE NOT THE FIRST TO PUKE IT UP ON THIS JOB.
AND YOU WON'T BE THE LAST.

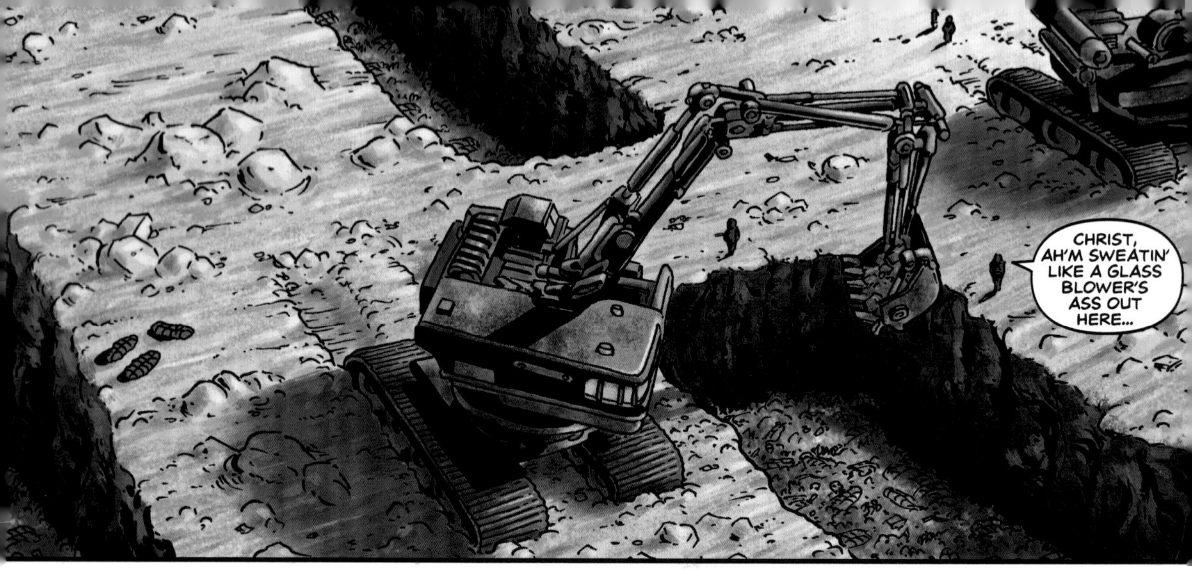
CHRIST, AH'M SWEATIN' LIKE A GLASS BLOWER'S ASS OUT HERE...

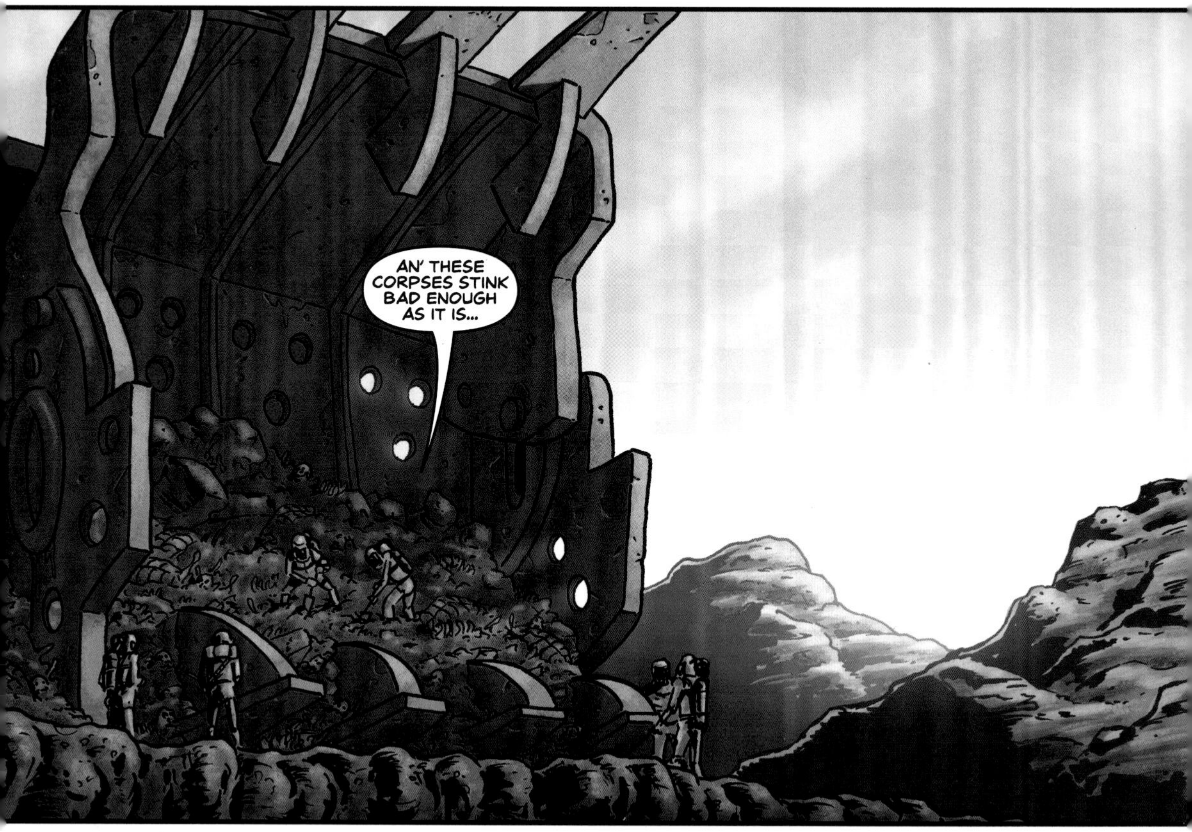
AN' THESE CORPSES STINK BAD ENOUGH AS IT IS...

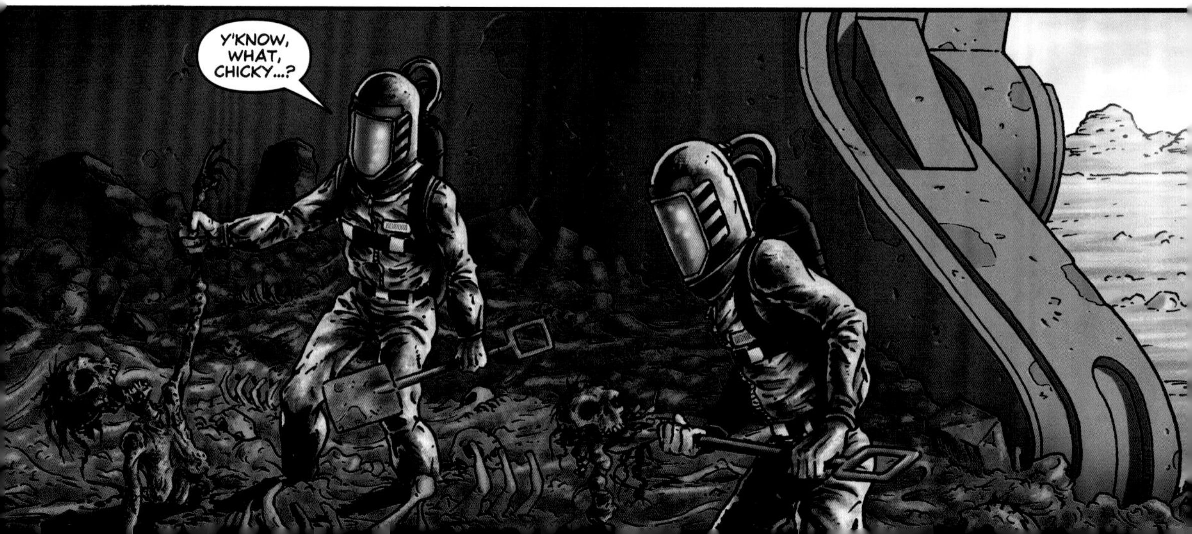
Y'KNOW, WHAT, CHICKY...?

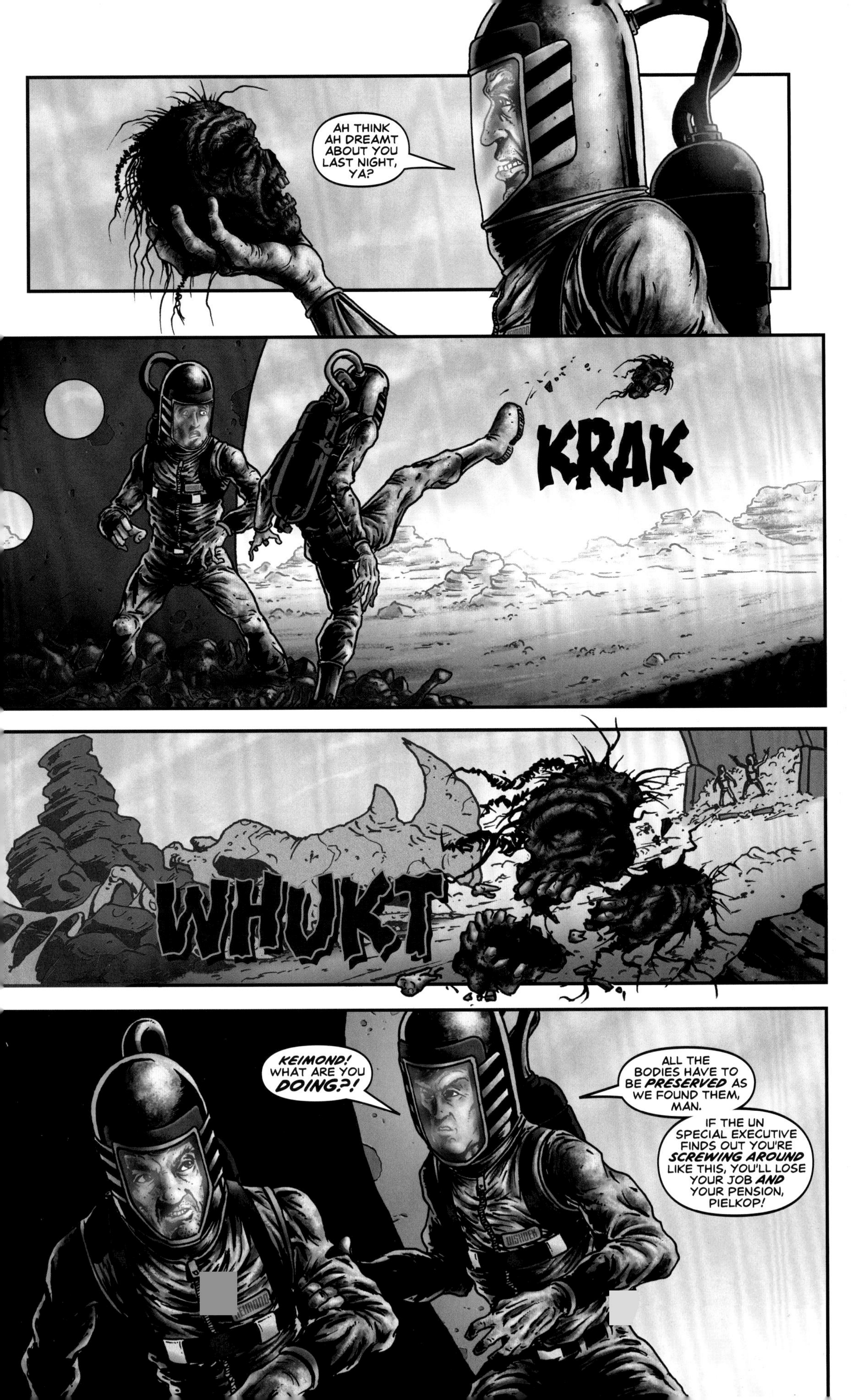
AH THINK AH DREAMT ABOUT YOU LAST NIGHT, YA?
KRAK
WHUKT
KEIMOND! WHAT ARE YOU DOING?!
ALL THE BODIES HAVE TO BE PRESERVED AS WE FOUND THEM, MAN.
IF THE UN SPECIAL EXECUTIVE FINDS OUT YOU'RE SCREWING AROUND LIKE THIS, YOU'LL LOSE YOUR JOB AND YOUR PENSION, PIELKOP!

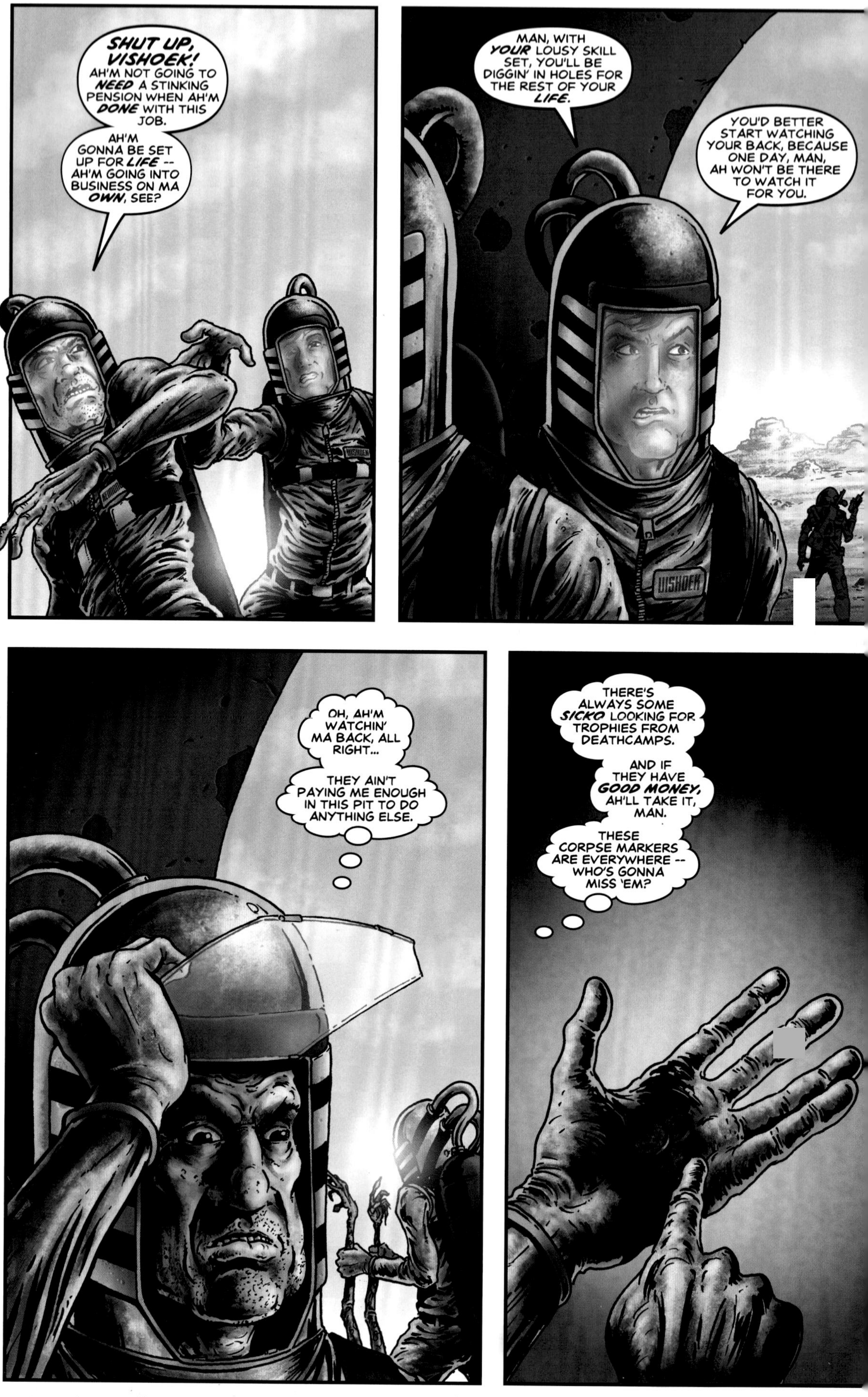
SHUT UP, VISHOEK! AH'M NOT GOING TO NEED A STINKING PENSION WHEN AH'M DONE WITH THIS JOB.
AH'M GONNA BE SET UP FOR LIFE -- AH'M GOING INTO BUSINESS ON MA OWN, SEE?
MAN, WITH YOUR LOUSY SKILL SET, YOU'LL BE DIGGIN' IN HOLES FOR THE REST OF YOUR LIFE.
YOU'D BETTER START WATCHING YOUR BACK, BECAUSE ONE DAY, MAN, AH WON'T BE THERE TO WATCH IT FOR YOU.
OH, AH'M WATCHIN' MA BACK, ALL RIGHT...
THEY AIN'T PAYING ME ENOUGH IN THIS PIT TO DO ANYTHING ELSE.
THERE'S ALWAYS SOME SICKO LOOKING FOR TROPHIES FROM DEATHCAMPS.
AND IF THEY HAVE GOOD MONEY, AH'LL TAKE IT, MAN.
THESE CORPSE MARKERS ARE EVERYWHERE -- WHO'S GONNA MISS 'EM?

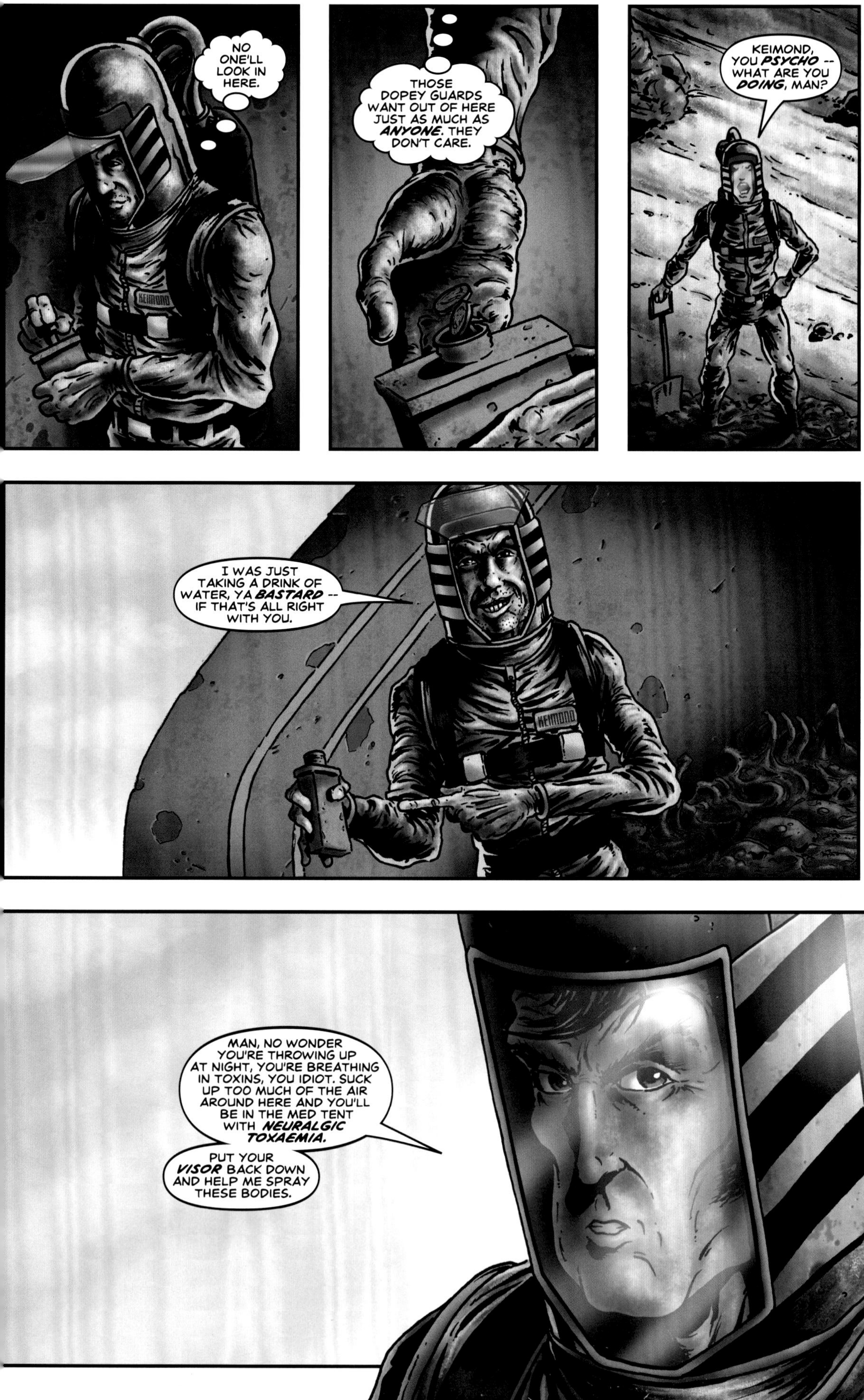
NO ONE'LL LOOK IN HERE.
THOSE DOPEY GUARDS WANT OUT OF HERE JUST AS MUCH AS ANYONE. THEY DON'T CARE.
KEIMOND, YOU PSYCHO -- WHAT ARE YOU DOING, MAN?
I WAS JUST TAKING A DRINK OF WATER, YA BASTARD -- IF THAT'S ALL RIGHT WITH YOU.
MAN, NO WONDER YOU'RE THROWING UP AT NIGHT, YOU'RE BREATHING IN TOXINS, YOU IDIOT. SUCK UP TOO MUCH OF THE AIR AROUND HERE AND YOU'LL BE IN THE MED TENT WITH NEURALGIC TOXAEMIA.
PUT YOUR VISOR BACK DOWN AND HELP ME SPRAY THESE BODIES.

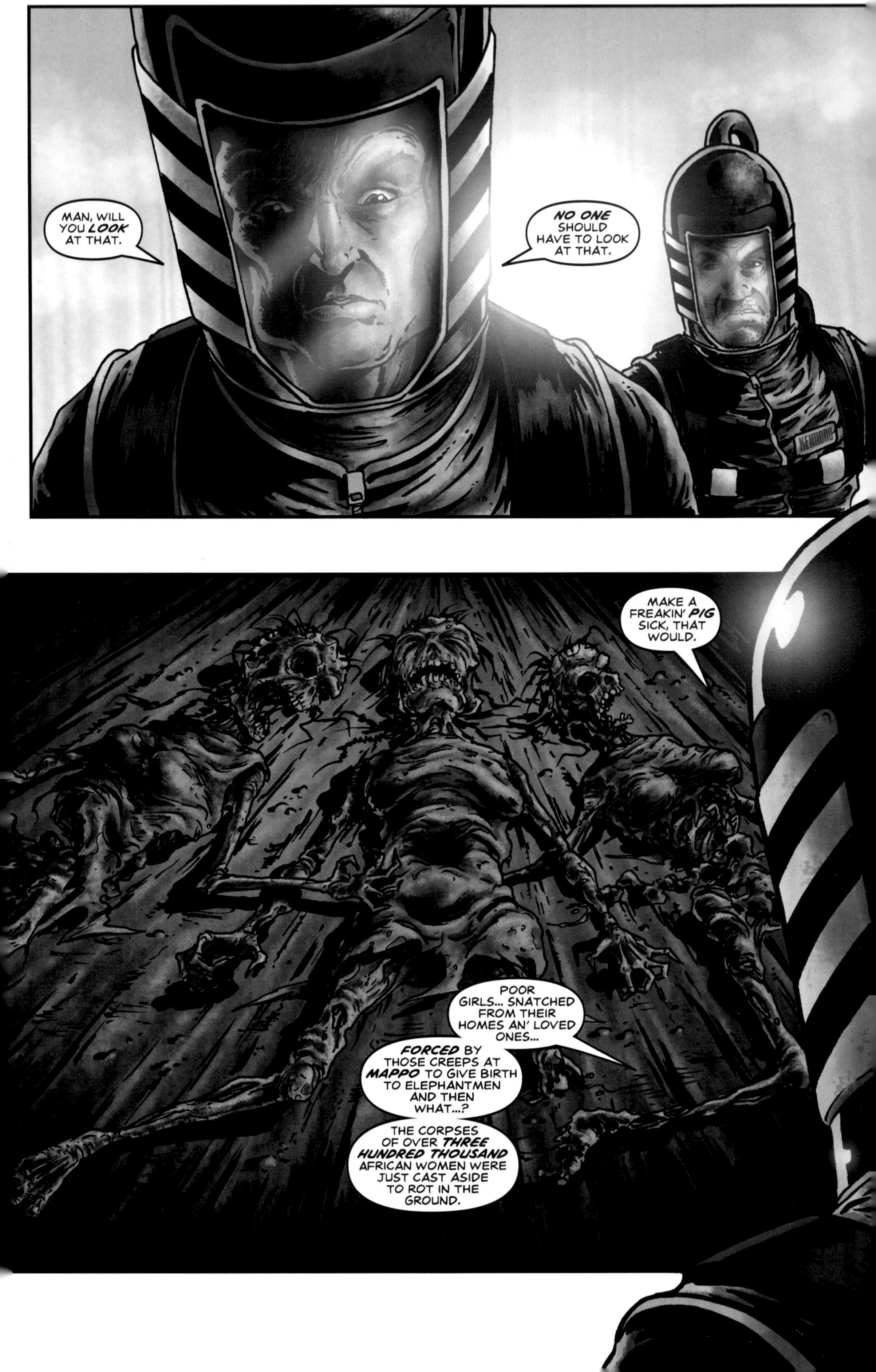
MAN, WILL YOU LOOK AT THAT.
NO ONE SHOULD HAVE TO LOOK AT THAT.
MAKE A FREAKIN' PIG SICK, THAT WOULD.
POOR GIRLS... SNATCHED FROM THEIR HOMES AN' LOVED ONES...
FORCED BY THOSE CREEPS AT MAPPO TO GIVE BIRTH TO ELEPHANTMEN AND THEN WHAT...?
THE CORPSES OF OVER THREE HUNDRED THOUSAND AFRICAN WOMEN WERE JUST CAST ASIDE TO ROT IN THE GROUND.

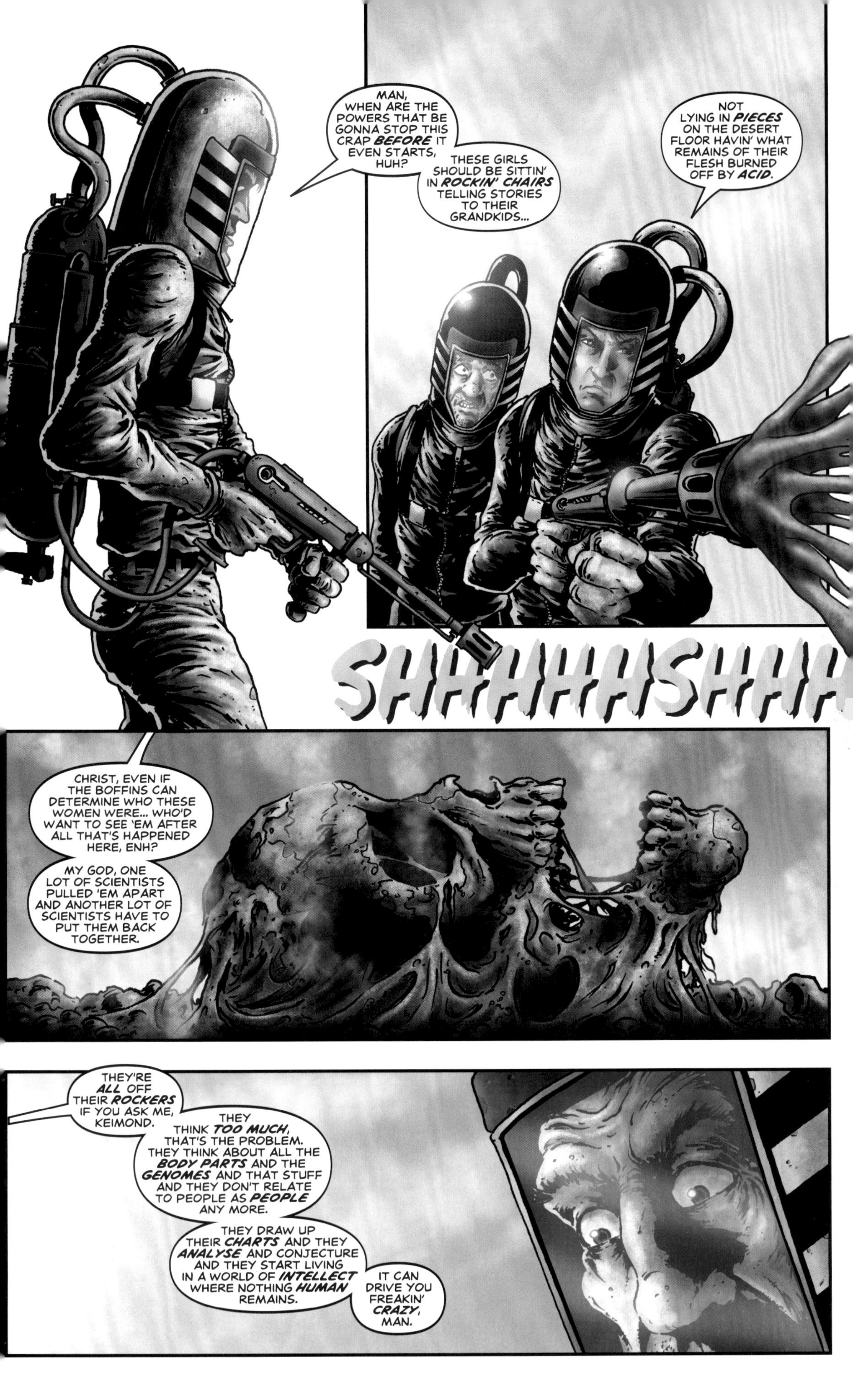
MAN, WHEN ARE THE POWERS THAT BE GONNA STOP THIS CRAP BEFORE IT EVEN STARTS, HUH?
THESE GIRLS SHOULD BE SITTIN' IN ROCKIN' CHAIRS TELLING STORIES TO THEIR GRANDKIDS...
NOT LYING IN PIECES ON THE DESERT FLOOR HAVIN' WHAT REMAINS OF THEIR FLESH BURNED OFF BY ACID.
SHHHHHSHHH
CHRIST, EVEN IF THE BOFFINS CAN DETERMINE WHO THESE WOMEN WERE... WHO'D WANT TO SEE 'EM AFTER ALL THAT'S HAPPENED HERE, ENH?
MY GOD, ONE LOT OF SCIENTISTS PULLED 'EM APART AND ANOTHER LOT OF SCIENTISTS HAVE TO PUT THEM BACK TOGETHER.
THEY'RE ALL OFF THEIR ROCKERS IF YOU ASK ME, KEIMOND.
THEY THINK TOO MUCH, THAT'S THE PROBLEM. THEY THINK ABOUT ALL THE BODY PARTS AND THE GENOMES AND THAT STUFF AND THEY DON'T RELATE TO PEOPLE AS PEOPLE ANY MORE.
THEY DRAW UP THEIR CHARTS AND THEY ANALYSE AND CONJECTURE AND THEY START LIVING IN A WORLD OF INTELLECT WHERE NOTHING HUMAN REMAINS.
IT CAN DRIVE YOU FREAKIN' CRAZY, MAN.

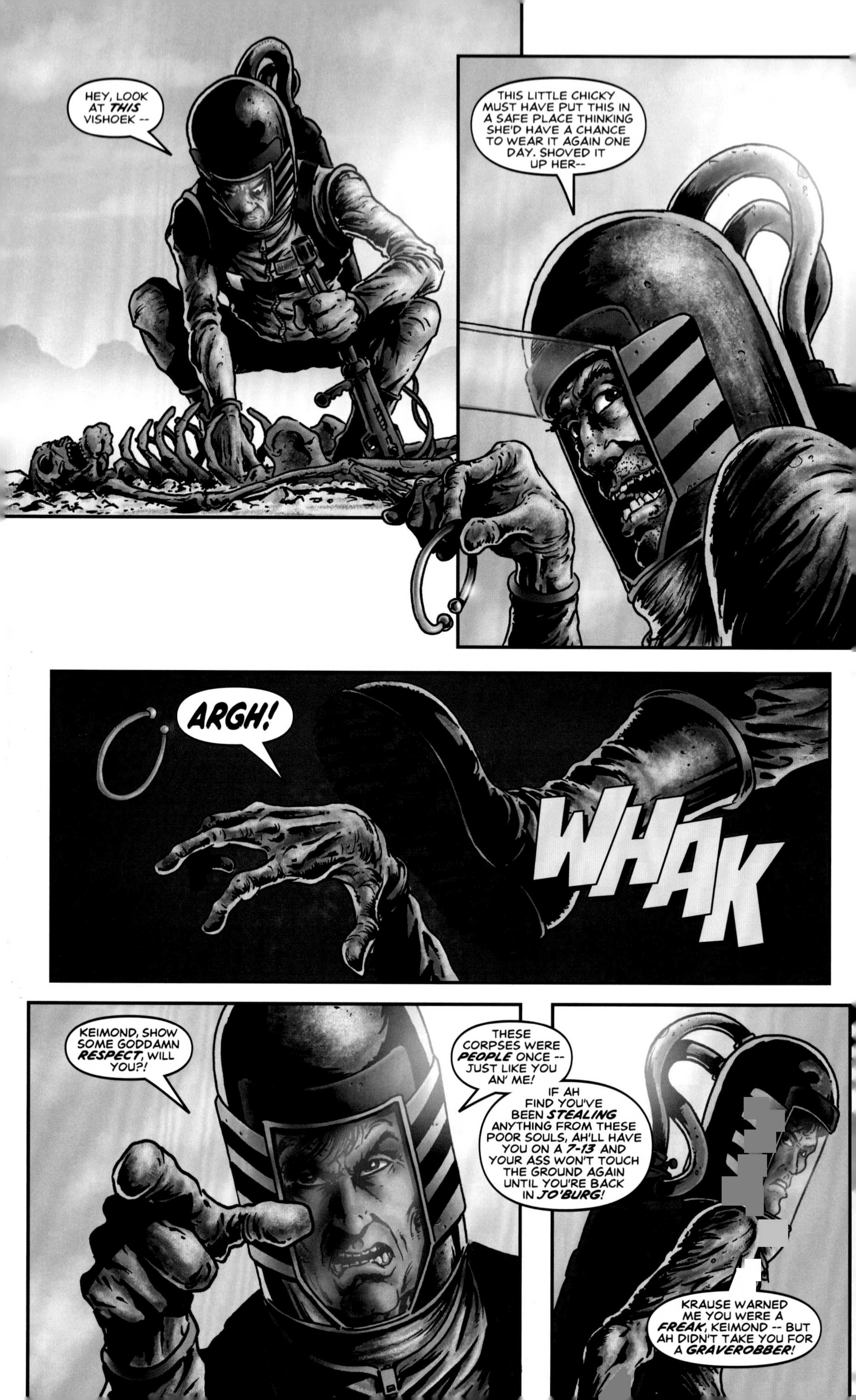
HEY, LOOK AT THIS VISHOEK --
THIS LITTLE CHICKY MUST HAVE PUT THIS IN A SAFE PLACE THINKING SHE'D HAVE A CHANCE TO WEAR IT AGAIN ONE DAY. SHOVED IT UP HER--
ARGH!
WHAK
KEIMOND, SHOW SOME GODDAMN RESPECT, WILL YOU?!
THESE CORPSES WERE PEOPLE ONCE -- JUST LIKE YOU AN' ME!
IF AH FIND YOU'VE BEEN STEALING ANYTHING FROM THESE POOR SOULS, AH'LL HAVE YOU ON A 7-13 AND YOUR ASS WON'T TOUCH THE GROUND AGAIN UNTIL YOU'RE BACK IN JO'BURG!
KRAUSE WARNED ME YOU WERE A FREAK, KEIMOND -- BUT AH DIDN'T TAKE YOU FOR A GRAVEROBBER!

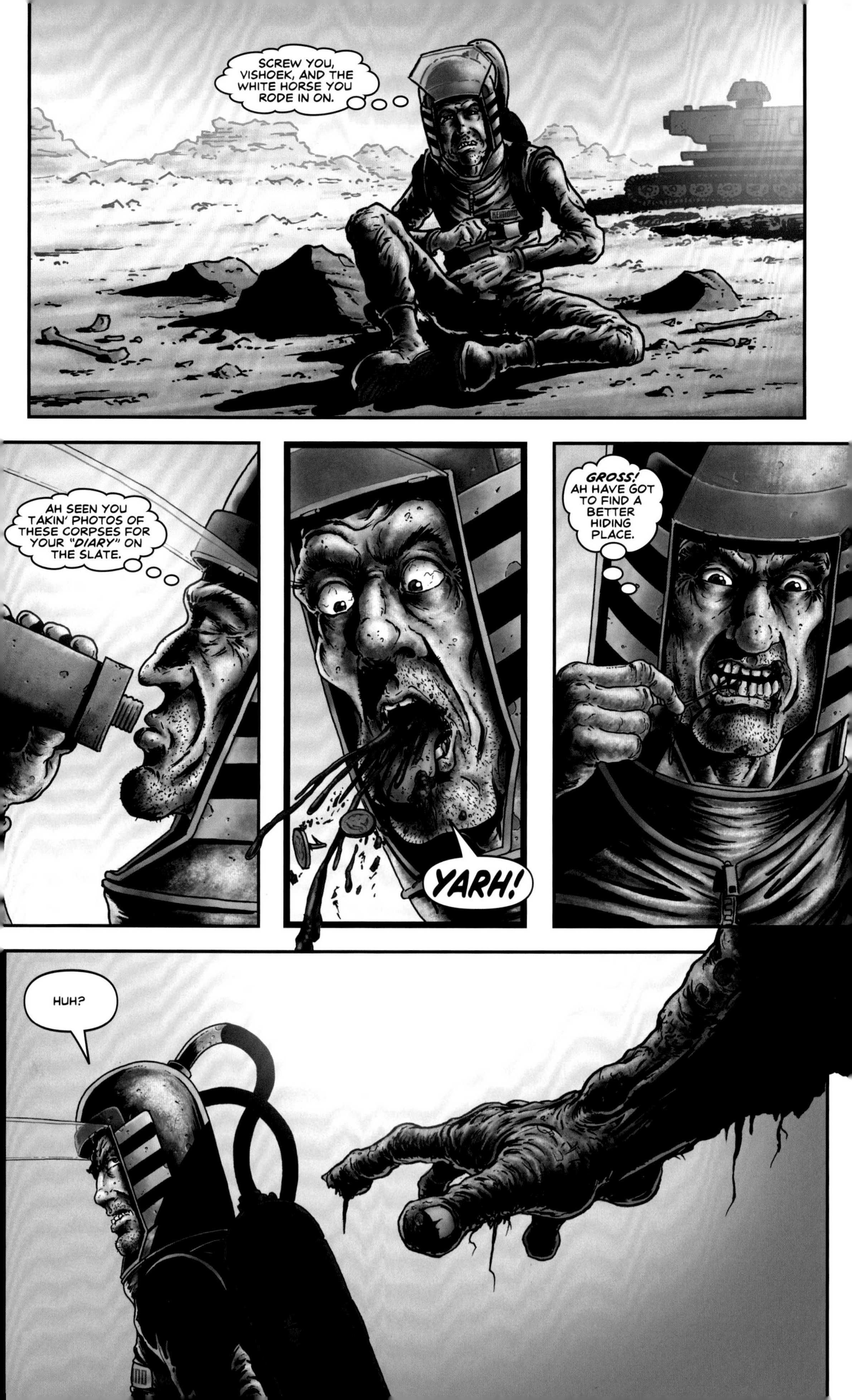
SCREW YOU, VISHOEK, AND THE WHITE HORSE YOU RODE IN ON.
AH SEEN YOU TAKIN' PHOTOS OF THESE CORPSES FOR YOUR "DIARY" ON THE SLATE.
YARH!
GROSS! AH HAVE GOT TO FIND A BETTER HIDING PLACE.
HUH?

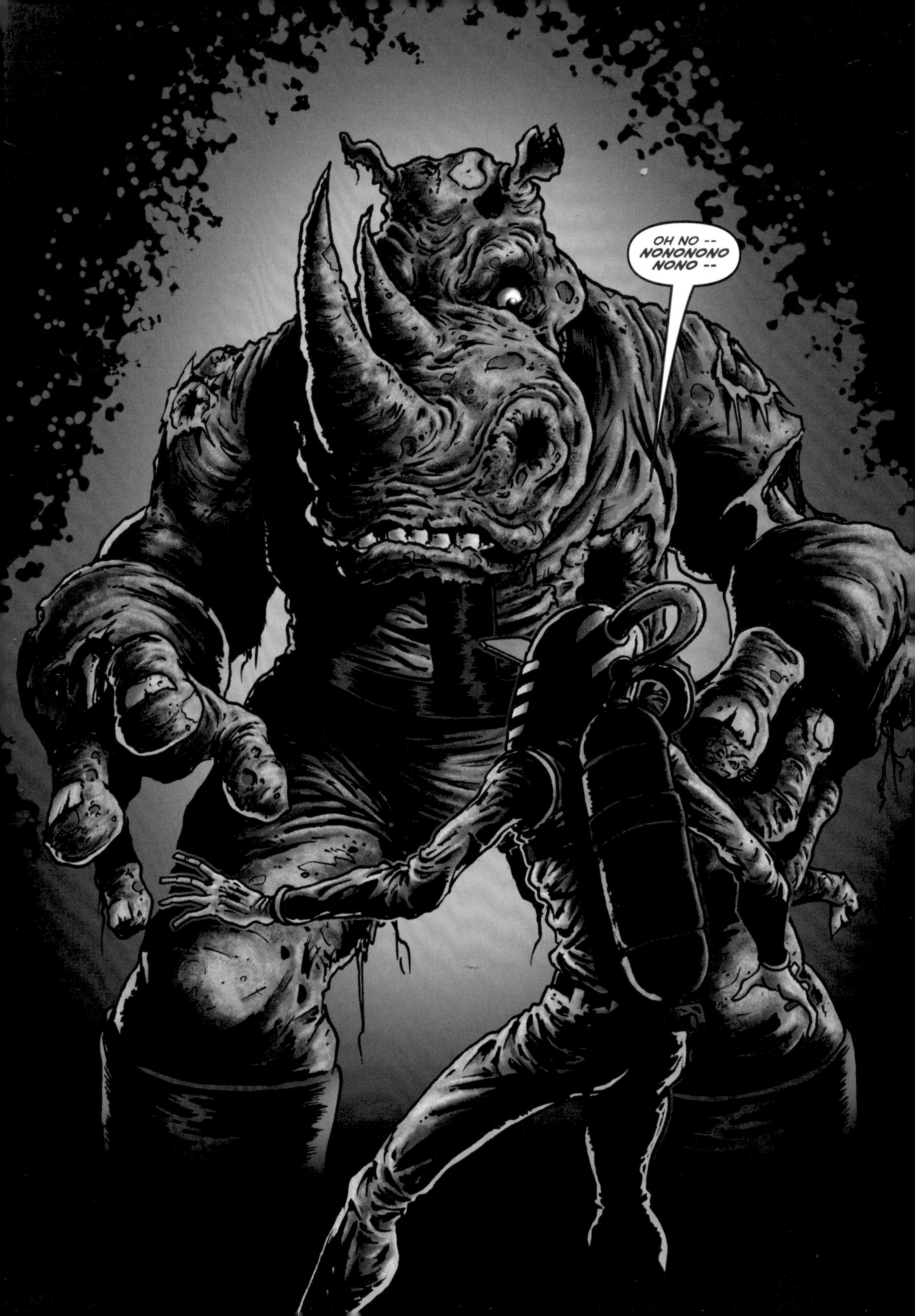
OH NO -- NONONONO NONO --

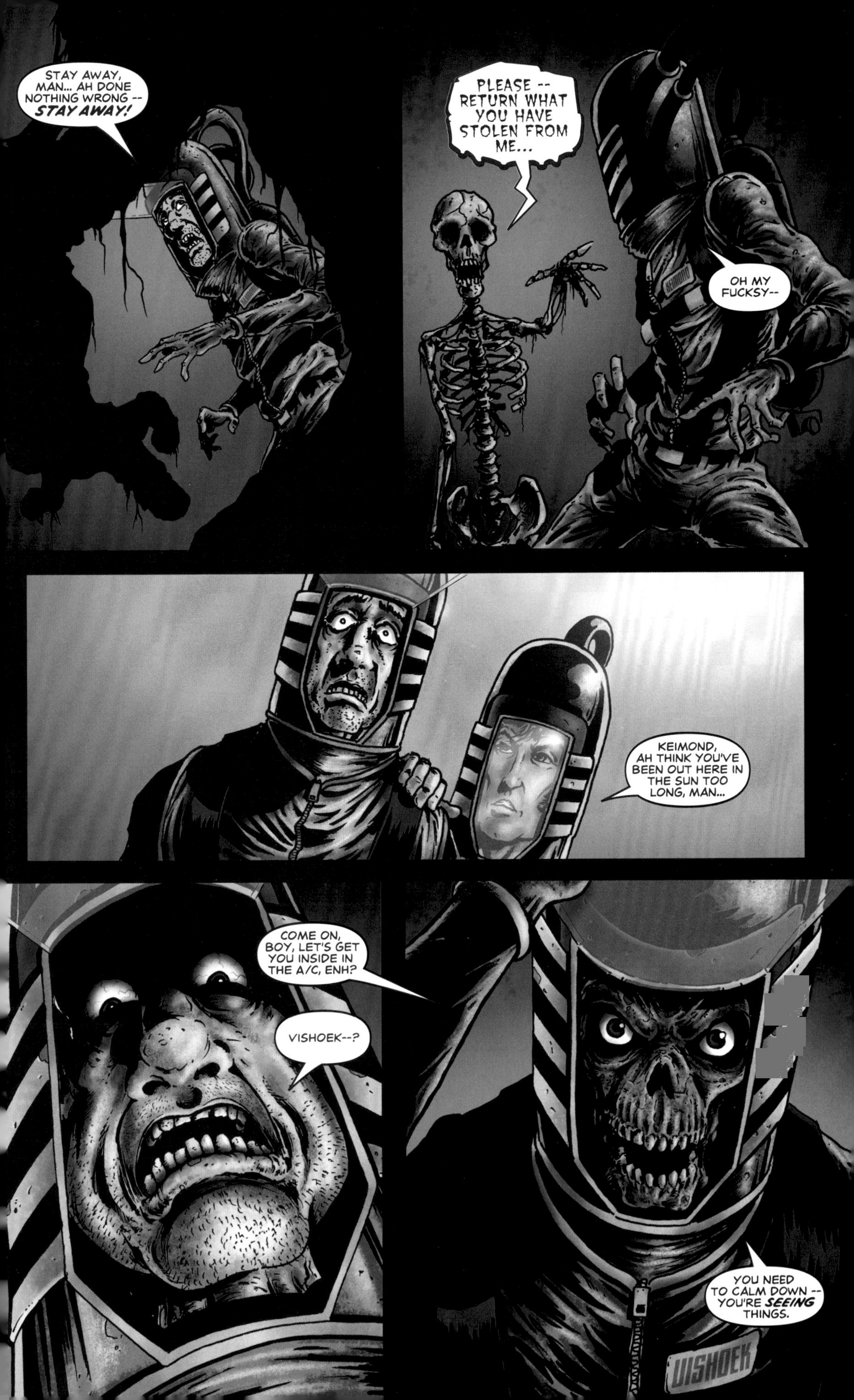
STAY AWAY, MAN... AH DONE NOTHING WRONG -- *STAY AWAY!*
PLEASE -- RETURN WHAT YOU HAVE STOLEN FROM ME...
OH MY FUCKSY--
KEIMOND, AH THINK YOU'VE BEEN OUT HERE IN THE SUN TOO LONG, MAN...
COME ON, BOY, LET'S GET YOU INSIDE IN THE A/C, ENH?
VISHOEK--?
YOU NEED TO CALM DOWN -- YOU'RE *SEEING* THINGS.
VISHOEK

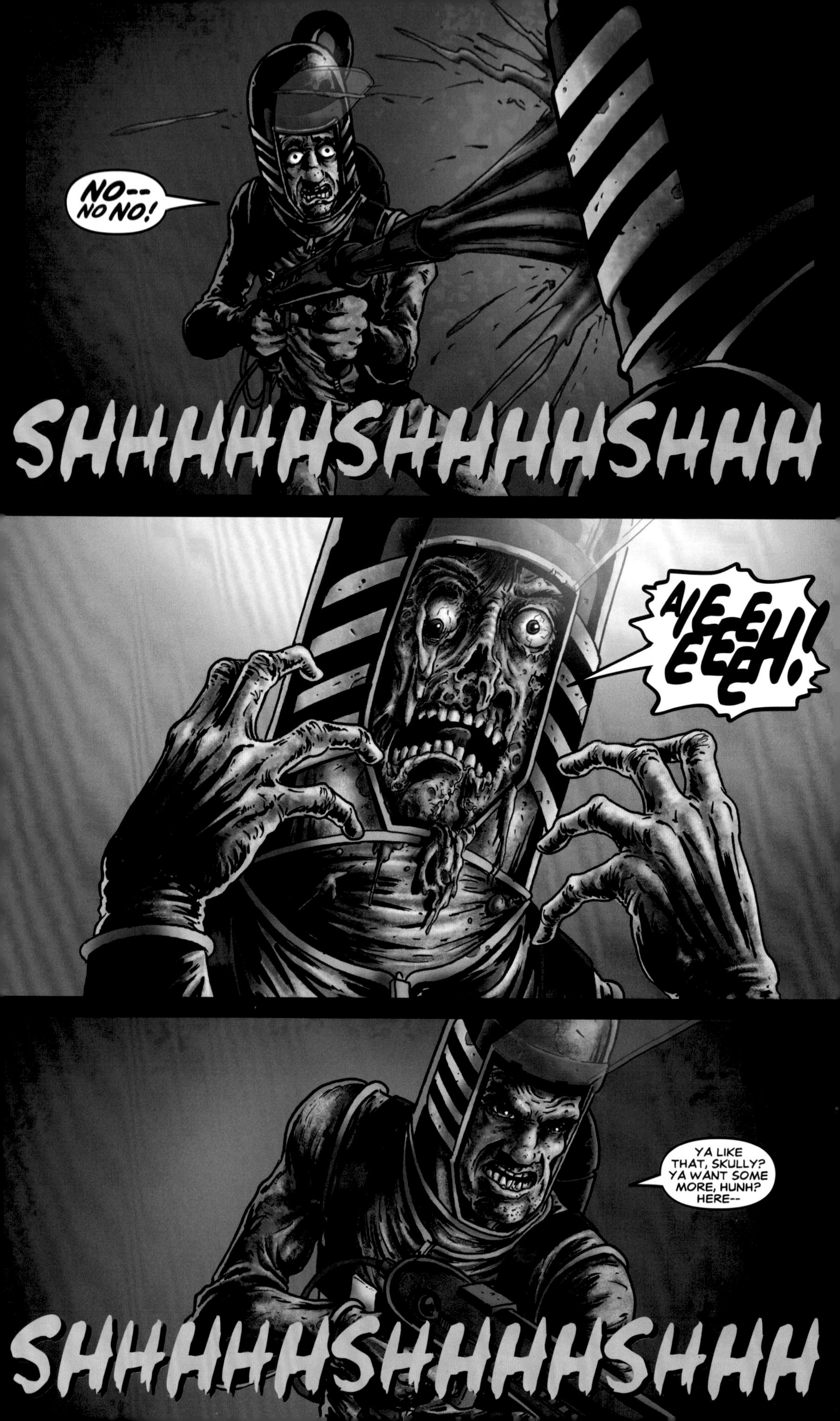
NO--
NO NO!
SHHHHSHHHHSHHH
AIEEEEH! EEEEH!
YA LIKE THAT, SKULLY? YA WANT SOME MORE, HUNH? HERE--
SHHHHSHHHHSHHH

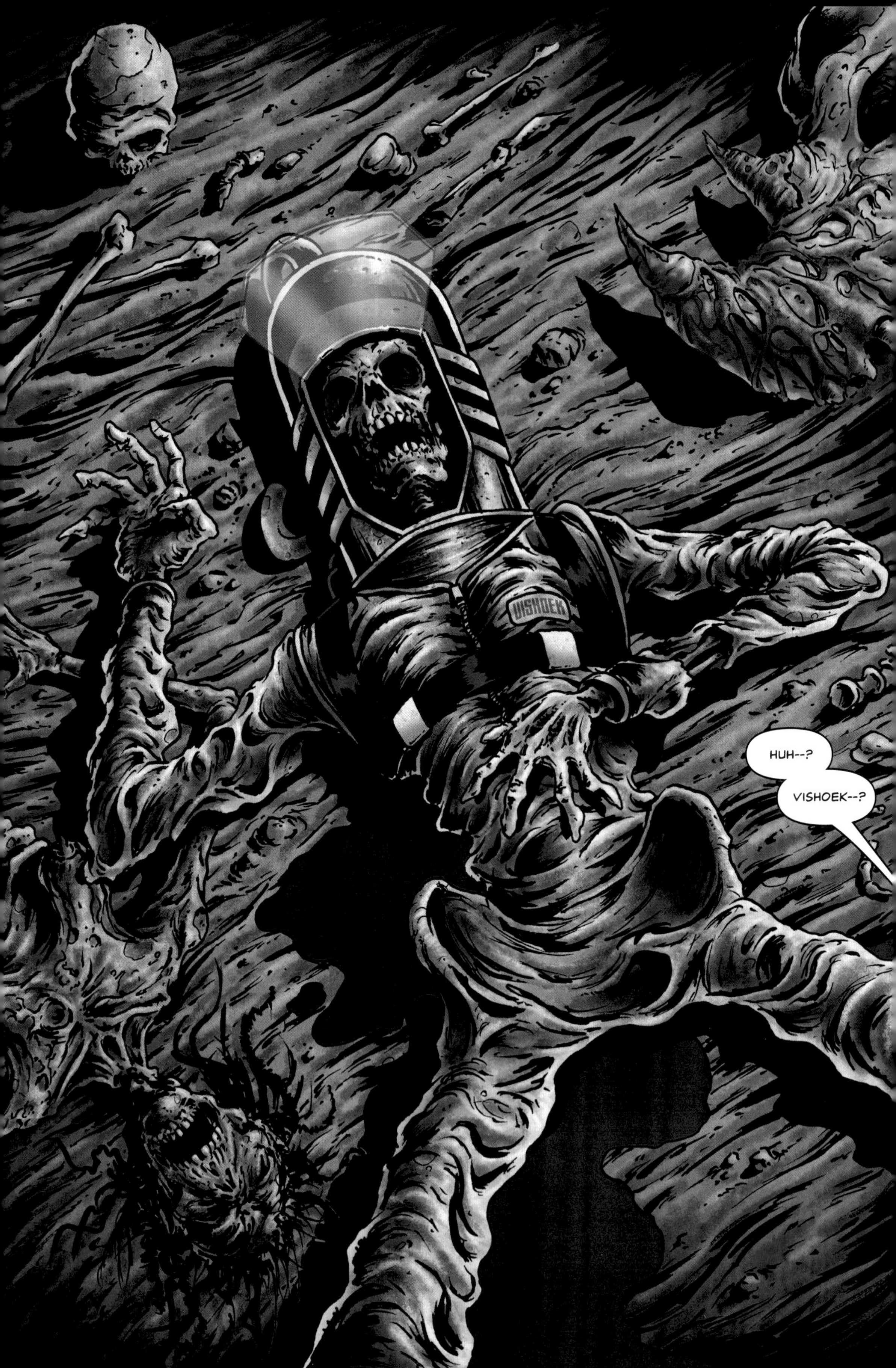
HUH--?
VISHOEK--?
VISHOEK

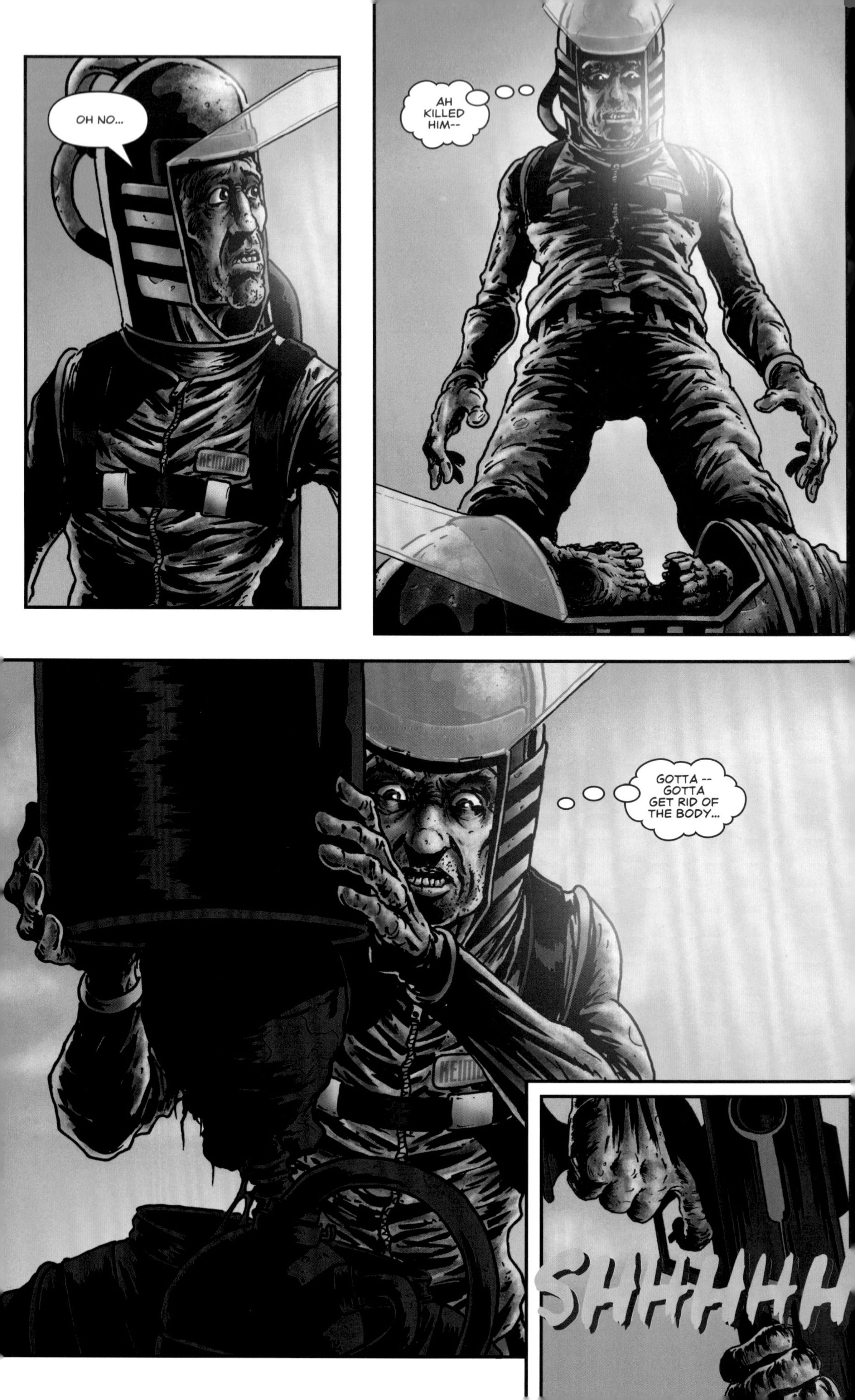
OH NO...
AH KILLED HIM--
GOTTA -- GOTTA GET RID OF THE BODY...
SHHHHH

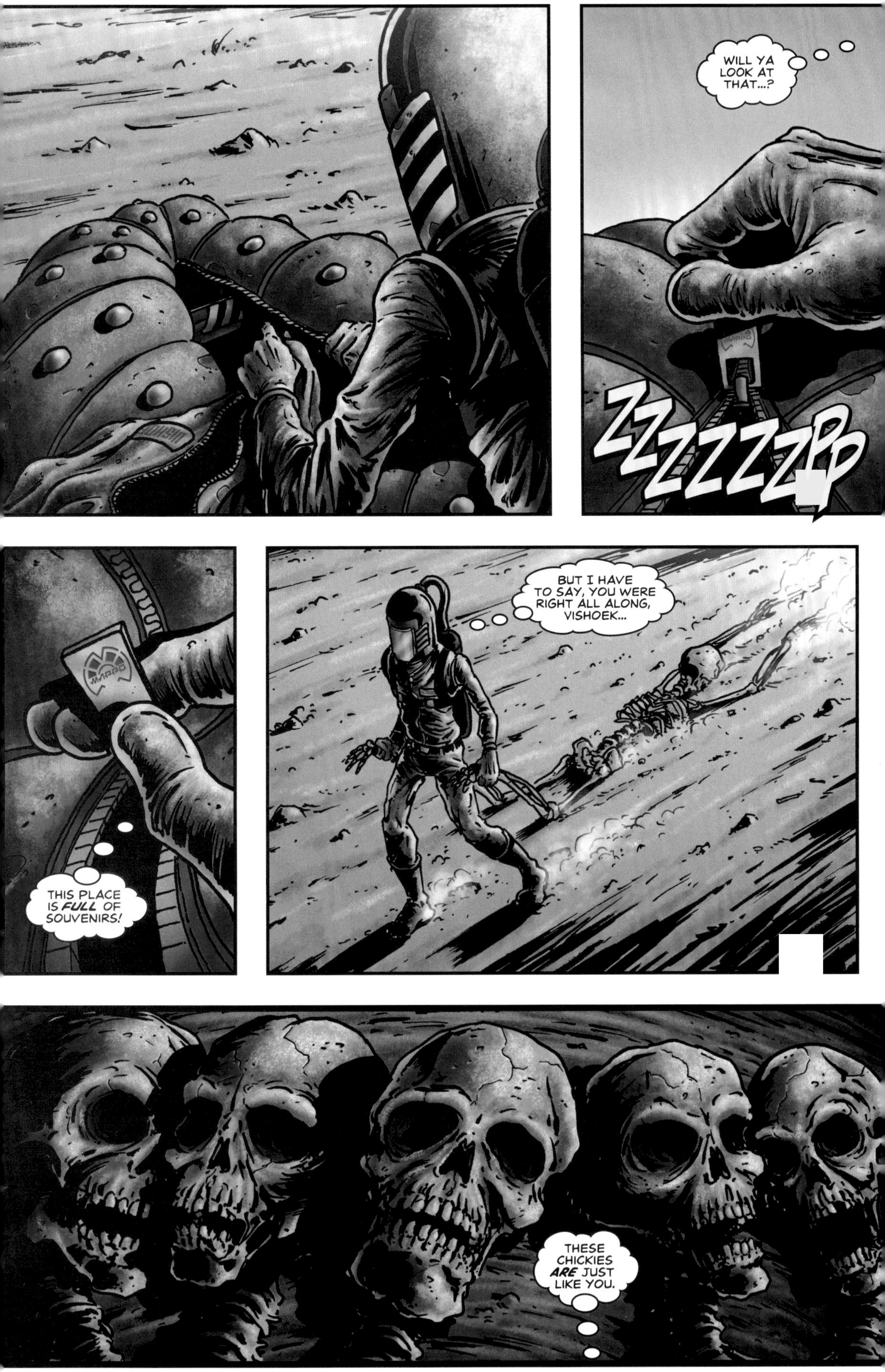
WILL YA LOOK AT THAT...?
ZZZZZZPP
THIS PLACE IS FULL OF SOUVENIRS!
BUT I HAVE TO SAY, YOU WERE RIGHT ALL ALONG, VISHOEK...
THESE CHICKIES ARE JUST LIKE YOU.

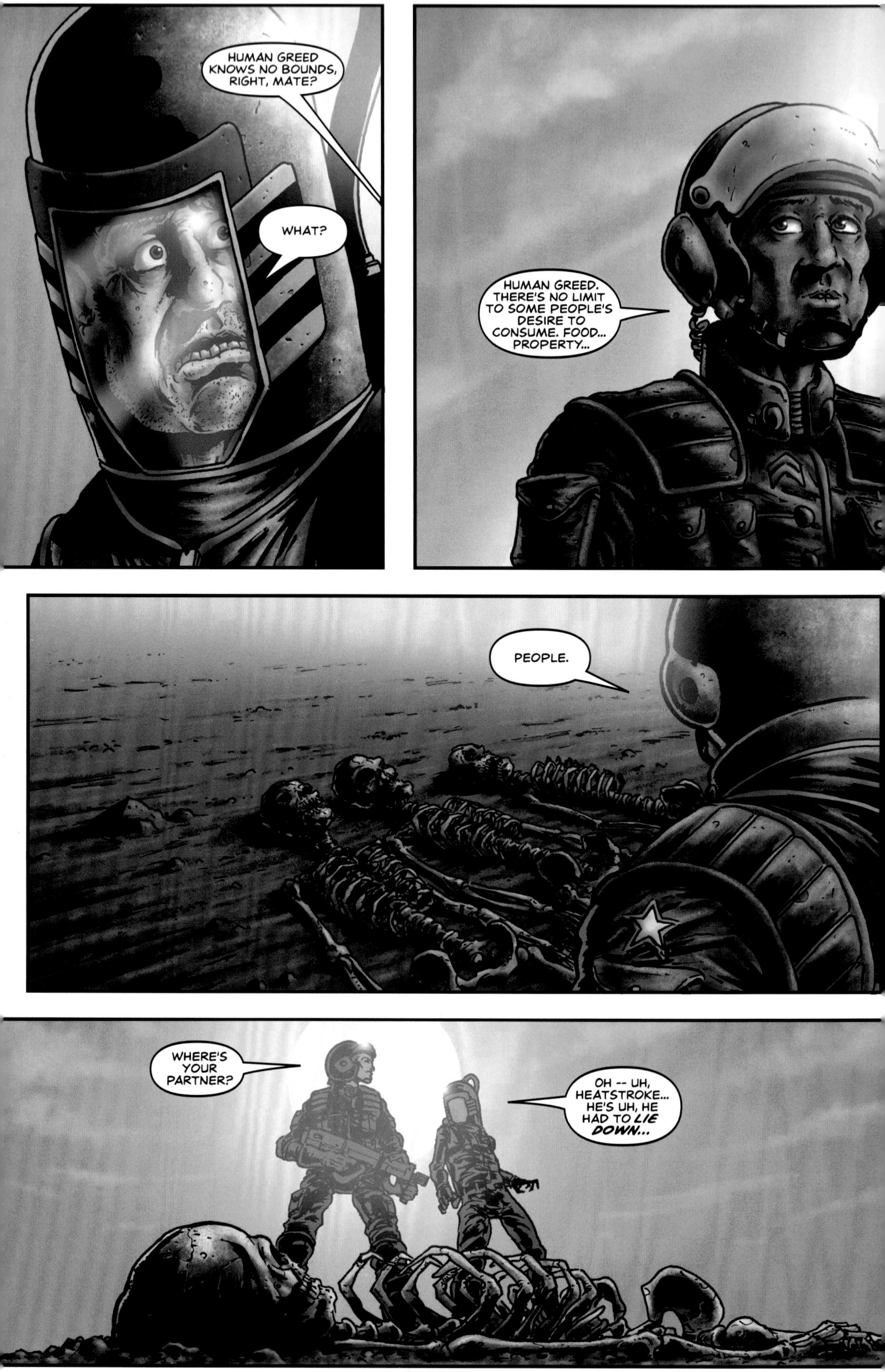
HUMAN GREED KNOWS NO BOUNDS, RIGHT, MATE?
WHAT?
HUMAN GREED. THERE'S NO LIMIT TO SOME PEOPLE'S DESIRE TO CONSUME. FOOD... PROPERTY...
PEOPLE.
WHERE'S YOUR PARTNER?
OH -- UH, HEATSTROKE... HE'S UH, HE HAD TO *LIE DOWN...*

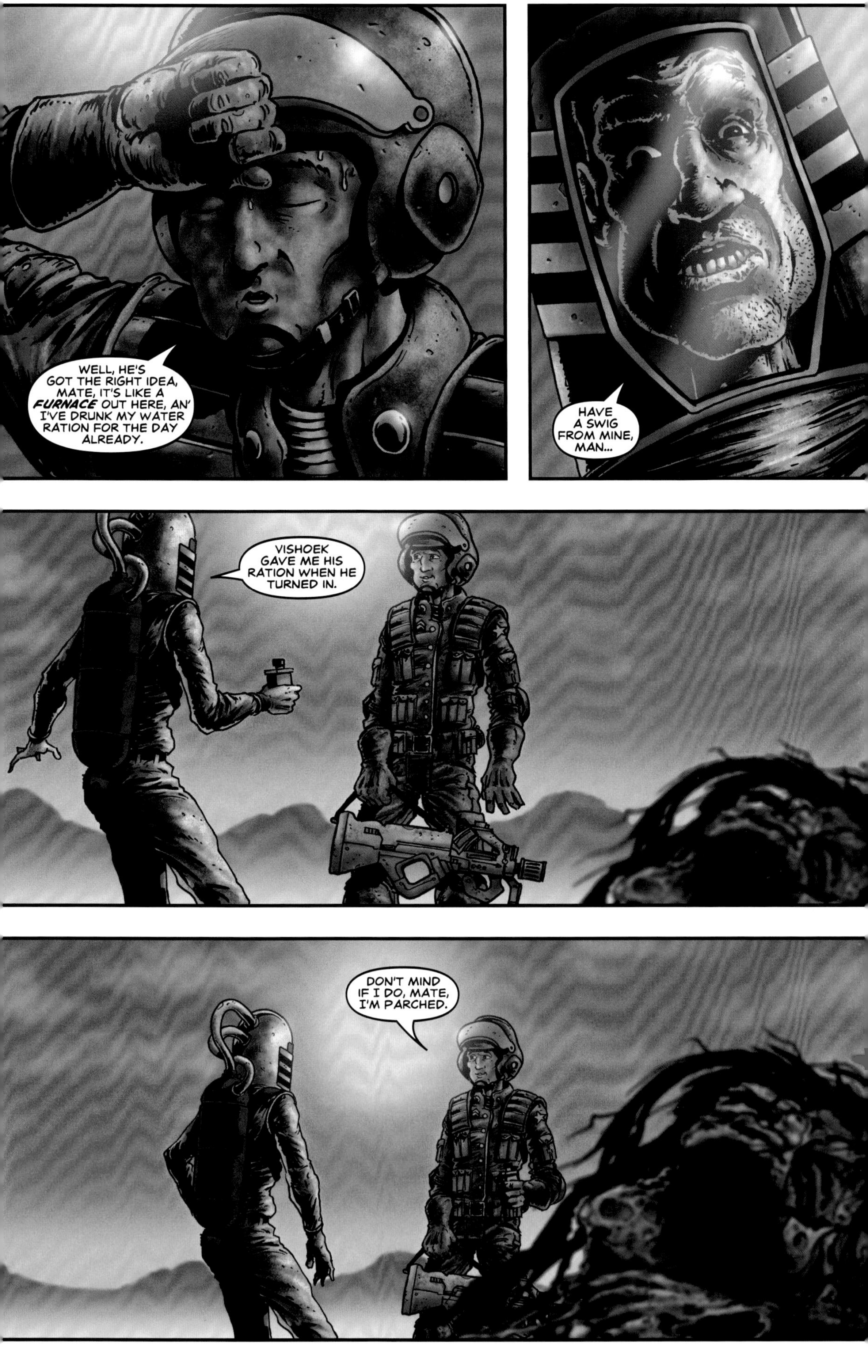
WELL, HE'S GOT THE RIGHT IDEA, MATE, IT'S LIKE A FURNACE OUT HERE, AN' I'VE DRUNK MY WATER RATION FOR THE DAY ALREADY.
HAVE A SWIG FROM MINE, MAN...
VISHOEK GAVE ME HIS RATION WHEN HE TURNED IN.
DON'T MIND IF I DO, MATE, I'M PARCHED.

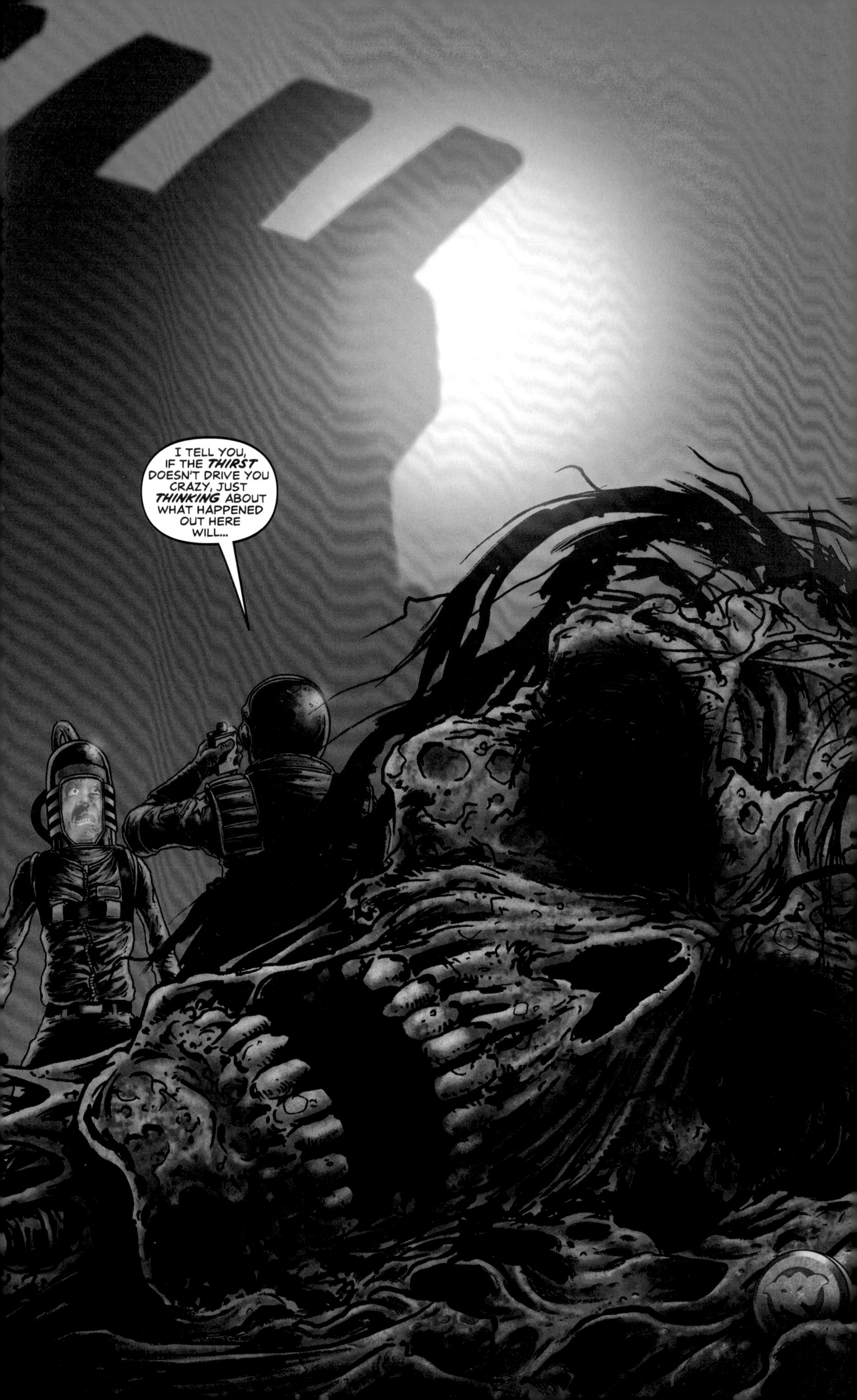
I TELL YOU, IF THE *THIRST* DOESN'T DRIVE YOU CRAZY, JUST *THINKING* ABOUT WHAT HAPPENED OUT HERE WILL...

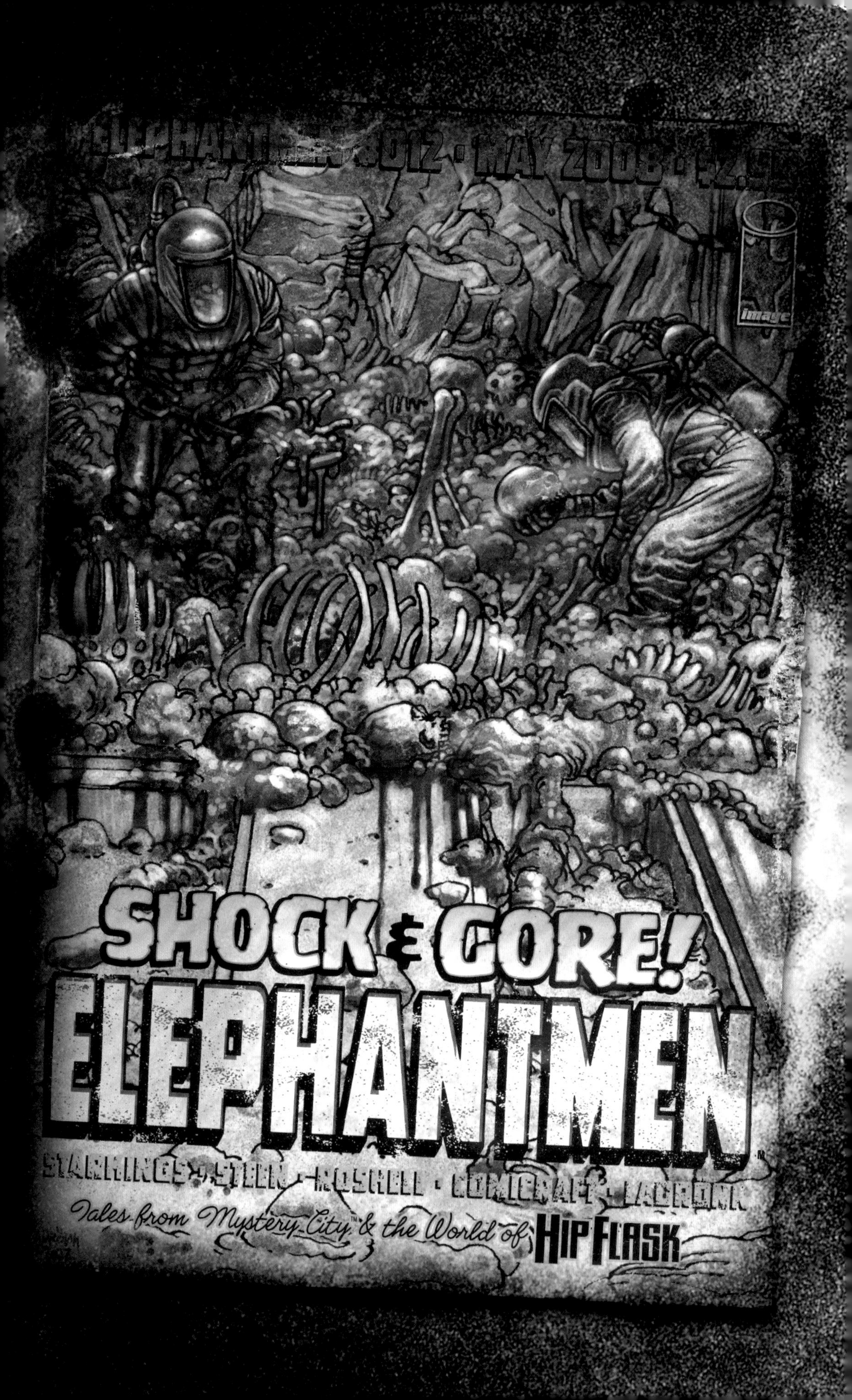
SHOCK & GORE!
ELEPHANTMEN
Tales from Mystery City™ & the World of HIP FLASK

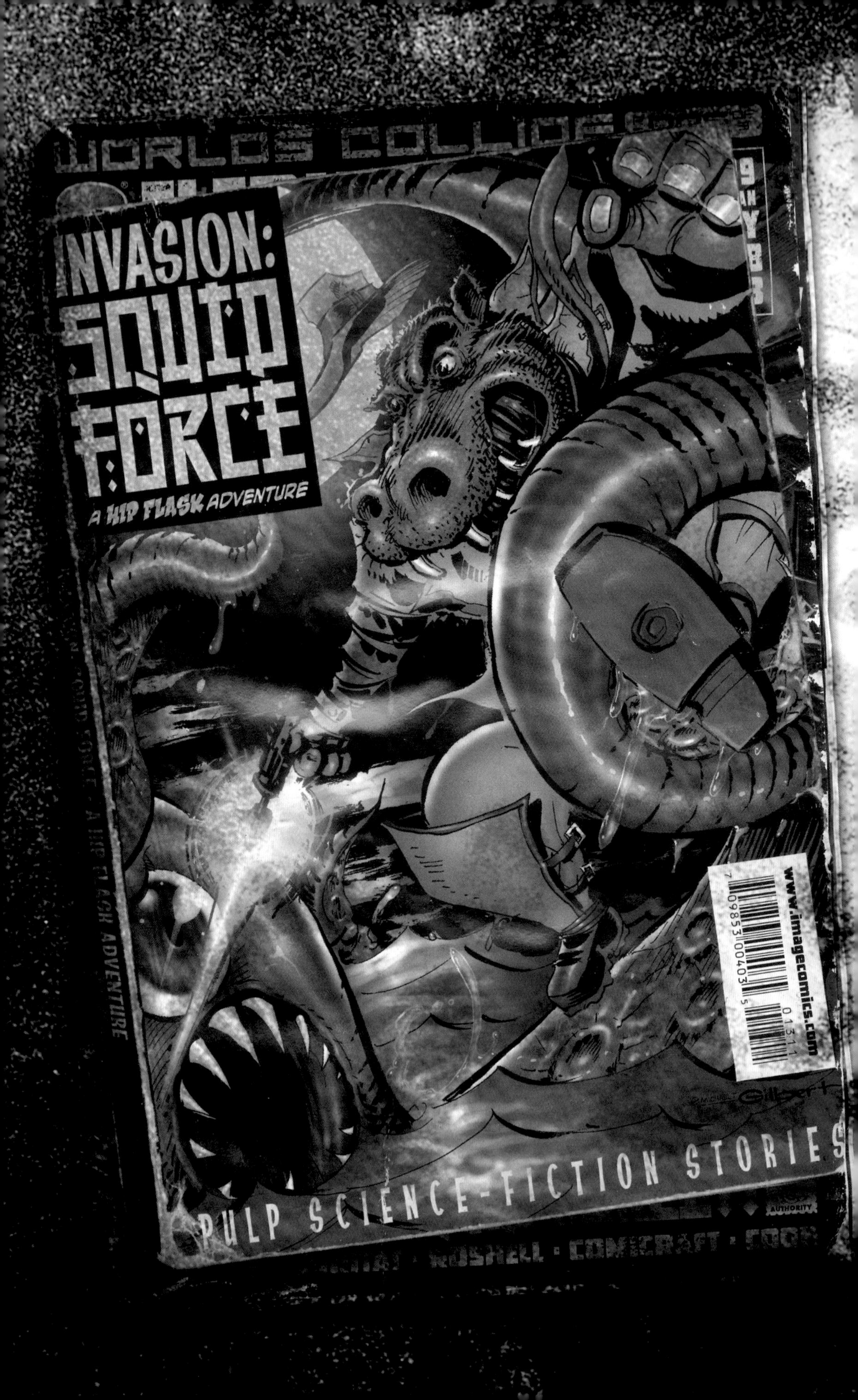
WORLDS COLLIDE
INVASION: SQUID FORCE
A HIP FLASK ADVENTURE
www.imagecomics.com
PULP SCIENCE-FICTION STORIES
AUTHORITY
ROSHELL · COMICRAFT ·

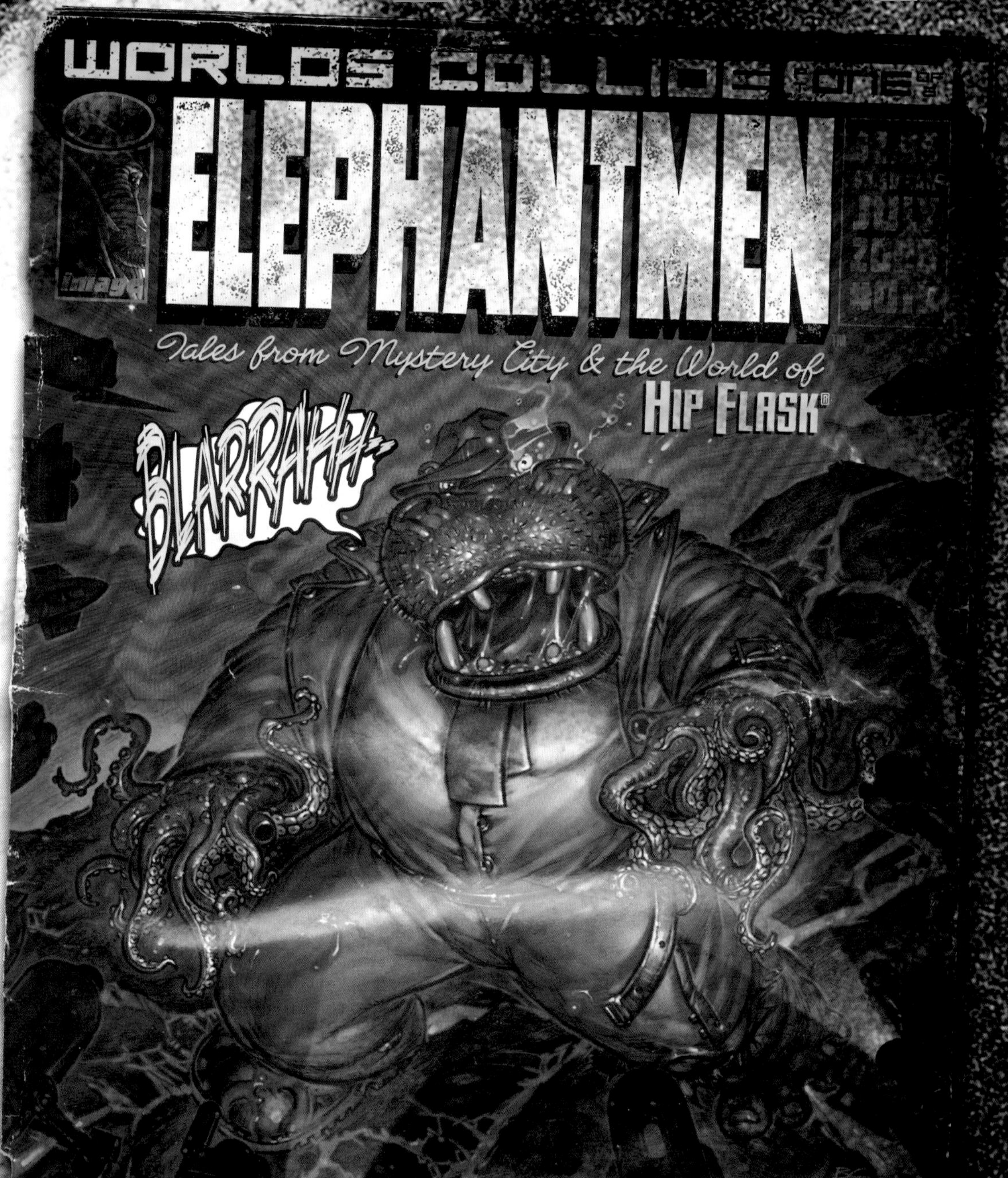
WORLDS COLLIDE
ELEPHANTMEN
Tales from Mystery City & the World of
HIP FLASK
BLARRAHH
INVASION: SQUID FORCE?!

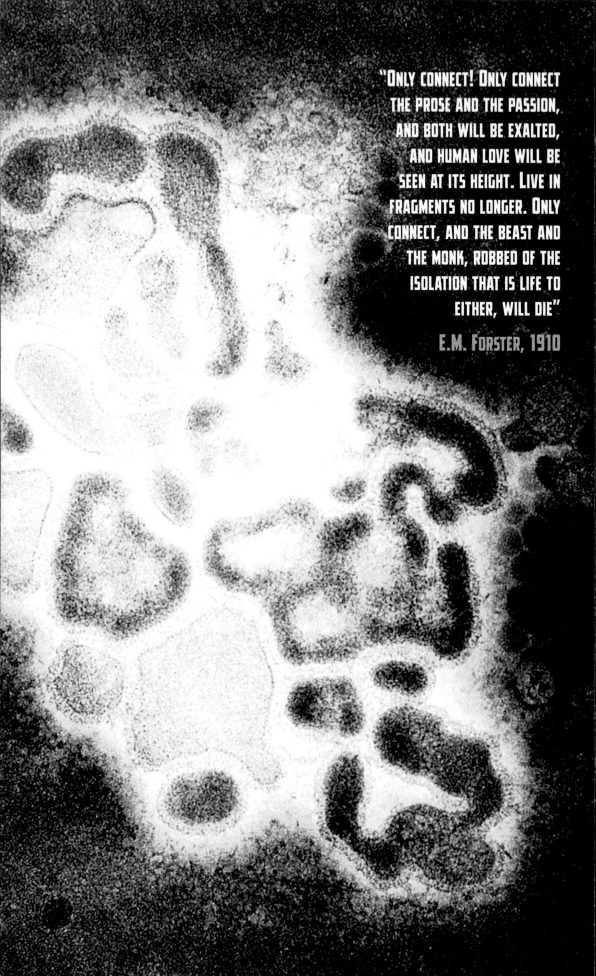

"ONLY CONNECT! ONLY CONNECT THE PROSE AND THE PASSION, AND BOTH WILL BE EXALTED, AND HUMAN LOVE WILL BE SEEN AT ITS HEIGHT. LIVE IN FRAGMENTS NO LONGER. ONLY CONNECT, AND THE BEAST AND THE MONK, ROBBED OF THE ISOLATION THAT IS LIFE TO EITHER, WILL DIE"

E.M. FORSTER, 1910

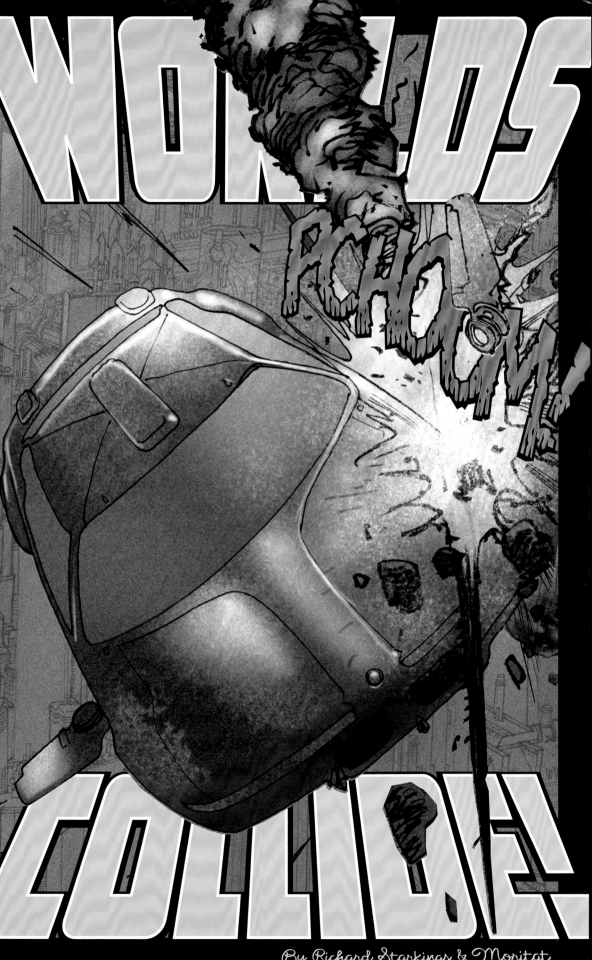

WORLDS COLLIDE!

PCHOOM!

By Richard Starkings & Moritat

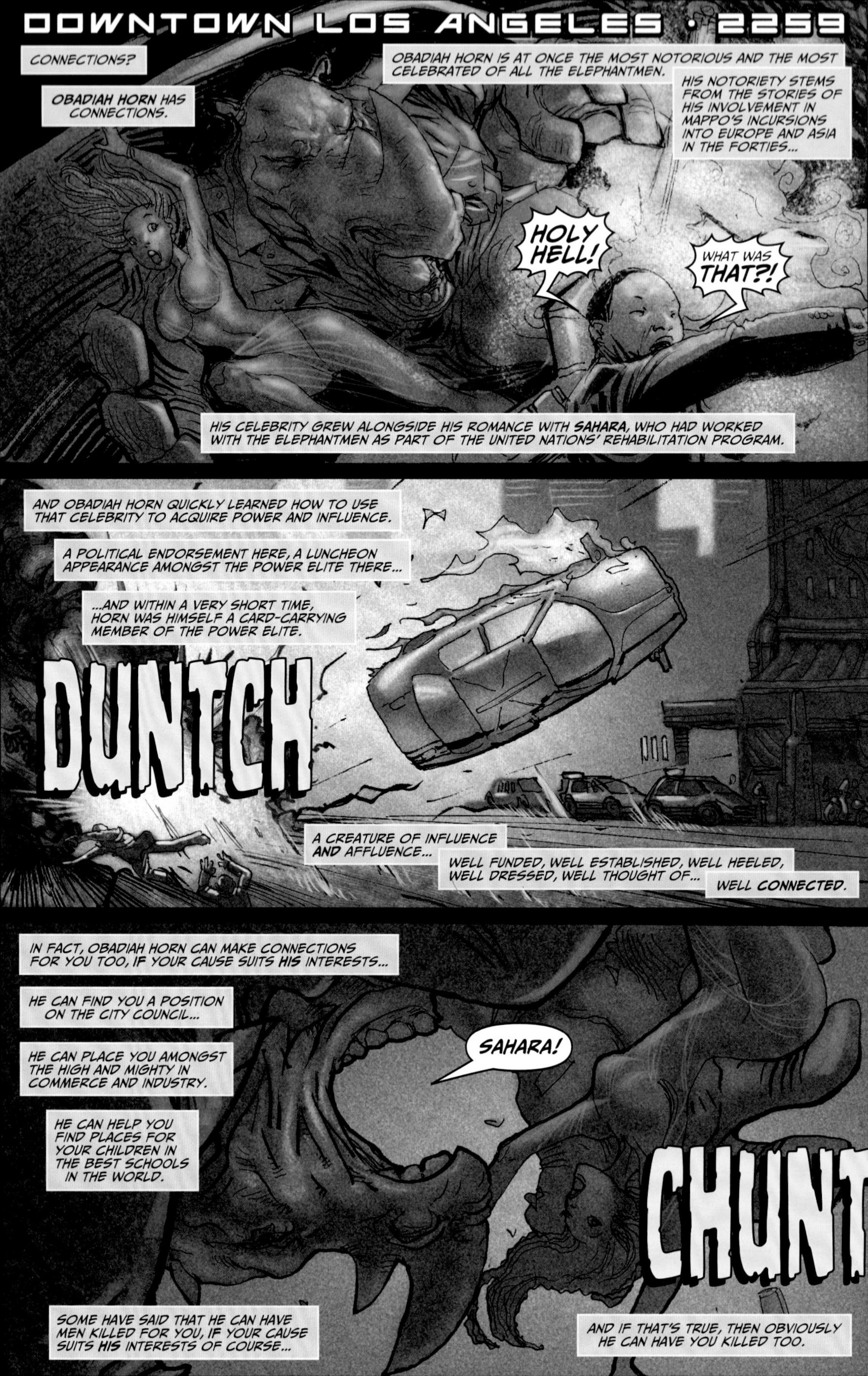
DOWNTOWN LOS ANGELES · 2259
CONNECTIONS?
OBADIAH HORN HAS CONNECTIONS.
OBADIAH HORN IS AT ONCE THE MOST NOTORIOUS AND THE MOST CELEBRATED OF ALL THE ELEPHANTMEN.
HIS NOTORIETY STEMS FROM THE STORIES OF HIS INVOLVEMENT IN MAPPO'S INCURSIONS INTO EUROPE AND ASIA IN THE FORTIES...
HOLY HELL!
WHAT WAS THAT?!
HIS CELEBRITY GREW ALONGSIDE HIS ROMANCE WITH SAHARA, WHO HAD WORKED WITH THE ELEPHANTMEN AS PART OF THE UNITED NATIONS' REHABILITATION PROGRAM.
AND OBADIAH HORN QUICKLY LEARNED HOW TO USE THAT CELEBRITY TO ACQUIRE POWER AND INFLUENCE.
A POLITICAL ENDORSEMENT HERE, A LUNCHEON APPEARANCE AMONGST THE POWER ELITE THERE...
...AND WITHIN A VERY SHORT TIME, HORN WAS HIMSELF A CARD-CARRYING MEMBER OF THE POWER ELITE.
DUNTCH
A CREATURE OF INFLUENCE AND AFFLUENCE...
WELL FUNDED, WELL ESTABLISHED, WELL HEELED, WELL DRESSED, WELL THOUGHT OF...
WELL CONNECTED.
IN FACT, OBADIAH HORN CAN MAKE CONNECTIONS FOR YOU TOO, IF YOUR CAUSE SUITS HIS INTERESTS...
HE CAN FIND YOU A POSITION ON THE CITY COUNCIL...
HE CAN PLACE YOU AMONGST THE HIGH AND MIGHTY IN COMMERCE AND INDUSTRY.
HE CAN HELP YOU FIND PLACES FOR YOUR CHILDREN IN THE BEST SCHOOLS IN THE WORLD.
SAHARA!
CHUNT
SOME HAVE SAID THAT HE CAN HAVE MEN KILLED FOR YOU, IF YOUR CAUSE SUITS HIS INTERESTS OF COURSE...
AND IF THAT'S TRUE, THEN OBVIOUSLY HE CAN HAVE YOU KILLED TOO.

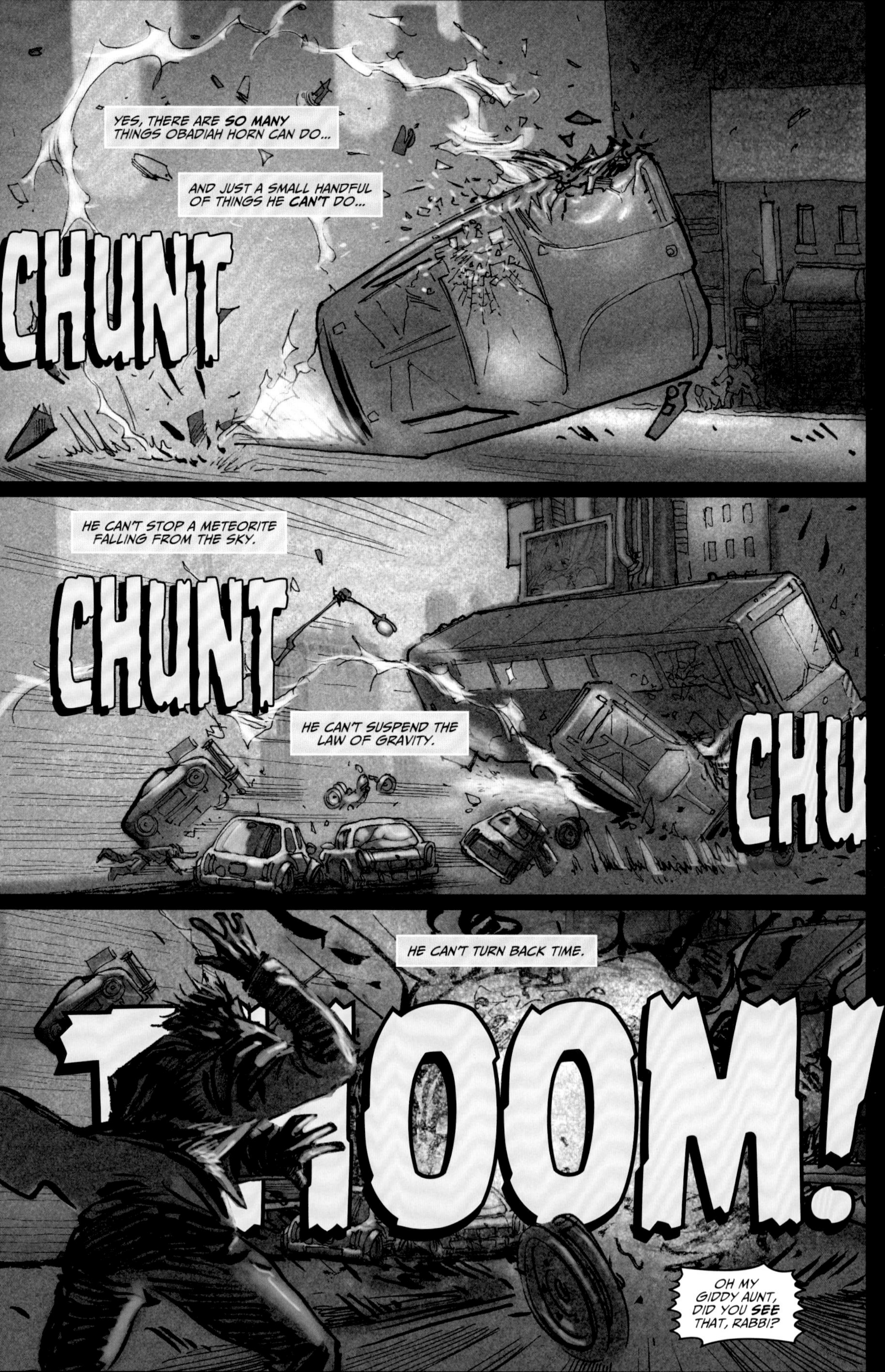

YES, THERE ARE SO MANY THINGS OBADIAH HORN CAN DO...
AND JUST A SMALL HANDFUL OF THINGS HE CAN'T DO...
CHUNT
HE CAN'T STOP A METEORITE FALLING FROM THE SKY.
CHUNT
HE CAN'T SUSPEND THE LAW OF GRAVITY.
HE CAN'T TURN BACK TIME.
OOM!
OH MY GIDDY AUNT, DID YOU SEE THAT, RABBI?

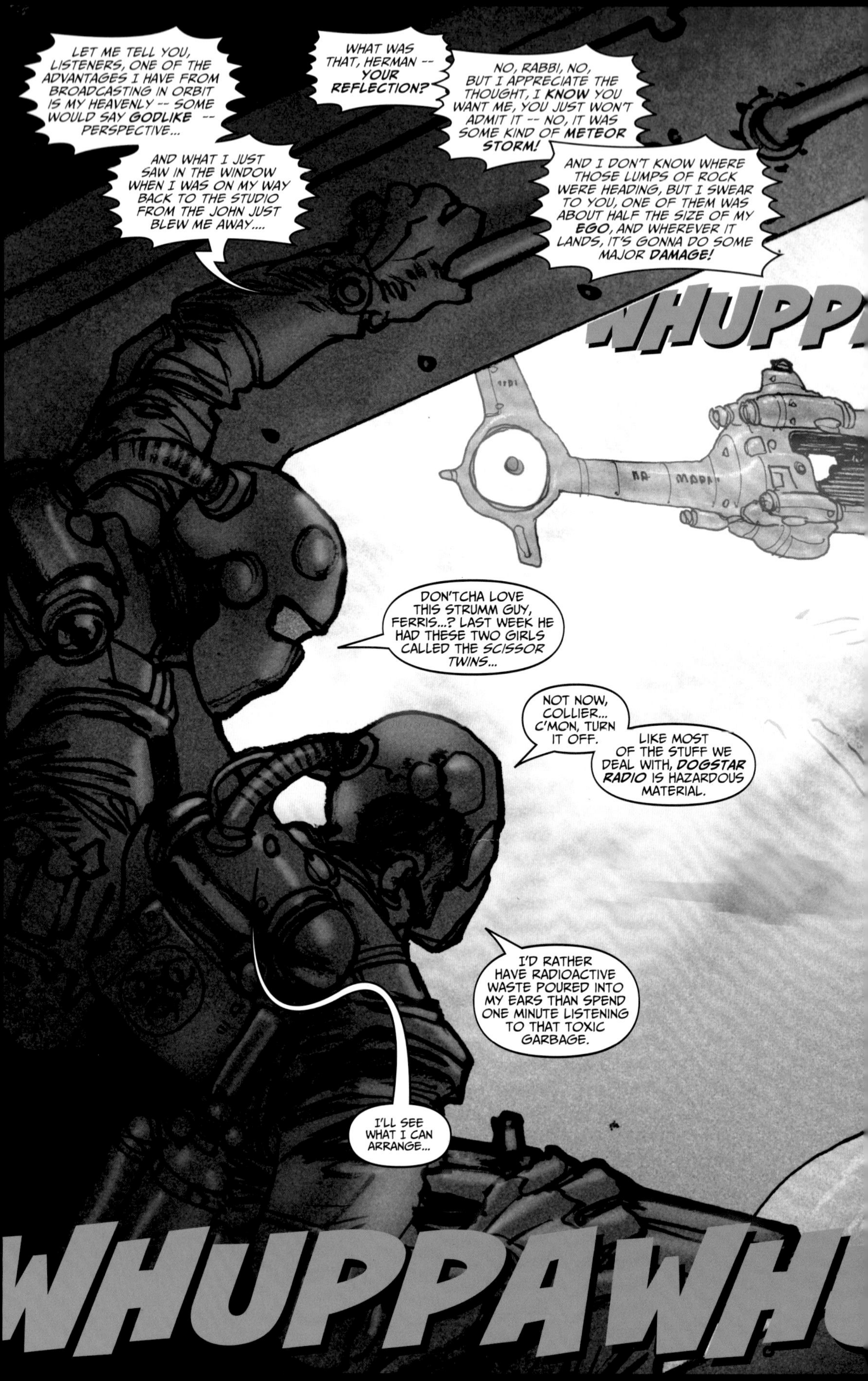

LET ME TELL YOU, LISTENERS, ONE OF THE ADVANTAGES I HAVE FROM BROADCASTING IN ORBIT IS MY HEAVENLY -- SOME WOULD SAY GODLIKE -- PERSPECTIVE...
AND WHAT I JUST SAW IN THE WINDOW WHEN I WAS ON MY WAY BACK TO THE STUDIO FROM THE JOHN JUST BLEW ME AWAY....
WHAT WAS THAT, HERMAN -- YOUR REFLECTION?
NO, RABBI, NO, BUT I APPRECIATE THE THOUGHT, I KNOW YOU WANT ME, YOU JUST WON'T ADMIT IT -- NO, IT WAS SOME KIND OF METEOR STORM!
AND I DON'T KNOW WHERE THOSE LUMPS OF ROCK WERE HEADING, BUT I SWEAR TO YOU, ONE OF THEM WAS ABOUT HALF THE SIZE OF MY EGO, AND WHEREVER IT LANDS, IT'S GONNA DO SOME MAJOR DAMAGE!
WHUPP
DON'TCHA LOVE THIS STRUMM GUY, FERRIS...? LAST WEEK HE HAD THESE TWO GIRLS CALLED THE SCISSOR TWINS...
NOT NOW, COLLIER... C'MON, TURN IT OFF.
LIKE MOST OF THE STUFF WE DEAL WITH, DOGSTAR RADIO IS HAZARDOUS MATERIAL.
I'D RATHER HAVE RADIOACTIVE WASTE POURED INTO MY EARS THAN SPEND ONE MINUTE LISTENING TO THAT TOXIC GARBAGE.
I'LL SEE WHAT I CAN ARRANGE...
WHUPPAWH

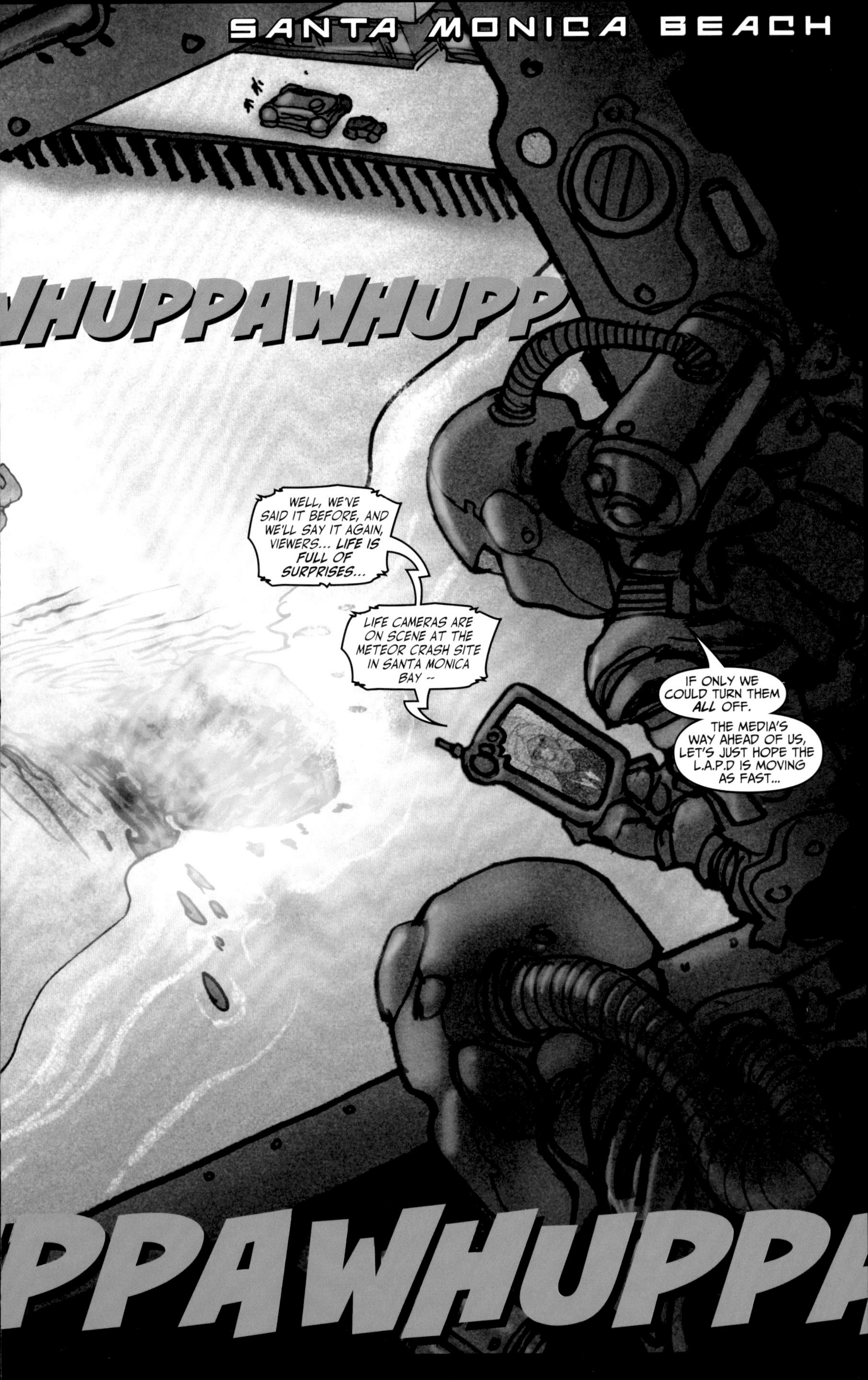
SANTA MONICA BEACH
WHUPPAWHUPP
WELL, WE'VE SAID IT BEFORE, AND WE'LL SAY IT AGAIN, VIEWERS... LIFE IS FULL OF SURPRISES...
LIFE CAMERAS ARE ON SCENE AT THE METEOR CRASH SITE IN SANTA MONICA BAY --
IF ONLY WE COULD TURN THEM ALL OFF.
THE MEDIA'S WAY AHEAD OF US, LET'S JUST HOPE THE L.A.P.D IS MOVING AS FAST...
PPAWHUPPA

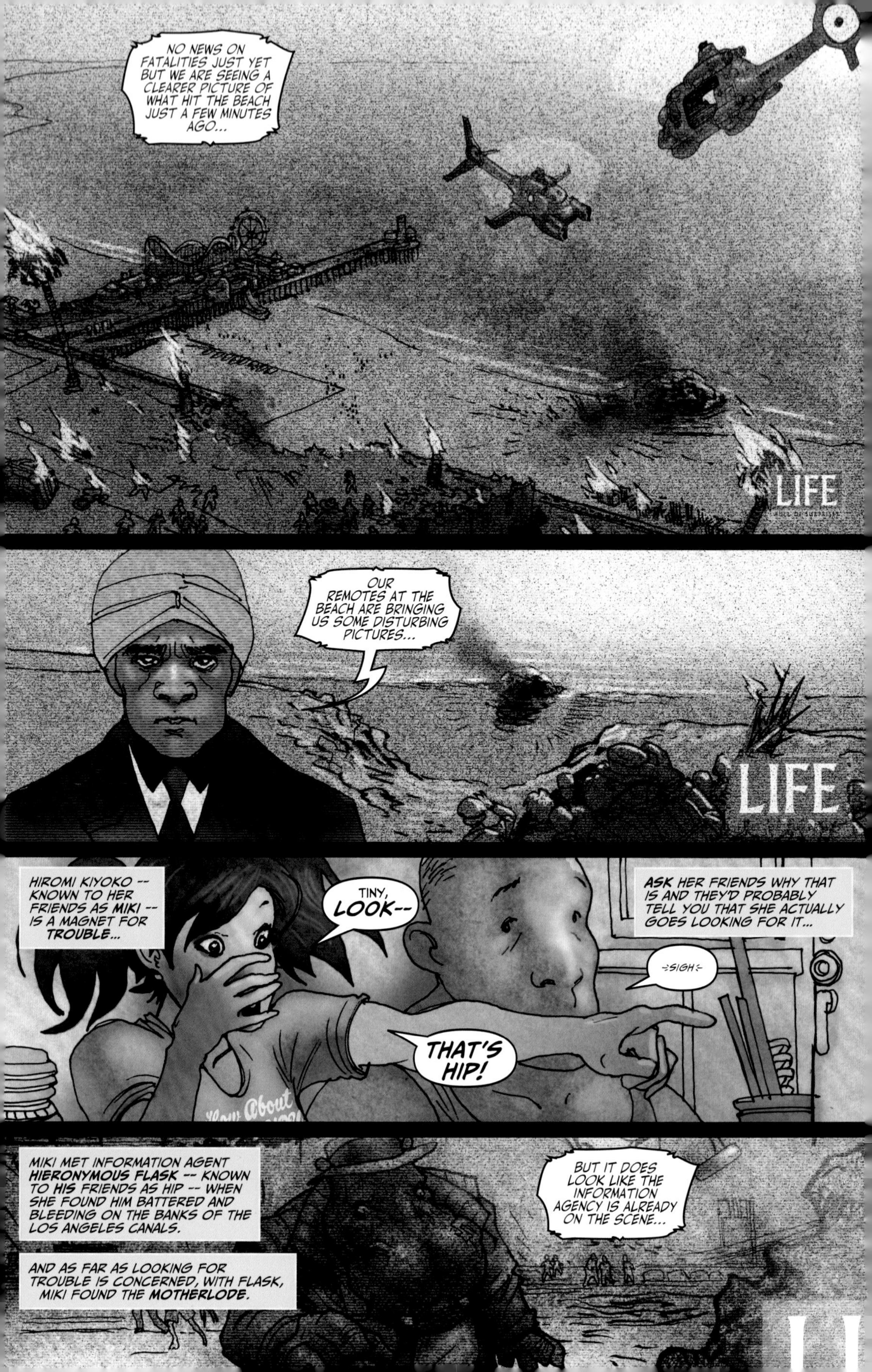
NO NEWS ON FATALITIES JUST YET BUT WE ARE SEEING A CLEARER PICTURE OF WHAT HIT THE BEACH JUST A FEW MINUTES AGO...
LIFE
OUR REMOTES AT THE BEACH ARE BRINGING US SOME DISTURBING PICTURES...
LIFE
HIROMI KIYOKO -- KNOWN TO HER FRIENDS AS MIKI -- IS A MAGNET FOR TROUBLE...
TINY, LOOK--
ASK HER FRIENDS WHY THAT IS AND THEY'D PROBABLY TELL YOU THAT SHE ACTUALLY GOES LOOKING FOR IT...
SIGH
THAT'S HIP!
MIKI MET INFORMATION AGENT HIERONYMOUS FLASK -- KNOWN TO HIS FRIENDS AS HIP -- WHEN SHE FOUND HIM BATTERED AND BLEEDING ON THE BANKS OF THE LOS ANGELES CANALS.
AND AS FAR AS LOOKING FOR TROUBLE IS CONCERNED, WITH FLASK, MIKI FOUND THE MOTHERLODE.
BUT IT DOES LOOK LIKE THE INFORMATION AGENCY IS ALREADY ON THE SCENE...

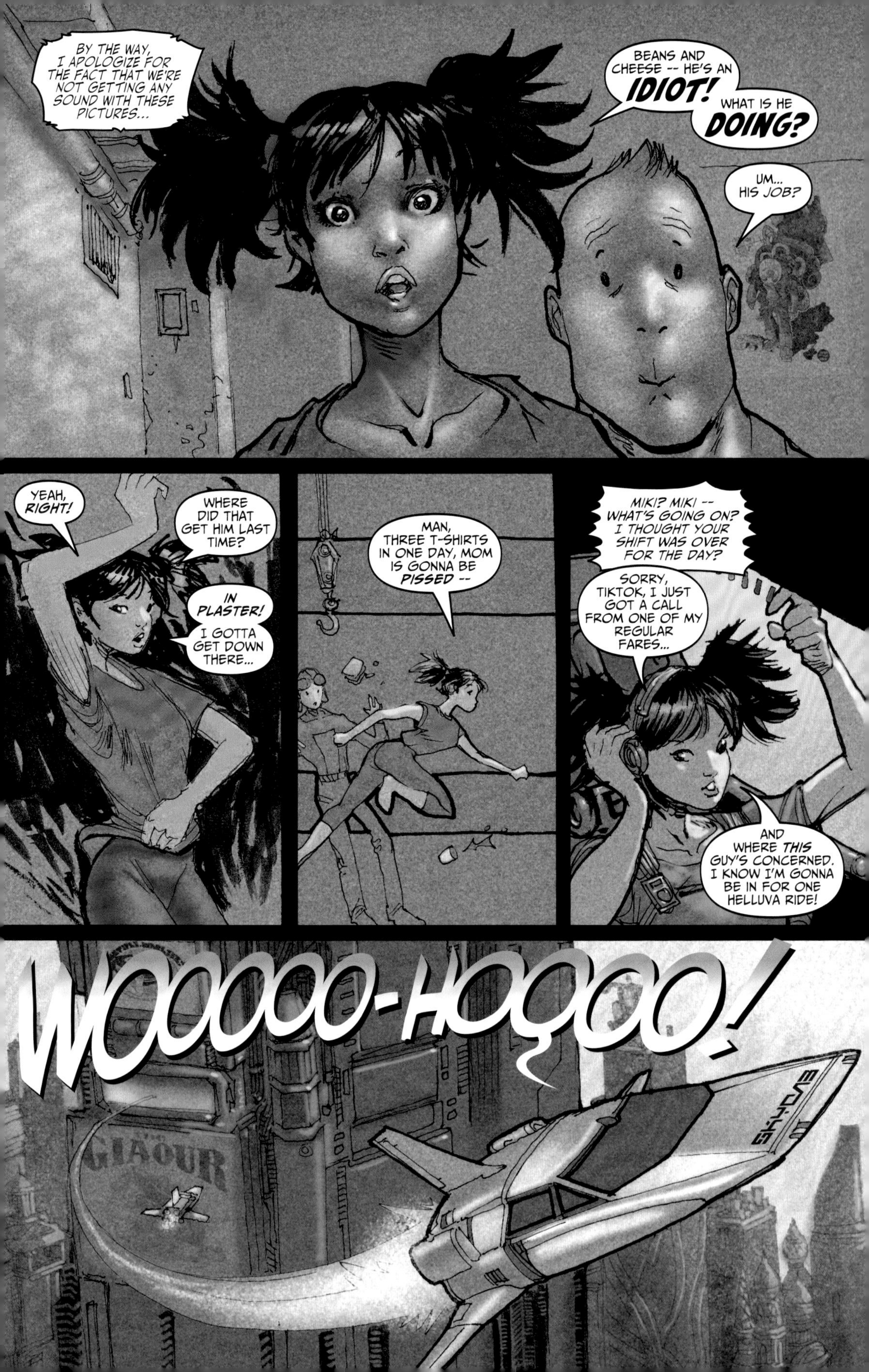
BY THE WAY, I APOLOGIZE FOR THE FACT THAT WE'RE NOT GETTING ANY SOUND WITH THESE PICTURES...
BEANS AND CHEESE -- HE'S AN IDIOT!
WHAT IS HE DOING?
UM... HIS JOB?
YEAH, RIGHT!
WHERE DID THAT GET HIM LAST TIME?
IN PLASTER!
I GOTTA GET DOWN THERE...
MAN, THREE T-SHIRTS IN ONE DAY, MOM IS GONNA BE PISSED --
MIKI? MIKI -- WHAT'S GOING ON? I THOUGHT YOUR SHIFT WAS OVER FOR THE DAY?
SORRY, TIKTOK, I JUST GOT A CALL FROM ONE OF MY REGULAR FARES...
AND WHERE THIS GUY'S CONCERNED, I KNOW I'M GONNA BE IN FOR ONE HELLUVA RIDE!
WOOOOO-HOOOOO!
GIAOUR

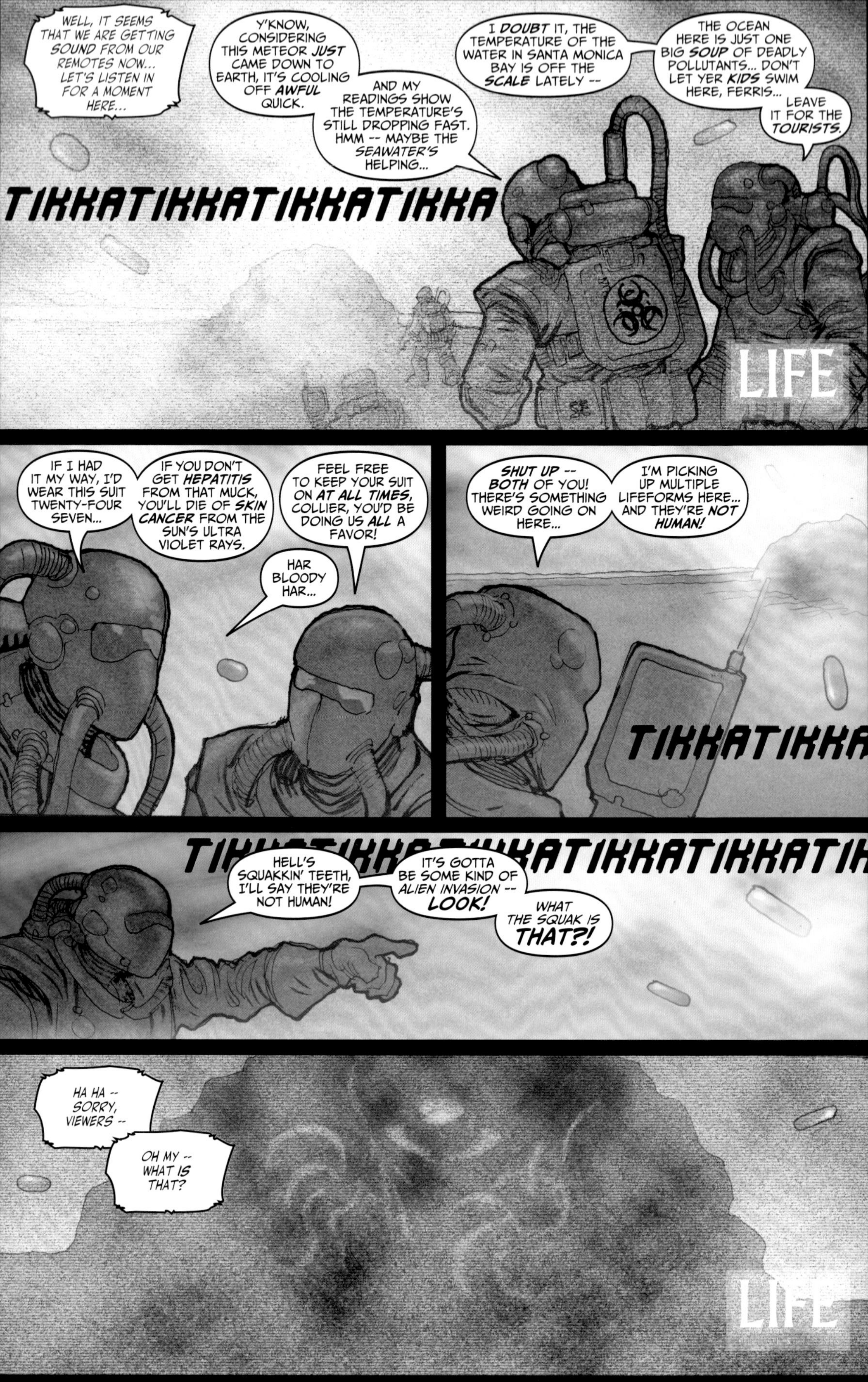
WELL, IT SEEMS THAT WE ARE GETTING SOUND FROM OUR REMOTES NOW... LET'S LISTEN IN FOR A MOMENT HERE...
Y'KNOW, CONSIDERING THIS METEOR JUST CAME DOWN TO EARTH, IT'S COOLING OFF AWFUL QUICK.
AND MY READINGS SHOW THE TEMPERATURE'S STILL DROPPING FAST. HMM -- MAYBE THE SEAWATER'S HELPING...
I DOUBT IT, THE TEMPERATURE OF THE WATER IN SANTA MONICA BAY IS OFF THE SCALE LATELY --
THE OCEAN HERE IS JUST ONE BIG SOUP OF DEADLY POLLUTANTS... DON'T LET YER KIDS SWIM HERE, FERRIS...
LEAVE IT FOR THE TOURISTS.
TIKKATIKKATIKKATIKKA
LIFE
IF I HAD IT MY WAY, I'D WEAR THIS SUIT TWENTY-FOUR SEVEN...
IF YOU DON'T GET HEPATITIS FROM THAT MUCK, YOU'LL DIE OF SKIN CANCER FROM THE SUN'S ULTRA VIOLET RAYS.
FEEL FREE TO KEEP YOUR SUIT ON AT ALL TIMES, COLLIER, YOU'D BE DOING US ALL A FAVOR!
HAR BLOODY HAR...
SHUT UP -- BOTH OF YOU! THERE'S SOMETHING WEIRD GOING ON HERE...
I'M PICKING UP MULTIPLE LIFEFORMS HERE... AND THEY'RE NOT HUMAN!
TIKKATIKKA
HELL'S SQUAKKIN' TEETH, I'LL SAY THEY'RE NOT HUMAN!
IT'S GOTTA BE SOME KIND OF ALIEN INVASION -- LOOK!
WHAT THE SQUAK IS THAT?!
HA HA -- SORRY, VIEWERS --
OH MY -- WHAT IS THAT?
LIFE

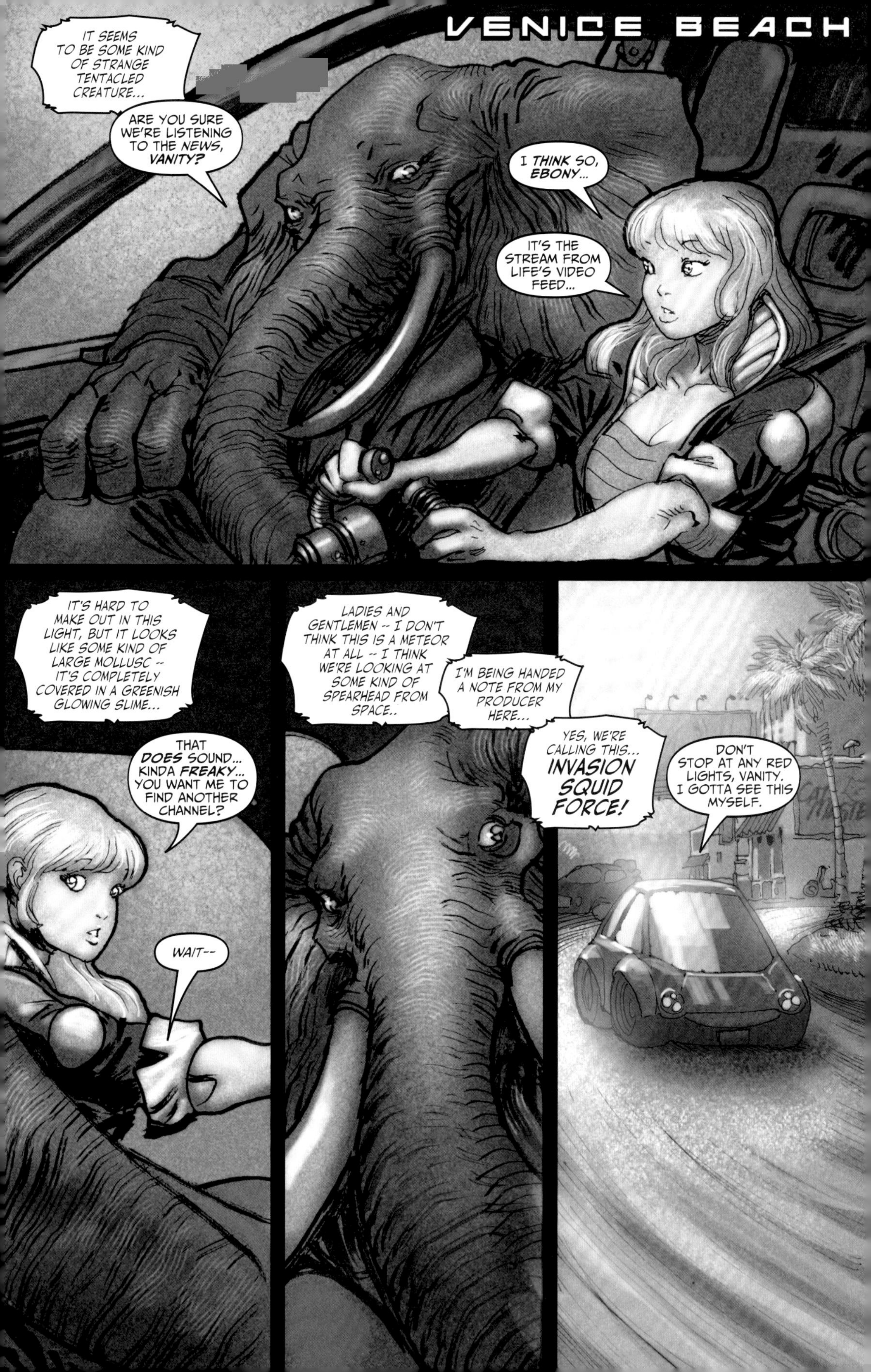
VENICE BEACH
IT SEEMS TO BE SOME KIND OF STRANGE TENTACLED CREATURE...
ARE YOU SURE WE'RE LISTENING TO THE NEWS, VANITY?
I THINK SO, EBONY...
IT'S THE STREAM FROM LIFE'S VIDEO FEED...
IT'S HARD TO MAKE OUT IN THIS LIGHT, BUT IT LOOKS LIKE SOME KIND OF LARGE MOLLUSC -- IT'S COMPLETELY COVERED IN A GREENISH GLOWING SLIME...
THAT DOES SOUND... KINDA FREAKY... YOU WANT ME TO FIND ANOTHER CHANNEL?
WAIT--
LADIES AND GENTLEMEN -- I DON'T THINK THIS IS A METEOR AT ALL -- I THINK WE'RE LOOKING AT SOME KIND OF SPEARHEAD FROM SPACE..
I'M BEING HANDED A NOTE FROM MY PRODUCER HERE...
YES, WE'RE CALLING THIS... INVASION SQUID FORCE!
DON'T STOP AT ANY RED LIGHTS, VANITY. I GOTTA SEE THIS MYSELF.

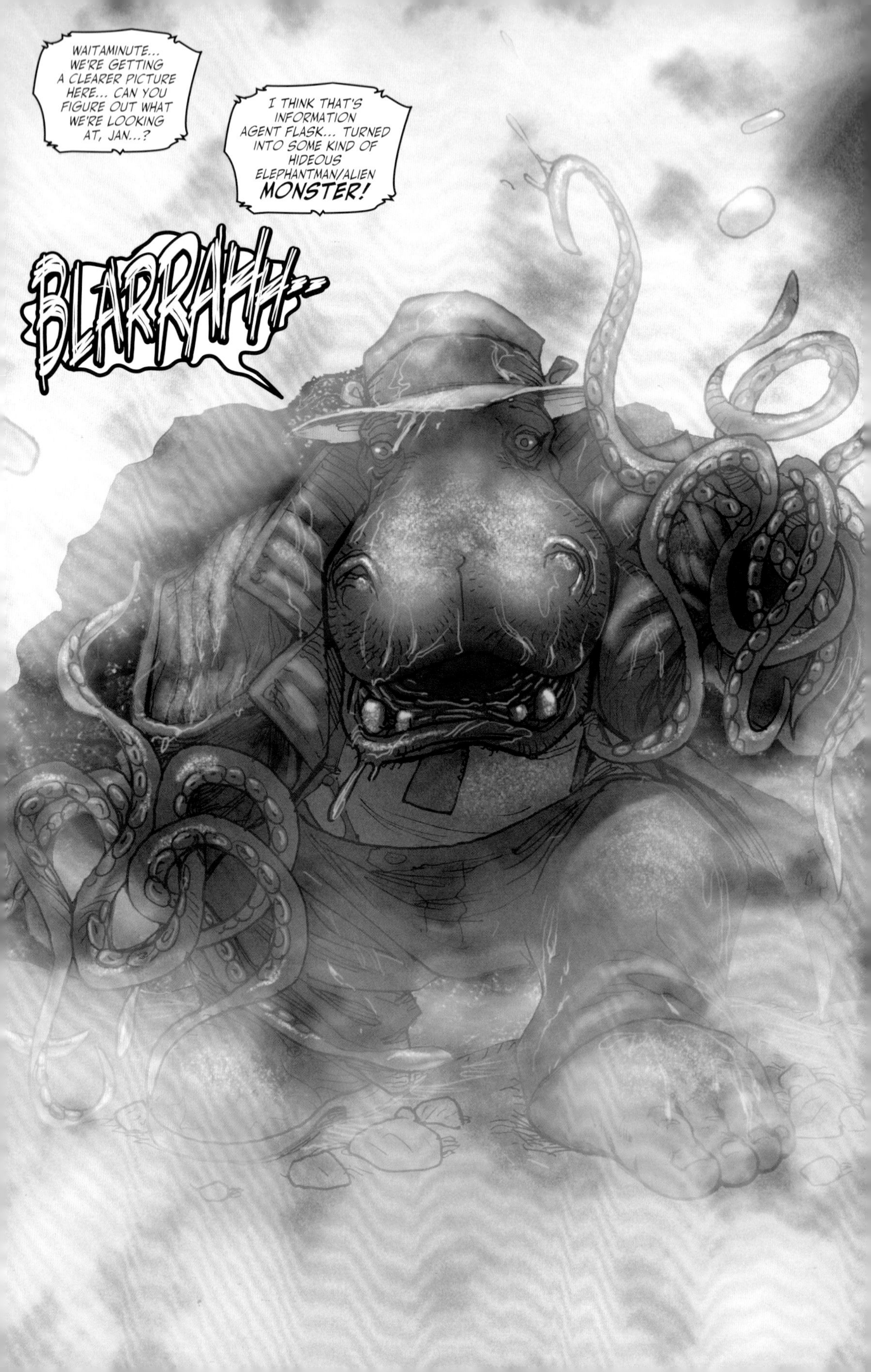
WAITAMINUTE... WE'RE GETTING A CLEARER PICTURE HERE... CAN YOU FIGURE OUT WHAT WE'RE LOOKING AT, JAN...?
I THINK THAT'S INFORMATION AGENT FLASK... TURNED INTO SOME KIND OF HIDEOUS ELEPHANTMAN/ALIEN MONSTER!
BLARRAHH--

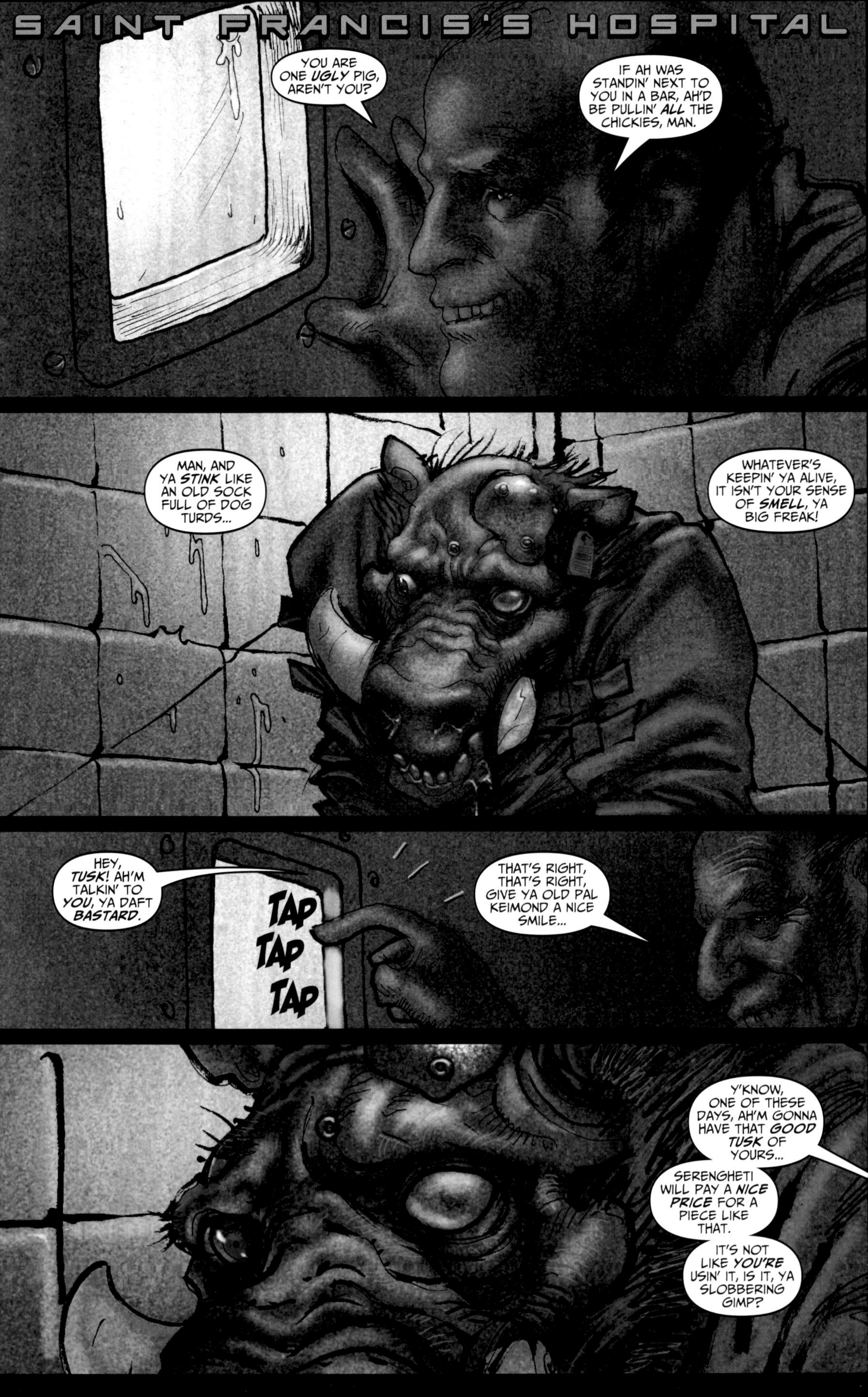
SAINT FRANCIS'S HOSPITAL
YOU ARE ONE UGLY PIG, AREN'T YOU?
IF AH WAS STANDIN' NEXT TO YOU IN A BAR, AH'D BE PULLIN' ALL THE CHICKIES, MAN.
MAN, AND YA STINK LIKE AN OLD SOCK FULL OF DOG TURDS...
WHATEVER'S KEEPIN' YA ALIVE, IT ISN'T YOUR SENSE OF SMELL, YA BIG FREAK!
HEY, TUSK! AH'M TALKIN' TO YOU, YA DAFT BASTARD.
TAP TAP TAP
THAT'S RIGHT, THAT'S RIGHT, GIVE YA OLD PAL KEIMOND A NICE SMILE...
Y'KNOW, ONE OF THESE DAYS, AH'M GONNA HAVE THAT GOOD TUSK OF YOURS...
SERENGHETI WILL PAY A NICE PRICE FOR A PIECE LIKE THAT.
IT'S NOT LIKE YOU'RE USIN' IT, IS IT, YA SLOBBERING GIMP?

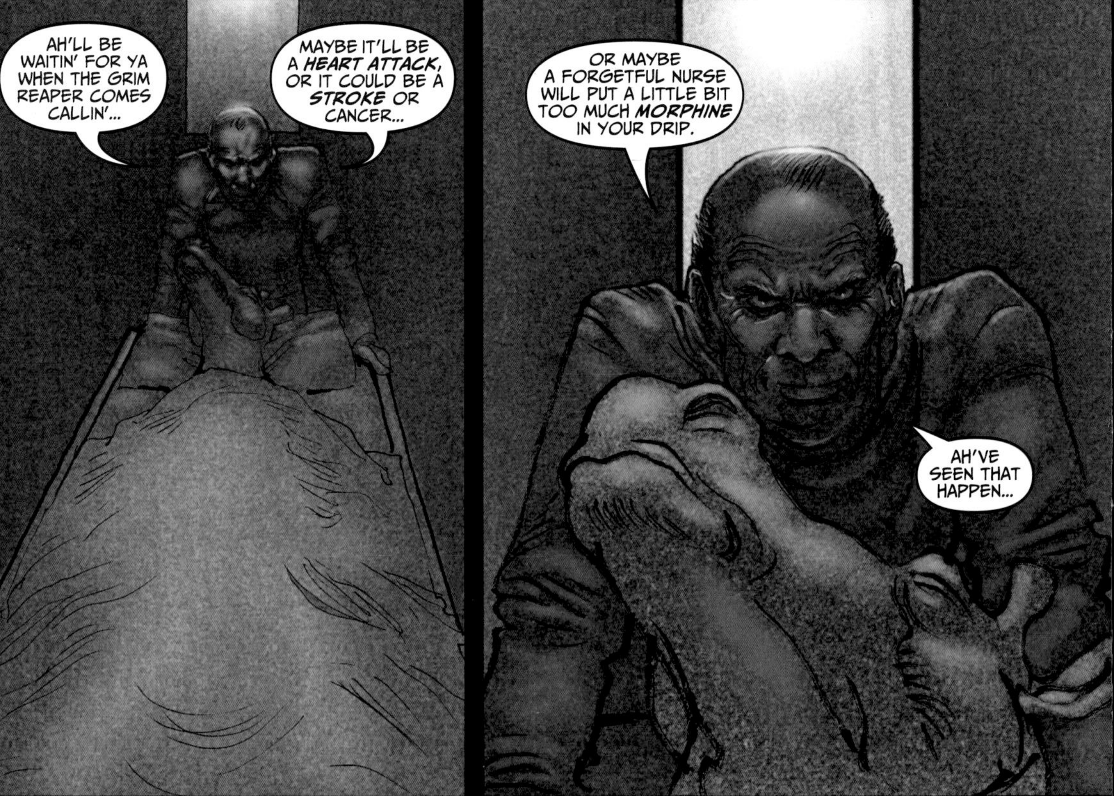
AH'LL BE WAITIN' FOR YA WHEN THE GRIM REAPER COMES CALLIN'...
MAYBE IT'LL BE A **HEART ATTACK**, OR IT COULD BE A **STROKE** OR CANCER...
OR MAYBE A FORGETFUL NURSE WILL PUT A LITTLE BIT TOO MUCH **MORPHINE** IN YOUR DRIP.
AH'VE SEEN THAT HAPPEN...

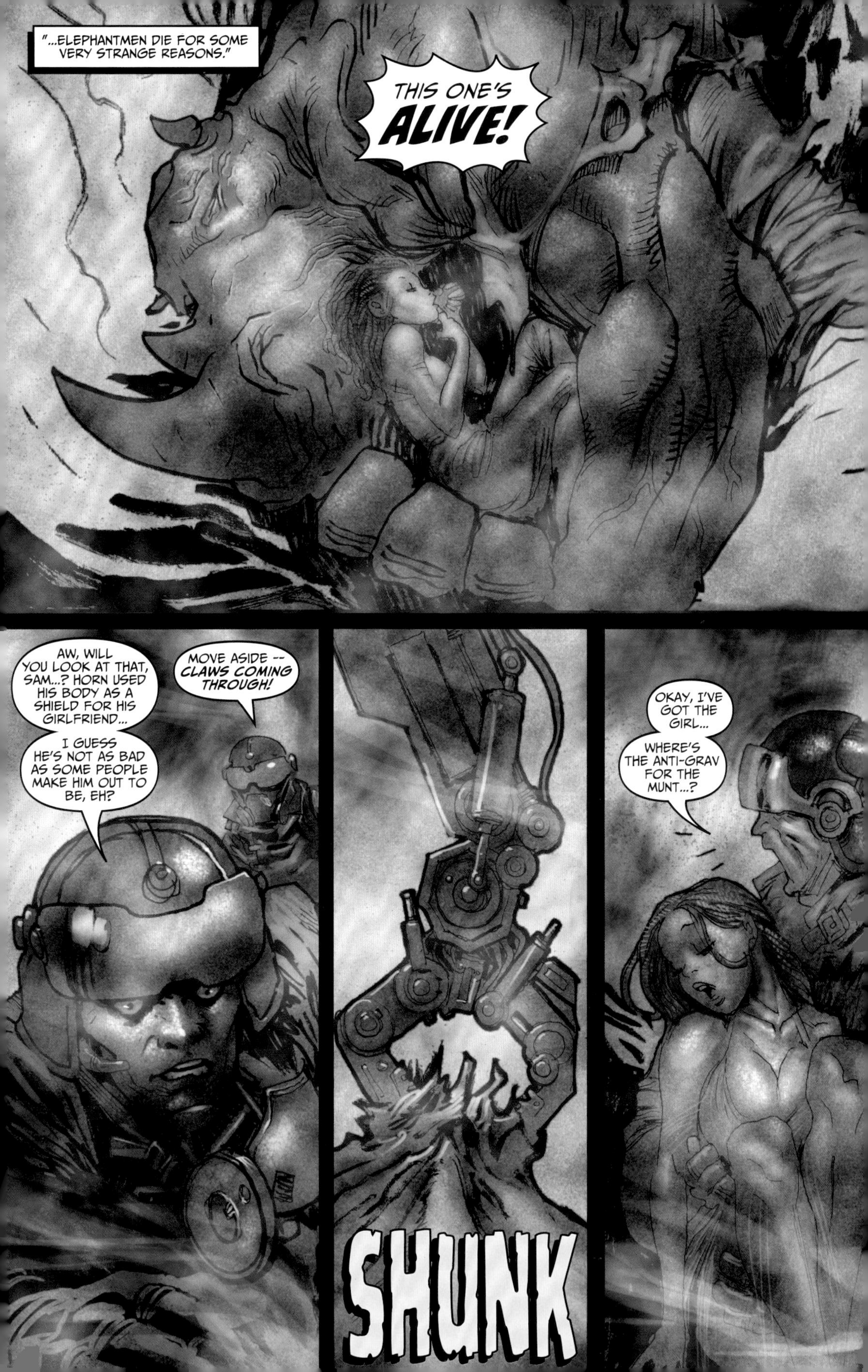
"...ELEPHANTMEN DIE FOR SOME VERY STRANGE REASONS."
THIS ONE'S ALIVE!
AW, WILL YOU LOOK AT THAT, SAM...? HORN USED HIS BODY AS A SHIELD FOR HIS GIRLFRIEND...
I GUESS HE'S NOT AS BAD AS SOME PEOPLE MAKE HIM OUT TO BE, EH?
MOVE ASIDE -- CLAWS COMING THROUGH!
SHUNK
OKAY, I'VE GOT THE GIRL...
WHERE'S THE ANTI-GRAV FOR THE MUNT...?

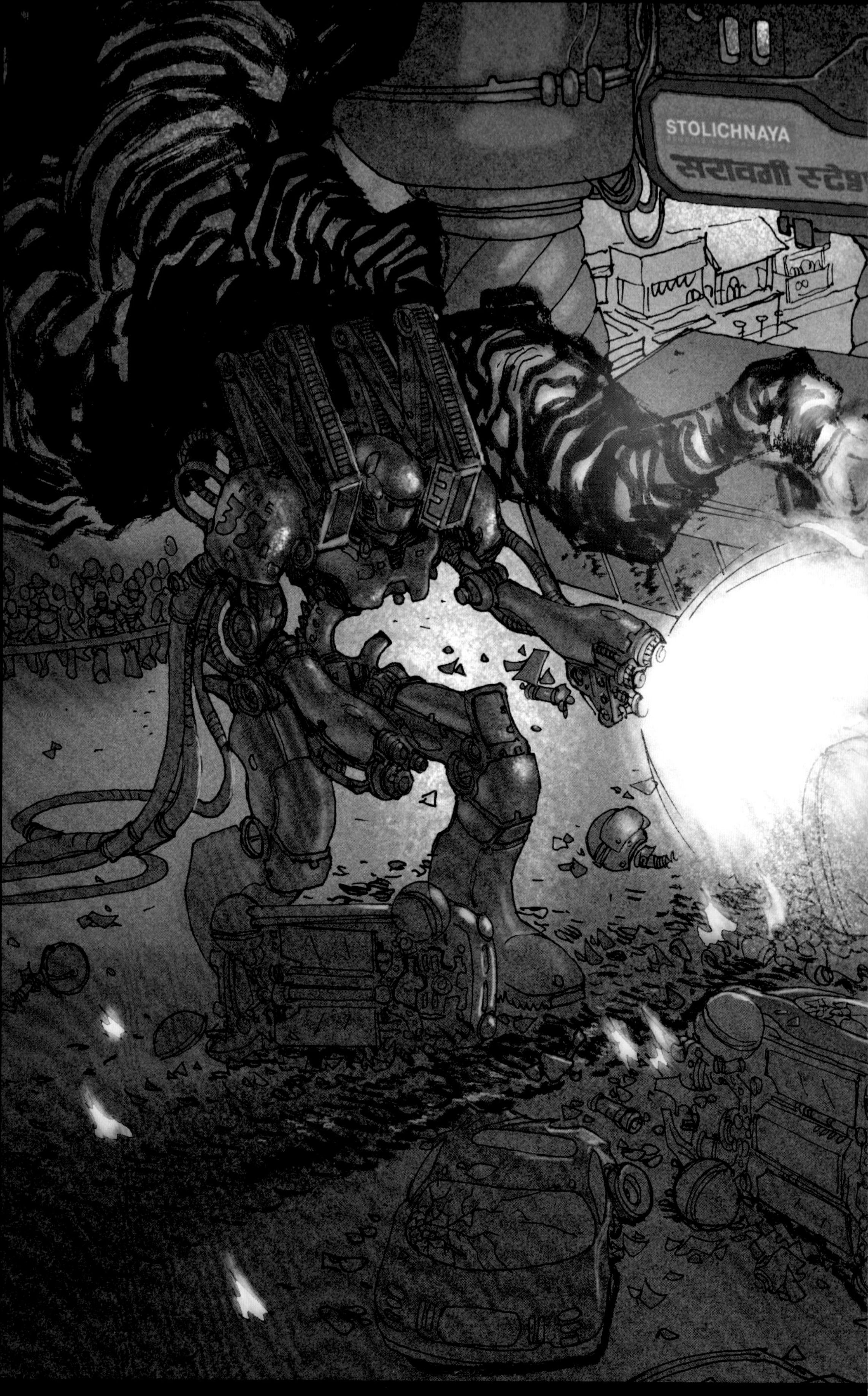
STOLICHNAYA
FIRE

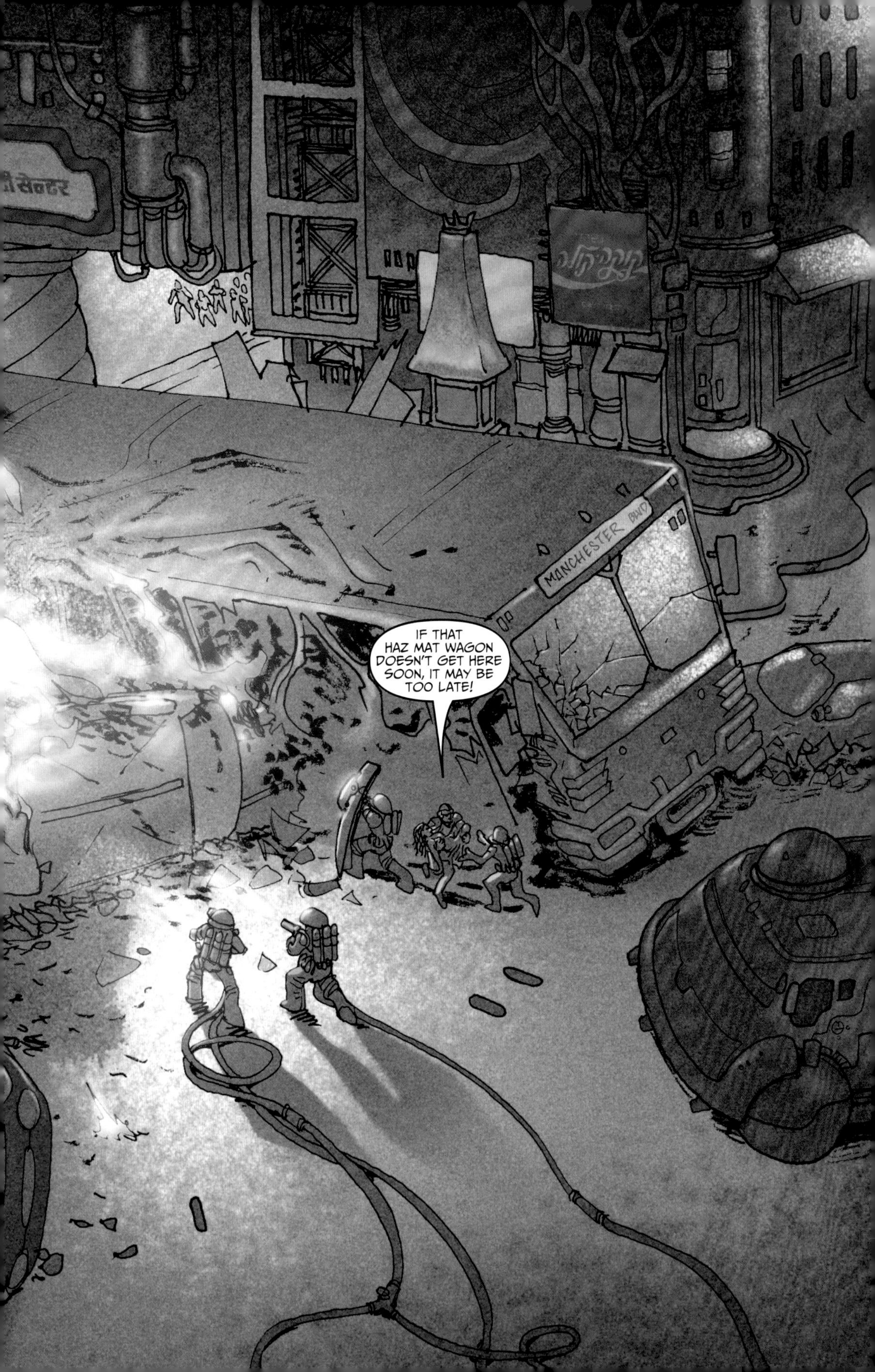
MANCHESTER BLVD
IF THAT HAZ MAT WAGON DOESN'T GET HERE SOON, IT MAY BE TOO LATE!

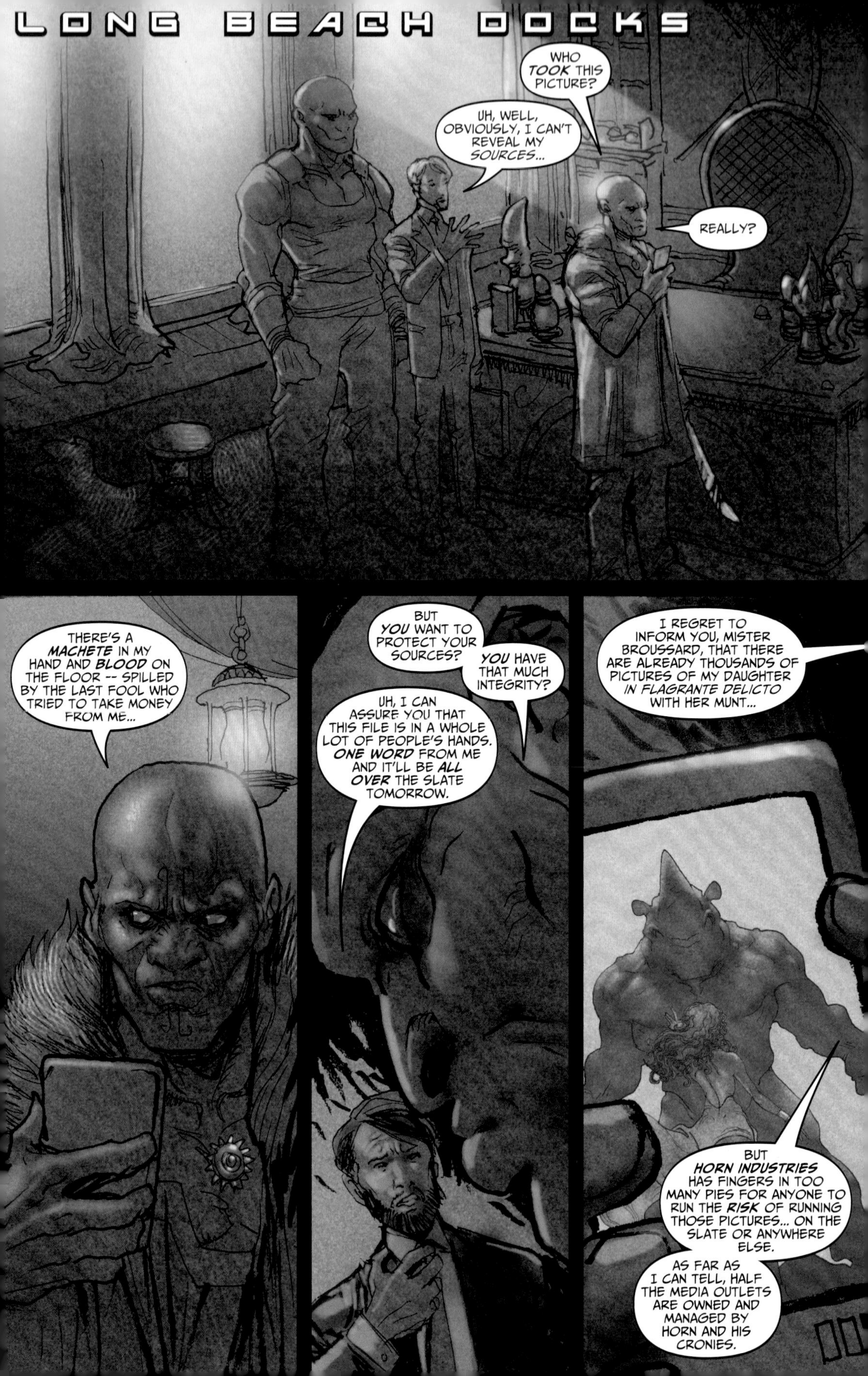
LONG BEACH DOCKS
WHO TOOK THIS PICTURE?
UH, WELL, OBVIOUSLY, I CAN'T REVEAL MY SOURCES...
REALLY?
THERE'S A MACHETE IN MY HAND AND BLOOD ON THE FLOOR -- SPILLED BY THE LAST FOOL WHO TRIED TO TAKE MONEY FROM ME...
BUT YOU WANT TO PROTECT YOUR SOURCES?
YOU HAVE THAT MUCH INTEGRITY?
UH, I CAN ASSURE YOU THAT THIS FILE IS IN A WHOLE LOT OF PEOPLE'S HANDS. ONE WORD FROM ME AND IT'LL BE ALL OVER THE SLATE TOMORROW.
I REGRET TO INFORM YOU, MISTER BROUSSARD, THAT THERE ARE ALREADY THOUSANDS OF PICTURES OF MY DAUGHTER IN FLAGRANTE DELICTO WITH HER MUNT...
BUT HORN INDUSTRIES HAS FINGERS IN TOO MANY PIES FOR ANYONE TO RUN THE RISK OF RUNNING THOSE PICTURES... ON THE SLATE OR ANYWHERE ELSE.
AS FAR AS I CAN TELL, HALF THE MEDIA OUTLETS ARE OWNED AND MANAGED BY HORN AND HIS CRONIES.

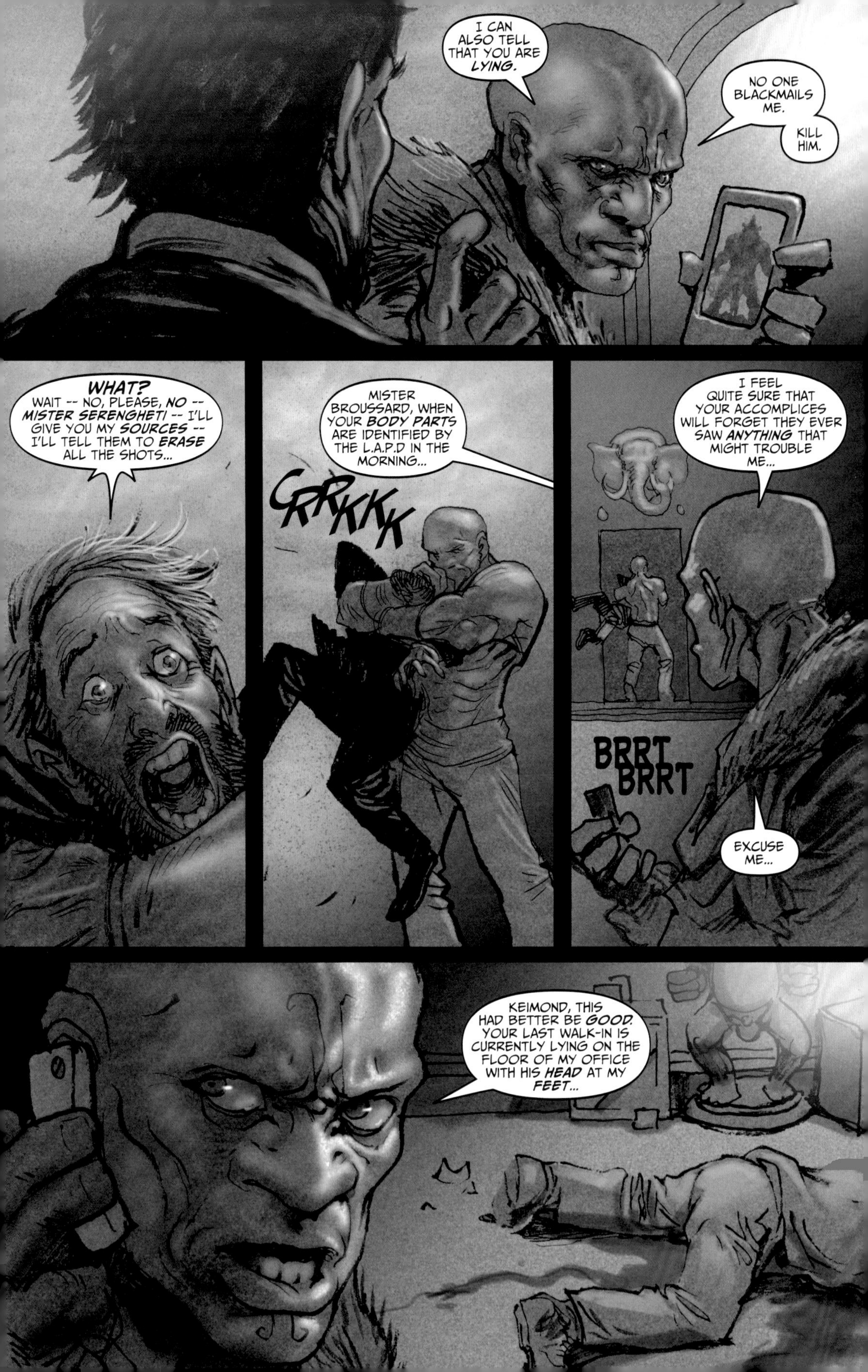
I CAN ALSO TELL THAT YOU ARE *LYING.*
NO ONE BLACKMAILS ME.
KILL HIM.
WHAT? WAIT -- NO, PLEASE, *NO* -- *MISTER SERENGHETI* -- I'LL GIVE YOU MY *SOURCES* -- I'LL TELL THEM TO *ERASE* ALL THE SHOTS...
MISTER BROUSSARD, WHEN YOUR *BODY PARTS* ARE IDENTIFIED BY THE L.A.P.D IN THE MORNING...
CRRKKKK
I FEEL QUITE SURE THAT YOUR ACCOMPLICES WILL FORGET THEY EVER SAW *ANYTHING* THAT MIGHT TROUBLE ME...
BRRT BRRT
EXCUSE ME...
KEIMOND, THIS HAD BETTER BE *GOOD.* YOUR LAST WALK-IN IS CURRENTLY LYING ON THE FLOOR OF MY OFFICE WITH HIS *HEAD* AT MY *FEET*...

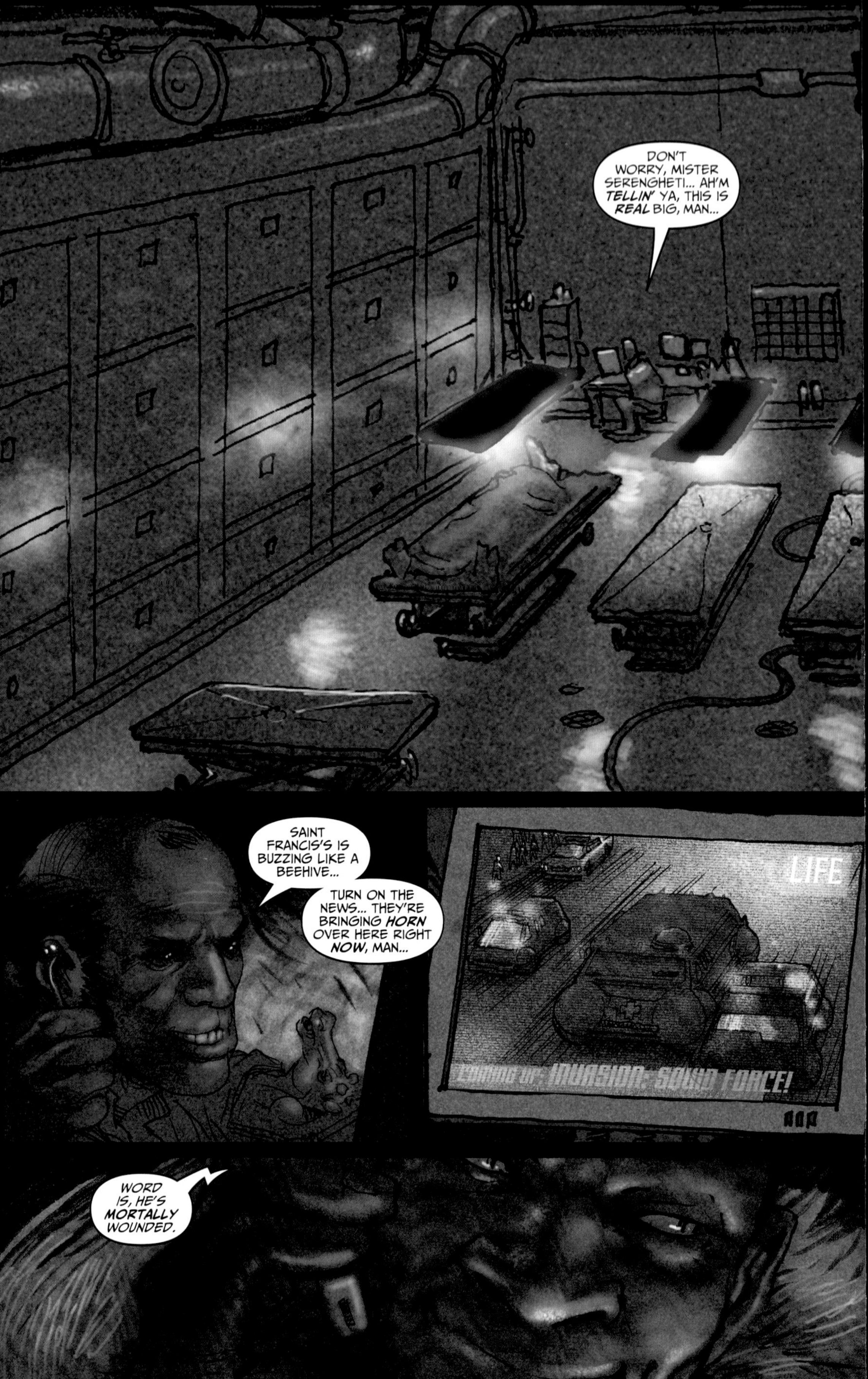
DON'T WORRY, MISTER SERENGHETI... AH'M TELLIN' YA, THIS IS REAL BIG, MAN...
SAINT FRANCIS'S IS BUZZING LIKE A BEEHIVE...
TURN ON THE NEWS... THEY'RE BRINGING HORN OVER HERE RIGHT NOW, MAN...
LIFE
COMING UP: INVASION: SOLID FORCE!
WORD IS, HE'S MORTALLY WOUNDED.

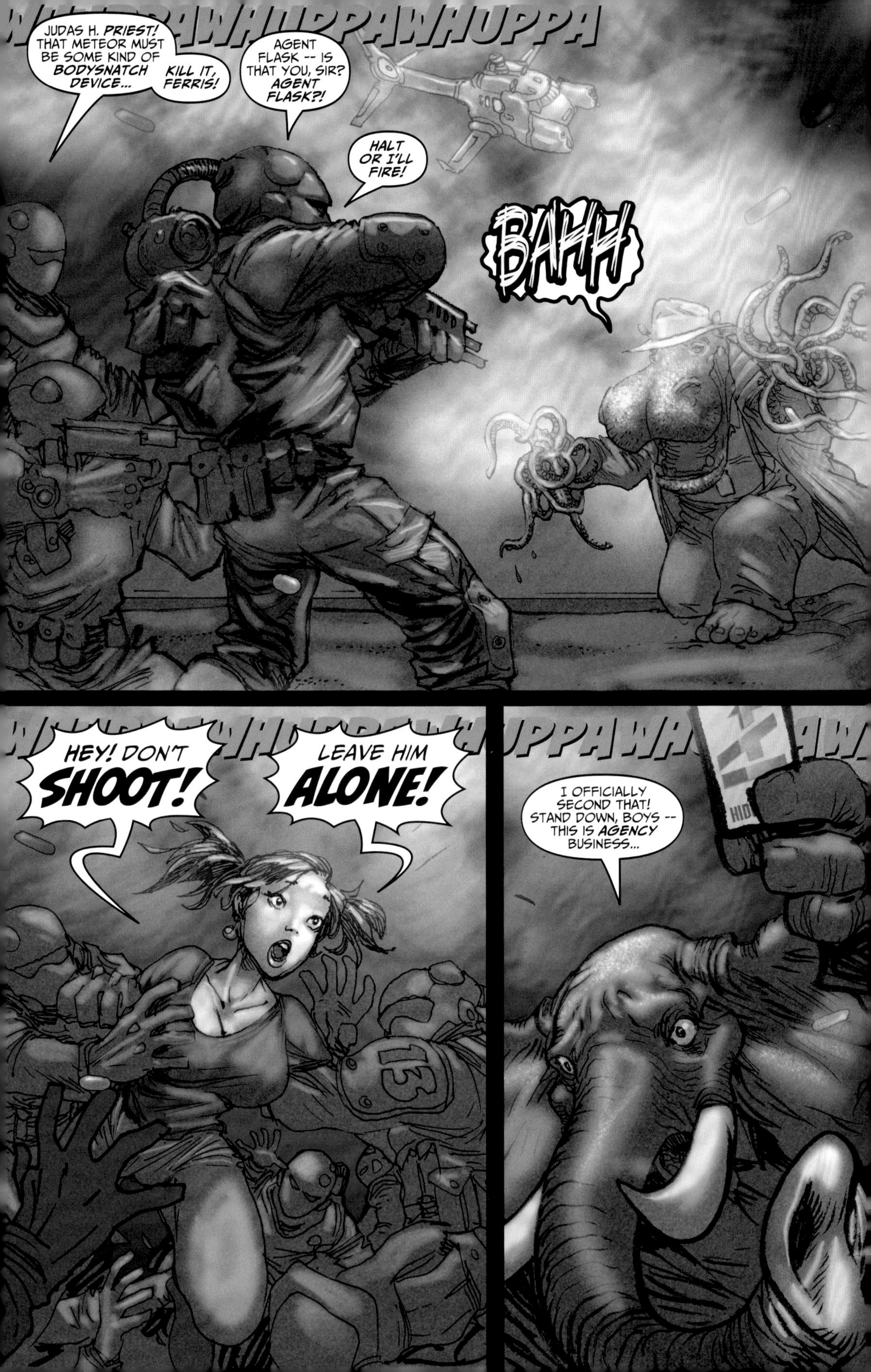

WHUPPAWHUPPAWHUPPA
JUDAS H. PRIEST! THAT METEOR MUST BE SOME KIND OF BODYSNATCH DEVICE...
KILL IT, FERRIS!
AGENT FLASK -- IS THAT YOU, SIR? AGENT FLASK?!
HALT OR I'LL FIRE!
BAHH
HEY! DON'T SHOOT!
LEAVE HIM ALONE!
I OFFICIALLY SECOND THAT! STAND DOWN, BOYS -- THIS IS AGENCY BUSINESS...

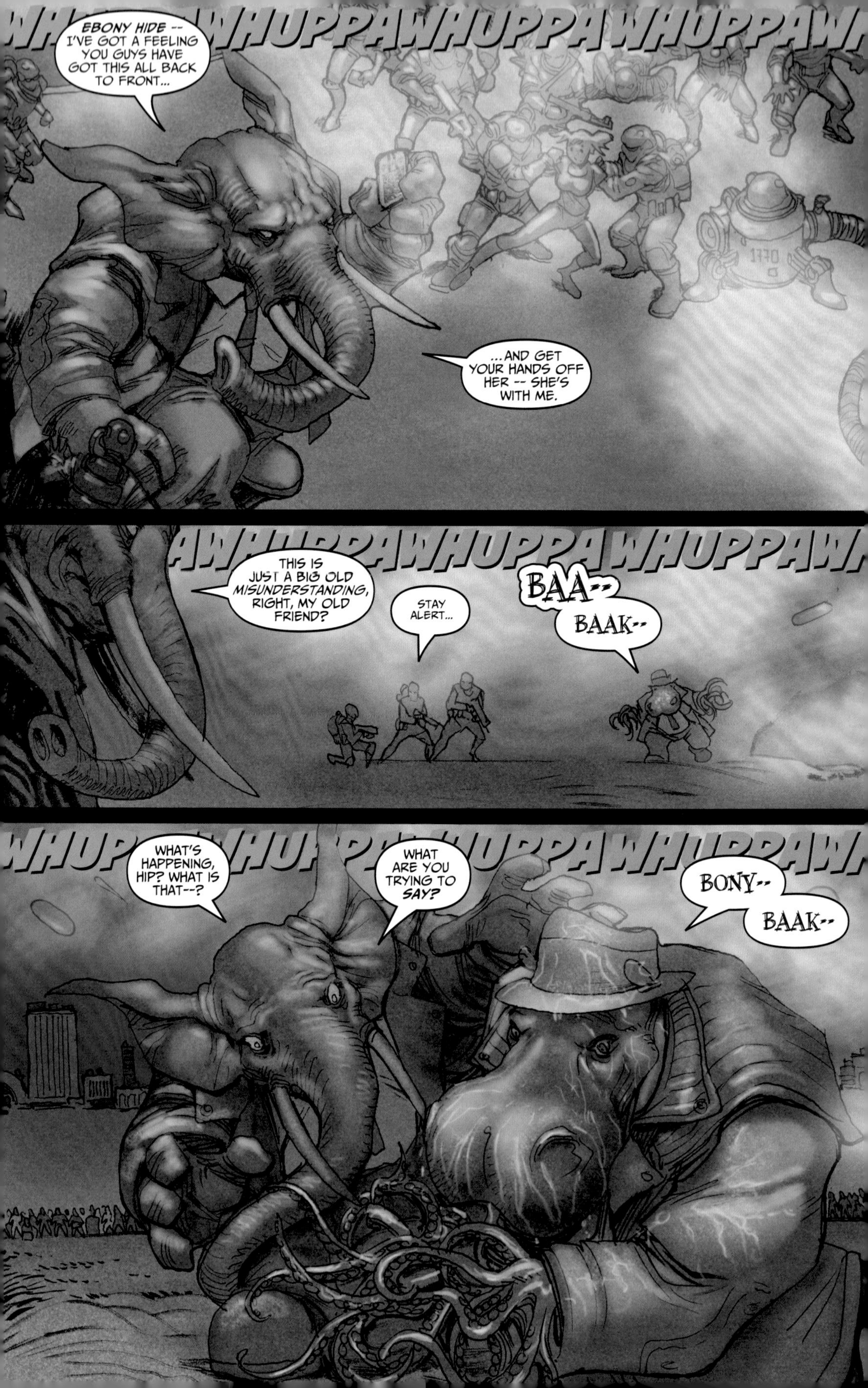
WHUPPAWHUPPAWHUPPAWH
EBONY HIDE -- I'VE GOT A FEELING YOU GUYS HAVE GOT THIS ALL BACK TO FRONT...
...AND GET YOUR HANDS OFF HER -- SHE'S WITH ME.
AWHUPPAWHUPPAWHUPPAW
THIS IS JUST A BIG OLD MISUNDERSTANDING, RIGHT, MY OLD FRIEND?
STAY ALERT...
BAA--
BAAK--
WHUPPAWHUPPAWHUPPAW
WHAT'S HAPPENING, HIP? WHAT IS THAT--?
WHAT ARE YOU TRYING TO SAY?
BONY--
BAAK--

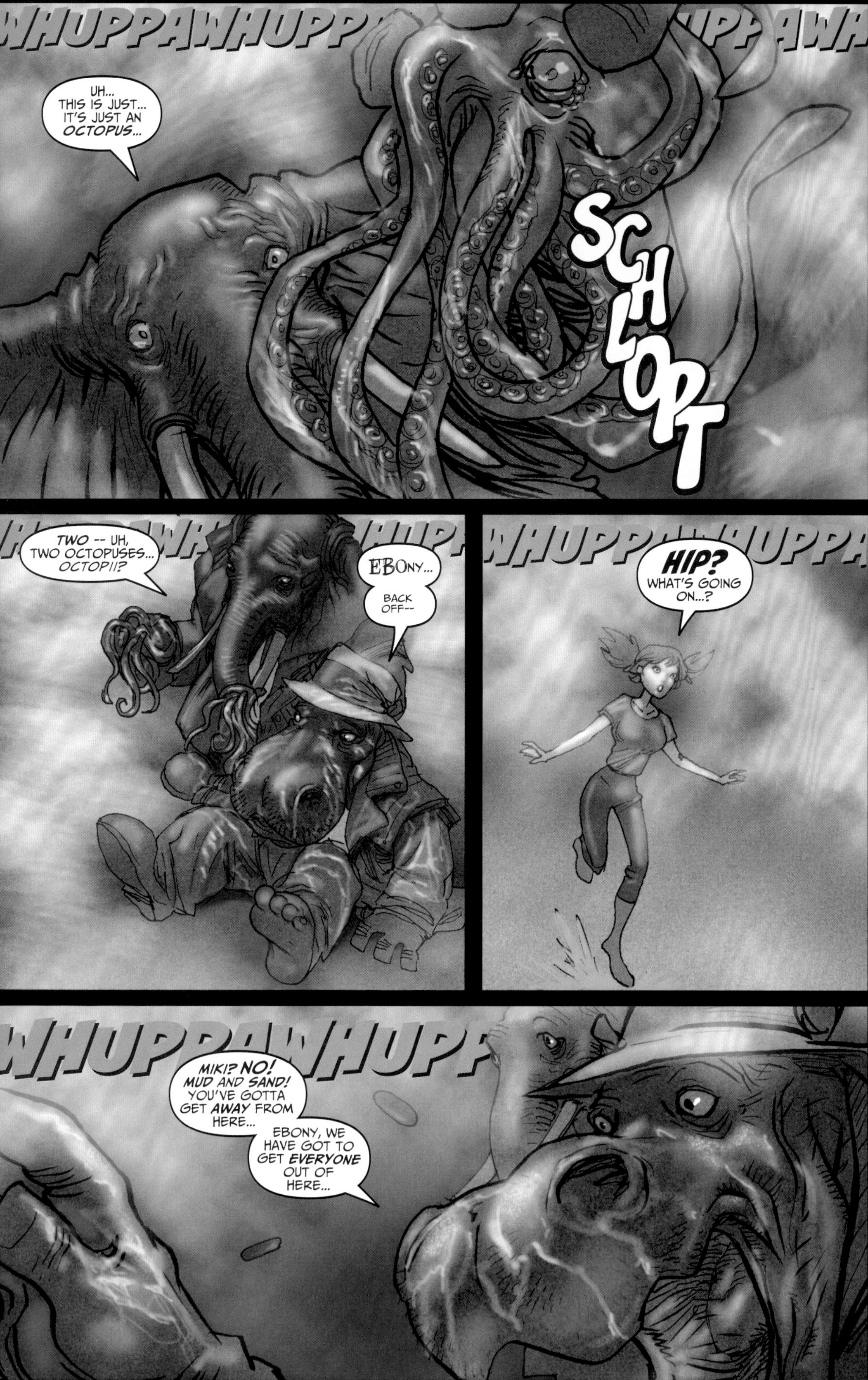
WHUPPAWHUPPAWHUPPAWH
UH... THIS IS JUST... IT'S JUST AN OCTOPUS...
SCHLOPT
TWO -- UH, TWO OCTOPUSES... OCTOPII?
EBONY...
BACK OFF--
HIP? WHAT'S GOING ON...?
MIKI? NO! MUD AND SAND! YOU'VE GOTTA GET AWAY FROM HERE...
EBONY, WE HAVE GOT TO GET EVERYONE OUT OF HERE...

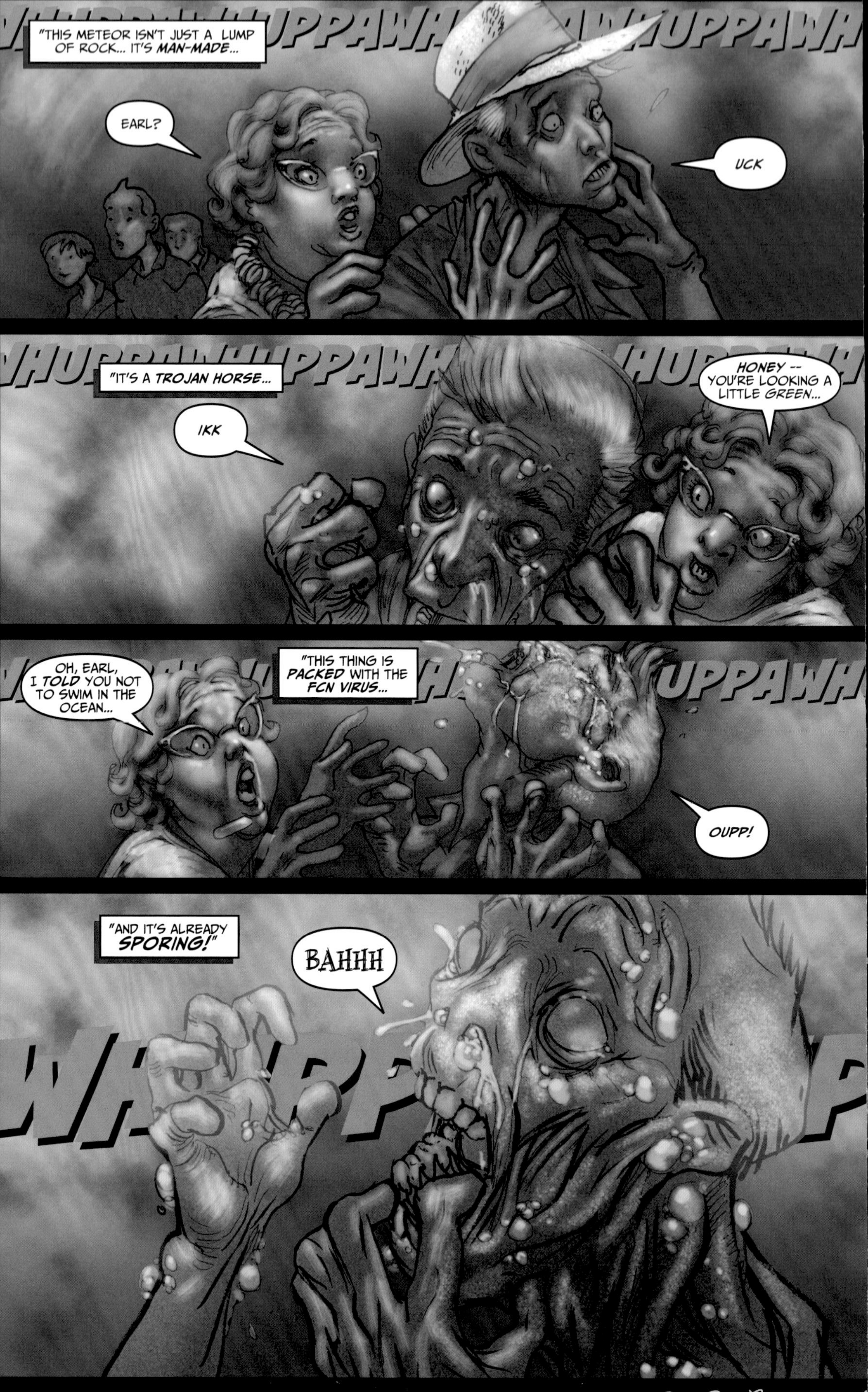

WHUPPAWHUPPAWHUPPAWHUPPAWH
"THIS METEOR ISN'T JUST A LUMP OF ROCK... IT'S MAN-MADE...
EARL?
UCK
"IT'S A TROJAN HORSE...
IKK
HONEY -- YOU'RE LOOKING A LITTLE GREEN...
OH, EARL, I TOLD YOU NOT TO SWIM IN THE OCEAN...
"THIS THING IS PACKED WITH THE FCN VIRUS...
OUPP!
"AND IT'S ALREADY SPORING!"
BAHHH
WHUPP

To Be Continued!

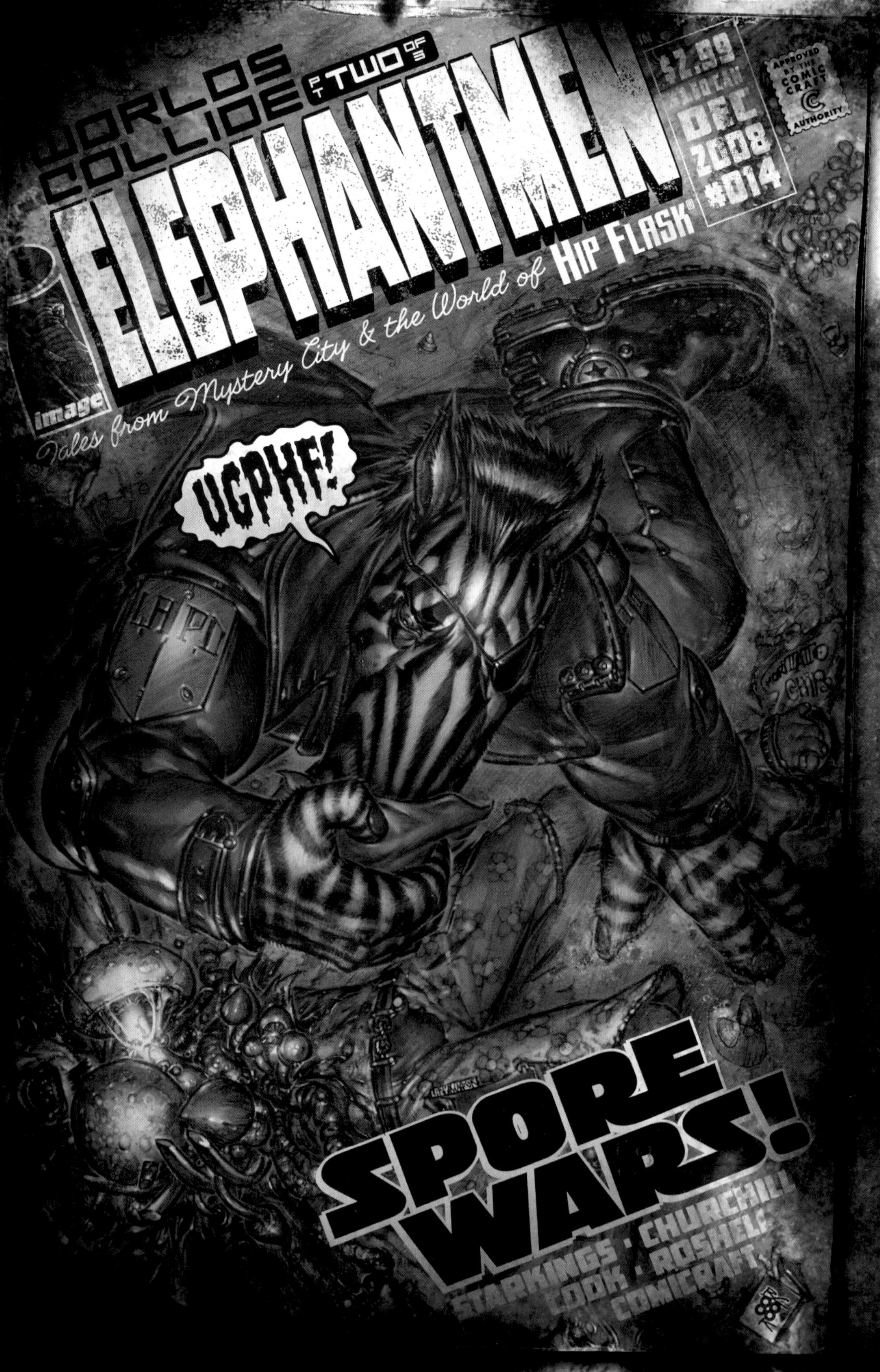

WORLDS COLLIDE
PT TWO OF 3
ELEPHANTMEN
Tales from Mystery City & the World of HIP FLASK
$2.99
DEC 2008 #014
APPROVED BY THE COMIC CRAFT AUTHORITY
image
UGPHF!
SPORE WARS!
STARKINGS · CHURCHILL
COOK · ROSHELL
COMICRAFT

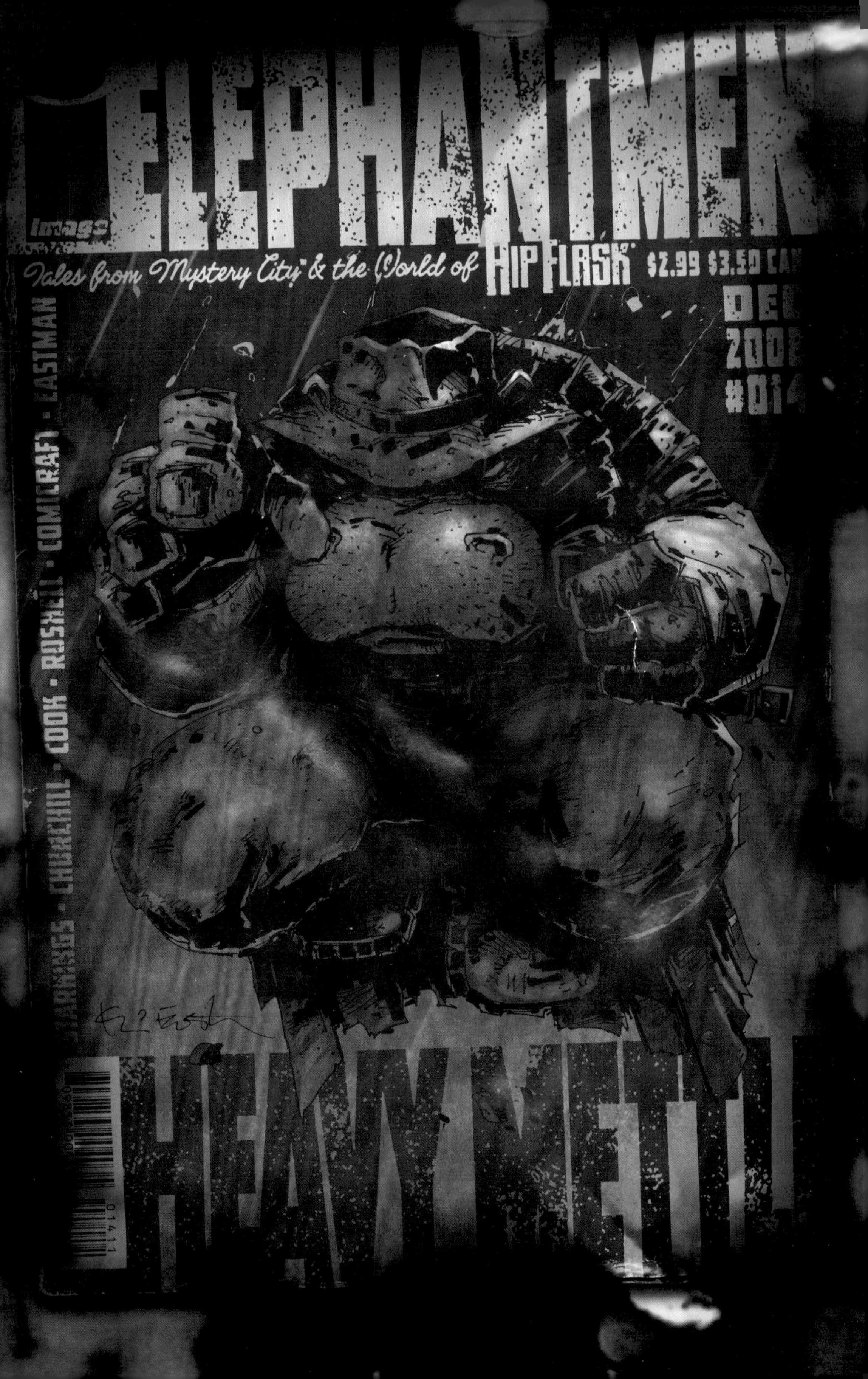
ELEPHANTMEN
image
Tales from Mystery City & the World of HIP FLASK
$2.99 $3.50 CAN
DEC 2008 #014
CHURCHILL · COOK · ROSHELL · COMICRAFT · EASTMAN
HEAVY METAL

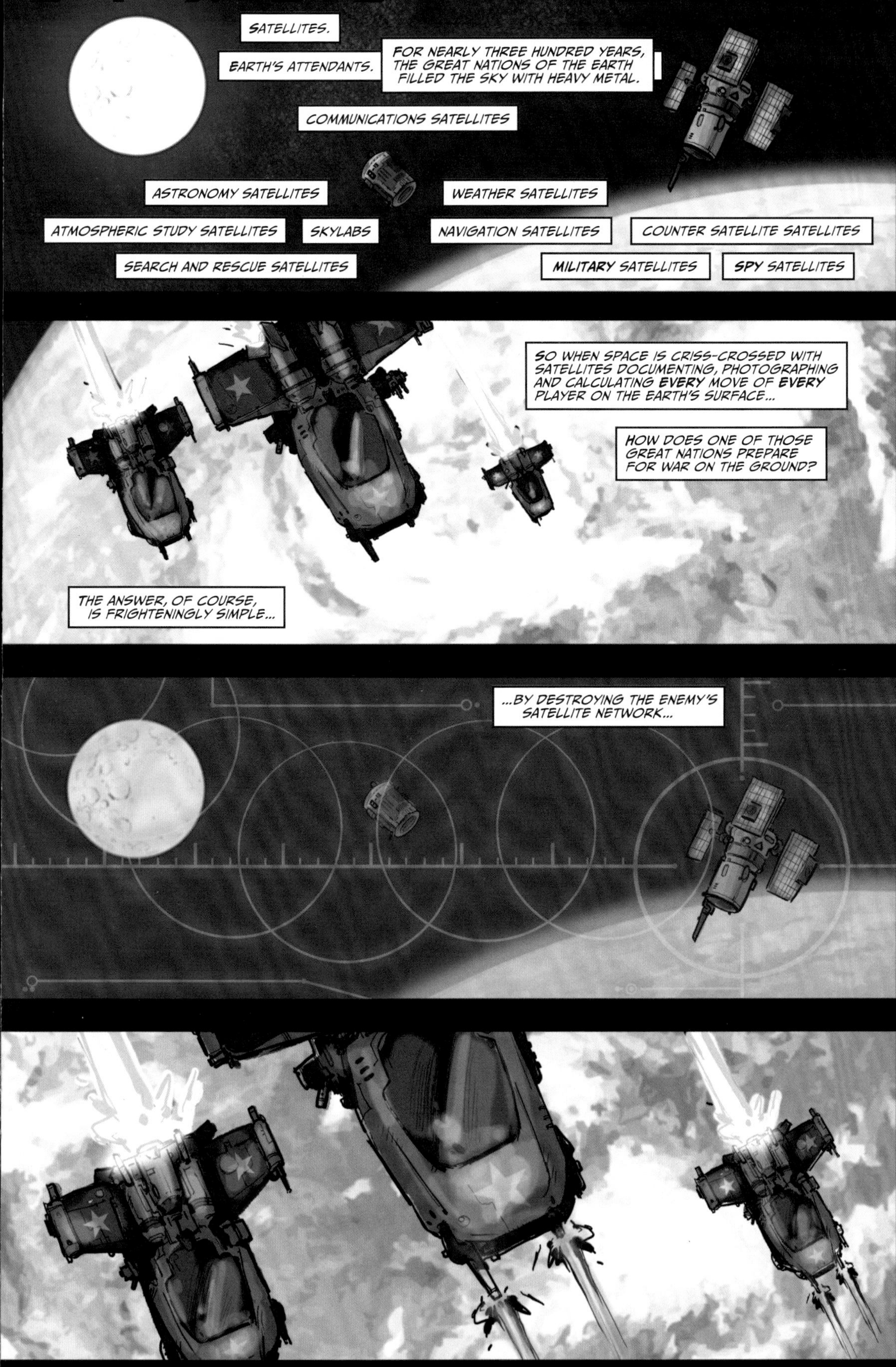
SATELLITES.
EARTH'S ATTENDANTS.
FOR NEARLY THREE HUNDRED YEARS, THE GREAT NATIONS OF THE EARTH FILLED THE SKY WITH HEAVY METAL.
COMMUNICATIONS SATELLITES
ASTRONOMY SATELLITES
WEATHER SATELLITES
ATMOSPHERIC STUDY SATELLITES
SKYLABS
NAVIGATION SATELLITES
COUNTER SATELLITE SATELLITES
SEARCH AND RESCUE SATELLITES
MILITARY SATELLITES
SPY SATELLITES
SO WHEN SPACE IS CRISS-CROSSED WITH SATELLITES DOCUMENTING, PHOTOGRAPHING AND CALCULATING EVERY MOVE OF EVERY PLAYER ON THE EARTH'S SURFACE...
HOW DOES ONE OF THOSE GREAT NATIONS PREPARE FOR WAR ON THE GROUND?
THE ANSWER, OF COURSE, IS FRIGHTENINGLY SIMPLE...
...BY DESTROYING THE ENEMY'S SATELLITE NETWORK...

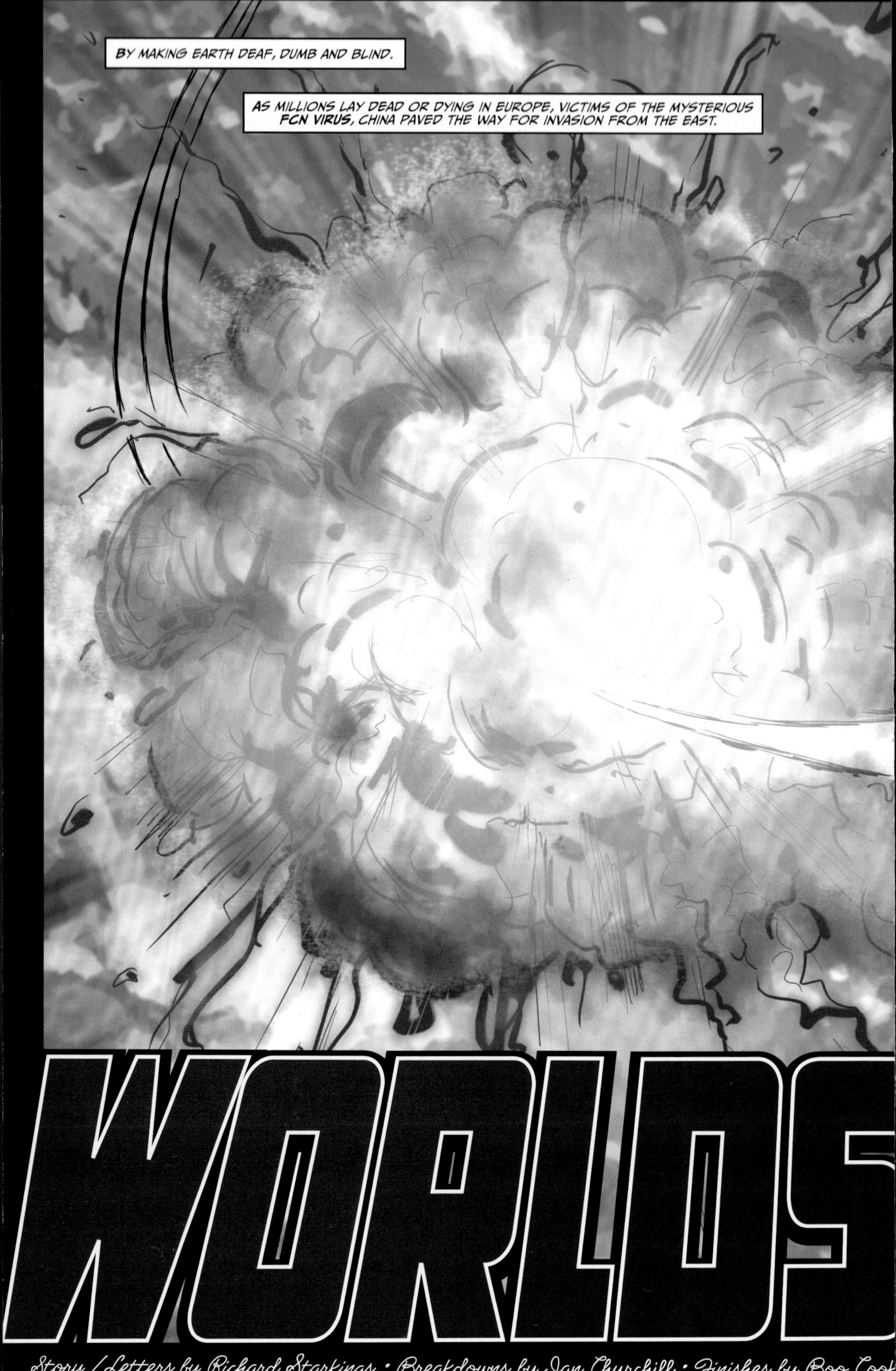
BY MAKING EARTH DEAF, DUMB AND BLIND.
AS MILLIONS LAY DEAD OR DYING IN EUROPE, VICTIMS OF THE MYSTERIOUS FCN VIRUS, CHINA PAVED THE WAY FOR INVASION FROM THE EAST.
WORLDS
Story / Letters by Richard Starkings • Breakdowns by Ian Churchill • Finishes by Boo Cook

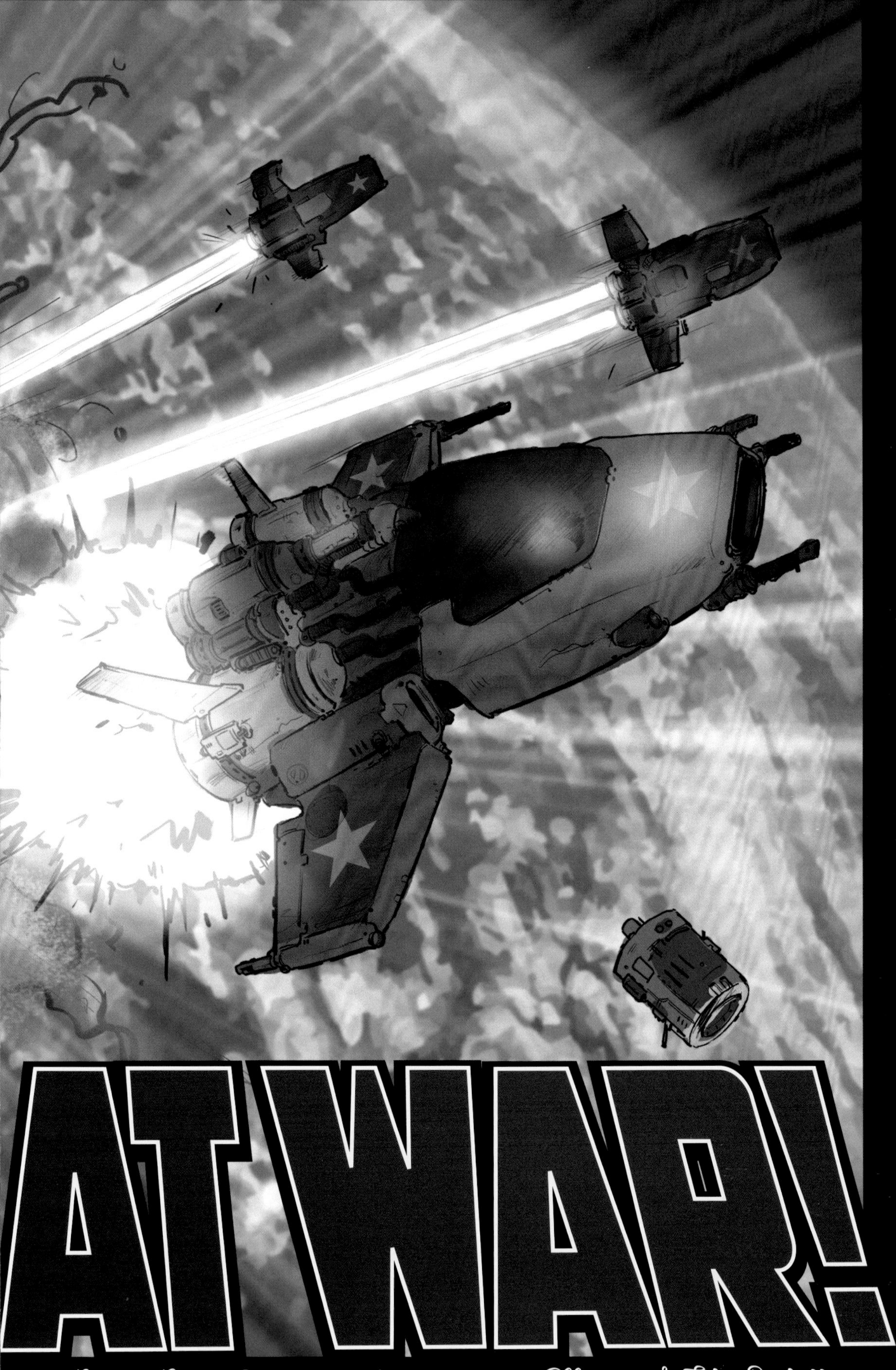
AT WAR!

Color by Gabriel Bautista with Special Thanks to Moritat & John Roshell

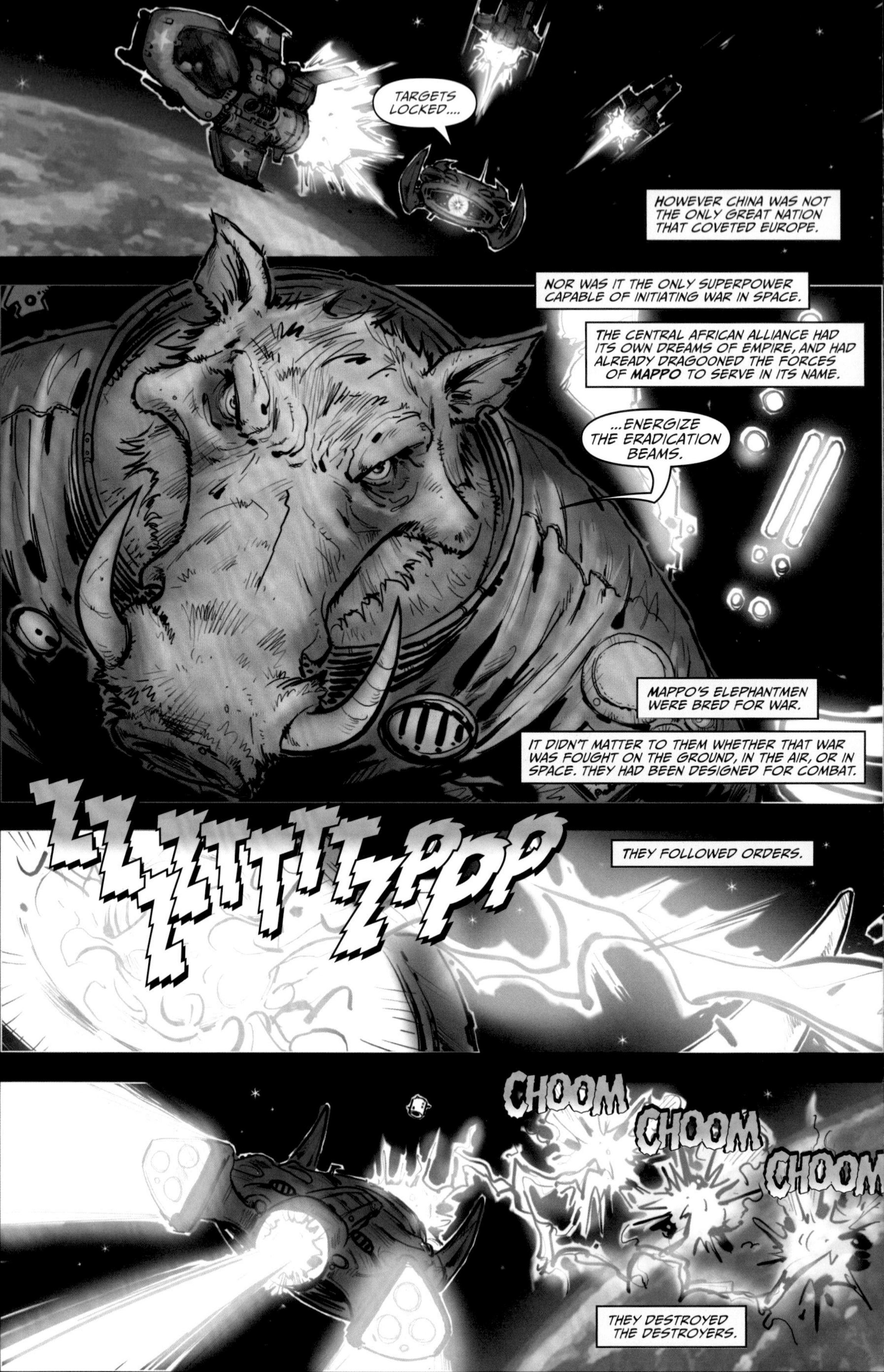
TARGETS LOCKED....
HOWEVER CHINA WAS NOT THE ONLY GREAT NATION THAT COVETED EUROPE.
NOR WAS IT THE ONLY SUPERPOWER CAPABLE OF INITIATING WAR IN SPACE.
THE CENTRAL AFRICAN ALLIANCE HAD ITS OWN DREAMS OF EMPIRE, AND HAD ALREADY DRAGOONED THE FORCES OF MAPPO TO SERVE IN ITS NAME.
...ENERGIZE THE ERADICATION BEAMS.
MAPPO'S ELEPHANTMEN WERE BRED FOR WAR.
IT DIDN'T MATTER TO THEM WHETHER THAT WAR WAS FOUGHT ON THE GROUND, IN THE AIR, OR IN SPACE. THEY HAD BEEN DESIGNED FOR COMBAT.
ZZZZTTTTTZPPP
THEY FOLLOWED ORDERS.
CHOOM
CHOOM
CHOOM
THEY DESTROYED THE DESTROYERS.

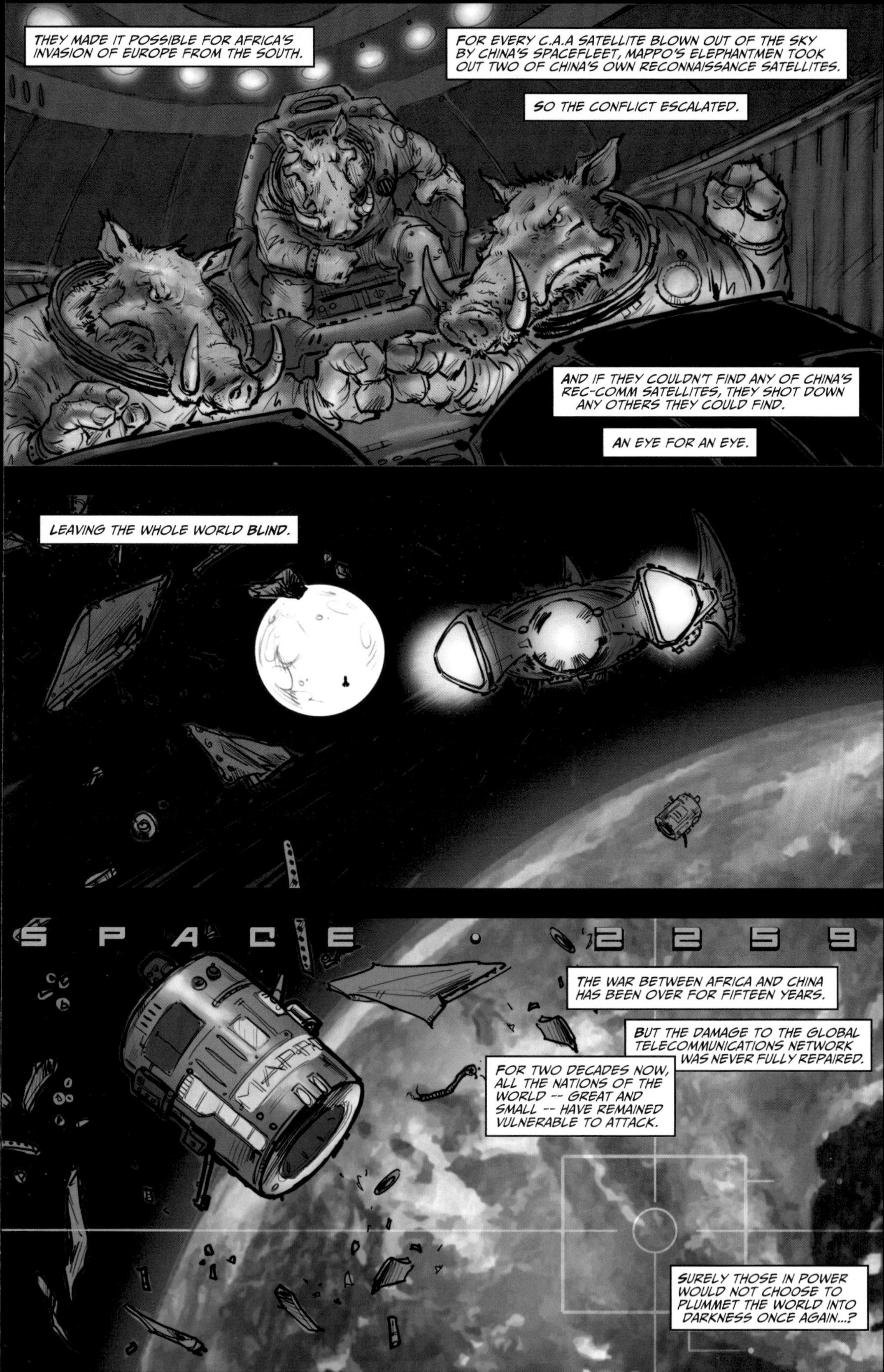

THEY MADE IT POSSIBLE FOR AFRICA'S INVASION OF EUROPE FROM THE SOUTH.
FOR EVERY C.A.A SATELLITE BLOWN OUT OF THE SKY BY CHINA'S SPACEFLEET, MAPPO'S ELEPHANTMEN TOOK OUT TWO OF CHINA'S OWN RECONNAISSANCE SATELLITES.
SO THE CONFLICT ESCALATED.
AND IF THEY COULDN'T FIND ANY OF CHINA'S REC-COMM SATELLITES, THEY SHOT DOWN ANY OTHERS THEY COULD FIND.
AN EYE FOR AN EYE.
LEAVING THE WHOLE WORLD BLIND.
SPACE · 2259
THE WAR BETWEEN AFRICA AND CHINA HAS BEEN OVER FOR FIFTEEN YEARS.
BUT THE DAMAGE TO THE GLOBAL TELECOMMUNICATIONS NETWORK WAS NEVER FULLY REPAIRED.
FOR TWO DECADES NOW, ALL THE NATIONS OF THE WORLD -- GREAT AND SMALL -- HAVE REMAINED VULNERABLE TO ATTACK.
SURELY THOSE IN POWER WOULD NOT CHOOSE TO PLUMMET THE WORLD INTO DARKNESS ONCE AGAIN...?

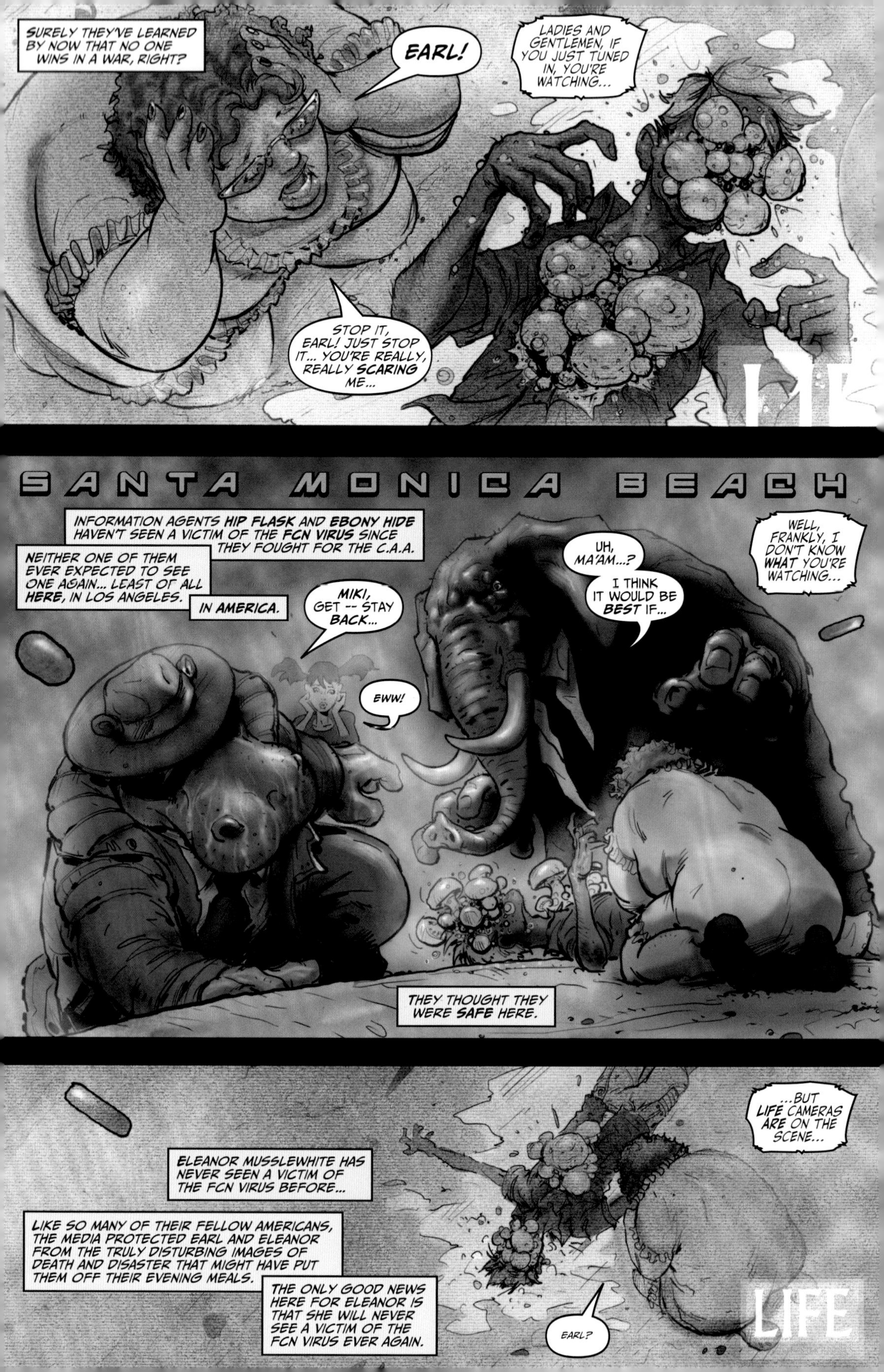
SURELY THEY'VE LEARNED BY NOW THAT NO ONE WINS IN A WAR, RIGHT?
EARL!
LADIES AND GENTLEMEN, IF YOU JUST TUNED IN, YOU'RE WATCHING...
STOP IT, EARL! JUST STOP IT... YOU'RE REALLY, REALLY SCARING ME...
LIFE
SANTA MONICA BEACH
INFORMATION AGENTS HIP FLASK AND EBONY HIDE HAVEN'T SEEN A VICTIM OF THE FCN VIRUS SINCE THEY FOUGHT FOR THE C.A.A.
NEITHER ONE OF THEM EVER EXPECTED TO SEE ONE AGAIN... LEAST OF ALL HERE, IN LOS ANGELES.
IN AMERICA.
MIKI, GET -- STAY BACK...
UH, MA'AM...?
I THINK IT WOULD BE BEST IF...
WELL, FRANKLY, I DON'T KNOW WHAT YOU'RE WATCHING...
EWW!
THEY THOUGHT THEY WERE SAFE HERE.
...BUT LIFE CAMERAS ARE ON THE SCENE...
ELEANOR MUSSLEWHITE HAS NEVER SEEN A VICTIM OF THE FCN VIRUS BEFORE...
LIKE SO MANY OF THEIR FELLOW AMERICANS, THE MEDIA PROTECTED EARL AND ELEANOR FROM THE TRULY DISTURBING IMAGES OF DEATH AND DISASTER THAT MIGHT HAVE PUT THEM OFF THEIR EVENING MEALS.
THE ONLY GOOD NEWS HERE FOR ELEANOR IS THAT SHE WILL NEVER SEE A VICTIM OF THE FCN VIRUS EVER AGAIN.
EARL?
LIFE

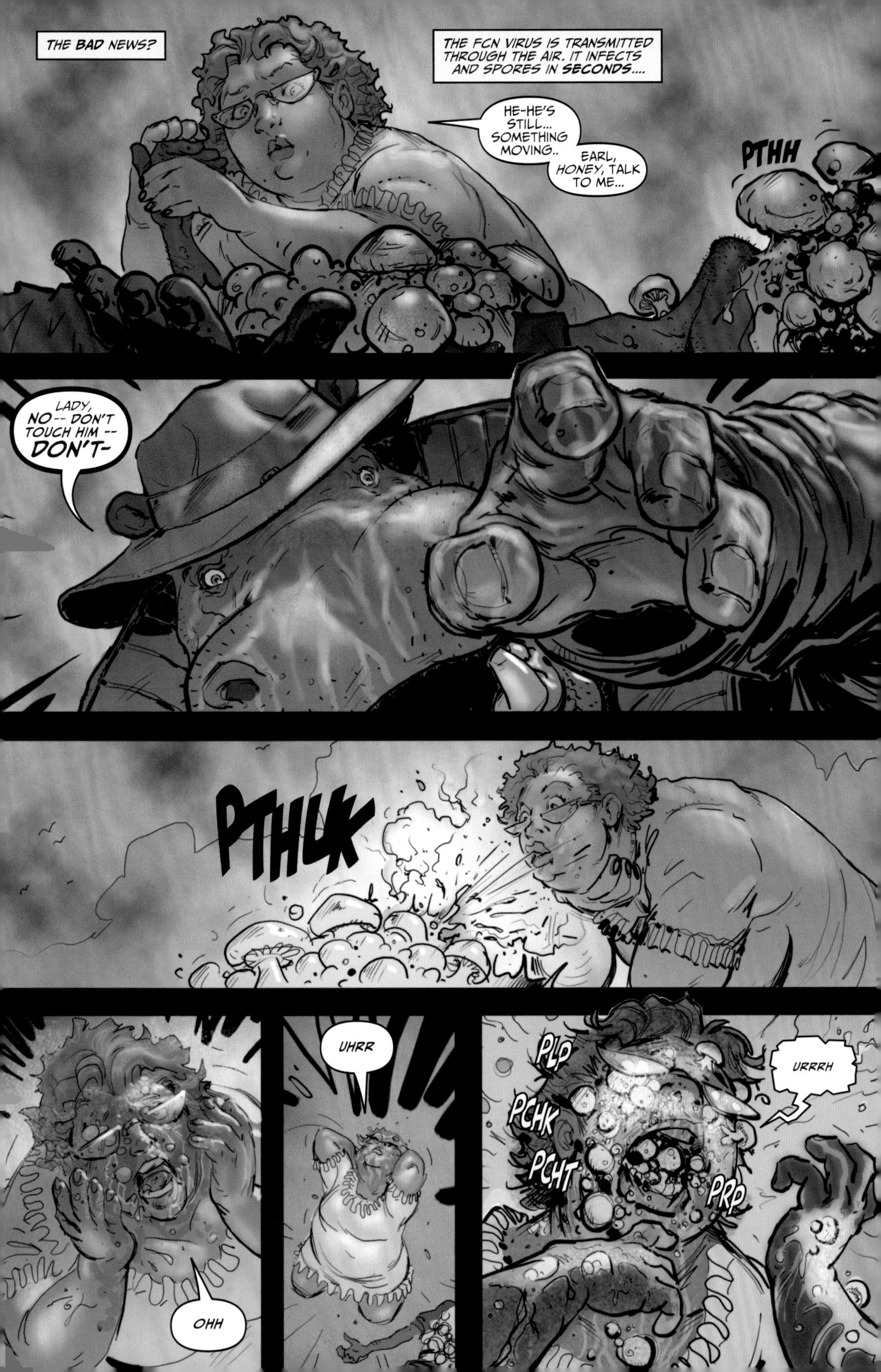
THE BAD NEWS?
THE FCN VIRUS IS TRANSMITTED THROUGH THE AIR. IT INFECTS AND SPORES IN SECONDS....
HE-HE'S STILL... SOMETHING MOVING..
EARL, HONEY, TALK TO ME...
PTHH
LADY, NO-- DON'T TOUCH HIM -- DON'T-
PTHUK
OHH
UHRR
PLP
PCHK
PCHT
PRP
URRRH

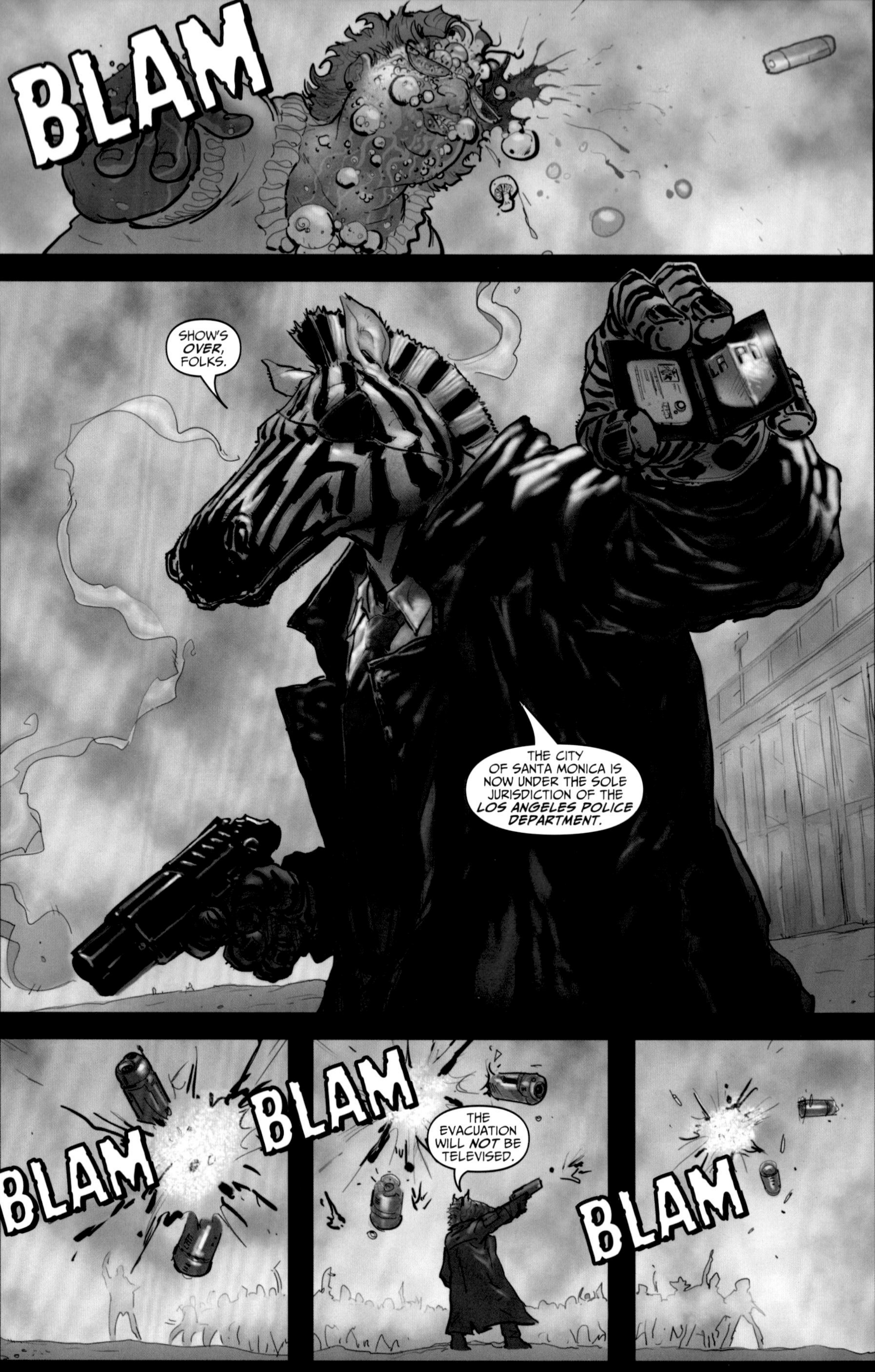
BLAM
SHOW'S OVER, FOLKS.
THE CITY OF SANTA MONICA IS NOW UNDER THE SOLE JURISDICTION OF THE LOS ANGELES POLICE DEPARTMENT.
BLAM
BLAM
THE EVACUATION WILL NOT BE TELEVISED.
BLAM

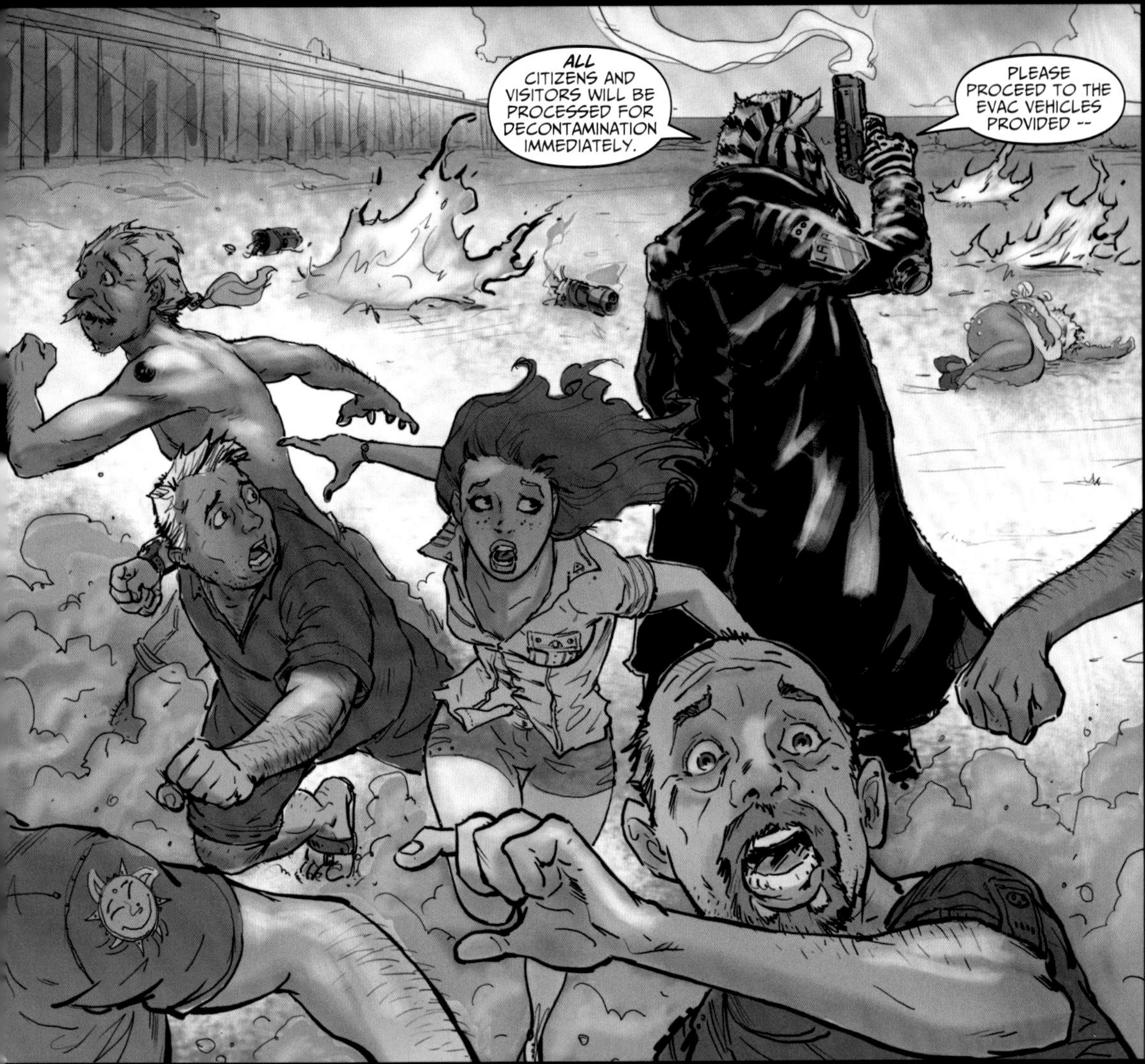
ALL CITIZENS AND VISITORS WILL BE PROCESSED FOR DECONTAMINATION IMMEDIATELY.
PLEASE PROCEED TO THE EVAC VEHICLES PROVIDED --

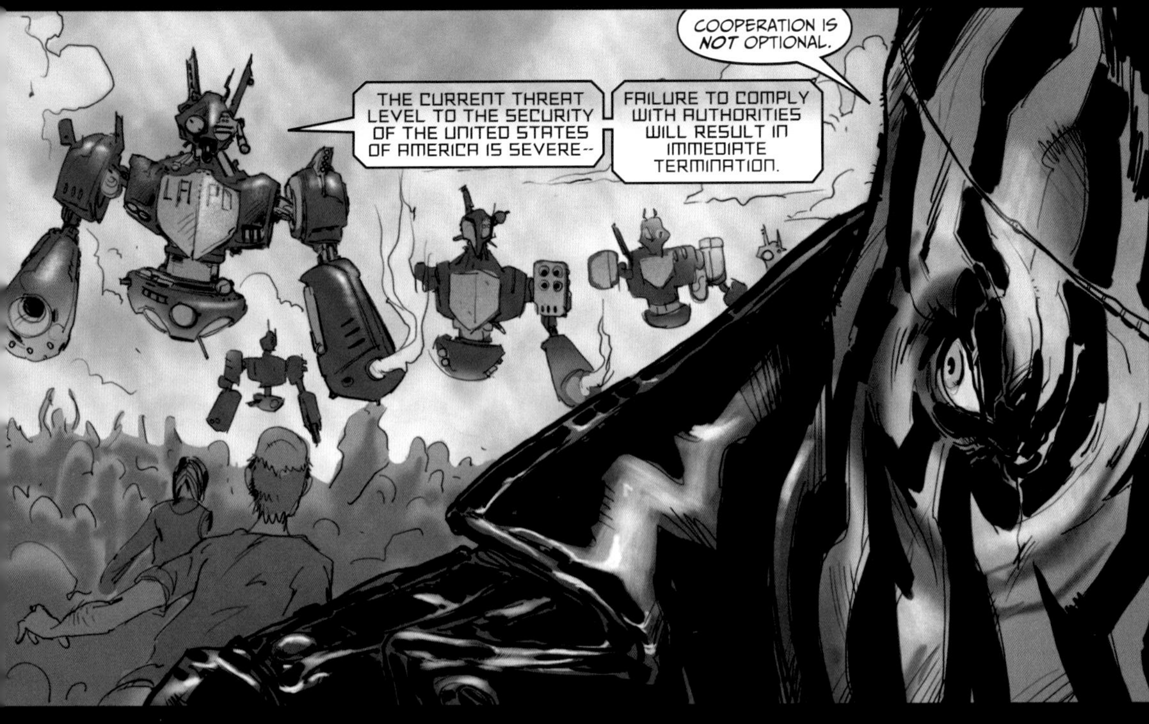
THE CURRENT THREAT LEVEL TO THE SECURITY OF THE UNITED STATES OF AMERICA IS SEVERE--
FAILURE TO COMPLY WITH AUTHORITIES WILL RESULT IN IMMEDIATE TERMINATION.
COOPERATION IS NOT OPTIONAL.

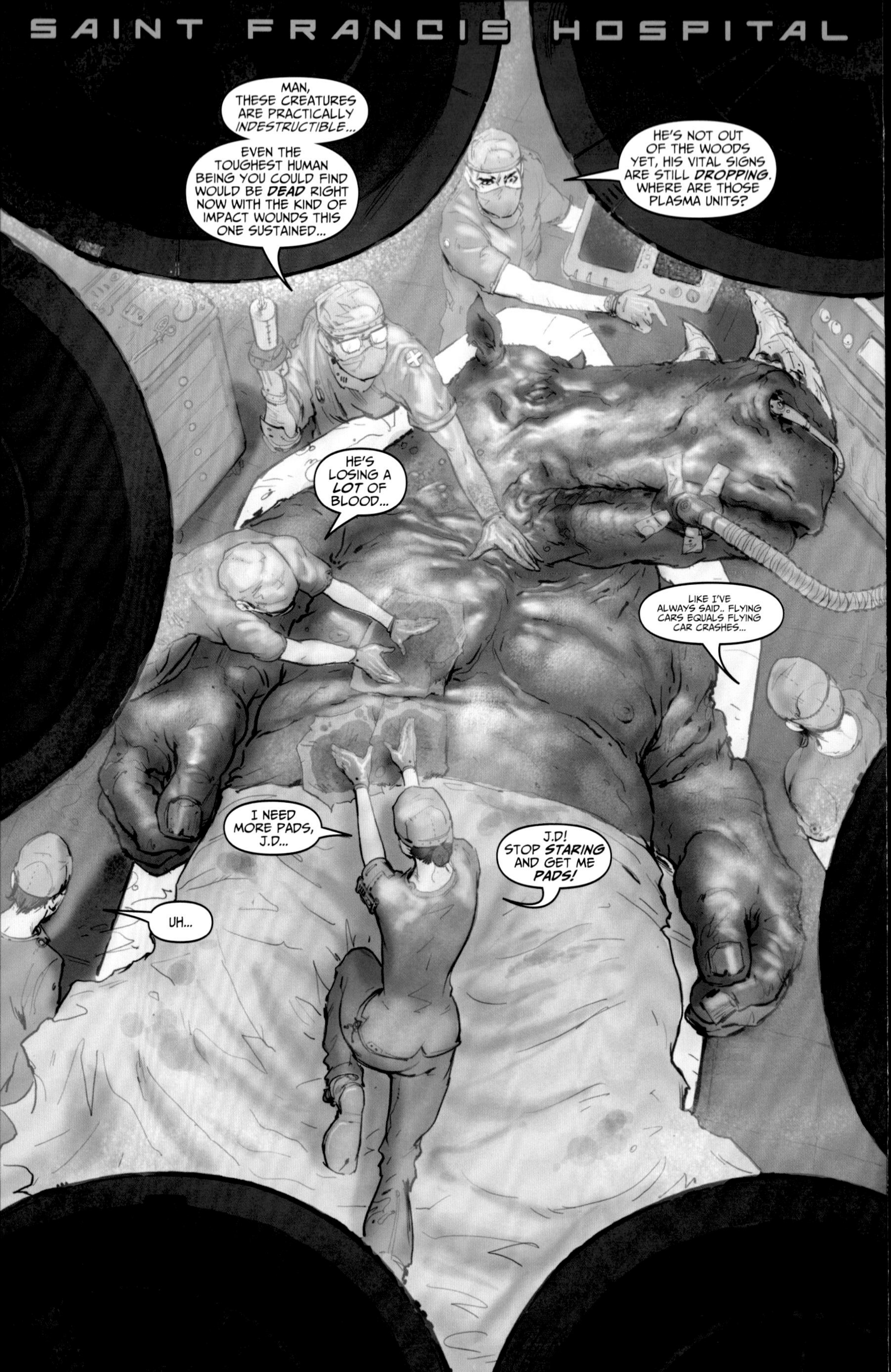
SAINT FRANCIS HOSPITAL
MAN, THESE CREATURES ARE PRACTICALLY INDESTRUCTIBLE...
EVEN THE TOUGHEST HUMAN BEING YOU COULD FIND WOULD BE DEAD RIGHT NOW WITH THE KIND OF IMPACT WOUNDS THIS ONE SUSTAINED...
HE'S NOT OUT OF THE WOODS YET, HIS VITAL SIGNS ARE STILL DROPPING. WHERE ARE THOSE PLASMA UNITS?
HE'S LOSING A LOT OF BLOOD...
LIKE I'VE ALWAYS SAID.. FLYING CARS EQUALS FLYING CAR CRASHES...
I NEED MORE PADS, J.D...
J.D! STOP STARING AND GET ME PADS!
UH...

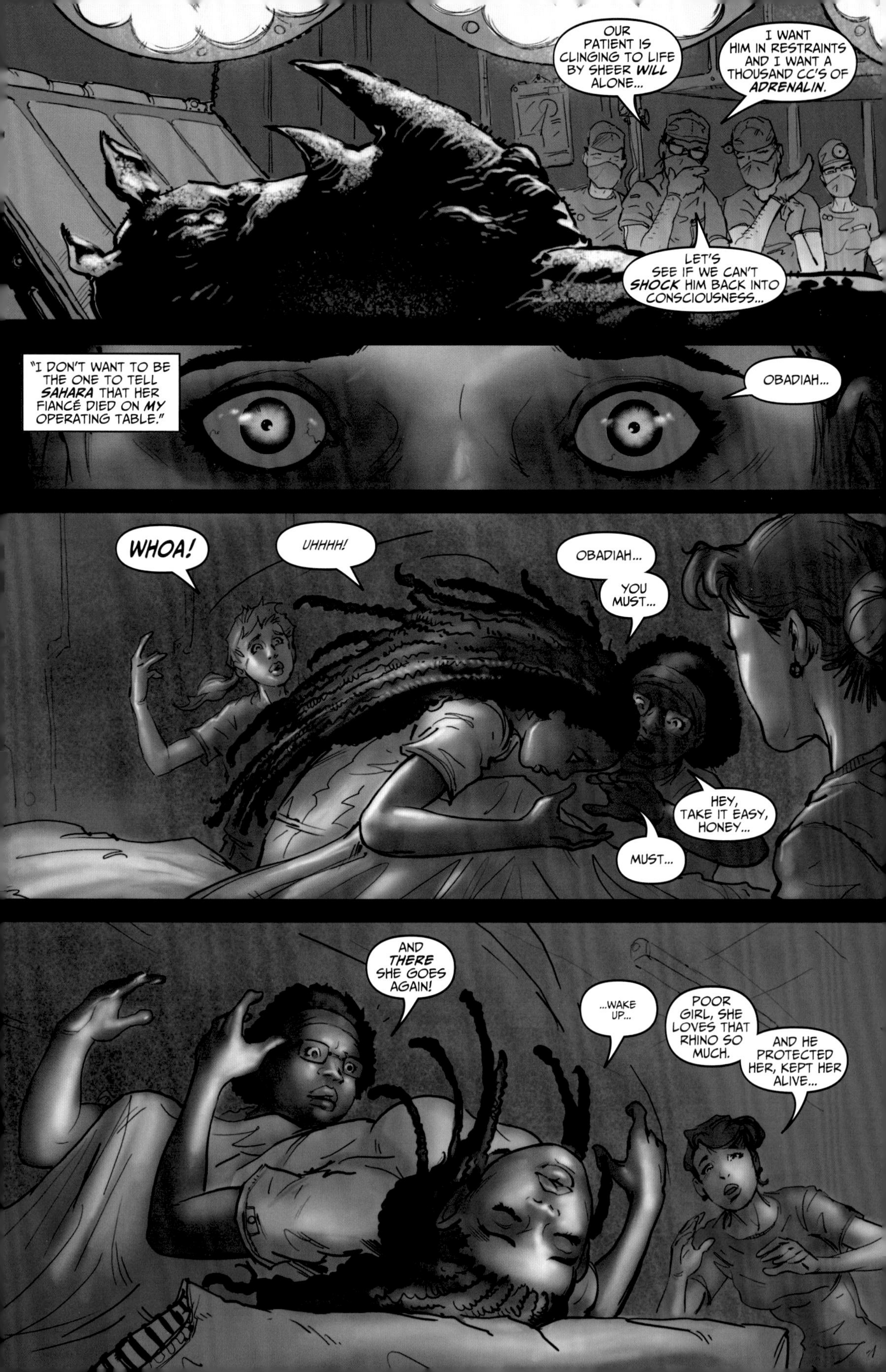

OUR PATIENT IS CLINGING TO LIFE BY SHEER WILL ALONE...
I WANT HIM IN RESTRAINTS AND I WANT A THOUSAND CC'S OF ADRENALIN.
LET'S SEE IF WE CAN'T SHOCK HIM BACK INTO CONSCIOUSNESS...
"I DON'T WANT TO BE THE ONE TO TELL SAHARA THAT HER FIANCÉ DIED ON MY OPERATING TABLE."
OBADIAH...
WHOA!
UHHHH!
OBADIAH...
YOU MUST...
HEY, TAKE IT EASY, HONEY...
MUST...
AND THERE SHE GOES AGAIN!
...WAKE UP...
POOR GIRL, SHE LOVES THAT RHINO SO MUCH.
AND HE PROTECTED HER, KEPT HER ALIVE...

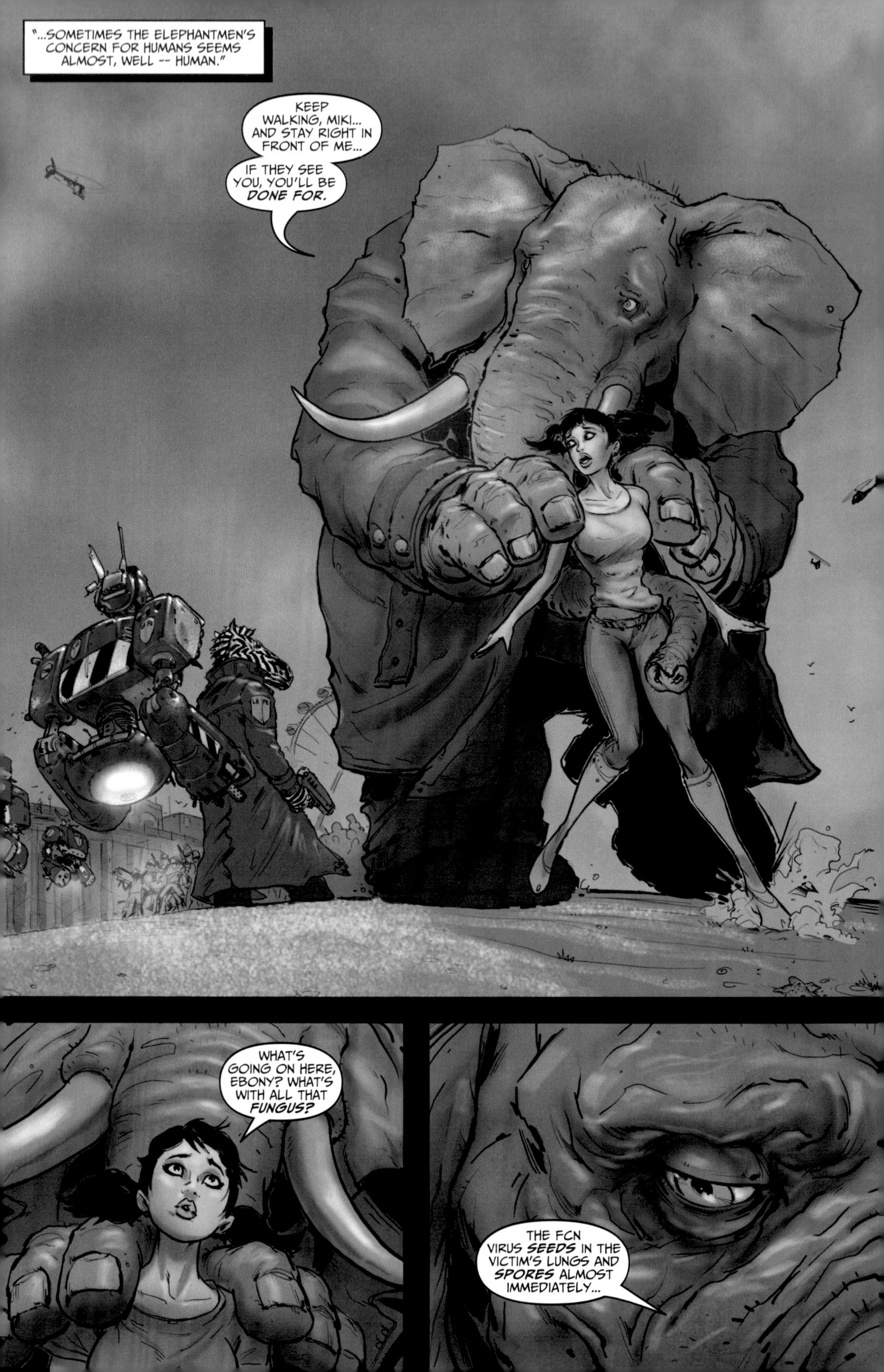
"...SOMETIMES THE ELEPHANTMEN'S CONCERN FOR HUMANS SEEMS ALMOST, WELL -- HUMAN."
KEEP WALKING, MIKI... AND STAY RIGHT IN FRONT OF ME...
IF THEY SEE YOU, YOU'LL BE *DONE FOR.*
WHAT'S GOING ON HERE, EBONY? WHAT'S WITH ALL THAT *FUNGUS?*
THE FCN VIRUS *SEEDS* IN THE VICTIM'S LUNGS AND *SPORES* ALMOST IMMEDIATELY...

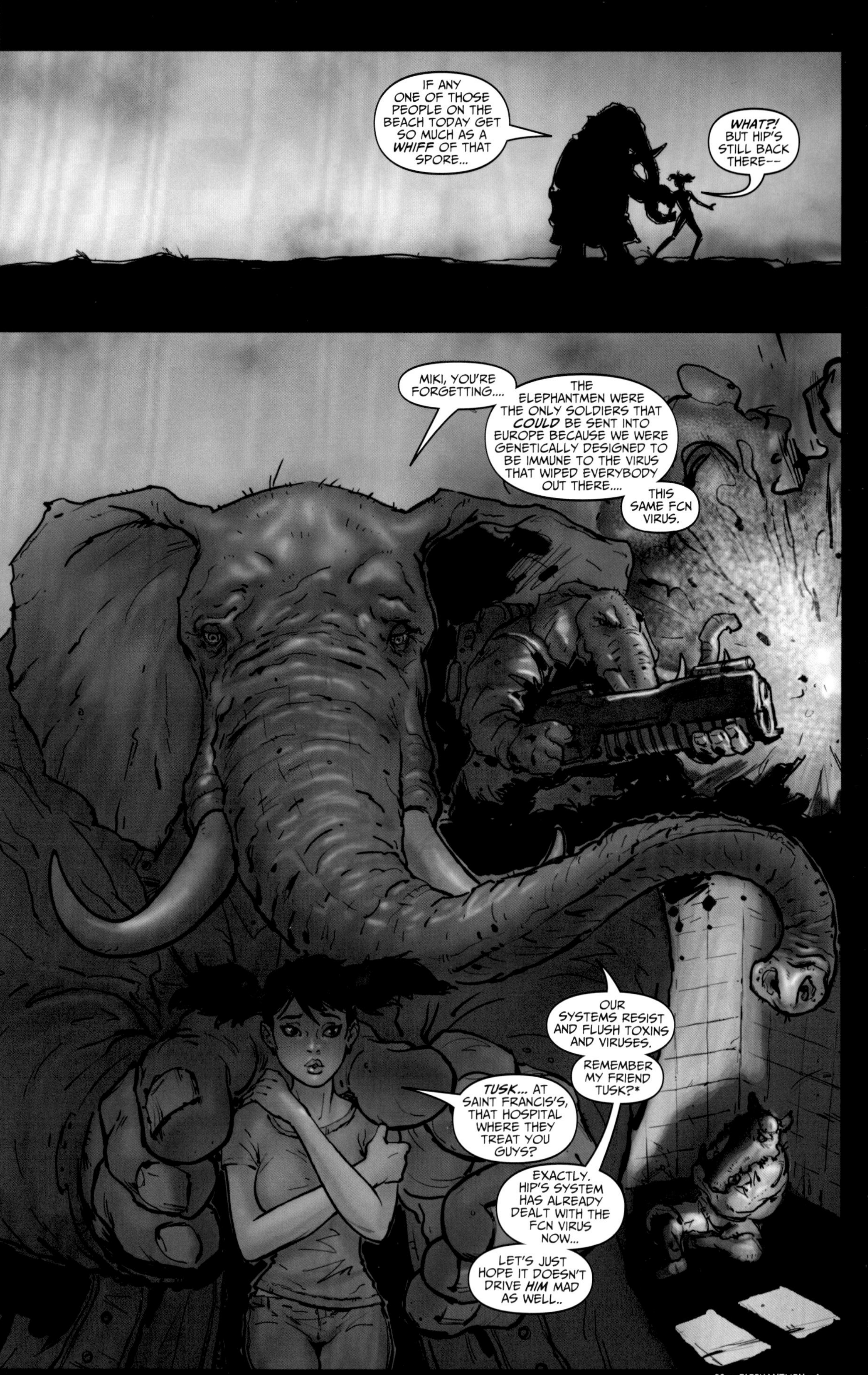
IF ANY ONE OF THOSE PEOPLE ON THE BEACH TODAY GET SO MUCH AS A WHIFF OF THAT SPORE...
WHAT?! BUT HIP'S STILL BACK THERE--
MIKI, YOU'RE FORGETTING....
THE ELEPHANTMEN WERE THE ONLY SOLDIERS THAT COULD BE SENT INTO EUROPE BECAUSE WE WERE GENETICALLY DESIGNED TO BE IMMUNE TO THE VIRUS THAT WIPED EVERYBODY OUT THERE....
THIS SAME FCN VIRUS.
OUR SYSTEMS RESIST AND FLUSH TOXINS AND VIRUSES.
REMEMBER MY FRIEND TUSK?*
TUSK... AT SAINT FRANCIS'S, THAT HOSPITAL WHERE THEY TREAT YOU GUYS?
EXACTLY. HIP'S SYSTEM HAS ALREADY DEALT WITH THE FCN VIRUS NOW...
LET'S JUST HOPE IT DOESN'T DRIVE HIM MAD AS WELL..

*See ELEPHANTMEN #4

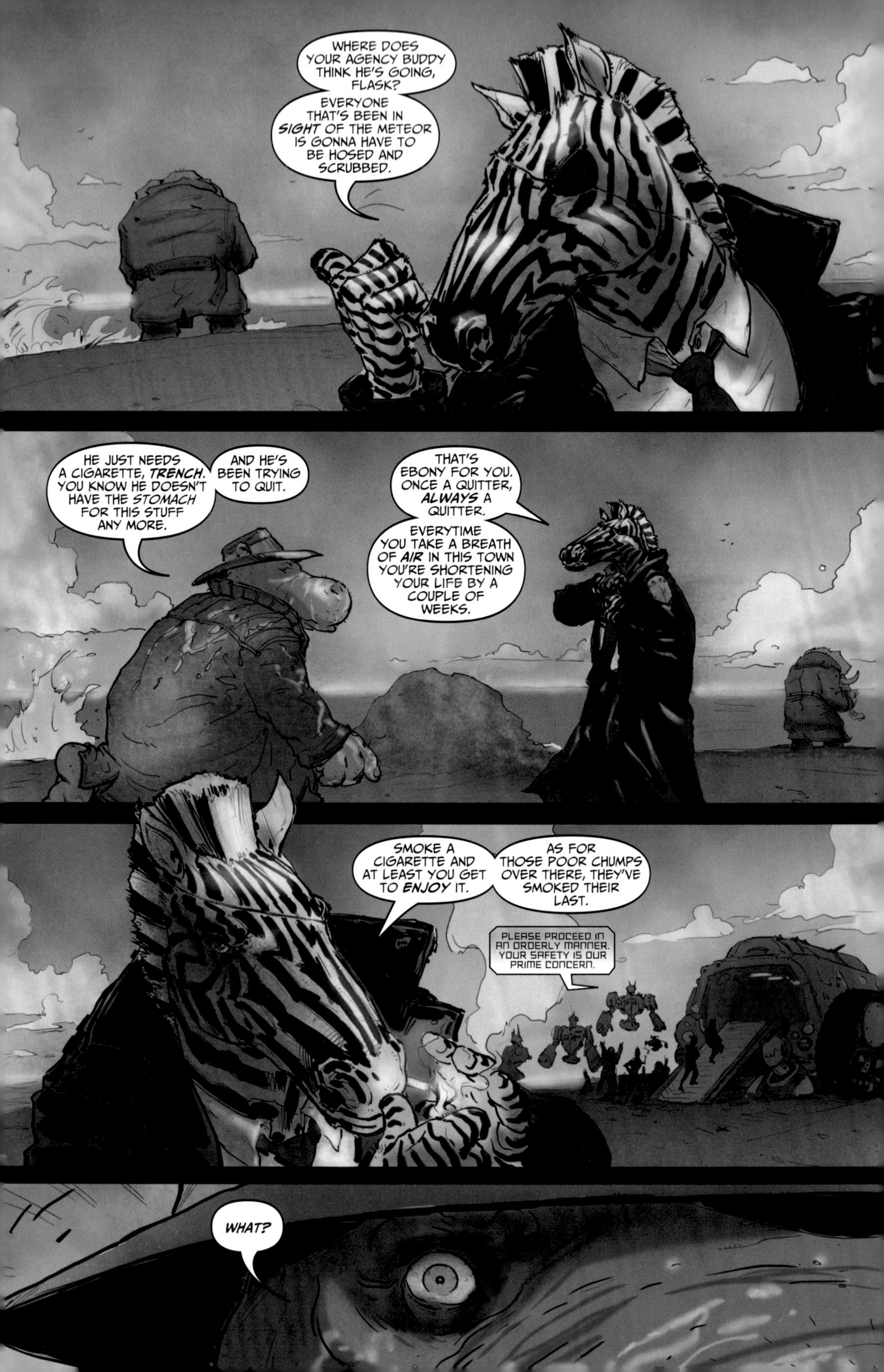
WHERE DOES YOUR AGENCY BUDDY THINK HE'S GOING, FLASK?
EVERYONE THAT'S BEEN IN SIGHT OF THE METEOR IS GONNA HAVE TO BE HOSED AND SCRUBBED.
HE JUST NEEDS A CIGARETTE, TRENCH. YOU KNOW HE DOESN'T HAVE THE STOMACH FOR THIS STUFF ANY MORE.
AND HE'S BEEN TRYING TO QUIT.
THAT'S EBONY FOR YOU. ONCE A QUITTER, ALWAYS A QUITTER.
EVERYTIME YOU TAKE A BREATH OF AIR IN THIS TOWN YOU'RE SHORTENING YOUR LIFE BY A COUPLE OF WEEKS.
SMOKE A CIGARETTE AND AT LEAST YOU GET TO ENJOY IT.
AS FOR THOSE POOR CHUMPS OVER THERE, THEY'VE SMOKED THEIR LAST.
PLEASE PROCEED IN AN ORDERLY MANNER. YOUR SAFETY IS OUR PRIME CONCERN.
WHAT?

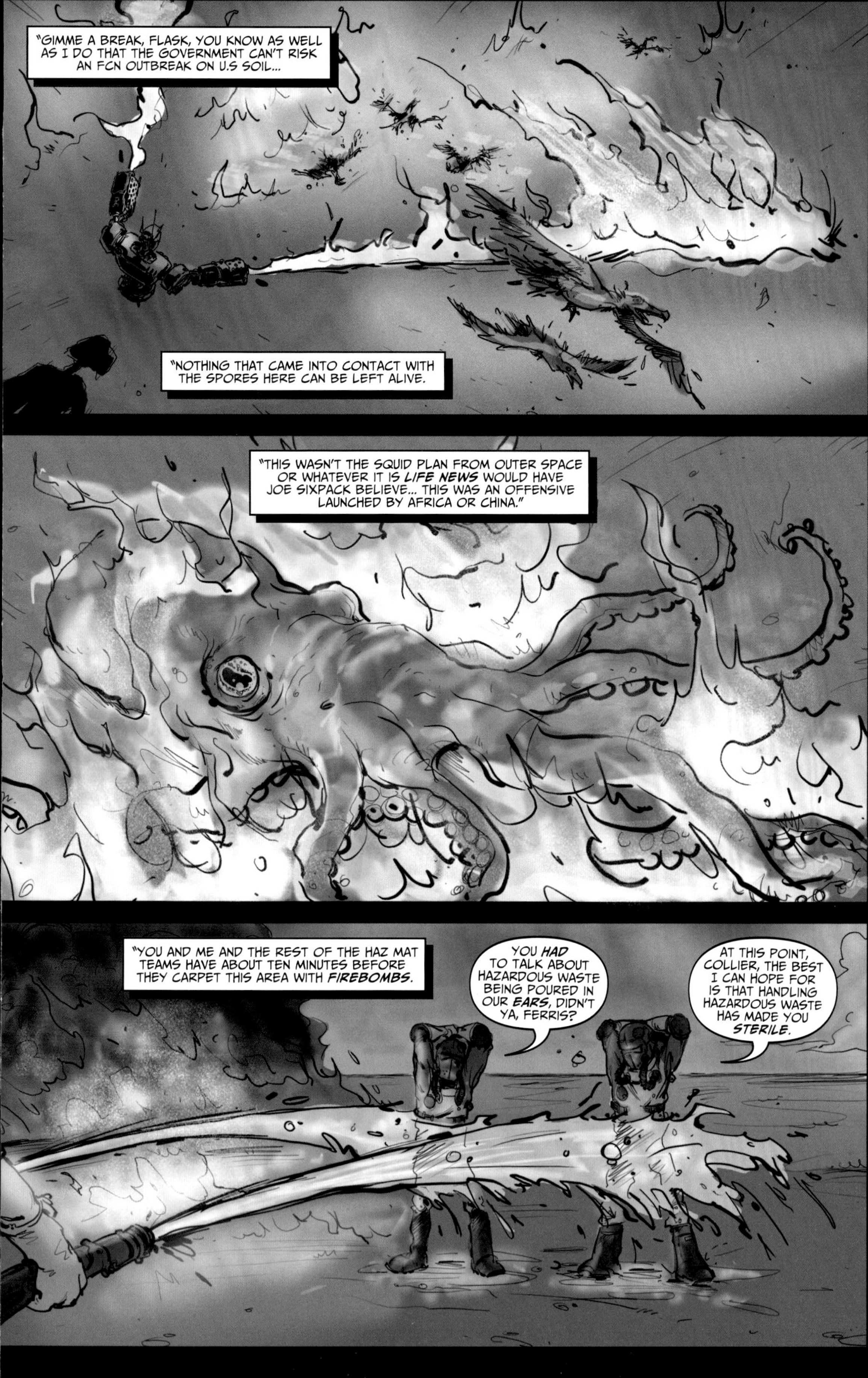
"GIMME A BREAK, FLASK, YOU KNOW AS WELL AS I DO THAT THE GOVERNMENT CAN'T RISK AN FCN OUTBREAK ON U.S SOIL...
"NOTHING THAT CAME INTO CONTACT WITH THE SPORES HERE CAN BE LEFT ALIVE.
"THIS WASN'T THE SQUID PLAN FROM OUTER SPACE OR WHATEVER IT IS LIFE NEWS WOULD HAVE JOE SIXPACK BELIEVE... THIS WAS AN OFFENSIVE LAUNCHED BY AFRICA OR CHINA."
"YOU AND ME AND THE REST OF THE HAZ MAT TEAMS HAVE ABOUT TEN MINUTES BEFORE THEY CARPET THIS AREA WITH FIREBOMBS.
YOU HAD TO TALK ABOUT HAZARDOUS WASTE BEING POURED IN OUR EARS, DIDN'T YA, FERRIS?
AT THIS POINT, COLLIER, THE BEST I CAN HOPE FOR IS THAT HANDLING HAZARDOUS WASTE HAS MADE YOU STERILE.

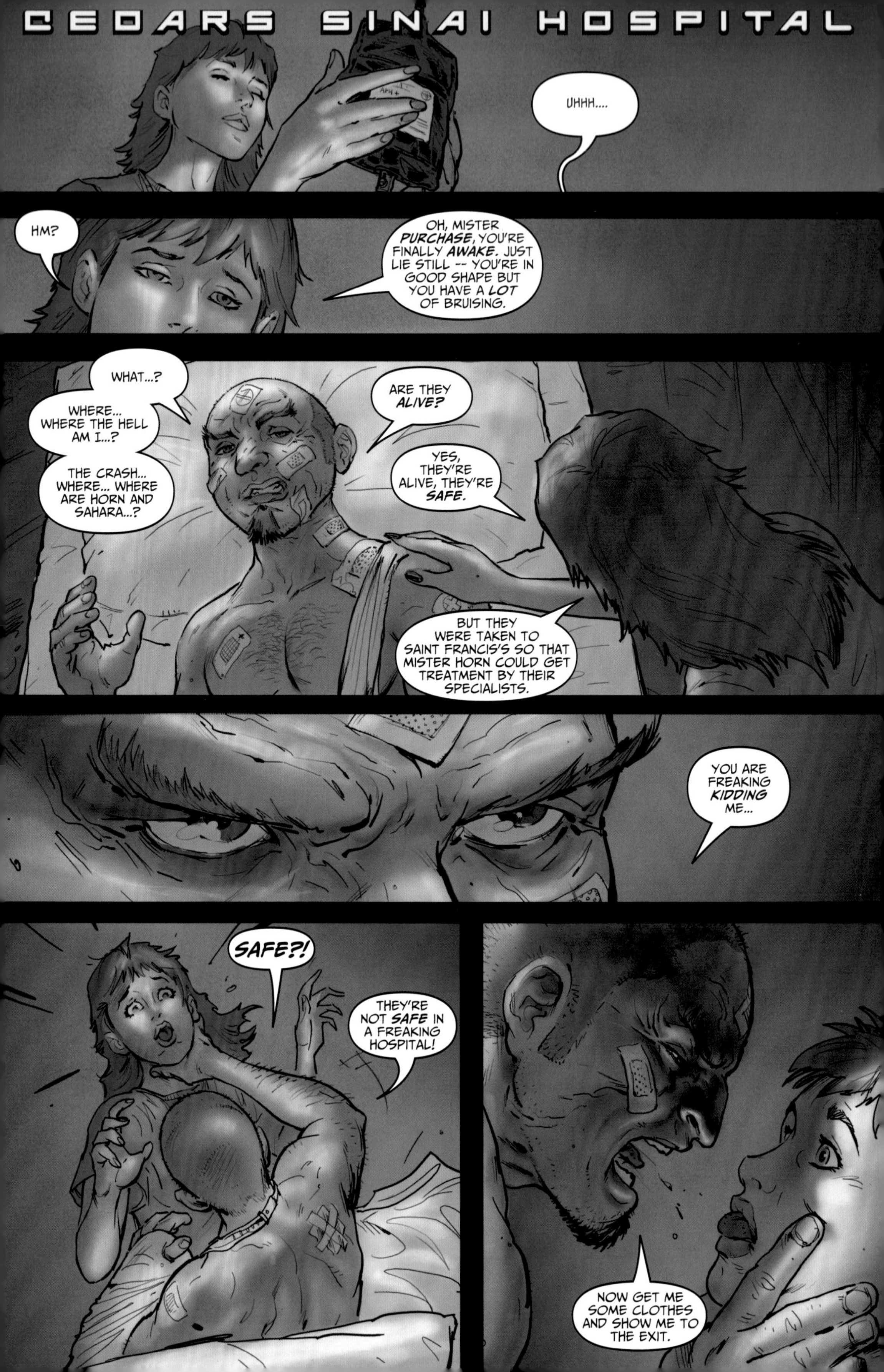
CEDARS SINAI HOSPITAL
UHHH....
HM?
OH, MISTER PURCHASE, YOU'RE FINALLY AWAKE. JUST LIE STILL -- YOU'RE IN GOOD SHAPE BUT YOU HAVE A LOT OF BRUISING.
WHAT...?
WHERE... WHERE THE HELL AM I...?
THE CRASH... WHERE... WHERE ARE HORN AND SAHARA...?
ARE THEY ALIVE?
YES, THEY'RE ALIVE, THEY'RE SAFE.
BUT THEY WERE TAKEN TO SAINT FRANCIS'S SO THAT MISTER HORN COULD GET TREATMENT BY THEIR SPECIALISTS.
YOU ARE FREAKING KIDDING ME...
SAFE?!
THEY'RE NOT SAFE IN A FREAKING HOSPITAL!
NOW GET ME SOME CLOTHES AND SHOW ME TO THE EXIT.

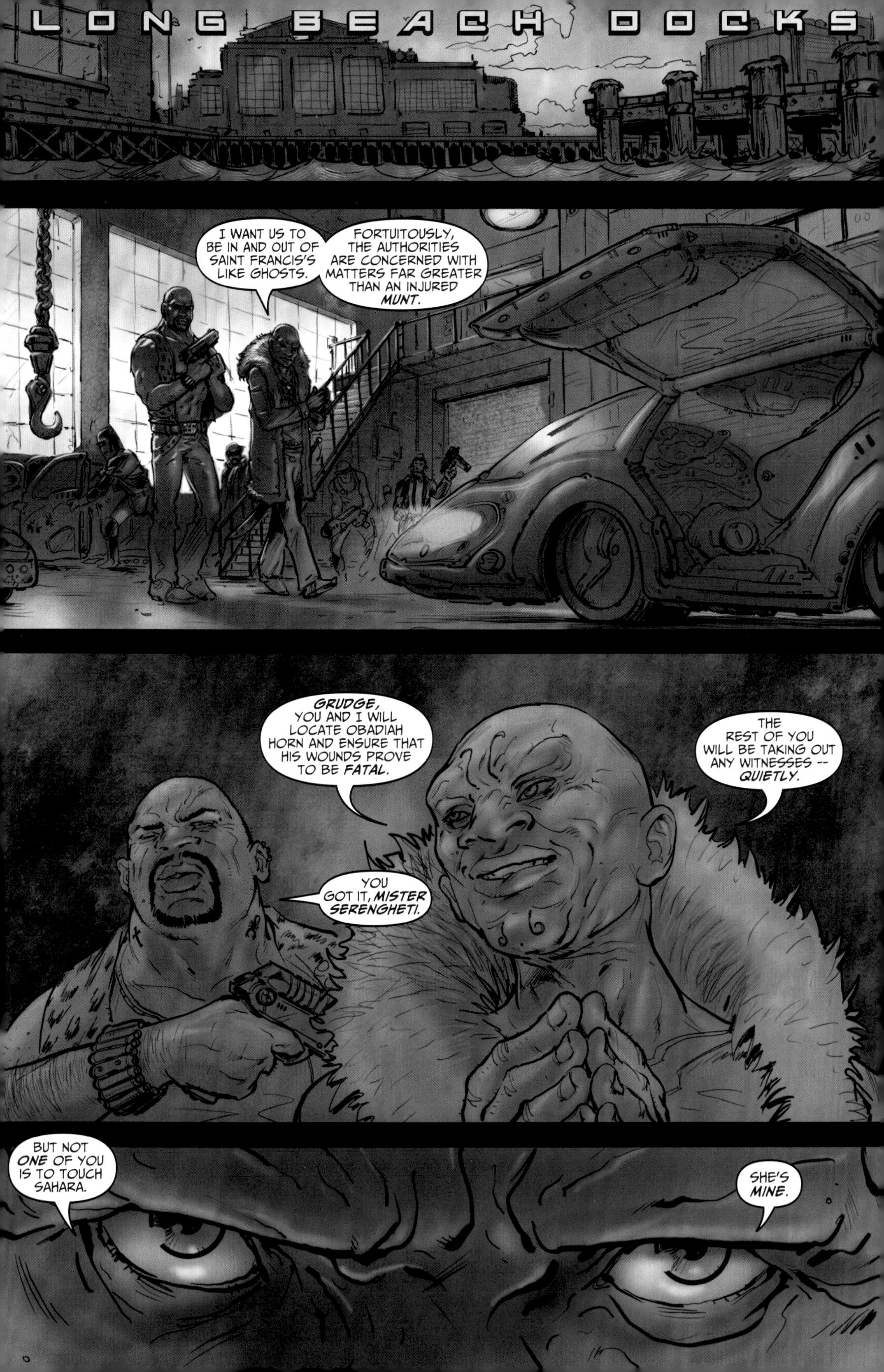
LONG BEACH DOCKS
I WANT US TO BE IN AND OUT OF SAINT FRANCIS'S LIKE GHOSTS.
FORTUITOUSLY, THE AUTHORITIES ARE CONCERNED WITH MATTERS FAR GREATER THAN AN INJURED MUNT.
GRUDGE, YOU AND I WILL LOCATE OBADIAH HORN AND ENSURE THAT HIS WOUNDS PROVE TO BE FATAL.
THE REST OF YOU WILL BE TAKING OUT ANY WITNESSES -- QUIETLY.
YOU GOT IT, MISTER SERENGHETI.
BUT NOT ONE OF YOU IS TO TOUCH SAHARA.
SHE'S MINE.

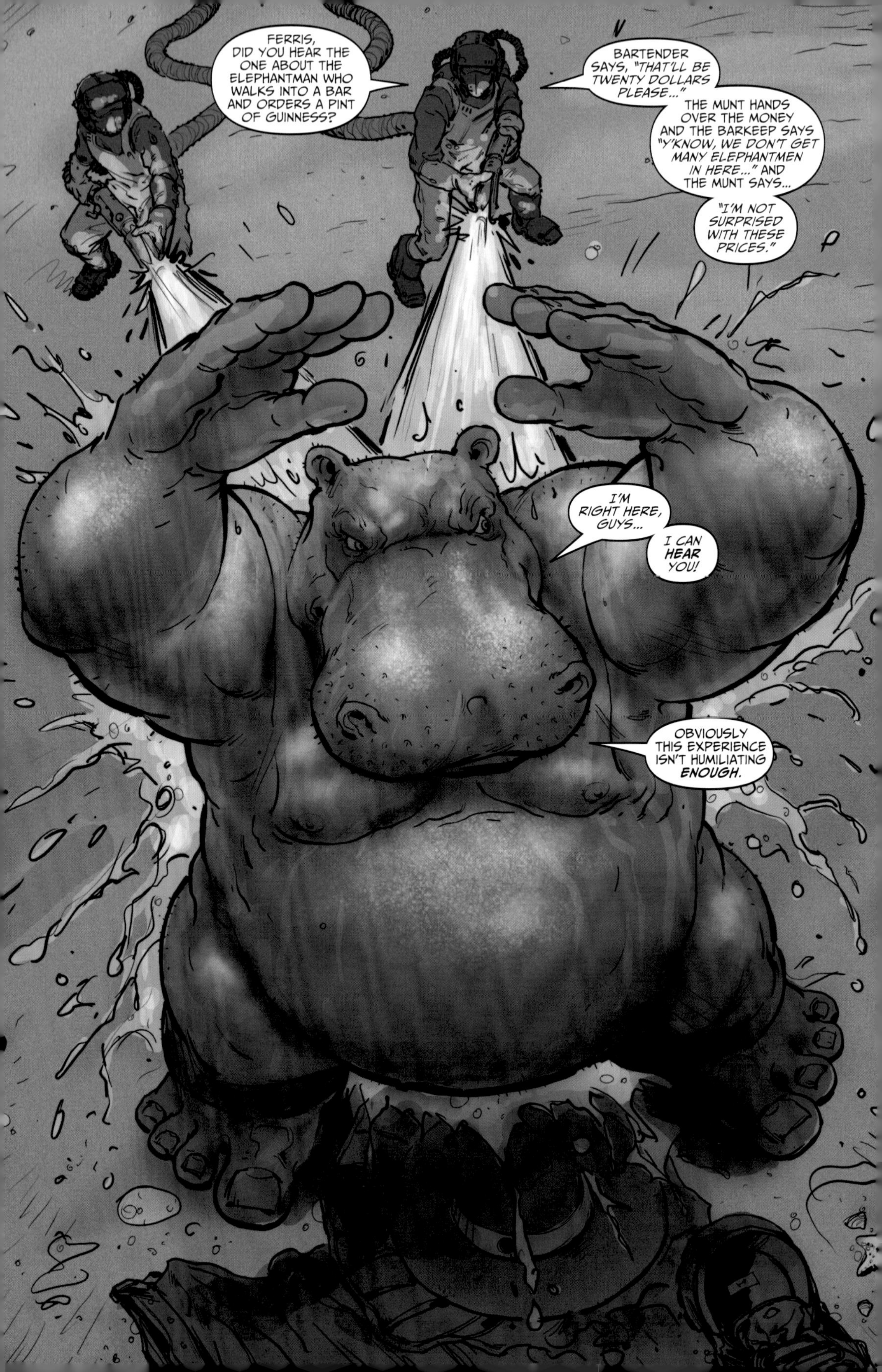
FERRIS, DID YOU HEAR THE ONE ABOUT THE ELEPHANTMAN WHO WALKS INTO A BAR AND ORDERS A PINT OF GUINNESS?
BARTENDER SAYS, "THAT'LL BE TWENTY DOLLARS PLEASE..."
THE MUNT HANDS OVER THE MONEY AND THE BARKEEP SAYS "Y'KNOW, WE DON'T GET MANY ELEPHANTMEN IN HERE..." AND THE MUNT SAYS...
"I'M NOT SURPRISED WITH THESE PRICES."
I'M RIGHT HERE, GUYS...
I CAN **HEAR** YOU!
OBVIOUSLY THIS EXPERIENCE ISN'T HUMILIATING **ENOUGH**.

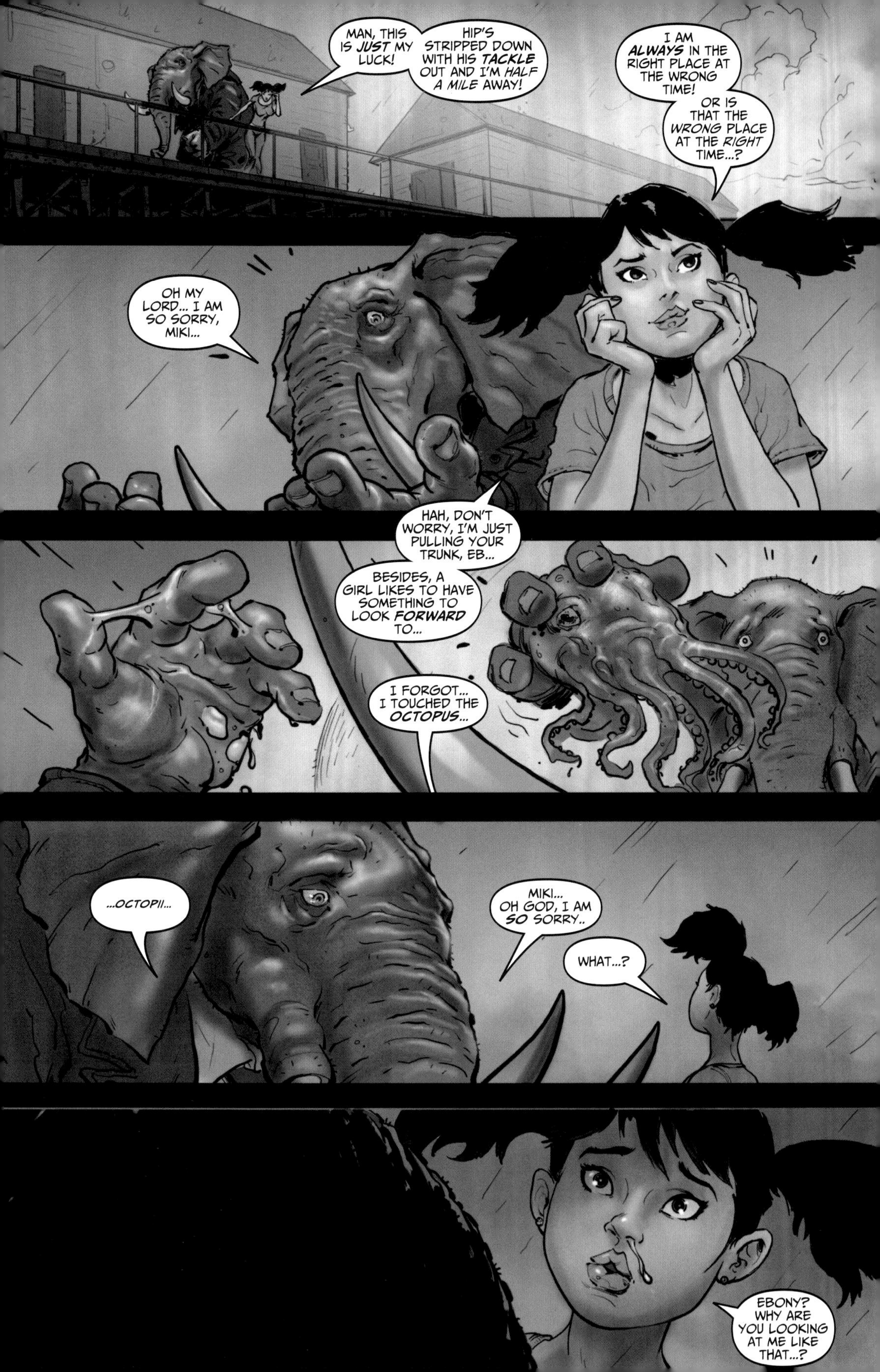
MAN, THIS IS JUST MY LUCK!
HIP'S STRIPPED DOWN WITH HIS TACKLE OUT AND I'M HALF A MILE AWAY!
I AM ALWAYS IN THE RIGHT PLACE AT THE WRONG TIME!
OR IS THAT THE WRONG PLACE AT THE RIGHT TIME...?
OH MY LORD... I AM SO SORRY, MIKI...
HAH, DON'T WORRY, I'M JUST PULLING YOUR TRUNK, EB...
BESIDES, A GIRL LIKES TO HAVE SOMETHING TO LOOK FORWARD TO...
I FORGOT... I TOUCHED THE OCTOPUS...
...OCTOPII...
MIKI... OH GOD, I AM SO SORRY..
WHAT...?
EBONY? WHY ARE YOU LOOKING AT ME LIKE THAT...?

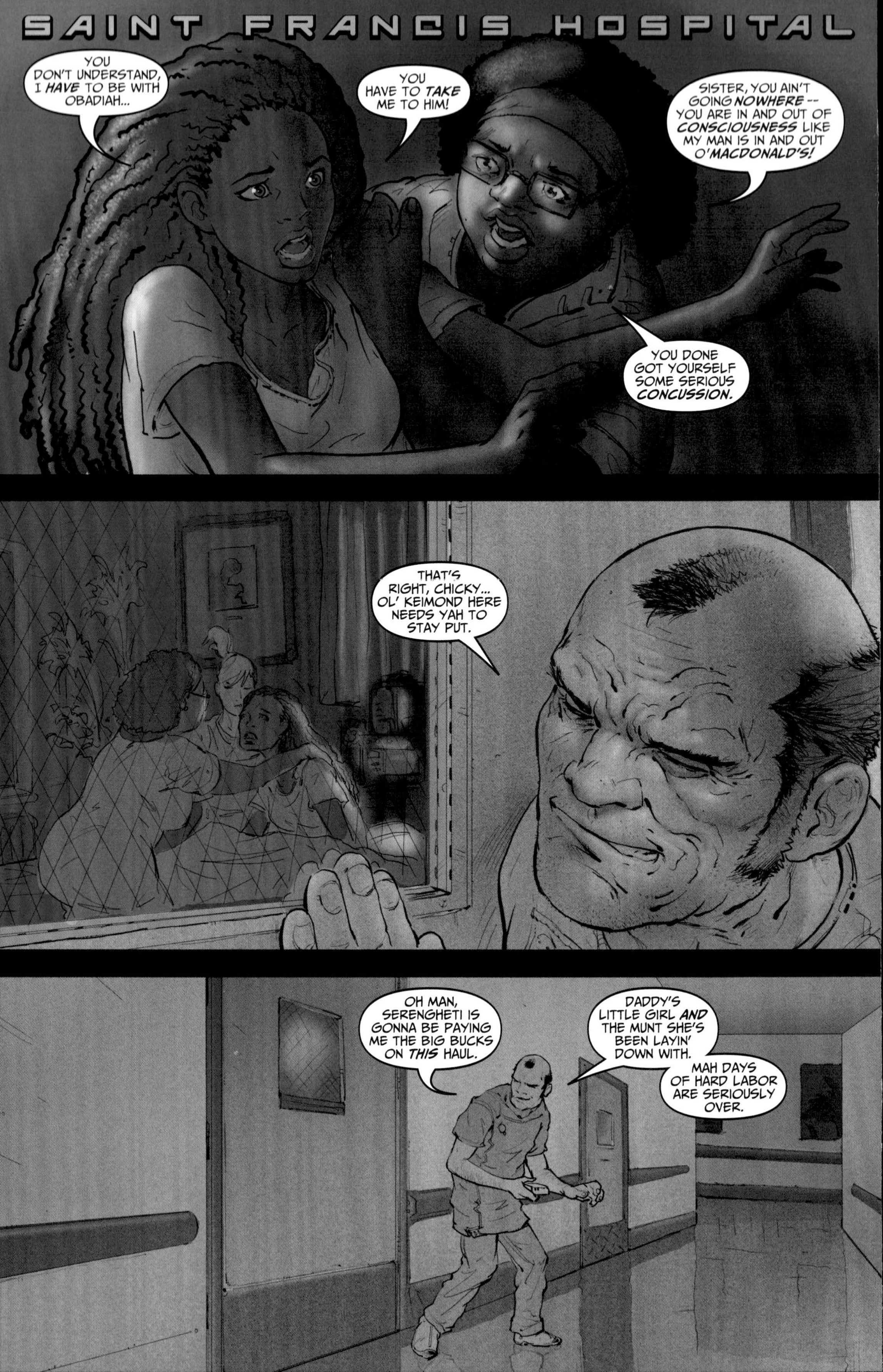
SAINT FRANCIS HOSPITAL
YOU DON'T UNDERSTAND, I HAVE TO BE WITH OBADIAH...
YOU HAVE TO TAKE ME TO HIM!
SISTER, YOU AIN'T GOING NOWHERE -- YOU ARE IN AND OUT OF CONSCIOUSNESS LIKE MY MAN IS IN AND OUT O'MACDONALD'S!
YOU DONE GOT YOURSELF SOME SERIOUS CONCUSSION.
THAT'S RIGHT, CHICKY... OL' KEIMOND HERE NEEDS YAH TO STAY PUT.
OH MAN, SERENGHETI IS GONNA BE PAYING ME THE BIG BUCKS ON THIS HAUL.
DADDY'S LITTLE GIRL AND THE MUNT SHE'S BEEN LAYIN' DOWN WITH.
MAH DAYS OF HARD LABOR ARE SERIOUSLY OVER.

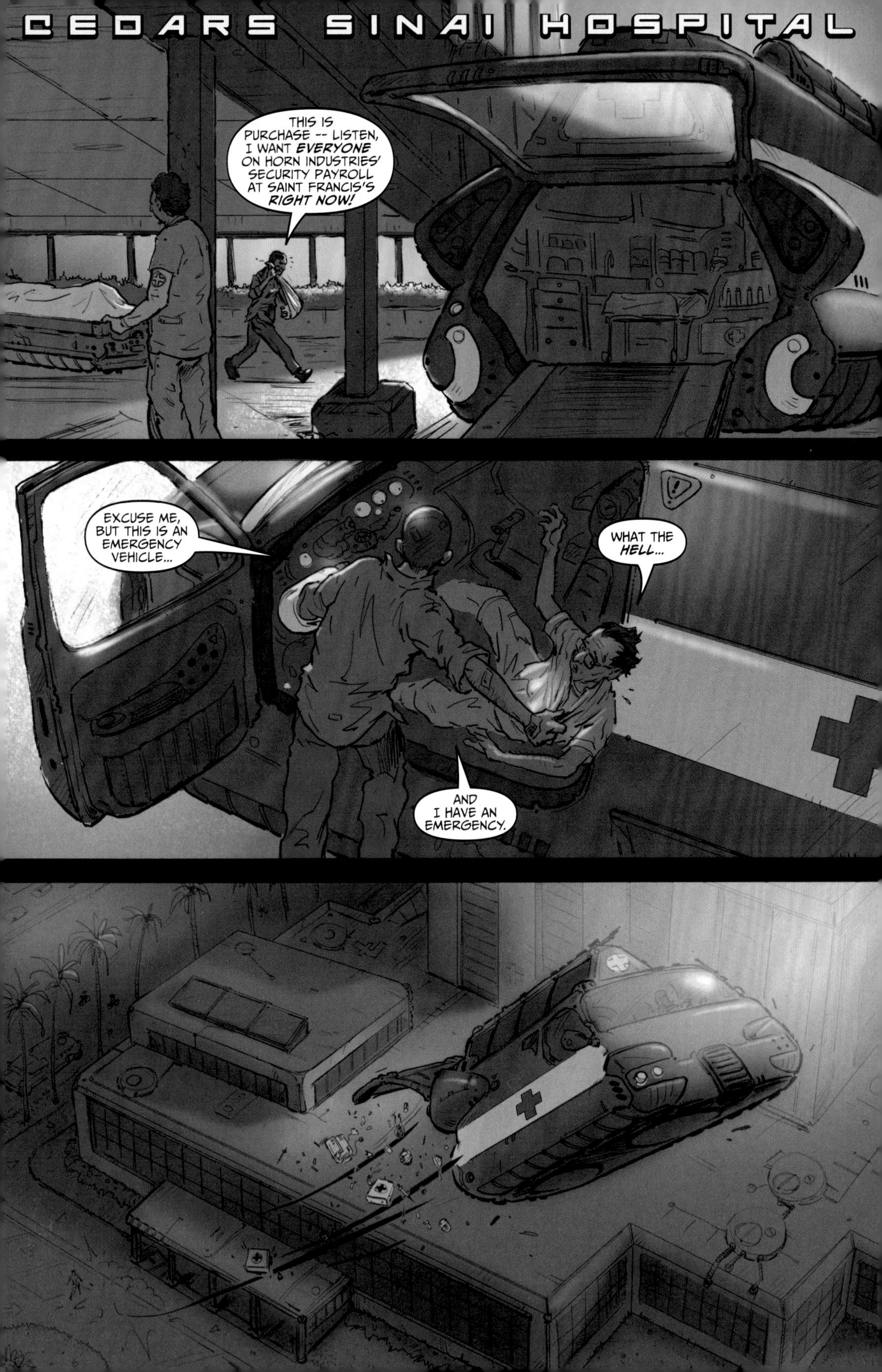
CEDARS SINAI HOSPITAL
THIS IS PURCHASE -- LISTEN, I WANT EVERYONE ON HORN INDUSTRIES' SECURITY PAYROLL AT SAINT FRANCIS'S RIGHT NOW!
EXCUSE ME, BUT THIS IS AN EMERGENCY VEHICLE...
WHAT THE HELL...
AND I HAVE AN EMERGENCY.

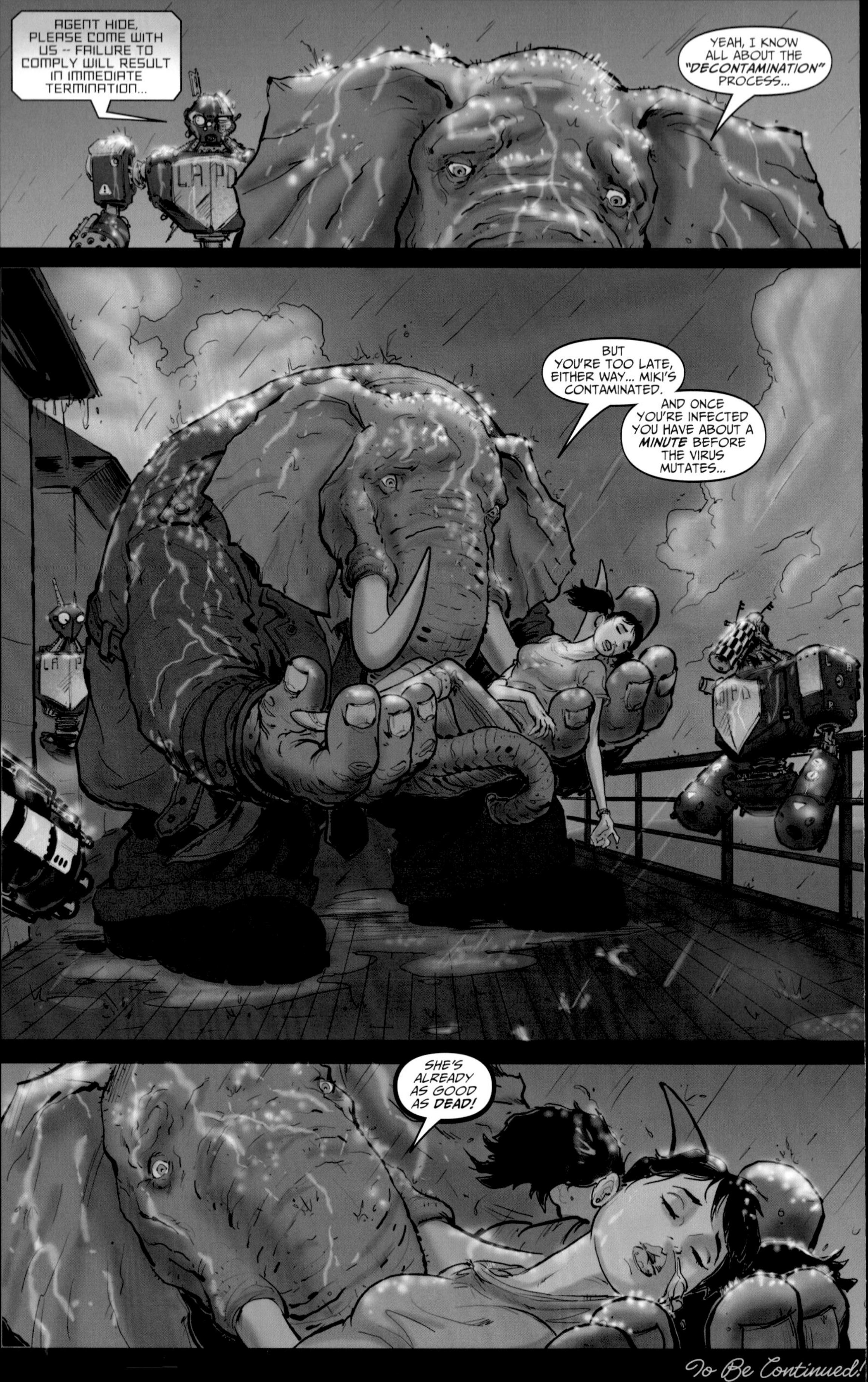
AGENT HIDE, PLEASE COME WITH US -- FAILURE TO COMPLY WILL RESULT IN IMMEDIATE TERMINATION...
YEAH, I KNOW ALL ABOUT THE "DECONTAMINATION" PROCESS...
BUT YOU'RE TOO LATE, EITHER WAY... MIKI'S CONTAMINATED.
AND ONCE YOU'RE INFECTED YOU HAVE ABOUT A MINUTE BEFORE THE VIRUS MUTATES...
SHE'S ALREADY AS GOOD AS DEAD!
To Be Continued!

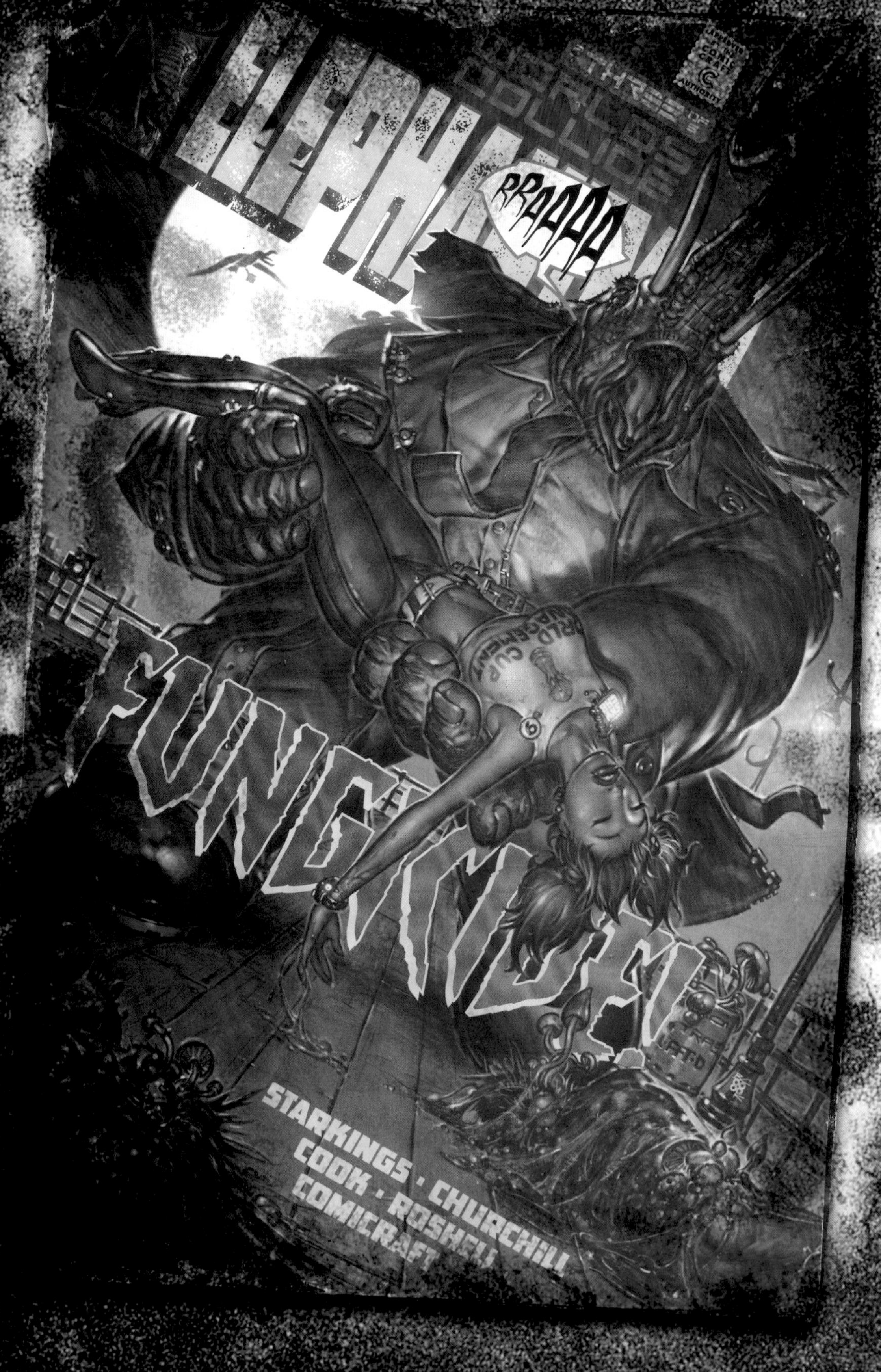
APPROVED BY THE COMIC CRAFT AUTHORITY
RRAAAA
STARKINGS · CHURCHILL
COOK · ROSHELL
COMICRAFT

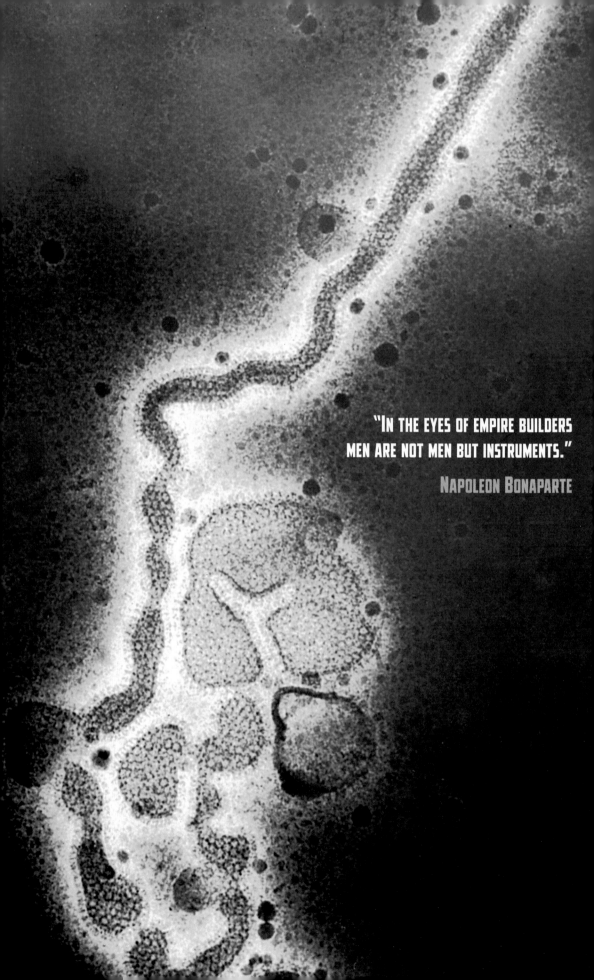

"IN THE EYES OF EMPIRE BUILDERS
MEN ARE NOT MEN BUT INSTRUMENTS."

NAPOLEON BONAPARTE

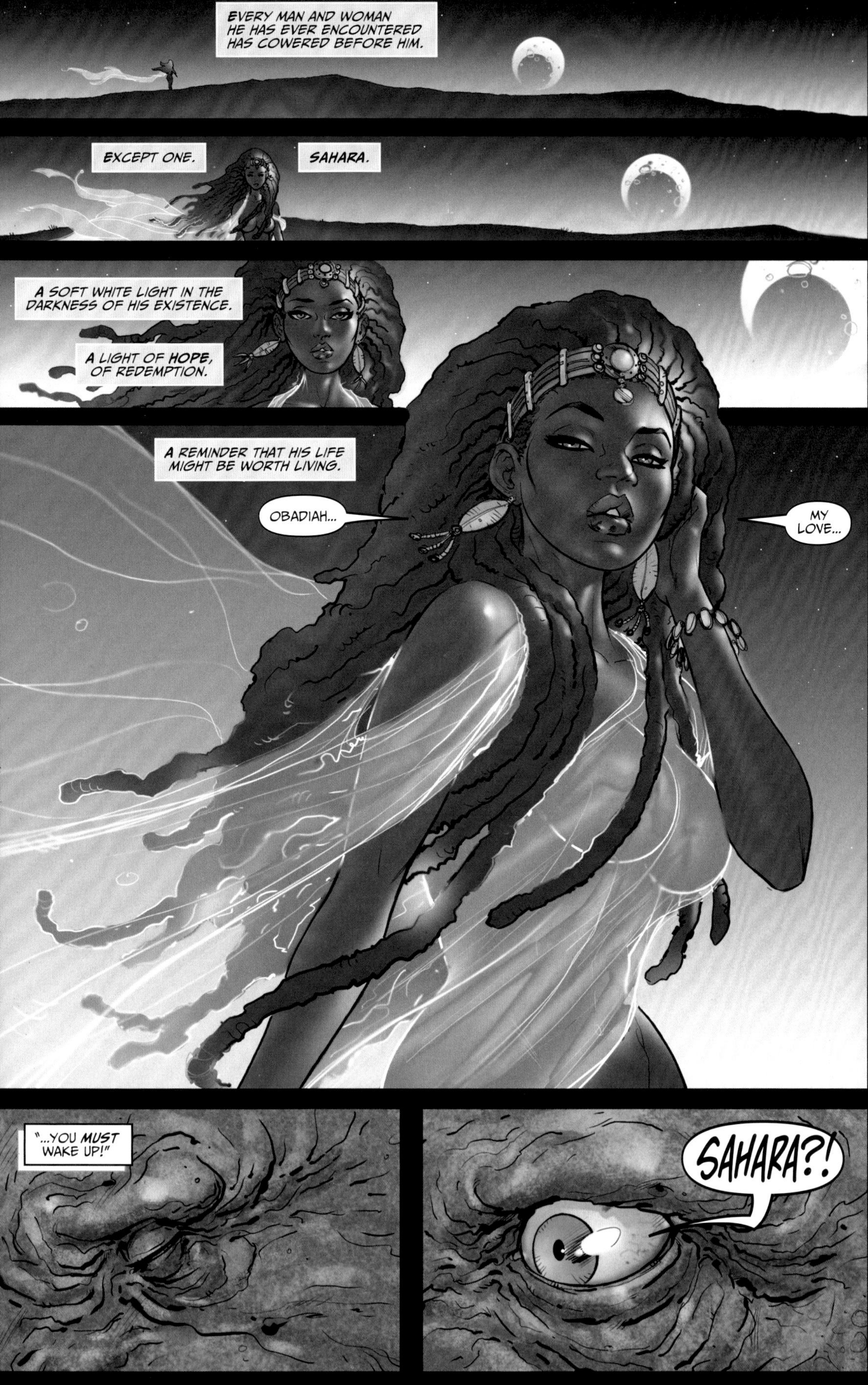

EVERY MAN AND WOMAN HE HAS EVER ENCOUNTERED HAS COWERED BEFORE HIM.
EXCEPT ONE.
SAHARA.
A SOFT WHITE LIGHT IN THE DARKNESS OF HIS EXISTENCE.
A LIGHT OF HOPE, OF REDEMPTION.
A REMINDER THAT HIS LIFE MIGHT BE WORTH LIVING.
OBADIAH...
MY LOVE...
"...YOU MUST WAKE UP!"
SAHARA?!

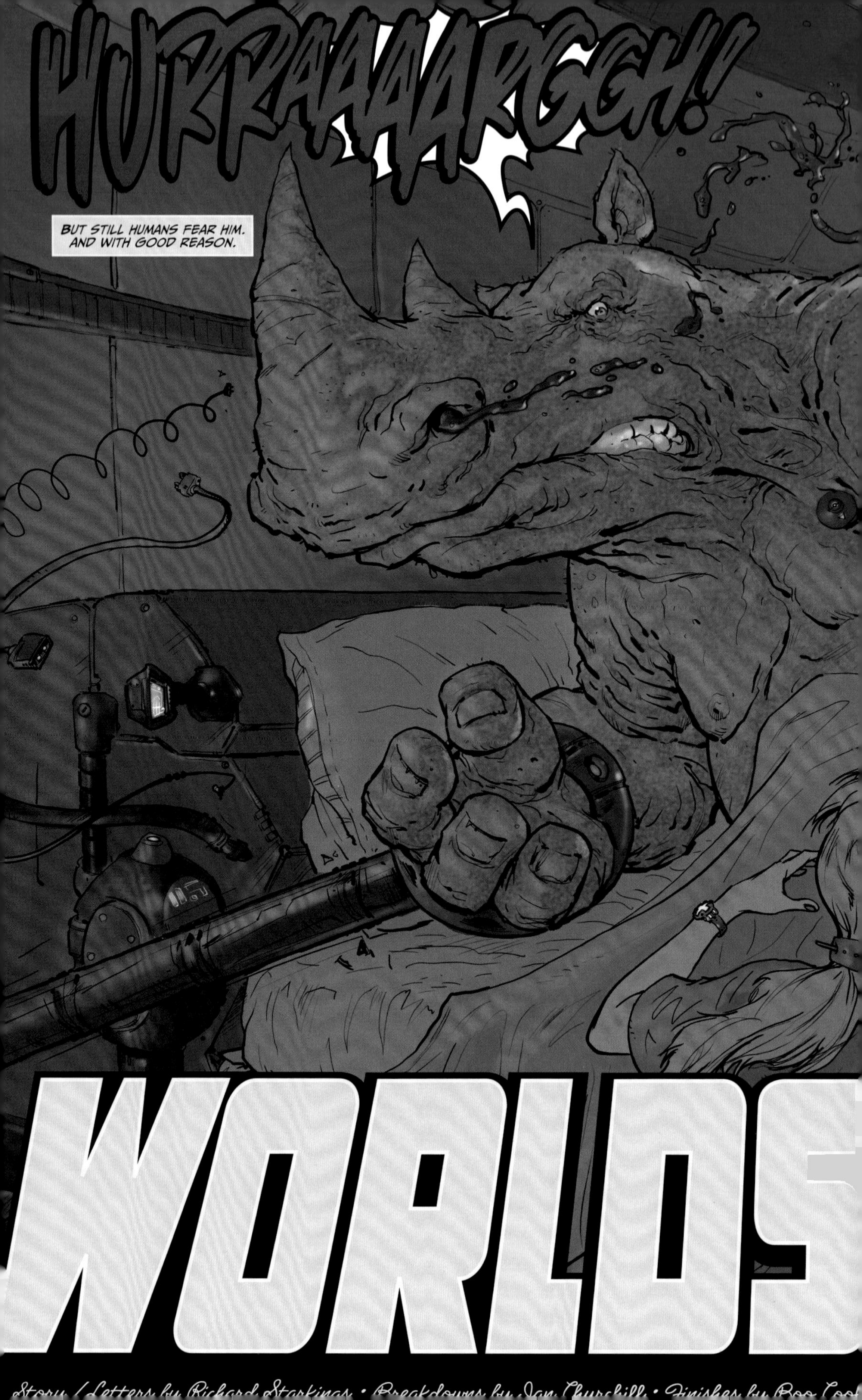
HURRAAAARGGH!
BUT STILL HUMANS FEAR HIM. AND WITH GOOD REASON.
WORLDS
Story / Letters by Richard Starkings • Breakdowns by Ian Churchill • Finishes by Boo Coo

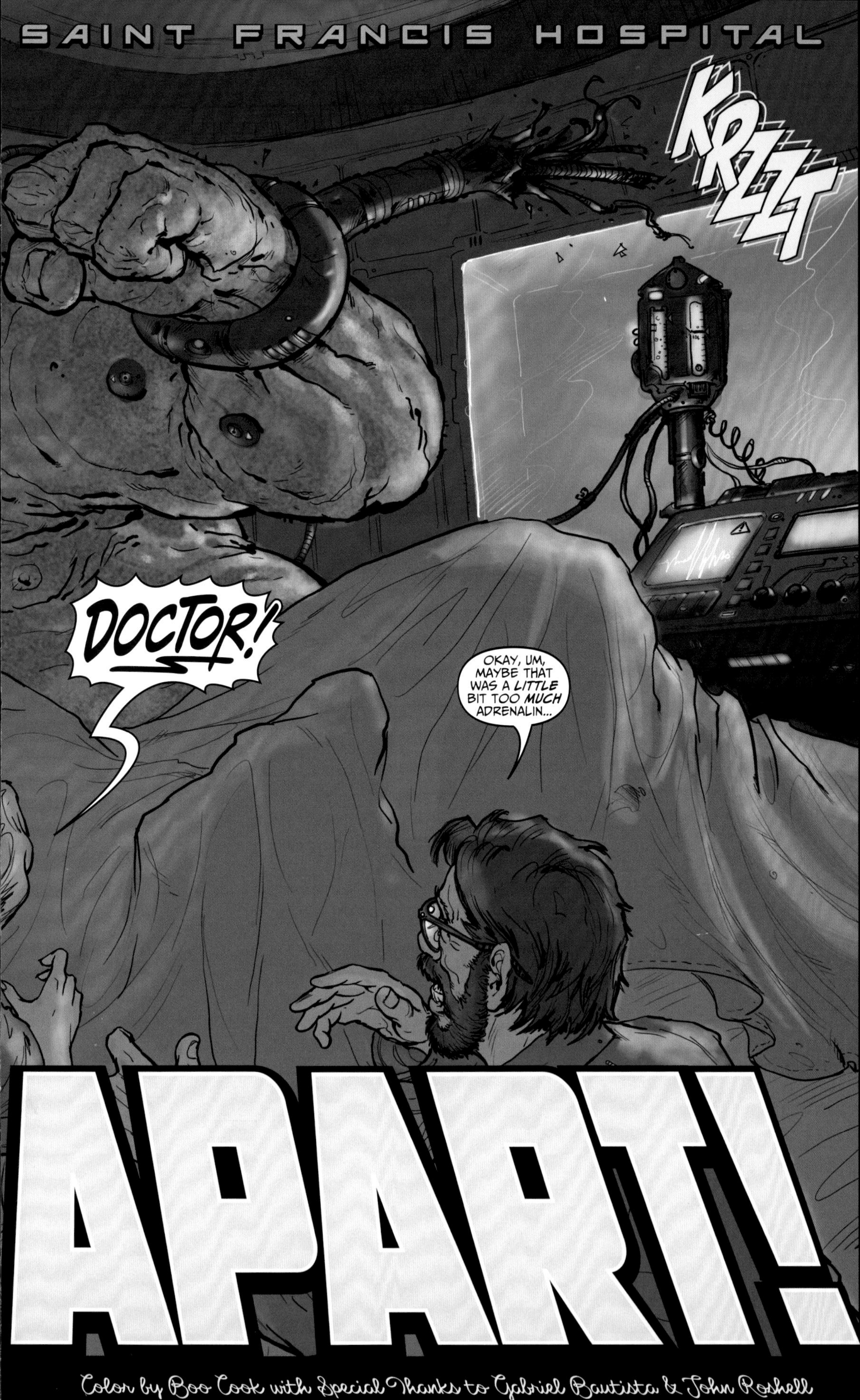
SAINT FRANCIS HOSPITAL
KRZZZT
DOCTOR!
OKAY, UM, MAYBE THAT WAS A *LITTLE* BIT TOO *MUCH* ADRENALIN...
APART!
Color by Boo Cook with Special Thanks to Gabriel Bautista & John Roshell

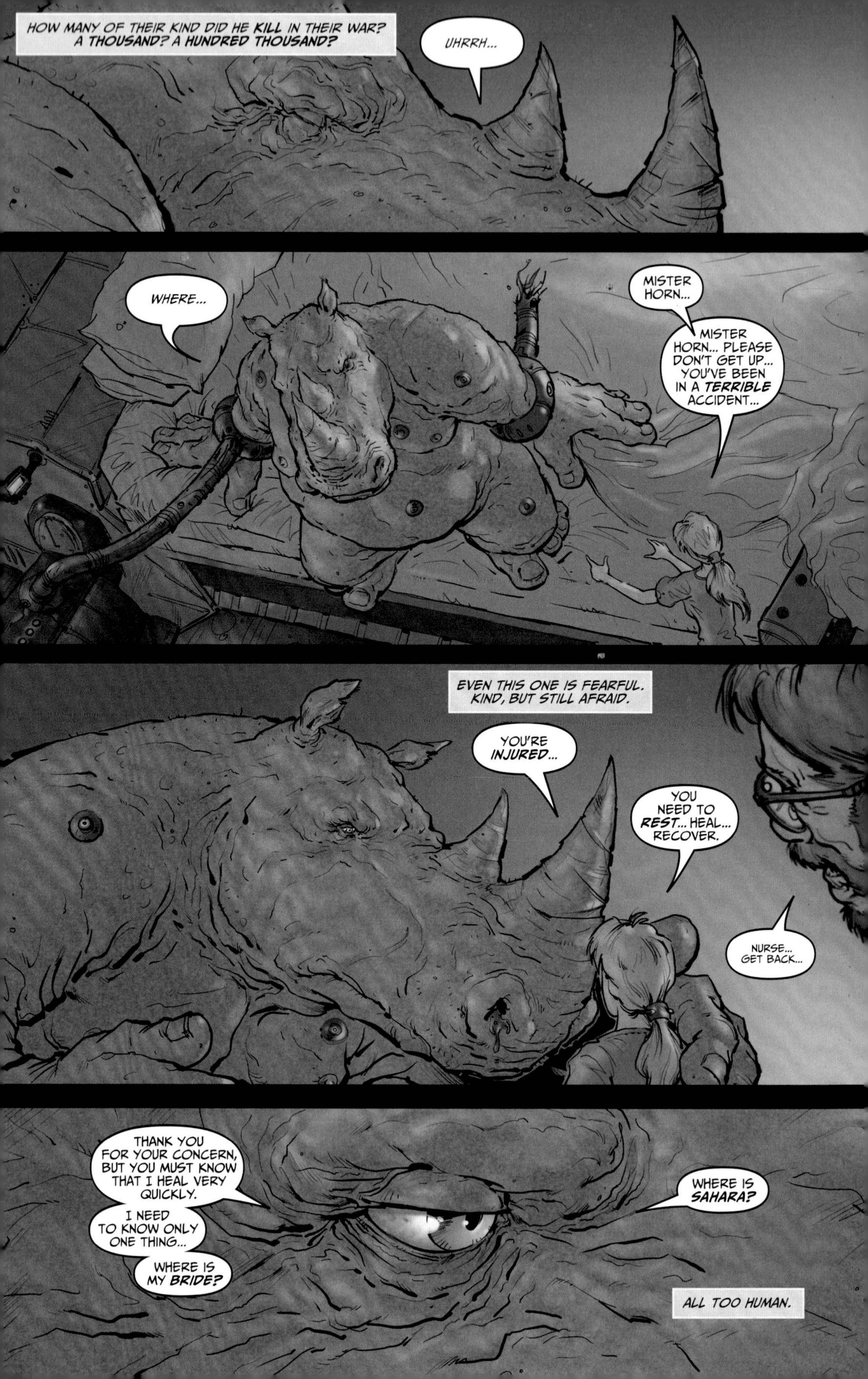
HOW MANY OF THEIR KIND DID HE KILL IN THEIR WAR? A THOUSAND? A HUNDRED THOUSAND?
UHRRH...
WHERE...
MISTER HORN...
MISTER HORN... PLEASE DON'T GET UP... YOU'VE BEEN IN A TERRIBLE ACCIDENT...
EVEN THIS ONE IS FEARFUL. KIND, BUT STILL AFRAID.
YOU'RE INJURED...
YOU NEED TO REST... HEAL... RECOVER.
NURSE... GET BACK...
THANK YOU FOR YOUR CONCERN, BUT YOU MUST KNOW THAT I HEAL VERY QUICKLY.
I NEED TO KNOW ONLY ONE THING...
WHERE IS MY BRIDE?
WHERE IS SAHARA?
ALL TOO HUMAN.

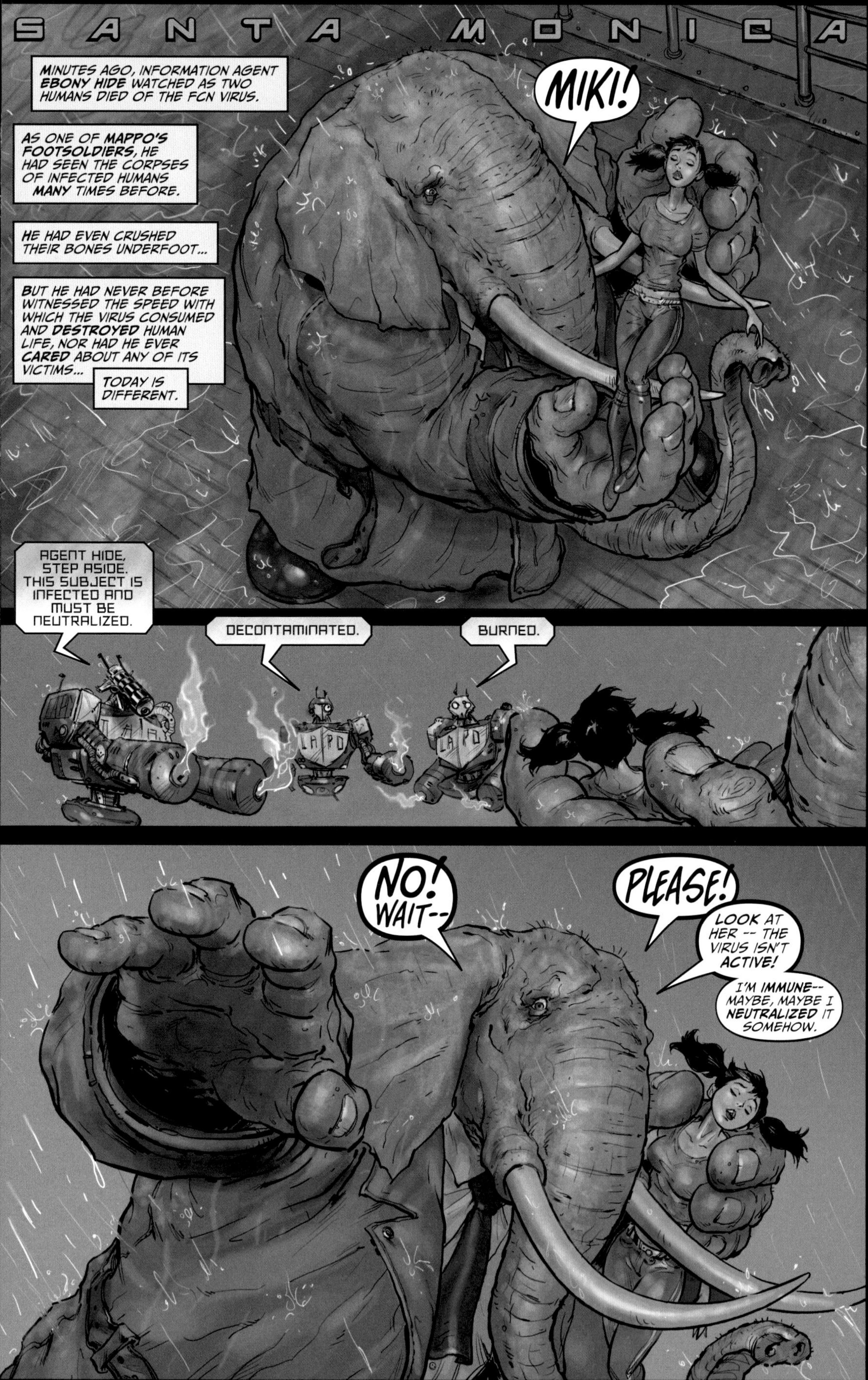
SANTA MONICA
MINUTES AGO, INFORMATION AGENT EBONY HIDE WATCHED AS TWO HUMANS DIED OF THE FCN VIRUS.
AS ONE OF MAPPO'S FOOTSOLDIERS, HE HAD SEEN THE CORPSES OF INFECTED HUMANS MANY TIMES BEFORE.
HE HAD EVEN CRUSHED THEIR BONES UNDERFOOT...
BUT HE HAD NEVER BEFORE WITNESSED THE SPEED WITH WHICH THE VIRUS CONSUMED AND DESTROYED HUMAN LIFE, NOR HAD HE EVER CARED ABOUT ANY OF ITS VICTIMS...
TODAY IS DIFFERENT.
MIKI!
AGENT HIDE, STEP ASIDE. THIS SUBJECT IS INFECTED AND MUST BE NEUTRALIZED.
DECONTAMINATED.
BURNED.
NO! WAIT--
PLEASE!
LOOK AT HER -- THE VIRUS ISN'T ACTIVE!
I'M IMMUNE-- MAYBE, MAYBE I NEUTRALIZED IT SOMEHOW.

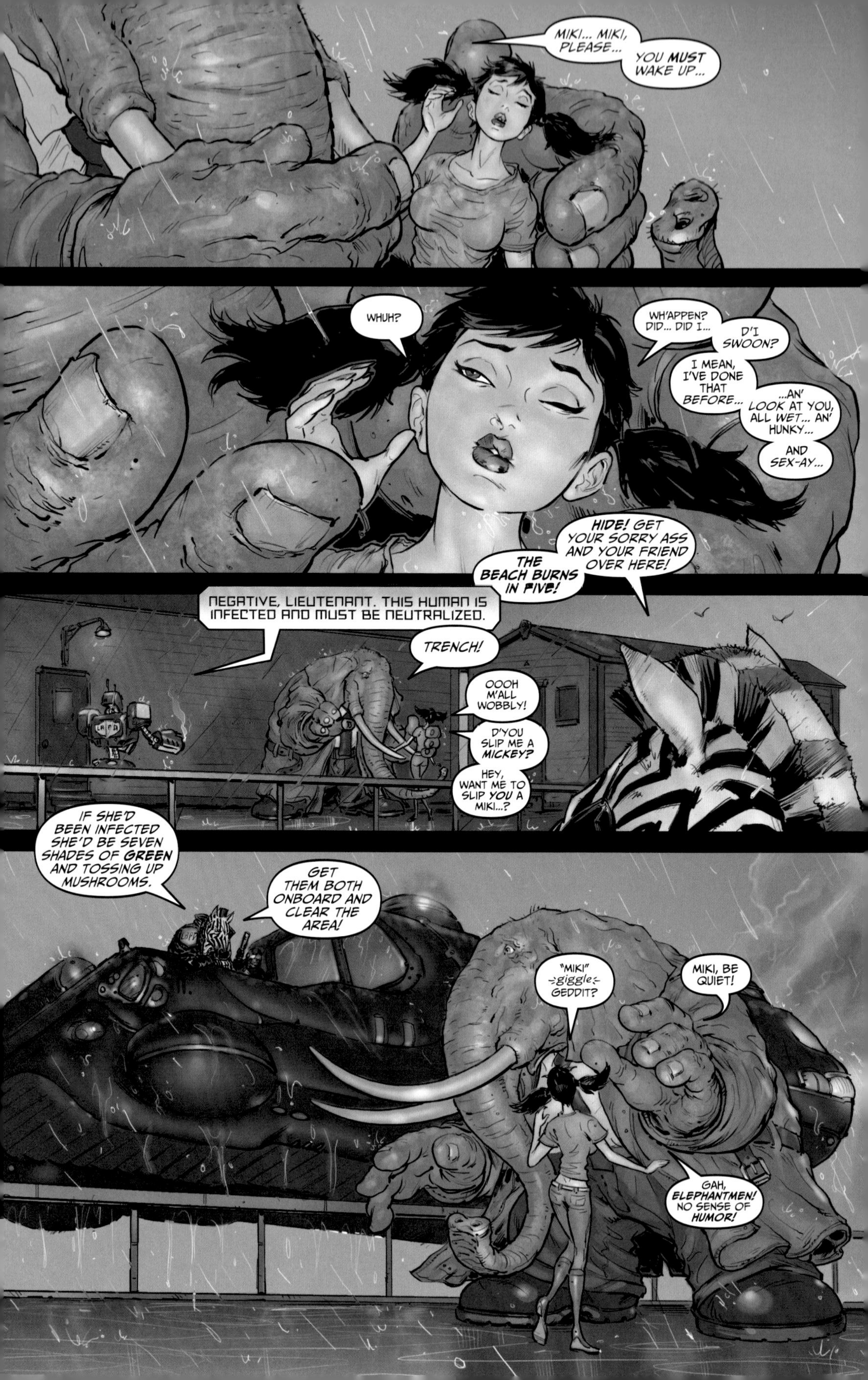
MIKI... MIKI, PLEASE...
YOU MUST WAKE UP...
WHUH?
WH'APPEN? DID... DID I...
D'I SWOON?
I MEAN, I'VE DONE THAT BEFORE...
...AN' LOOK AT YOU, ALL WET... AN' HUNKY...
AND SEX-AY...
HIDE! GET YOUR SORRY ASS AND YOUR FRIEND OVER HERE!
THE BEACH BURNS IN FIVE!
NEGATIVE, LIEUTENANT. THIS HUMAN IS INFECTED AND MUST BE NEUTRALIZED.
TRENCH!
OOOH M'ALL WOBBLY!
D'YOU SLIP ME A MICKEY?
HEY, WANT ME TO SLIP YOU A MIKI...?
IF SHE'D BEEN INFECTED SHE'D BE SEVEN SHADES OF GREEN AND TOSSING UP MUSHROOMS.
GET THEM BOTH ONBOARD AND CLEAR THE AREA!
"MIKI" -giggle- GEDDIT?
MIKI, BE QUIET!
GAH, ELEPHANTMEN! NO SENSE OF HUMOR!

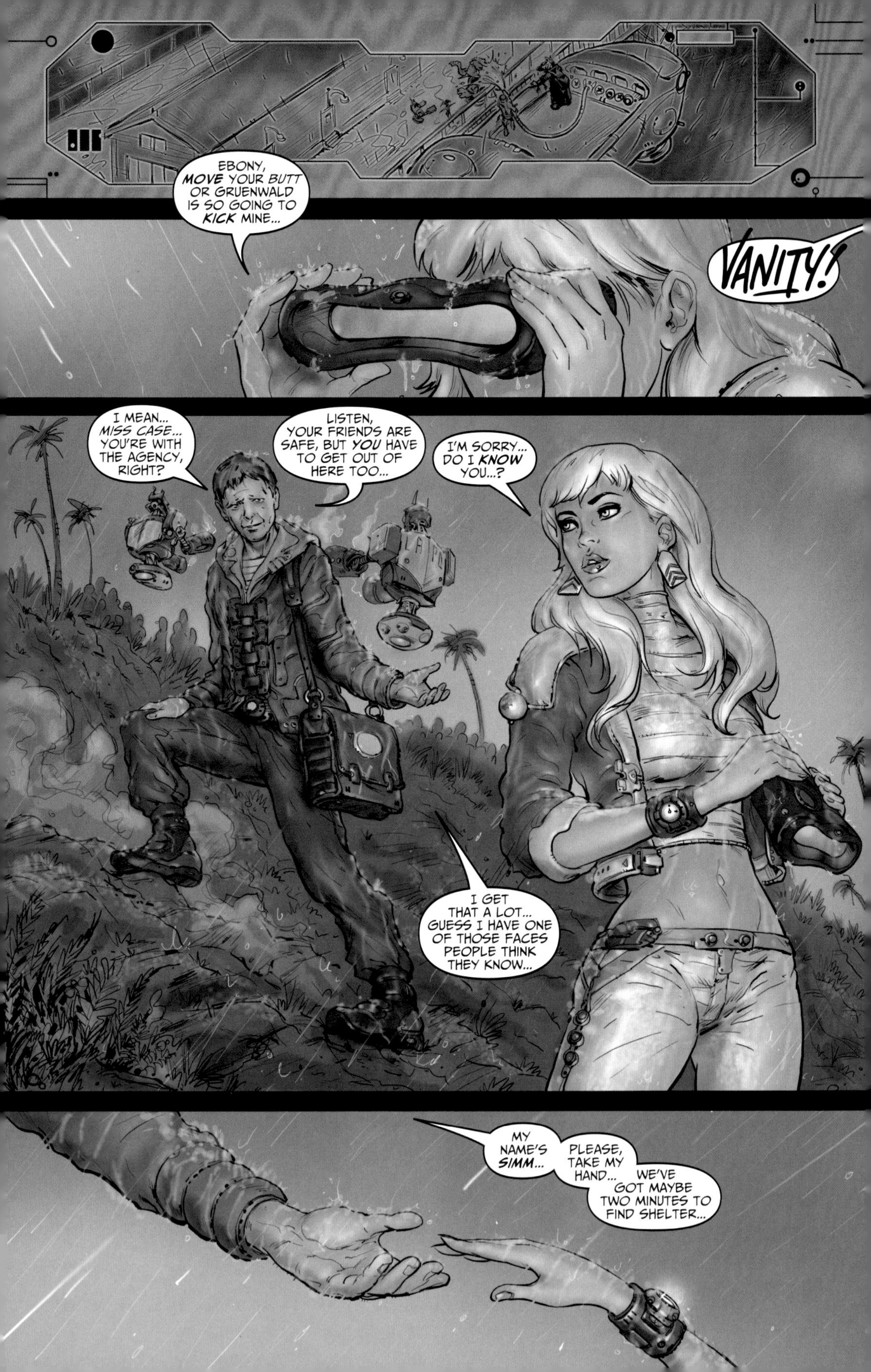

EBONY, MOVE YOUR BUTT OR GRUENWALD IS SO GOING TO KICK MINE...
VANITY!
I MEAN... MISS CASE... YOU'RE WITH THE AGENCY, RIGHT?
LISTEN, YOUR FRIENDS ARE SAFE, BUT YOU HAVE TO GET OUT OF HERE TOO...
I'M SORRY... DO I KNOW YOU...?
I GET THAT A LOT... GUESS I HAVE ONE OF THOSE FACES PEOPLE THINK THEY KNOW...
MY NAME'S SIMM...
PLEASE, TAKE MY HAND...
WE'VE GOT MAYBE TWO MINUTES TO FIND SHELTER...

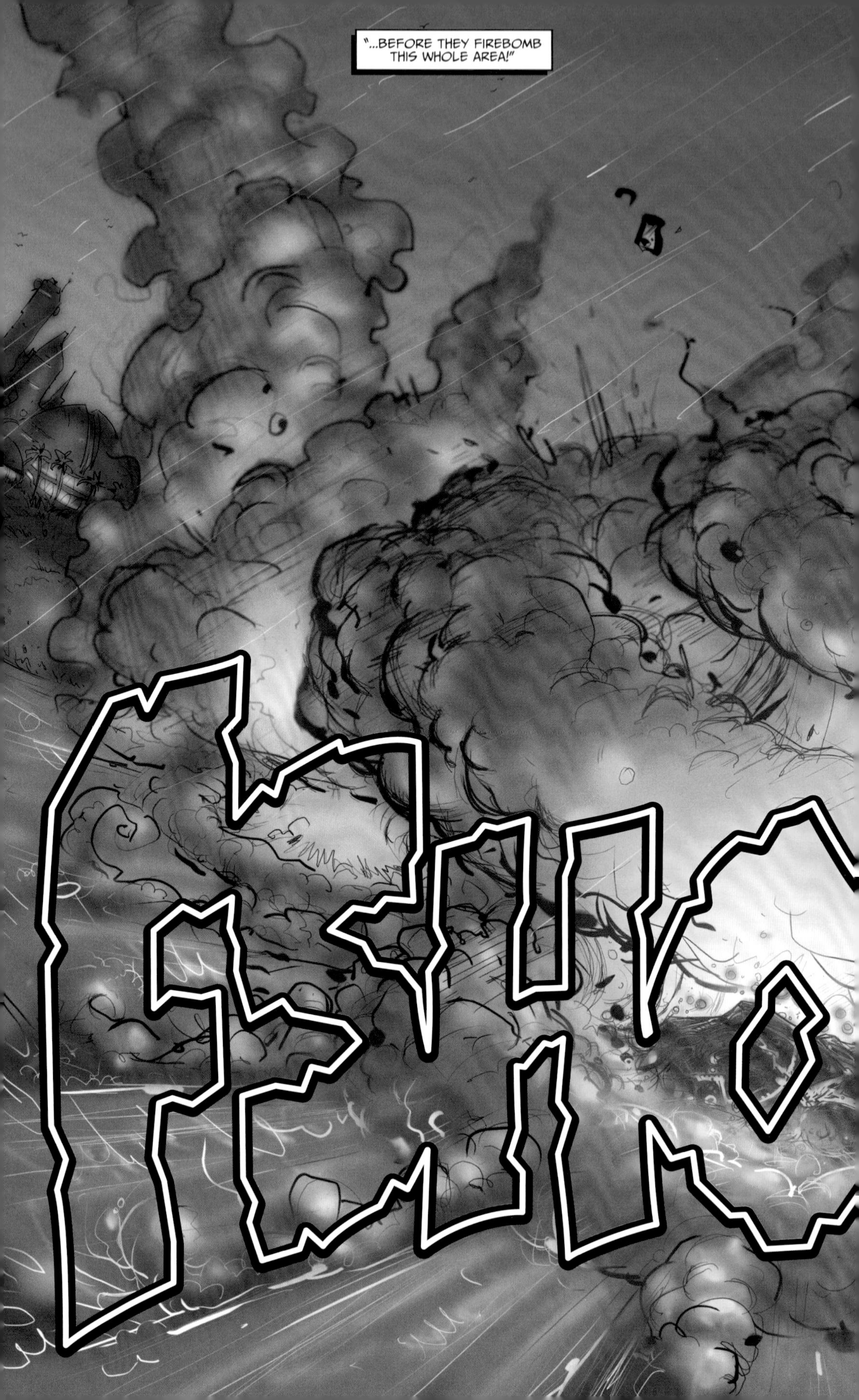
"...BEFORE THEY FIREBOMB THIS WHOLE AREA!"

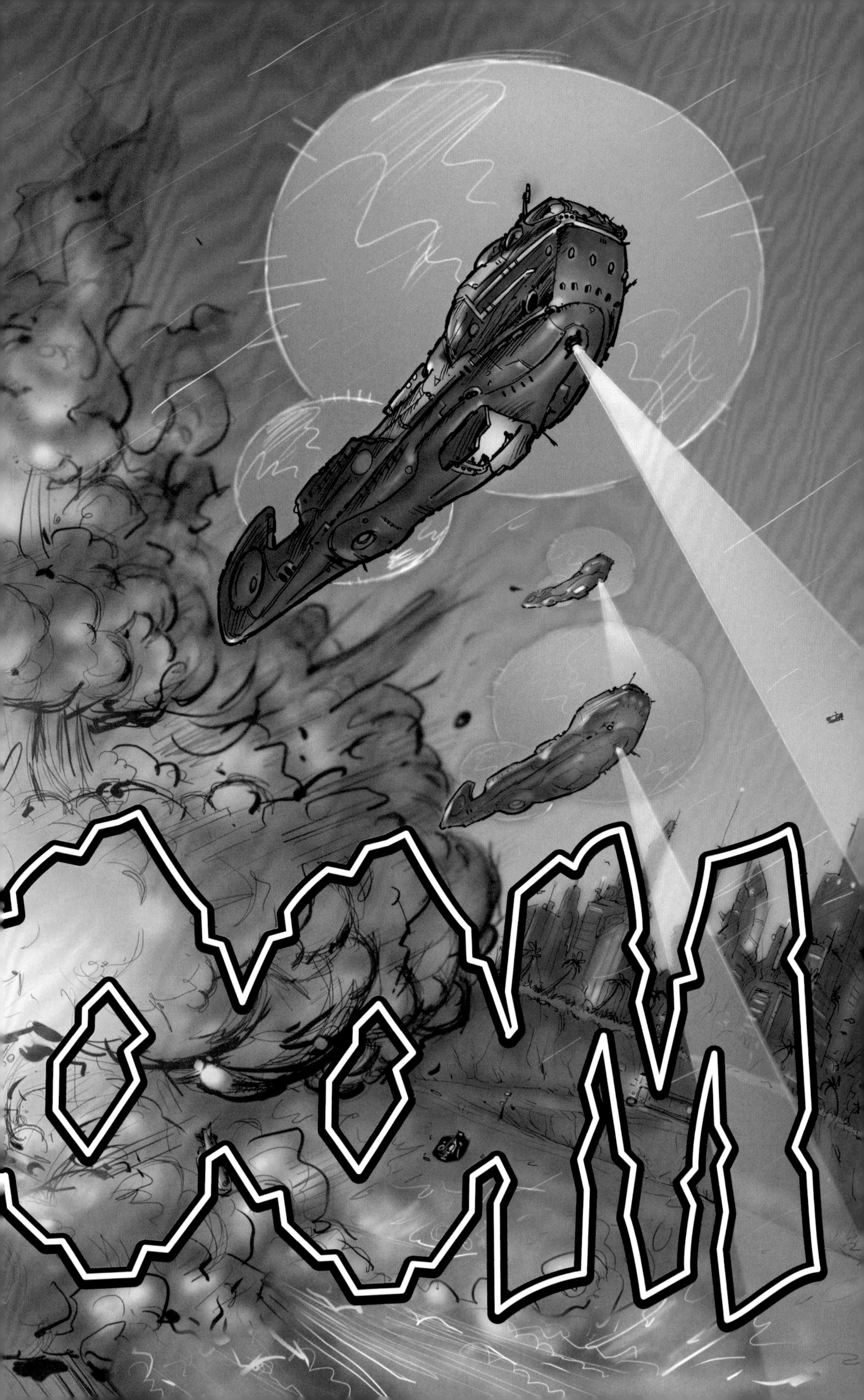

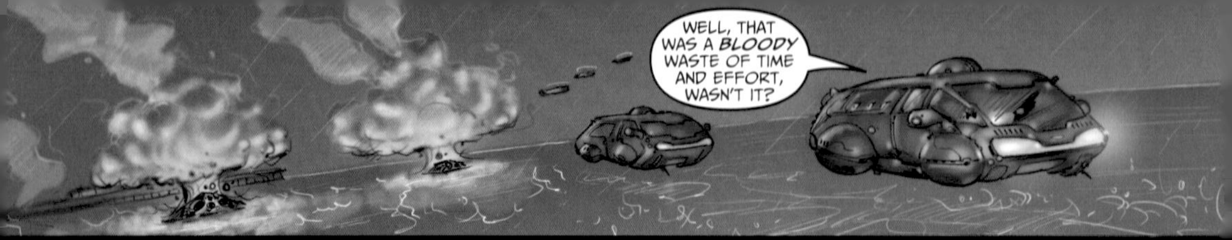
WELL, THAT WAS A BLOODY WASTE OF TIME AND EFFORT, WASN'T IT?

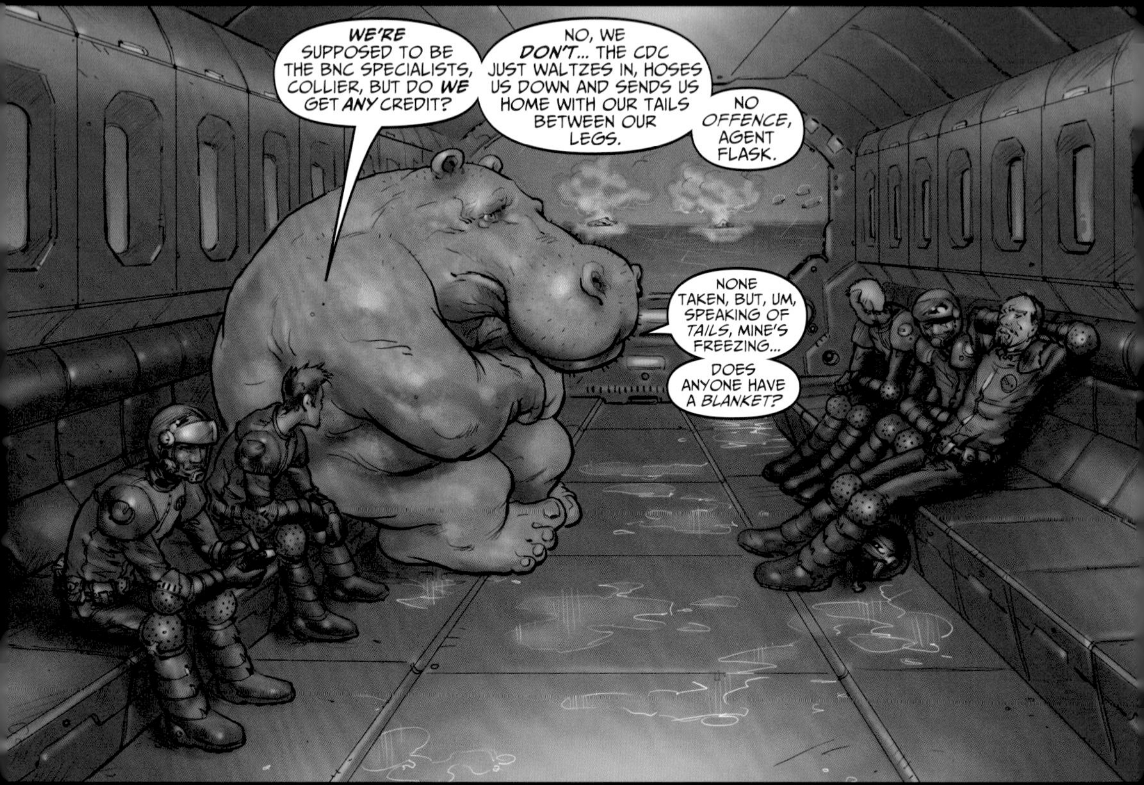
WE'RE SUPPOSED TO BE THE BNC SPECIALISTS, COLLIER, BUT DO WE GET ANY CREDIT?
NO, WE DON'T... THE CDC JUST WALTZES IN, HOSES US DOWN AND SENDS US HOME WITH OUR TAILS BETWEEN OUR LEGS.
NO OFFENCE, AGENT FLASK.
NONE TAKEN, BUT, UM, SPEAKING OF TAILS, MINE'S FREEZING...
DOES ANYONE HAVE A BLANKET?

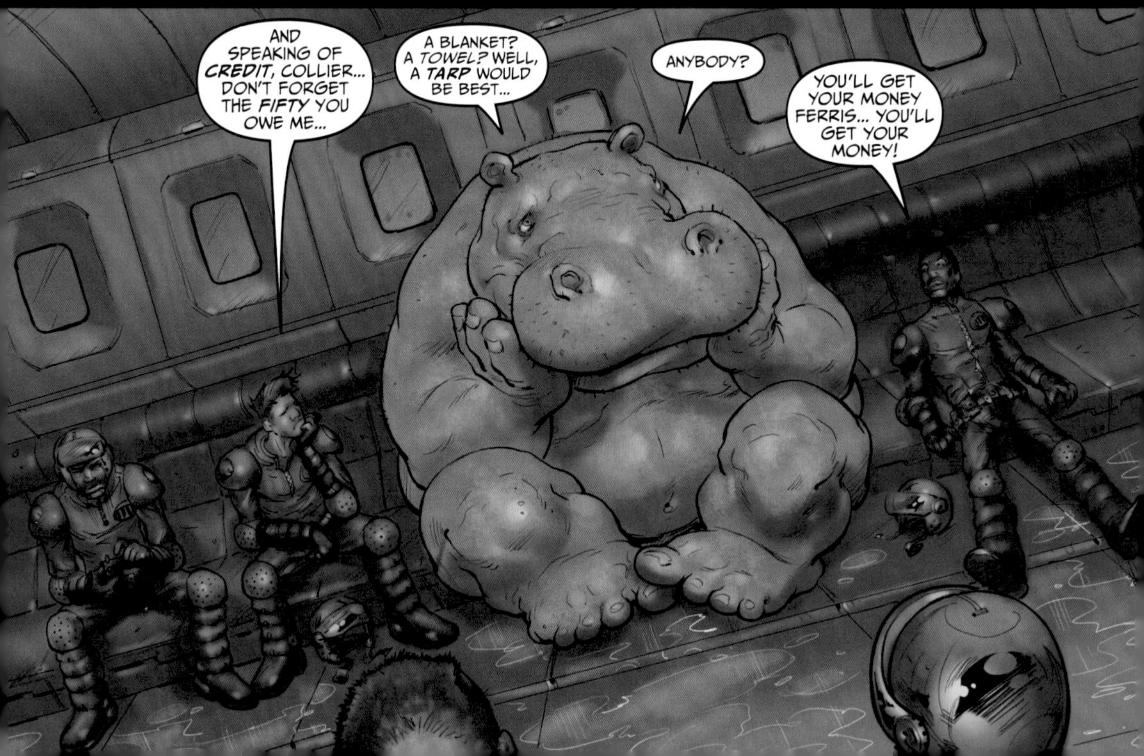
AND SPEAKING OF CREDIT, COLLIER... DON'T FORGET THE FIFTY YOU OWE ME...
A BLANKET? A TOWEL? WELL, A TARP WOULD BE BEST...
ANYBODY?
YOU'LL GET YOUR MONEY FERRIS... YOU'LL GET YOUR MONEY!

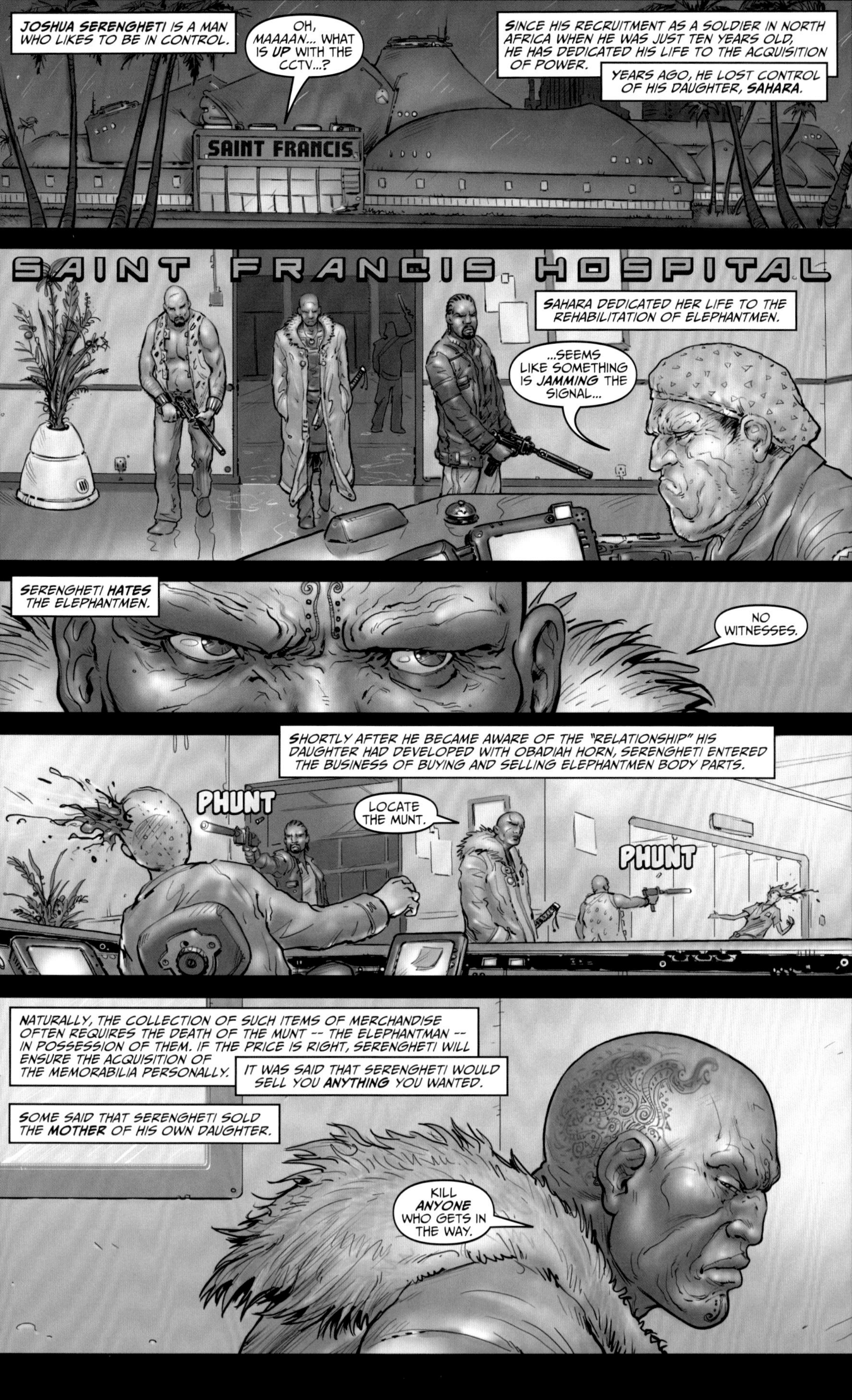
JOSHUA SERENGHETI IS A MAN WHO LIKES TO BE IN CONTROL.
OH, MAAAAN... WHAT IS UP WITH THE CCTV...?
SINCE HIS RECRUITMENT AS A SOLDIER IN NORTH AFRICA WHEN HE WAS JUST TEN YEARS OLD, HE HAS DEDICATED HIS LIFE TO THE ACQUISITION OF POWER.
YEARS AGO, HE LOST CONTROL OF HIS DAUGHTER, SAHARA.
SAINT FRANCIS
SAINT FRANCIS HOSPITAL
SAHARA DEDICATED HER LIFE TO THE REHABILITATION OF ELEPHANTMEN.
...SEEMS LIKE SOMETHING IS JAMMING THE SIGNAL...
SERENGHETI HATES THE ELEPHANTMEN.
NO WITNESSES.
SHORTLY AFTER HE BECAME AWARE OF THE "RELATIONSHIP" HIS DAUGHTER HAD DEVELOPED WITH OBADIAH HORN, SERENGHETI ENTERED THE BUSINESS OF BUYING AND SELLING ELEPHANTMEN BODY PARTS.
PHUNT
LOCATE THE MUNT.
PHUNT
NATURALLY, THE COLLECTION OF SUCH ITEMS OF MERCHANDISE OFTEN REQUIRES THE DEATH OF THE MUNT -- THE ELEPHANTMAN -- IN POSSESSION OF THEM. IF THE PRICE IS RIGHT, SERENGHETI WILL ENSURE THE ACQUISITION OF THE MEMORABILIA PERSONALLY.
IT WAS SAID THAT SERENGHETI WOULD SELL YOU ANYTHING YOU WANTED.
SOME SAID THAT SERENGHETI SOLD THE MOTHER OF HIS OWN DAUGHTER.
KILL ANYONE WHO GETS IN THE WAY.

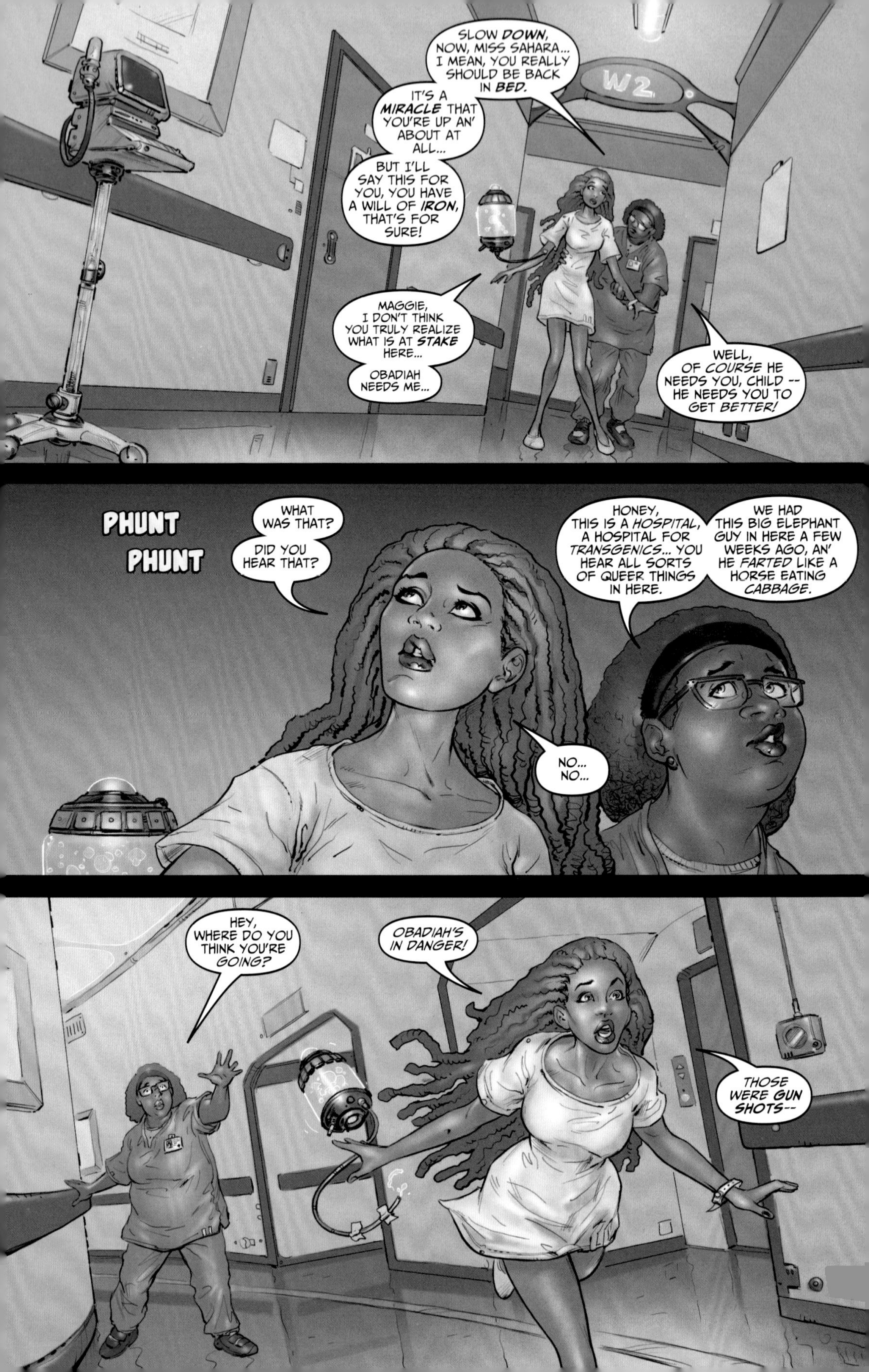
SLOW DOWN, NOW, MISS SAHARA... I MEAN, YOU REALLY SHOULD BE BACK IN BED.
W2
IT'S A MIRACLE THAT YOU'RE UP AN' ABOUT AT ALL...
BUT I'LL SAY THIS FOR YOU, YOU HAVE A WILL OF IRON, THAT'S FOR SURE!
MAGGIE, I DON'T THINK YOU TRULY REALIZE WHAT IS AT STAKE HERE...
OBADIAH NEEDS ME...
WELL, OF COURSE HE NEEDS YOU, CHILD -- HE NEEDS YOU TO GET BETTER!
PHUNT
PHUNT
WHAT WAS THAT?
DID YOU HEAR THAT?
HONEY, THIS IS A HOSPITAL, A HOSPITAL FOR TRANSGENICS... YOU HEAR ALL SORTS OF QUEER THINGS IN HERE.
WE HAD THIS BIG ELEPHANT GUY IN HERE A FEW WEEKS AGO, AN' HE FARTED LIKE A HORSE EATING CABBAGE.
NO... NO...
HEY, WHERE DO YOU THINK YOU'RE GOING?
OBADIAH'S IN DANGER!
THOSE WERE GUN SHOTS--

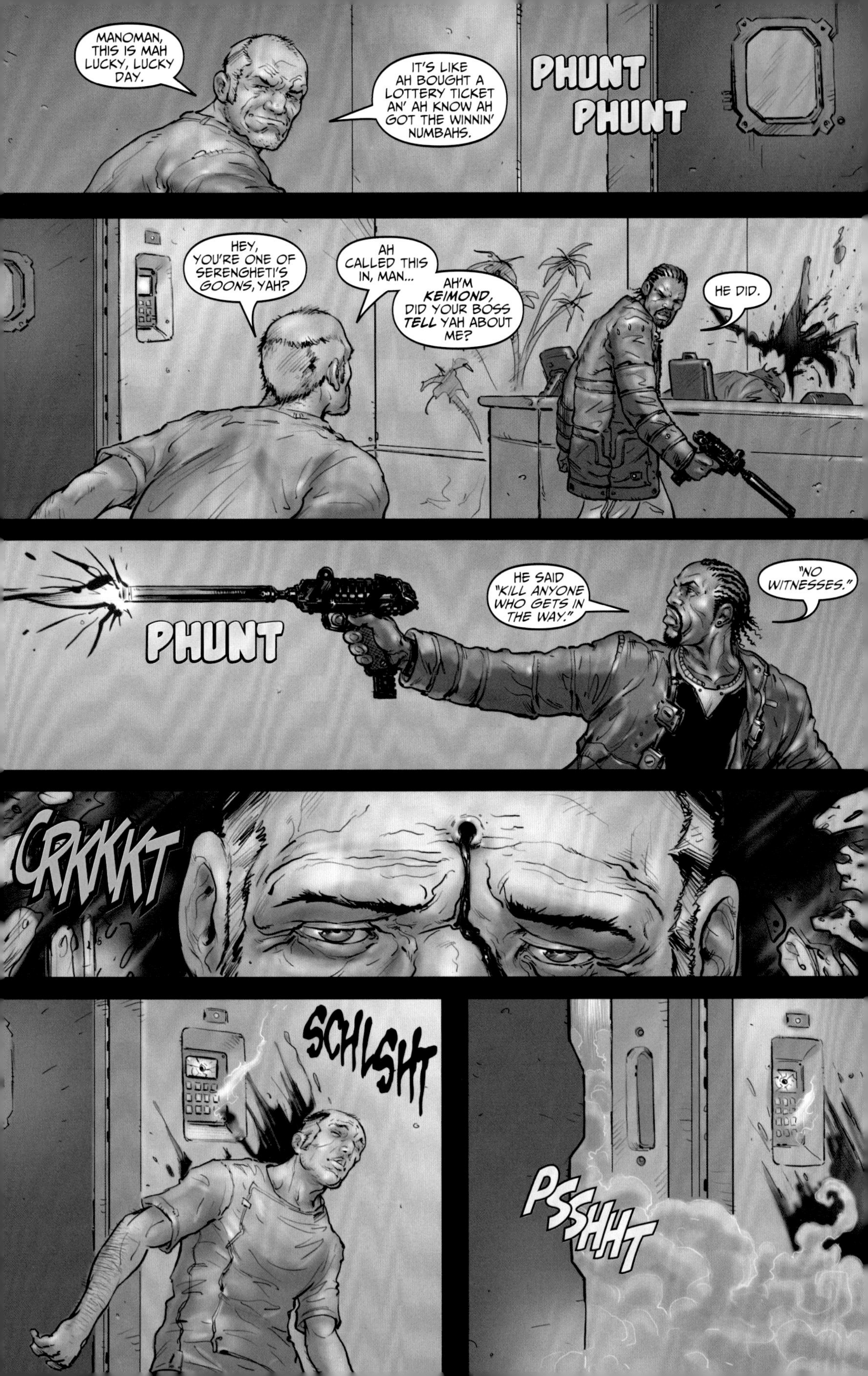

MANOMAN, THIS IS MAH LUCKY, LUCKY DAY.
IT'S LIKE AH BOUGHT A LOTTERY TICKET AN' AH KNOW AH GOT THE WINNIN' NUMBAHS.
PHUNT PHUNT
HEY, YOU'RE ONE OF SERENGHETI'S GOONS, YAH?
AH CALLED THIS IN, MAN...
AH'M KEIMOND, DID YOUR BOSS TELL YAH ABOUT ME?
HE DID.
PHUNT
HE SAID "KILL ANYONE WHO GETS IN THE WAY."
"NO WITNESSES."
CRKKKT
SCHLSHT
PSSHHT

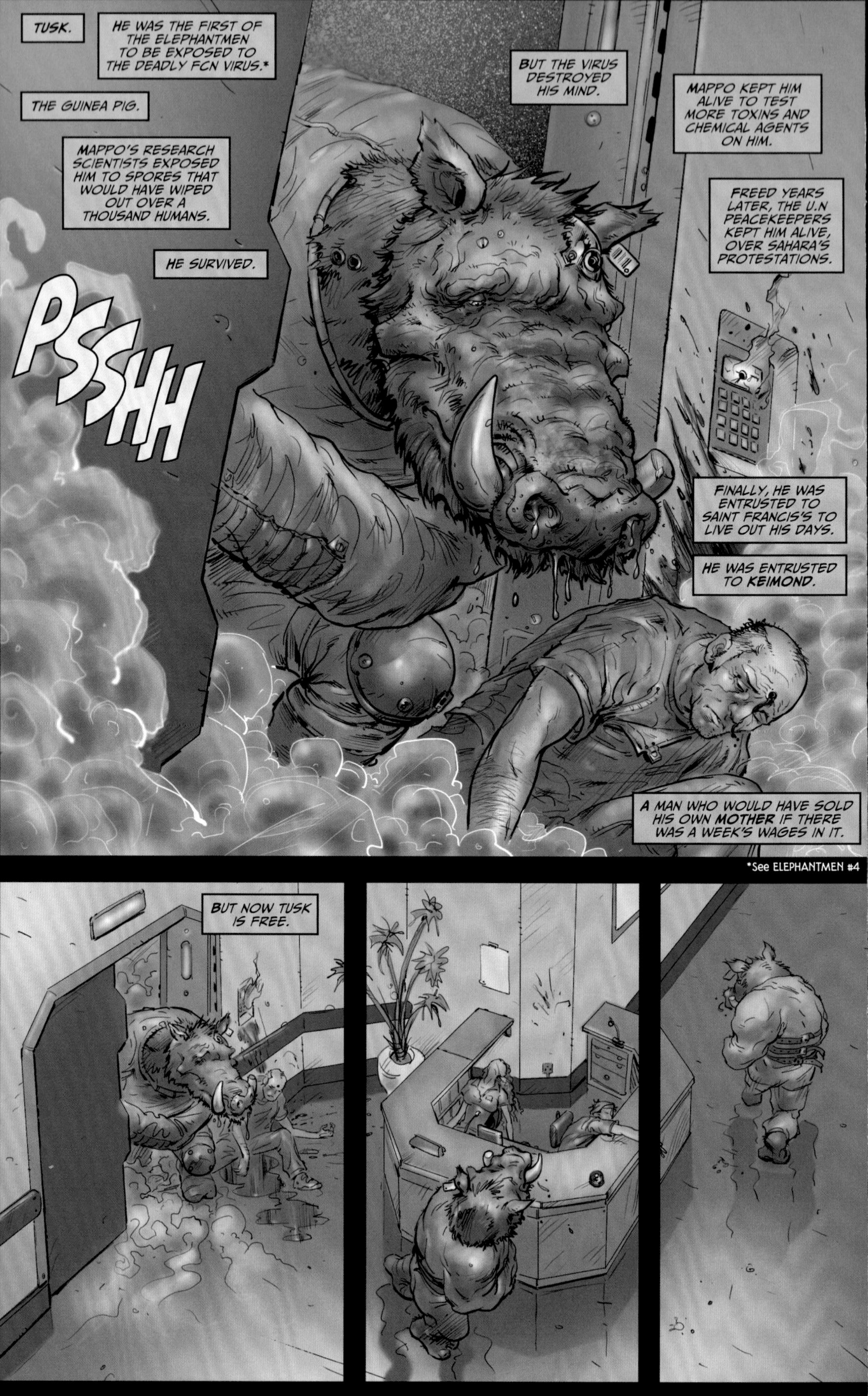
TUSK.
HE WAS THE FIRST OF THE ELEPHANTMEN TO BE EXPOSED TO THE DEADLY FCN VIRUS.*
THE GUINEA PIG.
MAPPO'S RESEARCH SCIENTISTS EXPOSED HIM TO SPORES THAT WOULD HAVE WIPED OUT OVER A THOUSAND HUMANS.
HE SURVIVED.
PSSHH
BUT THE VIRUS DESTROYED HIS MIND.
MAPPO KEPT HIM ALIVE TO TEST MORE TOXINS AND CHEMICAL AGENTS ON HIM.
FREED YEARS LATER, THE U.N PEACEKEEPERS KEPT HIM ALIVE, OVER SAHARA'S PROTESTATIONS.
FINALLY, HE WAS ENTRUSTED TO SAINT FRANCIS'S TO LIVE OUT HIS DAYS.
HE WAS ENTRUSTED TO KEIMOND.
A MAN WHO WOULD HAVE SOLD HIS OWN MOTHER IF THERE WAS A WEEK'S WAGES IN IT.
*See ELEPHANTMEN #4
BUT NOW TUSK IS FREE.

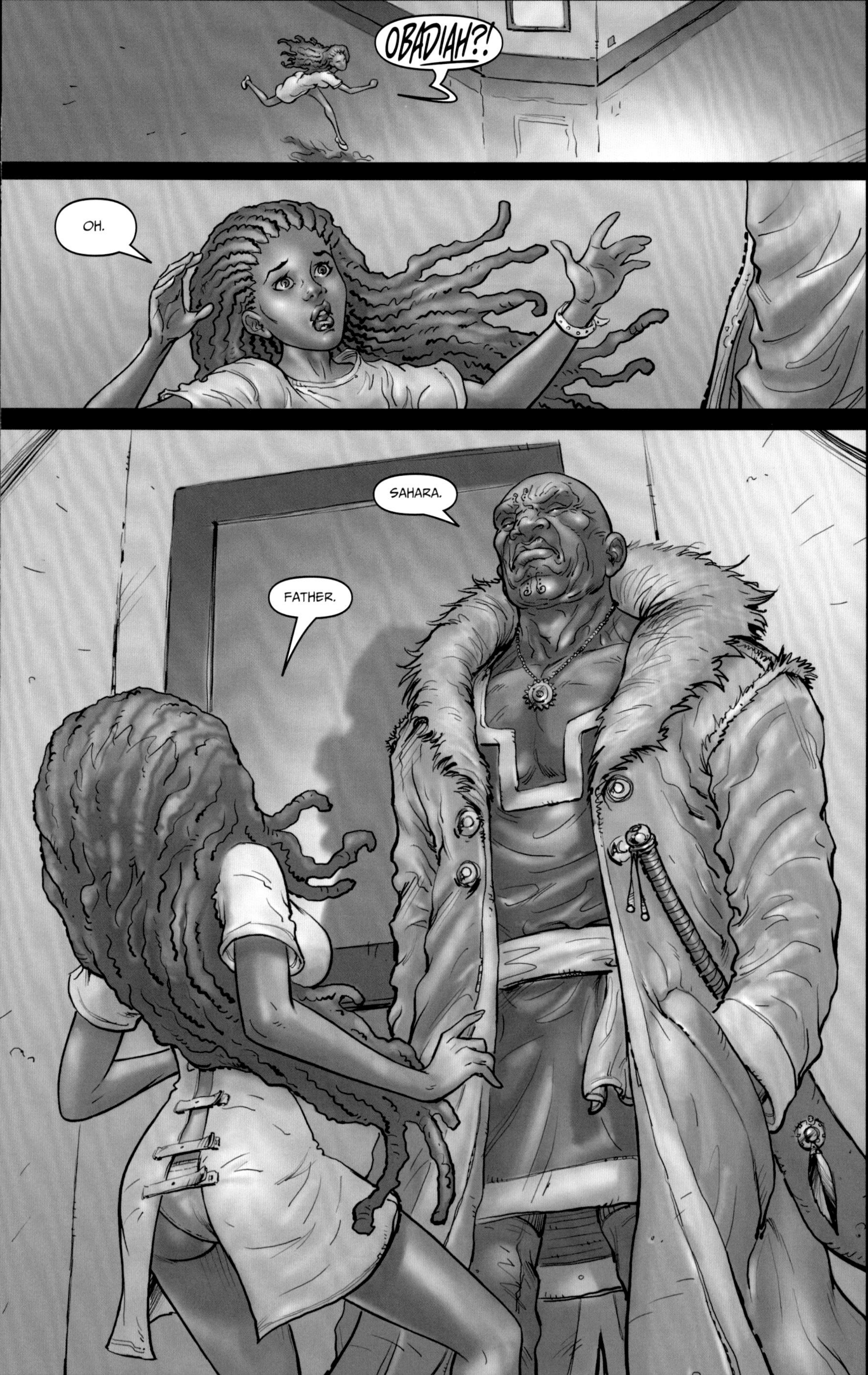
OBADIAH?!
OH.
SAHARA.
FATHER.

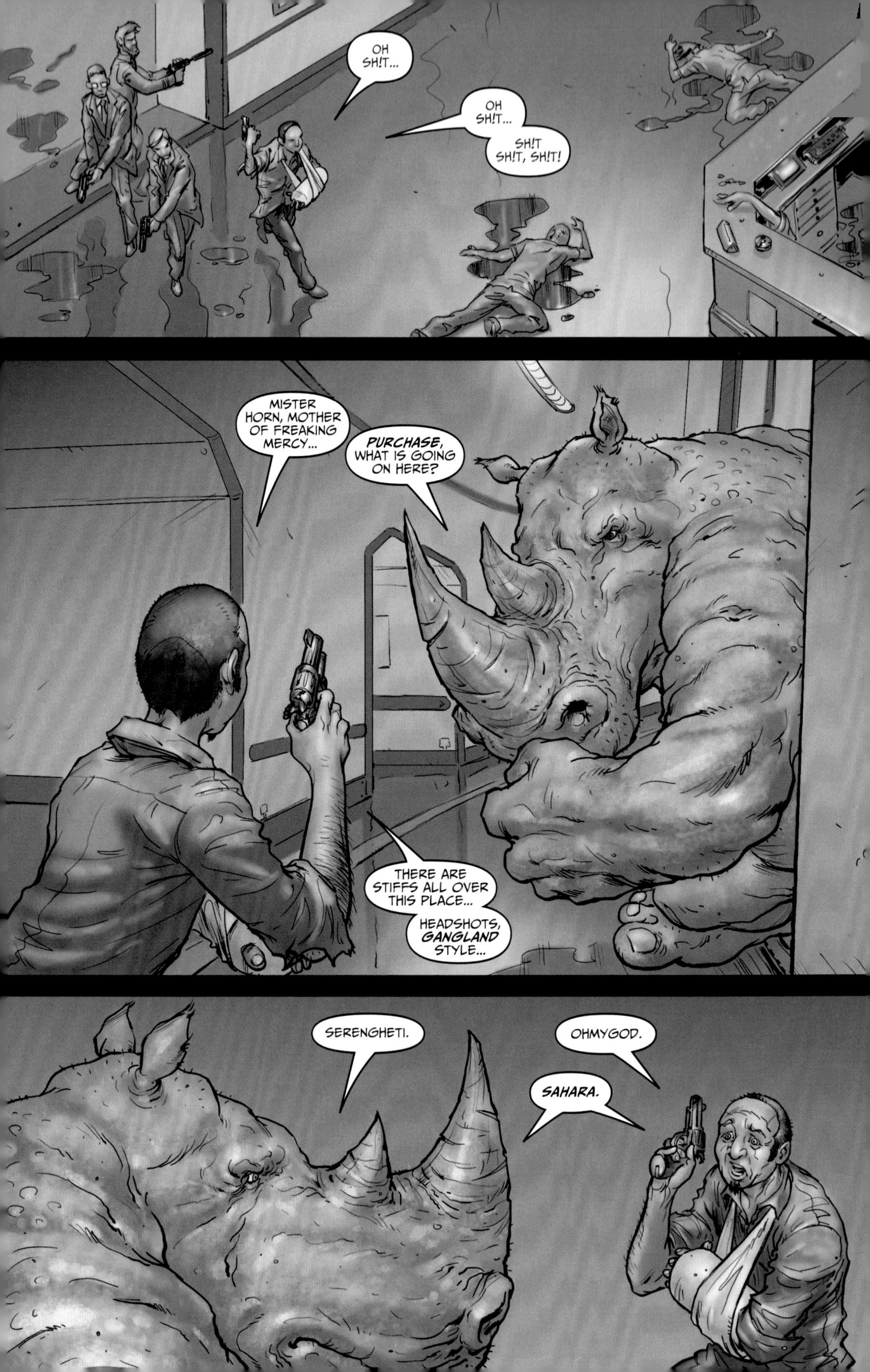
OH SH!T...
OH SH!T...
SH!T SH!T, SH!T!
MISTER HORN, MOTHER OF FREAKING MERCY...
PURCHASE, WHAT IS GOING ON HERE?
THERE ARE STIFFS ALL OVER THIS PLACE...
HEADSHOTS, *GANGLAND* STYLE...
SERENGHETI.
OHMYGOD.
SAHARA.

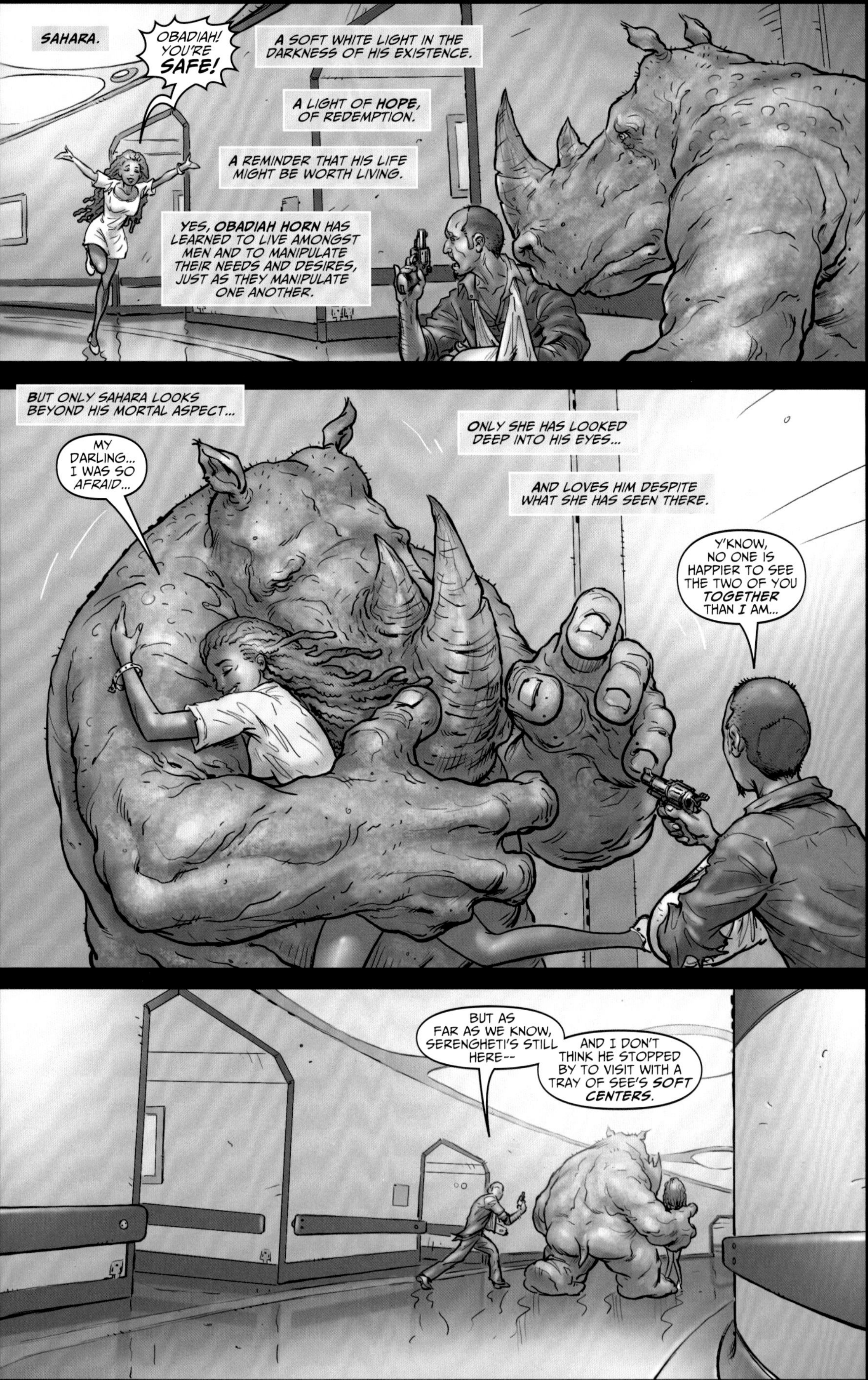
SAHARA.
OBADIAH! YOU'RE SAFE!
A SOFT WHITE LIGHT IN THE DARKNESS OF HIS EXISTENCE.
A LIGHT OF HOPE, OF REDEMPTION.
A REMINDER THAT HIS LIFE MIGHT BE WORTH LIVING.
YES, OBADIAH HORN HAS LEARNED TO LIVE AMONGST MEN AND TO MANIPULATE THEIR NEEDS AND DESIRES, JUST AS THEY MANIPULATE ONE ANOTHER.
BUT ONLY SAHARA LOOKS BEYOND HIS MORTAL ASPECT...
MY DARLING... I WAS SO AFRAID...
ONLY SHE HAS LOOKED DEEP INTO HIS EYES...
AND LOVES HIM DESPITE WHAT SHE HAS SEEN THERE.
Y'KNOW, NO ONE IS HAPPIER TO SEE THE TWO OF YOU TOGETHER THAN I AM...
BUT AS FAR AS WE KNOW, SERENGHETI'S STILL HERE--
AND I DON'T THINK HE STOPPED BY TO VISIT WITH A TRAY OF SEE'S SOFT CENTERS.

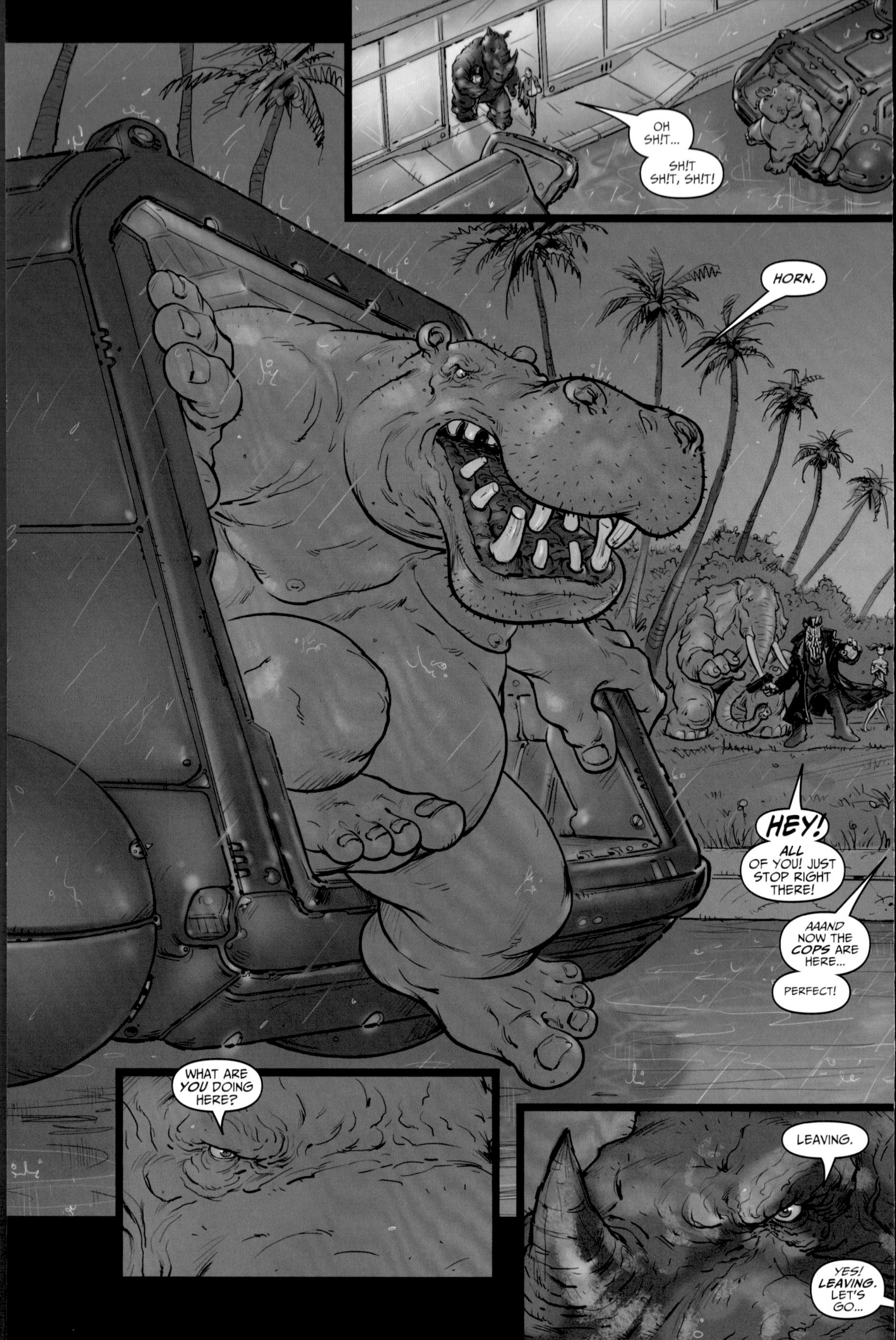
OH SH!T...
SH!T SH!T, SH!T!
HORN.
HEY! ALL OF YOU! JUST STOP RIGHT THERE!
AAAND NOW THE COPS ARE HERE...
PERFECT!
WHAT ARE YOU DOING HERE?
LEAVING.
YES! LEAVING. LET'S GO...

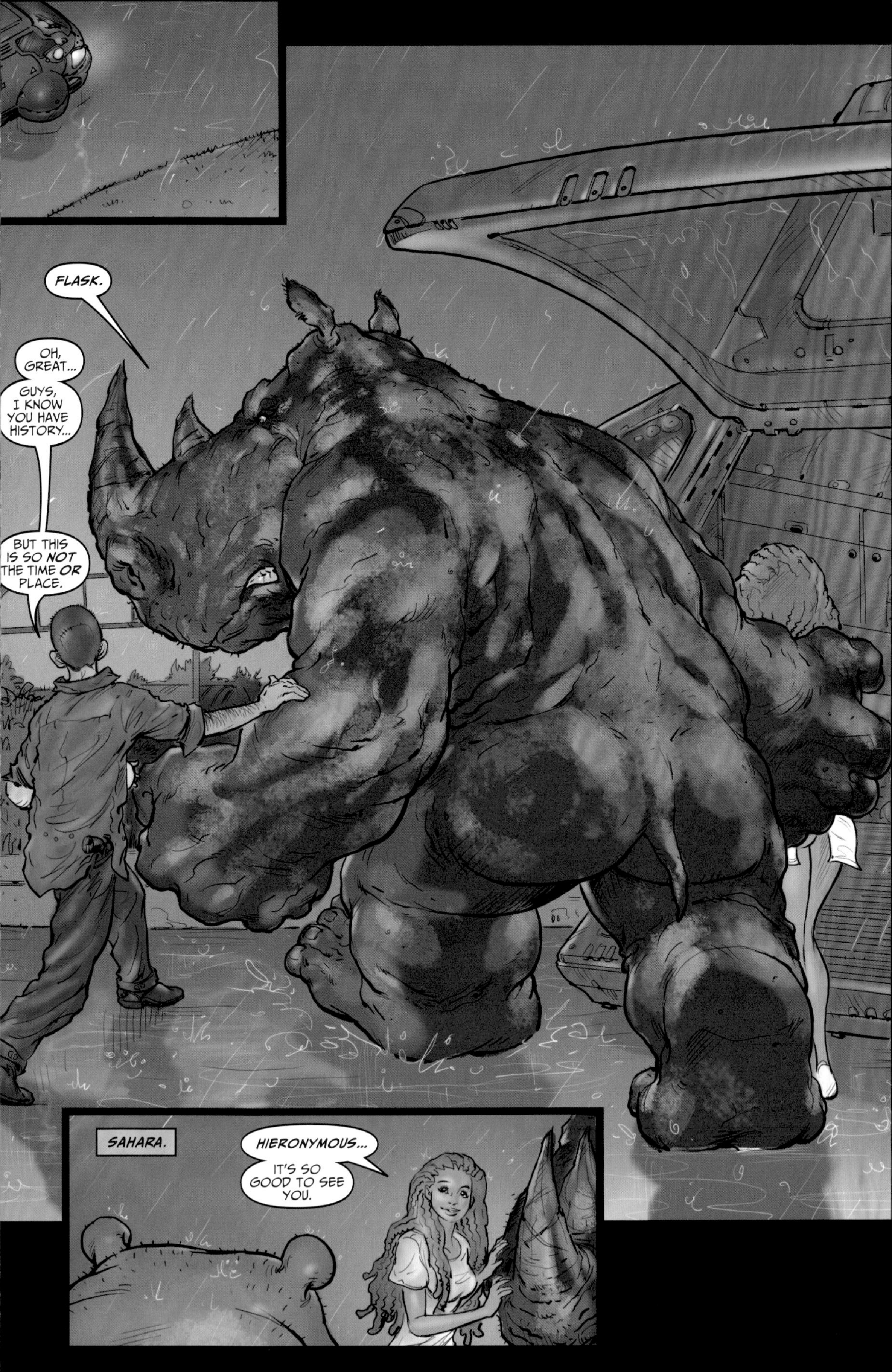
FLASK.
OH, GREAT...
GUYS, I KNOW YOU HAVE HISTORY...
BUT THIS IS SO NOT THE TIME OR PLACE.
SAHARA.
HIERONYMOUS...
IT'S SO GOOD TO SEE YOU.

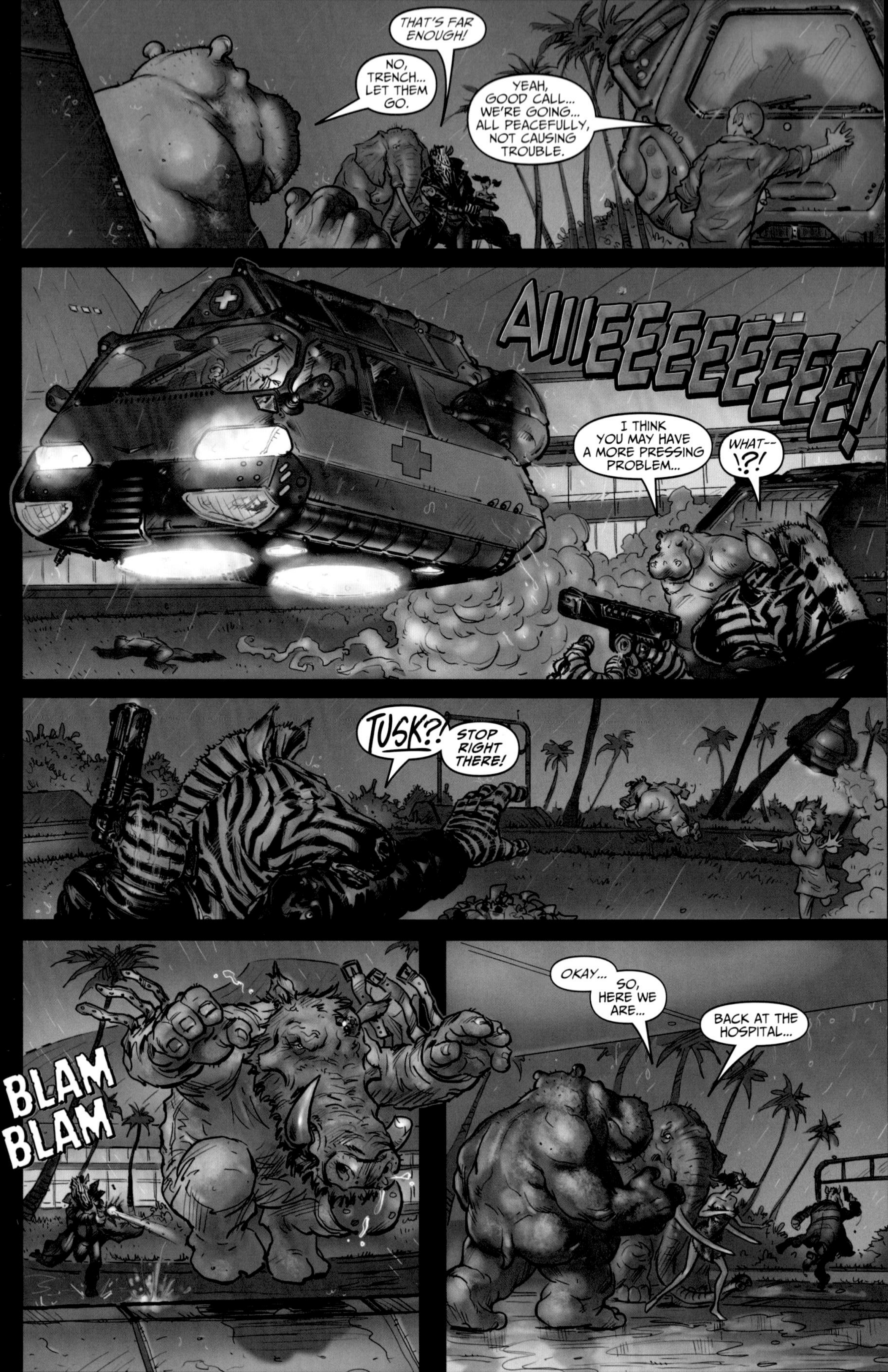
THAT'S FAR ENOUGH!
NO, TRENCH... LET THEM GO.
YEAH, GOOD CALL... WE'RE GOING... ALL PEACEFULLY, NOT CAUSING TROUBLE.
AIIIEEEEEEEEEE!
I THINK YOU MAY HAVE A MORE PRESSING PROBLEM...
WHAT-- !?!
TUSK?!
STOP RIGHT THERE!
BLAM BLAM
OKAY... SO, HERE WE ARE...
BACK AT THE HOSPITAL...

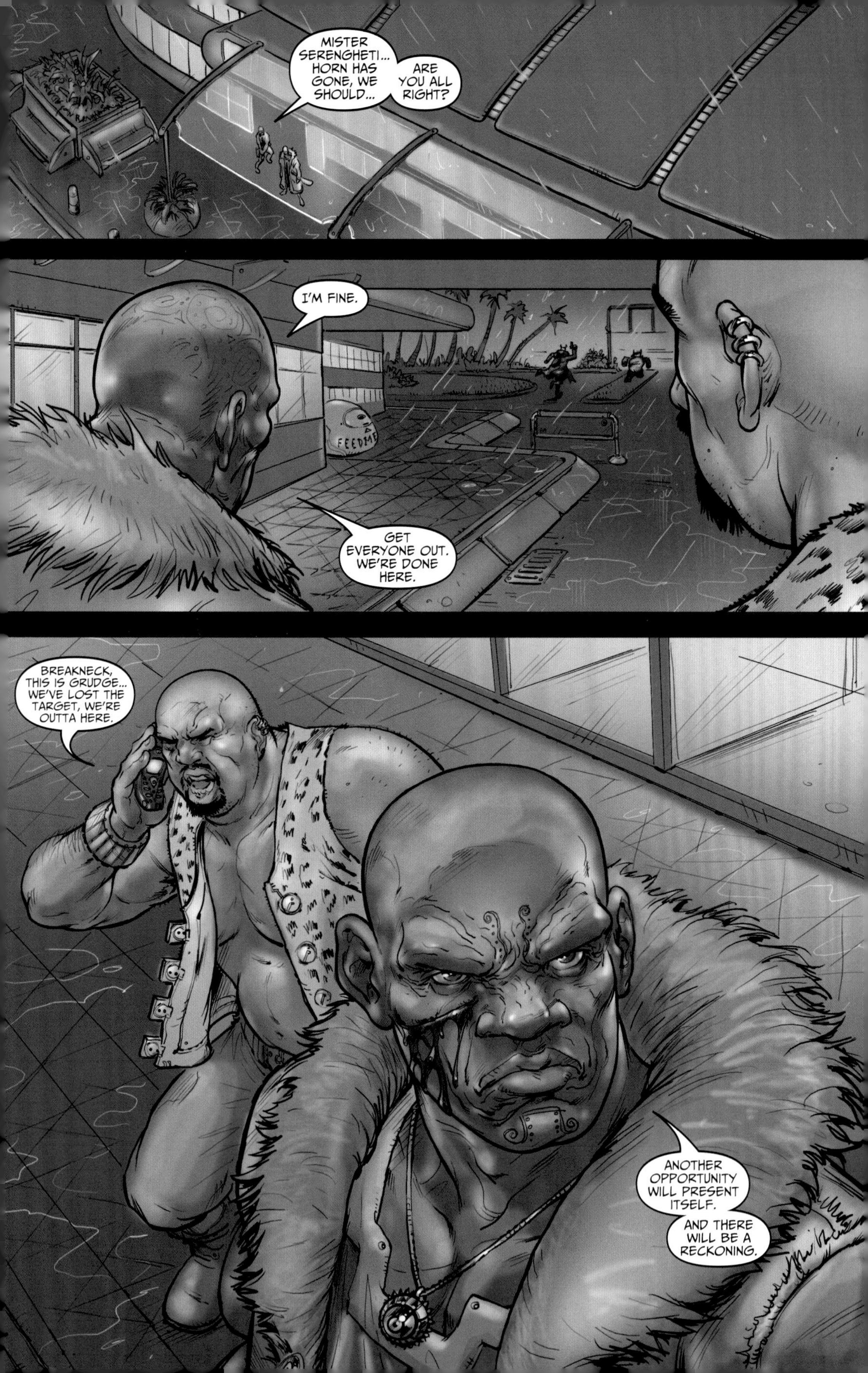
MISTER SERENGHETI... HORN HAS GONE, WE SHOULD...
ARE YOU ALL RIGHT?
I'M FINE.
GET EVERYONE OUT. WE'RE DONE HERE.
BREAKNECK, THIS IS GRUDGE... WE'VE LOST THE TARGET, WE'RE OUTTA HERE.
ANOTHER OPPORTUNITY WILL PRESENT ITSELF.
AND THERE WILL BE A RECKONING.
FEEDME

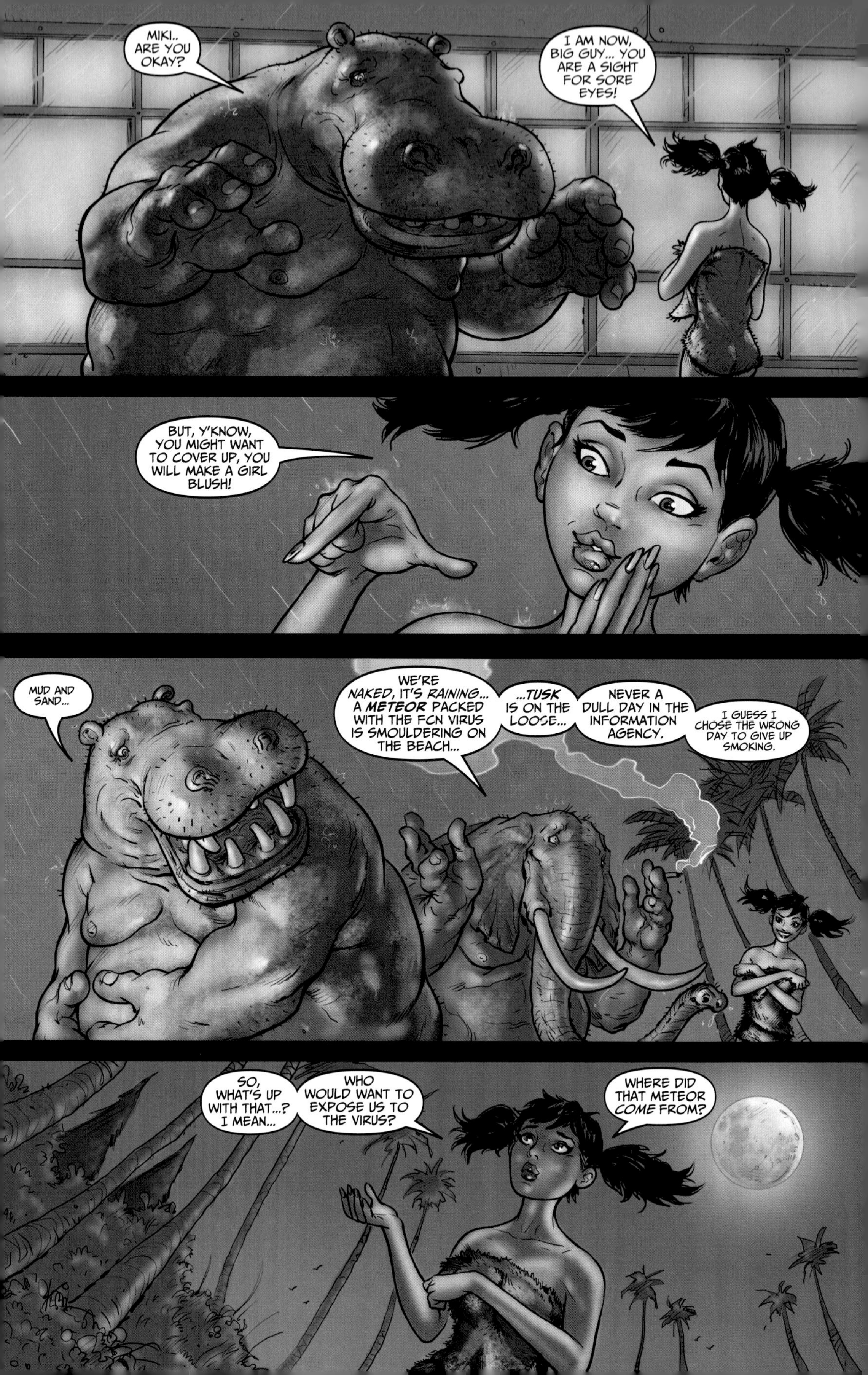
MIKI.. ARE YOU OKAY?
I AM NOW, BIG GUY... YOU ARE A SIGHT FOR SORE EYES!
BUT, Y'KNOW, YOU MIGHT WANT TO COVER UP, YOU WILL MAKE A GIRL BLUSH!
MUD AND SAND...
WE'RE *NAKED*, IT'S *RAINING*... A ***METEOR*** PACKED WITH THE FCN VIRUS IS SMOULDERING ON THE BEACH...
...***TUSK*** IS ON THE LOOSE...
NEVER A DULL DAY IN THE INFORMATION AGENCY.
I GUESS I CHOSE THE WRONG DAY TO GIVE UP SMOKING.
SO, WHAT'S UP WITH THAT...? I MEAN...
WHO WOULD WANT TO EXPOSE US TO THE VIRUS?
WHERE DID THAT METEOR *COME* FROM?

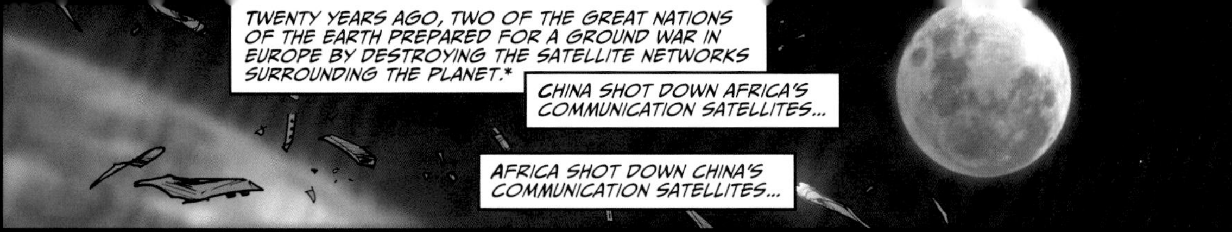
TWENTY YEARS AGO, TWO OF THE GREAT NATIONS OF THE EARTH PREPARED FOR A GROUND WAR IN EUROPE BY DESTROYING THE SATELLITE NETWORKS SURROUNDING THE PLANET.*
CHINA SHOT DOWN AFRICA'S COMMUNICATION SATELLITES...
AFRICA SHOT DOWN CHINA'S COMMUNICATION SATELLITES...

*See ELEPHANTMEN #14

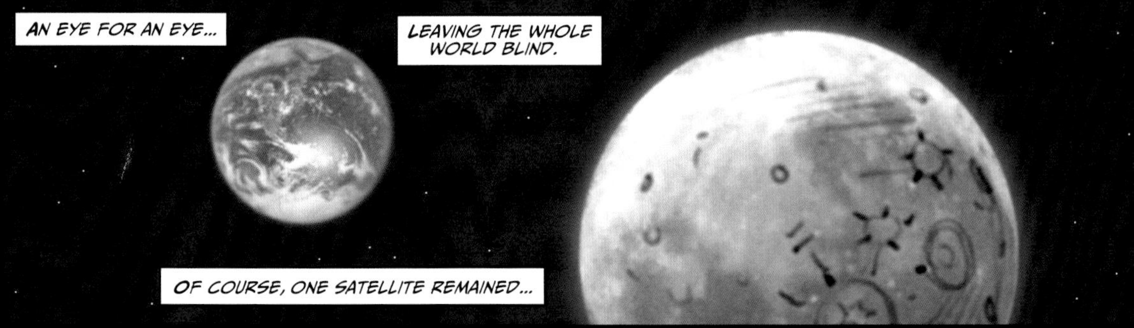
AN EYE FOR AN EYE...
LEAVING THE WHOLE WORLD BLIND.
OF COURSE, ONE SATELLITE REMAINED...

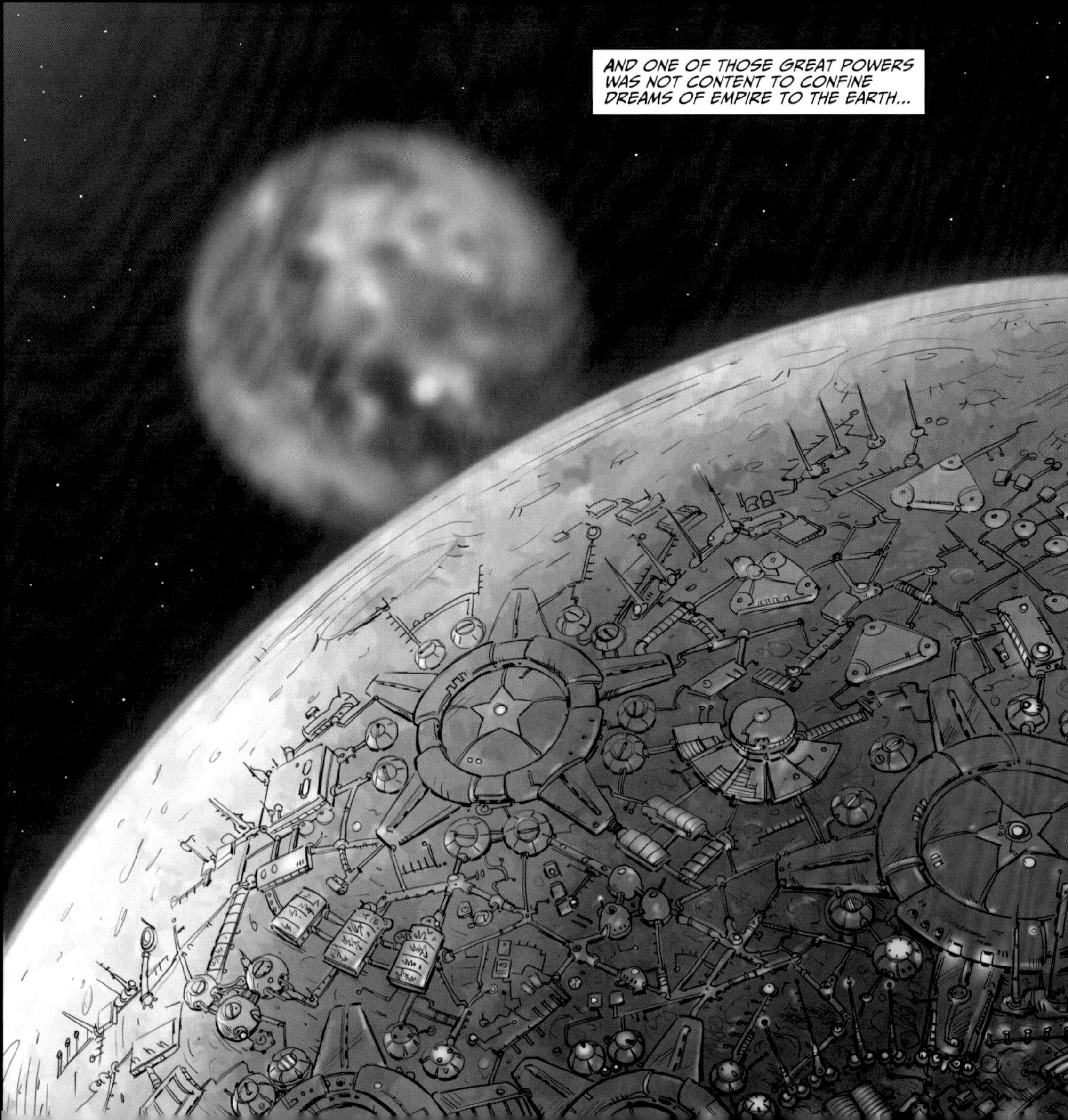
AND ONE OF THOSE GREAT POWERS WAS NOT CONTENT TO CONFINE DREAMS OF EMPIRE TO THE EARTH...

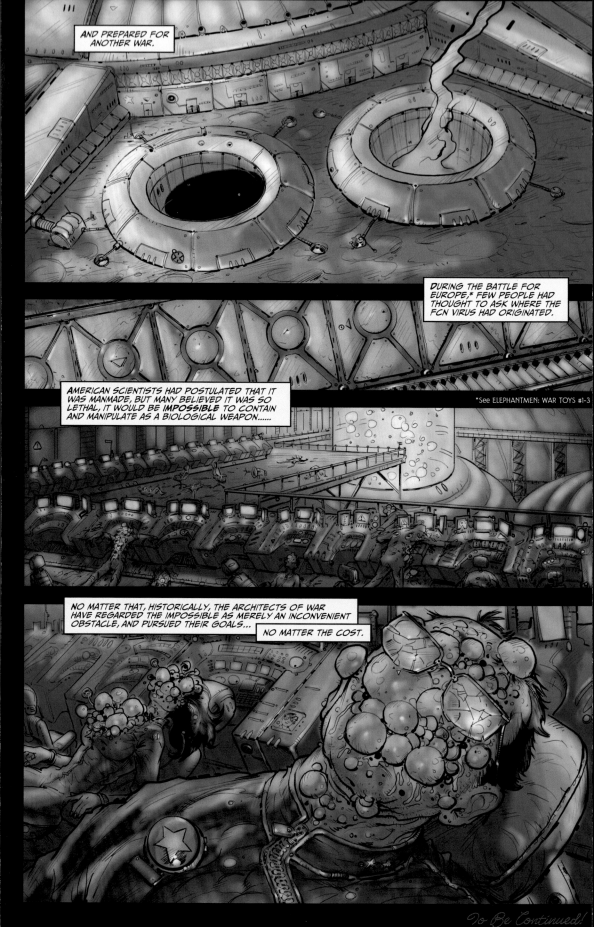

AND PREPARED FOR ANOTHER WAR.

DURING THE BATTLE FOR EUROPE,* FEW PEOPLE HAD THOUGHT TO ASK WHERE THE FCN VIRUS HAD ORIGINATED.

AMERICAN SCIENTISTS HAD POSTULATED THAT IT WAS MANMADE, BUT MANY BELIEVED IT WAS SO LETHAL, IT WOULD BE **IMPOSSIBLE** TO CONTAIN AND MANIPULATE AS A BIOLOGICAL WEAPON......

*See ELEPHANTMEN: WAR TOYS #1-3

NO MATTER THAT, HISTORICALLY, THE ARCHITECTS OF WAR HAVE REGARDED THE IMPOSSIBLE AS MERELY AN INCONVENIENT OBSTACLE, AND PURSUED THEIR GOALS...

NO MATTER THE COST.

To Be Continued!

"A VISITOR FROM MARS
COULD EASILY PICK OUT
THE CIVILIZED NATIONS.
THEY HAVE THE BEST
IMPLEMENTS OF WAR."

HERBERT V. PROCHNOW
1897-1998

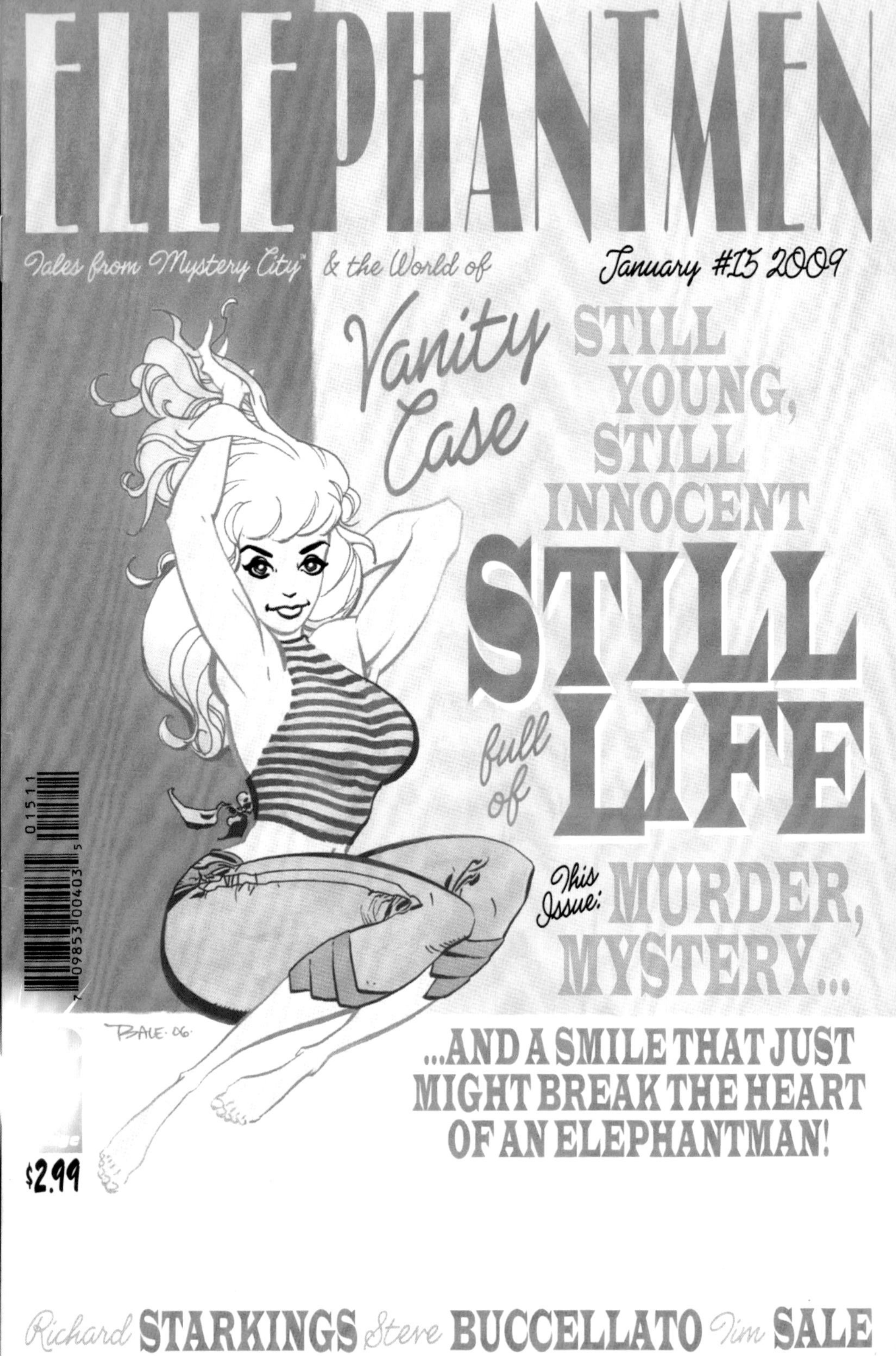
ELEPHANTMEN
Tales from Mystery City™ & the World of
January #15 2009
Vanity Case
STILL YOUNG, STILL INNOCENT
STILL full of LIFE
This Issue: MURDER, MYSTERY...
...AND A SMILE THAT JUST MIGHT BREAK THE HEART OF AN ELEPHANTMAN!
SALE · 06
$2.99
Richard STARKINGS Steve BUCCELLATO Tim SALE

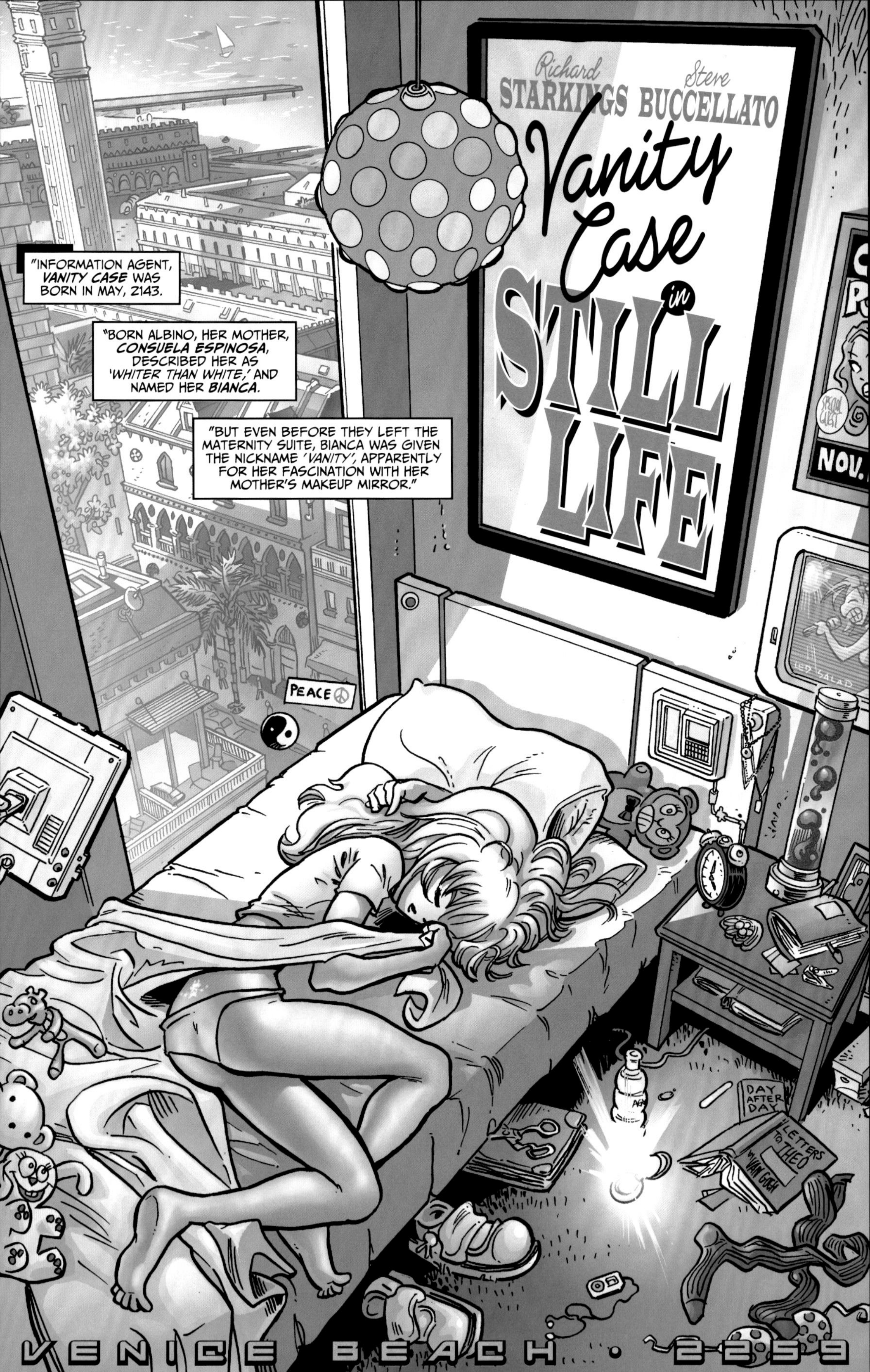

"INFORMATION AGENT, VANITY CASE WAS BORN IN MAY, 2143.
"BORN ALBINO, HER MOTHER, CONSUELA ESPINOSA, DESCRIBED HER AS 'WHITER THAN WHITE,' AND NAMED HER BIANCA.
"BUT EVEN BEFORE THEY LEFT THE MATERNITY SUITE, BIANCA WAS GIVEN THE NICKNAME 'VANITY', APPARENTLY FOR HER FASCINATION WITH HER MOTHER'S MAKEUP MIRROR."
Richard STARKINGS Steve BUCCELLATO
Vanity Case in STILL LIFE
NOV.
PEACE
DAY AFTER DAY
LETTERS TO THEO by VAN GOGH
VENICE BEACH • 2259

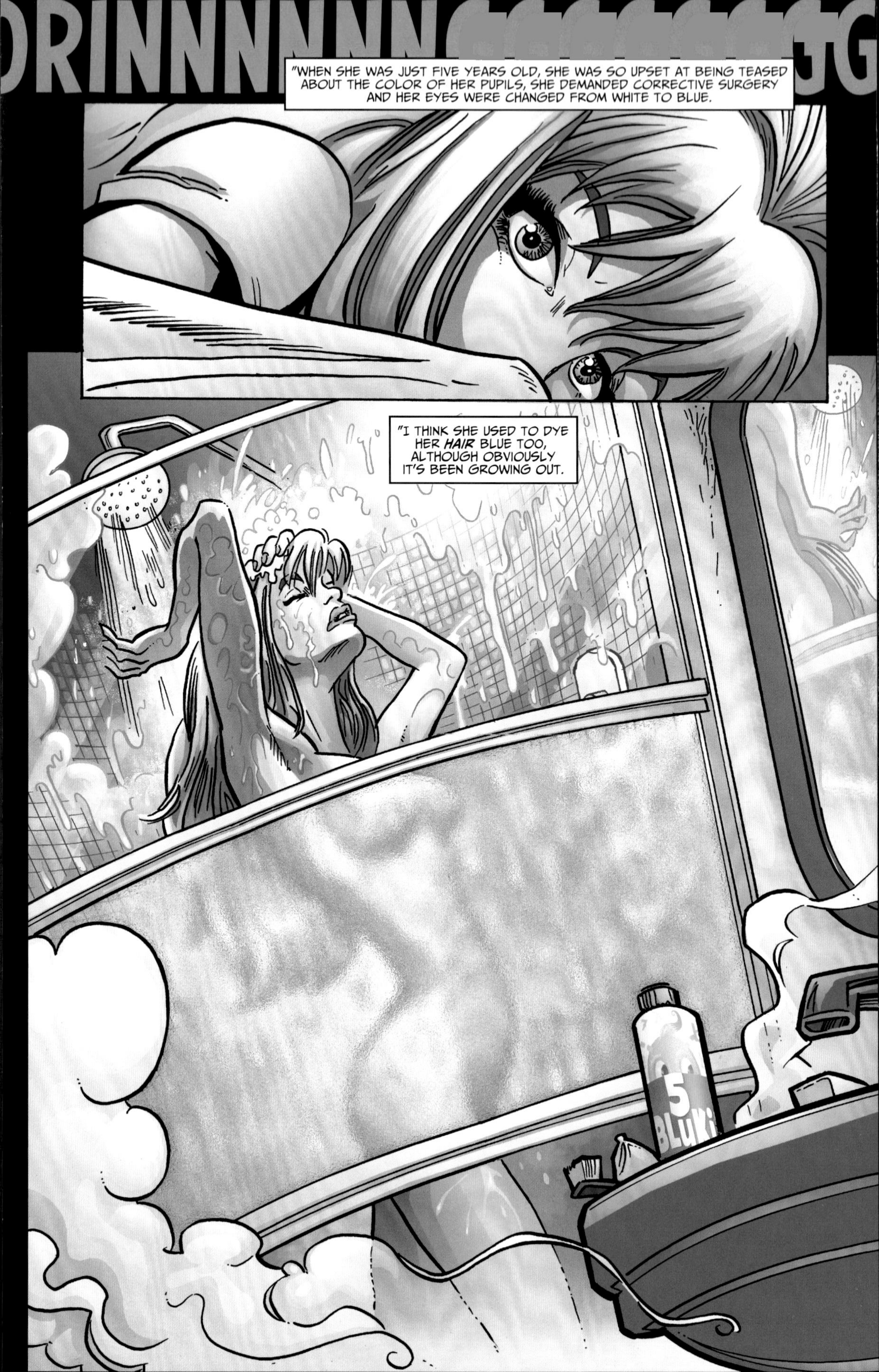
DRINNNNNNGGGGGGGG
"WHEN SHE WAS JUST FIVE YEARS OLD, SHE WAS SO UPSET AT BEING TEASED ABOUT THE COLOR OF HER PUPILS, SHE DEMANDED CORRECTIVE SURGERY AND HER EYES WERE CHANGED FROM WHITE TO BLUE.
"I THINK SHE USED TO DYE HER *HAIR* BLUE TOO, ALTHOUGH OBVIOUSLY IT'S BEEN GROWING OUT.
5
BLUKI

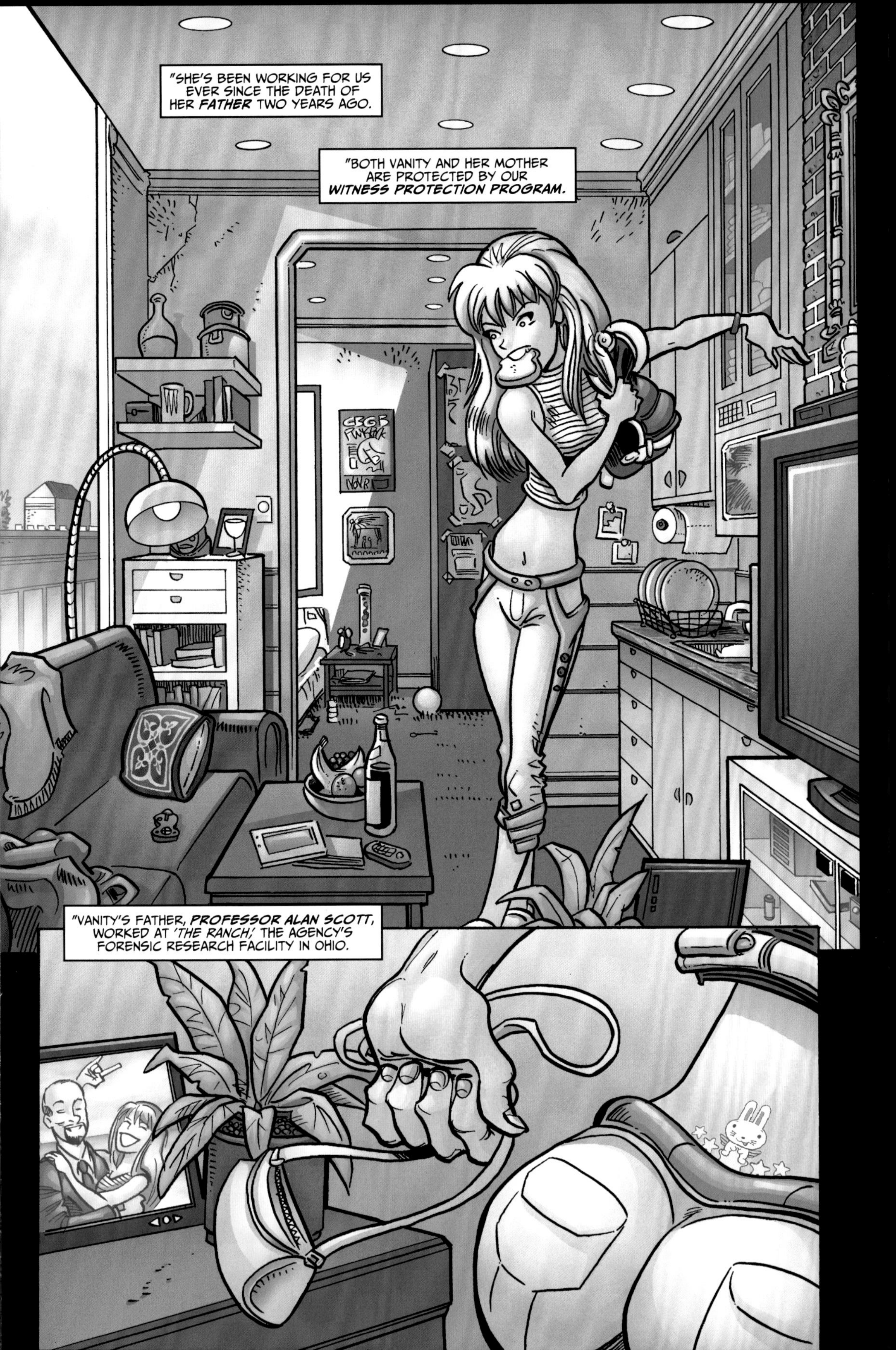
"SHE'S BEEN WORKING FOR US EVER SINCE THE DEATH OF HER FATHER TWO YEARS AGO.
"BOTH VANITY AND HER MOTHER ARE PROTECTED BY OUR WITNESS PROTECTION PROGRAM.
CBGB
"VANITY'S FATHER, PROFESSOR ALAN SCOTT, WORKED AT 'THE RANCH,' THE AGENCY'S FORENSIC RESEARCH FACILITY IN OHIO.

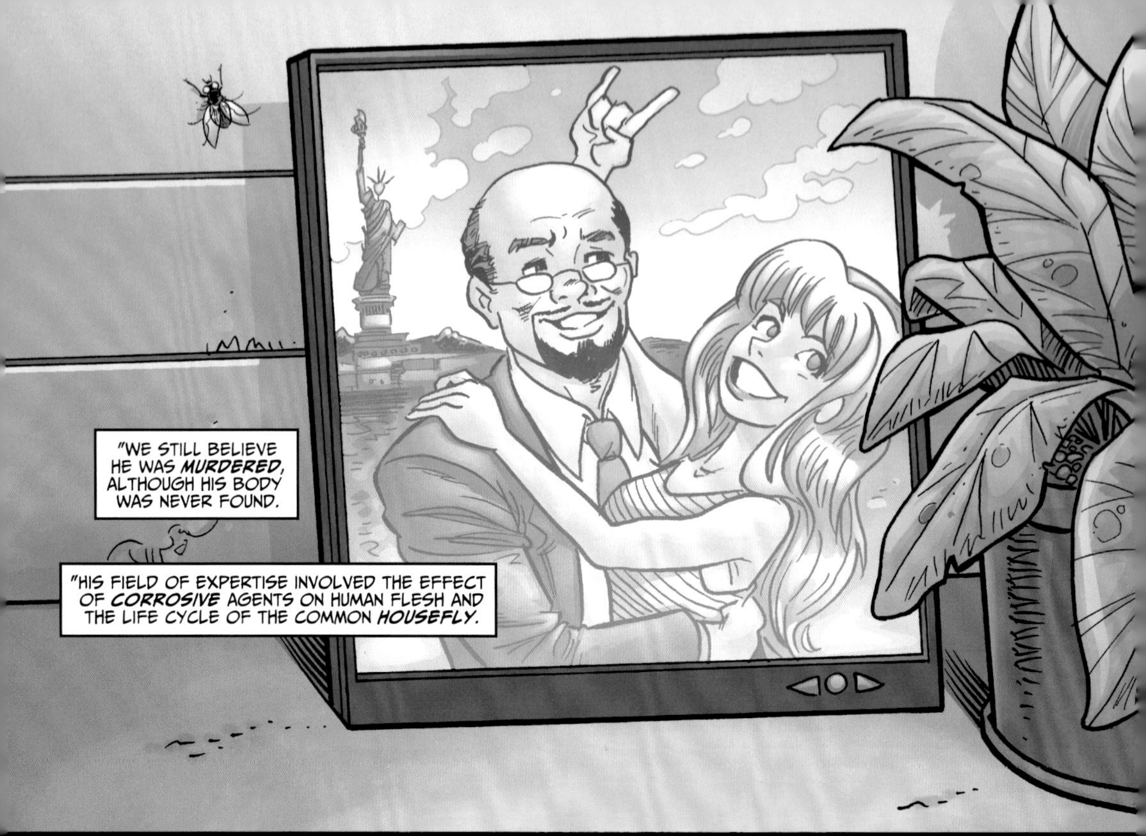
"WE STILL BELIEVE HE WAS MURDERED, ALTHOUGH HIS BODY WAS NEVER FOUND.
"HIS FIELD OF EXPERTISE INVOLVED THE EFFECT OF CORROSIVE AGENTS ON HUMAN FLESH AND THE LIFE CYCLE OF THE COMMON HOUSEFLY.

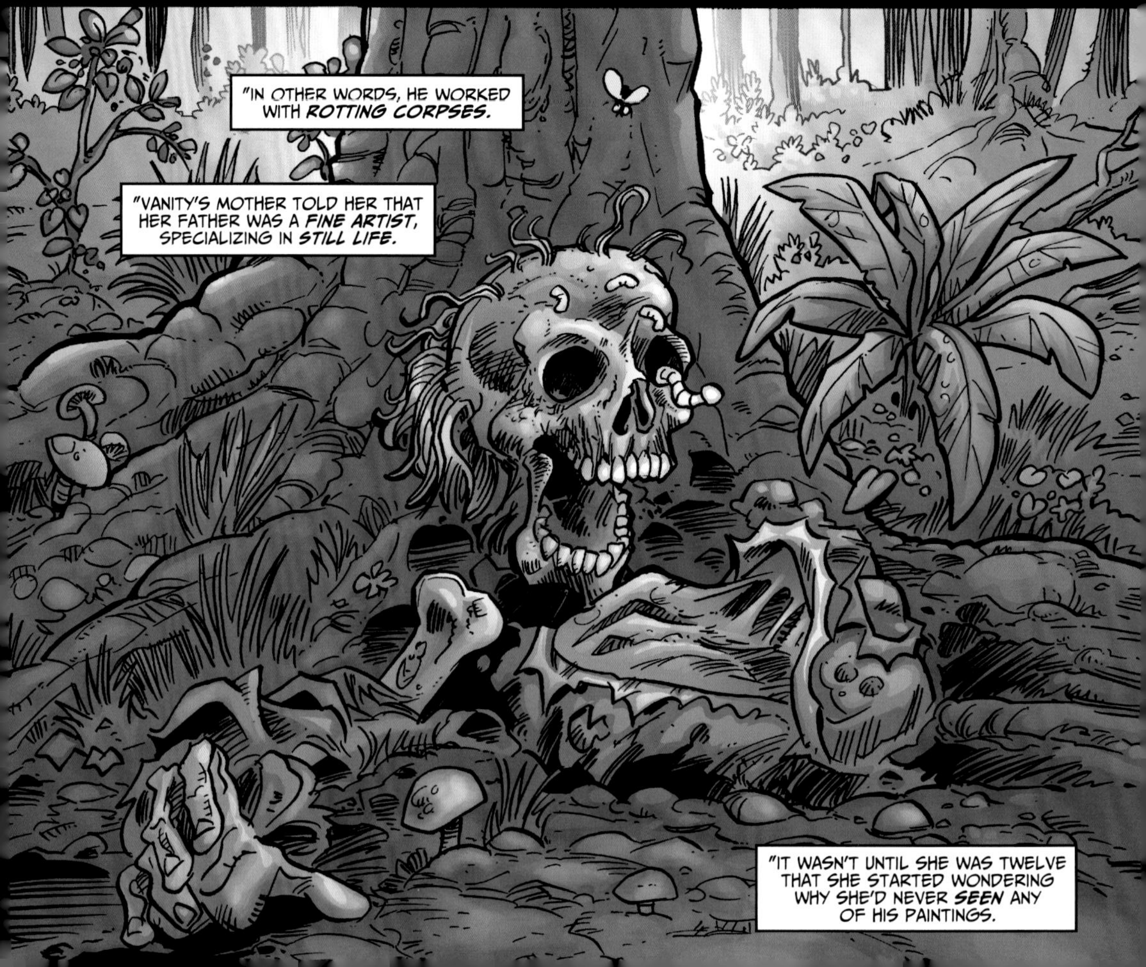
"IN OTHER WORDS, HE WORKED WITH ROTTING CORPSES.
"VANITY'S MOTHER TOLD HER THAT HER FATHER WAS A FINE ARTIST, SPECIALIZING IN STILL LIFE.
"IT WASN'T UNTIL SHE WAS TWELVE THAT SHE STARTED WONDERING WHY SHE'D NEVER SEEN ANY OF HIS PAINTINGS.

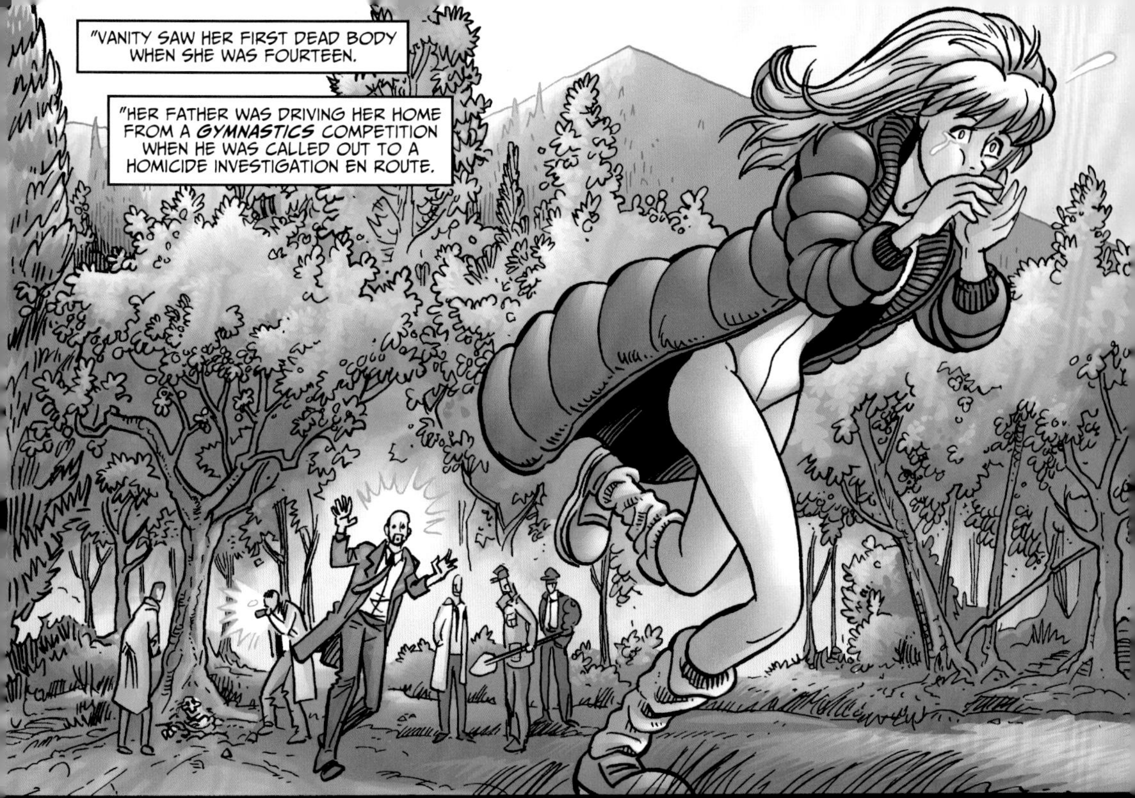
"VANITY SAW HER FIRST DEAD BODY WHEN SHE WAS FOURTEEN.
"HER FATHER WAS DRIVING HER HOME FROM A *GYMNASTICS* COMPETITION WHEN HE WAS CALLED OUT TO A HOMICIDE INVESTIGATION EN ROUTE.

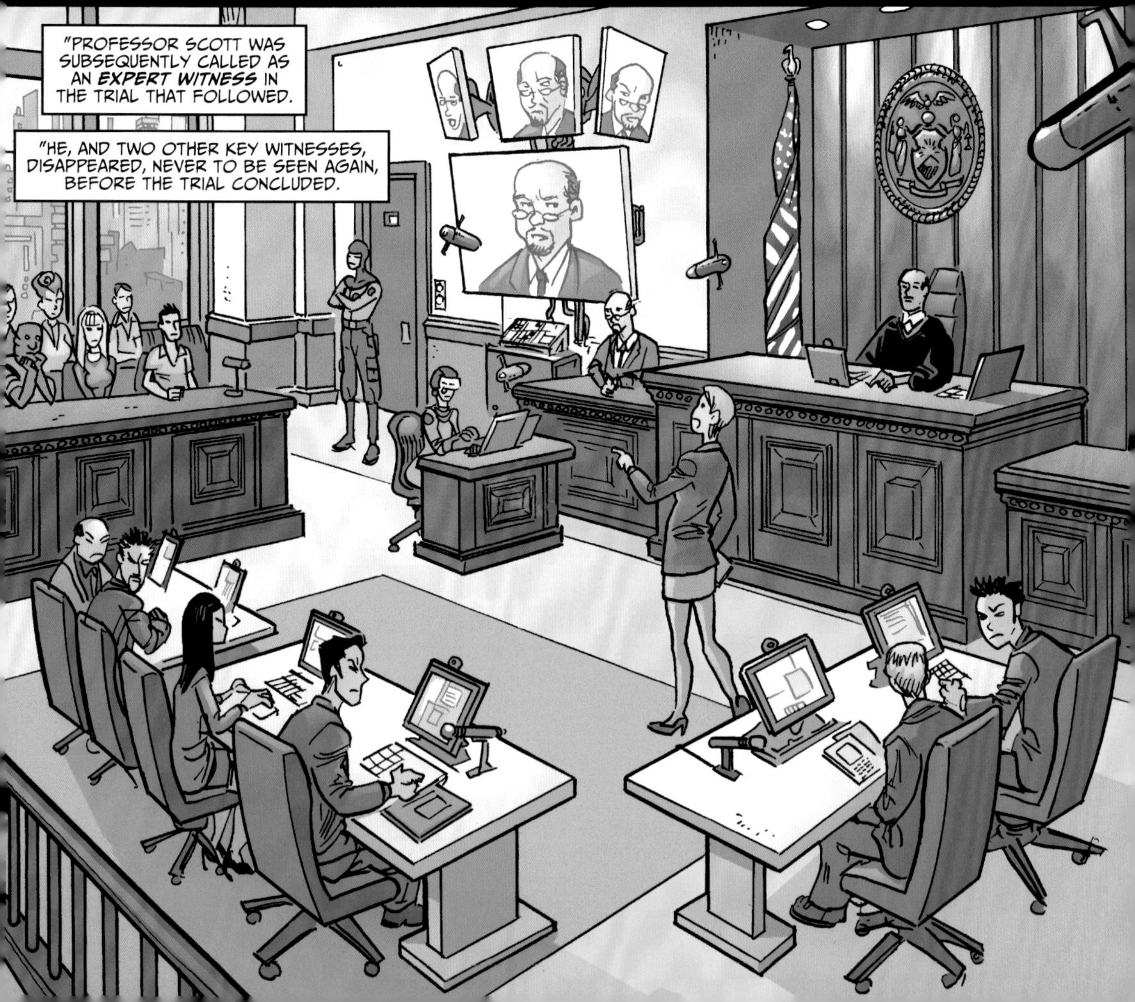
"PROFESSOR SCOTT WAS SUBSEQUENTLY CALLED AS AN *EXPERT WITNESS* IN THE TRIAL THAT FOLLOWED.
"HE, AND TWO OTHER KEY WITNESSES, DISAPPEARED, NEVER TO BE SEEN AGAIN, BEFORE THE TRIAL CONCLUDED.

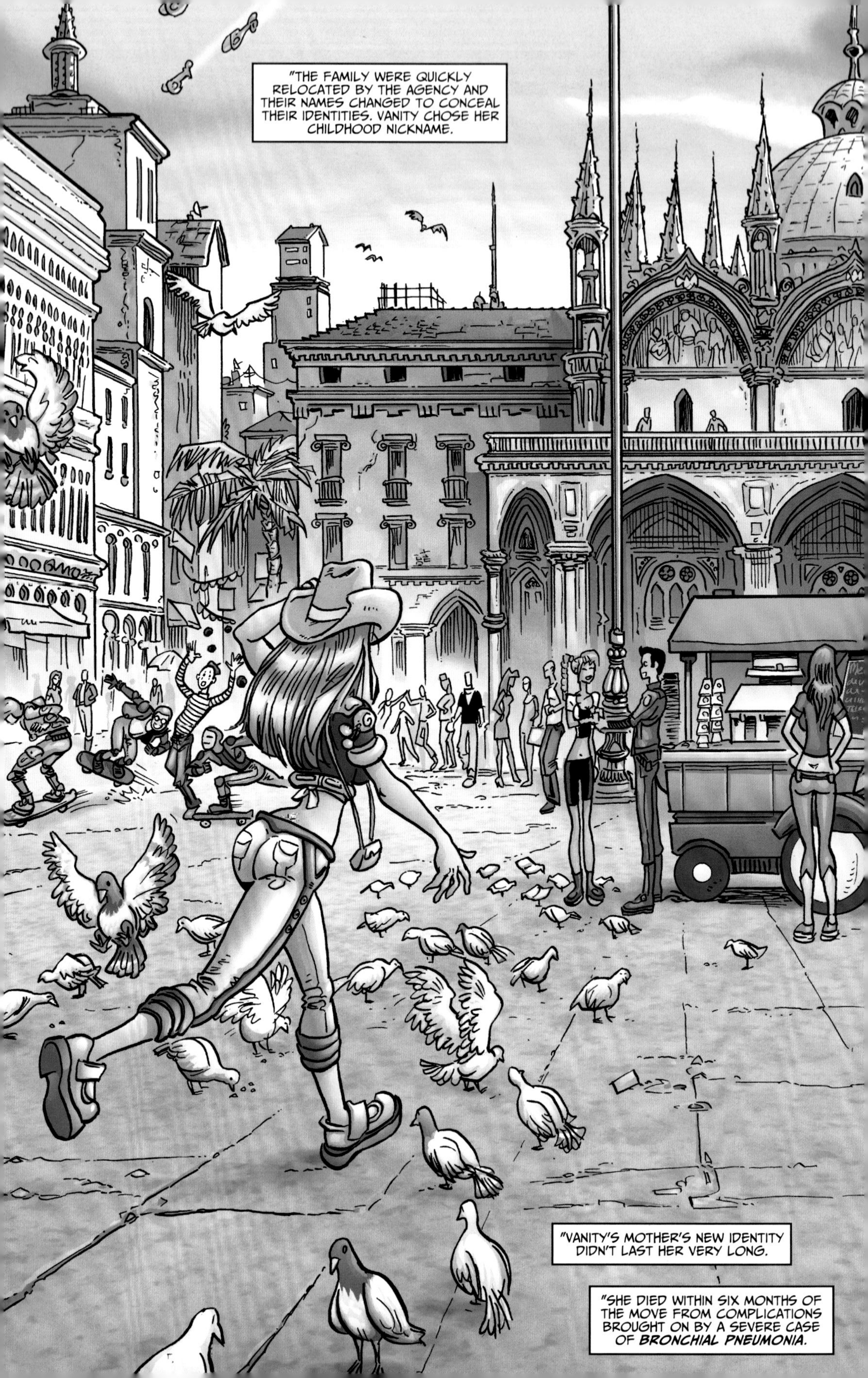
"THE FAMILY WERE QUICKLY RELOCATED BY THE AGENCY AND THEIR NAMES CHANGED TO CONCEAL THEIR IDENTITIES. VANITY CHOSE HER CHILDHOOD NICKNAME.
"VANITY'S MOTHER'S NEW IDENTITY DIDN'T LAST HER VERY LONG.
"SHE DIED WITHIN SIX MONTHS OF THE MOVE FROM COMPLICATIONS BROUGHT ON BY A SEVERE CASE OF ***BRONCHIAL PNEUMONIA.***

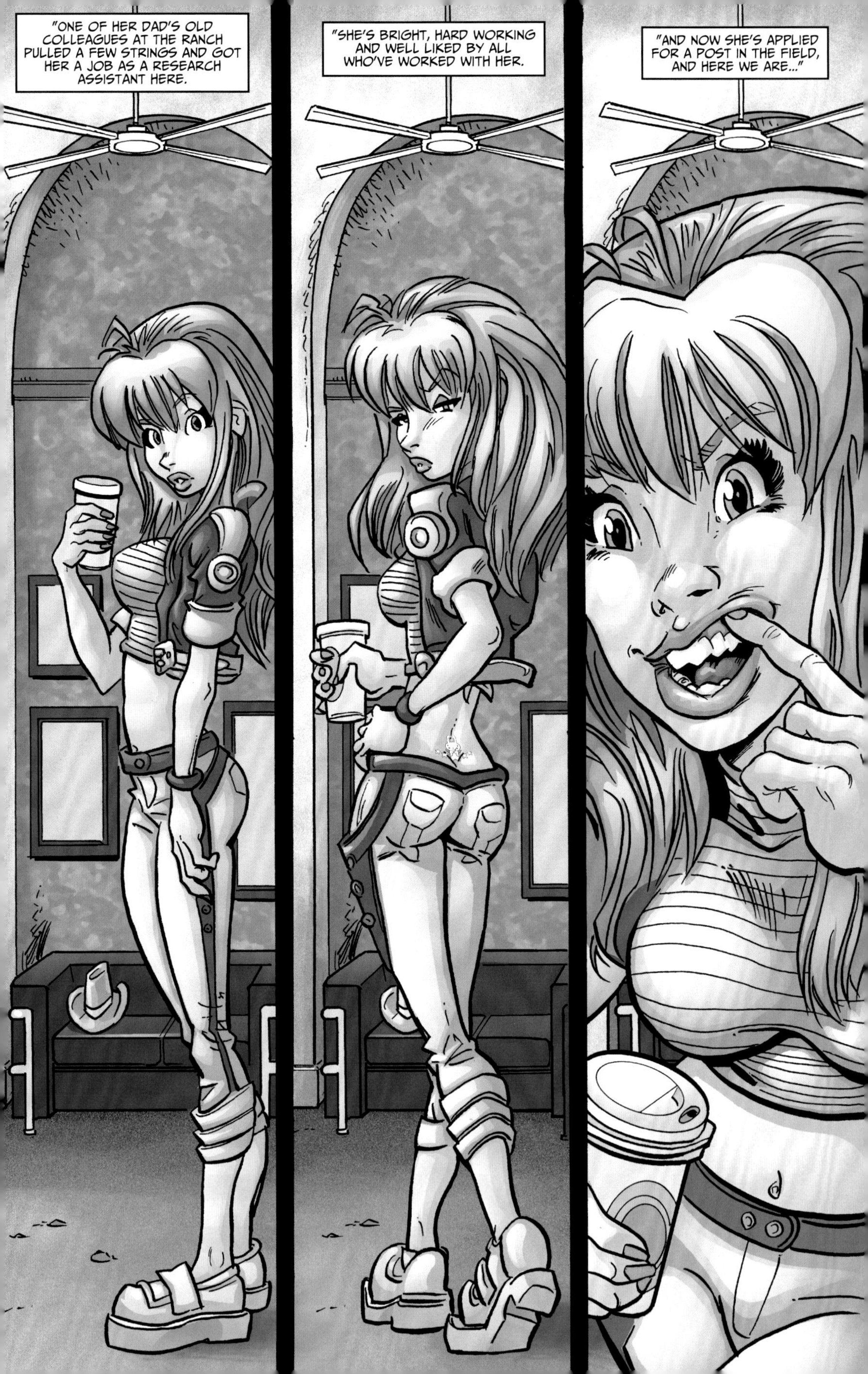
"ONE OF HER DAD'S OLD COLLEAGUES AT THE RANCH PULLED A FEW STRINGS AND GOT HER A JOB AS A RESEARCH ASSISTANT HERE.
"SHE'S BRIGHT, HARD WORKING AND WELL LIKED BY ALL WHO'VE WORKED WITH HER.
"AND NOW SHE'S APPLIED FOR A POST IN THE FIELD, AND HERE WE ARE..."

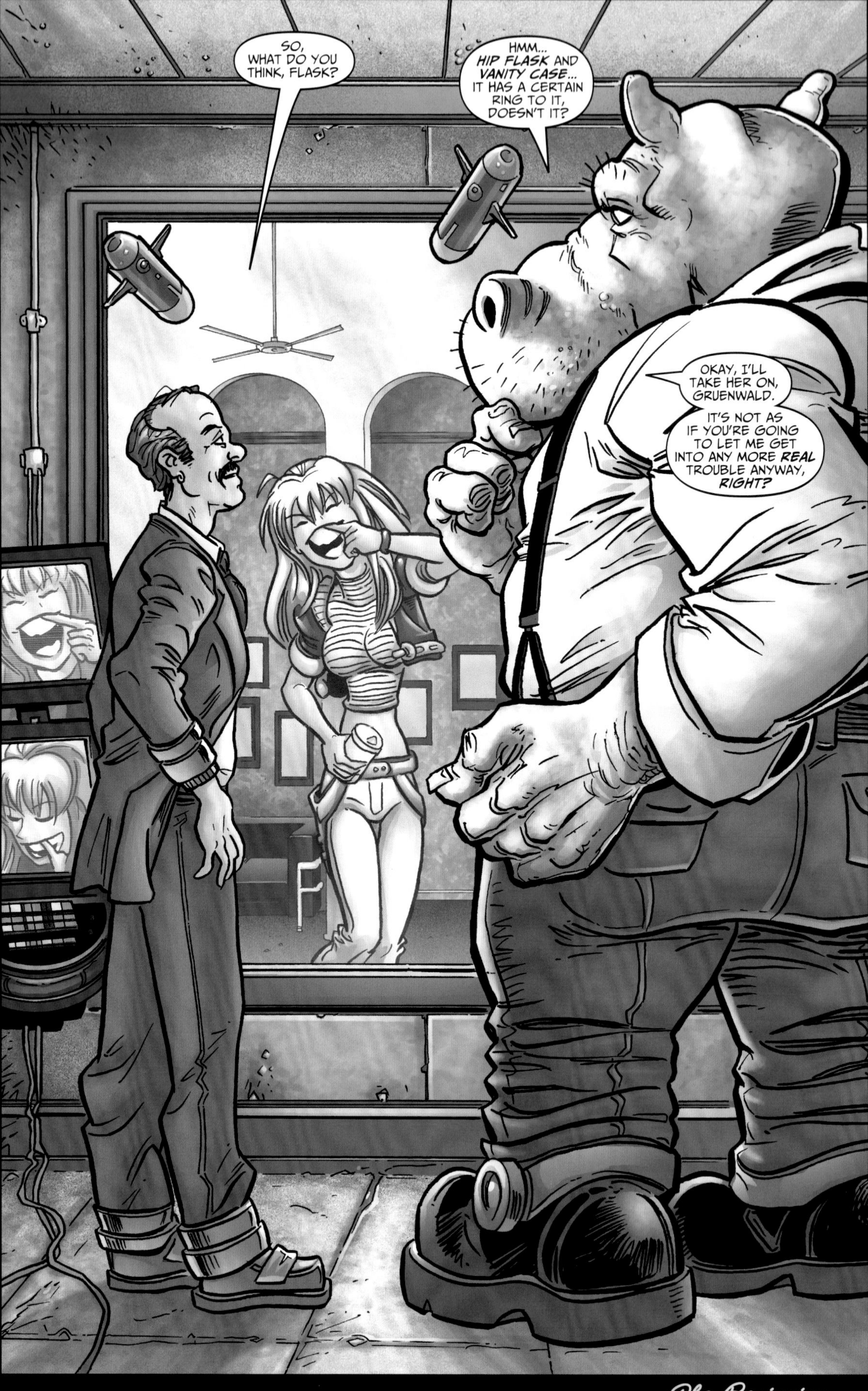
SO, WHAT DO YOU THINK, FLASK?
HMM... *HIP FLASK* AND *VANITY CASE*... IT HAS A CERTAIN RING TO IT, DOESN'T IT?
OKAY, I'LL TAKE HER ON, GRUENWALD.
IT'S NOT AS IF YOU'RE GOING TO LET ME GET INTO ANY MORE *REAL* TROUBLE ANYWAY, *RIGHT?*

The Beginning...

"The woman who appeals to a man's vanity may stimulate him, the woman who appeals to his heart may attract him, but it is the woman who appeals to his imagination who gets him."

Helen Rowland
1875-1950

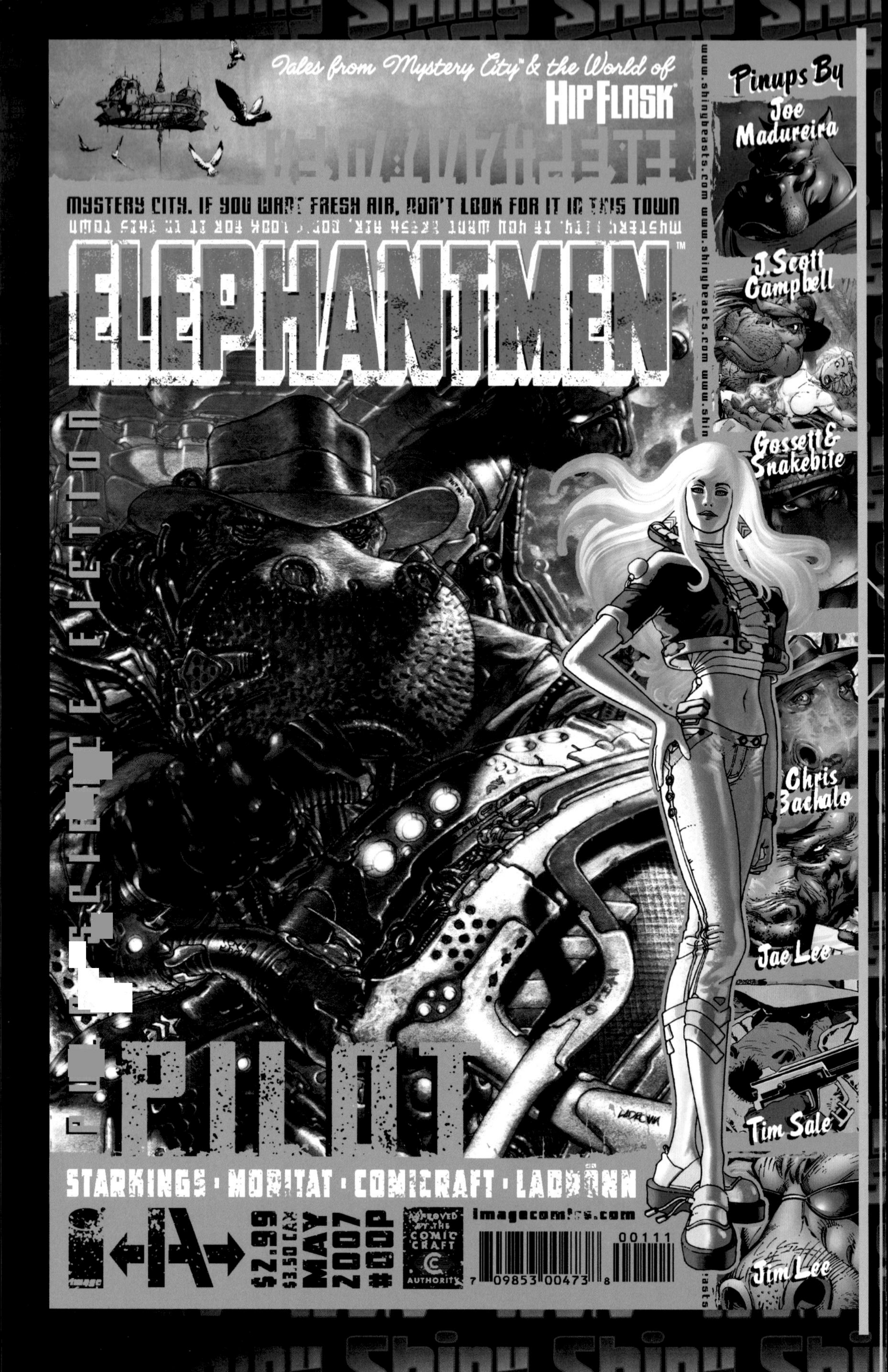

Tales from Mystery City™ & the World of
HIP FLASK™
MYSTERY CITY. IF YOU WANT FRESH AIR, DON'T LOOK FOR IT IN THIS TOWN
ELEPHANTMEN™
PILOT
STARKINGS · MORITAT · COMICRAFT · LADRÖNN
$2.99
$3.50 CAN
MAY 2007
#00P
APPROVED BY THE COMICRAFT AUTHORITY
imagecomics.com
www.shinybeasts.com
Pinups By
Joe Madureira
J. Scott Campbell
Gossett & Snakebite
Chris Bachalo
Jae Lee
Tim Sale
Jim Lee

PERTINENT POINTS PERTAINING TO PILOTS, PIECES and PULCHRITUDE

Previously... When I started working with Ladrönn on **ELEPHANTMEN**'s parent title, **HIP FLASK** in the year [not the comic] 2000AD, the first thing he did was create a number of concept drawings and figure sketches based on the story direction we were discussing.* When I was considering ideas for cover designs, I grabbed the three most finished drawings I had from Ladrönn at the time and threw them together with some abandoned cover graphics I had submitted to Joe Quesada for his old company **EVENT COMICS**. The cover you see opposite is pretty much the same as the one I threw together seven years ago, albeit with a little extra polish [or tarnish] provided by Ladrönn and Comicraft's Secret Weapon, JG. The cover within a cover that precedes the issue that fits inbetween issues #9 and #10 in this collection is the second version [there's also a third] of a piece Intrepid Ian Churchill created for a poster we published in 1998 to promote our ever-growing line of fonts. Over the page is the original **HIP FLASK** cover mock up which I intended to submit to Image Comics in 1999, when Ian had tentatively agreed to work on the series with me. It's fitting that this volume features Ian's first work on the **ELEPHANTMEN** series proper.

Perhaps you're looking at the cover opposite and thinking, "Okay, I know that a Zero issue is generally an origin story, I know that a Half issue is usually a teaser or prologue story... but **ELEPHANTMEN** had a 'P' issue?!? What's up with that?!"

The answer is very simple -- the 'P' issue was an excuse to publish 44 pages of pulsating, power-packed potboilers and pinups by a panoply of premium pencil pushers and purveyors of purple prose! And if that's not already enough Ps for you, here's one more; Pilot.

Y'see, as many of you may already know, in television the first episode of a TV series is referred to as the Pilot. That episode is regarded as a test flight for a possible series and orders are placed by networks on the strength of that first flight. Twelve years ago, when **HIP FLASK** was little more than a mascot for the **COMICRAFT** line of comic book fonts [find 'em at ComicBookFonts.com, natch'!] I occasionally engaged artists I was working with to help me flesh out the character with a pinup here and a t-shirt design there. This was an extension of what I used to refer to as my working-for-Raisin-and-Biscuit-Yorkies phase. When I was but a humble art assistant at Marvel UK in London in the 80's, fellow editors would coax me to help them out with logos for their books by offering me bars of chocolate. The Raisin and Biscuit Yorkie was a favorite of mine at the time, and word got around -- Richard will work for chocolate. This is still true today, but in the mid 90's I had enough money to buy chocolate for myself... so if an old colleague like top cover artist Brian Bolland approached me for a selection of fonts, I bartered with him for a **HIP FLASK** t-shirt design in return. On occasion I even paid for artwork, but after a couple of years, other artists started asking me why I hadn't asked them to create a **HIP FLASK** pinup, and

*See Unhuman: The Elephantmen Art of Ladrönn

pretty soon I had more art than I knew what to do with... enough to fill a whole comic book even!

However, as the **HIP FLASK** storyline started to take shape, it became clear to me that a lot of the artwork sitting in my drawer just didn't fit the dark, dystopian Pulp Science Fiction action/adventure scenario I was developing with Ladrönn. I think it's particularly interesting to note that, for some reason, don't ask me why, almost every artist who gave me a **HIP FLASK** pinup or portfolio piece, preferred to picture our particular pachyderm with a preponderance of pistols or pieces, and paired him with plucky and perky partners with prominent pudenda! Or, as Miki might say, "What's with all the Guns and Boobs?"

So there we were, nine issues into the **ELEPHANTMEN** story, and some of our more fervent readers out there -- having visited the **HIP FLASK** website [www.HipFlask.com] -- wanted to know why they hadn't seen Jae Lee's piece in print -- or they'd seen Ian Churchill's strip in **COMIC BOOK LETTERING THE COMICRAFT WAY** [still on sale in all good comic book shops, bookstores or at Amazon.com] but wanted to see it in the pages of **ELEPHANTMEN**. Pax Pachyderm Proselytes! The 'P' issue represented pretty much all the **HIP FLASK** extant material and even included one or two pieces no one had seen before! So the 'P' issue was the **PILOT** issue -- the one where Captain Pike sits in the command chair of the Enterprise, Spock shows way too much emotion and Nurse Chapel has long dark hair and never cracks a smile. And, in Classic **STAR TREK** style, we wrapped everything up in a special framing sequence featuring the lovely Miki with art by Moritat himself and a story of sorts by yours truly.

Kurt Busiek and Stuart Immonen, bless 'em, created the seven page story featured in **THE PILOT** issue in exchange for **COMICRAFT**'s work on the late, lamented **GORILLA COMICS** website, and John JG Roshell's sterling design work on their **SHOCKROCKETS** title [still available in trade paperback form from those awfully nice chaps at **DARK HORSE**]. Joe Kelly gave us Dungburgers in exchange for work on the **MAN OF ACTION** website [www.ManOfAction.tv] and our other contributors provided pinups and covers for a number of reasons which, quite honestly, I've completely forgotten. Special thanks to Jeph Loeb and Tim Sale, Peter Gross and Ryan Kelly for their work and a big **HIP FLASK** tip of the hat to my grate mate, Ian Churchill, whose awesome artwork and cheeky British enthusiasm brought a lot of power and majesty to both Hip Flask and Obadiah Horn when they were but a twinkle in my eye, and continues to do so to this day -- take a look at the double page spread at the end of issue #15 and tell me you don't agree! Seems Ian has something of an an eye for guns and boobs too. As Miki would say...*Tt Tt Tt... Boys, boys, boys...*

Richard Starkings

COMICRAFT
STARKINGS · CHURCHILL · LIQUID!
image
HIP FLASK
PULP SCIENCE FICTION
CRIMETIME IS OVER

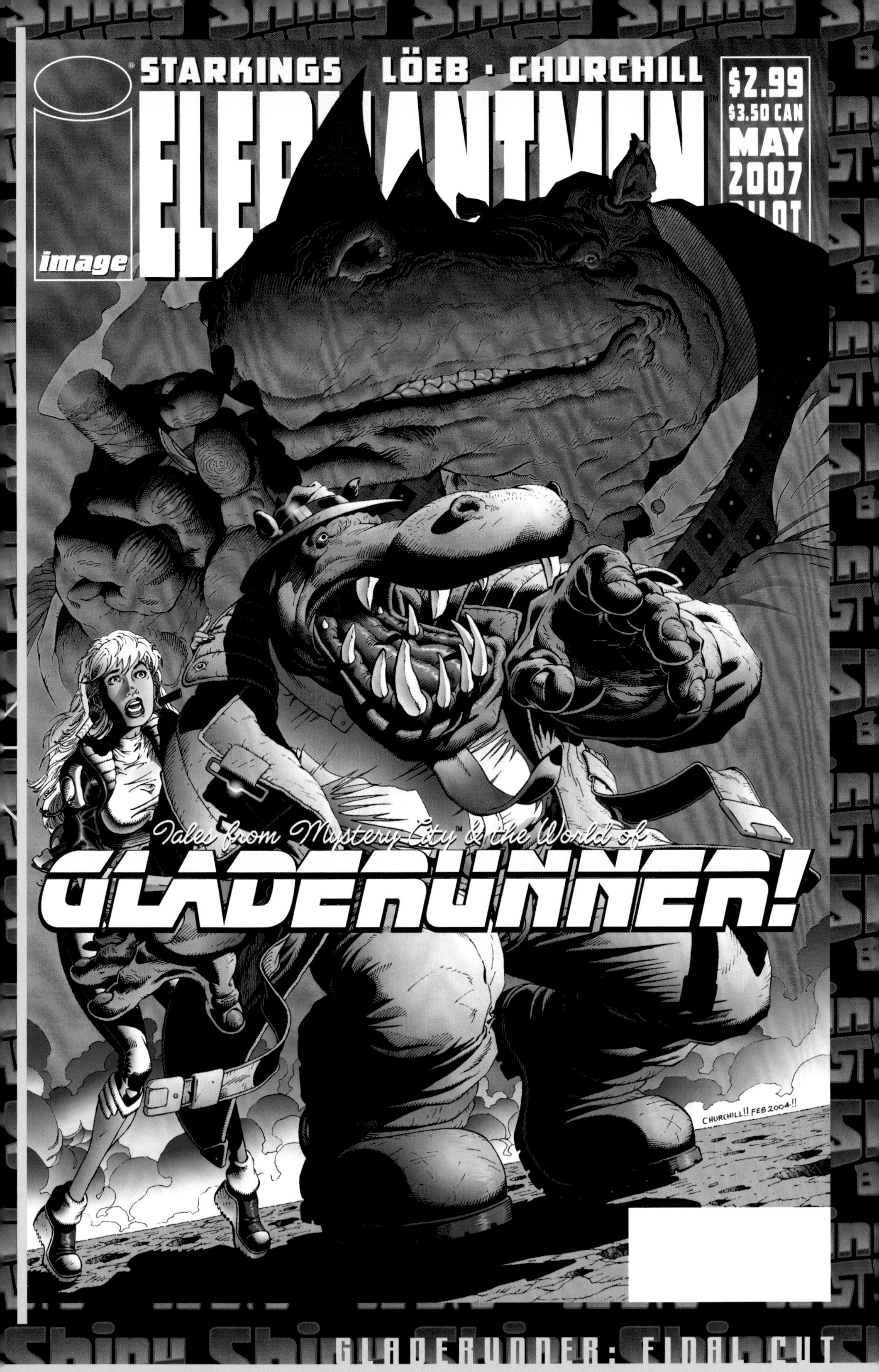

STARKINGS LÖEB · CHURCHILL
$2.99
$3.50 CAN
MAY
2007
image
Tales from Mystery City & the World of
GLADERUNNER!
CHURCHILL!! FEB 2004!!

GLADERUNNER: FINAL CUT

by Ian Churchill

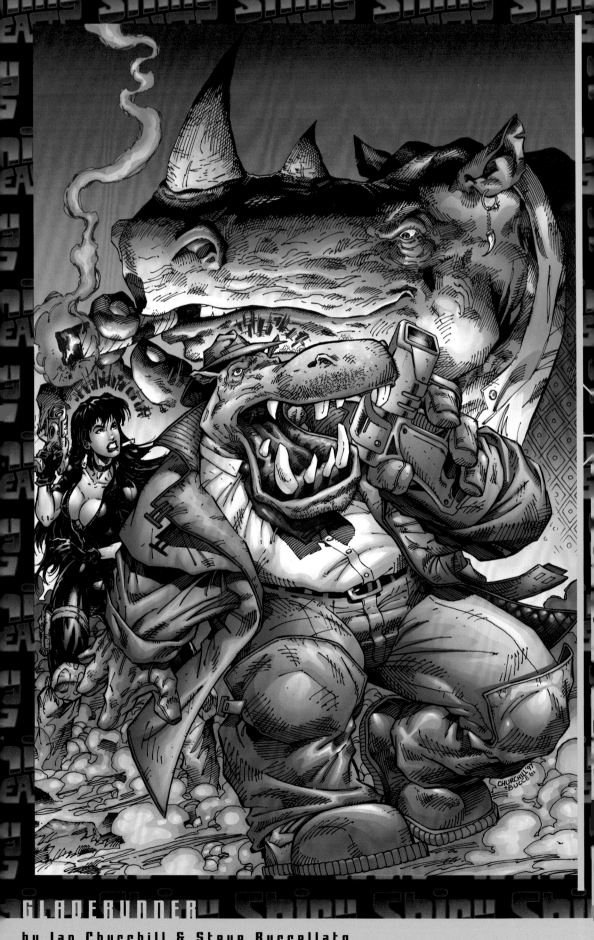

GLADERUNNER

by Ian Churchill & Steve Buccellato

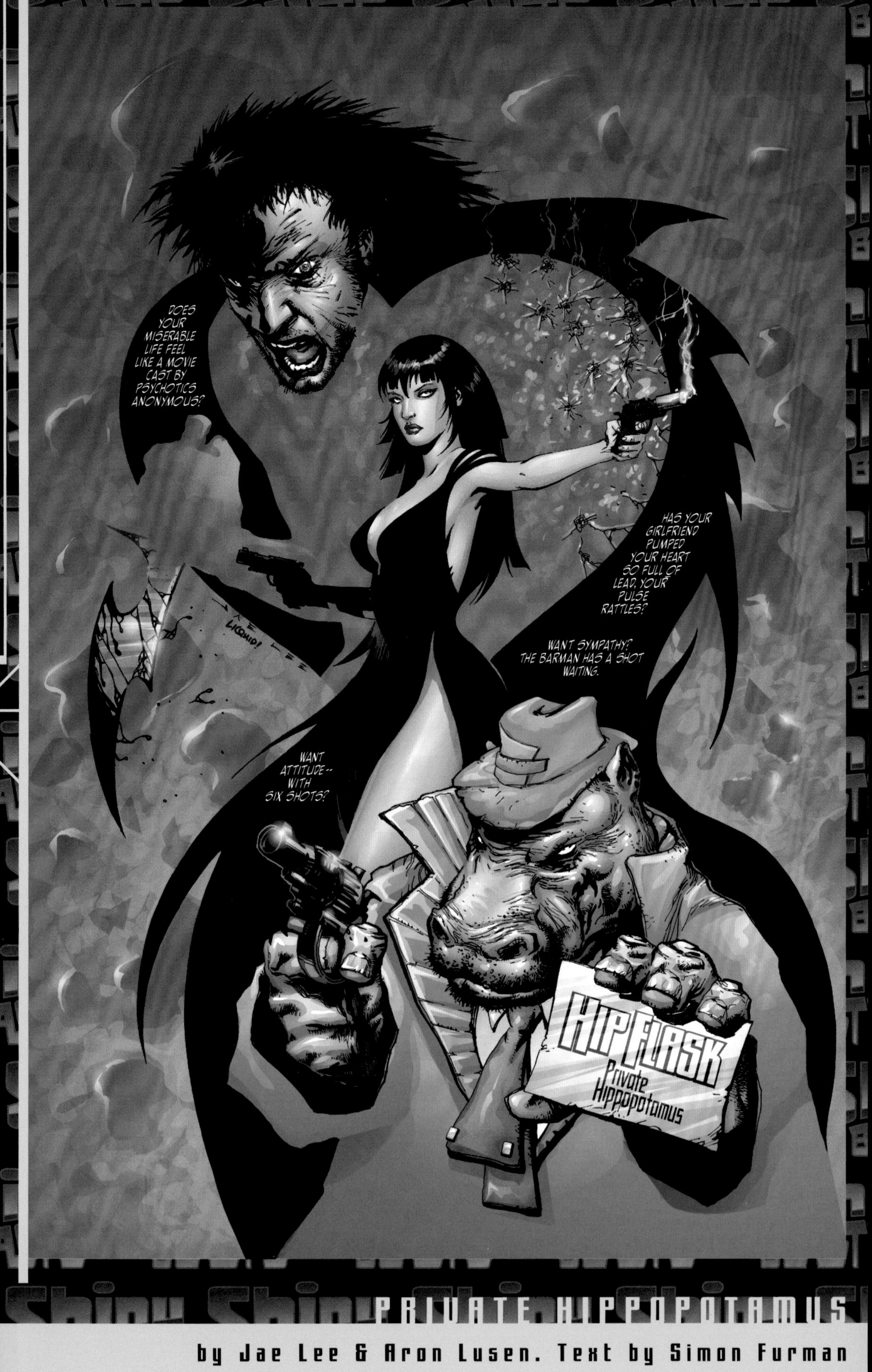
DOES YOUR MISERABLE LIFE FEEL LIKE A MOVIE CAST BY PSYCHOTICS ANONYMOUS?
HAS YOUR GIRLFRIEND PUMPED YOUR HEART SO FULL OF LEAD, YOUR PULSE RATTLES?
WANT SYMPATHY? THE BARMAN HAS A SHOT WAITING.
WANT ATTITUDE-- WITH SIX SHOTS?
HIP FLASK
Private Hippopotamus

PRIVATE HIPPOPOTAMUS

by Jae Lee & Aron Lusen. Text by Simon Furman

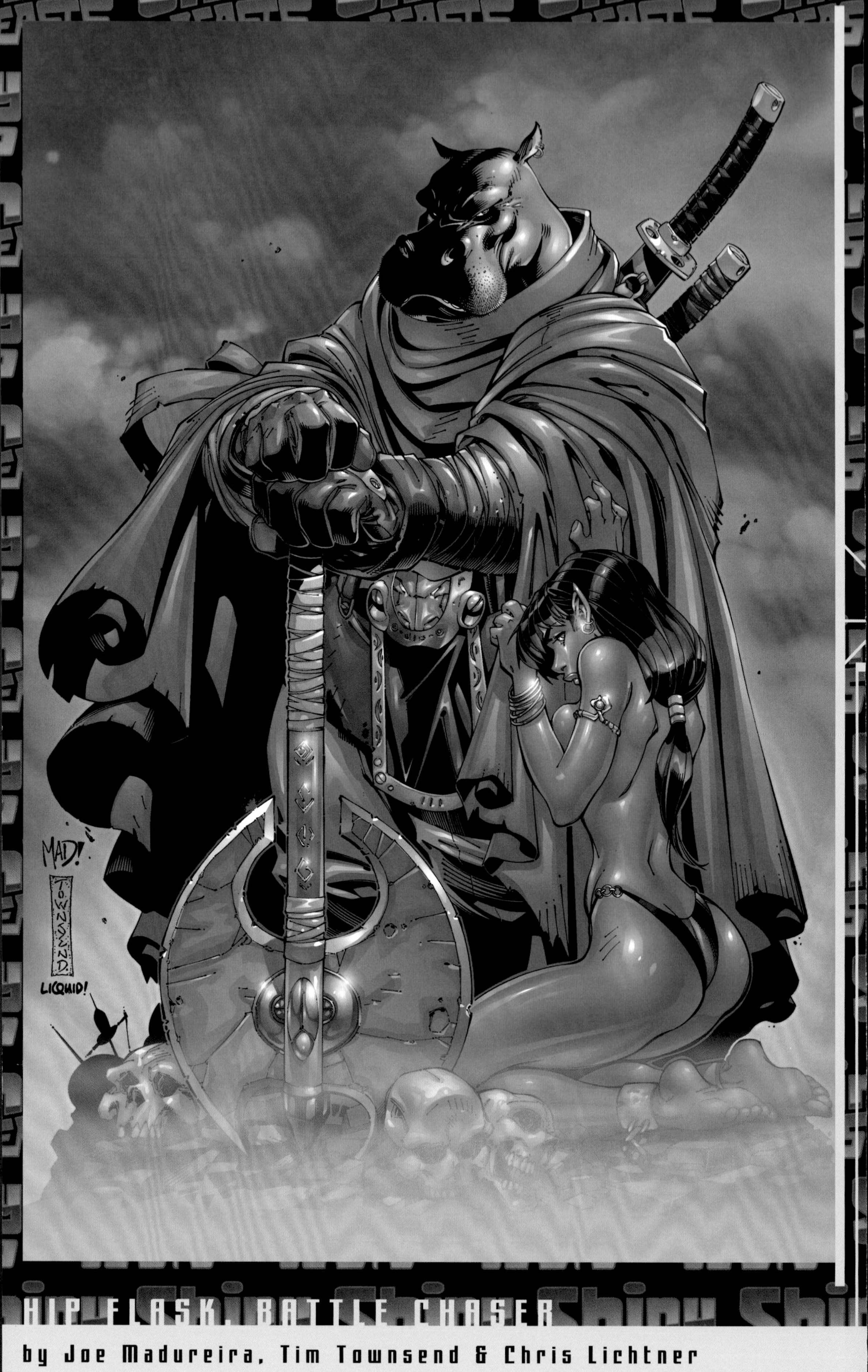
MAD!
TOWNSEND
LICQUID!

HIP FLASK, BATTLE CHASER

by Joe Madureira, Tim Townsend & Chris Lichtner

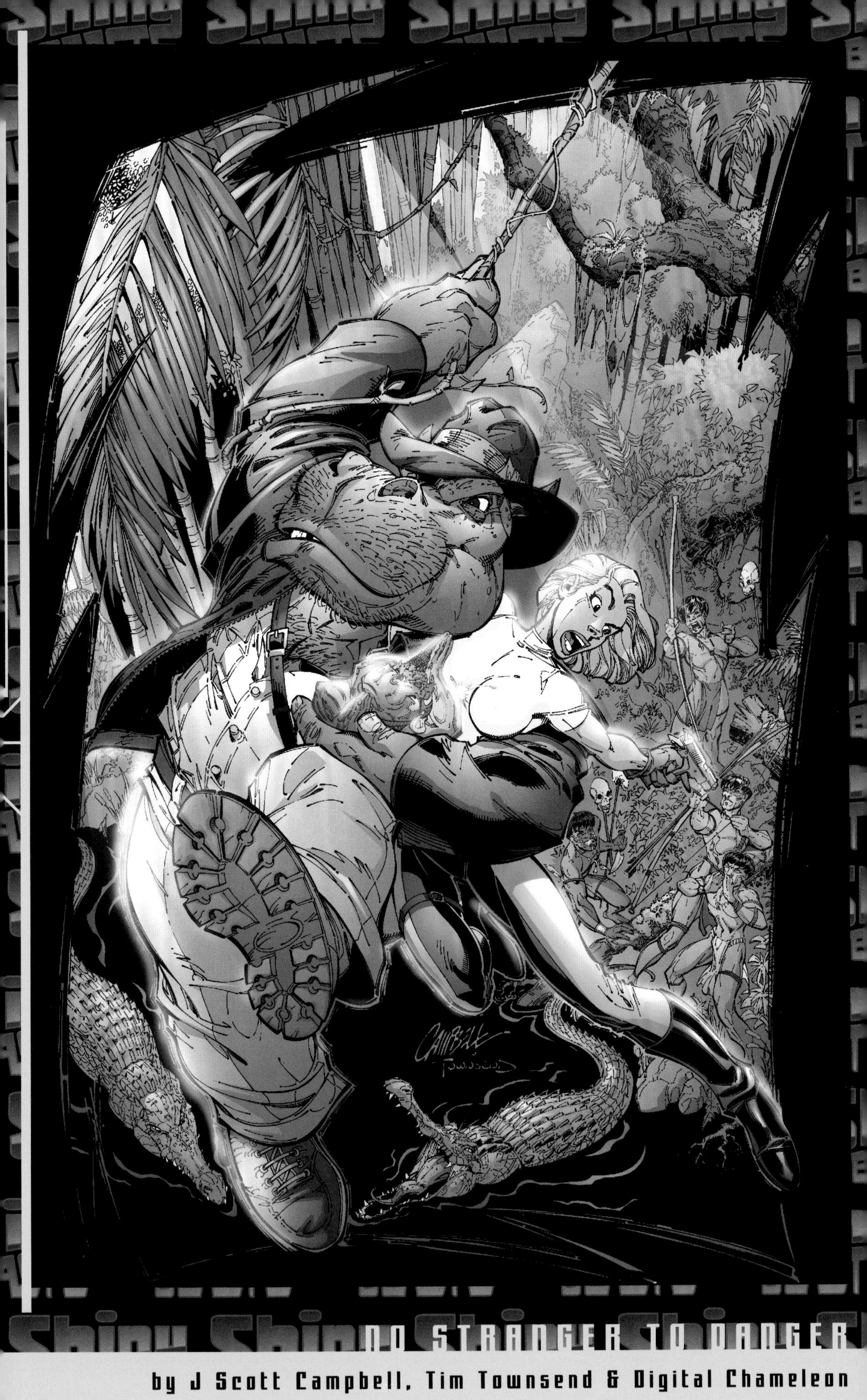

NO STRANGER TO DANGER

by J Scott Campbell, Tim Townsend & Digital Chameleon

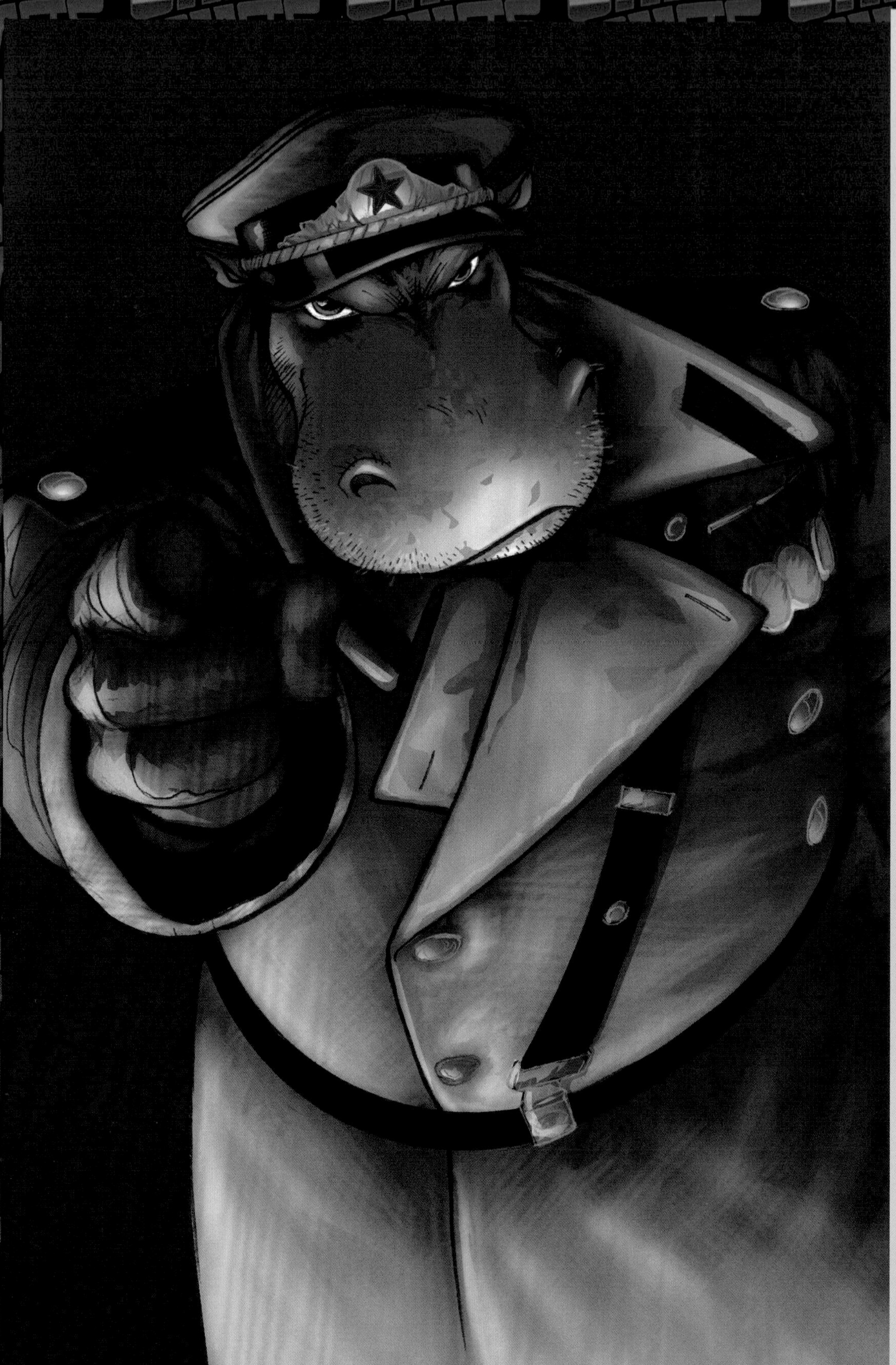

COMRADE FLASK

by Christian Gossett vs Snakebite!

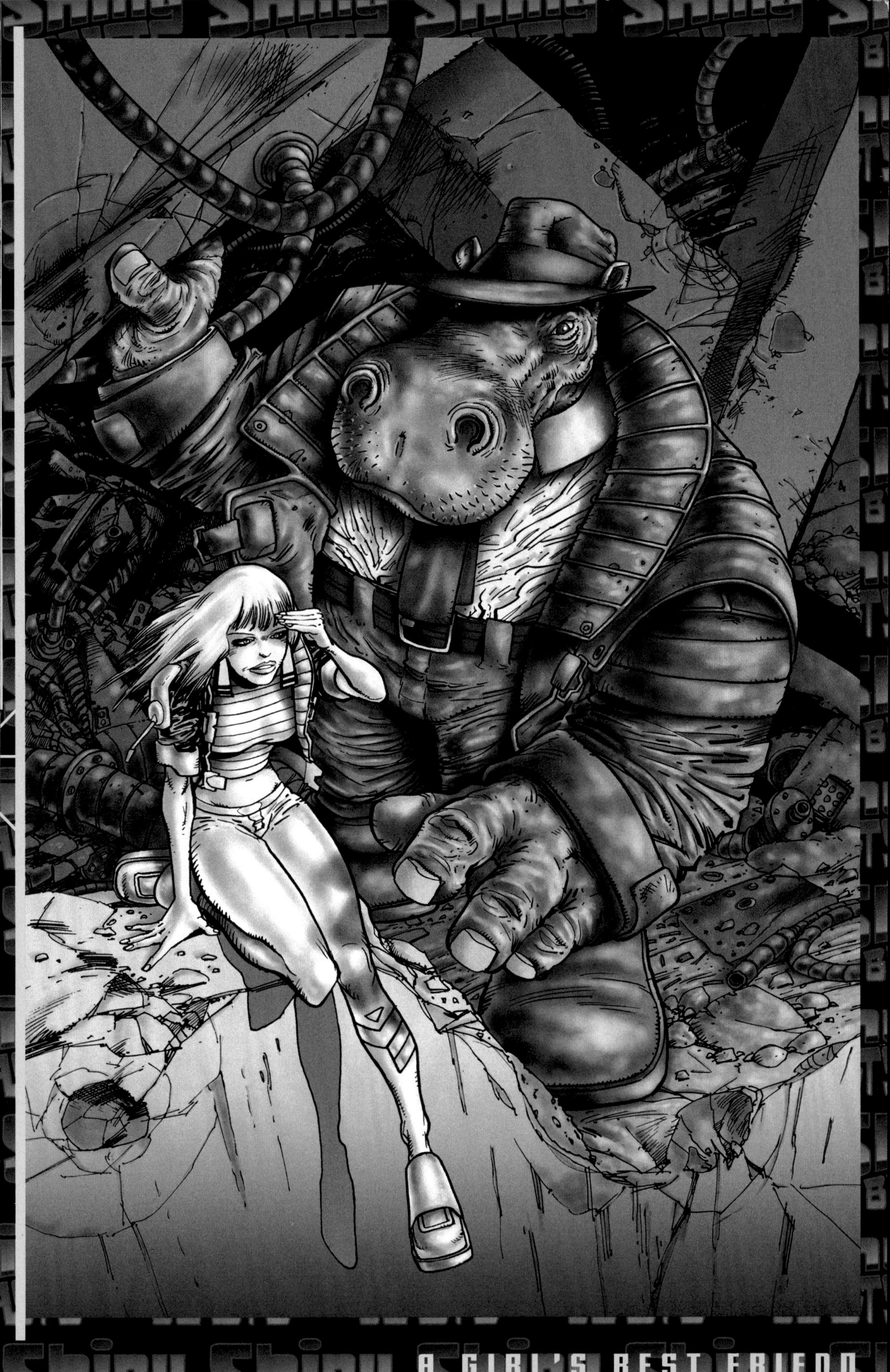

A GIRL'S BEST FRIEND

by Henry Flint & Rob Steen

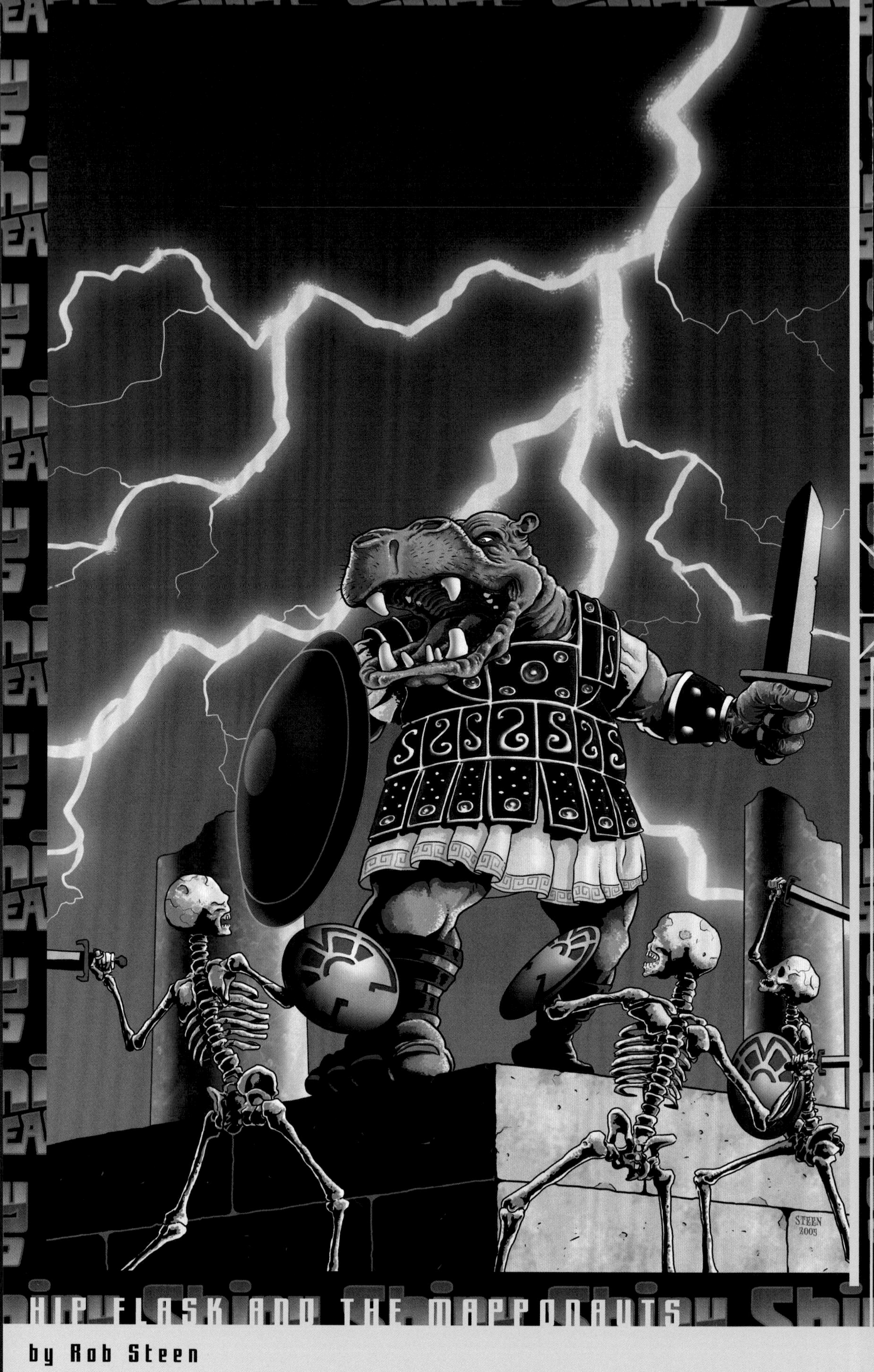
STEEN
2005

HIP FLASK AND THE MAPPONAUTS

by Rob Steen

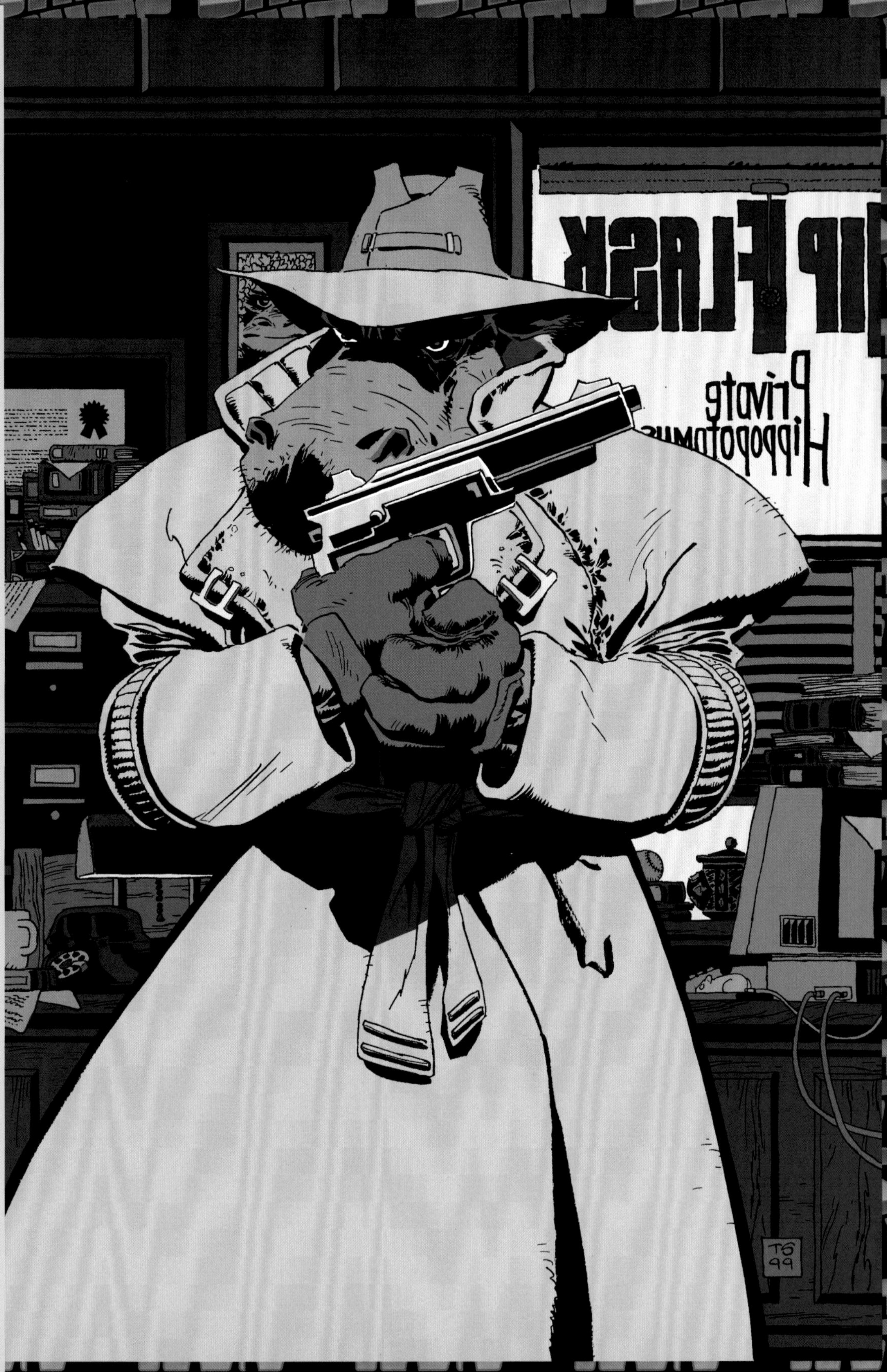

THE LONG HOT SUMMER

by Tim Sale & Gregory Wright

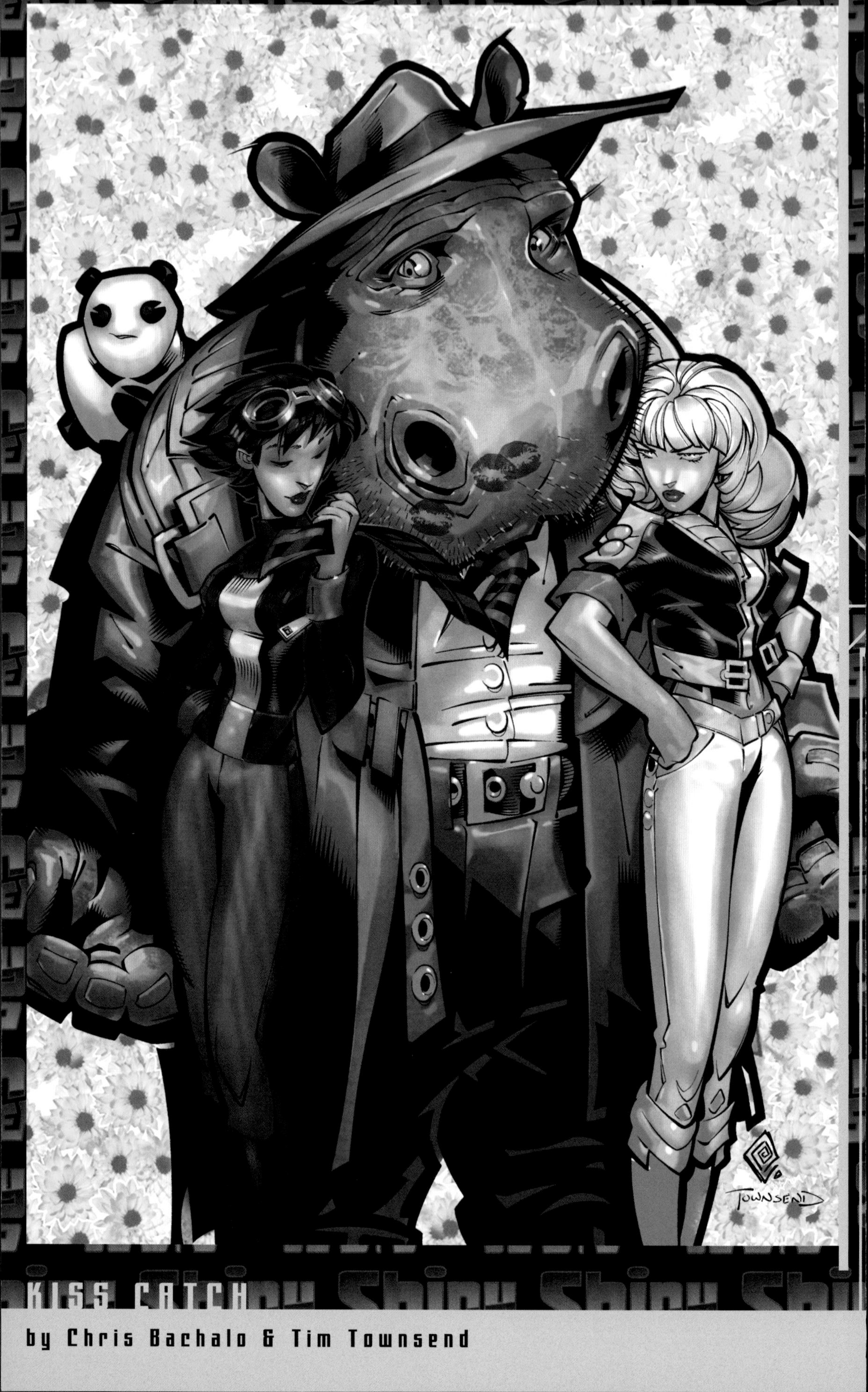
TOWNSEND

KISS CATCH

by Chris Bachalo & Tim Townsend

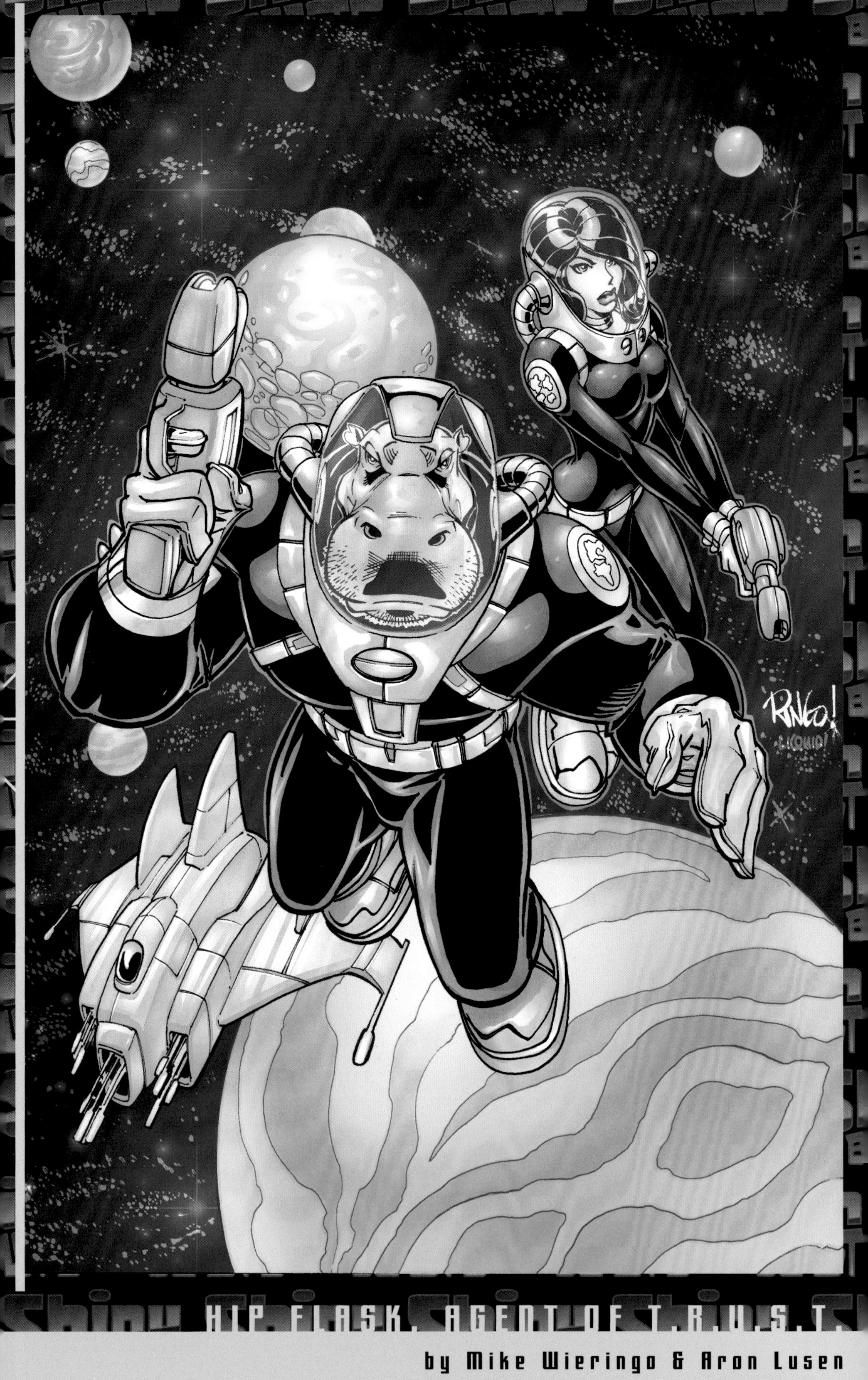

RINGO!
LIQUID!

HIP FLASK, AGENT OF T.R.U.S.T.

by Mike Wieringo & Aron Lusen

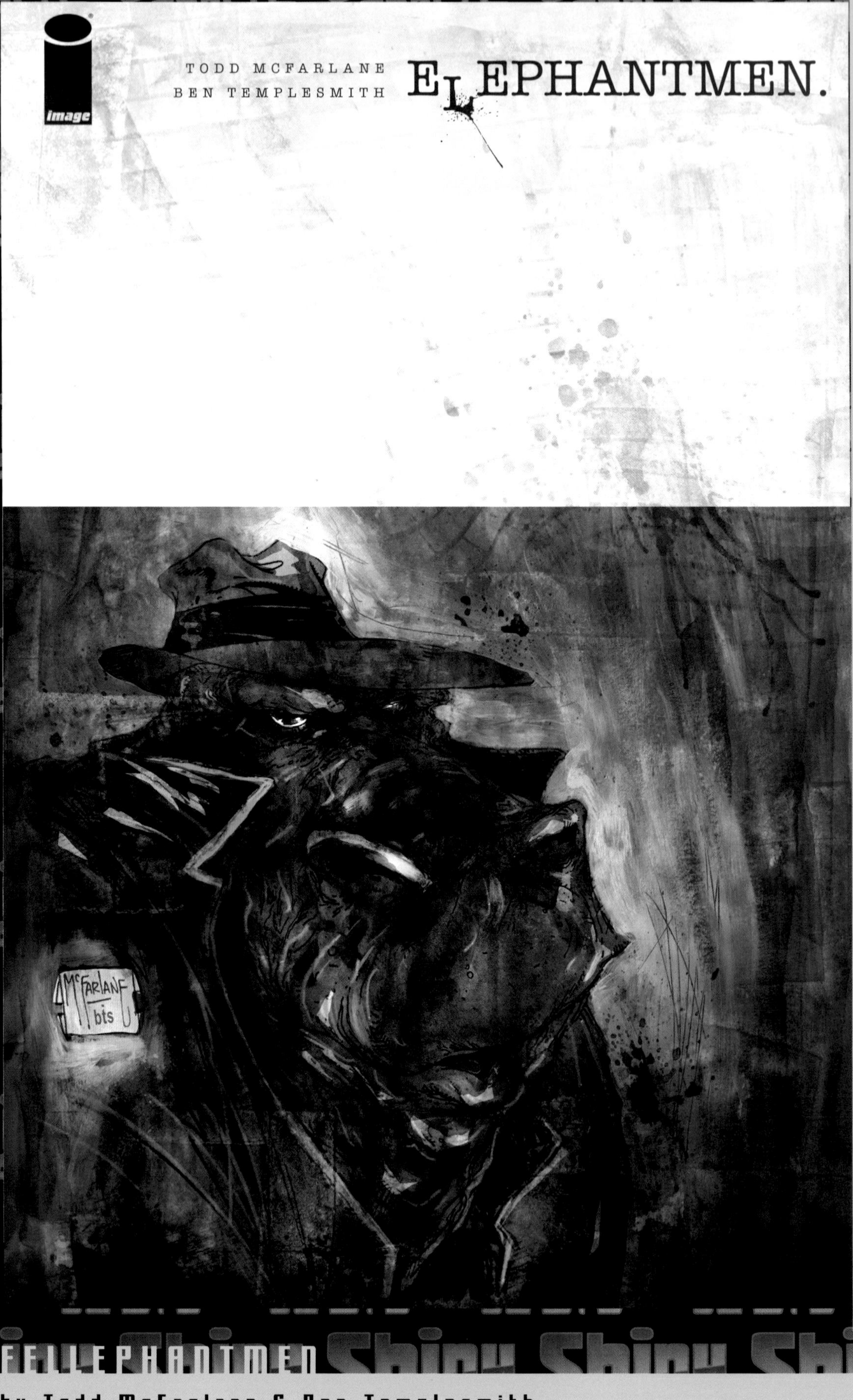
TODD MCFARLANE
BEN TEMPLESMITH
ELEPHANTMEN.
image
McFARLANE
bts

FELLEPHANTMEN

by Todd McFarlane & Ben Templesmith

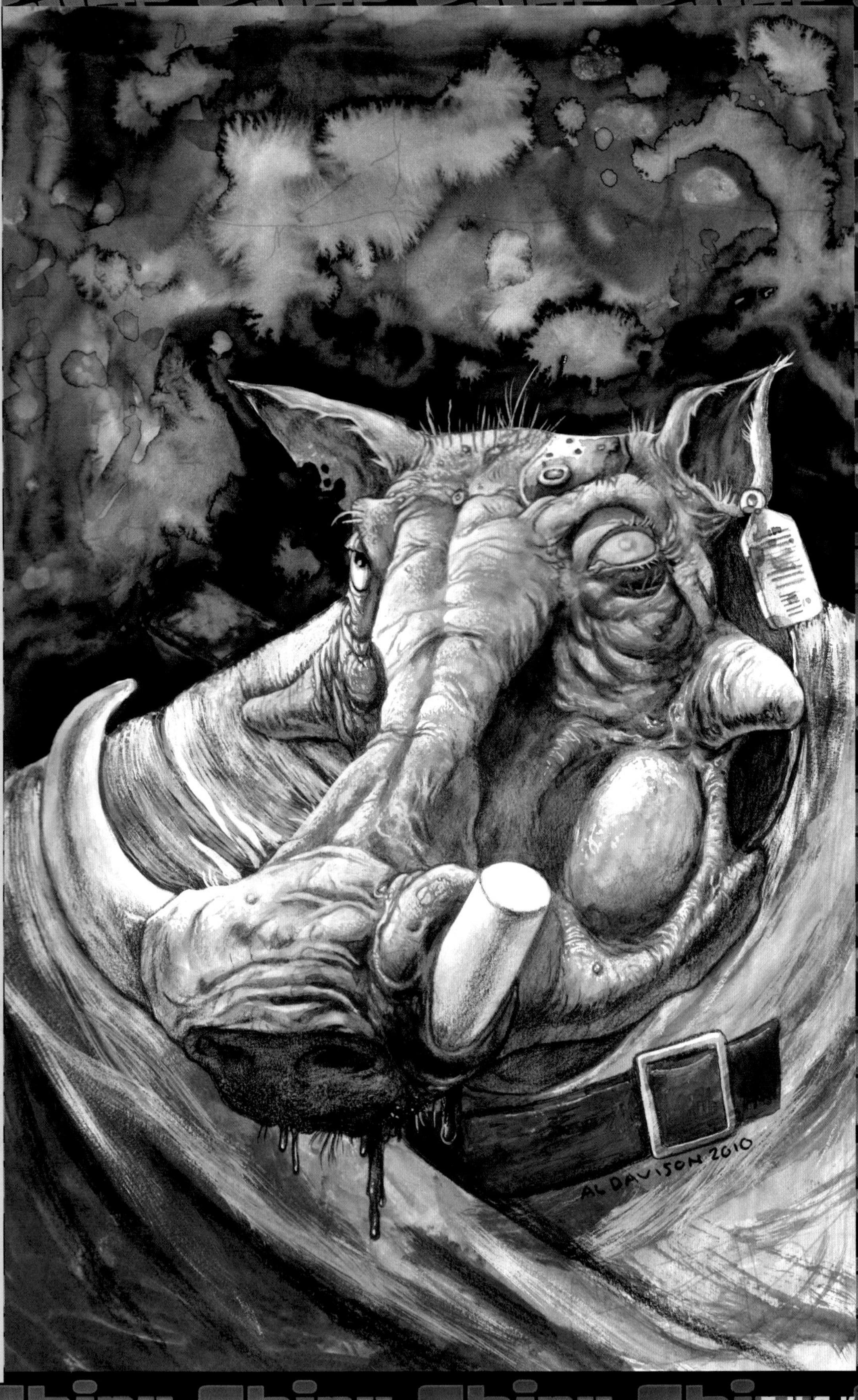
AL DAVISON 2010

TUSK

by Al Davison

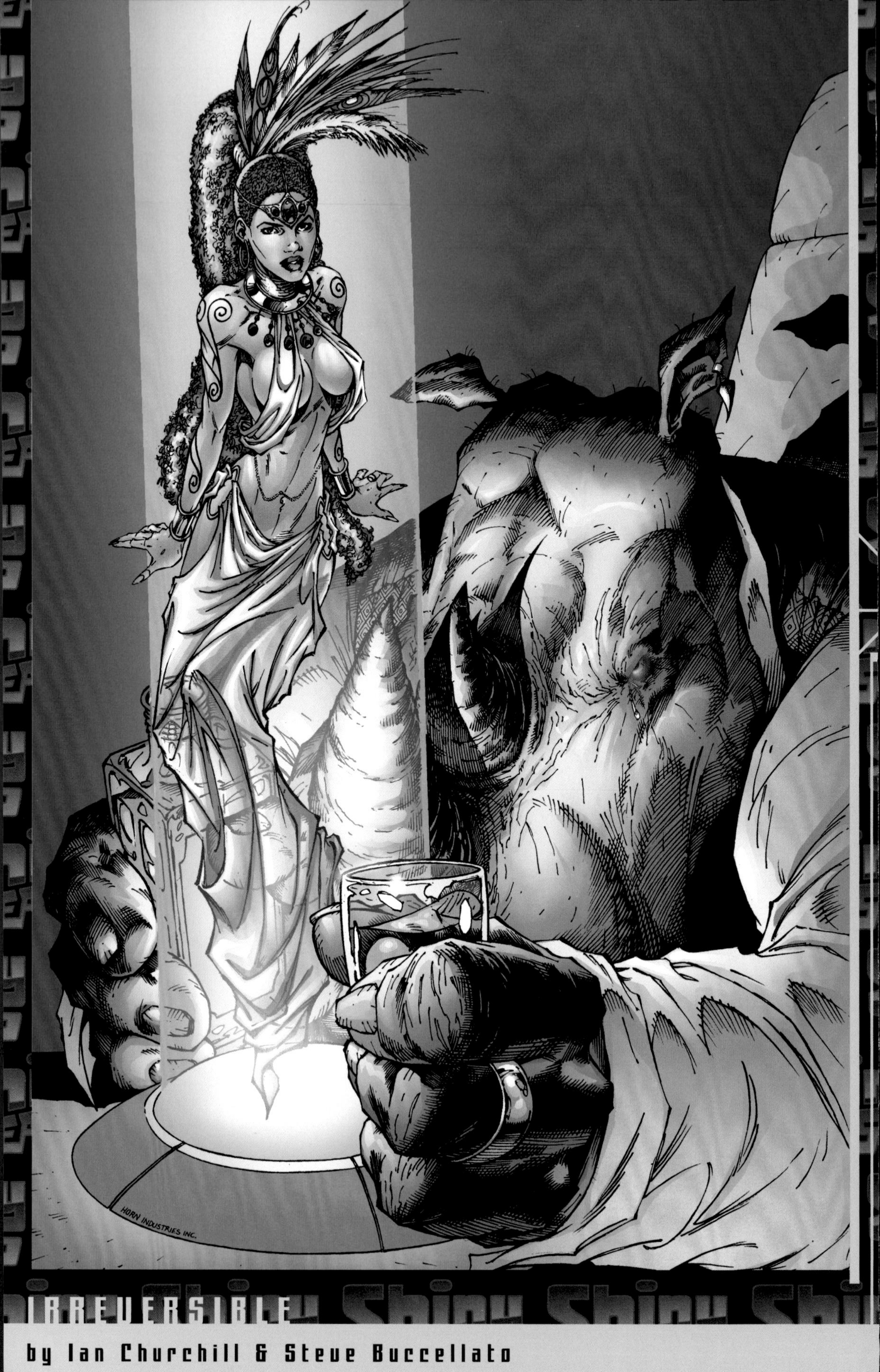
HORN INDUSTRIES INC.

IRREVERSIBLE

by Ian Churchill & Steve Buccellato

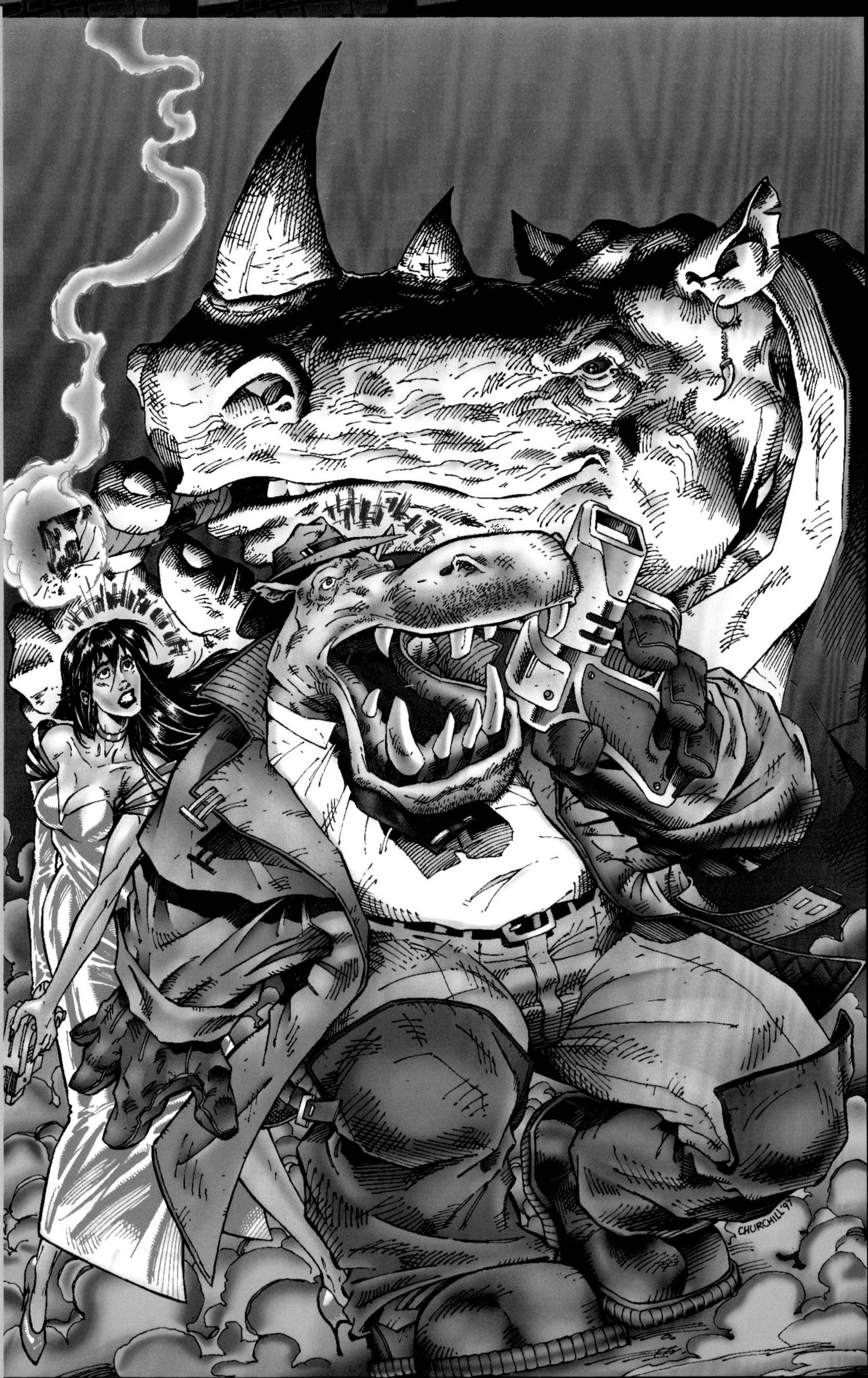
CHURCHILL'97

GLADERUNNER: ROUGH CUT

by Ian Churchill & JG Roshell

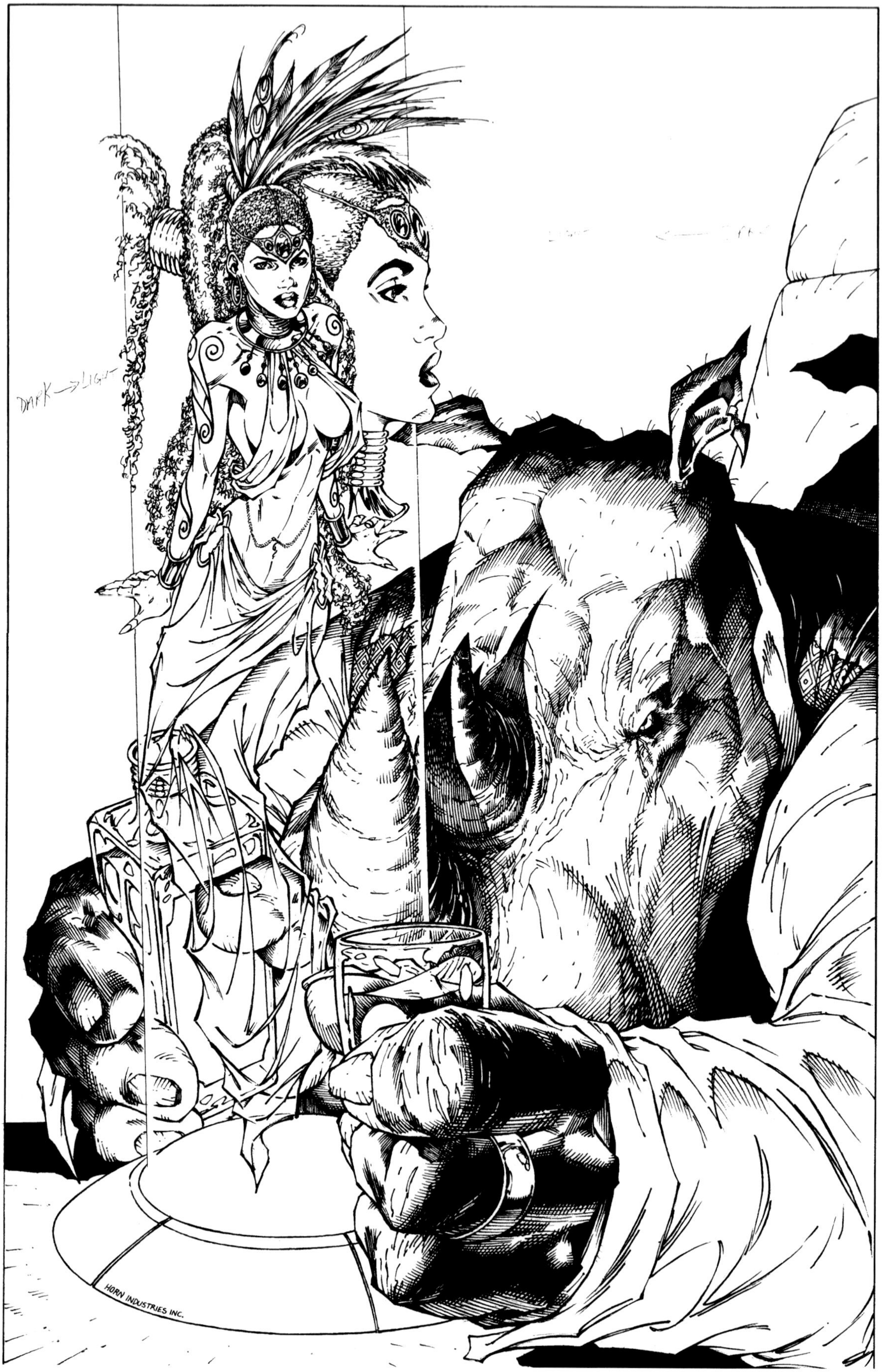
DARK → LIGHT
HORN INDUSTRIES INC.

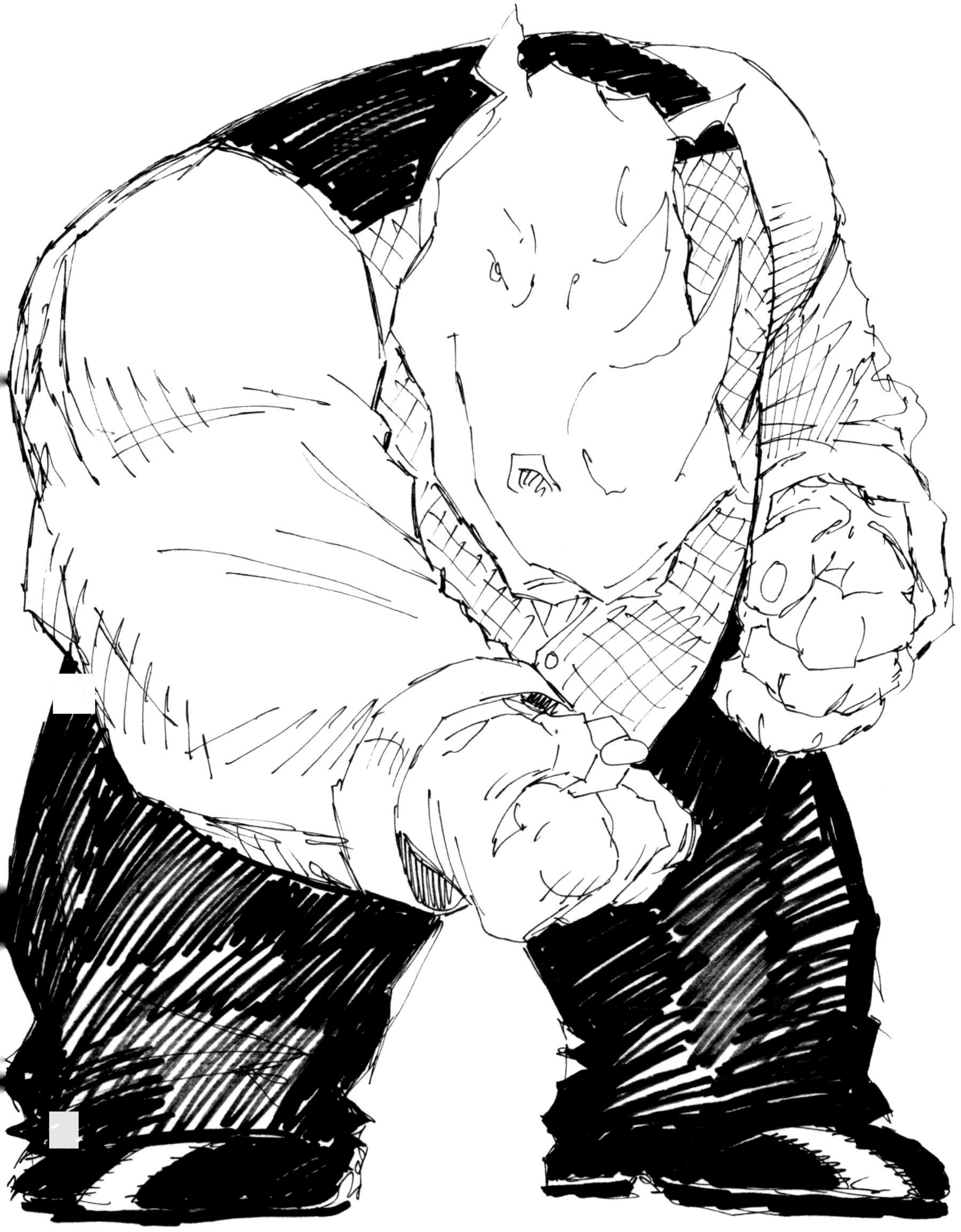

THE HORNS OF A DILEMMA!

MORITAT was exhausted... at the end of issue #13 he decided to take a much deserved break from ELEPHANTMEN... right in the middle of our three part finale... but who could possibly jump into the story and maintain the integrity of the characters and meet the high standard Moritat had established? Who already knew the series like the back of his hand and would have fun drawing not only Hip and Horn, but also Sahara, Vanity, Ebony, Miki, Tusk, Trench and Serengheti? As soon as these questions ran through my mind I instantly knew it could only be IAN CHURCHILL!

PIGS IN SPACE!

MORITAT had made a start on #14, but Ian wanted to take a crack at the script from page 1, which included designing the Warthogs' space cruiser, below right.

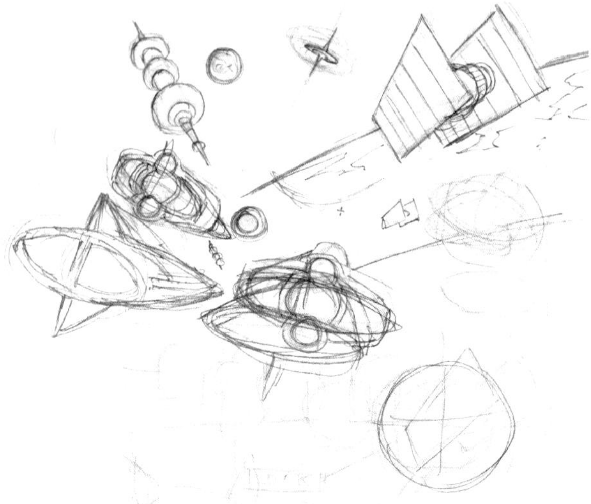

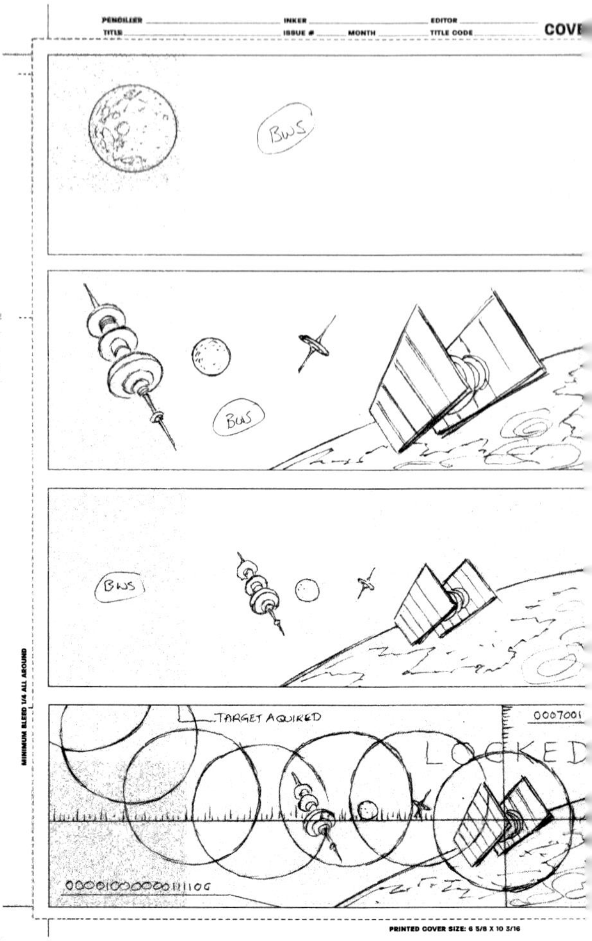

PENCILLER
INKER
EDITOR
TITLE
ISSUE #
MONTH
TITLE CODE
COVE
BWS
BWS
BWS
TARGET AQUIRED
0007001
LOCKED
MINIMUM BLEED 1/4 ALL AROUND
PRINTED COVER SIZE: 6 5/8 X 10 3/16

The pages you see opposite were lightly pencilled on sheets of A4 (8.5 x 11") before being scanned and sent to Boo Cook for digital inks.

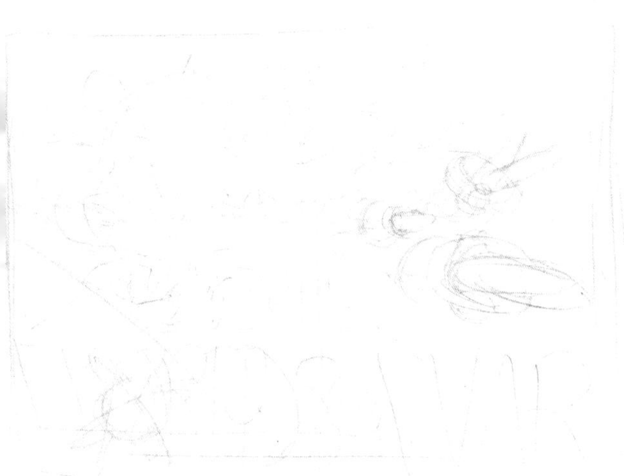

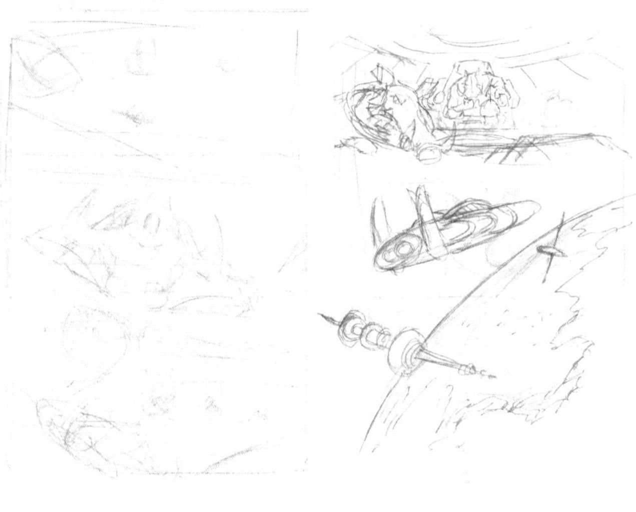

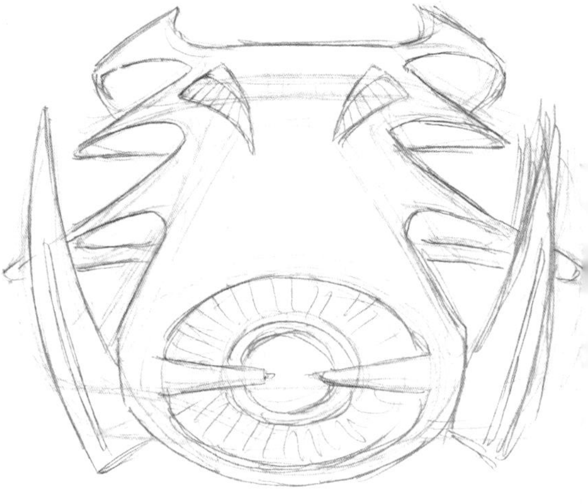

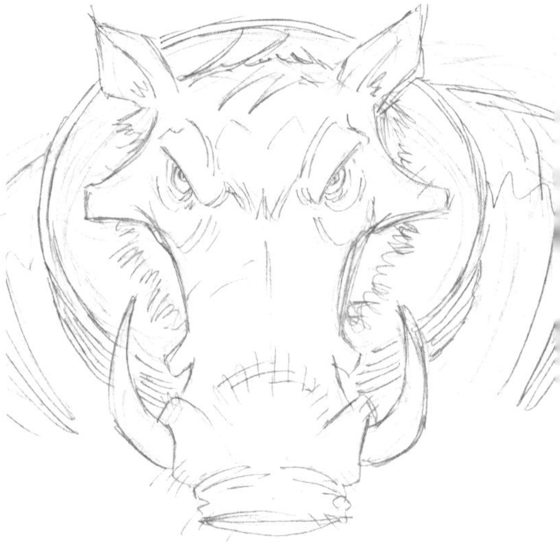

PENCILLER INKER EDITOR
TITLE ISSUE # MONTH TITLE CODE COVER

PENCILLER INKER EDITOR
TITLE ISSUE # MONTH TITLE CODE COVER

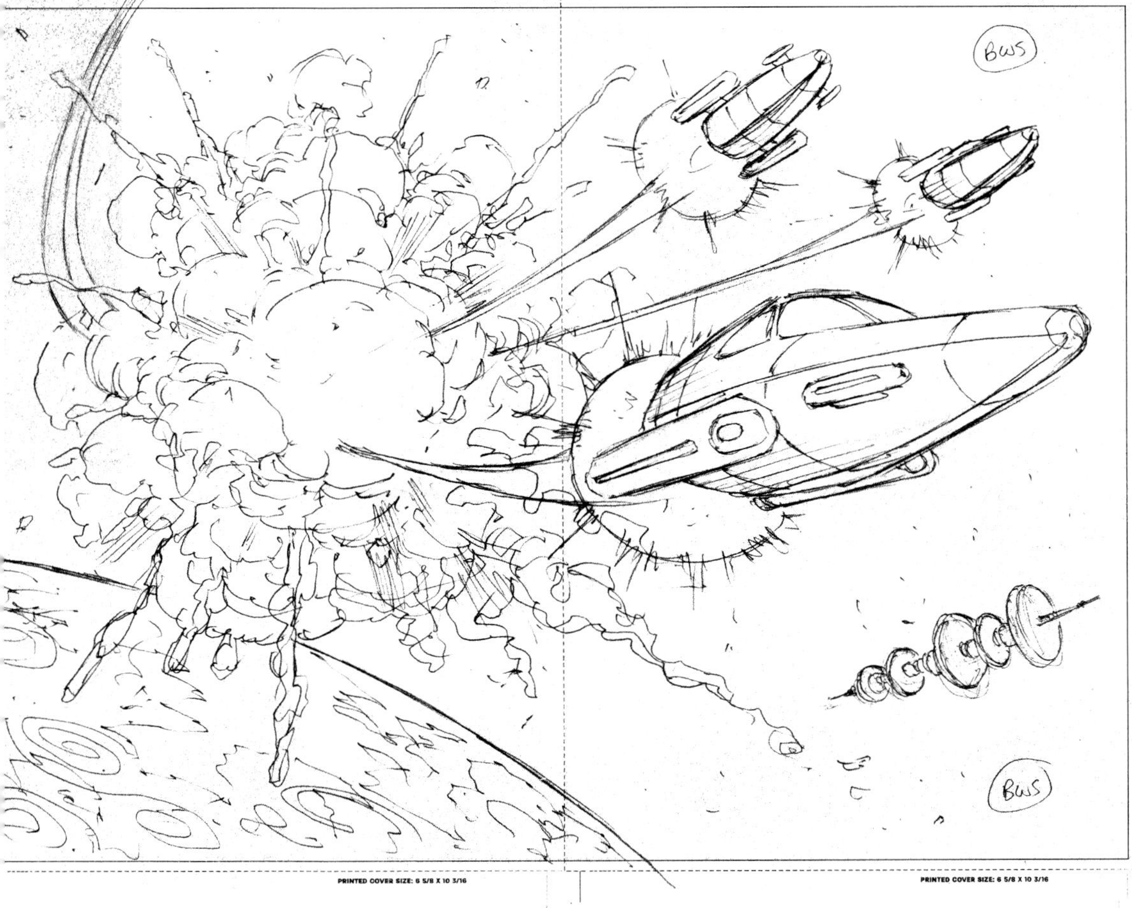
BWS
BWS

LOGO AREA

PRINTED COVER SIZE: 6 5/8 X 10 3/16

PRINTED COVER SIZE: 6 5/8 X 10 3/16

PENCILLER INKER EDITOR
TITLE ISSUE # MONTH TITLE CODE COVER

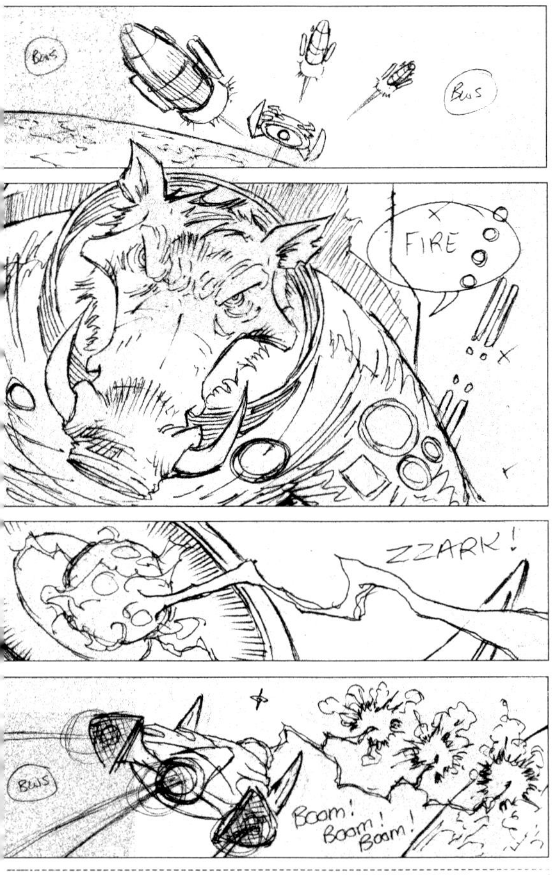
BWS
BWS
FIRE
ZZARK!
BWS
Boom!
Boom!
Boom!

LOGO AREA

PRINTED COVER SIZE: 6 5/8 X 10 3/16

PENCILLER INKER EDITOR
TITLE ISSUE # MONTH TITLE CODE COVER

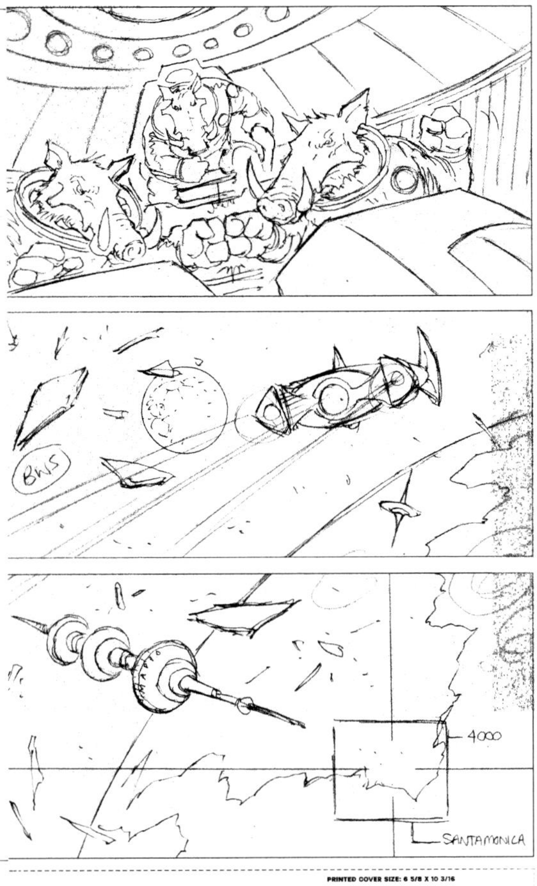
BWS
4000
SANTAMONICA

LOGO AREA

PRINTED COVER SIZE: 6 5/8 X 10 3/16

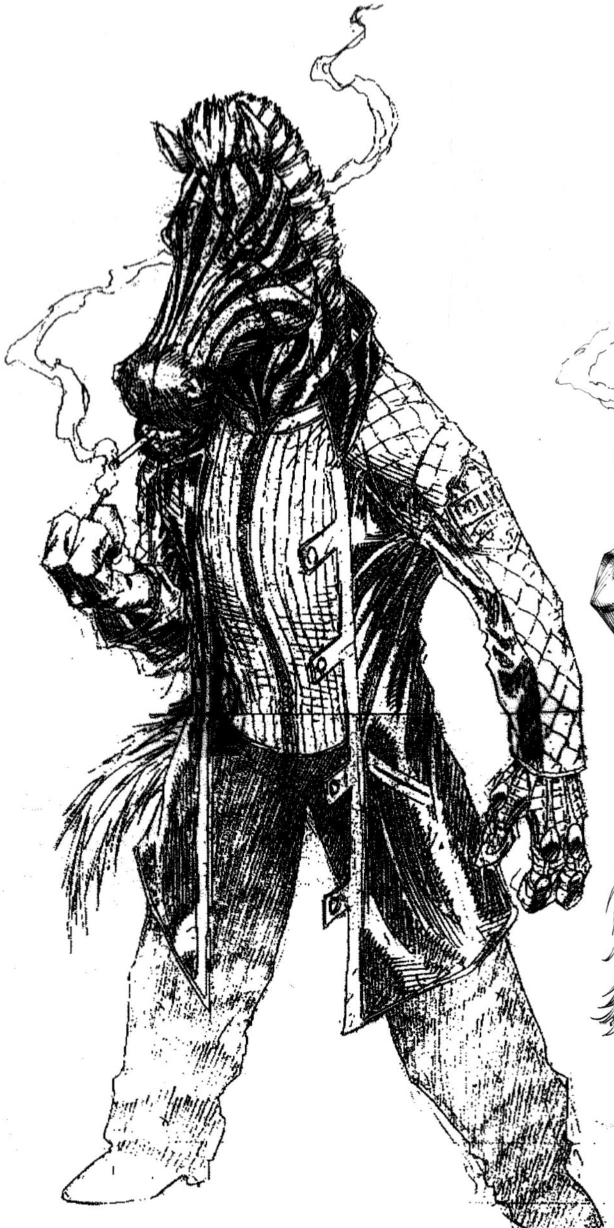

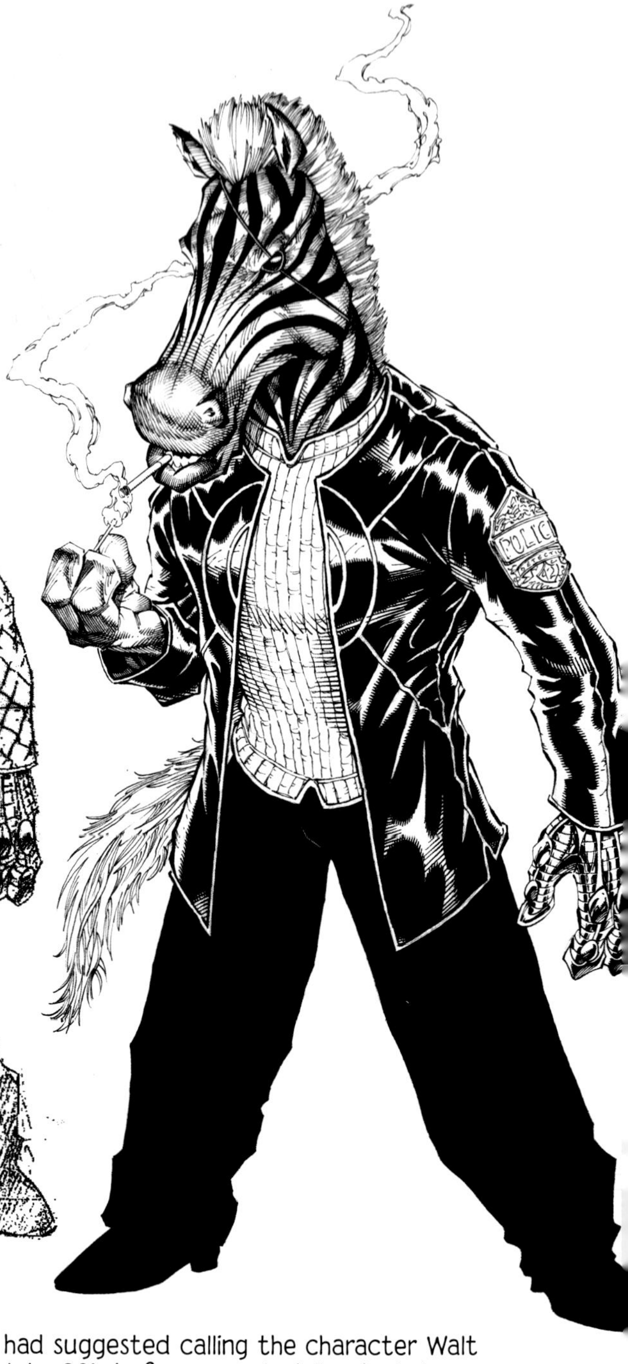

TRENCH

Ian had helped design Lieutenant Trench (he had suggested calling the character Walt Zebraski, but I quickly shot it down!) in the late 90's before even Ladrönn had drawn him, so it was fun to see Ian draw Trench's appearance in the WORLDS COLLIDE arc.

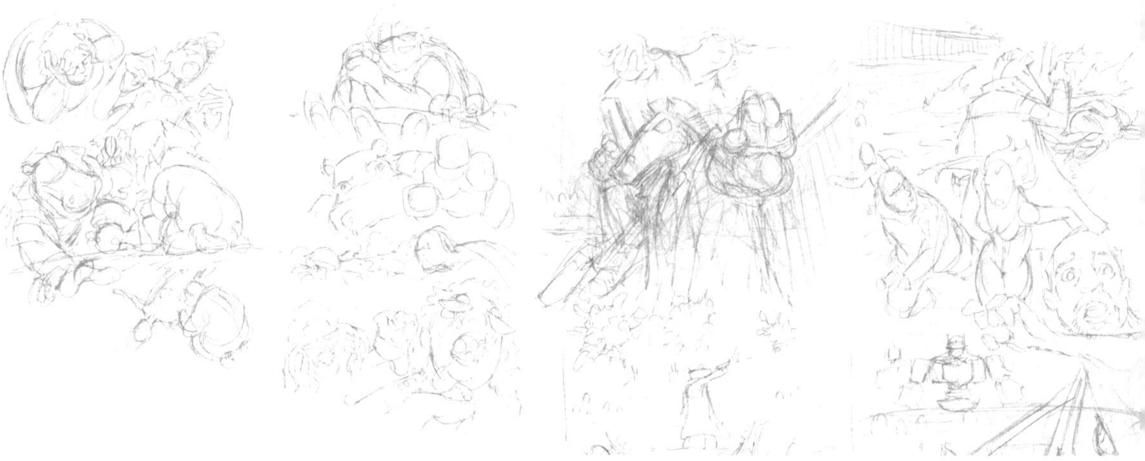

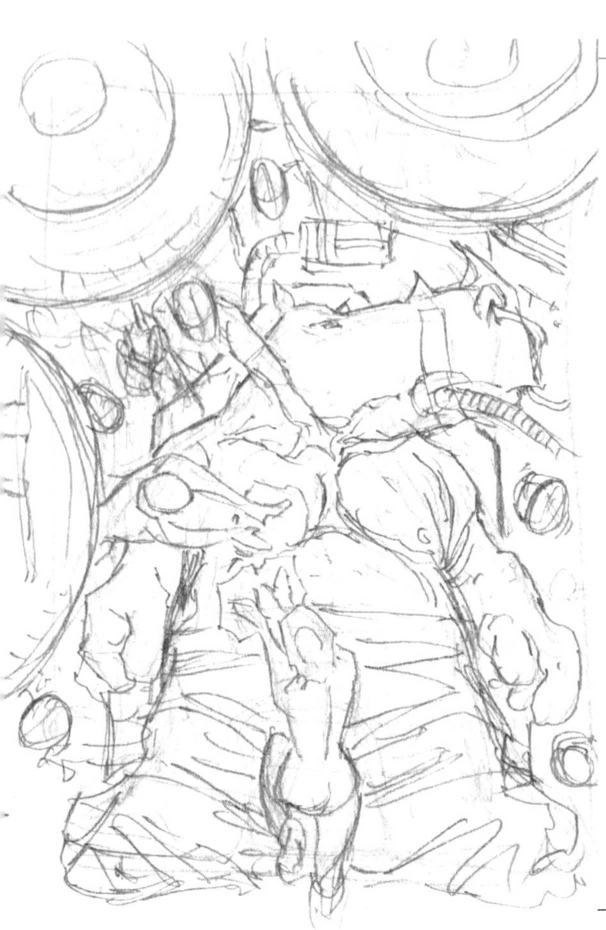

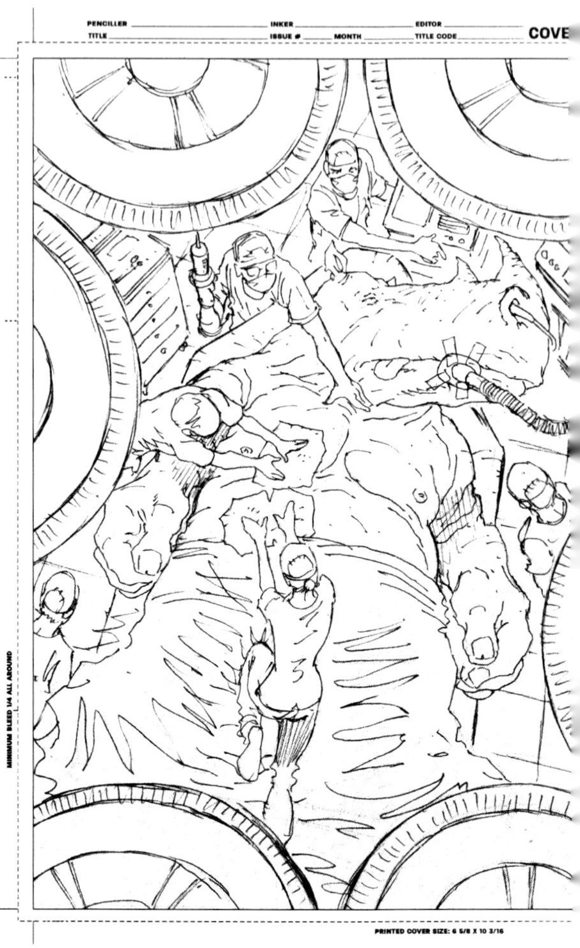
PENCILLER
INKER
EDITOR
TITLE
ISSUE #
MONTH
TITLE CODE
COVE
MINIMUM BLEED 1/4 ALL AROUND
PRINTED COVER SIZE: 6 5/8 X 10 3/16

INTENSIVE CARE

Initially, I had asked Ian to draw thumbnails from which Boo could create finished art...

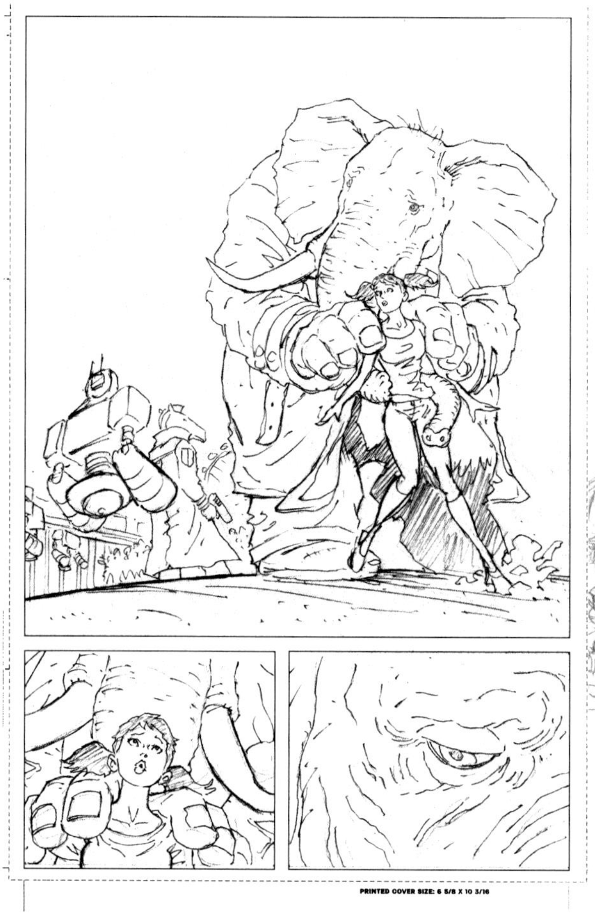
PRINTED COVER SIZE: 6 5/8 X 10 3/16

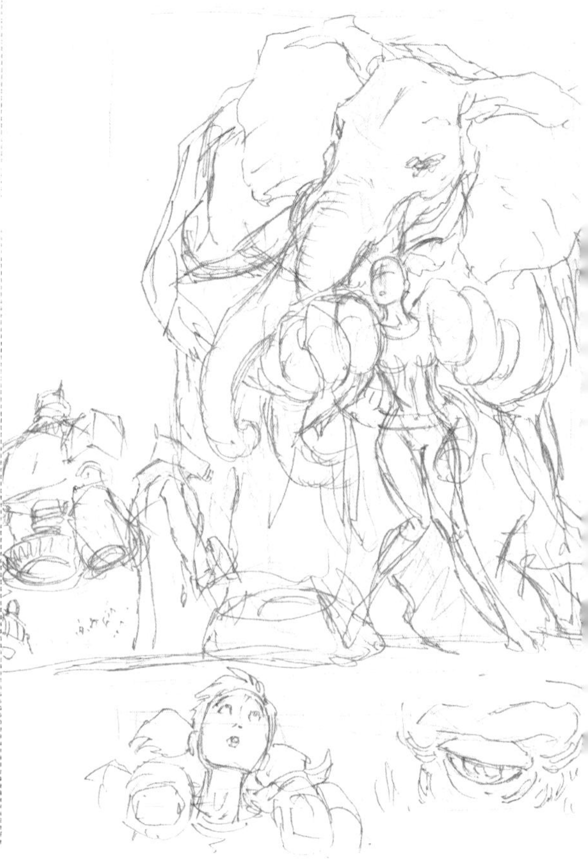

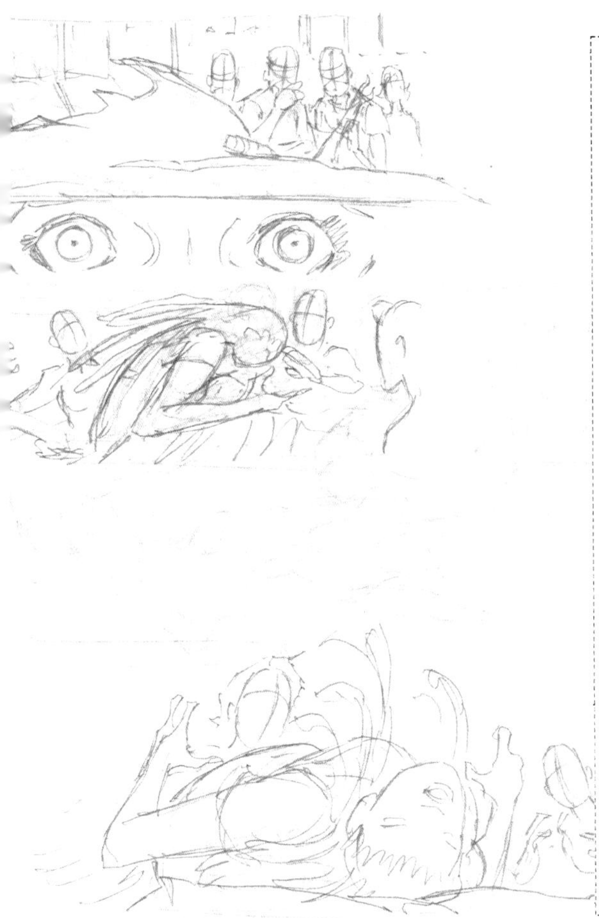

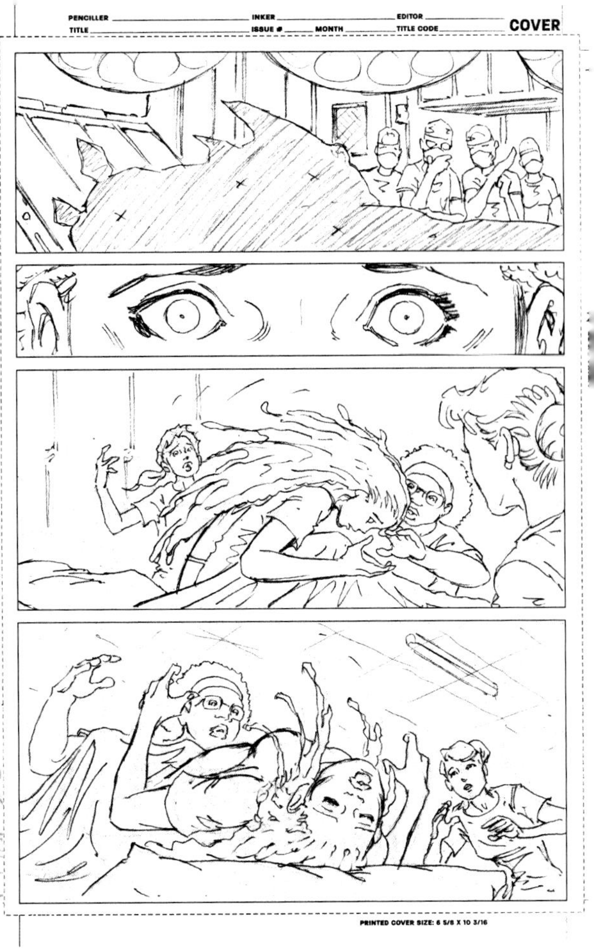

PENCILLER INKER EDITOR
TITLE ISSUE # MONTH TITLE CODE
COVER
PRINTED COVER SIZE: 6 5/8 X 10 3/16

Imagine my surprise when, after completing the issue, Ian sent me the lovely blue pencil sketches that preceded his “thumbnails.” What a professional!

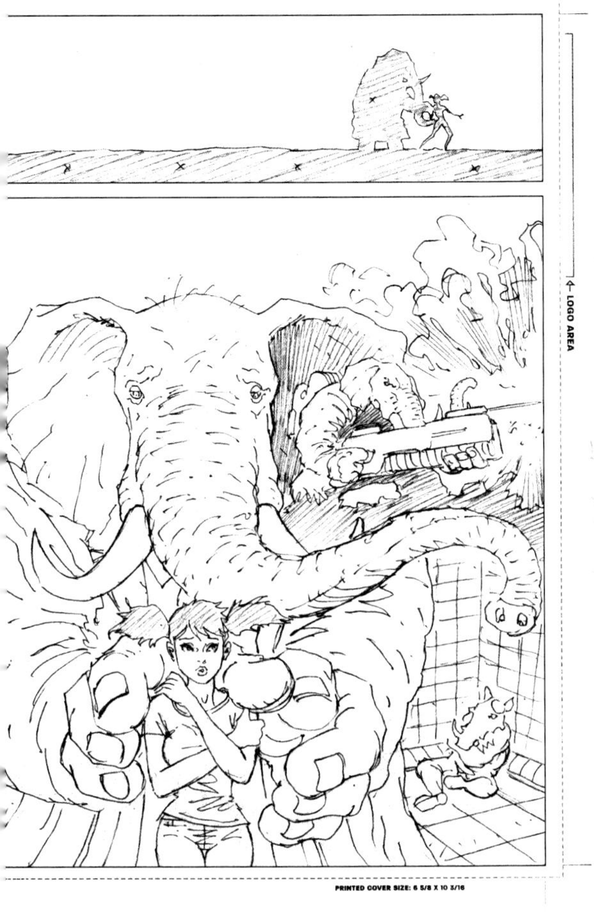

LOGO AREA
PRINTED COVER SIZE: 6 5/8 X 10 3/16

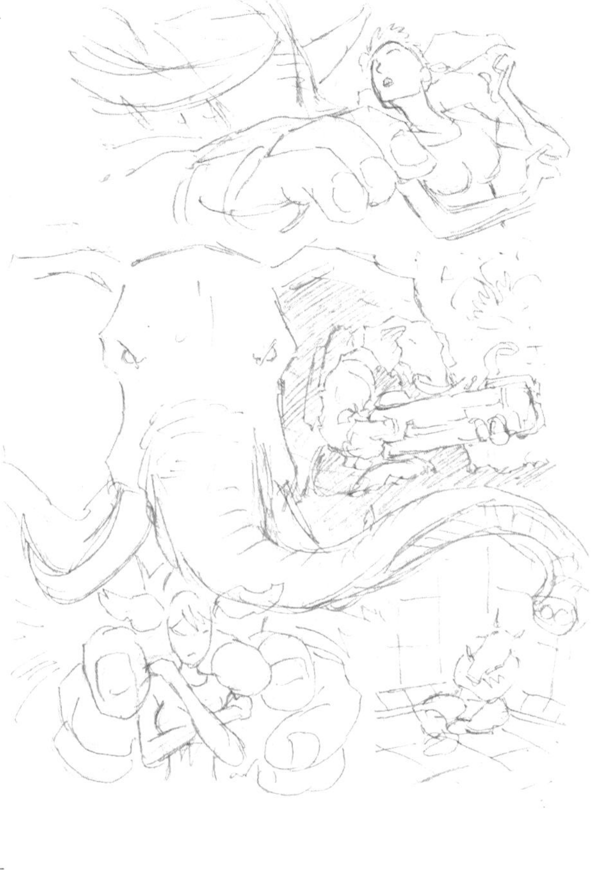

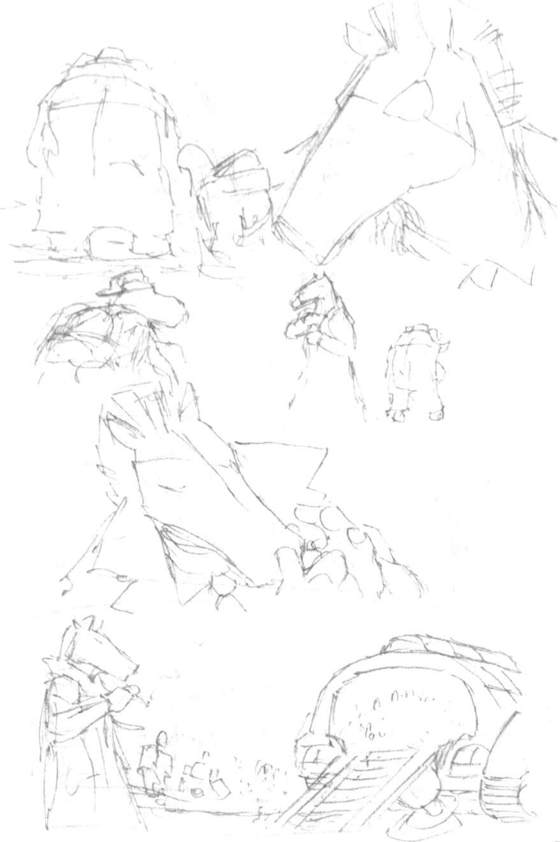

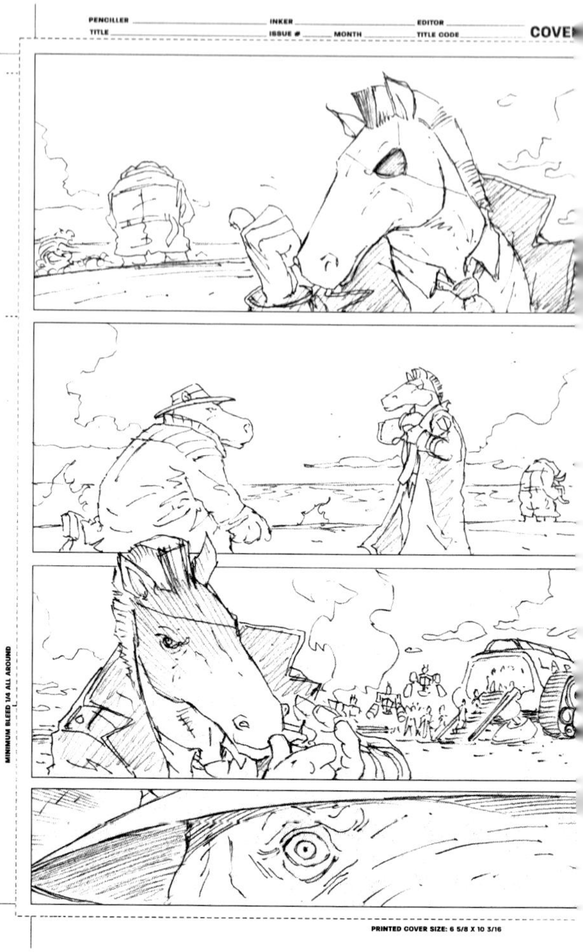
PENCILLER
INKER
EDITOR
TITLE
ISSUE #
MONTH
TITLE CODE
COVE
MINIMUM BLEED 1/4 ALL AROUND
PRINTED COVER SIZE: 6 5/8 X 10 3/16

BEACH BUM

"Don't worry," I'd said... "there'll be no backgrounds -- it's all on the beach!" But, c'mon, if IAN CHURCHILL is drawing your book...

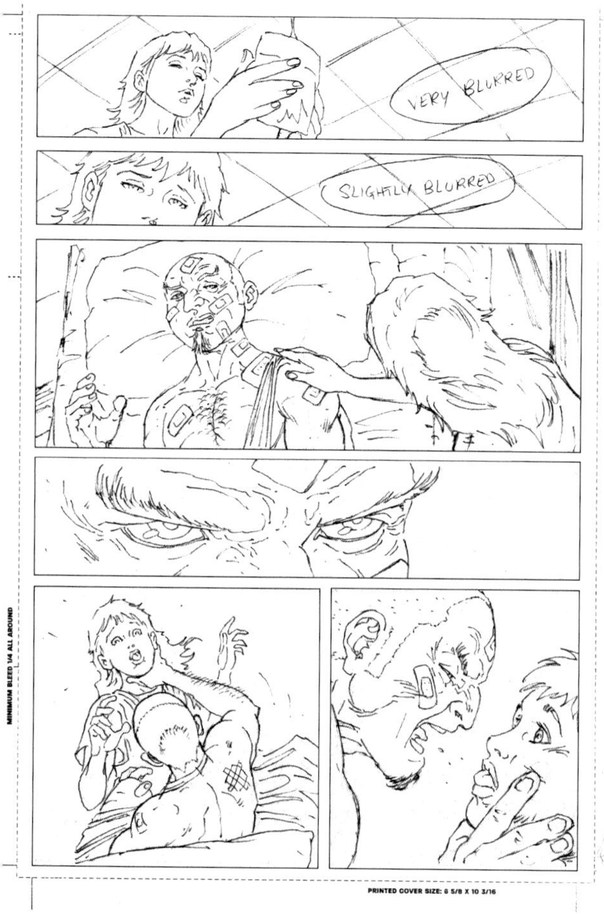
VERY BLURRED
SLIGHTLY BLURRED
MINIMUM BLEED 1/4 ALL AROUND
PRINTED COVER SIZE: 6 5/8 X 10 3/16

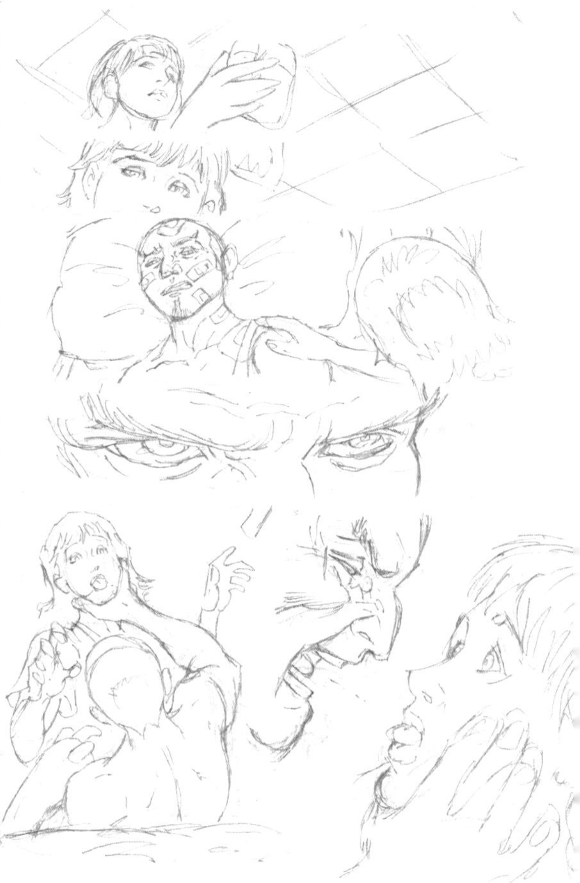

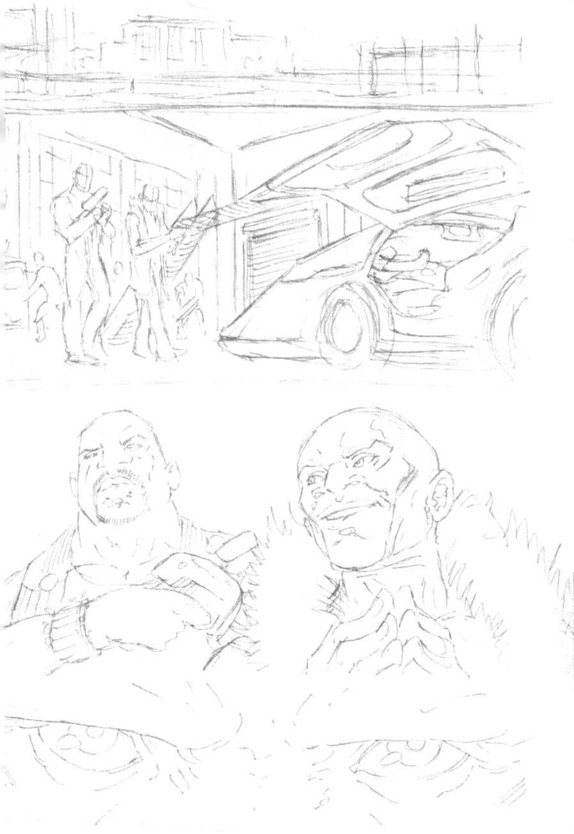

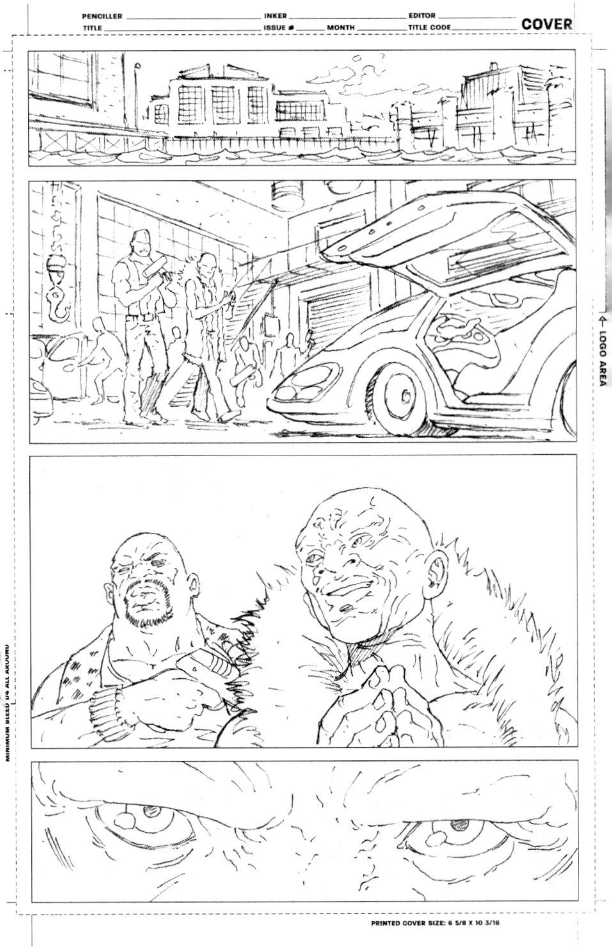
PENCILLER
INKER
EDITOR
COVER
TITLE
ISSUE #
MONTH
TITLE CODE
LOGO AREA
MINIMUM BLEED 1/4 ALL AROUND
PRINTED COVER SIZE: 6 5/8 X 10 3/16

Ian later wrote... "I'll tell you what, the NEXT time you tell me 'no backgrounds, it's all on the beach, mate...' I shan't believe you for an instant!" Tee Hee.

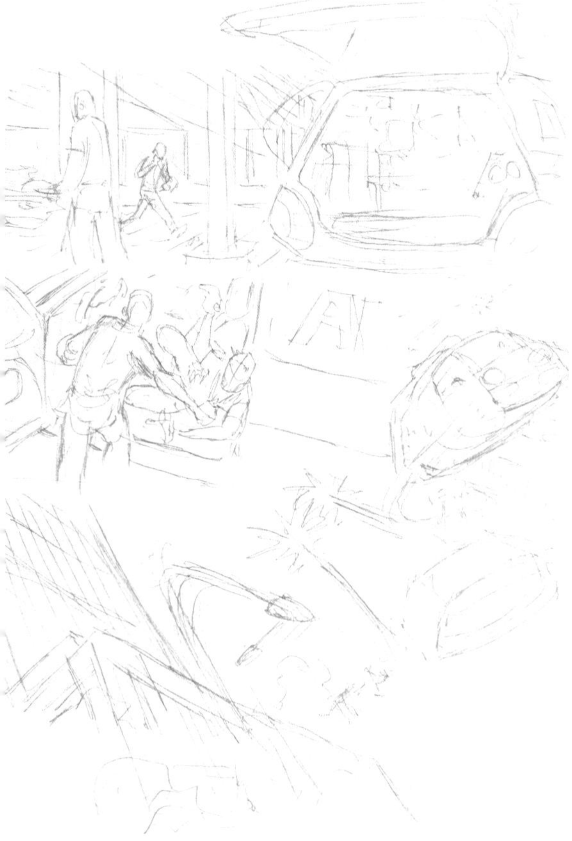

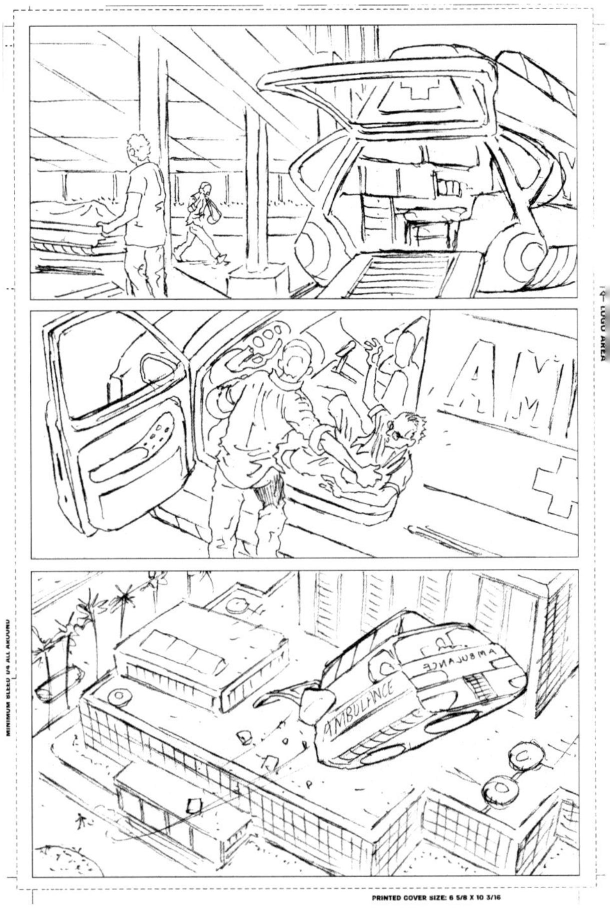
LOGO AREA
MINIMUM BLEED 1/4 ALL AROUND
AMBULANCE
PRINTED COVER SIZE: 6 5/8 X 10 3/16

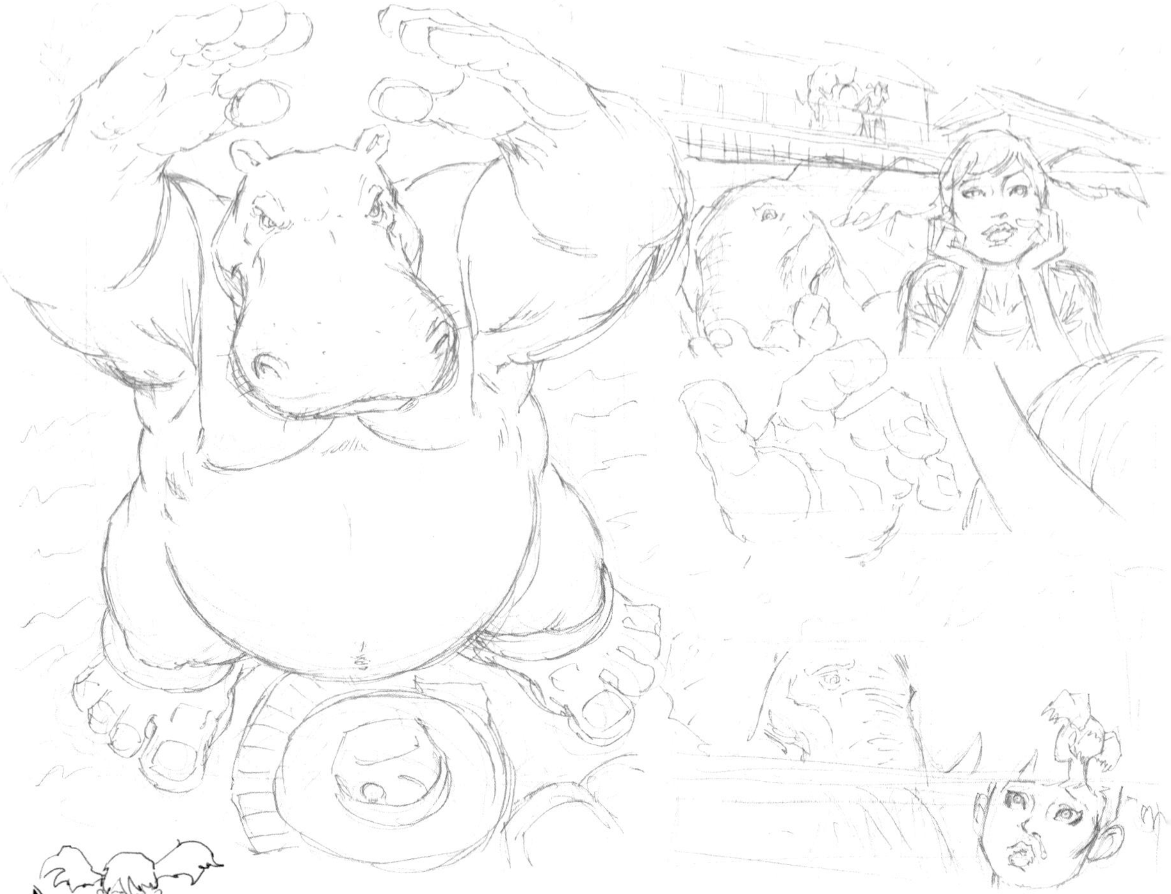

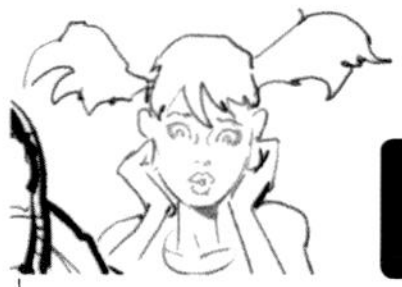

OH, MIKI!

Ian really took a liking to Miki, and Ebony Hide... he even proposed a series with just the two of them!

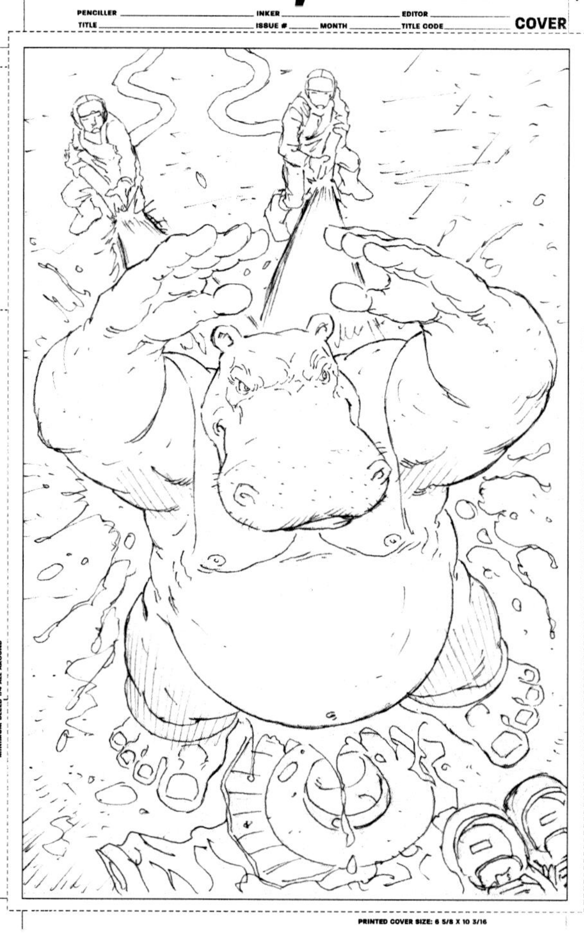
PENCILLER
INKER
EDITOR
TITLE
ISSUE #
MONTH
TITLE CODE
COVER
MINIMUM BLEED 1/4 ALL AROUND
PRINTED COVER SIZE: 6 5/8 X 10 3/16

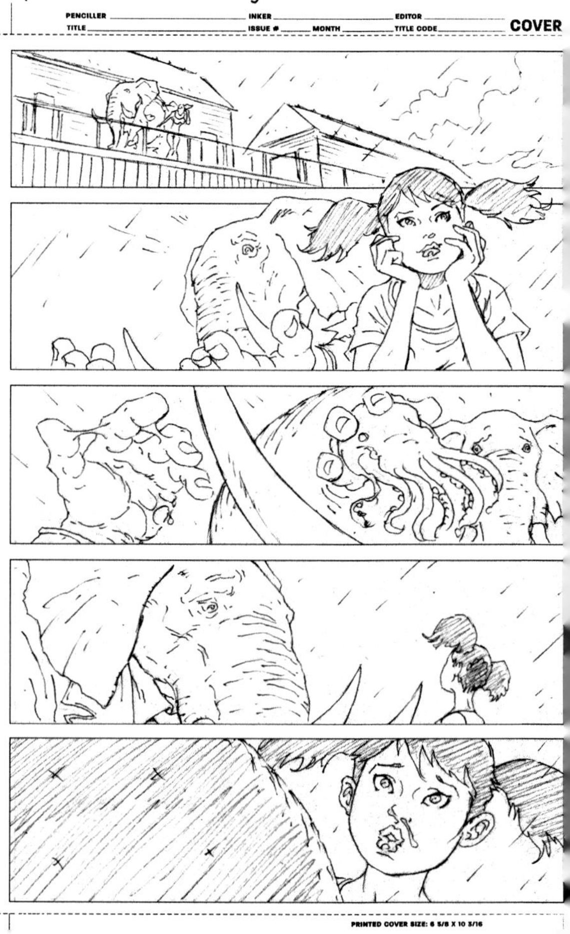
PENCILLER
INKER
EDITOR
TITLE
ISSUE #
MONTH
TITLE CODE
COVER
PRINTED COVER SIZE: 6 5/8 X 10 3/16

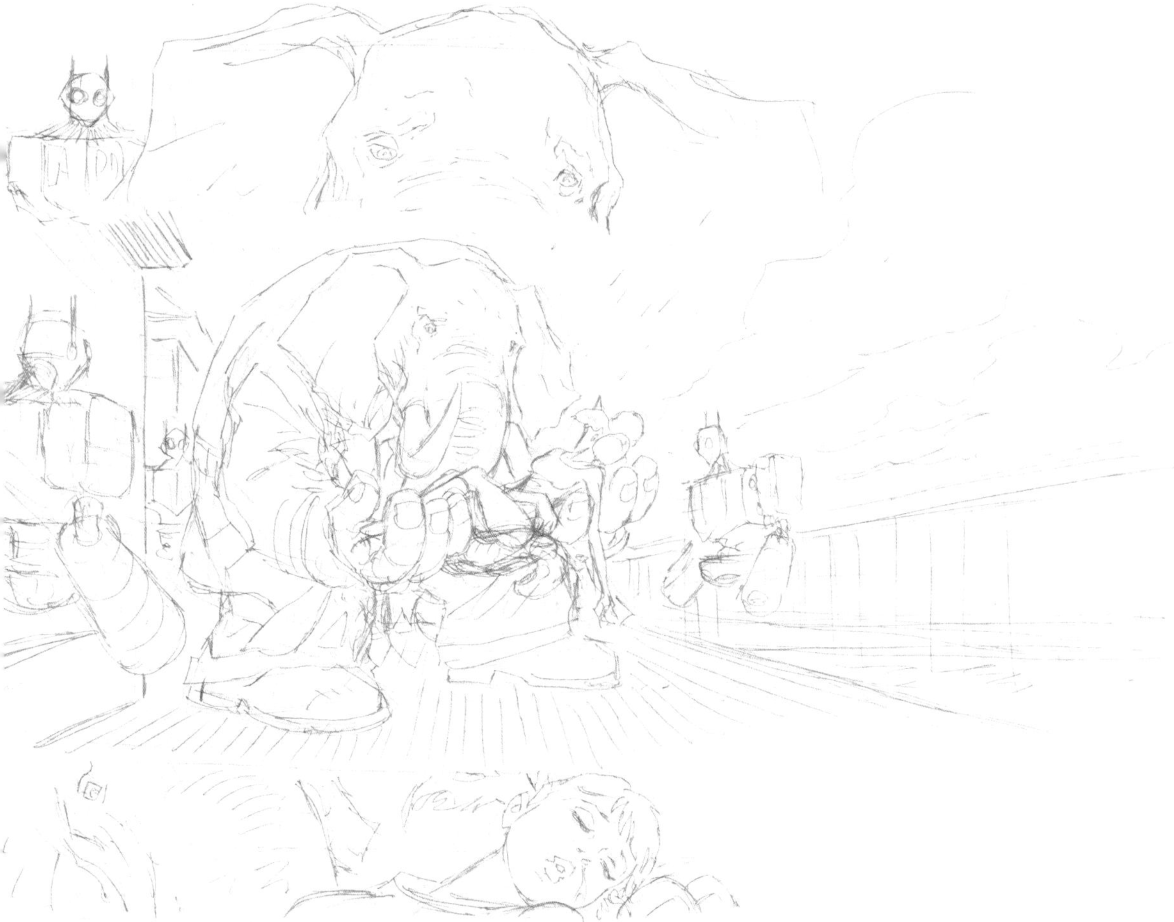
LA PD

Ian's been busy on his Eisner nominated, all ages Image series MARINEMAN, but perhaps one day...

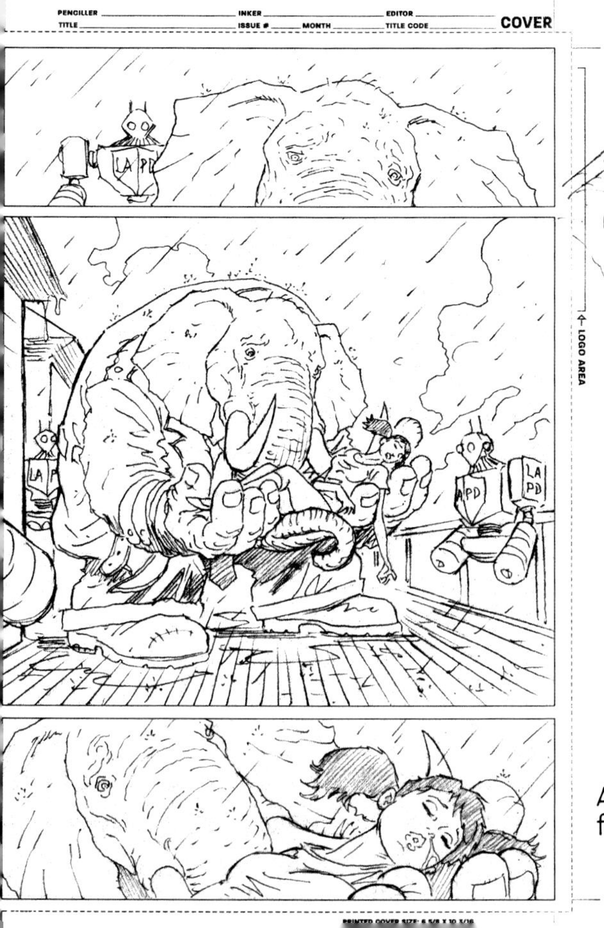
PENCILLER
INKER
EDITOR
TITLE
ISSUE #
MONTH
TITLE CODE
COVER
LA PD
LA PD
APD
LA PD
LOGO AREA

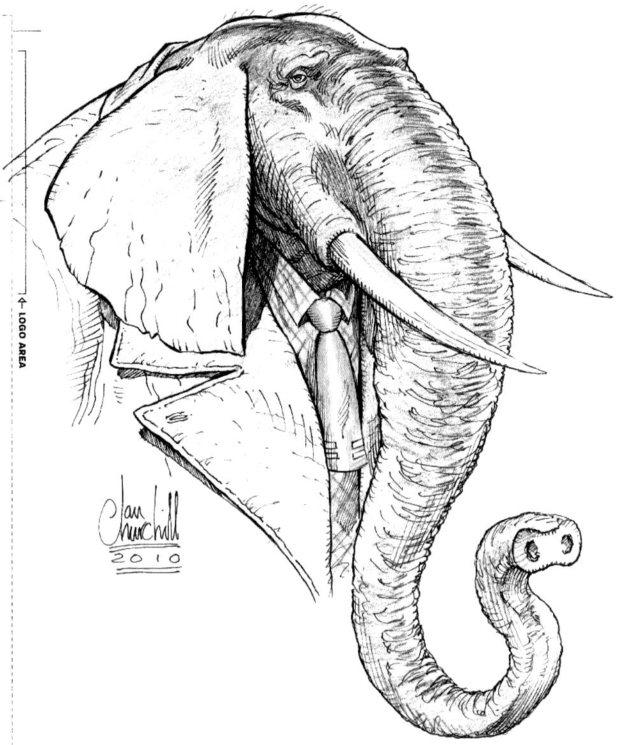
2010

Above: A drawing of Ebony Ian created for a fan at a comic convention.

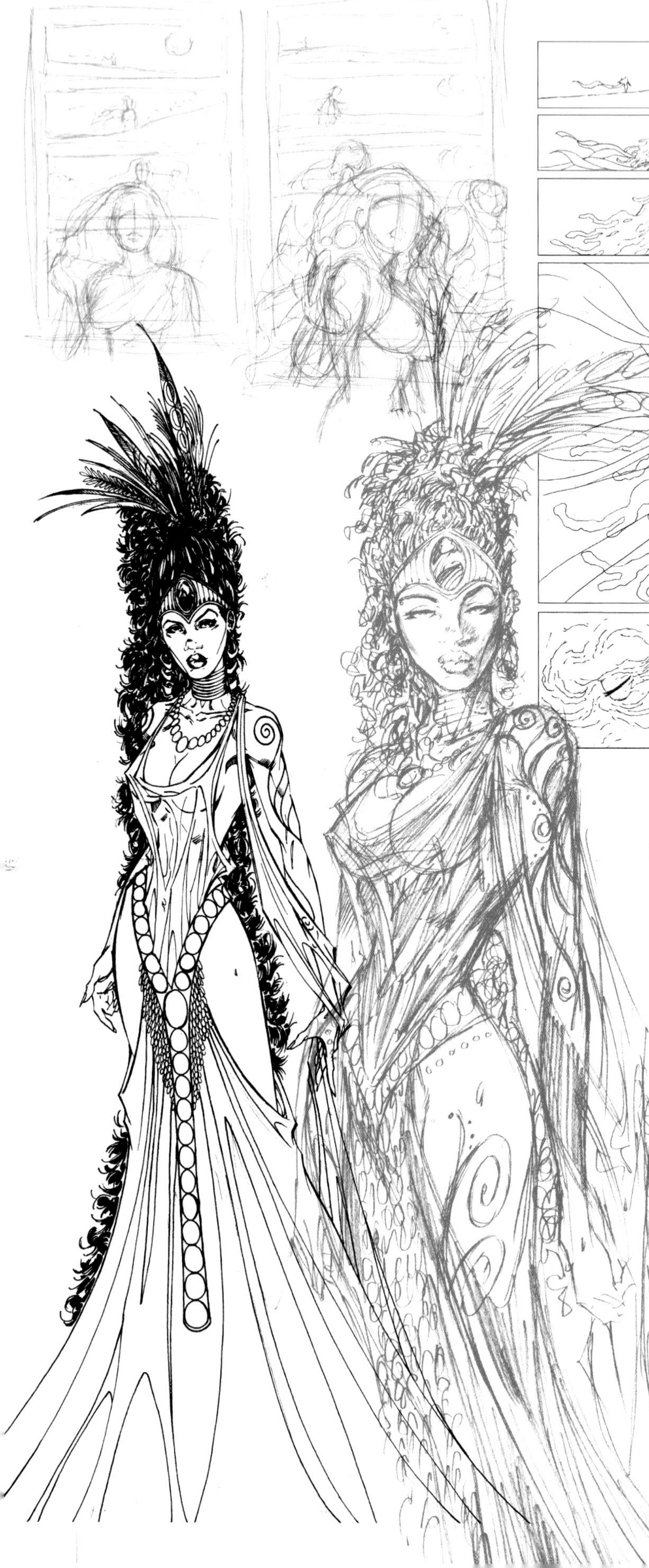

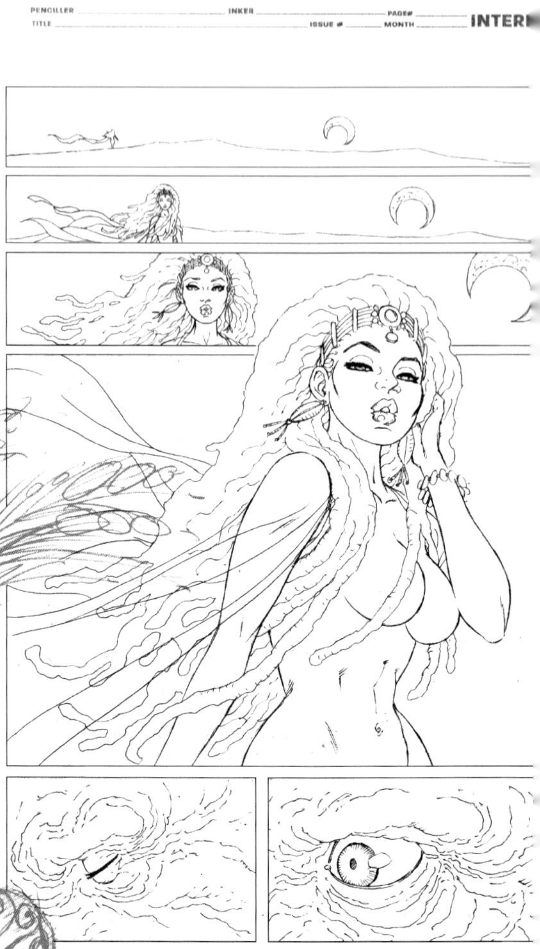
PENCILLER
INKER
PAGE#
TITLE
ISSUE #
MONTH

SAHARA

Ian was sitting in my Santa Monica office when I first came up with the idea of a consort for Horn by the name of Sahara.. He created the sketches you see on the left here in just a couple of hours, so, once again, it was nice to give him the opportunity to draw her properly in ELEPHANTMEN

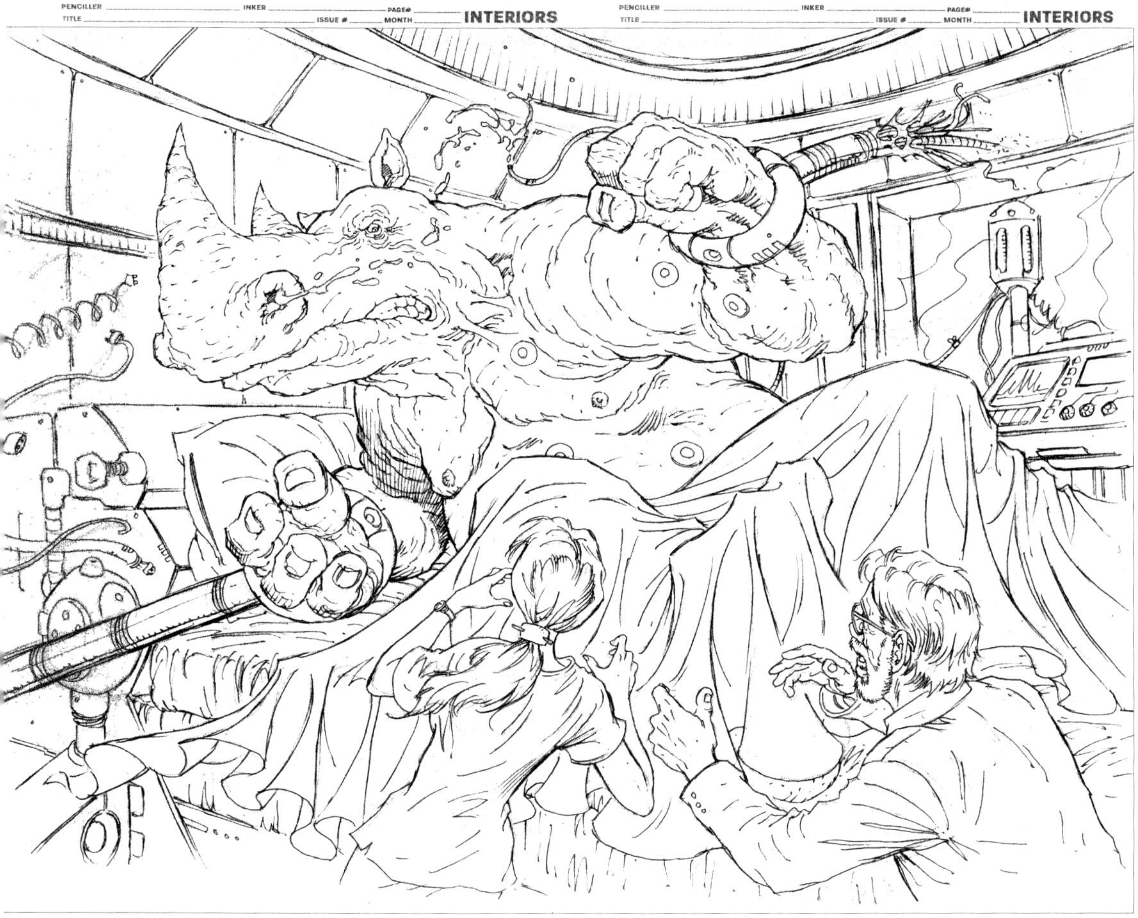
PENCILLER
INKER
PAGE#
TITLE
ISSUE #
MONTH
INTERIORS
PENCILLER
INKER
PAGE#
TITLE
ISSUE #
MONTH
INTERIORS

AND HORN

Horn first appeared in HIP FLASK #1/2, which we reprinted in this collection as part of our PILOT issue (see my notes some pages back!) When Ladrönn first drew the character, he struggled with the head-to-body proportions for some time before admitting to me that Ian had got them exactly right.

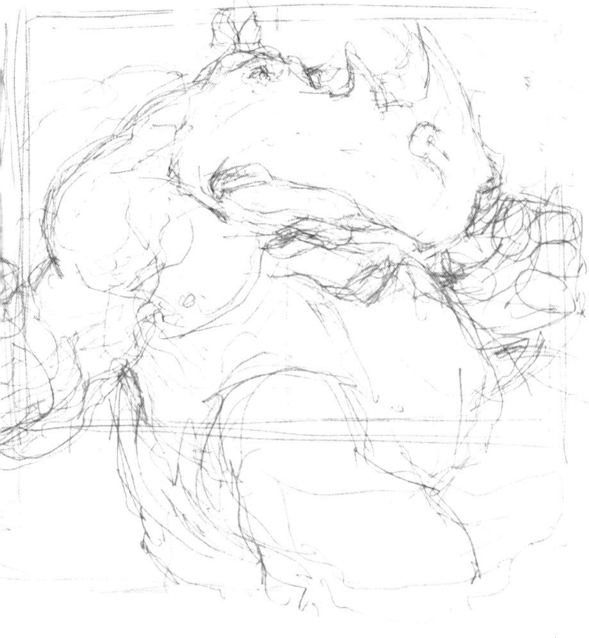

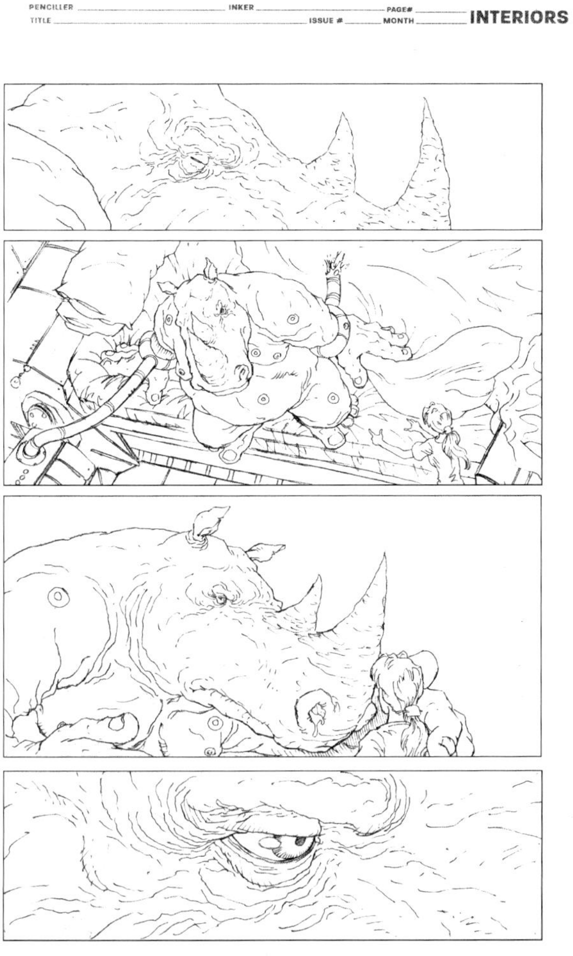
PENCILLER
INKER
PAGE#
TITLE
ISSUE #
MONTH
INTERIORS

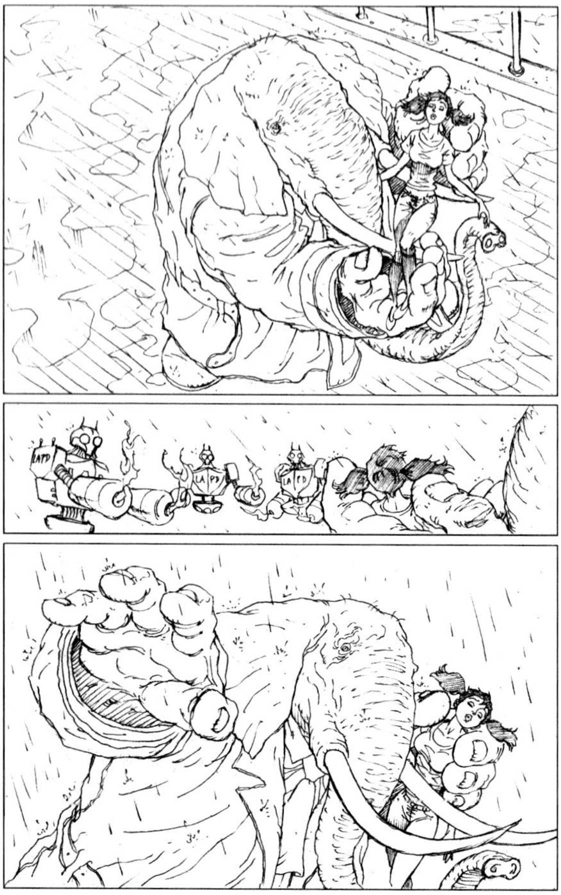

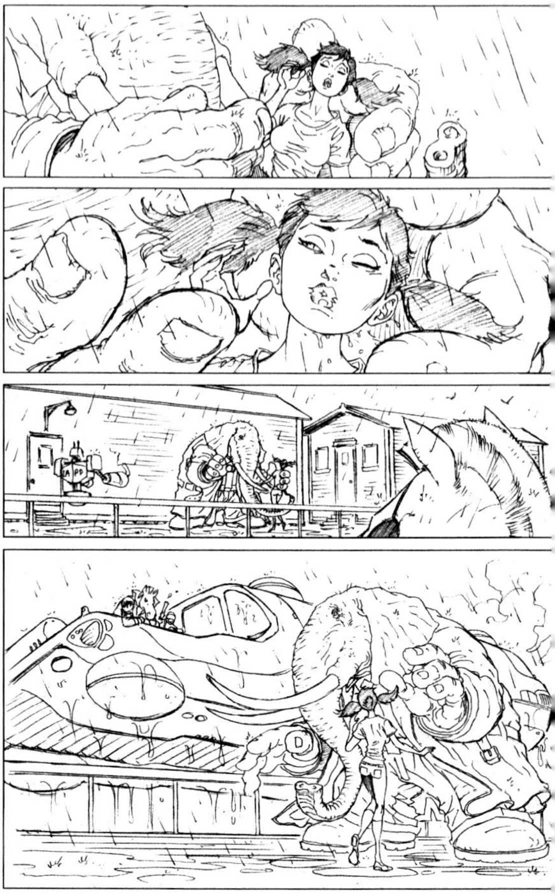

VANITY

THEN & NOW: Ian created the pages that follow for a mini series that never was. I never liked the costume he originally gave her... sorry, mate!

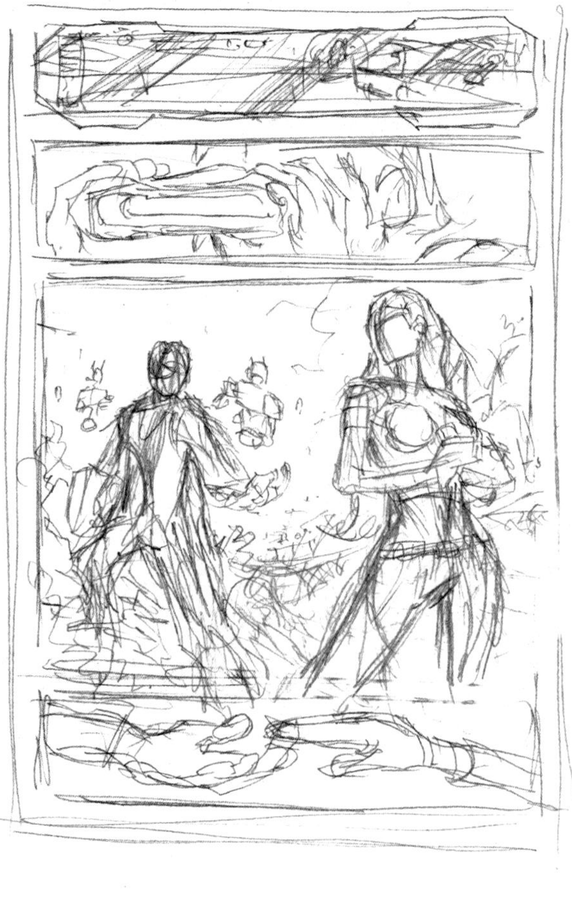

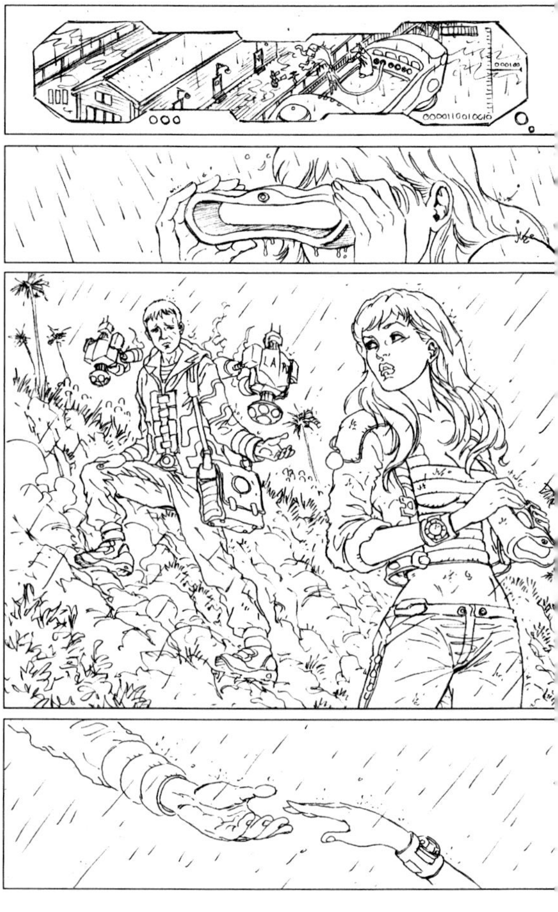

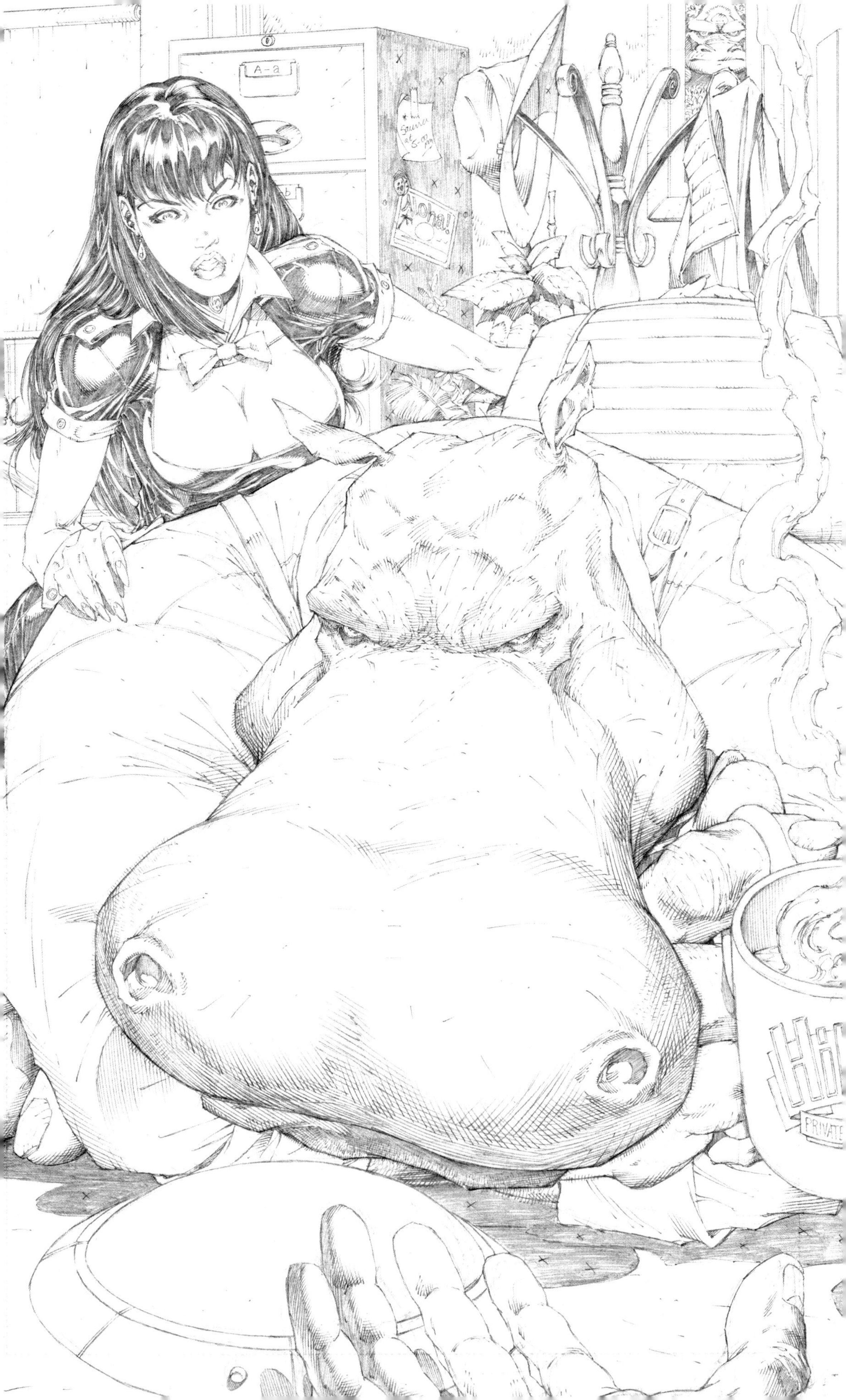
A-a
Aloha!
PRIVATE

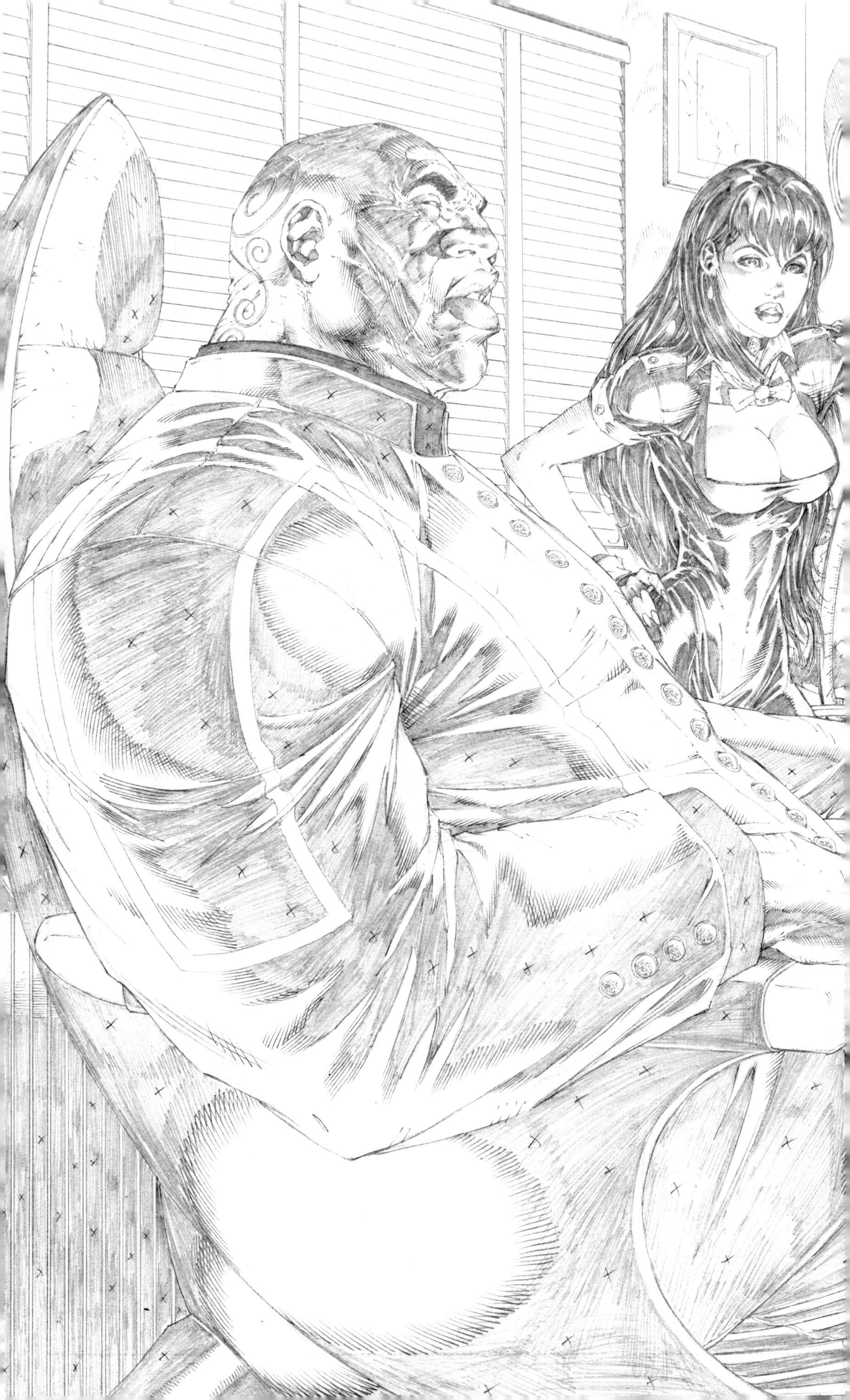

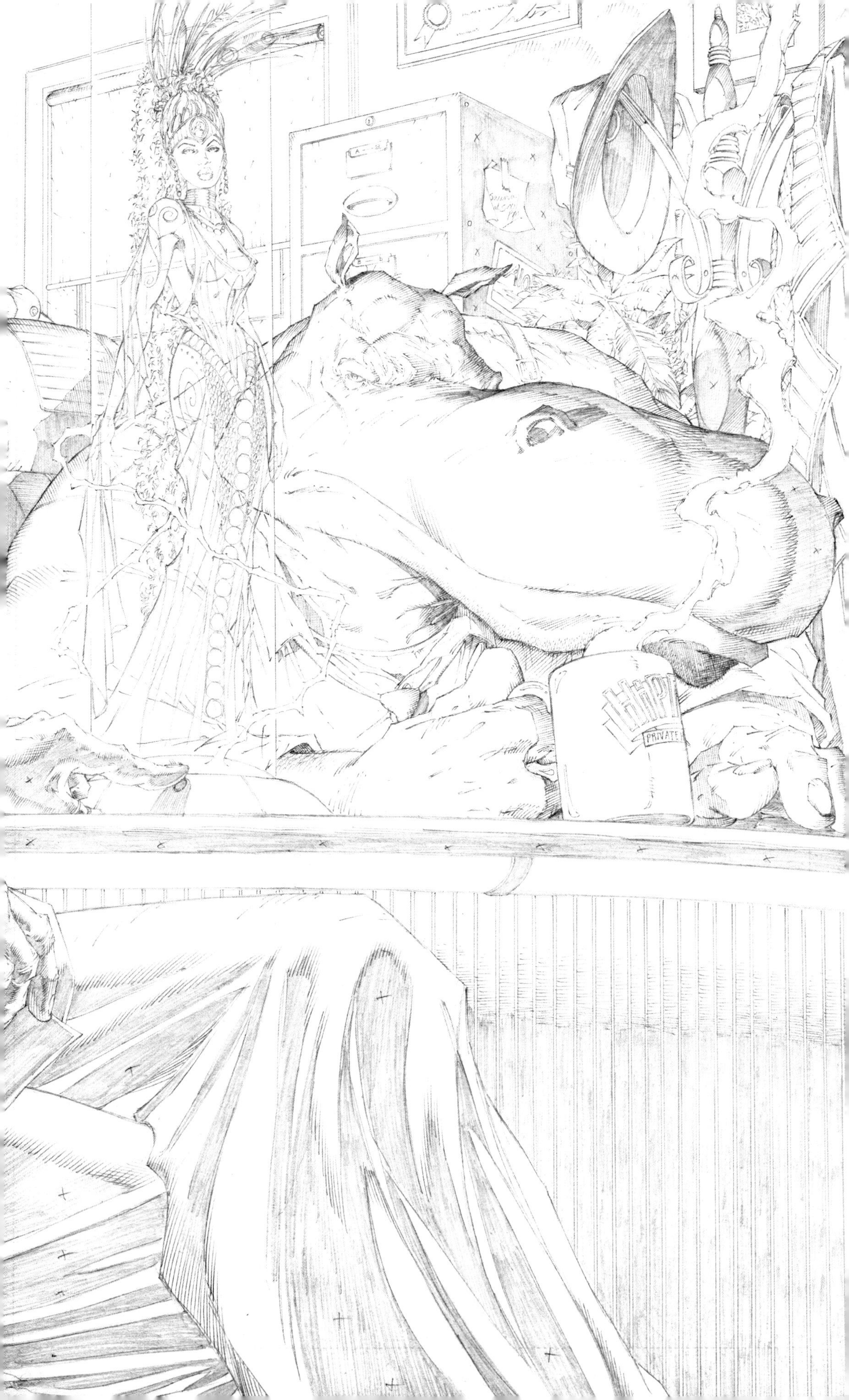
PRIVATE

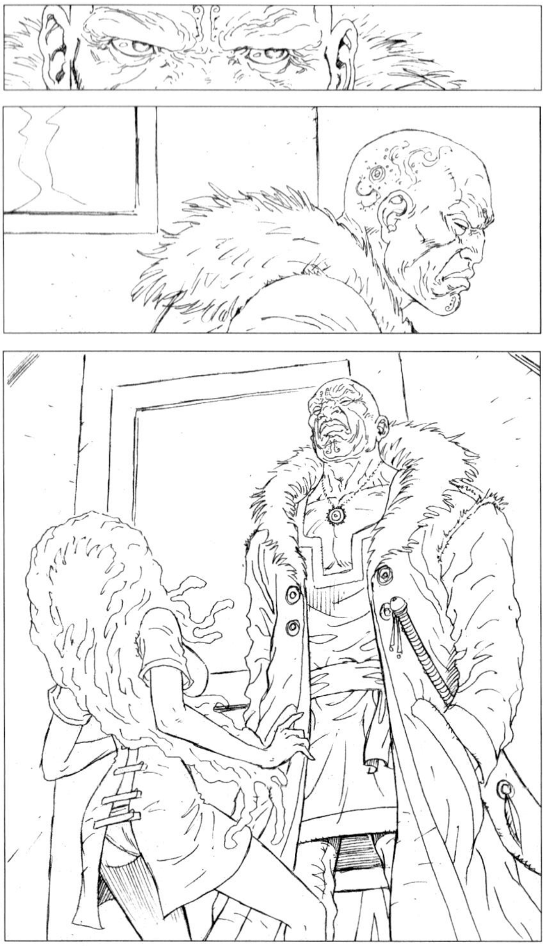

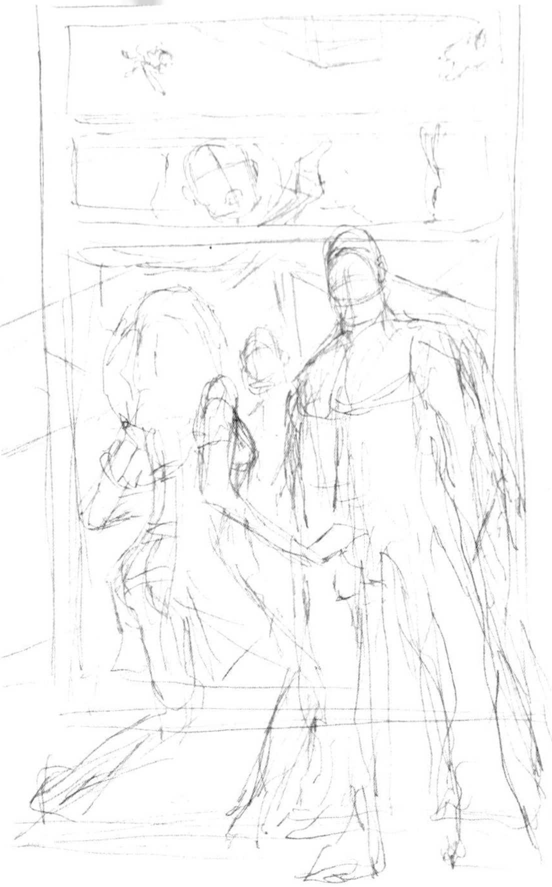

SERENGHETI

However, Ian pretty much nailed my concept for Sahara's father (previous spread), and only his clothing changed over time.

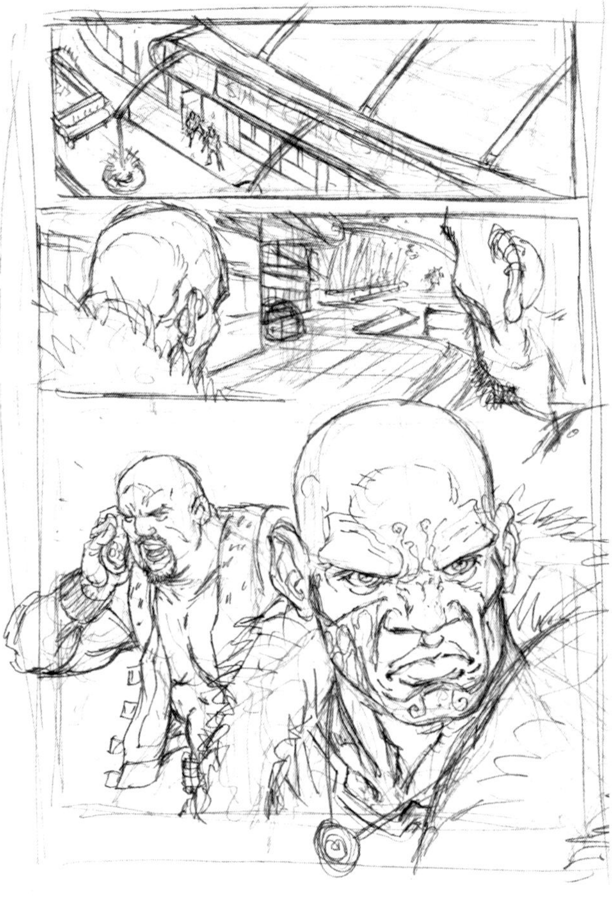

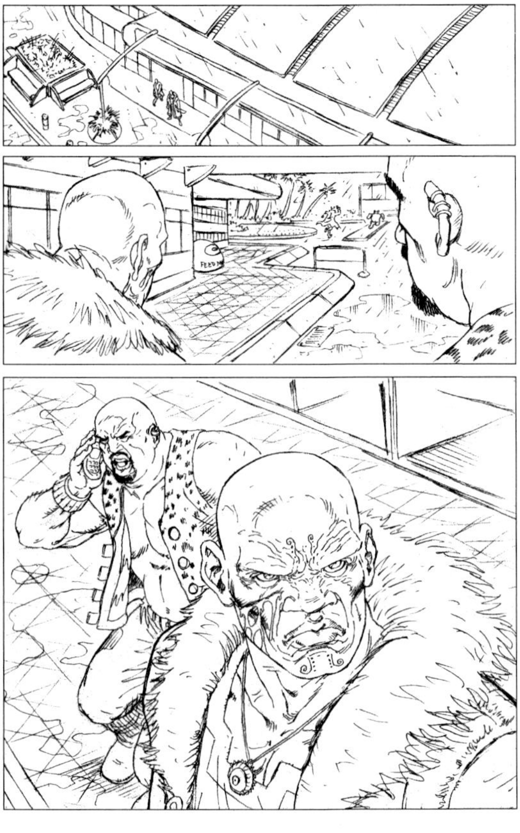

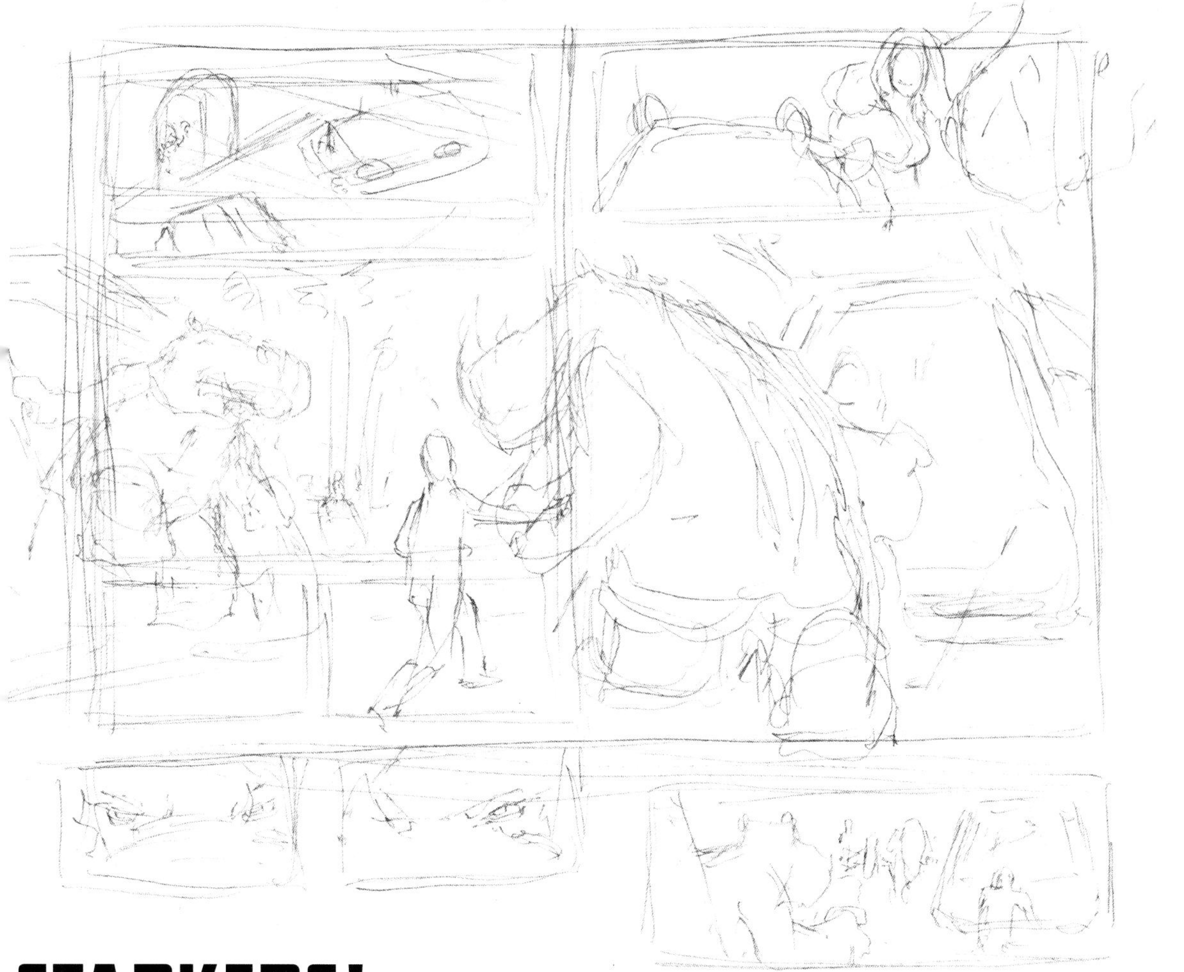

STARKERS!

Meteors, Octopii, Flying Cars, Robocops and Robbers and all the lead characters naked! Is there nothing Ian can't draw?

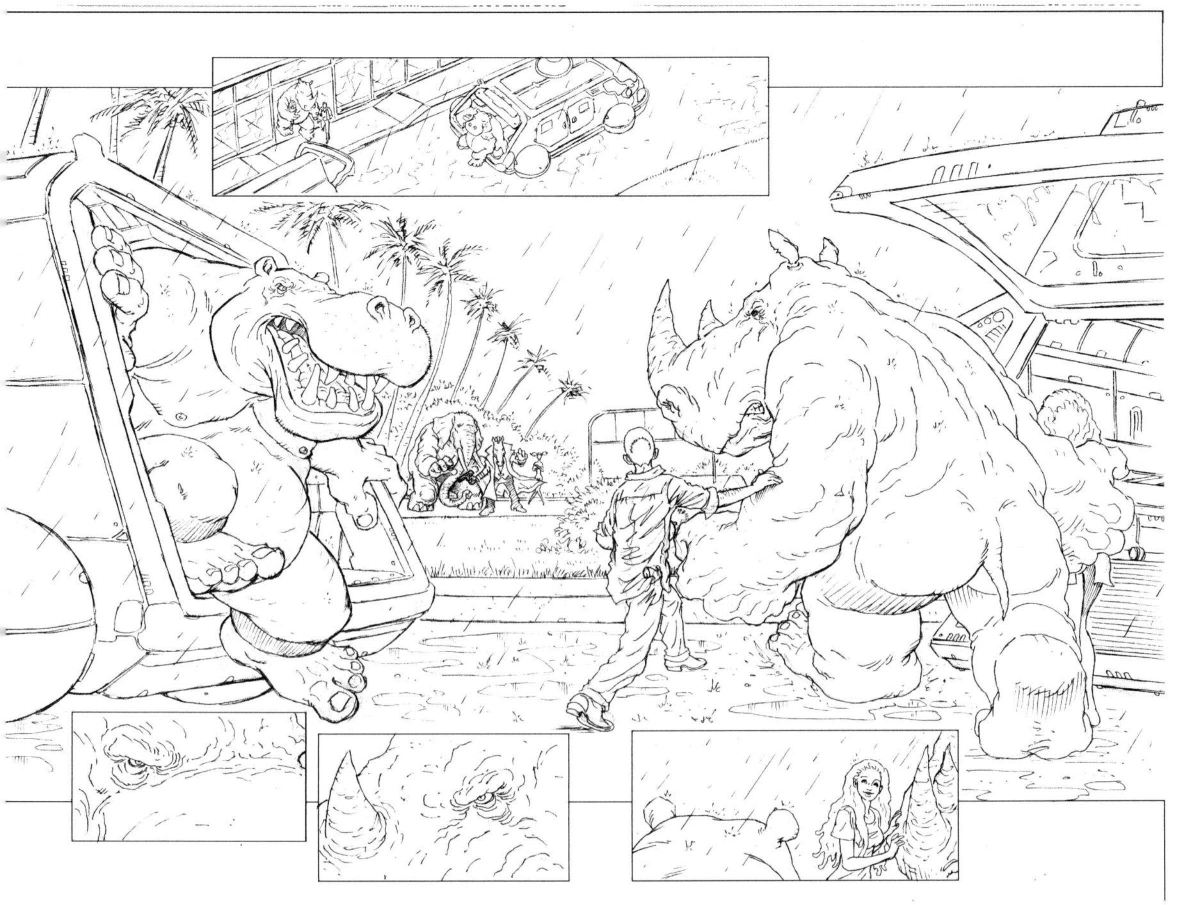

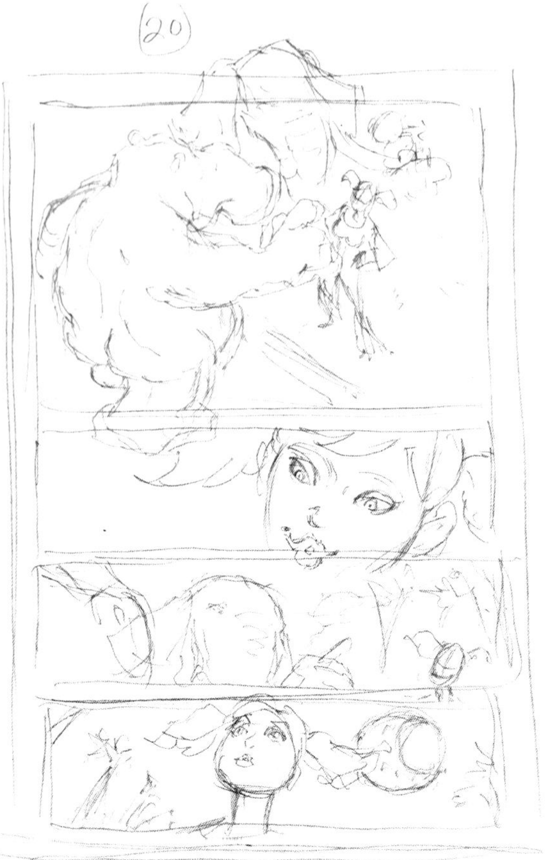

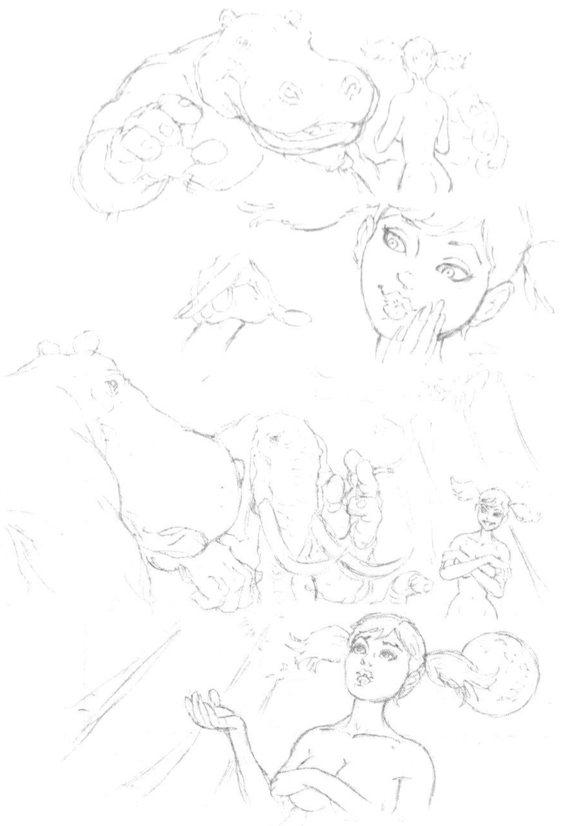

MOONING

Seriously though, it takes an artist of incredible skill and range to pull off Action, Adventure, Drama, Melodrama, Humour and Clothing. I am proud to have Ian as my friend and collaborator! Opposite... another unused page from the late 90's!

Rich!

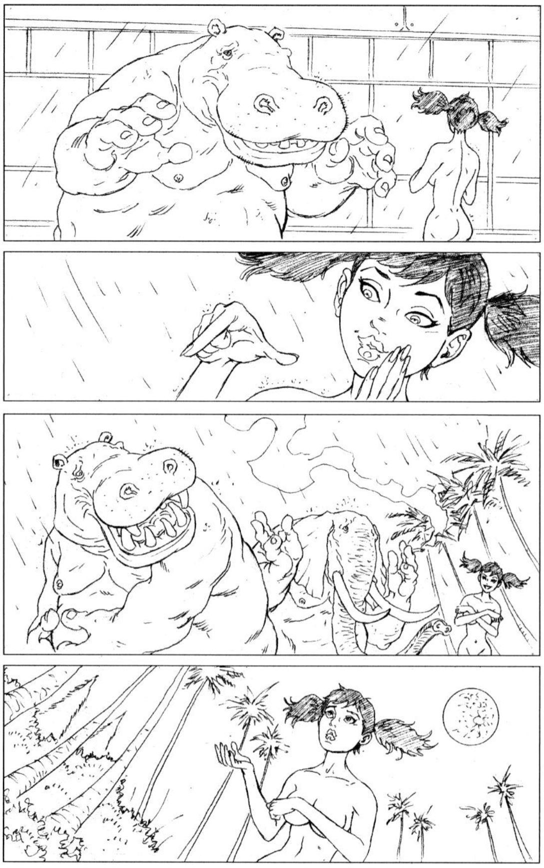

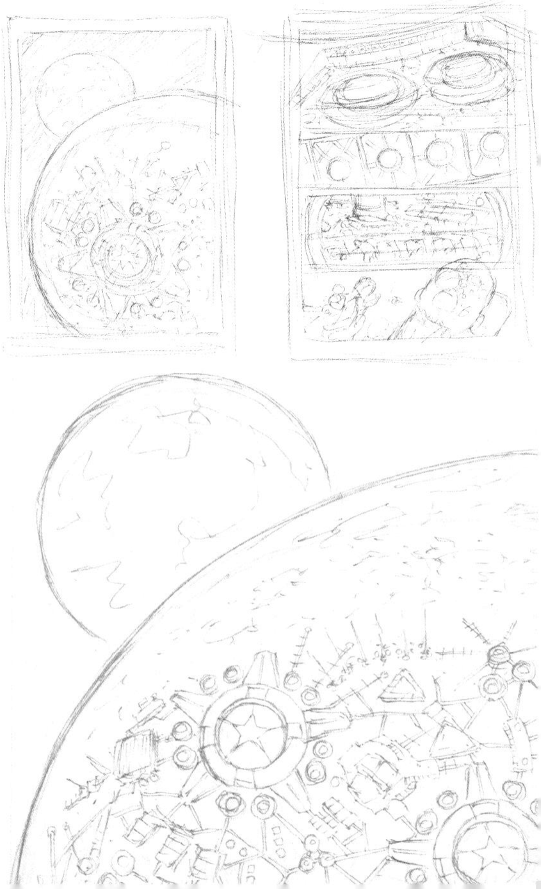

IAN NORM

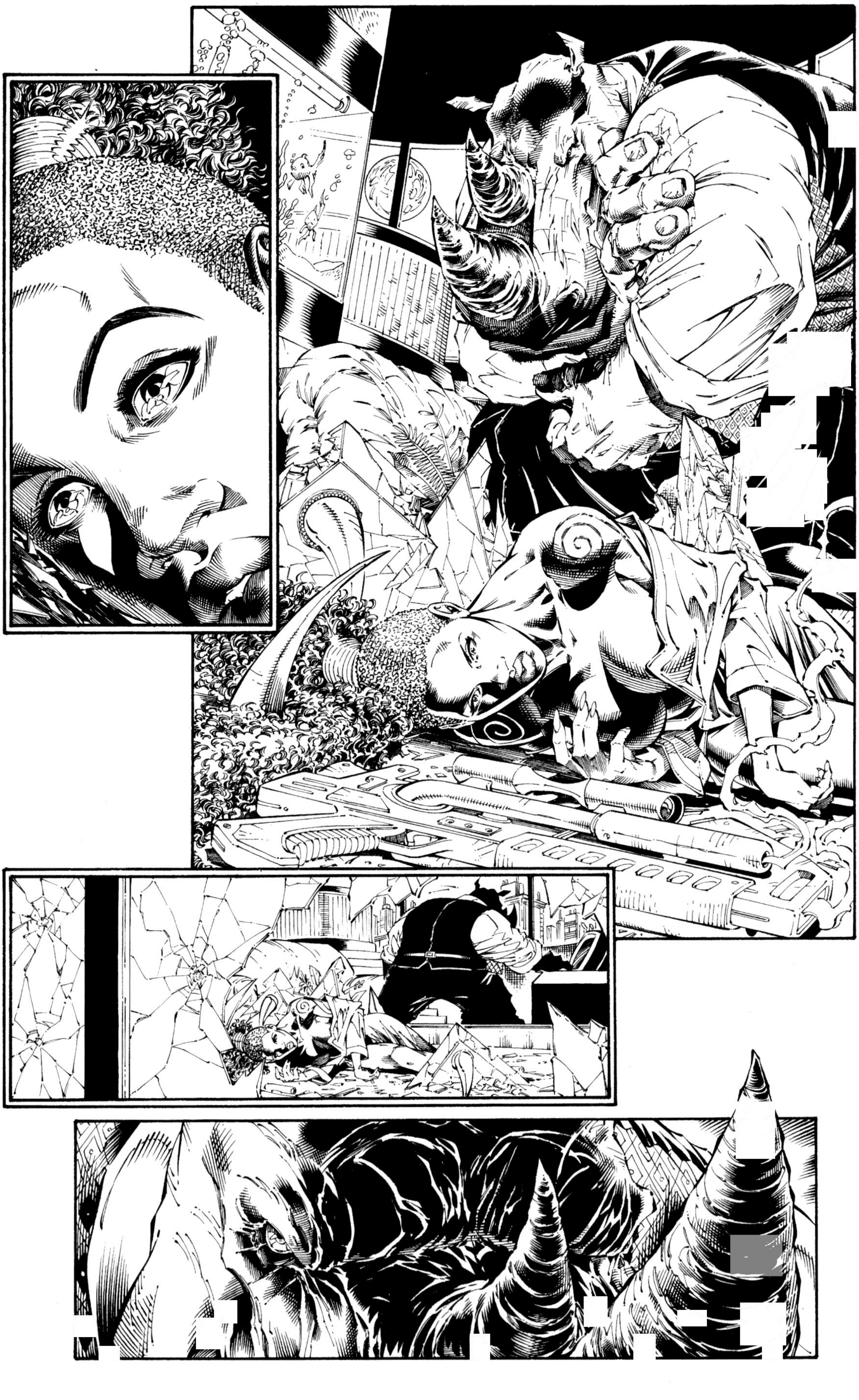

ABOUT *the*

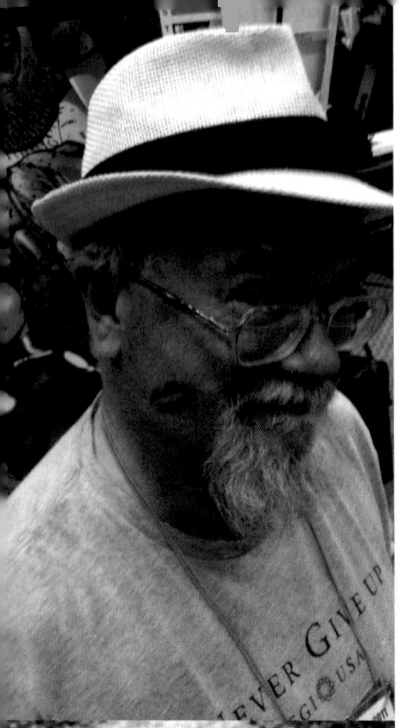

RICHARD STARKINGS is the creator of **HIP FLASK** and **ELEPHANTMEN**. Born and raised in England, Starkings worked for five years at Marvel UK's London offices as editor, designer and occasional writer of **ZOIDS**, **GHOSTBUSTERS**, **TRANSFORMERS** and the **DOCTOR WHO** comic strip. He is perhaps best known for his work with the award-winning Comicraft design and lettering studio, which he founded in 1992 with John 'JG' Roshell. Starkings & Roshell also co-authored the best-selling books **COMIC BOOK LETTERING THE COMICRAFT WAY** and **TIM SALE: BLACK AND WHITE**.

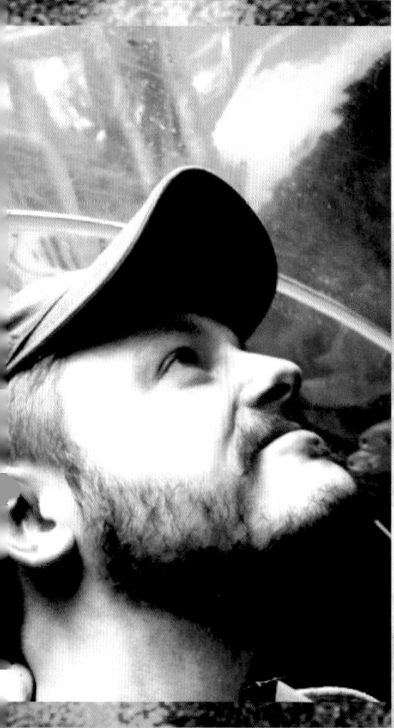

BOO COOK lives in Brighton, England with his lovely wife Gemma. He has worked on **2000AD** for Tharg the Mighty in Blighty for eleven years now, drawing favorites such as **JUDGE DREDD**, **JUDGE ANDERSON**, **A.B.C WARRIORS** and a basketcase of covers including a run on Marvel's **X-FACTOR** series. If you want to track down a big chunk of Boo, look for the **ASYLUM** collection, and if it leaves you begging for more, ask him about **BLUNT**. Boo's most recent work for **ELEPHANTMEN** -- **WAR TOYS II: ENEMY SPECIES** -- appears in issues #34 and 35!

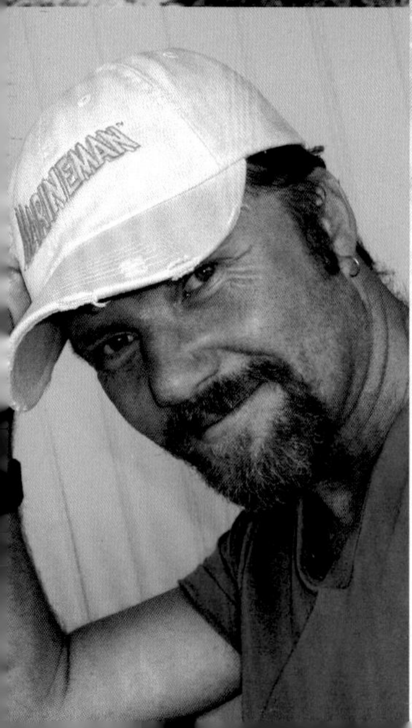
MARINEMAN

IAN CHURCHILL left a career in graphic design to work professionally in comics in 1994, when he was hired on the spot at a London comic convention by Marvel's editor-in-chief at the time, Bob Harras. Alongside Jeph Loeb, Churchill took Marvel's X-Men title, **CABLE** to new heights shortly before Joe Casey and Ladrönn created their memorable run on the book. Most recently, he launched his creator owned series, the Eisner-nominated **MARINEMAN**, with Image.

CREATORS

MORITAT, a.k.a. "Justin Norman," has suffered from kidney stones, carpal tunnel syndrome and had his gall bladder removed during the course of the ELEPHANTMEN series. He is still recovering from being the artist of STRAY MOONBEAMS, ATTRACTIVE FORCES, THE 3RD DEGREE, SOLSTICE and DC's THE SPIRIT. Some people see JONAH HEX in his future.

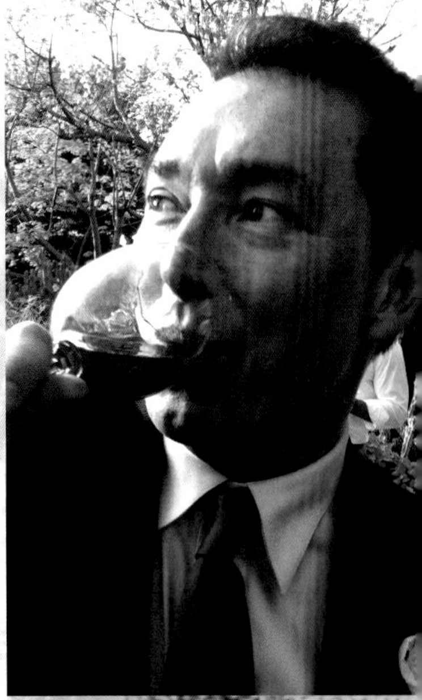

AXEL MEDELLIN was born in 1975 in Guadalajara, Mexico. Axel was a straight A-student until he graduated as an industrial designer and decided he wanted to draw comic books for a living, which in Mexico is like signing a suicide note. After working in advertising, illustration, storyboards and comic books in Mexico, Axel's first U.S. work appeared in METAL HURLANT, followed by stories for HEAVY METAL, FABLEWOOD, Zenoscope's GRIMM FAIRY TALES and Boom! Studios' MR STUFFINS. Look out for his work on Image Comics' 50 GIRLS 50, previewed in ELEPHANTMEN #31! Axel is happily married to Aurora, "the most beautiful woman in the whole wide world," and together they have a daughter, Alexa.

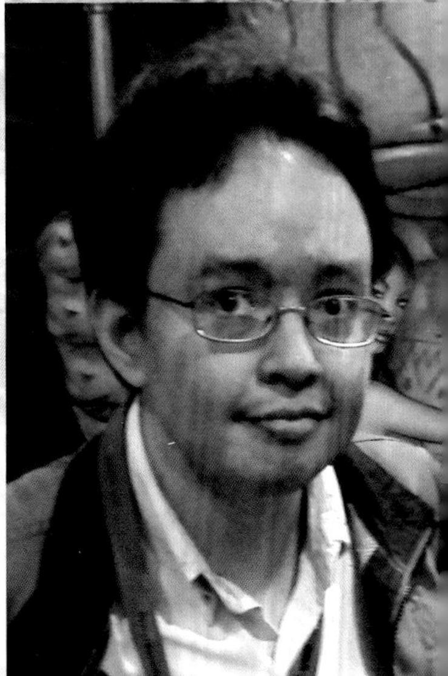

JOHN ROSHELL, a.k.a. "JG", a.k.a. "Mr. Fontastic", a.k.a. "Comicraft's Secret Weapon", grew up nary an iPod's throw from Apple headquarters in Northern California. These days he uses the Mac to create fonts and design books, logos and websites, including the official ELEPHANTMEN site at HipFlask.com. He also writes CHARLEY LOVES ROBOTS and plays a mean guitar.

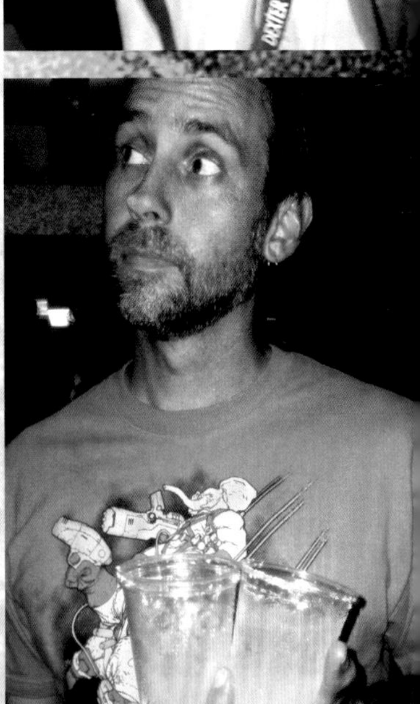

A B O U T *the*

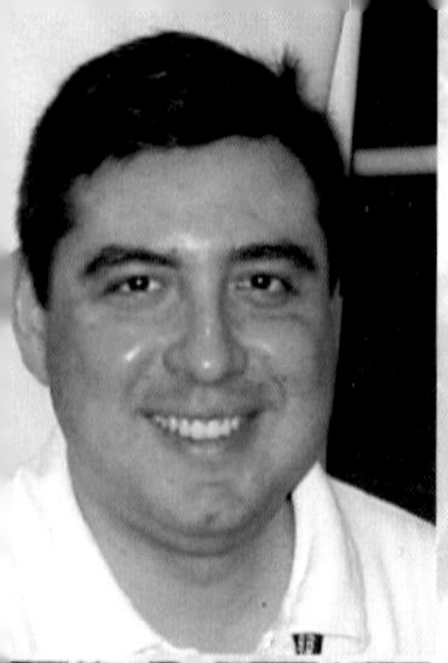

LADRÖNN was born and raised in Veracruz, Mexico, and never considered creating comics, especially not for the American market, until after he visited the San Diego Comic Con in 1995. His incredible painted work was first published in a short story for the **THOR 2000** Annual before he started work on **THE INHUMANS**. He was twice nominated for Eisner awards for his work on **HIP FLASK**, and finally received the Eisner award for best painter for **HIP FLASK: MYSTERY CITY** [collected by Image Comics in **HIP FLASK: CONCRETE JUNGLE**]. His covers have recently graced DC's **GREEN ARROW/BLACK CANARY** and **THE SPIRIT**, and he is currently working on **HIP FLASK: OUROBOROUS**.

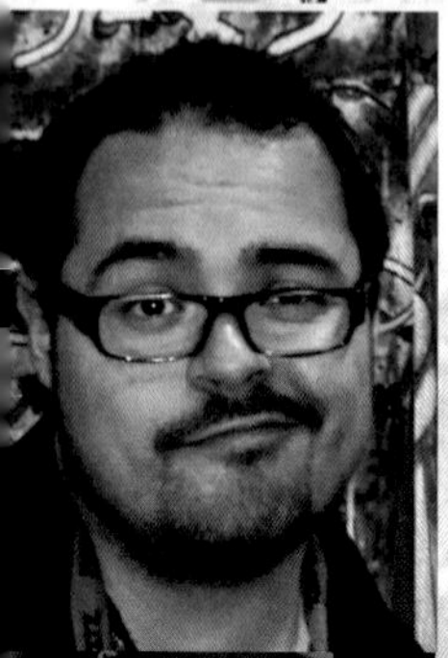

GABRIEL "GALVO" BAUTISTA is from the northwest burbs of Chicago, home of the true wind wakers. **HE IS A SILVERBACK COMIX GORILLA KNOCKING DOWN TREES IN THE JUNGLE OF ART.**

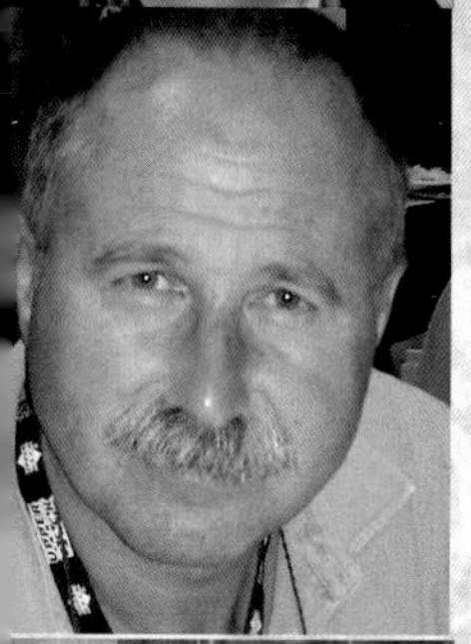

BRIAN BOLLAND self-published his first comics work, **SUDDENLY AT TWO O'CLOCK IN THE MORNING** shortly after he left art college in 1974. He is best known for his work on **2000AD**, for which he illustrated a string of covers and short stories before eventually being assigned to the strip with which he would become most closely associated, **JUDGE DREDD**. Bolland's work has also graced the pages of **MYSTERY IN SPACE**, **CAMELOT 3000** and **DETECTIVE COMICS**, but he is best known for his collaboration, heh, with letterer -- and **HIP FLASK** creator -- Richard Starkings, on **BATMAN: THE KILLING JOKE**, written by some other British guy who probably wouldn't want to be named as the author of the work any moore, um, more. If you haven't already tracked down Brian's **STRIPS** or Image's huge **THE ART OF BRIAN BOLLAND**, do so immediately -- and don't forget to lick every page.

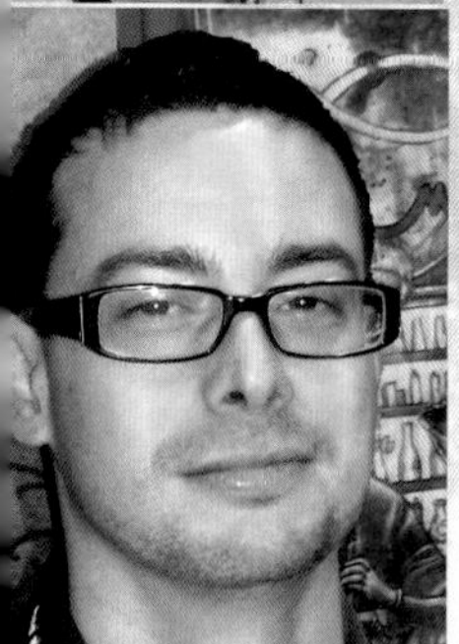

STEVE BUCCELLATO is a freelance artist living in Los Angeles with his wife, son and a hypoallergenic dog that would be the envy of the Obama family, if only they knew about her. Recent projects include his original manga, **BATTLE OF THE BANDS** [TokyoPop], **RONALD REAGAN: A GRAPHIC BIOGRAPHY** [HILL & WANG], AND Amazing Stories of Polio, featured in Rotary International's The Rotarian. For more about Steve, his work, or his dog, please visit www.stevebuccellato.com.

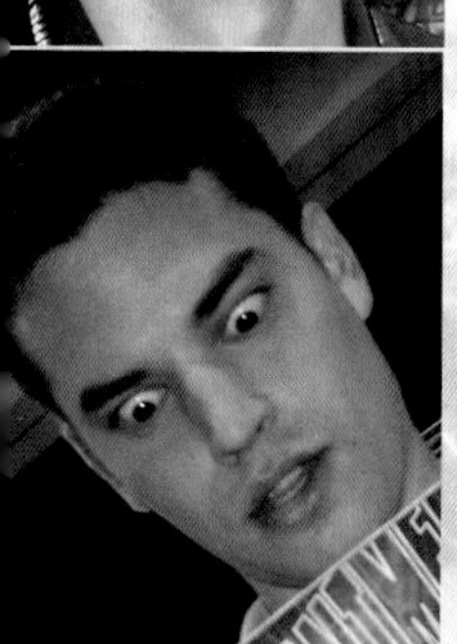

CHRIS BURNHAM is too young to be working on a biography for this page. I bet when he's drawing **ULTIMATES** volume 11 with Jeph Loeb, his entry on Wikipedia won't even mention **ELEPHANTMEN**. Of course by that time he won't be grinning any more either, he'll be hunched over, grey-haired, bitter and twisted. He'll probably keep a .45 near his front door and peer at callers through the mailbox. "Remember when Chris was happy," I'll say, "Yeah, before you ruined his life by giving him his first big break in comics," you'll reply.

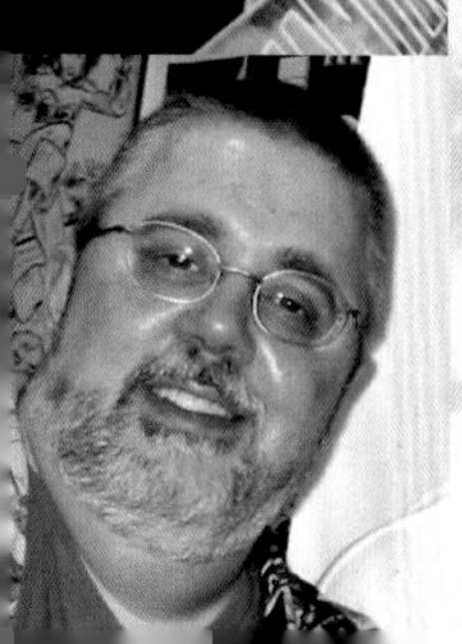

KURT BUSIEK is the creator and writer of the award-winning **ASTRO CITY** series. One of the industry's most prolific and talented writers, his work includes **ARROWSMITH**, **THE AVENGERS**, **IRON MAN**, **NINJAK**, **SHOCKROCKETS**, **SUPERMAN**, **SUPERSTAR**, **THUNDERBOLTS**, **A WIZARD'S TALE** and, of course, the award-winning **MARVELS** series and its sequel, **EYE OF THE CAMERA** -- all lettered by those awfully nice chaps at Comicraft. Anything else doesn't really count, does it, Kurt?

CREATORS

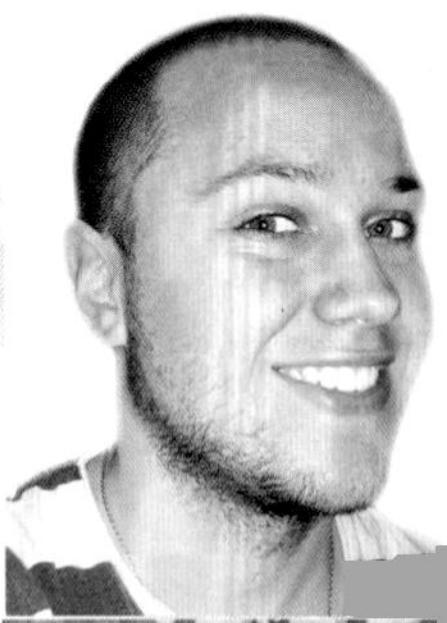

NICOLAS CHAPUIS was born in 1985 in Freiburg, Germany. He has been a huge comic fan since he has been a little kid. He has been coloring for Image comics, Tokyopop, Cereal Geek Magazine and other independent comics in the US and Europe. Feel free to visit his online portfolio at http://booom.deviantart.com/

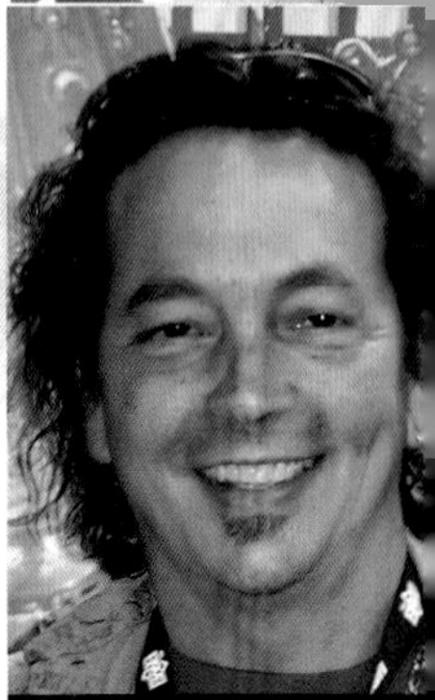

KEVIN EASTMAN's first known drawings were on the walls of the farm he grew up on. Inspired by Jack Kirby, Richard Corben, Frank Miller, and Dave Sim, he began writing and drawing his own comics as an adolescent, and after meeting Peter Laird in 1983, self-published the TEENAGE MUTANT NINJA TURTLES in 1984. Using most of his good fortune, he formed the creator friendly Tundra Publishing, the Words and Pictures Museum and bought HEAVY METAL magazine. The first two are gone, while the third continues to thrive after more than thirty years. Today he juggles the magazine, entertainment projects, some personal creative work, two families, and thirteen dogs. Visit him online at www.metaltv.com

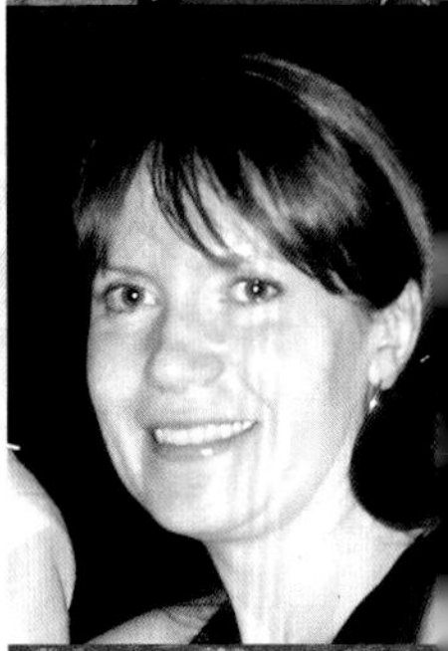

JILL FRESHNEY spent her childhood in the idyllic English countryside before moving to London to become part of the wonderful world of publishing. In 2000AD [the year, not the comic] she moved to California where she was Managing Editor for a Los Angeles-based manga/graphic novel publisher which may or may not have been TokyoPop. She now lives in New York City with a psychotic cat, Minnie and a slightly less psychotic husband. She hopes, one day, to be the proud owner of her very own iFrog.

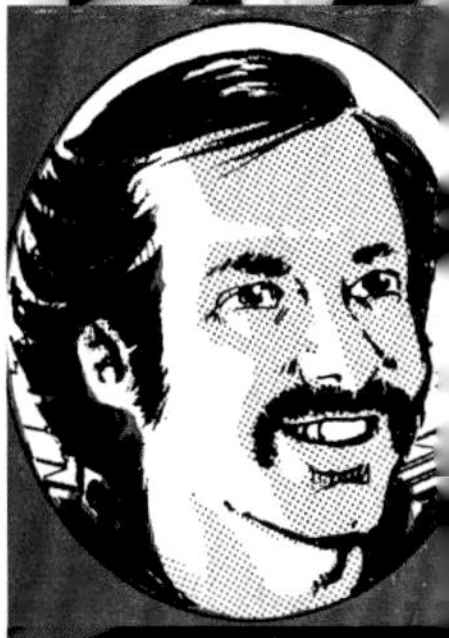

The Spirit, Elric, The Wraith, Doctor Strange, Superman, Batman, Mickey Mouse and Donald Duck are just a few of the characters **MICHAEL T. GILBERT** has either written or drawn during his 30-year comic book career. However, his most famous character remains the monster-fighting superhero, MR. MONSTER, which he created for Pacific Comics in 1984. In recent years, Michael has scripted the adventures of DONALD DUCK and the rest of the Disney crew for Egmont Comics in Denmark, published in America by Gemstone Comics. In addition, Michael writes a monthly column on comic book history for ALTER EGO magazine, MR. MONSTER'S Comic Crypt! He lives in Eugene, Oregon, with his wife Janet, and maintains the distinction of having the coolest business card in all of comicdom.

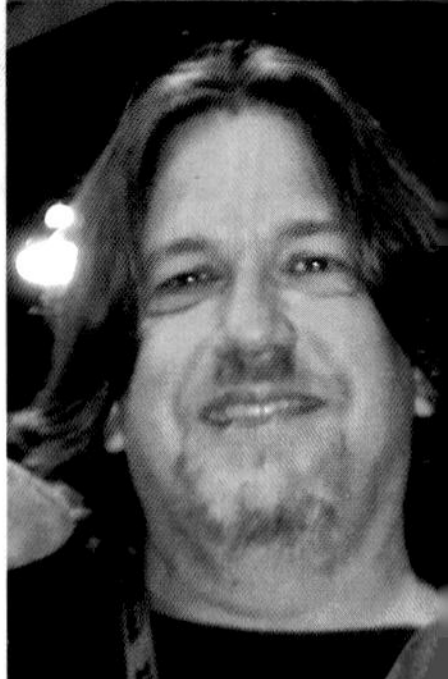

PETER GROSS is best known for his work on Vertigo's BOOKS OF MAGIC series which he wrote and drew for many years. He continues to write and draw but does not seem to have his own Wikipedia entry and is terribly hard to get hold of...

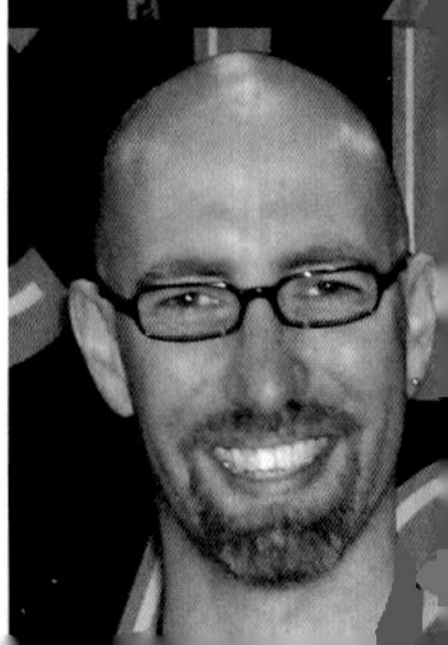

JOE KELLY is a New York based writer working in comic books and animation. His runs on X-MEN, ACTION COMICS, SUPERGIRL, JLA and SPACE GHOST stand as "exceptional works of genre-busting and emotional subterfuge," according to his elementary school aged children, and a hot dog vendor who bears a remarkable resemblance to Orson Welles. Joe is 1/4 of MAN OF ACTION Studios [www.manofaction.tv], the creative juggernaut behind life-changing-mega-hit BEN 10 on Cartoon Network. By most accounts his life is swell, bordering on rapturous. Check out his well lovely Image Comics' mini series I KILL GIANTS.

A B O U T *the*

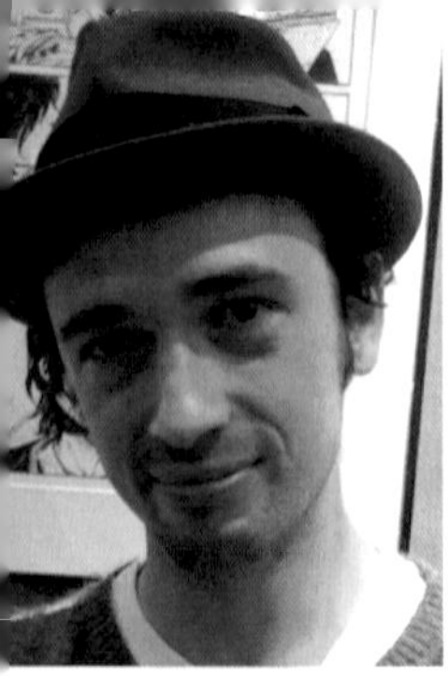

RYAN KELLY graduated from the Minneapolis College of Art and Design in 1998, where he studied under comic book artist Peter Gross, whom he worked with on the DC/Vertigo comic books **LUCIFER** and **BOOKS OF MAGIC**. He then moved on to inking and penciling responsibilities on **AMERICAN VIRGIN** and penciling for AiT/PlanetLar's **GIANT WARRIOR ROBOTS** with Stuart Moore. He is now on the **MCAD** staff, teaching the occasional inking class as well as classes for younger students, while working on **NORTHLANDERS** with Brian Wood for Vertigo.

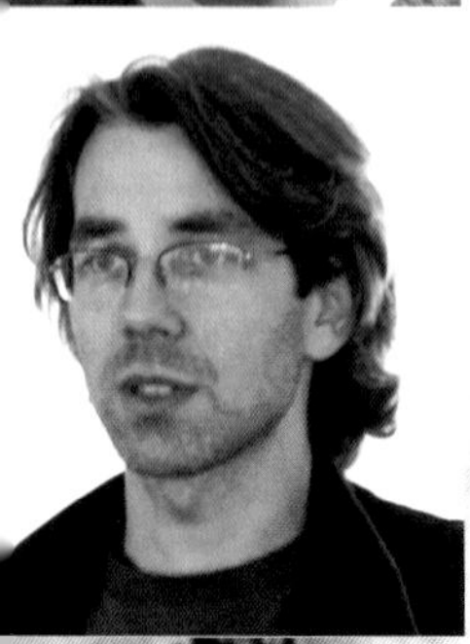

STUART IMMONEN has drawn such high-profile characters as **SUPERMAN, HULK, THE LEGION OF SUPER-HEROES,** and **THE X-MEN.** His recent work includes stints on the titles **ULTIMATE FANTASTIC FOUR** and **ULTIMATE X-MEN** with writers Warren Ellis and Brian K. Vaughan, as well as a 12-issue run pencilling Ellis's **NEXTWAVE.** In 2005, Immonen published **50 REASONS TO STOP SKETCHING AT CONVENTIONS**, a series of fifty strips that gently detail why he no longer sketches for fans... he also maintains a webcomic called **NEVER AS BAD AS YOU THINK** which is co-authored by his wife, Kathryn.

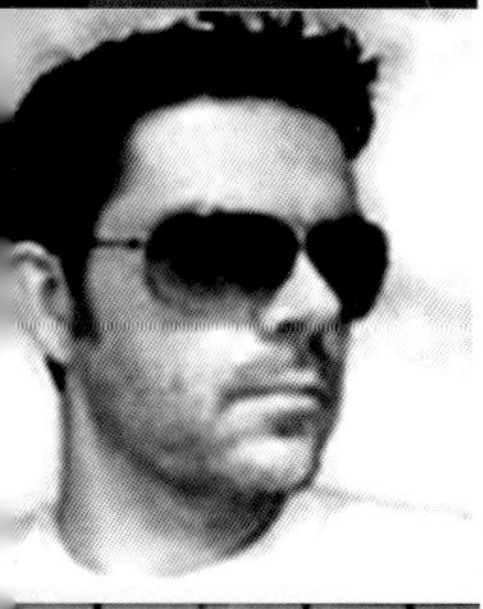

CHRISTIAN LICHTNER is one of the most groundbreaking colorists in the comic industry. With Aron Lusen, he formed Liquid! in the mid-'90s, and their use of digital coloring provided a look never before seen in comics and quickly became a sensation. Christian worked closely with Joe Madureira on **BATTLE CHASERS** before both took their talents to the video-game industry. In 2008, he reunited with Madureira on **ULTIMATES 3**, with writerJeph Loeb.

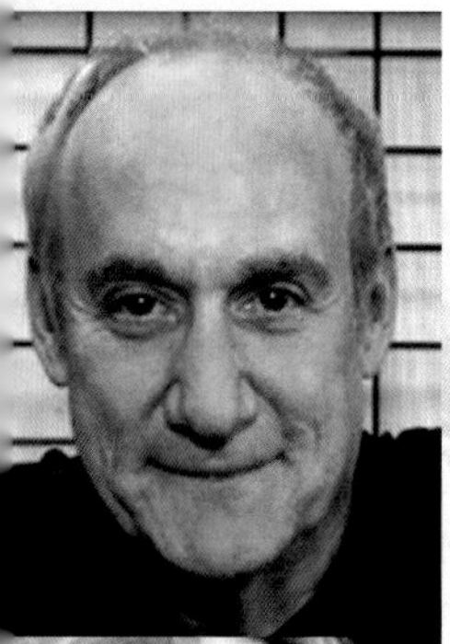

JEPH LOEB is an Emmy and four-time Eisner award-winning writer/producer. In television, his many credits include **HEROES, LOST** and **SMALLVILLE**, and in film, **TEEN WOLF** and **COMMANDO.** In comics, Jeph has written nearly every major icon including Hulk, Iron Man, Spider-Man, Wolverine, Batman and Superman.

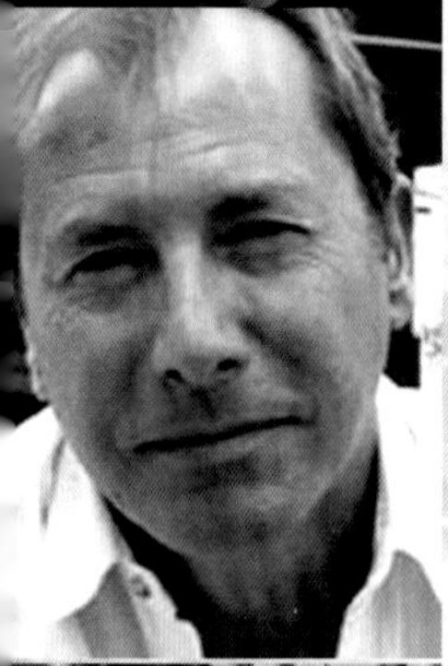

DAVID LLOYD trained as a commercial artist in an advertising firm before becoming a strip cartoonist in 1977. His big break was a book of stories and strips from the **LOGAN'S RUN TV** series. He later drew the pulp adventure series **NIGHT RAVEN** for Marvel UK, and a range of stories featuring the many villains of **DOCTOR WHO.** In 1980 he began collaborating with Alan Moore on the series **V FOR VENDETTA**, which was published as a graphic novel in 1990 and successfully adapted for the cinema in 2005. David's other work has included **HELLBLAZER, SLAINE, WAR STORIES, GLOBAL FREQUENCY, ALIENS: GLASS CORRIDOR, MARLOWE, NIGHT RAVEN: HOUSE OF CARDS,** and many short stories. His latest work is the 96-page crime-noir thriller **KICKBACK.**

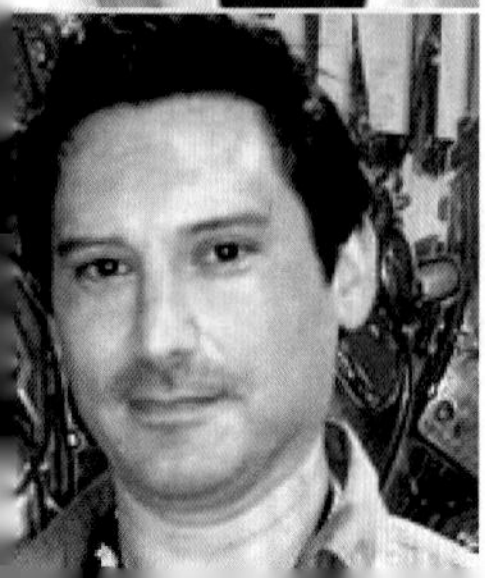

ARON LUSEN is not only the creator and writer of **E.V.E. PROTOMECHA** and **DEAD SAMURAI**, but one of the founders of the award winning **LIQUID! GRAPHICS** studio, often described as the Industrial Light and Magic of comic book coloring. Aron's work has graced the pages of **UNCANNY X-MEN, THE FANTASTIC FOUR** and Joe Madureira's **BATTLE CHASERS.** Aron was recently working for **GOOGLE** in Southern California but has since moved silently on, like a ninja, his whereabouts currently unknown.

CREATORS

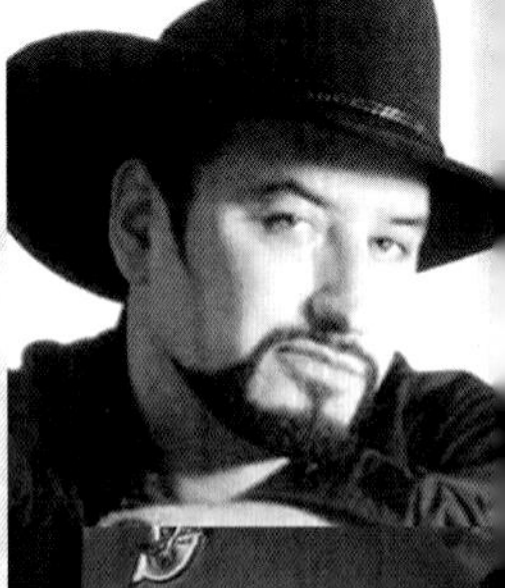

DREW POSADA began his career when he was hired by Image Comics as a colorist in the spring of 1994. Posada's coloring work won him acclaim, but in 1999 he abruptly switched gears and worked to become recognized as a pin-up artist, inspired by two legends of cheesecake pin-ups, Hajime Sorayama and Olivia De Berardinis. Sadly, Drew died from pancreatitis in January 2007, but not before accomplishing his dream of earning a living as a pin-up artist -- hunt down a copy of his art book, or enter his name in Google to see his amazing work.

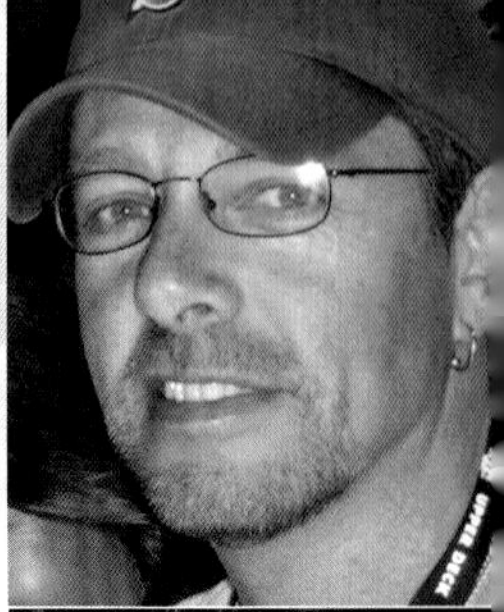

TIM SALE lives in southern California with his aged dogs, Hotspur and Shelby. Raised in Seattle, he still finds California an odd place, though he hopes that will change someday. Tim is the artist on BATMAN: DARK VICTORY, CATWOMAN: WHEN IN ROME, BATMAN: THE LONG HALLOWEEN and SUPERMAN FOR ALL SEASONS among many other titles. From 2006-2008, Tim was the artist for the hit NBC television series HEROES.

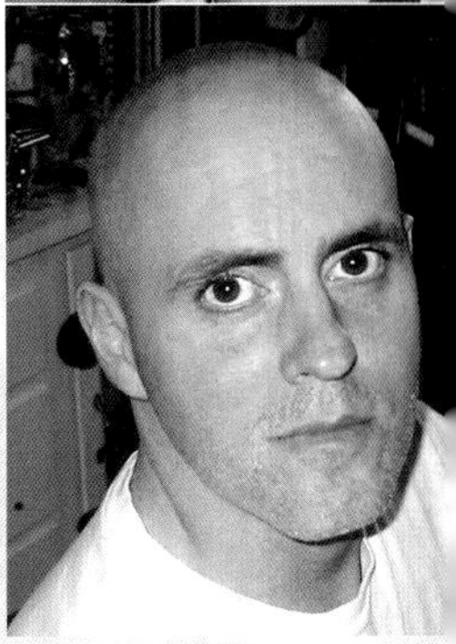

ROB STEEN arrived at his current profession in illustration after careers as a musician, morgue technician, record store clerk, graphic designer and electronic technician. After graduating from The University of Comicraft under the guidance of Professor Richard Starkings, he eventually settled on a sedentary life of drawing. For the last few years he has devoted his life to the study of Flanimals which have produced four books so far with the latest, FLANIMALS: THE DAY OF THE BLETCHLING in stores now. He currently resides in New York and likes to fill his spare time with Guinness.

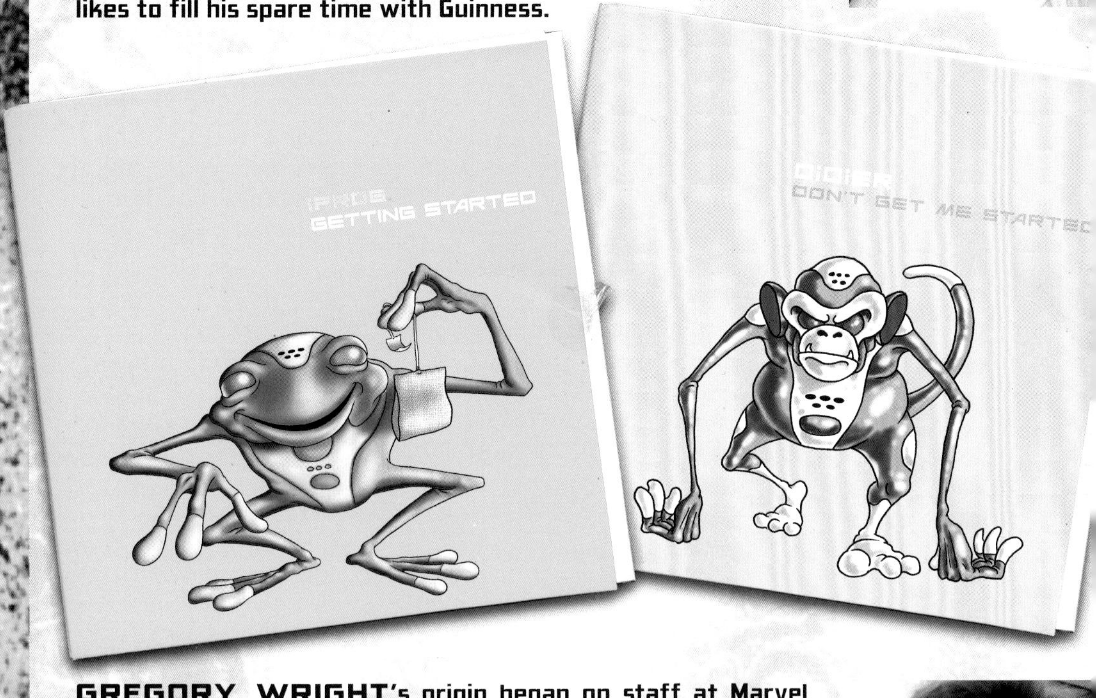
GETTING STARTED
DON'T GET ME STARTED

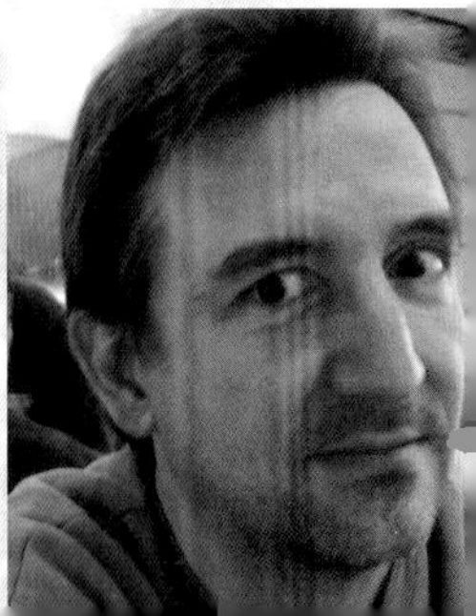

GREGORY WRIGHT's origin began on staff at Marvel comics. A Marvel/Epic Comic editor known to wield a small bat when discussing deadlines, he found that freelance writing and coloring was much less stressful and far more fulfilling. Greg has worked on everything from SPIDER-MAN to BATMAN to ROBOCOP to DEATHLOK and SILVER SABLE. His favorite color work is BATMAN: THE LONG HALLOWEEN. To the surprise of many of his friends, he's actually happily married with a daughter who reportedly has many of his most annoying traits.

ALSO AVAILABLE

THE ORIGIN

STARKINGS · CASEY · LADRONN
HIP FLASK
UNNATURAL SELECTION

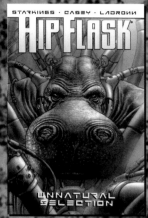

HIP FLASK VOL. 1: UNNATURAL SELECTION

2218: The birth of Hieronymous Flask and the Elephantmen, and their eventual liberation from the torturous world of MAPPO.

ISBN 0-97405-670-7
Diamond #STAR19898

THE MYSTERY

STARKINGS · CASEY · LADRONN
HIP FLASK
CONCRETE JUNGLE

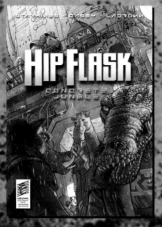

HIP FLASK VOL. 2: CONCRETE JUNGLE

2262: The broken and bloody body of an unidentifiable man sets Hip Flask and Vanity Case on a trail that leads them to Casbah Joe and The Eye of the Needle.

ISBN 1-58240-679-0
Diamond #NOV06 1859

THE SURVIVORS

ELEPHANTMEN
VOLUME 01 WOUNDED ANIMALS
STARKINGS · MORITAT · LADRONN · ROSHELL · COOK

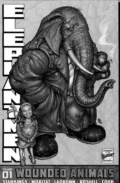

ELEPHANTMEN VOL. 1: WOUNDED ANIMALS

2259: Nikken's creations struggle for survival and acceptance in the world of man. TPB collects issues #0-7.

SOFTCOVER:
ISBN 978-160706-337-7
Diamond #SEP10 0455

HARDCOVER [#1-7]:
ISBN 978-1-60706-088-8
Diamond #JAN07 1927

ELEPHANTMEN
WOUNDED ANIMALS
STARKINGS · MORITAT · COMICRAFT · LADRONN

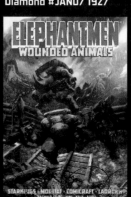

THE ENEMIES

ELEPHANTMEN
INTRODUCTION BY JANET ZUCKER
VOLUME 02 FATAL DISEASES
STARKINGS · MORITAT · CHURCHILL · ROSHELL · COOK

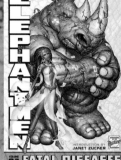

ELEPHANTMEN VOL. 2: FATAL DISEASES

A meteor falls in Santa Monica Bay, with far-reaching consequences for all. Collects issues #8-15 and PILOT.

SOFTCOVER:
ISBN 978-1-60706-394-0
Diamond #MAY11 0455

HARDCOVER:
ISBN 978-1-60706-088-8
Diamond #AUG08 2238

ELEPHANTMEN
FATAL DISEASES
STARKINGS · MORITAT · CHURCHILL · ROSHELL · COOK

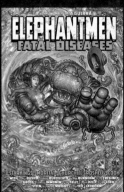

THE DARKNESS

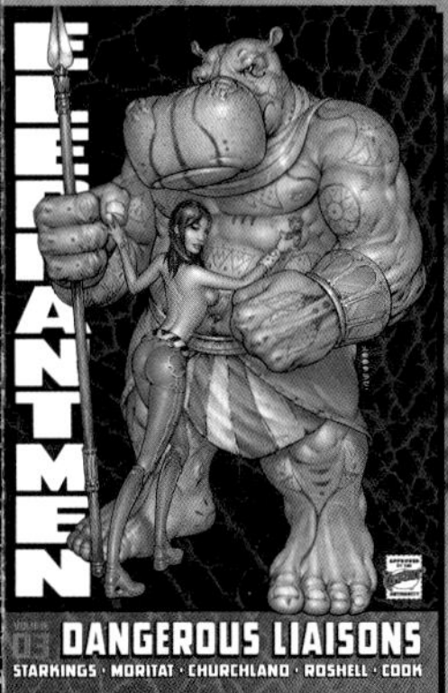
ELEPHANTMEN
VOLUME 03 DANGEROUS LIAISONS
STARKINGS · MORITAT · CHURCHLAND · ROSHELL · COOK

ELEPHANTMEN VOL. 3: DANGEROUS LIAISONS

Hip Flask, Ebony Hide and Obadiah Horn go about their business in Los Angeles, 2259, unaware a MAPPO sleeper cell has plans for them. Collects issues #16-23.

SOFTCOVER:
ISBN 978-1-60706-268-4
Diamond #MAY10 0439

HARDCOVER:
ISBN 978-1-60706-250-9
Diamond #FEB10 0355

THE CASUALTIES

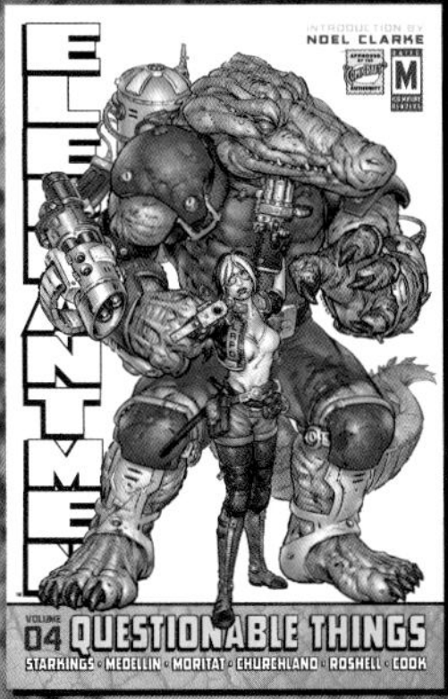
INTRODUCTION BY NOEL CLARKE
ELEPHANTMEN
VOLUME 04 QUESTIONABLE THINGS
STARKINGS · MEDELLIN · MORITAT · CHURCHLAND · ROSHELL · COOK

ELEPHANTMEN VOL. 4: QUESTIONABLE THINGS

A MAPPO sleeper cell has been reactivating Elephantmen. Collects issues #24-30

SOFTCOVER:
ISBN 978-1-60706-393-3

HARDCOVER:
ISBN 978-1-60706-364-3
Diamond #JAN11 0550

THE FANTASY

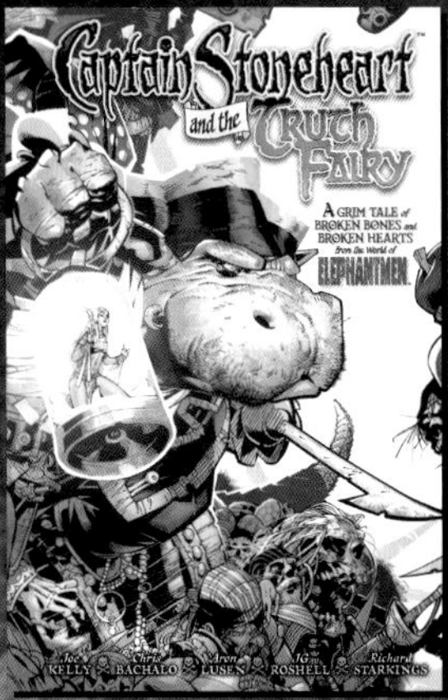
Captain Stoneheart and the Truth Fairy
A GRIM TALE of BROKEN BONES and BROKEN HEARTS from the World of ELEPHANTMEN
Joe KELLY · Chris BACHALO · Aron LUSEN · JG ROSHELL · Richard STARKINGS

CAPTAIN STONEHEART AND THE TRUTH FAIRY

Joe Kelly and Chris Bachalo craft a grim but beautiful fairy tale of broken bones and broken hearts. Includes the full script, pencil artwork and audio CD.

ISBN 1-58240-865-3
DIAMOND #JAN07 1927

THE REALITY

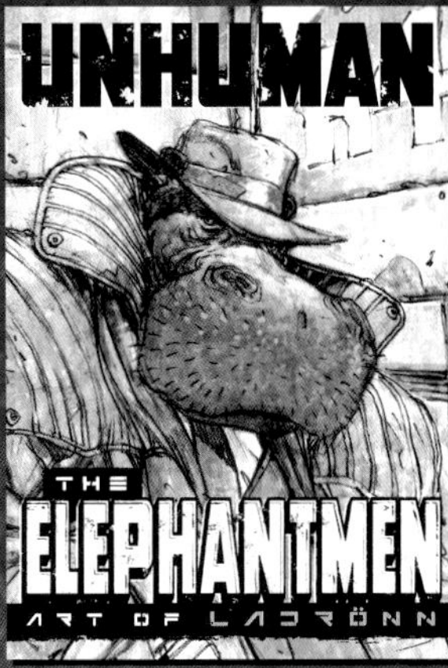
UNHUMAN
THE ELEPHANTMEN
ART OF LADRÖNN

UNHUMAN: THE ELEPHANTMEN ART OF LADRÖNN

Unpublished art, sketches and drawings by Ladrönn show the development of the HIP FLASK universe in a beautiful oversized hardcover volume.

ISBN 1-58240-882-3
Diamond #SEP07 1961

ALL-NEW DUSTJACKETS FOR VOLUME 1 & 2 HARDCOVERS AVAILABLE AT COMICRAZY.COM!

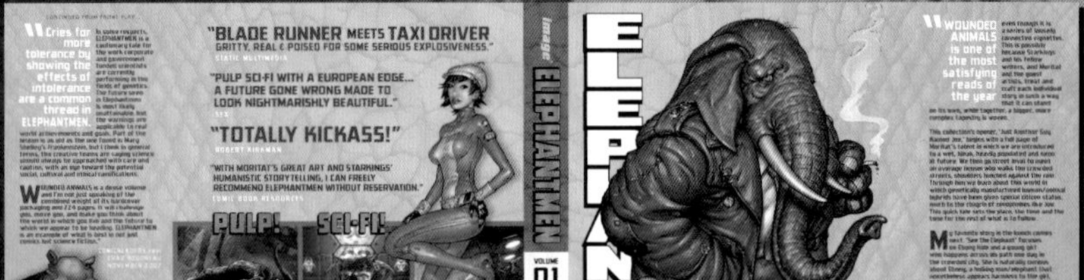
"BLADE RUNNER MEETS TAXI DRIVER
GRITTY, REAL & POISED FOR SOME SERIOUS EXPLOSIVENESS."
"PULP SCI-FI WITH A EUROPEAN EDGE... A FUTURE GONE WRONG MADE TO LOOK NIGHTMARISHLY BEAUTIFUL."
"TOTALLY KICKASS!"
PULP! SCI-FI!
ELEPHANTMEN
VOLUME 01 WOUNDED ANIMALS
STARKINGS · MORITAT · LADRÖNN · ROSHELL · COOK

BY THE SAME CREATORS

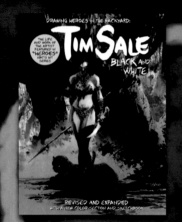

TIM SALE: BLACK AND WHITE REVISED & EXPANDED

HEROES artist Tim Sale discusses his life and work in this comprehensive and lavishly illustrated 272 page volume.

ISBN 1-58240-880-7
Diamond #OCT07 1973

STRANGE EMBRACE AND OTHER NIGHTMARES

David Hine's tortured modern gothic tale of pain and sorrow, obsession and damnation is not for the nervous!

ISBN 1-58240-914-5
DIAMOND #APR08 2187

HIP FLASK 1000 PIECE JIGSAW PUZZLE BY LADRÖNN

PREVIEWS #JUN07 1880

COMIC BOOK LETTERING THE COMICRAFT WAY

ISBN #0-97405-673-1
PREVIEWS #JAN03 1884

BY STEVEN T. SEAGLE AND JUSTIN NORMAN

ISBN #0-97667-611-7
PREVIEWS #APR05Z512

ALSO FROM IMAGE COMICS

THE BULLETPROOF COFFIN
978-1-60706-368-1

CHEW, VOL. 1 TP
978-1-60706-159-5

GIRLS
VOL. 1: CONCEPTION TP
978-1-58240-529-2
VOL. 2: EMERGENCE TP
978-1-58240-608-4
VOL. 3: SURVIVAL TP
978-1-58240-703-6
VOL. 4: EXTINCTION
978-1-58240-753-1

JACK STAFF
VOL. 1: EVERYTHING USED TO BE BLACK AND WHITE TP
987-7-58240-335-9
VOL. 2: SOLDIERS TP
978-1-58240-392-2
VOL. 3: ECHOES OF TOMORROW TP
978-1-58240-719-7

JERSEY GODS
VOL. 1 TP
978-1-60706-063-5
VOL. 2 TP
978-1-60706-117-5
VOL. 3 TP
978-1-60706-262-2

PHONOGRAM, VOL. 1:
RUE BRITANNIA TP
978-1-58240-694-7

POPGUN
VOL. 1
978-1-58240-824-8
VOL. 2
978-1-58240-920-7
VOL. 3
978-1-58240-974-0
VOL. 4
978-1-60706-188-5

PROOF
VOL. 1: GOATSUCKER TP
978-158240-944-3
VOL. 2: THE COMPANY OF MEN TP
978-160706-017-8
VOL. 3: THUNDERBIRDS ARE GO TP
978-160706-134-2

THE SWORD
VOL. 1 TP
978-1-58240-879-8
VOL. 2 TP
978-1-58240-976-4
VOL. 3 TP
978-1-60706-073-4
VOL. 4 TP
978-1-60706-168-7

WATERLOO SUNSET
978-158240-668-8